James Oliver Curwood, best novels

In this book:
The River's End
Kazan
The Grizzly King
The Alaskan

James Oliver "Jim" Curwood (1878 – 1927) was an American action-adventure writer and conservationist. His books ranked among Publisher's Weekly top-ten best sellers in the United States in the early 1920s. At least eighteen motion pictures have been based on or directly inspired by his novels and short stories. At the time of his death, he was the highest paid (per word) author in the world. His writing studio, Curwood Castle, is now a museum in Owosso, Michigan. His most successful work was his 1920 novel, The River's End. The book sold more than 100,000 copies and was the fourth best-selling title of the year in the United States, according to Publisher's Weekly.

In this book:

The River's End

I

Between Conniston, of His Majesty's Royal Northwest Mounted Police, and Keith, the outlaw, there was a striking physical and facial resemblance. Both had observed it, of course. It gave them a sort of confidence in each other. Between them it hovered in a subtle and unanalyzed presence that was constantly suggesting to Conniston a line of action that would have made him a traitor to his oath of duty. For nearly a month he had crushed down the whispered temptings of this thing between them. He represented the law. He was the law. For twenty-seven months he had followed Keith, and always there had been in his mind that parting injunction of the splendid service of which he was a part—"Don't come back until you get your man, dead or alive." Otherwise—

A racking cough split in upon his thoughts. He sat up on the edge of the cot, and at the gasping cry of pain that came with the red stain of blood on his lips Keith went to him and with a strong arm supported his shoulders. He said nothing, and after a moment Conniston wiped the stain away and laughed softly, even before the shadow of pain had faded from his eyes. One of his hands rested on a wrist that still bore the ring-mark of a handcuff. The sight of it brought him back to grim reality. After all, fate was playing whimsically as well as tragically with their destinies.

"Thanks, old top," he said. "Thanks."

His fingers closed over the manacle-marked wrist.

Over their heads the arctic storm was crashing in a mighty fury, as if striving to beat down the little cabin that had dared to rear itself in the dun-gray emptiness at the top of the world, eight hundred miles from civilization. There were curious waitings, strange screeching sounds, and heart-breaking meanings in its strife, and when at last its passion died away and there followed a strange quiet, the two men could feel the frozen earth under their feet shiver with the rumbling reverberations of the crashing and breaking fields of ice out in Hudson's Bay. With it came a dull and steady roar, like the incessant rumble of a far battle, broken now and then—when an ice mountain split asunder—with a report like that of a sixteen-inch gun. Down through the Roes Welcome into Hudson's Bay countless billions of tons of ice were rending their way like Hunnish armies in the break-up.

"You'd better lie down," suggested Keith.

Conniston, instead, rose slowly to his feet and went to a table on which a seal-oil lamp was burning. He swayed a little as he walked. He sat down, and Keith seated himself opposite him. Between them lay a worn deck of cards. As Conniston fumbled them in his fingers, he looked straight across at Keith and grinned.

"It's queer, devilish queer," he said.

"Don't you think so, Keith?" He was an Englishman, and his blue eyes shone with a grim, cold humor. "And funny," he added.

"Queer, but not funny," partly agreed Keith.

"Yes, it is funny," maintained Conniston. "Just twenty-seven months ago, lacking three days, I was sent out to get you, Keith. I was told to bring you in dead or alive—and at the end of the twenty-sixth month I got you, alive. And as a sporting proposition you deserve a hundred years of life instead of the noose, Keith, for you led me a chase that took me through seven different kinds of hell before I landed you. I froze, and I starved, and I drowned. I haven't seen a white woman's face in eighteen months. It was terrible. But I beat you at last. That's the jolly good part of it, Keith—I beat you and GOT you, and there's the proof of it on your wrists this minute. I won. Do you concede that? You must be fair, old top, because this is the last big game I'll ever play." There was a break, a yearning that was almost plaintive, in his voice.

Keith nodded. "You won," he said.

"You won so square that when the frost got your lung—"

"You didn't take advantage of me," interrupted Conniston. "That's the funny part of it, Keith. That's where the humor comes in. I had you all tied up and scheduled for the hangman when— bing!—along comes a cold snap that bites a corner of my lung, and the tables are turned. And instead of doing to me as I was going to do to you, instead of killing me or making your getaway while I was helpless—Keith—old pal—YOU'VE TRIED TO NURSE ME BACK TO LIFE! Isn't that funny? Could anything be funnier?"

He reached a hand across the table and gripped Keith's. And then, for a few moments, he bowed his head while his body was convulsed by another racking cough. Keith sensed the pain of it in the convulsive clutching of Conniston's fingers about his own. When Conniston raised his face, the red stain was on his lips again.

"You see, I've got it figured out to the day," he went on, wiping away the stain with a cloth already dyed red. "This is Thursday. I won't see another Sunday. It'll come Friday night or some time Saturday. I've seen this frosted lung business a dozen times. Understand? I've got two sure days ahead of me, possibly a third. Then you'll have to dig a hole and bury me. After that you will no longer be held by the word of honor you gave me when I slipped off your manacles. And I'm asking you—WHAT ARE YOU GOING TO DO?"

In Keith's face were written deeply the lines of suffering and of tragedy. Yesterday they had compared ages.

He was thirty-eight, only a little younger than the man who had run him down and who in the hour of his achievement was dying. They had not put the fact plainly before. It had been a matter of some little embarrassment for Keith, who at another time had found it easier to kill a man than to tell this man that he was going to die. Now that Conniston had measured his own span definitely and with most amazing coolness, a load was lifted from Keith's shoulders. Over the table they looked into each other's eyes, and this time it was Keith's fingers that tightened about Conniston's. They looked like brothers in the sickly glow of the seal-oil lamp.

"What are you going to do?" repeated Conniston.

Keith's face aged even as the dying Englishman stared at him. "I suppose—I'll go back," he said heavily.

"You mean to Coronation Gulf? You'll return to that stinking mess of Eskimo igloos? If you do, you'll go mad!"

"I expect to," said Keith. "But it's the only thing left. You know that. You of all men must know how they've hunted me. If I went south—"

It was Conniston's turn to nod his head, slowly and thoughtfully. "Yes, of course," he agreed. "They're hunting you hard, and you're giving 'em a bully chase. But they'll get you, even up there. And I'm—sorry."

Their hands unclasped. Conniston filled his pipe and lighted it. Keith noticed that he held the lighted taper without a tremor. The nerve of the man was magnificent.

"I'm sorry," he said again. "I—like you. Do you know, Keith, I wish we'd been born brothers and you hadn't killed a man. That night I slipped the ring-dogs on you I felt almost like a devil. I wouldn't say it if it wasn't for this bally lung. But what's the use of keeping it back now? It doesn't seem fair to keep a man up in that place for three years, running from hole to hole like a rat, and then take him down for a hanging. I know it isn't fair in your case. I feel it. I don't mean to be inquisitive, old chap, but I'm not believing Departmental 'facts' any more. I'd make a topping good wager you're not the sort they make you out. And so I'd like to know—just why—you killed Judge Kirkstone?"

Keith's two fists knotted in the center of the table. Conniston saw his blue eyes darken for an instant with a savage fire. In that moment there came a strange silence over the cabin, and in that silence the incessant and maddening yapping of the little white foxes rose shrilly over the distant booming and rumbling of the ice.

II

"Why did I kill Judge Kirkstone?" Keith repeated the words slowly.

His clenched hands relaxed, but his eyes held the steady glow of fire. "What do the Departmental 'facts' tell you, Conniston?"

"That you murdered him in cold blood, and that the honor of the Service is at stake until you are hung."

"There's a lot in the view-point, isn't there? What if I said I didn't kill Judge Kirkstone?"

Conniston leaned forward a little too eagerly. The deadly paroxysm shook his frame again, and when it was over his breath came pantingly, as if hissing through a sieve. "My God, not Sunday—or Saturday," he breathed. "Keith, it's coming TOMORROW!"

"No, no, not then," said Keith, choking back something that rose in his throat. "You'd better lie down again."

Conniston gathered new strength. "And die like a rabbit? No, thank you, old chap! I'm after facts, and you can't lie to a dying man. Did you kill Judge Kirkstone?"

"I—don't—know," replied Keith slowly, looking steadily into the other's eyes. "I think so, and yet I am not positive. I went to his home that night with the determination to wring justice from him or kill him. I wish you could look at it all with my eyes, Conniston. You could if you had known my father. You see, my mother died when I was a little chap, and my father and I grew up together, chums. I don't believe I ever thought of him as just simply a father. Fathers are common. He was more than that. From the time I was ten years old we were inseparable. I guess I was twenty before he told me of the deadly feud that existed between him and Kirkstone, and it never troubled me much—because I didn't think anything would ever come of it—until Kirkstone got him. Then I realized that all through the years the old rattlesnake had been watching for his chance. It was a frame-up from beginning to end, and my father stepped into the trap. Even then he thought that his political enemies, and not Kirkstone, were at the bottom of it. We soon discovered the truth. My father got ten years. He was innocent. And the only man on earth who could prove his innocence was Kirkstone, the man who was gloating like a Shylock over his pound of flesh. Conniston, if you had known these things and had been in my shoes, what would you have done?"

Conniston, lighting another taper over the oil flame, hesitated and answered: "I don't know yet, old chap. What did you do?"

"I fairly got down on my knees to the scoundrel," resumed Keith. "If ever a man begged for another man's life, I begged for my father's—for the few words from Kirkstone that would set him free. I offered everything I had in the world, even my body and soul. God, I'll never forget that night! He sat there, fat and oily, two big rings on his stubby fingers—a monstrous toad in human form—and he chuckled and laughed at me in his joy, as though I were a mountebank playing amusing tricks for him—and there my soul was bleeding itself out before his eyes! And his son came in, fat and oily and accursed like his father, and HE laughed at me. I didn't know that such hatred could exist in the world, or that vengeance could bring such hellish joy. I could still hear their gloating laughter when I stumbled out into the night. It haunted me. I heard it in the trees. It came in the wind. My brain was filled with it—and suddenly I turned back, and I went into that house again without knocking, and I faced the two of them alone once more in that room. And this time, Conniston, I went back to get justice—or to kill. Thus far it was premeditated, but I went with my naked hands. There was a key in the door, and I locked it. Then I made my demand. I wasted no words—"

Keith rose from the table and began to pace back and forth. The wind had died again. They could hear the yapping of the foxes and the low thunder of the ice.

"The son began it," said Keith. "He sprang at me. I struck him. We grappled, and then the beast himself leaped at me with some sort of weapon in his hand. I couldn't see what it was, but it was heavy. The first blow almost broke my shoulder. In the scuffle I wrenched it from his hand, and then I found it was a long, rectangular bar of copper made for a paper-weight. In that same instant I saw the son snatch up a similar object from the table, and in the act he smashed the table light. In darkness we fought. I did not feel that I was fighting men. They were monsters and gave me the horrible sensation of being in darkness with crawling serpents. Yes, I struck hard. And the son was striking, and neither of us could see. I felt my weapon hit, and it was then that Kirkstone crumpled down with a blubbery wheeze. You know what happened after that. The next morning only one copper weight was found in that room. The son had done away with the other. And the one that was left was covered with Kirkstone's blood and hair. There was no chance for me. So I got away. Six months later my father died in prison, and for three years I've been hunted as a fox is hunted by the hounds. That's all, Conniston. Did I kill Judge Kirkstone? And, if I killed him, do you think I'm sorry for it, even though I hang?"

"Sit down!"

The Englishman's voice was commanding. Keith dropped back to his seat, breathing hard. He saw a strange light in the steely blue eyes of Conniston.

"Keith, when a man knows he's going to live, he is blind to a lot of things. But when he knows he's going to die, it's different. If you had told me that story a month ago, I'd have taken you down to the hangman just the same. It would have been my duty, you know, and I might have argued you were lying. But you can't lie to me—now. Kirkstone deserved to die. And so I've made up my mind what you're going to do. You're not going back to Coronation Gulf. You're going south. You're going back into God's country again. And you're not going as John Keith, the murderer, but as Derwent Conniston of His Majesty's Royal Northwest Mounted Police! Do you get me, Keith? Do you understand?"

Keith simply stared. The Englishman twisted a mustache, a half-humorous gleam in his eyes. He had been thinking of this plan of his for some time, and he had foreseen just how it would take Keith off his feet.

"Quite a scheme, don't you think, old chap? I like you. I don't mind saying I think a lot of you, and there isn't any reason on earth why you shouldn't go on living in my shoes. There's no moral objection. No one will miss me. I was the black sheep back in England—younger brother and all that—and when I had to choose between Africa and Canada, I chose Canada. An Englishman's pride is the biggest fool thing on earth, Keith, and I suppose all of them over there think I'm dead. They haven't heard from me in six or seven years. I'm forgotten. And the beautiful thing about this scheme is that we look so deucedly alike, you know. Trim that mustache and beard of yours a little, add a bit of a scar over your right eye, and you can walk in on old McDowell himself, and I'll wager he'll jump up and say, 'Bless my heart, if it isn't Conniston!' That's all I've got to leave you, Keith, a dead man's clothes and name. But you're welcome. They'll be of no more use to me after tomorrow."

"Impossible!" gasped Keith. "Conniston, do you know what you are saying?"

"Positively, old chap. I count every word, because it hurts when I talk. So you won't argue with me, please. It's the biggest sporting thing that's ever come my way. I'll be dead. You can bury me under this floor, where the foxes can't get at me. But my name will go on living and you'll wear my clothes back to civilization and tell McDowell how you got your man and how he died up here with a frosted lung. As proof of it you'll lug your own clothes down in a bundle along with any other little identifying things you may have, and there's a sergeancy waiting. McDowell promised it to you—if you got your man. Understand? And McDowell hasn't seen me for two years and three months, so if I MIGHT look a bit different to him, it would be natural, for you and I have been on the rough edge of the world all that time. The jolly good part of it all is that we look so much alike. I say the idea is splendid!"

Conniston rose above the presence of death in the thrill of the great gamble he was projecting. And Keith, whose heart was pounding like an excited fist, saw in a flash the amazing audacity of the thing that was in Conniston's mind, and felt the responsive thrill of its possibilities. No one down there would recognize in him the John Keith of four years ago. Then he was smooth-faced, with shoulders that stooped a little and a body that was not too strong. Now he was an animal! A four years' fight with the raw things of life had made him that, and inch for inch he measured up with Conniston. And Conniston, sitting opposite him, looked enough like him to be a twin brother. He seemed to read the thought in Keith's mind. There was an amused glitter in his eyes.

"I suppose it's largely because of the hair on our faces," he said. "You know a beard can cover a multitude of physical sins—and differences, old chap. I wore mine two years before I started out after you, vandyked rather carefully, you understand, so you'd better not use a razor. Physically you won't run a ghost of a chance of being caught. You'll look the part. The real fun is coming in other ways. In the next twenty-four hours you've got to learn by heart the history of Derwent Conniston from the day he joined the Royal Mounted. We won't go back further than that, for it wouldn't interest you, and ancient history won't turn up to trouble you. Your biggest danger will be with McDowell, commanding F Division at Prince Albert. He's a human fox of the old military school, mustaches and all, and he can see through boiler-plate. But he's got a big heart. He has been a good friend of mine, so along with Derwent Conniston's story you've got to load up with a lot about McDowell, too. There are many things—OH, GOD—"

He flung a hand to his chest. Grim horror settled in the little cabin as the cough convulsed him. And over it the wind shrieked again, swallowing up the yapping of the foxes and the rumble of the ice.

That night, in the yellow sputter of the seal-oil lamp, the fight began. Grim-faced—one realizing the nearness of death and struggling to hold it back, the other praying for time—two men went through the amazing process of trading their identities. From the beginning it was Conniston's fight. And Keith, looking at him, knew that in this last mighty effort to die game the Englishman was narrowing the slight margin of hours ahead of him. Keith had loved but one man, his father. In this fight he learned to love another, Conniston. And once he cried out bitterly that it was unfair, that Conniston should live and he should die. The dying Englishman smiled and laid a hand on his, and Keith felt that the hand was damp with a cold sweat.

Through the terrible hours that followed Keith felt the strength and courage of the dying man becoming slowly a part of himself. The thing was epic. Conniston, throttling his own agony, was magnificent. And Keith felt his warped and despairing soul swelling with a new life and a new hope, and he was thrilled by the thought of what he must do to live up to the mark of the Englishman. Conniston's story was of the important things first. It began with his acquaintance with McDowell. And then, between the paroxysms that stained his lips red, he filled in with incident and smiled wanly as he told how McDowell had sworn him to secrecy once in the matter of an incident which the chief did not want the barracks to know—and laugh over. A very sensitive man in some ways was McDowell! At the end of the first hour Keith stood up in the middle of the floor, and with his arms resting on the table and his shoulders sagging Conniston put him through the drill. After that he gave Keith his worn Service Manual and commanded him to study while he rested. Keith helped him to his bunk, and for a time after that tried to read the Service book. But his eyes blurred, and his brain refused to obey. The agony in the Englishman's low breathing oppressed him with a physical pain. Keith felt himself choking and rose at last from the table and went out into the gray, ghostly twilight of the night.

His lungs drank in the ice-tanged air. But it was not cold. Kwaske-hoo—the change—had come. The air was filled with the tumult of the last fight of winter against the invasion of spring, and the forces of winter were crumbling. The earth under Keith's feet trembled in the mighty throes of their dissolution. He could hear more clearly the roar and snarl and rending thunder of the great fields of ice as they swept down with the arctic current into Hudson's Bay. Over him hovered a strange night. It was not black but a weird and wraith-like gray, and out of this sepulchral chaos came strange sounds and the moaning of a wind high up. A little while longer, Keith thought, and the thing would have driven him mad. Even now he fancied he heard the screaming and wailing of voices far up under the hidden stars. More than once in the past months he had listened to the sobbing of little children, the agony of weeping women, and the taunting of wind voices that were either tormenting or crying out in a ghoulish triumph; and more than once in those months he had seen Eskimos—born in that hell but driven mad in the torture of its long night—rend the clothes from their bodies and plunge naked out into the pitiless gloom and cold to die. Conniston would never know how near the final breakdown his brain had been in that hour when he made him a prisoner. And Keith had not told him. The man-hunter had saved him from going mad. But Keith had kept that secret to himself.

Even now he shrank down as a blast of wind shot out of the chaos above and smote the cabin with a shriek that had in it a peculiarly penetrating note. And then he squared his shoulders and laughed, and the yapping of the foxes no longer filled him with a shuddering torment. Beyond them he was seeing home. God's country! Green forests and waters spattered with golden sun—things he had almost forgotten; once more the faces of women who were white. And with those faces he heard the voice of his people and the song of birds and felt under his feet the velvety touch of earth that was bathed in the aroma of flowers. Yes, he had almost forgotten those things. Yesterday they had been with him only as moldering skeletons— phantasmal dream-things—because he was going mad, but now they were real, they were just off there to the south, and he was going to them. He stretched up his arms, and a cry rose out of his throat. It was of triumph, of final exaltation. Three years of THAT—and he had lived through it! Three years of dodging from burrow to burrow, just as Conniston had said, like a hunted fox; three years of starvation, of freezing, of loneliness so great that his soul had broken—and now he was going home!

He turned again to the cabin, and when he entered the pale face of the dying Englishman greeted him from the dim glow of the yellow light at the table. And Conniston was smiling in a quizzical, distressed sort of way, with a hand at his chest. His open watch on the table pointed to the hour of midnight when the lesson went on.

Still later he heated the muzzle of his revolver in the flame of the seal-oil.

"It will hurt, old chap—putting this scar over your eye. But it's got to be done. I say, won't it be a ripping joke on McDowell?" Softly he repeated it, smiling into Keith's eyes. "A ripping joke—on McDowell!"

III

Dawn—the dusk of another night—and Keith raised his haggard face from Conniston's bedside with a woman's sob on his lips. The Englishman had died as he knew that he would die, game to the last threadbare breath that came out of his body. For with this last breath he whispered the words which he had repeated a dozen times before, "Remember, old chap, you win or lose the moment McDowell first sets his eyes on you!" And then, with a strange kind of sob in his chest, he was gone, and Keith's eyes were blinded by the miracle of a hot flood of tears, and there rose in him a mighty pride in the name of Derwent Conniston.

It was his name now. John Keith was dead. It was Derwent Conniston who was living. And as he looked down into the cold, still face of the heroic Englishman, the thing did not seem so strange to him after all. It would not be difficult to bear Conniston's name; the difficulty would be in living up to the Conniston code.

That night the rumble of the ice fields was clearer because there was no wind to deaden their tumult. The sky was cloudless, and the stars were like glaring, yellow eyes peering through holes in a vast, overhanging curtain of jet black. Keith, out to fill his lungs with air, looked up at the phenomenon of the polar night and shuddered. The stars were like living things, and they were looking at him. Under their sinister glow the foxes were holding high carnival. It seemed to Keith that they had drawn a closer circle about the cabin and that there was a different note in their yapping now, a note that was more persistent, more horrible. Conniston had foreseen that closing-in of the little white beasts of the night, and Keith, reentering the cabin, set about the fulfillment of his promise. Ghostly dawn found his task completed.

Half an hour later he stood in the edge of the scrub timber that rimmed in the arctic plain, and looked for the last time upon the little cabin under the floor of which the Englishman was buried. It stood there splendidly unafraid in its terrible loneliness, a proud monument to a dead man's courage and a dead man's soul. Within its four walls it treasured a thing which gave to it at last a reason for being, a reason for fighting against dissolution as long as one log could hold upon another. Conniston's spirit had become a living part of it, and the foxes might yap everlastingly, and the winds howl, and winter follow winter, and long night follow long night—and it would stand there in its pride fighting to the last, a memorial to Derwent Conniston, the Englishman.

Looking back at it, Keith bared his head in the raw dawn. "God bless you, Conniston," he whispered, and turned slowly away and into the south.

Ahead of him was eight hundred miles of wilderness—eight hundred miles between him and the little town on the Saskatchewan where McDowell commanded Division of the Royal Mounted. The thought of distance did not appall him. Four years at the top of the earth had accustomed him to the illimitable and had inured him to the lack of things. That winter Conniston had followed him with the tenacity of a ferret for a thousand miles along the rim of the Arctic, and it had been a miracle that he had not killed the Englishman. A score of times he might have ended the exciting chase without staining his own hands. His Eskimo friends would have performed the deed at a word. But he had let the Englishman live, and Conniston, dead, was sending him back home. Eight hundred miles was but the step between.

He had no dogs or sledge. His own team had given up the ghost long ago, and a treacherous Kogmollock from the Roes Welcome had stolen the Englishman's outfit in the last lap of their race down from Fullerton's Point. What he carried was Conniston's, with the exception of his rifle and his own parka and hood. He even wore Conniston's watch. His pack was light. The chief articles it contained were a little flour, a three-pound tent, a sleeping-bag, and certain articles of identification to prove the death of John Keith, the outlaw. Hour after hour of that first day the zip, zip, zip of his snowshoes beat with deadly monotony upon his brain. He could not think. Time and again it seemed to him that something was pulling him back, and always he was hearing Conniston's voice and seeing Conniston's face in the gray gloom of the day about him. He passed through the slim finger of scrub timber that a strange freak of nature had flung across the plain, and once more was a moving speck in a wide and wind-swept barren. In the afternoon he made out a dark rim on the southern horizon and knew it was timber, real timber, the first he had seen since that day, a year and a half ago, when the last of the Mackenzie River forest had faded away behind him! It gave him, at last, something tangible to grip. It was a thing beckoning to him, a sentient, living wall beyond which was his other world. The eight hundred miles meant less to him than the space between himself and that growing, black rim on the horizon.

He reached it as the twilight of the day was dissolving into the deeper dusk of the night, and put up his tent in the shelter of a clump of gnarled and storm-beaten spruce. Then he gathered wood and built himself a fire. He did not count the sticks as he had counted them for eighteen months. He was wasteful, prodigal. He had traveled forty miles since morning but he felt no exhaustion. He gathered wood until he had a great pile of it, and the flames of his fire leaped higher and higher until the spruce needles crackled and hissed over his head. He boiled a pot of weak tea and made a supper of caribou meat and a bit of bannock. Then he sat with his back to a tree and stared into the flames.

The fire leaping and crackling before his eyes was like a powerful medicine. It stirred things that had lain dormant within him. It consumed the heavy dross of four years of stupefying torture and brought back to him vividly the happenings of a yesterday that had dragged itself on like a century. All at once he seemed unburdened of shackles that had weighted him down to the point of madness. Every fiber in his body responded to that glorious roar of the fire; a thing seemed to snap in his head, freeing it of an oppressive bondage, and in the heart of the flames he saw home, and hope, and life—the things familiar and precious long ago, which the scourge of the north had almost beaten dead in his memory. He saw the broad Saskatchewan shimmering its way through the yellow plains, banked in by the foothills and the golden mists of morning dawn; he saw his home town clinging to its shore on one side and with its back against the purple wilderness on the other; he heard the rhythmic chug, chug, chug of the old gold dredge and the rattle of its chains as it devoured its tons of sand for a few grains of treasure; over him there were lacy clouds in a blue heaven again, he heard the sound of voices, the tread of feet, laughter—life. His soul reborn, he rose to his feet and stretched his arms until the muscles snapped. No, they would not know him back there—now! He laughed softly as he thought of the old John Keith—"Johnny" they used to call him up and down the few balsam-scented streets—his father's right-hand man mentally but a little off feed, as his chum, Reddy McTabb, used to say, when it came to the matter of muscle and brawn. He could look back on things without excitement now. Even hatred had burned itself out, and he found himself wondering if old Judge Kirkstone's house looked the same on the top of the hill, and if Miriam Kirkstone had come back to live there after that terrible night when he had returned to avenge his father.

Four years! It was not so very long, though the years had seemed like a lifetime to him. There would not be many changes. Everything would be the same—everything—except—the old home. That home he and his father had planned, and they had overseen the building of it, a chateau of logs a little distance from the town, with the Saskatchewan sweeping below it and the forest at its doors. Masterless, it must have seen changes in those four years. Fumbling in his pocket, his fingers touched Conniston's watch. He drew it out and let the firelight play on the open dial. It was ten o'clock. In the back of the premier half of the case Conniston had at some time or another pasted a picture. It must have been a long time ago, for the face was faded and indistinct. The eyes alone were undimmed, and in the flash of the fire they took on a living glow as they looked at Keith. It was the face of a young girl—a schoolgirl, Keith thought, of ten or twelve. Yet the eyes seemed older; they seemed pleading with someone, speaking a message that had come spontaneously out of the soul of the child. Keith closed the watch. Its tick, tick, tick rose louder to his ears. He dropped it in his pocket. He could still hear it.

A pitch-filled spruce knot exploded with the startling vividness of a star bomb, and with it came a dull sort of mental shock to Keith. He was sure that for an instant he had seen Conniston's face and that the Englishman's eyes were looking at him as the eyes had looked at him out of the face in the watch. The deception was so real that it sent him back a step, staring, and then, his eyes striving to catch the illusion again, there fell upon him a realization of the tremendous strain he had been under for many hours. It had been days since he had slept soundly. Yet he was not sleepy now; he scarcely felt fatigue. The instinct of self-preservation made him arrange his sleeping-bag on a carpet of spruce boughs in the tent and go to bed.

Even then, for a long time, he lay in the grip of a harrowing wakefulness. He closed his eyes, but it was impossible for him to hold them closed. The sounds of the night came to him with painful distinctness—the crackling of the fire, the serpent-like hiss of the flaming pitch, the whispering of the tree tops, and the steady tick, tick, tick of Conniston's watch. And out on the barren, through the rim of sheltering trees, the wind was beginning to moan its everlasting whimper and sob of loneliness. In spite of his clenched hands and his fighting determination to hold it off, Keith fancied that he heard again—riding strangely in that wind—the sound of Conniston's voice. And suddenly he asked himself: What did it mean? What was it that Conniston had forgotten? What was it that Conniston had been trying to tell him all that day, when he had felt the presence of him in the gloom of the Barrens? Was it that Conniston wanted him to come back?

He tried to rid himself of the depressing insistence of that thought. And yet he was certain that in the last half-hour before death entered the cabin the Englishman had wanted to tell him something and had crucified the desire. There was the triumph of an iron courage in those last words, "Remember, old chap, you win or lose the moment McDowell first sets his eyes on you!"—but in the next instant, as death sent home its thrust, Keith had caught a glimpse of Conniston's naked soul, and in that final moment when speech was gone forever, he knew that Conniston was fighting to make his lips utter words which he had left unspoken until too late. And Keith, listening to the moaning of the wind and the crackling of the fire, found himself repeating over and over again, "What was it he wanted to say?"

In a lull in the wind Conniston's watch seemed to beat like a heart in its case, and swiftly its tick, tick, ticked to his ears an answer, "Come back, come back, come back!"

With a cry at his own pitiable weakness, Keith thrust the thing far under his sleeping-bag, and there its sound was smothered. At last sleep overcame him like a restless anesthesia.

With the break of another day he came out of his tent and stirred the fire. There were still bits of burning ember, and these he fanned into life and added to their flame fresh fuel. He could not easily forget last night's torture, but its significance was gone. He laughed at his own folly and wondered what Conniston himself would have thought of his nervousness. For the first time in years he thought of the old days down at college where, among other things, he had made a mark for himself in psychology. He had considered himself an expert in the discussion and understanding of phenomena of the mind. Afterward he had lived up to the mark and had profited by his beliefs, and the fact that a simple relaxation of his mental machinery had so disturbed him last night amused him now. The solution was easy. It was his mind struggling to equilibrium after four years of brain-fag. And he felt better. His brain was clearer. He listened to the watch and found its ticking natural. He braced himself to another effort and whistled as he prepared his breakfast.

After that he packed his dunnage and continued south. He wondered if Conniston ever knew his Manual as he learned it now. At the end of the sixth day he could repeat it from cover to cover. Every hour he made it a practice to stop short and salute the trees about him. McDowell would not catch him there.

"I am Derwent Conniston," he kept telling himself. "John Keith is dead—dead. I buried him back there under the cabin, the cabin built by Sergeant Trossy and his patrol in nineteen hundred and eight. My name is Conniston—Derwent Conniston."

In his years of aloneness he had grown into the habit of talking to himself—or with himself—to keep up his courage and sanity. "Keith, old boy, we've got to fight it out," he would say. Now it was, "Conniston, old chap, we'll win or die." After the third day, he never spoke of John Keith except as a man who was dead. And over the dead John Keith he spread Conniston's mantle. "John Keith died game, sir," he said to McDowell, who was a tree. "He was the finest chap I ever knew."

On this sixth day came the miracle. For the first time in many months John Keith saw the sun. He had seen the murky glow of it before this, fighting to break through the pall of fog and haze that hung over the Barrens, but this sixth day it was the sun, the real sun, bursting in all its glory for a short space over the northern world. Each day after this the sun was nearer and warmer, as the arctic vapor clouds and frost smoke were left farther behind, and not until he had passed beyond the ice fogs entirely did Keith swing westward. He did not hurry, for now that he was out of his prison, he wanted time in which to feel the first exhilarating thrill of his freedom. And more than all else he knew that he must measure and test himself for the tremendous fight ahead of him.

Now that the sun and the blue sky had cleared his brain, he saw the hundred pit-falls in his way, the hundred little slips that might be made, the hundred traps waiting for any chance blunder on his part. Deliberately he was on his way to the hangman. Down there—every day of his life—he would rub elbows with him as he passed his fellow men in the street. He would never completely feel himself out of the presence of death. Day and night he must watch himself and guard himself, his tongue, his feet, his thoughts, never knowing in what hour the eyes of the law would pierce the veneer of his disguise and deliver his life as the forfeit. There were times when the contemplation of these things appalled him, and his mind turned to other channels of escape. And then—always—he heard Conniston's cool, fighting voice, and the red blood fired up in his veins, and he faced home.

He was Derwent Conniston. And never for an hour could he put out of his mind the one great mystifying question in this adventure of life and death, who was Derwent Conniston? Shred by shred he pieced together what little he knew, and always he arrived at the same futile end. An Englishman, dead to his family if he had one, an outcast or an expatriate—and the finest, bravest gentleman he had ever known. It was the WHYFORE of these things that stirred within him an emotion which he had never experienced before. The Englishman had grimly and determinedly taken his secret to the grave with him. To him, John Keith—who was now Derwent Conniston—he had left an heritage of deep mystery and the mission, if he so chose, of discovering who he was, whence he had come—and why. Often he looked at the young girl's picture in the watch, and always he saw in her eyes something which made him think of Conniston as he lay in the last hour of his life. Undoubtedly the girl had grown into a woman now.

Days grew into weeks, and under Keith's feet the wet, sweet-smelling earth rose up through the last of the slush snow. Three hundred miles below the Barrens, he was in the Reindeer Lake country early in May. For a week he rested at a trapper's cabin on the Burntwood, and after that set out for Cumberland House. Ten days later he arrived at the post, and in the sunlit glow of the second evening afterward he built his camp-fire on the shore of the yellow Saskatchewan.

The mighty river, beloved from the days of his boyhood, sang to him again, that night, the wonderful things that time and grief had dimmed in his heart. The moon rose over it, a warm wind drifted out of the south, and Keith, smoking his pipe, sat for a long time listening to the soft murmur of it as it rolled past at his feet. For him it had always been more than the river. He had grown up with it, and it had become a part of him; it had mothered his earliest dreams and ambitions; on it he had sought his first adventures; it had been his chum, his friend, and his comrade, and the fancy struck him that in the murmuring voice of it tonight there was a gladness, a welcome, an exultation in his return. He looked out on its silvery bars shimmering in the moonlight, and a flood of memories swept upon him. Thirty years was not so long ago that he could not remember the beautiful mother who had told him stories as the sun went down and bedtime drew near. And vividly there stood out the wonderful tales of Kistachiwun, the river; how it was born away over in the mystery of the western mountains, away from the eyes and feet of men; how it came down from the mountains into the hills, and through the hills into the plains, broadening and deepening and growing mightier with every mile, until at last it swept past their door, bearing with it the golden grains of sand that made men rich. His father had pointed out the deep-beaten trails of buffalo to him and had told him stories of the Indians and of the land before white men came, so that between father and mother the river became his book of fables, his wonderland, the never-ending source of his treasured tales of childhood. And tonight the river was the one thing left to him. It was the one friend he could claim again, the one comrade he could open his arms to without fear of betrayal. And with the grief for things that once had lived and were now dead, there came over him a strange sort of happiness, the spirit of the great river itself giving him consolation.

Stretching out his arms, he cried: "My old river—it's me—Johnny Keith! I've come back!"

And the river, whispering, seemed to answer him: "It's Johnny Keith! And he's come back! He's come back!"

IV

For a week John Keith followed up the shores of the Saskatchewan. It was a hundred and forty miles from the Hudson's Bay Company's post of Cumberland House to Prince Albert as the crow would fly, but Keith did not travel a homing line. Only now and then did he take advantage of a portage trail. Clinging to the river, his journey was lengthened by some sixty miles. Now that the hour for which Conniston had prepared him was so close at hand, he felt the need of this mighty, tongueless friend that had played such an intimate part in his life. It gave to him both courage and confidence, and in its company he could think more clearly. Nights he camped on its golden-yellow bars with the open stars over his head when he slept; his ears drank in the familiar sounds of long ago, for which he had yearned to the point of madness in his exile—the soft cries of the birds that hunted and mated in the glow of the moon, the friendly twit, twit, twit of the low-flying sand-pipers, the hoot of the owls, and the splash and sleepy voice of wildfowl already on their way up from the south. Out of that south, where in places the plains swept the forest back almost to the river's edge, he heard now and then the doglike barking of his little yellow friends of many an exciting horseback chase, the coyotes, and on the wilderness side, deep in the forest, the sinister howling of wolves. He was traveling, literally, the narrow pathway between two worlds. The river was that pathway. On the one hand, not so very far away, were the rolling prairies, green fields of grain, settlements and towns and the homes of men; on the other the wilderness lay to the water's edge with its doors still open to him. The seventh day a new sound came to his ears at dawn. It was the whistle of a train at Prince Albert.

There was no change in that whistle, and every nerve-string in his body responded to it with crying thrill. It was the first voice to greet his home-coming, and the sound of it rolled the yesterdays back upon him in a deluge. He knew where he was now; he recalled exactly what he would find at the next turn in the river. A few minutes later he heard the wheezy chug, chug, chug of the old gold dredge at McCoffin's Bend. It would be the Betty M., of course, with old Andy Duggan at the windlass, his black pipe in mouth, still scooping up the shifting sands as he had scooped them up for more than twenty years. He could see Andy sitting at his post, clouded in a halo of tobacco smoke, a red-bearded, shaggy-headed giant of a man whom the town affectionately called the River Pirate. All his life Andy had spent in digging gold out of the mountains or the river, and like grim death he had hung to the bars above and below McCoffin's Bend. Keith smiled as he remembered old Andy's passion for bacon. One could always find the perfume of bacon about the Betty M., and when Duggan went to town, there were those who swore they could smell it in his whiskers.

Keith left the river trail now for the old logging road. In spite of his long fight to steel himself for what Conniston had called the "psychological moment," he felt himself in the grip of an uncomfortable mental excitement. At last he was face to face with the great gamble. In a few hours he would play his one card. If he won, there was life ahead of him again, if he lost—death. The old question which he had struggled to down surged upon him. Was it worth the chance? Was it in an hour of madness that he and Conniston had pledged themselves to this amazing adventure? The forest was still with him. He could turn back. The game had not yet gone so far that he could not withdraw his hand—and for a space a powerful impulse moved him. And then, coming suddenly to the edge of the clearing at McCoffin's Bend, he saw the dredge close inshore, and striding up from the beach Andy Duggan himself! In another moment Keith had stepped forth and was holding up a hand in greeting.

He felt his heart thumping in an unfamiliar way as Duggan came on. Was it conceivable that the riverman would not recognize him? He forgot his beard, forgot the great change that four years had wrought in him. He remembered only that Duggan had been his friend, that a hundred times they had sat together in the quiet glow of long evenings, telling tales of the great river they both loved. And always Duggan's stories had been of that mystic paradise hidden away in the western mountains—the river's end, the paradise of golden lure, where the Saskatchewan was born amid towering peaks, and where Duggan—a long time ago—had quested for the treasure which he knew was hidden somewhere there. Four years had not changed Duggan. If anything his beard was redder and thicker and his hair shaggier than when Keith had last seen him. And then, following him from the Betsy M., Keith caught the everlasting scent of bacon. He devoured it in deep breaths. His soul cried out for it. Once he had grown tired of Duggan's bacon, but now he felt that he could go on eating it forever. As Duggan advanced, he was moved by a tremendous desire to stretch out his hand and say: "I'm John Keith. Don't you know me, Duggan?" Instead, he choked back his desire and said, "Fine morning!"

Duggan nodded uncertainly. He was evidently puzzled at not being able to place his man. "It's always fine on the river, rain 'r shine. Anybody who says it ain't is a God A'mighty liar!"

He was still the old Duggan, ready to fight for his river at the drop of a hat! Keith wanted to hug him. He shifted his pack and said:

"I've slept with it for a week—just to have it for company—on the way down from Cumberland House. Seems good to get back!" He took off his hat and met the riverman's eyes squarely. "Do you happen to know if McDowell is at barracks?" he asked.

"He is," said Duggan.

That was all. He was looking at Keith with a curious directness. Keith held his breath. He would have given a good deal to have seen behind Duggan's beard. There was a hard note in the riverman's voice, too. It puzzled him. And there was a flash of sullen fire in his eyes at the mention of McDowell's name. "The Inspector's there—sittin' tight," he added, and to Keith's amazement brushed past him without another word and disappeared into the bush.

This, at least, was not like the good-humored Duggan of four years ago. Keith replaced his hat and went on. At the farther side of the clearing he turned and looked back. Duggan stood in the open roadway, his hands thrust deep in his pockets, staring after him. Keith waved his hand, but Duggan did not respond. He stood like a sphinx, his big red beard glowing in the early sun, and watched Keith until he was gone.

To Keith this first experiment in the matter of testing an identity was a disappointment. It was not only disappointing but filled him with apprehension. It was true that Duggan had not recognized him as John Keith, BUT NEITHER HAD HE RECOGNIZED HIM AS DERWENT CONNISTON! And Duggan was not a man to forget in three or four years—or half a lifetime, for that matter. He saw himself facing a new and unexpected situation. What if McDowell, like Duggan, saw in him nothing more than a stranger? The Englishman's last words pounded in his head again like little fists beating home a truth, "You win or lose the moment McDowell first sets his eyes on you." They pressed upon him now with a deadly significance. For the first time he understood all that Conniston had meant. His danger was not alone in the possibility of being recognized as John Keith; it lay also in the hazard of NOT being recognized as Derwent Conniston.

If the thought had come to him to turn back, if the voice of fear and a premonition of impending evil had urged him to seek freedom in another direction, their whispered cautions were futile in the thrill of the greater excitement that possessed him now. That there was a third hand playing in this game of chance in which Conniston had already lost his life, and in which he was now staking his own, was something which gave to Keith a new and entirely unlooked-for desire to see the end of the adventure. The mental vision of his own certain fate, should he lose, dissolved into a nebulous presence that no longer oppressed nor appalled him. Physical instinct to fight against odds, the inspiration that presages the uncertainty of battle, fired his blood with an exhilarating eagerness. He was anxious to stand face to face with McDowell. Not until then would the real fight begin. For the first time the fact seized upon him that the Englishman was wrong—he would NOT win or lose in the first moment of the Inspector's scrutiny. In that moment he could lose—McDowell's cleverly trained eyes might detect the fraud; but to win, if the game was not lost at the first shot, meant an exciting struggle. Today might be his Armageddon, but it could not possess the hour of his final triumph.

He felt himself now like a warrior held in leash within sound of the enemy's guns and the smell of his powder. He held his old world to be his enemy, for civilization meant people, and the people were the law—and the law wanted his life. Never had he possessed a deeper hatred for the old code of an eye for an eye and a tooth for a tooth than in this hour when he saw up the valley a gray mist of smoke rising over the roofs of his home town. He had never conceded within himself that he was a criminal. He believed that in killing Kirkstone he had killed a serpent who had deserved to die, and a hundred times he had told himself that the job would have been much more satisfactory from the view-point of human sanitation if he had sent the son in the father's footsteps. He had rid the people of a man not fit to live—and the people wanted to kill him for it. Therefore the men and women in that town he had once loved, and still loved, were his enemies, and to find friends among them again he was compelled to perpetrate a clever fraud.

He remembered an unboarded path from this side of the town, which entered an inconspicuous little street at the end of which was a barber shop. It was the barber shop which he must reach first He was glad that it was early in the day when he came to the street an hour later, for he would meet few people. The street had changed considerably. Long, open spaces had filled in with houses, and he wondered if the anticipated boom of four years ago had come. He smiled grimly as the humor of the situation struck him. His father and he had staked their future in accumulating a lot of "outside" property. If the boom had materialized, that property was "inside" now—and worth a great deal. Before he reached the barber shop he realized that the dream of the Prince Albertites had come true. Prosperity had advanced upon them in mighty leaps. The population of the place had trebled. He was a rich man! And also, it occurred to him, he was a dead one—or would be when he reported officially to McDowell. What a merry scrap there would be among the heirs of John Keith, deceased!

The old shop still clung to its corner, which was valuable as "business footage" now. But it possessed a new barber. He was alone. Keith gave his instructions in definite detail and showed him Conniston's photograph in his identification book. The beard and mustache must be just so, very smart, decidedly English, and of military neatness, his hair cut not too short and brushed smoothly back. When the operation was over, he congratulated the barber and himself. Bronzed to the color of an Indian by wind and smoke, straight as an arrow, his muscles swelling with the brute strength of the wilderness, he smiled at himself in the mirror when he compared the old John Keith with this new Derwent Conniston! Before he went out he tightened his belt a notch. Then he headed straight for the barracks of His Majesty's Royal Northwest Mounted Police.

His way took him up the main street, past the rows of shops that had been there four years ago, past the Saskatchewan Hotel and the little Board of Trade building which, like the old barber shop, still hung to its original perch at the edge of the high bank which ran precipitously down to the river. And there, as sure as fate, was Percival Clary, the little English Secretary! But what a different Percy!

He had broadened out and straightened up. He had grown a mustache, which was immaculately waxed. His trousers were immaculately creased, his shoes were shining, and he stood before the door of his now important office resting lightly on a cane. Keith grinned as he witnessed how prosperity had bolstered up Percival along with the town. His eyes quested for familiar faces as he went along. Here and there he saw one, but for the most part he encountered strangers, lively looking men who were hustling as if they had a mission in hand. Glaring real estate signs greeted him from every place of prominence, and automobiles began to hum up and down the main street that stretched along the river—twenty where there had been one not so long ago.

Keith found himself fighting to keep his eyes straight ahead when he met a girl or a woman. Never had he believed fully and utterly in the angelhood of the feminine until now. He passed perhaps a dozen on the way to barracks, and he was overwhelmed with the desire to stop and feast his eyes upon each one of them. He had never been a lover of women; he admired them, he believed them to be the better part of man, he had worshiped his mother, but his heart had been neither glorified nor broken by a passion for the opposite sex. Now, to the bottom of his soul, he worshiped that dozen! Some of them were homely, some of them were plain, two or three of them were pretty, but to Keith their present physical qualifications made no difference. They were white women, and they were glorious, every one of them! The plainest of them was lovely. He wanted to throw up his hat and shout in sheer joy. Four years—and now he was back in angel land! For a space he forgot McDowell.

His head was in a whirl when he came to barracks. Life was good, after all. It was worth fighting for, and he was bound fight. He went straight to McDowell's office. A moment after his knock on the door the Inspector's secretary appeared.

"The Inspector is busy, sir," he said in response to Keith's inquiry. "I'll tell him—"

"That I am here on a very important matter," advised Keith. "He will admit me when you tell him that I bring information regarding a certain John Keith."

The secretary disappeared through an inner door. It seemed not more than ten seconds before he was back. "The Inspector will see you, sir."

Keith drew a deep breath to quiet the violent beating of his heart. In spite of all his courage he felt upon him the clutch of a cold and foreboding hand, a hand that seemed struggling to drag him back. And again he heard Conniston's dying voice whispering to him, "REMEMBER, OLD CHAP, YOU WIN OR LOSE THE MOMENT MCDOWELL FIRST SETS HIS EYES ON YOU!"

Was Conniston right?

Win or lose, he would play the game as the Englishman would have played it. Squaring his shoulders he entered to face McDowell, the cleverest man-hunter in the Northwest.

V

Keith's first vision, as he entered the office of the Inspector of Police, was not of McDowell, but of a girl. She sat directly facing him as he advanced through the door, the light from a window throwing into strong relief her face and hair. The effect was unusual. She was strikingly handsome. The sun, giving to the room a soft radiance, lit up her hair with shimmering gold; her eyes, Keith saw, were a clear and wonderful gray—and they stared at him as he entered, while the poise of her body and the tenseness of her face gave evidence of sudden and unusual emotion. These things Keith observed in a flash; then he turned toward McDowell.

The Inspector sat behind a table covered with maps and papers, and instantly Keith was conscious of the penetrating inquisition of his gaze. He felt, for an instant, the disquieting tremor of the criminal. Then he met McDowell's eyes squarely. They were, as Conniston had warned him, eyes that could see through boiler-plate. Of an indefinable color and deep set behind shaggy, gray eyebrows, they pierced him through at the first glance. Keith took in the carefully waxed gray mustaches, the close-cropped gray hair, the rigidly set muscles of the man's face, and saluted.

He felt creeping over him a slow chill. There was no greeting in that iron-like countenance, for full a quarter-minute no sign of recognition. And then, as the sun had played in the girl's hair, a new emotion passed over McDowell's face, and Keith saw for the first time the man whom Derwent Conniston had known as a friend as well as a superior. He rose from his chair, and leaning over the table said in a voice in which were mingled both amazement and pleasure:

"We were just talking about the devil—and here you are, sir! Conniston, how are you?"

For a few moments Keith did not see. HE HAD WON! The blood pounded through his heart so violently that it confused his vision and his senses. He felt the grip of McDowell's hand; he heard his voice; a vision swam before his eyes—and it was the vision of Derwent Conniston's triumphant face. He was standing erect, his head was up, he was meeting McDowell shoulder to shoulder, even smiling, but in that swift surge of exultation he did not know. McDowell, still gripping his hand and with his other hand on his arm, was wheeling him about, and he found the girl on her feet, staring at him as if he had newly risen from the dead.

McDowell's military voice was snapping vibrantly, "Conniston, meet Miss Miriam Kirkstone, daughter of Judge Kirkstone!"

He bowed and held for a moment in his own the hand of the girl whose father he had killed. It was lifeless and cold. Her lips moved, merely speaking his name. His own were mute. McDowell was saying something about the glory of the service and the sovereignty of the law. And then, breaking in like the beat of a drum on the introduction, his voice demanded, "Conniston—DID YOU GET YOUR MAN?"

The question brought Keith to his senses. He inclined his head slightly and said, "I beg to report that John Keith is dead, sir."

He saw Miriam Kirkstone give a visible start, as if his words had carried a stab. She was apparently making a strong effort to hide her agitation as she turned swiftly away from him, speaking to McDowell.

"You have been very kind, Inspector McDowell. I hope very soon to have the pleasure of talking with Mr. Conniston—about—John Keith."

She left them, nodding slightly to Keith.

When she was gone, a puzzled look filled the Inspector's eyes. "She has been like that for the last six months," he explained. "Tremendously interested in this man Keith and his fate. I don't believe that I have watched for your return more anxiously than she has, Conniston. And the curious part of it is she seemed to have no interest in the matter at all until six months ago. Sometimes I am afraid that brooding over her father's death has unsettled her a little. A mighty pretty girl, Conniston. A mighty pretty girl, indeed! And her brother is a skunk. Pst! You haven't forgotten him?"

He drew a chair up close to his own and motioned Keith to be seated. "You're changed, Conniston!"

The words came out of him like a shot. So unexpected were they that Keith felt the effect of them in every nerve of his body. He sensed instantly what McDowell meant. He was NOT like the Englishman; he lacked his mannerisms, his cool and superior suavity, the inimitable quality of his nerve and sportsmanship. Even as he met the disquieting directness of the Inspector's eyes, he could see Conniston sitting in his place, rolling his mustache between his forefinger and thumb, and smiling as though he had gone into the north but yesterday and had returned today. That was what McDowell was missing in him, the soul of Conniston himself— Conniston, the ne plus ultra of presence and amiable condescension, the man who could look the Inspector or the High Commissioner himself between the eyes, and, serenely indifferent to Service regulations, say, "Fine morning, old top!" Keith was not without his own sense of humor. How the Englishman's ghost must be raging if it was in the room at the present moment! He grinned and shrugged his shoulders.

"Were you ever up there—through the Long Night—alone?" he asked. "Ever been through six months of living torture with the stars leering at you and the foxes barking at you all the time, fighting to keep yourself from going mad? I went through that twice to get John Keith, and I guess you're right. I'm changed. I don't think I'll ever be the same again. Something—has gone. I can't tell what it is, but I feel it. I guess only half of me pulled through. It killed John Keith. Rotten, isn't it?"

He felt that he had made a lucky stroke. McDowell pulled out a drawer from under the table and thrust a box of fat cigars under his nose.

"Light up, Derry—light up and tell us what happened. Bless my soul, you're not half dead! A week in the old town will straighten you out."

He struck a match and held it to the tip of Keith's cigar.

For an hour thereafter Keith told the story of the man-hunt. It was his Iliad. He could feel the presence of Conniston as words fell from his lips; he forgot the presence of the stern-faced man who was watching him and listening to him; he could see once more only the long months and years of that epic drama of one against one, of pursuit and flight, of hunger and cold, of the Long Nights filled with the desolation of madness and despair. He triumphed over himself, and it was Conniston who spoke from within him. It was the Englishman who told how terribly John Keith had been punished, and when he came to the final days in the lonely little cabin in the edge of the Barrens, Keith finished with a choking in his throat, and the words, "And that was how John Keith died—a gentleman and a MAN!"

He was thinking of the Englishman, of the calm and fearless smile in his eyes as he died, of his last words, the last friendly grip of his hand, and McDowell saw the thing as though he had faced it himself. He brushed a hand over his face as if to wipe away a film. For some moments after Keith had finished, he stood with his back to the man who he thought was Conniston, and his mind was swiftly adding twos and twos and fours and fours as he looked away into the green valley of the Saskatchewan. He was the iron man when he turned to Keith again, the law itself, merciless and potent, by some miracle turned into the form of human flesh.

"After two and a half years of THAT even a murderer must have seemed like a saint to you, Conniston. You have done your work splendidly. The whole story shall go to the Department, and if it doesn't bring you a commission, I'll resign. But we must continue to regret that John Keith did not live to be hanged."

"He has paid the price," said Keith dully.

"No, he has not paid the price, not in full. He merely died. It could have been paid only at the end of a rope. His crime was atrociously brutal, the culmination of a fiend's desire for revenge. We will wipe off his name. But I can not wipe away the regret. I would sacrifice a year of my life if he were in this room with you now. It would be worth it. God, what a thing for the Service—to have brought John Keith back to justice after four years!"

He was rubbing his hands and smiling at Keith even as he spoke. His eyes had taken on a filmy glitter. The law! It stood there, without heart or soul, coveting the life that had escaped it. A feeling of revulsion swept over Keith.

A knock came at the door.

McDowell's voice gave permission, and the door slowly opened. Cruze, the young secretary, thrust in his head.

"Shan Tung is waiting, sir," he said.

An invisible hand reached up suddenly and gripped at Keith's throat. He turned aside to conceal what his face might have betrayed. Shan Tung! He knew what it was now that had pulled him back, he knew why Conniston's troubled face had traveled with him over the Barrens, and there surged over him with a sickening foreboding, a realization of what it was that Conniston had remembered and wanted to tell him—when it was too late. THEY HAD FORGOTTEN SHAN TUNG, THE CHINAMAN!

VI

In the hall beyond the secretary's room Shan Tung waited. As McDowell was the iron and steel embodiment of the law, so Shan Tung was the flesh and blood spirit of the mysticism and immutability of his race. His face was the face of an image made of an unemotional living tissue in place of wood or stone, dispassionate, tolerant, patient. What passed in the brain behind his yellow-tinged eyes only Shan Tung knew. It was his secret. And McDowell had ceased to analyze or attempt to understand him. The law, baffled in its curiosity, had come to accept him as a weird and wonderful mechanism—a thing more than a man—possessed of an unholy power. This power was the oriental's marvelous ability to remember faces. Once Shan Tung looked at a face, it was photographed in his memory for years. Time and change could not make him forget—and the law made use of him.

Briefly McDowell had classified him at Headquarters. "Either an exiled prime minister of China or the devil in a yellow skin," he had written to the Commissioner. "Correct age unknown and past history a mystery. Dropped into Prince Albert in 1908 wearing diamonds and patent leather shoes. A stranger then and a stranger now. Proprietor and owner of the Shan Tung Cafe. Educated, soft-spoken, womanish, but the one man on earth I'd hate to be in a dark room with, knives drawn. I use him, mistrust him, watch him, and would fear him under certain conditions. As far as we can discover, he is harmless and law-abiding. But such a ferret must surely have played his game somewhere, at some time."

This was the man whom Conniston had forgotten and Keith now dreaded to meet. For many minutes Shan Tung had stood at a window looking out upon the sunlit drillground and the broad sweep of green beyond. He was toying with his slim hands caressingly. Half a smile was on his lips. No man had ever seen more than that half smile illuminate Shan Tung's face. His black hair was sleek and carefully trimmed. His dress was immaculate. His slimness, as McDowell had noted, was the slimness of a young girl.

When Cruze came to announce that McDowell would see him, Shan Tung was still visioning the golden-headed figure of Miriam Kirkstone as he had seen her passing through the sunshine. There was something like a purr in his breath as he stood interlacing his tapering fingers. The instant he heard the secretary's footsteps the finger play stopped, the purr died, the half smile was gone. He turned softly. Cruze did not speak. He simply made a movement of his head, and Shan Tung's feet fell noiselessly. Only the slight sound made by the opening and closing of a door gave evidence of his entrance into the Inspector's room. Shan Tung and no other could open and close a door like that. Cruze shivered. He always shivered when Shan Tung passed him, and always he swore that he could smell something in the air, like a poison left behind.

Keith, facing the window, was waiting. The moment the door was opened, he felt Shan Tung's presence. Every nerve in his body was keyed to an uncomfortable tension. The thought that his grip on himself was weakening, and because of a Chinaman, maddened him. And he must turn. Not to face Shan Tung now would be but a postponement of the ordeal and a confession of cowardice. Forcing his hand into Conniston's little trick of twisting a mustache, he turned slowly, leveling his eyes squarely to meet Shan Tung's.

To his surprise Shan Tung seemed utterly oblivious of his presence. He had not, apparently, taken more than a casual glance in his direction. In a voice which one beyond the door might have mistaken for a woman's, he was saying to McDowell:

"I have seen the man you sent me to see, Mr. McDowell. It is Larsen. He has changed much in eight years. He has grown a beard. He has lost an eye. His hair has whitened. But it is Larsen." The faultlessness of his speech and the unemotional but perfect inflection of his words made Keith, like the young secretary, shiver where he stood. In McDowell's face he saw a flash of exultation.

"He had no suspicion of you, Shan Tung?"

"He did not see me to suspect. He will be there—when—" Slowly he faced Keith. "—When Mr. Conniston goes to arrest him," he finished.

He inclined his head as he backed noiselessly toward the door. His yellow eyes did not leave Keith's face. In them Keith fancied that he caught a sinister gleam. There was the faintest inflection of a new note in his voice, and his fingers were playing again, but not as when he had looked out through the window at Miriam Kirkstone. And then—in a flash, it seemed to Keith—the Chinaman's eyes closed to narrow slits, and the pupils became points of flame no larger than the sharpened ends of a pair of pencils. The last that Keith was conscious of seeing of Shan Tung was the oriental's eyes. They had seemed to drag his soul half out of his body.

"A queer devil," said McDowell. "After he is gone, I always feel as if a snake had been in the room. He still hates you, Conniston. Three years have made no difference. He hates you like poison. I believe he would kill you, if he had a chance to do it and get away with the Business. And you—you blooming idiot—simply twiddle your mustache and laugh at him! I'd feel differently if I were in your boots."

Inwardly Keith was asking himself why it was that Shan Tung had hated Conniston.

McDowell added nothing to enlighten him. He was gathering up a number of papers scattered on his desk, smiling with a grim satisfaction. "It's Larsen all right if Shan Tung says so," he told Keith. And then, as if he had only thought of the matter, he said, "You're going to reenlist, aren't you, Conniston?"

"I still owe the Service a month or so before my term expires, don't I? After that—yes—I believe I shall reenlist."

"Good!" approved the Inspector. "I'll have you a sergeancy within a month. Meanwhile you're off duty and may do anything you please. You know Brady, the Company agent? He's up the Mackenzie on a trip, and here's the key to his shack. I know you'll appreciate getting under a real roof again, and Brady won't object as long as I collect his thirty dollars a month rent. Of course Barracks is open to you, but it just occurred to me you might prefer this place while on furlough. Everything is there from a bathtub to nutcrackers, and I know a little Jap in town who is hunting a job as a cook. What do you say?"

"Splendid!" cried Keith. "I'll go up at once, and if you'll hustle the Jap along, I'll appreciate it. You might tell him to bring up stuff for dinner," he added.

McDowell gave him a key. Ten minutes later he was out of sight of barracks and climbing a green slope that led to Brady's bungalow.

In spite of the fact that he had not played his part brilliantly, he believed that he had scored a triumph. Andy Duggan had not recognized him, and the riverman had been one of his most intimate friends. McDowell had accepted him apparently without a suspicion. And Shan Tung—

It was Shan Tung who weighed heavily upon his mind, even as his nerves tingled with the thrill of success. He could not get away from the vision of the Chinaman as he had backed through the Inspector's door, the flaming needle-points of his eyes piercing him as he went. It was not hatred he had seen in Shan Tung's face. He was sure of that. It was no emotion that he could describe. It was as if a pair of mechanical eyes fixed in the head of an amazingly efficient mechanical monster had focused themselves on him in those few instants. It made him think of an X-ray machine. But Shan Tung was human. And he was clever. Given another skin, one would not have taken him for what he was. The immaculateness of his speech and manners was more than unusual; it was positively irritating, something which no Chinaman should rightfully possess. So argued Keith as he went up to Brady's bungalow.

He tried to throw off the oppression of the thing that was creeping over him, the growing suspicion that he had not passed safely under the battery of Shan Tung's eyes. With physical things he endeavored to thrust his mental uneasiness into the background. He lighted one of the half-dozen cigars McDowell had dropped into his pocket. It was good to feel a cigar between his teeth again and taste its flavor. At the crest of the slope on which Brady's bungalow stood, he stopped and looked about him. Instinctively his eyes turned first to the west. In that direction half of the town lay under him, and beyond its edge swept the timbered slopes, the river, and the green pathways of the plains. His heart beat a little faster as he looked. Half a mile away was a tiny, parklike patch of timber, and sheltered there, with the river running under it, was the old home. The building was hidden, but through a break in the trees he could see the top of the old red brick chimney glowing in the sun, as if beckoning a welcome to him over the tree tops. He forgot Shan Tung; he forgot McDowell; he forgot that he was John Keith, the murderer, in the overwhelming sea of loneliness that swept over him. He looked out into the world that had once been his, and all that he saw was that red brick chimney glowing in the sun, and the chimney changed until at last it seemed to him like a tombstone rising over the graves of the dead. He turned to the door of the bungalow with a thickening in his throat and his eyes filmed by a mist through which for a few moments it was difficult for him to see.

The bungalow was darkened by drawn curtains when he entered. One after another he let them up, and the sun poured in. Brady had left his place in order, and Keith felt about him an atmosphere of cheer that was a mighty urge to his flagging spirits. Brady was a home man without a wife. The Company's agent had called his place "The Shack" because it was built entirely of logs, and a woman could not have made it more comfortable. Keith stood in the big living-room. At one end was a strong fireplace in which kindlings and birch were already laid, waiting the touch of a match. Brady's reading table and his easy chair were drawn up close; his lounging moccasins were on a footstool; pipes, tobacco, books and magazines littered the table; and out of this cheering disorder rose triumphantly the amber shoulder of a half-filled bottle of Old Rye.

Keith found himself chuckling. His grin met the lifeless stare of a pair of glass eyes in the huge head of an old bull moose over the mantel, and after that his gaze rambled over the walls ornamented with mounted heads, pictures, snowshoes, gun-racks and the things which went to make up the comradeship and business of Brady's picturesque life. Keith could look through into the little dining-room, and beyond that was the kitchen. He made an inventory of both and found that McDowell was right. There were nutcrackers in Brady's establishment. And he found the bathroom. It was not much larger than a piano box, but the tub was man's size, and Keith raised a window and poked his head out to find that it was connected with a rainwater tank built by a genius, just high enough to give weight sufficient for a water system and low enough to gather the rain as it fell from the eaves. He laughed outright, the sort of laugh that comes out of a man's soul not when he is amused but when he is pleased. By the time he had investigated the two bedrooms, he felt a real affection for Brady. He selected the agent's room for his own. Here, too, were pipes and tobacco and books and magazines, and a reading lamp on a table close to the bedside. Not until he had made a closer inspection of the living-room did he discover that the Shack also had a telephone.

By that time he noted that the sun had gone out. Driving up from the west was a mass of storm clouds. He unlocked a door from which he could look up the river, and the wind that was riding softly in advance of the storm ruffled his hair and cooled his face. In it he caught again the old fancy—the smells of the vast reaches of unpeopled prairie beyond the rim of the forest, and the luring chill of the distant mountain tops. Always storm that came down with the river brought to him voice from the river's end. It came to him from the great mountains that were a passion with him; it seemed to thunder to him the old stories of the mightiest fastnesses of the Rockies and stirred in him the child-bred yearning to follow up his beloved river until he came at last to the mystery of its birthplace in the cradle of the western ranges. And now, as he faced the storm, the grip of that desire held him like a strong hand.

The sky blackened swiftly, and with the rumbling of far-away thunder he saw the lightning slitting the dark heaven like bayonets, and the fire of the electrical charges galloped to him and filled his veins. His heart all at once cried out words that his lips did not utter. Why should he not answer the call that had come to him through all the years? Now was the time—and why should he not go? Why tempt fate in the hazard of a great adventure where home and friends and even hope were dead to him, when off there beyond the storm was the place of his dreams?

He threw out his arms. His voice broke at last in a cry of strange ecstasy. Not everything was gone! Not everything was dead! Over the graveyard of his past there was sweeping a mighty force that called him, something that was no longer merely an urge and a demand but a thing that was irresistible. He would go! Tomorrow—today—tonight—he would begin making plans!

He watched the deluge as it came on with a roar of wind, a beating, hissing wall under which the tree tops down in the edge of the plain bent their heads like a multitude of people in prayer. He saw it sweeping up the slope in a mass of gray dragoons. It caught him before he had closed the door, and his face dripped with wet as he forced the last inch of it against the wind with his shoulder. It was the sort of storm Keith liked. The thunder was the rumble of a million giant cartwheels rolling overhead.

Inside the bungalow it was growing dark as though evening had come. He dropped on his knees before the pile of dry fuel in the fireplace and struck a match. For a space the blaze smoldered; then the birch fired up like oil-soaked tinder, and a yellow flame crackled and roared up the flue. Keith was sensitive in the matter of smoking other people's pipes, so he drew out his own and filled it with Brady's tobacco. It was an English mixture, rich and aromatic, and as the fire burned brighter and the scent of the tobacco filled the room, he dropped into Brady's big lounging chair and stretched out his legs with a deep breath of satisfaction. His thoughts wandered to the clash of the storm. He would have a place like this out there in the mystery of the trackless mountains, where the Saskatchewan was born. He would build it like Brady's place, even to the rain-water tank midway between the roof and the ground. And after a few years no one would remember that a man named John Keith had ever lived.

Something brought him suddenly to his feet. It was the ringing of the telephone. After four years the sound was one that roused with an uncomfortable jump every nerve in his body. Probably it was McDowell calling up about the Jap or to ask how he liked the place. Probably—it was that. He repeated the thought aloud as he laid his pipe on the table. And yet as his hand came in contact with the telephone, he felt an inclination to draw back. A subtle voice whispered him not to answer, to leave while the storm was dark, to go back into the wilderness, to fight his way to the western mountains.

With a jerk he unhooked the receiver and put it to his ear.

It was not McDowell who answered him. It was not Shan Tung. To his amazement, coming to him through the tumult of the storm, he recognized the voice of Miriam Kirkstone!

VII

Why should Miriam Kirkstone call him up in an hour when the sky was livid with the flash of lightning and the earth trembled with the roll of thunder? This was the question that filled Keith's mind as he listened to the voice at the other end of the wire. It was pitched to a high treble as if unconsciously the speaker feared that the storm might break in upon her words. She was telling him that she had telephoned McDowell but had been too late to catch him before he left for Brady's bungalow; she was asking him to pardon her for intruding upon his time so soon after his return, but she was sure that he would understand her. She wanted him to come up to see her that evening at eight o'clock. It was important—to her. Would he come?

Before Keith had taken a moment to consult with himself he had replied that he would. He heard her "thank you," her "good-by," and hung up the receiver, stunned. So far as he could remember, he had spoken no more than seven words. The beautiful young woman up at the Kirkstone mansion had clearly betrayed her fear of the lightning by winding up her business with him at the earliest possible moment. Why, then, had she not waited until the storm was over?

A pounding at the door interrupted his thought. He went to it and admitted an individual who, in spite of his water-soaked condition, was smiling all over. It was Wallie, the Jap. He was no larger than a boy of sixteen, and from eyes, ears, nose, and hair he was dripping streams, while his coat bulged with packages which he had struggled to protect, from the torrent through which he had forced his way up the hill. Keith liked him on the instant. He found himself powerless to resist the infection of Wallie's grin, and as Wallie hustled into the kitchen like a wet spaniel, he followed and helped him unload. By the time the little Jap had

19

disgorged his last package, he had assured Keith that the rain was nice, that his name was Wallie, that he expected five dollars a week and could cook "like heaven." Keith laughed outright, and Wallie was so delighted with the general outlook that he fairly kicked his heels together. Thereafter for an hour or so he was left alone in possession of the kitchen, and shortly Keith began to hear certain sounds and catch occasional odoriferous whiffs which assured him that Wallie was losing no time in demonstrating his divine efficiency in the matter of cooking.

Wallie's coming gave him an excuse to call up McDowell. He confessed to a disquieting desire to hear the inspector's voice again. In the back of his head was the fear of Shan Tung, and the hope that McDowell might throw some light on Miriam Kirkstone's unusual request to see her that night. The storm had settled down into a steady drizzle when he got in touch with him, and he was relieved to find there was no change in the friendliness of the voice that came over the telephone. If Shan Tung had a suspicion, he had kept it to himself.

To Keith's surprise it was McDowell who spoke first of Miss Kirkstone.

"She seemed unusually anxious to get in touch with you," he said. "I am frankly disturbed over a certain matter, Conniston, and I should like to talk with you before you go up tonight."

Keith sniffed the air. "Wallie is going to ring the dinner bell within half an hour. Why not slip on a raincoat and join me up here? I think it's going to be pretty good."

"I'll come," said McDowell. "Expect me any moment."

Fifteen minutes later Keith was helping him off with his wet slicker. He had expected McDowell to make some observation on the cheerfulness of the birch fire and the agreeable aromas that were leaking from Wallie's kitchen, but the inspector disappointed him. He stood for a few moments with his back to the fire, thumbing down the tobacco in his pipe, and he made no effort to conceal the fact that there was something in his mind more important than dinner and the cheer of a grate.

His eyes fell on the telephone, and he nodded toward it. "Seemed very anxious to see you, didn't she, Conniston? I mean Miss Kirkstone."

"Rather."

McDowell seated himself and lighted a match. "Seemed—a little—nervous—perhaps," he suggested between puffs. "As though something had happened—or was going to happen. Don't mind my questioning you, do you, Derry?"

"Not a bit," said Keith. "You see, I thought perhaps you might explain——"

There was a disquieting gleam in McDowell's eyes. "It was odd that she should call you up so soon—and in the storm—wasn't it? She expected to find you at my office. I could fairly hear the lightning hissing along the wires. She must have been under some unusual impulse."

"Perhaps."

McDowell was silent for a space, looking steadily at Keith, as if measuring him up to something.

"I don't mind telling you that I am very deeply interested in Miss Kirkstone," he said. "You didn't see her when the Judge was killed. She was away at school, and you were on John Keith's trail when she returned. I have never been much of a woman's man, Conniston, but I tell you frankly that up until six or eight months ago Miriam was one of the most beautiful girls I have ever seen. I would give a good deal to know the exact hour and date when the change in her began. I might be able to trace some event to that date. It was six months ago that she began to take an interest in the fate of John Keith. Since then the change in her has alarmed me, Conniston. I don't understand. She has betrayed nothing. But I have seen her dying by inches under my eyes. She is only a pale and drooping flower compared with what she was. I am positive it is not a sickness—unless it is mental. I have a suspicion. It is almost too terrible to put into words. You will be going up there tonight—you will be alone with her, will talk with her, may learn a great deal if you understand what it is that is eating like a canker in my mind. Will you help me to discover her secret?" He leaned toward Keith. He was no longer the man of iron. There was something intensely human in his face.

"There is no other man on earth I would confide this matter to," he went on slowly. "It will take—a gentleman—to handle it, someone who is big enough to forget if my suspicion is untrue, and who will understand fully what sacrilege means should it prove true. It is extremely delicate. I hesitate. And yet—I am waiting, Conniston. Is it necessary to ask you to pledge secrecy in the matter?"

Keith held out a hand. McDowell gripped it tight.

"It is—Shan Tung," he said, a peculiar hiss in his voice. "Shan Tung—and Miriam Kirkstone! Do you understand, Conniston? Does the horror of it get hold of you? Can you make yourself believe that it is possible? Am I mad to allow such a suspicion to creep into my brain? Shan Tung—Miriam Kirkstone! And she sees herself standing now at the very edge of the pit of hell, and it is killing her."

Keith felt his blood running cold as he saw in the inspector's face the thing which he did not put more plainly in word. He was shocked. He drew his hand from McDowell's grip almost fiercely.

"Impossible!" he cried. "Yes, you are mad. Such a thing would be inconceivable!"

"And yet I have told myself that it is possible," said McDowell. His face was returning into its iron-like mask. His two hands gripped the arms of his chair, and he stared at Keith again as if he were looking through him at something else, and to that something else he seemed to speak, slowly, weighing and measuring each word before it passed his lips. "I am not superstitious. It has always been a law with me to have conviction forced upon me. I do not believe unusual things until investigation proves them. I am making an exception in the case of Shan Tung. I have never regarded him as a man, like you and me, but as a sort of superphysical human machine possessed of a certain psychological power that is at times almost deadly. Do you begin to understand me? I believe that he has exerted the whole force of that influence upon Miriam Kirkstone—and she has surrendered to it. I believe—and yet I am not positive."

"And you have watched them for six months?"

"No. The suspicion came less than a month ago. No one that I know has ever had the opportunity of looking into Shan Tung's private life. The quarters behind his cafe are a mystery. I suppose they can be entered from the cafe and also from a little stairway at the rear. One night—very late—I saw Miriam Kirkstone come down that stairway. Twice in the last month she has visited Shan Tung at a late hour. Twice that I know of, you understand. And that is not all—quite."

Keith saw the distended veins in McDowell's clenched hands, and he knew that he was speaking under a tremendous strain.

"I watched the Kirkstone home—personally. Three times in that same month Shan Tung visited her there. The third time I entered boldly with a fraud message for the girl. I remained with her for an hour. In that time I saw nothing and heard nothing of Shan Tung. He was hiding—or got out as I came in."

Keith was visioning Miriam Kirkstone as he had seen her in the inspector's office. He recalled vividly the slim, golden beauty of her, the wonderful gray of her eyes, and the shimmer of her hair as she stood in the light of the window—and then he saw Shan Tung, effeminate, with his sly, creeping hands and his narrowed eyes, and the thing which McDowell had suggested rose up before him a monstrous impossibility.

"Why don't you demand an explanation of Miss Kirkstone?" he asked.

"I have, and she denies it all absolutely, except that Shan Tung came to her house once to see her brother. She says that she was never on the little stairway back of Shan Tung's place."

"And you do not believe her?"

"Assuredly not. I saw her. To speak the cold truth, Conniston, she is lying magnificently to cover up something which she does not want any other person on earth to know."

Keith leaned forward suddenly. "And why is it that John Keith, dead and buried, should have anything to do with this?" he demanded. "Why did this 'intense interest' you speak of in John Keith begin at about the same time your suspicions began to include Shan Tung?"

McDowell shook his head. "It may be that her interest was not so much in John Keith as in you, Conniston. That is for you to discover—tonight. It is an interesting situation. It has tragic possibilities. The instant you substantiate my suspicions we'll deal directly with Shan Tung. Just now—there's Wallie behind you grinning like a Cheshire cat. His dinner must be a success."

The diminutive Jap had noiselessly opened the door of the little dining-room in which the table was set for two.

Keith smiled as he sat down opposite the man who would have sent him to the executioner had he known the truth. After all, it was but a step from comedy to tragedy. And just now he was conscious of a bit of grisly humor in the situation.

VIII

The storm had settled into a steady drizzle when McDowell left the Shack at two o'clock. Keith watched the iron man, as his tall, gray figure faded away into the mist down the slope, with a curious undercurrent of emotion. Before the inspector had come up as his guest he had, he thought, definitely decided his future action. He would go west on his furlough, write McDowell that he had decided not to reenlist, and bury himself in the British Columbia mountains before an answer could get back to him, leaving the impression that he was going on to Australia or Japan. He was not so sure of himself now. He found himself looking ahead to the night, when he would see Miriam Kirkstone, and he no longer feared Shan Tung as he had feared him a few hours before. McDowell himself had given him new weapons. He was unofficially on Shan Tung's trail. McDowell had frankly placed the affair of Miriam Kirkstone in his hands. That it all had in some mysterious way something to do with himself—John Keith—urged him on to the adventure.

He waited impatiently for the evening. Wallie, smothered in a great raincoat, he sent forth on a general foraging expedition and to bring up some of Conniston's clothes. It was a quarter of eight when he left for Miriam Kirkstone's home.

Even at that early hour the night lay about him heavy and dark and saturated with a heavy mist. From the summit of the hill he could no longer make out the valley of the Saskatchewan. He walked down into a pit in which the scattered lights of the town burned dully like distant stars. It was a little after eight when he came to the Kirkstone house. It was set well back in an iron-fenced area thick with trees and shrubbery, and he saw that the porch light was burning to show him the way. Curtains were drawn, but a glow of warm light lay behind them.

He was sure that Miriam Kirkstone must have heard the crunch of his feet on the gravel walk, for he had scarcely touched the old-fashioned knocker on the door when the door itself was opened. It was Miriam who greeted him. Again he held her hand for a moment in his own.

It was not cold, as it had been in McDowell's office. It was almost feverishly hot, and the pupils of the girl's eyes were big, and dark, and filled with a luminous fire. Keith might have thought that coming in out of the dark night he had startled her. But it was not that. She was repressing something that had preceded him. He thought that he heard the almost noiseless closing of a door at the end of the long hall, and his nostrils caught the faint aroma of a strange perfume. Between him and the light hung a filmy veil of smoke. He knew that it had come from a cigarette. There was an uneasy note in Miss Kirkstone's voice as she invited him to hang his coat and hat on an old-fashioned rack near the door. He took his time, trying to recall where he had detected that perfume before. He remembered, with a sort of shock. It was after Shan Tung had left McDowell's office.

She was smiling when he turned, and apologizing again for making her unusual request that day.

"It was—quite unconventional. But I felt that you would understand, Mr. Conniston. I guess I didn't stop to think. And I am afraid of lightning, too. But I wanted to see you. I didn't want to wait until tomorrow to hear about what happened up there. Is it—so strange?"

Afterward he could not remember just what sort of answer he made. She turned, and he followed her through the big, square-cut door leading out of the hall. It was the same door with the great, sliding panel he had locked on that fateful night, years ago, when he had fought with her father and brother. In it, for a moment, her slim figure was profiled in a frame of vivid light. Her mother must have been beautiful. That was the thought that flashed upon him as the room and its tragic memory lay before him. Everything came back to him vividly, and he was astonished at the few changes in it. There was the big chair with its leather arms, in which the overfatted creature who had been her father was sitting when he came in. It was the same table, too, and it seemed to him that the same odds and ends were on the mantel over the cobblestone fireplace. And there was somebody's picture of the Madonna still hanging between two windows. The Madonna, like the master of the house, had been too fat to be beautiful. The son, an ogreish pattern of his father, had stood with his back to the Madonna, whose overfat arms had seemed to rest on his shoulders. He remembered that.

The girl was watching him closely when he turned toward her. He had frankly looked the room over, without concealing his intention. She was breathing a little unsteadily, and her hair was shimmering gloriously in the light of an overhead chandelier. She sat down with that light over her, motioning him to be seated opposite her—across the same table from which he had snatched the copper weight that had killed Kirkstone. He had never seen anything quite so steady, quite so beautiful as her eyes when they looked across at him. He thought of McDowell's suspicion and of Shan Tung and gripped himself hard. The same strange perfume hung subtly on the air he was breathing. On a small silver tray at his elbow lay the ends of three freshly burned cigarettes.

"Of course you remember this room?"

He nodded. "Yes. It was night when I came, like this. The next day I went after John Keith."

She leaned toward him, her hands clasped in front of her on the table. "You will tell me the truth about John Keith?" she asked in a low, tense voice. "You swear that it will be the truth?"

"I will keep nothing back from you that I have told Inspector McDowell," he answered, fighting to meet her eyes steadily. "I almost believe I may tell you more."

"Then—did you speak the truth when you reported to Inspector McDowell? IS JOHN KEITH DEAD?" Could Shan Tung meet those wonderful eyes as he was meeting them now, he wondered? Could he face them and master them, as McDowell had hinted? To McDowell the lie had come easily to his tongue. It stuck in his throat now. Without giving him time to prepare himself the girl had shot straight for the bull's-eye, straight to the heart of the thing that meant life or death to him, and for a moment he found no answer. Clearly he was facing suspicion. She could not have driven the shaft intuitively. The unexpectedness of the thing astonished him and then thrilled him, and in the thrill of it he found himself more than ever master of himself.

"Would you like to hear how utterly John Keith is dead and how he died?" he asked.

"Yes. That is what I must know."

He noticed that her hands had closed. Her slender fingers were clenched tight.

"I hesitate, because I have almost promised to tell you even more than I told McDowell," he went on. "And that will not be pleasant for you to hear. He killed your father. There can be no sympathy in your heart for John Keith. It will not be pleasant for you to hear that I liked the man, and that I am sorry he is dead."

"Go on—please."

Her hands unclasped. Her fingers lay limp. Something faded slowly out of her face. It was as if she had hoped for something, and that hope was dying. Could it be possible that she had hoped he would say that John Keith was alive?

"Did you know this man?" he asked.

"This John Keith?"

She shook her head. "No. I was away at school for many years. I don't remember him."

"But he knew you—that is, he had seen you," said Keith. "He used to talk to me about you in those days when he was helpless and dying. He said that he was sorry for you, and that only because of you did he ever regret the justice he brought upon your father. You see I speak his words. He called it justice. He never weakened on that point. You have probably never heard his part of the story."

"No."

The one word forced itself from her lips. She was expecting him to go on, and waited, her eyes never for an instant leaving his face.

He did not repeat the story exactly as he had told it to McDowell. The facts were the same, but the living fire of his own sympathy and his own conviction were in them now. He told it purely from Keith's point of view, and Miriam Kirkstone's face grew whiter, and her hands grew tense again, as she listened for the first time to Keith's own version of the tragedy of the room in which they were sitting. And then he followed Keith up into that land of ice and snow and gibbering Eskimos, and from that moment he was no longer Keith but spoke with the lips of Conniston. He described the sunless weeks and months of madness until the girl's eyes seemed to catch fire, and when at last he came to the little cabin in which Conniston had died, he was again John Keith. He could not have talked about himself as he did about the Englishman. And when he came to the point where he buried Conniston under the floor, a dry, broken sob broke in upon him from across the table. But there were no tears in the girl's eyes. Tears, perhaps, would have hidden from him the desolation he saw there. But she did not give in. Her white throat twitched. She tried to draw her breath steadily. And then she said:

"And that—was John Keith!"

He bowed his head in confirmation of the lie, and, thinking of Conniston, he said:

"He was the finest gentleman I ever knew. And I am sorry he is dead."

"And I, too, am sorry."

She was reaching a hand across the table to him, slowly, hesitatingly. He stared at her.

"You mean that?"

"Yes, I am sorry."

He took her hand. For a moment her fingers tightened about his own. Then they relaxed and drew gently away from him. In that moment he saw a sudden change come into her face. She was looking beyond him, over his right shoulder. Her eyes widened, her pupils dilated under his gaze, and she held her breath. With the swift caution of the man-hunted he turned. The room was empty behind him. There was nothing but a window at his back. The rain was drizzling against it, and he noticed that the curtain was not drawn, as they were drawn at the other windows. Even as he looked, the girl went to it and pulled down the shade. He knew that she had seen something, something that had startled her for a moment, but he did not question her. Instead, as if he had noticed nothing, he asked if he might light a cigar.

"I see someone smokes," he excused himself, nodding at the cigarette butts.

He was watching her closely and would have recalled the words in the next breath. He had caught her. Her brother was out of town. And there was a distinctly unAmerican perfume in the smoke that someone had left in the room. He saw the bit of red creeping up her throat into her cheeks, and his conscience shamed him. It was difficult for him not to believe McDowell now. Shan Tung had been there. It was Shan Tung who had left the hall as he entered. Probably it was Shan Tung whose face she had seen at the window.

What she said amazed him. "Yes, it is a shocking habit of mine, Mr. Conniston. I learned to smoke in the East. Is it so very bad, do you think?"

He fairly shook himself. He wanted to say, "You beautiful little liar, I'd like to call your bluff right now, but I won't, because I'm sorry for you!" Instead, he nipped off the end of his cigar, and said:

"In England, you know, the ladies smoke a great deal. Personally I may be a little prejudiced. I don't know that it is sinful, especially when one uses such good judgment—in orientals." And then he was powerless to hold himself back. He smiled at her frankly, unafraid. "I don't believe you smoke," he added.

He rose to his feet, still smiling across at her, like a big brother waiting for her confidence. She was not alarmed at the directness with which he had guessed the truth. She was no longer embarrassed. She seemed for a moment to be looking through him and into him, a strange and yearning desire glowing dully in her eyes. He saw her throat twitching again, and he was filled with an infinite compassion for this daughter of the man he had killed. But he kept it within himself. He had gone far enough. It was for her to speak. At the door she gave him her hand again, bidding him good-night. She looked pathetically helpless, and he thought that someone ought to be there with the right to take her in his arms and comfort her.

"You will come again?" she whispered.

"Yes, I am coming again," he said. "Good-night."

He passed out into the drizzle. The door closed behind him, but not before there came to him once more that choking sob from the throat of Miriam Kirkstone.

IX

Keith's hand was on the butt of his revolver as he made his way through the black night. He could not see the gravel path under his feet but could only feel it. Something that was more than a guess made him feel that Shan Tung was not far away, and he wondered if it was a premonition, and what it meant. With the keen instinct of a hound he was scenting for a personal danger. He passed through the gate and began the downward slope toward town, and not until then did he begin adding things together and analyzing the situation as it had transformed itself since he had stood in the door of the Shack, welcoming the storm from the western mountains. He thought that he had definitely made up his mind then; now it was chaotic. He could not leave Prince Albert immediately, as the inspiration had moved him a few hours before. McDowell had practically given him an assignment. And Miss Kirkstone was holding him. Also Shan Tung. He felt within himself the sensation of one who was traveling on very thin ice, yet he could not tell just where or why it was thin.

"Just a fool hunch," he assured himself.

"Why the deuce should I let a confounded Chinaman and a pretty girl get on my nerves at this stage of the game? If it wasn't for McDowell—"

And there he stopped. He had fought too long at the raw edge of things to allow himself to be persuaded by delusions, and he confessed that it was John Keith who was holding him, that in some inexplicable way John Keith, though officially dead and buried, was mixed up in a mysterious affair in which Miriam Kirkstone and Shan Tung were the moving factors. And inasmuch as he was now Derwent Conniston and no longer John Keith, he took the logical point of arguing that the affair was none of his business, and that he could go on to the mountains if he pleased. Only in that direction could he see ice of a sane and perfect thickness, to carry out the metaphor in his head. He could report indifferently to McDowell, forget Miss Kirkstone, and disappear from the menace of Shan Tung's eyes. John Keith, he repeated, would be officially dead, and being dead, the law would have no further interest in him.

He prodded himself on with this thought as he fumbled his way through darkness down into town. Miriam Kirkstone in her golden way was alluring; the mystery that shadowed the big house on the hill was fascinating to his hunting instincts; he had the desire, growing fast, to come at grips with Shan Tung. But he had not foreseen these things, and neither had Conniston foreseen them. They had planned only for the salvation of John Keith's precious neck, and tonight he had almost forgotten the existence of that unpleasant reality, the hangman. Truth settled upon him with depressing effect, and an infinite loneliness turned his mind again to the mountains of his dreams.

The town was empty of life. Lights glowed here and there through the mist; now and then a door opened; down near the river a dog howled forlornly. Everything was shut against him. There were no longer homes where he might call and be greeted with a cheery "Good evening, Keith. Glad to see you. Come in out of the wet." He could not even go to Duggan, his old river friend. He realized now that his old friends were the very ones he must avoid most carefully to escape self-betrayal. Friendship no longer existed for him; the town was a desert without an oasis where he might reclaim some of the things he had lost. Memories he had treasured gave place to bitter ones. His own townfolk, of all people, were his readiest enemies, and his loneliness clutched him tighter, until the air itself seemed thick and difficult to breathe. For the time Derwent Conniston was utterly submerged in the overwhelming yearnings of John Keith.

He dropped into a dimly lighted shop to purchase a box of cigars. It was deserted except for the proprietor. His elbow bumped into a telephone. He would call up Wallie and tell him to have a good fire waiting for him, and in the company of that fire he would do a lot of thinking before getting into communication with McDowell.

It was not Wallie who answered him, and he was about to apologize for getting the wrong number when the voice at the other end asked,

"Is that you, Conniston?"

It was McDowell. The discovery gave him a distinct shock. What could the Inspector be doing up at the Shack in his absence? Besides, there was an imperative demand in the question that shot at him over the wire. McDowell had half shouted it.

"Yes, it's I," he said rather feebly.

"I'm down-town, stocking up on some cigars. What's the excitement?"

"Don't ask questions but hustle up here," McDowell fired back. "I've got the surprise of your life waiting for you!"

Keith heard the receiver at the other end go up with a bang. Something had happened at the Shack, and McDowell was excited. He went out puzzled. For some reason he was in no great hurry to reach the top of the hill. He was beginning to expect things to happen—too many things—and in the stress of the moment he felt the incongruity of the friendly box of cigars tucked under his arm. The hardest luck he had ever run up against had never quite killed his sense of humor, and he chuckled. His fortunes were indeed at a low ebb when he found a bit of comfort in hugging a box of cigars still closer.

He could see that every room in the Shack was lighted, when he came to the crest of the slope, but the shades were drawn. He wondered if Wallie had pulled down the curtains, or if it was a caution on McDowell's part against possible espionage. Suspicion made him transfer the box of cigars to his left arm so that his right was free. Somewhere in the darkness Conniston's voice was urging him, as it had urged him up in the cabin on the Barren: "Don't walk into a noose. If it comes to a fight, FIGHT!"

And then something happened that brought his heart to a dead stop. He was close to the door. His ear was against it. And he was listening to a voice. It was not Wallie's, and it was not the iron man's. It was a woman's voice, or a girl's.

He opened the door and entered, taking swiftly the two or three steps that carried him across the tiny vestibule to the big room. His entrance was so sudden that the tableau in front of him was unbroken for a moment. Birch logs were blazing in the fireplace. In the big chair sat McDowell, partly turned, a smoking cigar poised in his fingers, staring at him. Seated on a footstool, with her chin in the cup of her hands, was a girl. At first, blinded a little by the light, Keith thought she was a child, a remarkably pretty child with wide-open, half-startled eyes and a wonderful crown of glowing, brown hair in which he could still see the shimmer of wet. He took off his hat and brushed the water from his eyes. McDowell did not move. Slowly the girl rose to her feet. It was then that Keith saw she was not a child. Perhaps she was eighteen, a slim, tired-looking, little thing, wonderfully pretty, and either on the verge of laughing or crying. Perhaps it was halfway between. To his growing discomfiture she came slowly toward him with a strange and wonderful look in her face. And McDowell still sat there staring.

His heart thumped with an emotion he had no time to question. In those wide-open, shining eyes of the girl he sensed unspeakable tragedy—for him. And then the girl's arms were reaching out to him, and she was crying in that voice that trembled and broke between sobs and laughter:

"Derry, don't you know me? Don't you know me?"

He stood like one upon whom had fallen the curse of the dumb. She was within arm's reach of him, her face white as a cameo, her eyes glowing like newly-fired stars, her slim throat quivering, and her arms reaching toward him.

"Derry, don't you know me? DON'T YOU KNOW ME?"

It was a sob, a cry. McDowell had risen. Overwhelmingly there swept upon Keith an impulse that rocked him to the depth of his soul. He opened his arms, and in an instant the girl was in them. Quivering, and sobbing, and laughing she was on his breast. He felt the crush of her soft hair against his face, her arms were about his neck, and she was pulling his head down and kissing him—not once or twice, but again and again, passionately and without shame. His own arms tightened. He heard McDowell's voice—a distant and non-essential voice it seemed to him now—saying that he would leave them alone and that he would see them again tomorrow. He heard the door open and close. McDowell was gone. And the soft little arms were still tight about his neck. The sweet crush of hair smothered his face, and on his breast she was crying now like a baby. He held her closer. A wild exultation seized upon him, and every fiber in his body responded to its thrill, as tautly-stretched wires respond to an electrical storm. It passed swiftly, burning itself out, and his heart was left dead. He heard a sound made by Wallie out in the kitchen. He saw the walls of the room again, the chair in which McDowell had sat, the blazing fire. His arms relaxed. The girl raised her head and put her two hands to his face, looking at him with eyes which Keith no longer failed to recognize. They were the eyes that had looked at him out of the faded picture in Conniston's watch.

"Kiss me, Derry!"

It was impossible not to obey. Her lips clung to him. There was love, adoration, in their caress.

And then she was crying again, with her arms around him tight and her face hidden against him, and he picked her up as he would have lifted a child, and carried her to the big chair in front of the fire. He put her in it and stood before her, trying to smile. Her hair had loosened, and the shining mass of it had fallen about her face and to her shoulders. She was more than ever like a little girl as she looked up at him, her eyes worshiping him, her lips trying to smile, and one little hand dabbing her eyes with a tiny handkerchief that was already wet and crushed.

"You—you don't seem very glad to see me, Derry."

"I—I'm just stunned," he managed to say. "You see—"

"It IS a shocking surprise, Derry. I meant it to be. I've been planning it for years and years and YEARS! Please take off your coat—it's dripping wet!—and sit down near me, on that stool!"

Again he obeyed. He was big for the stool.

"You are glad to see me, aren't you, Derry?"

She was leaning over the edge of the big chair, and one of her hands went to his damp hair, brushing it back. It was a wonderful touch. He had never felt anything like it before in his life, and involuntarily he bent his head a little. In a moment she had hugged it up close to her.

"You ARE glad, aren't you, Derry? Say 'yes.'"

"Yes," he whispered.

He could feel the swift, excited beating of her heart.

"And I'm never going back again—to THEM," he heard her say, something suddenly low and fierce in her voice. "NEVER! I'm going to stay with you always, Derry. Always!"

She put her lips close to his ear and whispered mysteriously. "They don't know where I am. Maybe they think I'm dead. But Colonel Reppington knows. I told him I was coming if I had to walk round the world to get here. He said he'd keep my secret, and gave me letters to some awfully nice people over here. I've been over six months. And when I saw your name in one of those dry-looking, blue-covered, paper books the Mounted Police get out, I just dropped down on my knees and thanked the good Lord, Derry. I knew I'd find you somewhere—sometime. I haven't slept two winks since leaving Montreal! And I guess I really frightened that big man with the terrible mustaches, for when I rushed in on him tonight, dripping wet, and said, 'I'm Miss Mary Josephine Conniston, and I want my brother,' his eyes grew bigger and bigger until I thought they were surely going to pop out at me. And then he swore. He said, 'My Gawd, I didn't know he had a sister!'"

Keith's heart was choking him. So this wonderful little creature was Derwent Conniston's sister! And she was claiming him. She thought he was her brother!

"—And I love him because he treated me so nicely," she was saying. "He really hugged me, Derry. I guess he didn't think I was away past eighteen. And he wrapped me up in a big oilskin, and we came up here. And—O Derry, Derry—why did you do it? Why didn't you let me know? Don't you—want me here?"

He heard, but his mind had swept beyond her to the little cabin in the edge of the Great Barren where Derwent Conniston lay dead. He heard the wind moaning, as it had moaned that night the Englishman died, and he saw again that last and unspoken yearning in Conniston's eyes. And he knew now why Conniston's face had followed him through the gray gloom and why he had felt the mysterious presence of him long after he had gone. Something that was Conniston entered into him now. In the throbbing chaos of his brain a voice was whispering, "She is yours, she is yours."

His arms tightened about her, and a voice that was not unlike John Keith's voice said: "Yes, I want you! I want you!"

X

For a space Keith did not raise his head. The girl's arms were about him close, and he could feel the warm pressure of her cheek against his hair. The realization of his crime was already weighing his soul like a piece of lead, yet out of that soul had come the cry, "I want you—I want you!" and it still beat with the voice of that immeasurable yearning even as his lips grew tight and he saw himself the monstrous fraud he was. This strange little, wonderful creature had come to him from out of a dead world, and her lips, and her arms, and the soft caress of her hands had sent his own world reeling about his head so swiftly that he had been drawn into a maelstrom to which he could find no bottom. Before McDowell she had claimed him. And before McDowell he had accepted her. He had lived the great lie as he had strengthened himself to live it, but success was no longer a triumph. There rushed into his brain like a consuming flame the desire to confess the truth, to tell this girl whose arms were about him that he was not Derwent Conniston, her brother, but John Keith, the murderer. Something drove it back, something that was still more potent, more demanding, the overwhelming urge of that fighting force in every man which calls for self-preservation.

Slowly he drew himself away from her, knowing that for this night at least his back was to the wall. She was smiling at him from out of the big chair, and in spite of himself he smiled back at her.

"I must send you to bed now, Mary Josephine, and tomorrow we will talk everything over," he said. "You're so tired you're ready to fall asleep in a minute."

Tiny, puckery lines came into her pretty forehead. It was a trick he loved at first sight.

"Do you know, Derry, I almost believe you've changed a lot. You used to call me 'Juddy.' But now that I'm grown up, I think I like Mary Josephine better, though you oughtn't to be quite so stiff about it. Derry, tell me honest—are you AFRAID of me?"

"Afraid of you!"

"Yes, because I'm grown up. Don't you like me as well as you did one, two, three, seven years ago? If you did, you wouldn't tell me to go to bed just a few minutes after you've seen me for the first time in all those—those—Derry, I'm going to cry! I AM!"

"Don't," he pleaded. "Please don't!"

He felt like a hundred-horned bull in a very small china shop. Mary Josephine herself saved the day for him by jumping suddenly from the big chair, forcing him into it, and snuggling herself on his knees.

"There!" She looked at a tiny watch on her wrist. "We're going to bed in two hours. We've got a lot to talk about that won't wait until tomorrow, Derry. You understand what I mean. I couldn't sleep until you've told me. And you must tell me the truth. I'll love you just the same, no matter what it is. Derry, Derry, WHY DID YOU DO IT?"

"Do what?" he asked stupidly.

The delicious softness went out of the slim little body on his knees. It grew rigid. He looked hopelessly into the fire, but he could feel the burning inquiry in the girl's eyes. He sensed a swift change passing through her. She seemed scarcely to breathe, and he knew that his answer had been more than inadequate. It either confessed or feigned an ignorance of something which it would have been impossible for him to forget had he been Conniston. He looked up at her at last. The joyous flush had gone out of her face. It was a little drawn. Her hand, which had been snuggling his neck caressingly, slipped down from his shoulder.

"I guess—you'd rather I hadn't come, Derry," she said, fighting to keep a break out of her voice. "And I'll go back, if you want to send me. But I've always dreamed of your promise, that some day you'd send for me or come and get me, and I'd like to know WHY before you tell me to go. Why have you hidden away from me all these years, leaving me among those who you knew hated me as they hated you? Was it because you didn't care? Or was it because— because—" She bent her head and whispered strangely, "Was it because you were afraid?"

"Afraid?" he repeated slowly, staring again into the fire. "Afraid—" He was going to add "Of what?" but caught the words and held them back.

The birch fire leaped up with a sudden roar into the chimney, and from the heart of the flame he caught again that strange and all-pervading thrill, the sensation of Derwent Conniston's presence very near to him. It seemed to him that for an instant he caught a flash of Conniston's face, and somewhere within him was a whispering which was Conniston's voice. He was possessed by a weird and masterful force that swept over him and conquered him, a thing that was more than intuition and greater than physical desire. It was inspiration. He knew that the Englishman would have him play the game as he was about to play it now.

The girl was waiting for him to answer. Her lips had grown a little more tense. His hesitation, the restraint in his welcome of her, and his apparent desire to evade that mysterious something which seemed to mean so much to her had brought a shining pain into her eyes. He had seen such a look in the eyes of creatures physically hurt. He reached out with his hands and brushed back the thick, soft hair from about her face. His fingers buried themselves in the silken disarray, and he looked for a moment straight into her eyes before he spoke.

"Little girl, will you tell me the truth?" he asked. "Do I look like the old Derwent Conniston, YOUR Derwent Conniston? Do I?"

Her voice was small and troubled, yet the pain was slowly fading out of her eyes as she felt the passionate embrace of his fingers in her hair. "No. You are changed."

"Yes, I am changed. A part of Derwent Conniston died seven years ago. That part of him was dead until he came through that door tonight and saw you. And then it flickered back into life. It is returning slowly, slowly. That which was dead is beginning to rouse itself, beginning to remember. See, little Mary Josephine. It was this!"

He drew a hand to his forehead and placed a finger on the scar. "I got that seven years ago. It killed a half of Derwent Conniston, the part that should have lived. Do you understand? Until tonight—"

Her eyes startled him, they were growing so big and dark and staring, living fires of understanding and horror. It was hard for him to go on with the lie. "For many weeks I was dead," he struggled on. "And when I came to life physically, I had forgotten a great deal. I had my name, my identity, but only ghastly dreams and visions of what had gone before. I remembered you, but it was in a dream, a strange and haunting dream that was with me always. It seems to me that for an age I have been seeking for a face, a voice, something I loved above all else on earth, something which was always near and yet was never found. It was you, Mary Josephine, you!"

Was it the real Derwent Conniston speaking now? He felt again that overwhelming force from within which was not his own. The thing that had begun as a lie struck him now as a thing that was truth. It was he, John Keith, who had been questing and yearning and hoping. It was John Keith, and not Conniston, who had returned into a world filled with a desolation of loneliness, and it was to John Keith that a beneficent God had sent this wonderful creature in an hour that was blackest in its despair. He was not lying now. He was fighting. He was fighting to keep for himself the one atom of humanity that meant more to him than all the rest of the human race, fighting to keep a great love that had come to him out of a world in which he no longer had a friend or a home, and to that fight his soul went out as a drowning man grips at a spar on a sea. As the girl's hands came to his face and he heard the yearning, grief-filled cry of his name on her lips, he no longer sensed the things he was saying, but held her close in his arms, kissing her mouth, and her eyes, and her hair, and repeating over and over again that now he had found her he would never give her up. Her arms clung to him. They were like two children brought together after a long separation, and Keith knew that Conniston's love for this girl who was his sister must have been a splendid thing. And his lie had saved Conniston as well as himself. There had been no time to question the reason for the Englishman's neglect— for his apparent desertion of the girl who had come across the sea to find him. Tonight it was sufficient that HE was Conniston, and that to him the girl had fallen as a precious heritage.

He stood up with her at last, holding her away from him a little so that he could look into her face wet with tears and shining with happiness. She reached up a hand to his face, so that it touched the scar, and in her eyes he saw an infinite pity, a luminously tender glow of love and sympathy and understanding that no measurements could compass. Gently her hand stroked his scarred forehead. He felt his old world slipping away from under his feet, and with his triumph there surged over him a thankfulness for that indefinable something that had come to him in time to give him the strength and the courage to lie. For she believed him, utterly and without the shadow of a suspicion she believed him.

"Tomorrow you will help me to remember a great many things," he said. "And now will you let me send you to bed, Mary Josephine?"

She was looking at the scar. "And all those years I didn't know," she whispered. "I didn't know. They told me you were dead, but I knew it was a lie. It was Colonel Reppington—" She saw something in his face that stopped her.

"Derry, DON'T YOU REMEMBER?"

"I shall—tomorrow. But tonight I can see nothing and think of nothing but you. Tomorrow—"

She drew his head down swiftly and kissed the brand made by the heated barrel of the Englishman's pistol. "Yes, yes, we must go to bed now, Derry," she cried quickly. "You must not think too much. Tonight it must just be of me. Tomorrow everything will come out right, everything. And now you may send me to bed. Do you remember—"

She caught herself, biting her lip to keep back the word.

"Tell me," he urged. "Do I remember what?"

"How you used to come in at the very last and tuck me in at night, Derry? And how we used to whisper to ourselves there in the darkness, and at last you would kiss me good-night? It was the kiss that always made me go to sleep."

He nodded. "Yes, I remember," he said.

He led her to the spare room, and brought in her two travel-worn bags, and turned on the light. It was a man's room, but Mary Josephine stood for a moment surveying it with delight.

"It's home, Derry, real home," she whispered.

He did not explain to her that it was a borrowed home and that this was his first night in it. Such unimportant details would rest until tomorrow. He showed her the bath and its water system and then explained to Wallie that his sister was in the house and he would have to bunk in the kitchen. At the last he knew what he was expected to do, what he must do. He kissed Mary Josephine good night. He kissed her twice. And Mary Josephine kissed him and gave him a hug the like of which he had never experienced until this night. It sent him back to the fire with blood that danced like a drunken man's.

He turned the lights out and for an hour sat in the dying glow of the birch. For the first time since he had come from Miriam Kirkstone's he had the opportunity to think, and in thinking he found his brain crowded with cold and unemotional fact. He saw his lie in all its naked immensity. Yet he was not sorry that he had lied. He had saved Conniston. He had saved himself. And he had saved Conniston's sister, to love, to fight for, to protect. It had not been a Judas lie but a lie with his heart and his soul and all the manhood in him behind it. To have told the truth would have made him his own executioner, it would have betrayed the dead Englishman who had given to him his name and all that he possessed, and it would have dragged to a pitiless grief the heart of a girl for whom the sun still continued to shine. No regret rose before him now. He felt no shame. All that he saw was the fight, the tremendous fight, ahead of him, his fight to make good as Conniston, his fight to play the game as Conniston would have him play it. The inspiration that had come to him as he stood facing the storm from the western mountains possessed him again. He would go to the river's end as he had planned to go before McDowell told him of Shan Tung and Miriam Kirkstone. And he would not go alone. Mary Josephine would go with him.

It was midnight when he rose from the big chair and went to his room. The door was closed. He opened it and entered. Even as his hand groped for the switch on the wall, his nostrils caught the scent of something which was familiar and yet which should not have been there. It filled the room, just as it had filled the big hall at the Kirkstone house, the almost sickening fragrance of agallochum burned in a cigarette. It hung like a heavy incense. Keith's eyes glared as he scanned the room under the lights, half expecting to see Shan Tung sitting there waiting for him. It was empty. His eyes leaped to the two windows. The shade was drawn at one, the other was up, and the window itself was open an inch or two above the sill. Keith's hand gripped his pistol as he went to it and drew the curtain. Then he turned to the table on which were the reading lamp and Brady's pipes and tobacco and magazines. On an ash-tray lay the stub of a freshly burned cigarette. Shan Tung had come secretly, but he had made no effort to cover his presence.

It was then that Keith saw something on the table which had not been there before. It was a small, rectangular, teakwood box no larger than a half of the palm of his hand. He had noticed Miriam Kirkstone's nervous fingers toying with just such a box earlier in the evening. They were identical in appearance. Both were covered with an exquisite fabric of oriental carving, and the wood was stained and polished until it shone with the dark luster of ebony. Instantly it flashed upon him that this was the same box he had seen at Miriam's. She had sent it to him, and Shan Tung had been her messenger. The absurd thought was in his head as he took up a small white square of card that lay on top of the box. The upper side of this card was blank; on the other side, in a script as exquisite in its delicacy as the carving itself, were the words:

"WITH THE COMPLIMENTS OF SHAN TUNG."

In another moment Keith had opened the box. Inside was a carefully folded slip of paper, and on this paper was written a single line. Keith's heart stopped beating, and his blood ran cold as he read what it held for him, a message of doom from Shan Tung in nine words:

"WHAT HAPPENED TO DERWENT CONNISTON? DID YOU KILL HIM?"

XI

Stunned by a shock that for a few moments paralyzed every nerve center in his body, John Keith stood with the slip of white paper in his hands. He was discovered! That was the one thought that pounded like a hammer in his brain. He was discovered in the very hour of his triumph and exaltation, in that hour when the world had opened its portals of joy and hope for him again and when life itself, after four years of hell, was once more worth the living. Had the shock come a few hours before, he would have taken it differently. He was expecting it then. He had expected it when he entered McDowell's office the first time. He was prepared for it afterward. Discovery, failure, and death were possibilities of the hazardous game he was playing, and he was unafraid, because he had only his life to lose, a life that was not much more than a hopeless derelict at most. Now it was different. Mary Josephine had come like some rare and wonderful alchemy to transmute for him all leaden things into gold. In a few minutes she had upset the world. She had literally torn aside for him the hopeless chaos in which he saw himself struggling, flooding him with the warm radiance of a great love and a still greater desire. On his lips he could feel the soft thrill of her good-night kiss and about his neck the embrace of her soft arms. She had not gone to sleep yet. Across in the other room she was thinking of him, loving him; perhaps she was on her knees praying for him, even as he held in his fingers Shan Tung's mysterious forewarning of his doom.

The first impulse that crowded in upon him was that of flight, the selfish impulse of personal salvation. He could get away. The night would swallow him up. A moment later he was mentally castigating himself for the treachery of that impulse to Mary Josephine. His floundering senses began to readjust themselves.

Why had Shan Tung given him this warning? Why had he not gone straight to Inspector McDowell with the astounding disclosure of the fact that the man supposed to be Derwent Conniston was not Derwent Conniston, but John Keith, the murderer of Miriam Kirkstone's father?

The questions brought to Keith a new thrill. He read the note again. It was a definite thing stating a certainty and not a guess. Shan Tung had not shot at random. He knew. He knew that he was not Derwent Conniston but John Keith. And he believed that he had killed the Englishman to steal his identity. In the face of these things he had not gone to McDowell! Keith's eyes fell upon the card again. "With the compliments of Shan Tung." What did the words mean? Why had Shan Tung written them unless—with his compliments—he was giving him a warning and the chance to save himself?

His immediate alarm grew less. The longer he contemplated the slip of paper in his hand, the more he became convinced that the inscrutable Shan Tung was the last individual in the world to stage a bit of melodrama without some good reason for it. There was but one conclusion he could arrive at. The Chinaman was playing a game of his own, and he had taken this unusual way of advising Keith to make a getaway while the going was good. It was evident that his intention had been to avoid the possibility of a personal discussion of the situation. That, at least, was Keith's first impression.

He turned to examine the window. There was no doubt that Shan Tung had come in that way. Both the sill and curtain bore stains of water and mud, and there was wet dirt on the floor. For once the immaculate oriental had paid no attention to his feet. At the door leading into the big room Keith saw where he had stood for some time, listening, probably when McDowell and Mary Josephine were in the outer room waiting for him. Suddenly his eyes riveted themselves on the middle panel of the door. Brady had intended his color scheme to be old ivory—the panel itself was nearly white—and on it Shan Tung had written heavily with a lead pencil the hour of his presence, "10.45 P.M." Keith's amazement found voice in a low exclamation. He looked at his watch. It was a quarter-hour after twelve. He had returned to the Shack before ten, and the clever Shan Tung was letting him know in this cryptic fashion that for more than three-quarters of an hour he had listened at the door and spied upon him and Mary Josephine through the keyhole.

Had even such an insignificant person as Wallie been guilty of that act, Keith would have felt like thrashing him. It surprised himself that he experienced no personal feeling of outrage at Shan Tung's frank confession of eavesdropping. A subtle significance began to attach itself more and more to the story his room was telling him. He knew that Shan Tung had left none of the marks of his presence out of bravado, but with a definite purpose. Keith's psychological mind was at all times acutely ready to seize upon possibilities, and just as his positiveness of Conniston's spiritual presence had inspired him to act his lie with Mary Josephine, so did the conviction possess him now that his room held for him a message of the most vital importance.

In such an emergency Keith employed his own method. He sat down, lighted his pipe again, and centered the full resource of his mind on Shan Tung, dissociating himself from the room and the adventure of the night as much as possible in his objective analysis of the man. Four distinct emotional factors entered into that analysis—fear, distrust, hatred, personal enmity. To his surprise he found himself drifting steadily into an unusual and unexpected mental attitude. From the time he had faced Shan Tung in the inspector's office, he had regarded him as the chief enemy of his freedom, his one great menace. Now he felt neither personal enmity nor hatred for him. Fear and distrust remained, but the fear was impersonal and the distrust that of one who watches a clever opponent in a game or a fight. His conception of Shan Tung changed. He found his occidental mind running parallel with the oriental, bridging the spaces which otherwise it never would have crossed, and at the end it seized upon the key. It proved to him that his first impulse had been wrong. Shan Tung had not expected him to seek safety in flight. He had given the white man credit for a larger understanding than that. His desire, first of all, had been to let Keith know that he was not the only one who was playing for big stakes, and that another, Shan Tung himself, was gambling a hazard of his own, and that the fraudulent Derwent Conniston was a trump card in that game.

To impress this upon Keith he had, first of all, acquainted him with the fact that he had seen through his deception and that he knew he was John Keith and not Derwent Conniston. He had also let him know that he believed he had killed the Englishman, a logical supposition under the circumstances. This information he had left for Keith was not in the form of an intimation. There was, indeed, something very near apologetic courtesy in the presence of the card bearing Shan Tung's compliments. The penciling of the hour on the panel of the door, without other notation, was a polite and suggestive hint. He wanted Keith to know that he understood his peculiar situation up until that particular time, that he had heard and possibly seen much that had passed between him and Mary Josephine. The partly opened window, the mud and wet on curtains and floor, and the cigarette stubs were all to call Keith's attention to the box on the table.

Keith could not but feel a certain sort of admiration for the Chinaman. The two questions he must answer now were, What was Shan Tung's game? and What did Shan Tung expect him to do?

Instantly Miriam Kirkstone flashed upon him as the possible motive for Shan Tung's visit. He recalled her unexpected and embarrassing question of that evening, in which she had expressed a suspicion and a doubt as to John Keith's death. He had gone to Miriam's at eight. It must have been very soon after that, and after she had caught a glimpse of the face at the window, that Shan Tung had hurried to the Shack.

Slowly but surely the tangled threads of the night's adventure were unraveling themselves for Keith. The main facts pressed upon him, no longer smothered in a chaos of theory and supposition. If there had been no Miriam Kirkstone in the big house on the hill, Shan Tung would have gone to McDowell, and he would have been in irons at the present moment. McDowell had been right after all. Miriam Kirkstone was fighting for something that was more than her existence. The thought of that "something" made Keith writhe and his hands clench. Shan Tung had triumphed but not utterly. A part of the fruit of his triumph was still just out of his reach, and the two—beautiful Miss Kirkstone and the deadly Shan Tung—were locked in a final struggle for its possession. In some mysterious way he, John Keith, was to play the winning hand. How or when he could not understand. But of one thing he was convinced; in exchange for whatever winning card he held Shan Tung had offered him his life. Tomorrow he would expect an answer.

That tomorrow had already dawned. It was one o'clock when Keith again looked at his watch. Twenty hours ago he had cooked his last camp-fire breakfast. It was only eighteen hours ago that he had filled himself with the smell of Andy Duggan's bacon, and still more recently that he had sat in the little barber shop on the corner wondering what his fate would be when he faced McDowell. It struck him as incongruous and impossible that only fifteen hours had passed since then. If he possessed a doubt of the reality of it all, the bed was there to help convince him. It was a real bed, and he had not slept in a real bed for a number of years. Wallie had made it ready for him. Its sheets were snow-white. There was a counterpane with a fringe on it and pillows puffed up with billowy invitation, as if they were on the point of floating away. Had they risen before his eyes, Keith would have regarded the phenomenon rather casually. After the swift piling up of the amazing events of those fifteen hours, a floating pillow would have seemed quite in the natural orbit of things. But they did not float. They remained where they were, their white breasts bared to him, urging upon him a common-sense perspective of the situation. He wasn't going to run away. He couldn't sit up all night. Therefore why not come to them and sleep?

There was something directly personal in the appeal of the pillows and the bed. It was not general; it was for him. And Keith responded.

He made another note of the time, a half-hour after one, when he turned in. He allotted himself four hours of sleep, for it was his intention to be up with the sun.

XII

Necessity had made of Keith a fairly accurate human chronometer. In the second year of his fugitivism he had lost his watch. At first it was like losing an arm, a part of his brain, a living friend. From that time until he came into possession of Conniston's timepiece he was his own hour-glass and his own alarm clock. He became proficient.

Brady's bed and the Circe-breasted pillows that supported his head were his undoing. The morning after Shan Tung's visit he awoke to find the sun flooding in through the eastern window of his room, The warmth of it as it fell full in his face, setting his eyes blinking, told him it was too late. He guessed it was eight o'clock. When he fumbled his watch out from under his pillow and looked at it, he found it was a quarter past. He got up quietly, his mind swiftly aligning itself to the happenings of yesterday. He stretched himself until his muscles snapped, and his chest expanded with deep breaths of air from the windows he had left open when he went to bed. He was fit. He was ready for Shan Tung, for McDowell. And over this physical readiness there surged the thrill of a glorious anticipation. It fairly staggered him to discover how badly he wanted to see Mary Josephine again.

He wondered if she was still asleep and answered that there was little possibility of her being awake—even at eight o'clock. Probably she would sleep until noon, the poor, tired, little thing! He smiled affectionately into the mirror over Brady's dressing-table. And then the unmistakable sound of voices in the outer room took him curiously to the door. They were subdued voices. He listened hard, and his heart pumped faster. One of them was Wallie's voice; the other was Mary Josephine's.

He was amused with himself at the extreme care with which he proceeded to dress. It was an entirely new sensation. Wallie had provided him with the necessaries for a cold sponge and in some mysterious interim since their arrival had brushed and pressed the most important of Conniston's things. With the Englishman's wardrobe he had brought up from barracks a small chest which was still locked. Until this morning Keith had not noticed it. It was less than half as large as a steamer trunk and had the appearance of being intended as a strong box rather than a traveling receptacle. It was ribbed by four heavy bands of copper, and the corners and edges were reinforced with the same metal. The lock itself seemed to be impregnable to one without a key. Conniston's name was heavily engraved on a copper tablet just above the lock.

Keith regarded the chest with swiftly growing speculation. It was not a thing one would ordinarily possess. It was an object which, on the face of it, was intended to be inviolate except to its master key, a holder of treasure, a guardian of mystery and of precious secrets. In the little cabin up on the Barren Conniston had said rather indifferently, "You may find something among my things down there that will help you out." The words flashed back to Keith. Had the Englishman, in that casual and uncommunicative way of his, referred to the contents of this chest? Was it not possible that it held for him a solution to the mystery that was facing him in the presence of Mary Josephine? A sense of conviction began to possess him. He examined the lock more closely and found that with proper tools it could be broken.

He finished dressing and completed his toilet by brushing his beard. On account of Mary Josephine he found himself regarding this hirsute tragedy with a growing feeling of disgust, in spite of the fact that it gave him an appearance rather distinguished and military. He wanted it off. Its chief crime was that it made him look older. Besides, it was inclined to be reddish. And it must tickle and prick like the deuce when——

He brought himself suddenly to salute with an appreciative grin. "You're there, and you've got to stick," he chuckled. After all, he was a likable-looking chap, even with that handicap. He was glad.

He opened his door so quietly that Mary Josephine did not see him at first. Her back was toward him as she bent over the dining-table. Her slim little figure was dressed in some soft stuff all crinkly from packing. Her hair, brown and soft, was piled up in shining coils on the top of her head. For the life of him Keith couldn't keep his eyes from traveling from the top of that glowing head to the little high-heeled feet on the floor. They were adorable, slim little, aristocratic feet with dainty ankles! He stood looking at her until she turned and caught him.

There was a change since last night. She was older. He could see it now, the utter impropriety of his cuddling her up like a baby in the big chair—the impossibility, almost.

Mary Josephine settled his doubt. With a happy little cry she ran to him, and Keith found her arms about him again and her lovely mouth held up to be kissed. He hesitated for perhaps the tenth part of a second, if hesitation could be counted in that space. Then his arms closed about her, and he kissed her. He felt the snuggle of her face against his breast again, the crush and sweetness of her hair against his lips and cheek. He kissed her again uninvited. Before he could stop the habit, he had kissed her a third time.

Then her hands were at his face, and he saw again that look in her eyes, a deep and anxious questioning behind the shimmer of love in them, something mute and understanding and wonderfully sympathetic, a mothering soul looking at him and praying as it looked. If his life had paid the forfeit the next instant, he could not have helped kissing her a fourth time.

If Mary Josephine had gone to bed with a doubt of his brotherly interest last night, the doubt was removed now. Her cheeks flushed. Her eyes shone. She was palpitantly, excitedly happy. "It's YOU, Derry," she cried. "Oh, it's you as you used to be!"

She seized his hand and drew him toward the table. Wallie thrust in his head from the kitchenette, grinning, and Mary Josephine flashed him back a meaning smile. Keith saw in an instant that Wallie had turned from his heathen gods to the worship of something infinitely more beautiful. He no longer looked to Keith for instructions.

Mary Josephine sat down opposite Keith at the table. She was telling him, with that warm laughter and happiness in her eyes, how the sun had wakened her, and how she had helped Wallie get breakfast. For the first time Keith was looking at her from a point of vantage; there was just so much distance between them, no more and no less, and the light was right. She was, to him, exquisite. The little puckery lines came into her smooth forehead when he apologized for his tardiness by explaining that he had not gone to bed until one o'clock. Her concern was delightful. She scolded him while Wallie brought in the breakfast, and inwardly he swelled with the irrepressible exultation of a great possessor. He had never had anyone to scold him like that before. It was a scolding which expressed Mary Josephine's immediate proprietorship of him, and he wondered if the pleasure of it made him look as silly as Wallie. His plans were all gone. He had intended to play the idiotic part of one who had partly lost his memory, but throughout the breakfast he exhibited no sign that he was anything but healthfully normal. Mary Josephine's delight at the improvement of his condition since last night shone in her face and eyes, and he could see that she was strictly, but with apparent unconsciousness, guarding herself against saying anything that might bring up the dread shadow between them. She had already begun to fight her own fight for him, and the thing was so beautiful that he wanted to go round to her, and get down on his knees, and put his head in her lap, and tell her the truth.

It was in the moment of that thought that the look came into his face which brought the questioning little lines into her forehead again. In that instant she caught a glimpse of the hunted man, of the soul that had traded itself, of desire beaten into helplessness by a thing she would never understand. It was gone swiftly, but she had caught it. And for her the scar just under his hair stood for its meaning. The responsive throb in her breast was electric. He felt it, saw it, sensed it to the depth of his soul, and his faith in himself stood challenged. She believed. And he—was a liar. Yet what a wonderful thing to lie for!

"—He called me up over the telephone, and when I told him to be quiet, that you were still asleep, I think he must have sworn—it sounded like it, but I couldn't hear distinctly—and then he fairly roared at me to wake you up and tell you that you didn't half deserve such a lovely little sister as I am. Wasn't that nice, Derry?"

"You—you're talking about McDowell?"

"To be sure I am talking about Mr. McDowell! And when I told him your injury troubled you more than usual, and that I was glad you were resting, I think I heard him swallow hard. He thinks a lot of you, Derry. And then he asked me WHICH injury it was that hurt you, and I told him the one in the head. What did he mean? Were you hurt somewhere else, Derry?"

Keith swallowed hard, too. "Not to speak of," he said. "You see, Mary Josephine, I've got a tremendous surprise for you, if you'll promise it won't spoil your appetite. Last night was the first night I've spent in a real bed for three years."

And then, without waiting for her questions, he began to tell her the epic story of John Keith. With her sitting opposite him, her beautiful, wide-open, gray eyes looking at him with amazement as she sensed the marvelous coincidence of their meeting, he told it as he had not told it to McDowell or even to Miriam Kirkstone. A third time the facts were the same. But it was John Keith now who was telling John Keith's story through the lips of an unreal and negative Conniston. He forgot his own breakfast, and a look of gloom settled on Wallie's face when he peered in through the door and saw that their coffee and toast were growing cold. Mary Josephine leaned a little over the table. Not once did she interrupt Keith. Never had he dreamed of a glory that might reflect his emotions as did her eyes. As he swept from pathos to storm, from the madness of long, black nights to starvation and cold, as he told of flight, of pursuit, of the merciless struggle that ended at last in the capture of John Keith, as he gave to these things words and life pulsing with the beat of his own heart, he saw them revisioned in those wonderful gray eyes, cold at times with fear, warm and glowing at other times with sympathy, and again shining softly with a glory of pride and love that was meant for him alone. With him she was present in the little cabin up in the big Barren. Until he told of those days and nights of hopeless desolation, of racking cough and the nearness of death, and of the comradeship of brothers that had come as a final benediction to the hunter and the hunted, until in her soul she was understanding and living those terrible hours as they two had lived them, he did not know how deep and dark and immeasurably tender that gray mystery of beauty in her eyes could be. From that hour he worshiped them as he worshiped no other part of her.

"And from all that you came back the same day I came," she said in a low, awed voice. "You came back from THAT!"

He remembered the part he must play.

"Yes, three years of it. If I could only remember as well, only half as well, things that happened before this—" He raised a hand to his forehead, to the scar.

"You will," she whispered swiftly. "Derry, darling, you will!"

Wallie sidled in and, with an adoring grin at Mary Josephine, suggested that he had more coffee and toast ready to serve, piping hot. Keith was relieved. The day had begun auspiciously, and over the bacon and eggs, done to a ravishing brown by the little Jap, he told Mary Josephine of some of his bills of fare in the north and how yesterday he had filled up on bacon smell at Andy Duggan's. Steak from the cheek of a walrus, he told her, was equal to porterhouse; seal meat wasn't bad, but one grew tired of it quickly unless he was an Eskimo; polar bear meat was filling but tough and strong. He liked whale meat, especially the tail-steaks of narwhal, and cold boiled blubber was good in the winter, only it was impossible to cook it because of lack of fuel, unless one was aboard ship or had an alcohol stove in his outfit. The tidbit of the Eskimo was birds' eggs, gathered by the ton in summer-time, rotten before cold weather came, and frozen solid as chunks of ice in winter. Through one starvation period of three weeks he had lived on them himself, crunching them raw in his mouth as one worries away with a piece of rock candy. The little lines gathered in Mary Josephine's forehead at this, but they smoothed away into laughter when he humorously described the joy of living on nothing at all but air. And he added to this by telling her how the gluttonous Eskimo at feast-time would lie out flat on their backs so that their womenfolk could feed them by dropping chunks of flesh into their open maws until their stomachs swelled up like the crops of birds overstuffed with grain.

It was a successful breakfast. When it was over, Keith felt that he had achieved a great deal. Before they rose from the table, he startled Mary Josephine by ordering Wallie to bring him a cold chisel and a hammer from Brady's tool-chest.

"I've lost the key that opens my chest, and I've got to break in," he explained to her.

Mary Josephine's little laugh was delicious. "After what you told me about frozen eggs, I thought perhaps you were going to eat some," she said.

She linked her arm in his as they walked into the big room, snuggling her head against his shoulder so that, leaning over, his lips were buried in one of the soft, shining coils of her hair. And she was making plans, enumerating them on the tips of her fingers. If he had business outside, she was going with him. Wherever he went she was going. There was no doubt in her mind about that. She called his attention to a trunk that had arrived while he slept, and assured him she would be ready for outdoors by the time he had opened his chest. She had a little blue suit she was going to wear. And her hair? Did it look good enough for his friends to see? She had put it up in a hurry.

"It is beautiful, glorious," he said.

Her face pinked under the ardency of his gaze. She put a finger to the tip of his nose, laughing at him. "Why, Derry, if you weren't my brother I'd think you were my lover! You said that as though you meant it TERRIBLY much. Do you?"

He felt a sudden dull stab of pain, "Yes, I mean it. It's glorious. And so are you, Mary Josephine, every bit of you."

On tiptoe she gave him the warm sweetness of her lips again. And then she ran away from him, joy and laughter in her face, and disappeared into her room. "You must hurry or I shall beat you," she called back to him.

XIII

In his own room, with the door closed and locked, Keith felt again that dull, strange pain that made his heart sick and the air about him difficult to breathe.

"IF YOU WEREN'T MY BROTHER."

The words beat in his brain. They were pounding at his heart until it was smothered, laughing at him and taunting him and triumphing over him just as, many times before, the raving voices of the weird wind-devils had scourged him from out of black night and arctic storm. HER BROTHER! His hand clenched until the nails bit into his flesh. No, he hadn't thought of that part of the fight! And now it swept upon him in a deluge. If he lost in the fight that was ahead of him, his life would pay the forfeit. The law would take him, and he would hang. And if he won—she would be his sister forever and to the end of all time! Just that, and no more. His SISTER! And the agony of truth gripped him that it was not as a brother that he saw the glory in her hair, the glory in her eyes and face, and the glory in her slim little, beautiful body—but as the lover. A merciless preordination had stacked the cards against him again. He was Conniston, and she was Conniston's sister.

A strong man, a man in whom blood ran red, there leaped up in him for a moment a sudden and unreasoning rage at that thing which he had called fate. He saw the unfairness of it all, the hopelessness of it, the cowardly subterfuge and trickery of life itself as it had played against him, and with tightly set lips and clenched hands he called mutely on God Almighty to play the game square. Give him a chance! Give him just one square deal, only one; let him see a way, let him fight a man's fight with a ray of hope ahead! In these red moments hope emblazoned itself before his eyes as a monstrous lie. Bitterness rose in him until he was drunk with it, and blasphemy filled his heart. Whichever way he turned, however hard he fought, there was no chance of winning. From the day he killed Kirkstone the cards had been stacked against him, and they were stacked now and would be stacked until the end. He had believed in God, he had believed in the inevitable ethics of the final reckoning of things, and he had believed strongly that an impersonal Something more powerful than man-made will was behind him in his struggles. These beliefs were smashed now. Toward them he felt the impulse of a maddened beast trampling hated things under foot. They stood for lies—treachery—cheating—yes, contemptible cheating! It was impossible for him to win. However he played, whichever way he turned, he must lose. For he was Conniston, and she was Conniston's sister, AND MUST BE TO THE END OF TIME.

Faintly, beyond the door, he heard Mary Josephine singing. Like a bit of steel drawn to a tension his normal self snapped back into place. His readjustment came with a lurch, a subtle sort of shock. His hands unclenched, the tense lines in his face relaxed, and because that God Almighty he had challenged had given to him an unquenchable humor, he saw another thing where only smirking ghouls and hypocrites had rent his brain with their fiendish exultations a moment before. It was Conniston's face, suave, smiling, dying, triumphant over life, and

Conniston was saying, just as he had said up there in the cabin on the Barren, with death reaching out a hand for him, "It's queer, old top, devilish queer—and funny!"

Yes, it was funny if one looked at it right, and Keith found himself swinging back into his old view-point. It was the hugest joke life had ever played on him. His sister! He could fancy Conniston twisting his mustaches, his cool eyes glimmering with silent laughter, looking on his predicament, and he could fancy Conniston saying: "It's funny, old top, devilish funny—but it'll be funnier still when some other man comes along and carries her off!"

And he, John Keith, would have to grin and bear it because he was her brother!

Mary Josephine was tapping at his door.

"Derwent Conniston," she called frigidly, "there's a female person on the telephone asking for you. What shall I say?"

"Er—why—tell her you're my sister, Mary Josephine, and if it's Miss Kirkstone, be nice to her and say I'm not able to come to the 'phone, and that you're looking forward to meeting her, and that we'll be up to see her some time today."

"Oh, indeed!"

"You see," said Keith, his mouth close to the door, "you see, this Miss Kirkstone—"

But Mary Josephine was gone.

Keith grinned. His illimitable optimism was returning. Sufficient for the day that she was there, that she loved him, that she belonged to him, that just now he was the arbiter of her destiny! Far off in the mountains he dreamed of, alone, just they two, what might not happen? Some day—

With the cold chisel and the hammer he went to the chest. His task was one that numbed his hands before the last of the three locks was broken. He dragged the chest more into the light and opened it. He was disappointed. At first glance he could not understand why Conniston had locked it at all. It was almost empty, so nearly empty that he could see the bottom of it, and the first object that met his eyes was an insult to his expectations—an old sock with a huge hole in the toe of it. Under the sock was an old fur cap not of the kind worn north of Montreal. There was a chain with a dog-collar attached to it, a hip-pocket pistol and a huge forty-five, and not less than a hundred cartridges of indiscriminate calibers scattered loosely about. At one end, bundled in carelessly, was a pair of riding-breeches, and under the breeches a pair of white shoes with rubber soles. There was neither sentiment nor reason to the collection in the chest. It was junk. Even the big forty-five had a broken hammer, and the pistol, Keith thought, might have stunned a fly at close range. He pawed the things over with the cold chisel, and the last thing he came upon—buried under what looked like a cast-off sport shirt—was a pasteboard shoe box. He raised the cover. The box was full of papers.

Here was promise. He transported the box to Brady's table and sat down. He examined the larger papers first. There were a couple of old game licenses for Manitoba, half a dozen pencil-marked maps, chiefly of the Peace River country, and a number of letters from the secretaries of Boards of Trade pointing out the incomparable possibilities their respective districts held for the homesteader and the buyer of land. Last of all came a number of newspaper clippings and a packet of letters.

Because they were loose he seized upon the clippings first, and as his eyes fell upon the first paragraph of the first clipping his body became suddenly tensed in the shock of unexpected discovery and amazed interest. There were six of the clippings, all from English papers, English in their terseness, brief as stock exchange reports, and equally to the point. He read the six in three minutes.

They simply stated that Derwent Conniston, of the Connistons of Darlington, was wanted for burglary—and that up to date he had not been found.

Keith gave a gasp of incredulity. He looked again to see that his eyes were not tricking him. And it was there in cold, implacable print. Derwent Conniston—that phoenix among men, by whom he had come to measure all other men, that Crichton of nerve, of calm and audacious courage, of splendid poise—a burglar! It was cheap, farcical, an impossible absurdity. Had it been murder, high treason, defiance of some great law, a great crime inspired by a great passion or a great ideal, but it was burglary, brigandage of the cheapest and most commonplace variety, a sneaking night-coward's plagiarism of real adventure and real crime. It was impossible. Keith gritted the words aloud. He might have accepted Conniston as a Dick Turpin, a Claude Duval or a Macheath, but not as a Jeremy Diddler or a Bill Sykes. The printed lines were lies. They must be. Derwent Conniston might have killed a dozen men, but he had never cracked a safe. To think it was to think the inconceivable.

He turned to the letters. They were postmarked Darlington, England. His fingers tingled as he opened the first. It was as he had expected, as he had hoped. They were from Mary Josephine. He arranged them—nine in all—in the sequence of their dates, which ran back

36

nearly eight years. All of them had been written within a period of eleven months. They were as legible as print. And as he passed from the first to the second, and from the second to the third, and then read on into the others, he forgot there was such a thing as time and that Mary Josephine was waiting for him. The clippings had told him one thing; here, like bits of driftage to be put together, a line in this place and half a dozen in that, in paragraphs that enlightened and in others that puzzled, was the other side of the story, a growing thing that rose up out of mystery and doubt in segments and fractions of segments adding themselves together piecemeal, welding the whole into form and substance, until there rode through Keith's veins a wild thrill of exultation and triumph.

And then he came to the ninth and last letter. It was in a different handwriting, brief, with a deadly specificness about it that gripped Keith as he read.

This ninth letter he held in his hand as he rose from the table, and out of his mouth there fell, unconsciously, Conniston's own words, "It's devilish queer, old top—and funny!"

There was no humor in the way he spoke them. His voice was hard, his eyes dully ablaze. He was looking back into that swirling, unutterable loneliness of the northland, and he was seeing Conniston again.

Fiercely he caught up the clippings, struck a match, and with a grim smile watched them as they curled up into flame and crumbled into ash. What a lie was life, what a malformed thing was justice, what a monster of iniquity the man-fabricated thing called law!

And again he found himself speaking, as if the dead Englishman himself were repeating the words, "It's devilish queer, old top—and funny!"

XIV

A quarter of an hour later, with Mary Josephine at his side, he was walking down the green slope toward the Saskatchewan. In that direction lay the rims of timber, the shimmering valley, and the broad pathways that opened into the plains beyond.

The town was at their backs, and Keith wanted it there. He wanted to keep McDowell, and Shan Tung, and Miriam Kirkstone as far away as possible, until his mind rode more smoothly in the new orbit in which it was still whirling a bit unsteadily. More than all else he wanted to be alone with Mary Josephine, to make sure of her, to convince himself utterly that she was his to go on fighting for. He sensed the nearness and the magnitude of the impending drama. He knew that today he must face Shan Tung, that again he must go under the battery of McDowell's eyes and brain, and that like a fish in treacherous waters he must swim cleverly to avoid the nets that would entangle and destroy him. Today was the day—the stage was set, the curtain about to be lifted, the play ready to be enacted. But before it was the prologue. And the prologue was Mary Josephine's.

At the crest of a dip halfway down the slope they had paused, and in this pause he stood a half-step behind her so that he could look at her for a moment without being observed. She was bareheaded, and it came upon him all at once how wonderful was a woman's hair, how beautiful beyond all other things beautiful and desirable. In twisted, glowing seductiveness it was piled up on Mary Josephine's head, transformed into brown and gold glories by the sun. He wanted to put forth his hand to it, and bury his fingers in it, and feel the thrill and the warmth and the crush of the palpitant life of it against his own flesh. And then, bending a little forward, he saw under her long lashes the sheer joy of life shining in her eyes as she drank in the wonderful panorama that lay below them to the west. Last night's rain had freshened it, the sun glorified it now, and the fragrance of earthly smells that rose up to them from it was the undefiled breath of a thing living and awake. Even to Keith the river had never looked more beautiful, and never had his yearnings gone out to it more strongly than in this moment, to the river and beyond—and to the back of beyond, where the mountains rose up to meet the blue sky and the river itself was born. And he heard Mary Josephine's voice, joyously suppressed, exclaiming softly,

"Oh, Derry!"

His heart was filled with gladness. She, too, was seeing what his eyes saw in that wonderland. And she was feeling it. Her hand, seeking his hand, crept into his palm, and the fingers of it clung to his fingers. He could feel the thrill of the miracle passing through her, the miracle of the open spaces, the miracle of the forests rising billow on billow to the purple mists of the horizon, the miracle of the golden Saskatchewan rolling slowly and peacefully in its slumbering sheen out of that mighty mysteryland that reached to the lap of the setting sun. He spoke to her of that land as she looked, wide-eyed, quick-breathing, her fingers closing still more tightly about his. This was but the beginning of the glory of the west and the north, he told her. Beyond that low horizon, where the tree tops touched the sky were the prairies—not the tiresome monotony which she had seen from the car windows, but the wide, glorious, God-given country of the Northwest with its thousands of lakes and rivers and its tens of thousands of square miles of forests; and beyond those things, still farther, were the foothills, and beyond the foothills the mountains. And in those mountains the river down there had its beginning.

She looked up swiftly, her eyes brimming with the golden flash of the sun. "It is wonderful! And just over there is the town!"

"Yes, and beyond the town are the cities."

"And off there—"

"God's country," said Keith devoutly.

Mary Josephine drew a deep breath. "And people still live in towns and cities!" she exclaimed in wondering credulity. "I've dreamed of 'over here,' Derry, but I never dreamed that. And you've had it for years and years, while I—oh, Derry!"

And again those two words filled his heart with gladness, words of loving reproach, atremble with the mysterious whisper of a great desire. For she was looking into the west. And her eyes and her heart and her soul were in the west, and suddenly Keith saw his way as though lighted by a flaming torch. He came near to forgetting that he was Conniston. He spoke of his dream, his desire, and told her that last night—before she came—he had made up his mind to go. She had come to him just in time. A little later and he would have been gone, buried utterly away from the world in the wonderland of the mountains. And now they would go together. They would go as he had planned to go, quietly, unobtrusively; they would slip away and disappear. There was a reason why no one should know, not even McDowell. It must be their secret. Some day he would tell her why. Her heart thumped excitedly as he went on like a boy planning a wonderful day. He could see the swifter beat of it in the flush that rose into her face and the joy glowing tremulously in her eyes as she looked at him. They would get ready quietly. They might go tomorrow, the next day, any time. It would be a glorious adventure, just they two, with all the vastness of that mountain paradise ahead of them.

"We'll be pals," he said. "Just you and me, Mary Josephine. We're all that's left."

It was his first experiment, his first reference to the information he had gained in the letters, and swift as a flash Mary Josephine's eyes turned up to him. He nodded, smiling. He understood their quick questioning, and he held her hand closer and began to walk with her down the slope.

"A lot of it came back last night and this morning, a lot of it," he explained. "It's queer what miracles small things can work sometimes, isn't it? Think what a grain of sand can do to a watch! This was one of the small things." He was still smiling as he touched the scar on his forehead. "And you, you were the other miracle. And I'm remembering. It doesn't seem like seven or eight years, but only yesterday, that the grain of sand got mixed up somewhere in the machinery in my head. And I guess there was another reason for my going wrong. You'll understand, when I tell you."

Had he been Conniston it could not have come from him more naturally, more sincerely. He was living the great lie, and yet to him it was no longer a lie. He did not hesitate, as shame and conscience might have made him hesitate. He was fighting that something beautiful might be raised up out of chaos and despair and be made to exist; he was fighting for life in place of death, for happiness in place of grief, for light in place of darkness—fighting to save where others would destroy. Therefore the great lie was not a lie but a thing without venom or hurt, an instrument for happiness and for all the things good and beautiful that went to make happiness. It was his one great weapon. Without it he would fail, and failure meant desolation. So he spoke convincingly, for what he said came straight from the heart though it was born in the shadow of that one master-falsehood. His wonder was that Mary Josephine believed him so utterly that not for an instant was there a questioning doubt in her eyes or on her lips.

He told her how much he "remembered," which was no more and no less than he had learned from the letters and the clippings. The story did not appeal to him as particularly unusual or dramatic. He had passed through too many tragic happenings in the last four years to regard it in that way. It was simply an unfortunate affair beginning in misfortune, and with its necessary whirlwind of hurt and sorrow. The one thing of shame he would not keep out of his mind was that he, Derwent Conniston, must have been a poor type of big brother in those days of nine or ten years ago, even though little Mary Josephine had worshiped him. He was well along in his twenties then. The Connistons of Darlington were his uncle and aunt, and his uncle was a more or less prominent figure in ship-building interests on the Clyde. With these people the three—himself, Mary Josephine, and his brother Egbert—had lived, "farmed out" to a hard-necked, flinty-hearted pair of relatives because of a brother's stipulation and a certain English law. With them they had existed in mutual discontent and dislike. Derwent, when he became old enough, had stepped over the traces. All this Keith had gathered from the letters, but there was a great deal that was missing. Egbert, he gathered, must have been a scapegrace. He was a cripple of some sort and seven or eight years his junior. In the letters Mary Josephine had spoken of him as "poor Egbert," pitying instead of condemning him, though it was Egbert who had brought tragedy and separation upon them. One night Egbert had broken open the Conniston safe and in the darkness had had a fight and a narrow escape from his uncle, who laid the crime upon Derwent. And Derwent, in whom Egbert must have confided, had fled to America that the cripple might be saved, with the promise that some day he would send for Mary Josephine. He was followed by the uncle's threat that if he ever returned to England, he would be jailed. Not long afterward "poor Egbert" was found dead in bed, fearfully contorted. Keith guessed there had been something mentally as well as physically wrong with him.

"—And I was going to send for you," he said, as they came to the level of the valley. "My plans were made, and I was going to send for you, when this came."

He stopped, and in a few tense, breathless moments Mary Josephine read the ninth and last letter he had taken from the Englishman's chest. It was from her uncle. In a dozen lines it stated that she, Mary Josephine, was dead, and it reiterated the threat against Derwent Conniston should he ever dare to return to England.

A choking cry came to her lips. "And that—THAT was it?"

"Yes, that—and the hurt in my head," he said, remembering the part he must play. "They came at about the same time, and the two of them must have put the grain of sand in my brain."

It was hard to lie now, looking straight into her face that had gone suddenly white, and with her wonderful eyes burning deep into his soul.

She did not seem, for an instant, to hear his voice or sense his words. "I understand now," she was saying, the letter crumpling in her fingers. "I was sick for almost a year, Derry. They thought I was going to die. He must have written it then, and they destroyed my letters to you, and when I was better they told me you were dead, and then I didn't write any more. And I wanted to die. And then, almost a year ago, Colonel Reppington came to me, and his dear old voice was so excited that it trembled, and he told me that he believed you were alive. A friend of his had just returned from British Columbia, and this friend told him that three years before, while on a grizzly shooting trip, he had met a man named Conniston, an Englishman. We wrote a hundred letters up there and found the man, Jack Otto, who was in the mountains with you, and then I knew you were alive. But we couldn't find you after that, and so I came—"

He would have wagered that she was going to cry, but she fought the tears back, smiling.

"And—and I've found you!" she finished triumphantly.

She snuggled close to him, and he slipped an arm about her waist, and they walked on. She told him about her arrival in Halifax, how Colonel Reppington had given her letters to nice people in Montreal and Winnipeg, and how it happened one day that she found his name in one of the Mounted Police blue books, and after that came on as fast as she could to surprise him at Prince Albert. When she came to that point, Keith pointed once more into the west and said:

"And there is our new world. Let us forget the old. Shall we, Mary Josephine?"

"Yes," she whispered, and her hand sought his again and crept into it, warm and confident.

XV

They went on through the golden morning, the earth damp under their feet, the air filled with its sweet incense, on past scattered clumps of balsams and cedars until they came to the river and looked down on its yellow sand-bars glistening in the sun. The town was hidden. They heard no sound from it. And looking up the great Saskatchewan, the river of mystery, of romance, of glamour, they saw before them, where the spruce walls seemed to meet, the wide-open door through which they might pass into the western land beyond. Keith pointed it out. And he pointed out the yellow bars, the glistening shores of sand, and told her how even as far as this, a thousand miles by river—those sands brought gold with them from the mountains, the gold whose treasure-house no man had ever found, and which must be hidden up there somewhere near the river's end. His dream, like Duggan's, had been to find it. Now they would search for it together.

Slowly he was picking his way so that at last they came to the bit of cleared timber in which was his old home. His heart choked him as they drew near. There was an uncomfortable tightness in his breath. The timber was no longer "clear." In four years younger generations of life had sprung up among the trees, and the place was jungle-ridden. They were within a few yards of the house before Mary Josephine saw it, and then she stopped suddenly with a little gasp. For this that she faced was not desertion, was not mere neglect. It was tragedy. She saw in an instant that there was no life in this place, and yet it stood as if tenanted. It was a log chateau with a great, red chimney rising at one end curtains and shades still hung at the windows. There were three chairs on the broad veranda that looked riverward. But two of the windows were broken, and the chairs were falling into ruin. There was no life. They were facing only the ghosts of life.

A swift glance into Keith's face told her this was so. His lips were set tight. There was a strange look in his face. Hand in hand they had come up, and her fingers pressed his tighter now.

"What is it?" she asked.

"It is John Keith's home as he left it four years ago," he replied.

The suspicious break in his voice drew her eyes from the chateau to his own again. She could see him fighting. There was a twitching in his throat. His hand was gripping hers until it hurt.

"John Keith?" she whispered softly.

"Yes, John Keith."

She inclined her head so that it rested lightly and affectionately against his arm.

"You must have thought a great deal of him, Derry."

"Yes."

He freed her hand, and his fists clenched convulsively. She could feel the cording of the muscles in his arm, his face was white, and in his eyes was a fixed stare that startled her. He fumbled in a pocket and drew out a key.

"I promised, when he died, that I would go in and take a last look for him," he said. "He loved this place. Do you want to go with me?"

She drew a deep breath. "Yes."

The key opened the door that entered on the veranda. As it swung back, grating on its rusty hinges, they found themselves facing the chill of a cold and lifeless air. Keith stepped inside. A glance told him that nothing was changed—everything was there in that room with the big fireplace, even as he had left it the night he set out to force justice from Judge Kirkstone. One thing startled him. On the dust-covered table was a bowl and a spoon. He remembered vividly how he had eaten his supper that night of bread and milk. It was the littleness of the thing, the simplicity of it, that shocked him. The bowl and spoon were still there after four years. He did not reflect that they were as imperishable as all the other things about; the miracle was that they were there on the table, as though he had used them only yesterday. The most trivial things in the room struck him deepest, and he found himself fighting hard, for a moment, to keep his nerve.

"He told me about the bowl and the spoon, John Keith did," he said, nodding toward them. "He told me just what I'd find here, even to that. You see, he loved the place greatly and everything that was in it. It was impossible for him to forget even the bowl and the spoon and where he had left them."

It was easier after that. The old home was whispering back its memories to him, and he told them to Mary Josephine as they went slowly from room to room, until John Keith was living there before her again, the John Keith whom Derwent Conniston had run to his death. It was this thing that gripped her, and at last what was in her mind found voice.

"It wasn't YOU who made him die, was it, Derry? It wasn't you?"

"No. It was the law. He died, as I told you, of a frosted lung. At the last I would have shared my life with him had it been possible. McDowell must never know that. You must never speak of John Keith before him."

"I—I understand, Derry."

"And he must not know that we came here. To him John Keith was a murderer whom it was his duty to hang."

She was looking at him strangely. Never had he seen her look at him in that way.

"Derry," she whispered.

"Yes?"

"Derry, IS JOHN KEITH ALIVE?"

He started. The shock of the question was in his face. He caught himself, but it was too late. And in an instant her hand was at his mouth, and she was whispering eagerly, almost fiercely:

"No, no, no—don't answer me, Derry! DON'T ANSWER ME! I know, and I understand, and I'm glad, glad, GLAD! He's alive, and it was you who let him live, the big, glorious brother I'm proud of! And everyone else thinks he's dead. But don't answer me, Derry, don't answer me!"

She was trembling against him. His arms closed about her, and he held her nearer to his heart, and longer, than he had ever held her before. He kissed her hair many times, and her lips once, and up about his neck her arms twined softly, and a great brightness was in her eyes.

"I understand," she whispered again. "I understand."

"And I—I must answer you," he said. "I must answer you, because I love you, and because you must know. Yes, John Keith is alive!"

XVI

An hour later, alone and heading for the inspector's office, Keith felt in battle trim. His head was fairly singing with the success of the morning. Since the opening of Conniston's chest many things had happened, and he was no longer facing a blank wall of mystery. His chief cause of exhilaration was Mary Josephine. She wanted to go away with him. She wanted to go with him anywhere, everywhere, as long as they were together. When she had learned that his term of enlistment was about to expire and that if he remained in the Service he would be away from her a great deal, she had pleaded with him not to reenlist. She did not question him when he told her that it might be necessary to go away very suddenly, without letting another soul know of their movements, not even Wallie. Intuitively she guessed that the reason had something to do with John Keith, for he had let the fear grow in her that McDowell might discover he had been a traitor to the Service, in which event the Law itself would take him away from her for a considerable number of years. And with that fear she was more than ever eager for the adventure, and planned with him for its consummation.

Another thing cheered Keith. He was no longer the absolute liar of yesterday, for by a fortunate chance he had been able to tell her that John Keith was alive. This most important of all truths he had confided to her, and the confession had roused in her a comradeship that had proclaimed itself ready to fight for him or run away with him. Not for an instant had she regretted the action he had taken in giving Keith his freedom. He was peculiarly happy because of that. She was glad John Keith was alive.

And now that she knew the story of the old home down in the clump of timber and of the man who had lived there, she was anxious to meet Miriam Kirkstone, daughter of the man he had killed. Keith had promised her they would go up that afternoon. Within himself he knew that he was not sure of keeping the promise. There was much to do in the next few hours, and much might happen. In fact there was but little speculation about it. This was the big day. Just what it held for him he could not be sure until he saw Shan Tung. Any instant might see him put to the final test.

Cruze was pacing slowly up and down the hall when Keith entered the building in which McDowell had his offices. The young secretary's face bore a perplexed and rather anxious expression. His hands were buried deep in his trousers pockets, and he was puffing a cigarette. At Keith's appearance he brightened up a bit.

"Don't know what to make of the governor this morning, by Jove I don't!" he explained, nodding toward the closed doors. "I've got instructions to let no one near him except you. You may go in."

"What seems to be the matter?" Keith felt out cautiously.

Cruze shrugged his thin shoulders, nipped the ash from his cigarette, and with a grimace said, "Shan Tung."

"Shan Tung?" Keith spoke the name in a sibilant whisper. Every nerve in him had jumped, and for an instant he thought he had betrayed himself. Shan Tung had been there early. And now McDowell was waiting for him and had given instructions that no other should be admitted. If the Chinaman had exposed him, why hadn't McDowell sent officers up to the Shack? That was the first question that jumped into his head. The answer came as quickly—

McDowell had not sent officers because, hating Shan Tung, he had not believed his story. But he was waiting there to investigate. A chill crept over Keith.

Cruze was looking at him intently.

"There's something to this Shan Tung business," he said. "It's even getting on the old man's nerves. And he's very anxious to see you, Mr. Conniston. I've called you up half a dozen times in the last hour."

He nipped away his cigarette, turned alertly, and moved toward the inspector's door. Keith wanted to call him back, to leap upon him, if necessary, and drag him away from that deadly door. But he neither moved nor spoke until it was too late. The door opened, he heard Cruze announce his presence, and it seemed to him the words were scarcely out of the secretary's mouth when McDowell himself stood in the door.

"Come in, Conniston," he said quietly. "Come in."

It was not McDowell's voice. It was restrained, terrible. It was the voice of a man speaking softly to cover a terrific fire raging within. Keith felt himself doomed. Even as he entered, his mind was swiftly gathering itself for the last play, the play he had set for himself if the crisis came. He would cover McDowell, bind and gag him even as Cruze sauntered in the hall, escape through a window, and with Mary Josephine bury himself in the forests before pursuit could overtake them. Therefore his amazement was unbounded when McDowell, closing the door, seized his hand in a grip that made him wince, and shook it with unfeigned gladness and relief.

"I'm not condemning you, of course," he said. "It was rather beastly of me to annoy your sister before you were up this morning. She flatly refused to rouse you, and by George, the way she said it made me turn the business of getting into touch with you over to Cruze. Sit down, Conniston. I'm going to explode a mine under you."

He flung himself into his swivel chair and twisted one of his fierce mustaches, while his eyes blazed at Keith. Keith waited. He saw the other was like an animal ready to spring and anxious to spring, the one evident stricture on his desire being that there was nothing to spring at unless it was himself.

"What happened last night?" he asked.

Keith's mind was already working swiftly. McDowell's question gave him the opportunity of making the first play against Shan Tung.

"Enough to convince me that I am going to see Shan Tung today," he said.

He noticed the slow clenching and unclenching of McDowell's fingers about the arms of his chair.

"Then—I was right?"

"I have every reason to believe you were—up to a certain point. I shall know positively when I have talked with Shan Tung."

He smiled grimly. McDowell's eyes were no harder than his own. The iron man drew a deep breath and relaxed a bit in his chair.

"If anything should happen," he said, looking away from Keith, as though the speech were merely casual, "if he attacks you—"

"It might be necessary to kill him in self-defense," finished Keith.

McDowell made no sign to show that he had heard, yet Keith thrilled with the conviction that he had struck home. He went on telling briefly what had happened at Miriam Kirkstone's house the preceding night. McDowell's face was purple when he described the evidences of Shan Tung's presence at the house on the hill, but with a mighty effort he restrained his passion.

"That's it, that's it," he exclaimed, choking back his wrath. "I knew he was there! And this morning both of them lie about it—both of them, do you understand! She lied, looking me straight in the eyes. And he lied, and for the first time in his life he laughed at me, curse me if he didn't! It was like the gurgle of oil. I didn't know a human could laugh that way. And on top of that he told me something that I WON'T believe, so help me God, I won't!"

He jumped to his feet and began pacing back and forth, his hands clenched behind him. Suddenly he whirled on Keith.

"Why in heaven's name didn't you bring Keith back with you, or, if not Keith, at least a written confession, signed by him?" he demanded.

This was a blow from behind for Keith. "What—what has Keith got to do with this?" he stumbled.

"More than I dare tell you, Conniston. But WHY didn't you bring back a signed confession from him? A dying man is usually willing to make that."

"If he is guilty, yes," agreed Keith. "But this man was a different sort. If he killed Judge Kirkstone, he had no regret. He did not consider himself a criminal. He felt that he had dealt out justice in his own way, and therefore, even when he was dying, he would not sign anything or state anything definitely."

McDowell subsided into his chair.

"And the curse of it is I haven't a thing on Shan Tung," he gritted. "Not a thing. Miriam Kirkstone is her own mistress, and in the eyes of the law he is as innocent of crime as I am. If she is voluntarily giving herself as a victim to this devil, it is her own business—legally, you understand. Morally—"

He stopped, his savagely gleaming eyes boring Keith to the marrow.

"He hates you as a snake hates fire-water. It is possible, if he thought the opportunity had come to him—"

Again he paused, cryptic, waiting for the other to gather the thing he had not spoken. Keith, simulating two of Conniston's tricks at the same time, shrugged a shoulder and twisted a mustache as he rose to his feet. He smiled coolly down at the iron man. For once he gave a passable imitation of the Englishman.

"And he's going to have the opportunity today," he said understandingly. "I think, old chap, I'd better be going. I'm rather anxious to see Shan Tung before dinner."

McDowell followed him to the door.

His face had undergone a change. There was a tense expectancy, almost an eagerness there. Again he gripped Keith's hand, and before the door opened he said,

"If trouble comes between you let it be in the open, Conniston—in the open and not on Shan Tung's premises."

Keith went out, his pulse quickening to the significance of the iron man's words, and wondering what the "mine" was that McDowell had promised to explode, but which he had not.

XVII

Keith lost no time in heading for Shan Tung's. He was like a man playing chess, and the moves were becoming so swift and so intricate that his mind had no rest. Each hour brought forth its fresh necessities and its new alternatives. It was McDowell who had given him his last cue, perhaps the surest and safest method of all for winning his game. The iron man, that disciple of the Law who was merciless in his demand of an eye for an eye and a tooth for a tooth, had let him understand that the world would be better off without Shan Tung. This man, who never in his life had found an excuse for the killer, now maneuvered subtly the suggestion for a killing.

Keith was both shocked and amazed. "If anything happens, let it be in the open and not on Shan Tung's premises," he had warned him. That implied in McDowell's mind a cool and calculating premeditation, the assumption that if Shan Tung was killed it would be in self-defense. And Keith's blood leaped to the thrill of it. He had not only found the depths of McDowell's personal interest in Miriam Kirkstone, but a last weapon had been placed in his hands, a weapon which he could use this day if it became necessary. Cornered, with no other hope of saving himself, he could as a last resort kill Shan Tung—and McDowell would stand behind him!

He went directly to Shan Tung's cafe and sauntered in. There were large changes in it since four years ago. The moment he passed through its screened vestibule, he felt its oriental exclusiveness, the sleek and mysterious quietness of it. One might have found such a place catering to the elite of a big city. It spoke sumptuously of a large expenditure of money, yet there was nothing bizarre or irritating to the senses. Its heavily-carved tables were almost oppressive in their solidity. Linen and silver, like Shan Tung himself, were immaculate. Magnificently embroidered screens were so cleverly arranged that one saw not all of the place at once, but caught vistas of it. The few voices that Keith heard in this pre-lunch hour were subdued, and the speakers were concealed by screens. Two orientals, as immaculate as the silver and linen, were moving about with the silence of velvet-padded lynxes. A third, far in the rear, stood motionless as one of the carven tables, smoking a cigarette and watchful as a ferret. This was Li King, Shan Tung's right-hand man.

Keith approached him. When he was near enough, Li King gave the slightest inclination to his head and took the cigarette from his mouth. Without movement or speech he registered the question, "What do you want?"

Keith knew this to be a bit of oriental guile. In his mind there was no doubt that Li King had been fully instructed by his master and that he had been expecting him, even watching for him. Convinced of this, he gave him one of Conniston's cards and said,

"Take this to Shan Tung. He is expecting me."

Li King looked at the card, studied it for a moment with apparent stupidity, and shook his head. "Shan Tung no home. Gone away."

That was all. Where he had gone or when he would return Keith could not discover from Li King. Of all other matters except that he had gone away the manager of Shan Tung's affairs was ignorant. Keith felt like taking the yellow-skinned hypocrite by the throat and choking something out of him, but he realized that Li King was studying and watching him, and that he would report to Shan Tung every expression that had passed over his face. So he looked at his watch, bought a cigar at the glass case near the cash register, and departed with a cheerful nod, saying that he would call again.

Ten minutes later he determined on a bold stroke. There was no time for indecision or compromise. He must find Shan Tung and find him quickly. And he believed that Miriam Kirkstone could give him a pretty good tip as to his whereabouts. He steeled himself to the demand he was about to make as he strode up to the house on the hill. He was disappointed again. Miss Kirkstone was not at home. If she was, she did not answer to his knocking and bell ringing.

He went to the depot. No one he questioned had seen Shan Tung at the west-bound train, the only train that had gone out that morning, and the agent emphatically disclaimed selling him a ticket. Therefore he had not gone far. Suspicion leaped red in Keith's brain. His imagination pictured Shan Tung at that moment with Miriam Kirkstone, and at the thought his disgust went out against them both. In this humor he returned to McDowell's office. He stood before his chief, leaning toward him over the desk table. This time he was the inquisitor.

"Plainly speaking, this liaison is their business," he declared. "Because he is yellow and she is white doesn't make it ours. I've just had a hunch. And I believe in following hunches, especially when one hits you good and hard, and this one has given me a jolt that means something. Where is that big fat brother of hers?"

McDowell hesitated. "It isn't a liaison," he temporized. "It's one-sided—a crime against—"

"WHERE IS THAT BIG FAT BROTHER?" With each word Keith emphasized his demand with a thud of his fist on the table. "WHERE IS HE?"

McDowell was deeply perturbed. Keith could see it and waited.

After a moment of silence the iron man rose from the swivel chair, walked to the window, gazed out for another moment, and walked back again, twisting one of his big gray mustaches in a way that betrayed the stress of his emotion. "Confound it, Conniston, you've got a mind for seeking out the trivialities, and little things are sometimes the most embarrassing."

"And sometimes most important," added Keith. "For instance, it strikes me as mighty important that we should know where Peter Kirkstone is and why he is not here fighting for his sister's salvation. Where is he?"

"I don't know. He disappeared from town a month ago. Miriam says he is somewhere in British Columbia looking over some old mining properties. She doesn't know just where."

"And you believe her?"

The eyes of the two men met. There was no longer excuse for equivocation. Both understood.

McDowell smiled in recognition of the fact. "No. I think, Conniston, that she is the most wonderful little liar that lives. And the beautiful part of it is, she is lying for a purpose. Imagine Peter Kirkstone, who isn't worth the powder to blow him to Hades, interested in old mines or anything else that promises industry or production! And the most inconceivable thing about the whole mess is that Miriam worships that fat and worthless pig of a brother. I've tried to find him in British Columbia. Failed, of course. Another proof that this affair between Miriam and Shan Tung isn't a voluntary liaison on her part. She's lying. She's walking on a pavement of lies. If she told the truth—"

"There are some truths which one cannot tell about oneself," interrupted Keith. "They must be discovered or buried. And I'm going deeper into this prospecting and undertaking business this afternoon. I've got another hunch. I think I'll have something interesting to report before night."

Ten minutes later, on his way to the Shack, he was discussing with himself the modus operandi of that "hunch." It had come to him in an instant, a flash of inspiration. That afternoon he would see Miriam Kirkstone and question her about Peter. Then he would return to McDowell, lay stress on the importance of the brother, tell him that he had a clew which he wanted to follow, and suggest finally a swift trip to British Columbia. He would take Mary Josephine, lie low until his term of service expired, and then report by letter to McDowell that he had failed and that he had made up his mind not to reenlist but to try his fortunes with Mary Josephine in Australia. Before McDowell received that letter, they could be on their way into the mountains. The "hunch" offered an opportunity for a clean getaway, and in his jubilation Miriam Kirkstone and her affairs were important only as a means to an end. He was John Keith now, fighting for John Keith's life—and Derwent Conniston's sister.

Mary Josephine herself put the first shot into the fabric of his plans. She must have been watching for him, for when halfway up the slope he saw her coming to meet him. She scolded him for being away from her, as he had expected her to do. Then she pulled his arm about her slim little waist and held the hand thus engaged in both her own as they walked up the winding path. He noticed the little wrinkles in her adorable forehead.

"Derry, is it the right thing for young ladies to call on their gentlemen friends over here?" she asked suddenly.

"Why—er—that depends, Mary Josephine. You mean—"

"Yes, I do, Derwent Conniston! She's pretty, and I don't blame you, but I can't help feeling that I don't like it!"

His arm tightened about her until she gasped. The fragile softness of her waist was a joy to him.

"Derry!" she remonstrated. "If you do that again, I'll break!"

"I couldn't help it," he pleaded. "I couldn't, dear. The way you said it just made my arm close up tight. I'm glad you didn't like it. I can love only one at a time, and I'm loving you, and I'm going on loving you all my life."

"I wasn't jealous," she protested, blushing. "But she called twice on the telephone and then came up. And she's pretty."

"I suppose you mean Miss Kirkstone?"

"Yes. She was frightfully anxious to see you, Derry."

"And what did you think of her, dear?"

She cast a swift look up into his face.

"Why, I like her. She's sweet and pretty, and I fell in love with her hair. But something was troubling her this morning. I'm quite sure of it, though she tried to keep it back."

"She was nervous, you mean, and pale, with sometimes a frightened look in her eyes. Was that it?"

"You seem to know, Derry. I think it was all that."

He nodded. He saw his horizon aglow with the smile of fortune. Everything was coming propitiously for him, even this unexpected visit of Miriam Kirkstone. He did not trouble himself to speculate as to the object of her visit, for he was grappling now with his own opportunity, his chance to get away, to win out for himself in one last master-stroke, and his mind was concentrated in that direction. The time was ripe to tell these things to Mary Josephine. She must be prepared.

On the flat table of the hill where Brady had built his bungalow were scattered clumps of golden birch, and in the shelter of one of the nearer clumps was a bench, to which Keith drew Mary Josephine. Thereafter for many minutes he spoke his plans. Mary Josephine's cheeks grew flushed. Her eyes shone with excitement and eagerness. She thrilled to the story he told her of what they would do in those wonderful mountains of gold and mystery, just they two alone. He made her understand even more definitely that his safety and their mutual happiness depended upon the secrecy of their final project, that in a way they were conspirators and must act as such. They might start for the west tonight or tomorrow, and she must get ready.

There he should have stopped. But with Mary Josephine's warm little hand clinging to his and her beautiful eyes shining at him like liquid stars, he felt within him an overwhelming faith and desire, and he went on, making a clean breast of the situation that was giving them the opportunity to get away. He felt no prick of conscience at thought of Miriam Kirkstone's affairs. Her destiny must be, as he had told McDowell, largely a matter of her own choosing. Besides, she had McDowell to fight for her. And the big fat brother, too. So without fear of its effect he told Mary Josephine of the mysterious liaison between Miriam Kirkstone and Shan Tung, of McDowell's suspicions, of his own beliefs, and how it was all working out for their own good.

Not until then did he begin to see the changing lights in her eyes. Not until he had finished did he notice that most of that vivid flush of joy had gone from her face and that she was looking at him in a strained, tense way. He felt then the reaction. She was not looking at the thing as he was looking at it. He had offered to her another woman's tragedy as THEIR opportunity, and her own woman's heart had responded in the way that has been woman's since the dawn of life. A sense of shame which he fought and tried to crush took possession of him. He was right. He must be right, for it was his life that was hanging in the balance. Yet Mary Josephine could not know that.

Her fingers had tightened about his, and she was looking away from him. He saw now that the color had almost gone from her face. There was the flash of a new fire in her yes.

"And THAT was why she was nervous and pale, with sometimes a frightened look in her eyes," she spoke softly, repeating his words. "It was because of this Chinese monster, Shan Tung—because he has some sort of power over her, you say—because—"

She snatched her hand from his with a suddenness that startled him. Her eyes, so beautiful and soft a few minutes before, scintillated fire. "Derry, if you don't fix this heathen devil—I WILL!"

She stood up before him, breathing quickly, and he beheld in her not the soft, slim-waisted little goddess of half an hour ago, but the fiercest fighter of all the fighting ages, a woman roused. And no longer fear, but a glory swept over him. She was Conniston's sister, AND SHE WAS CONNISTON. Even as he saw his plans falling about him, he opened his arms and held them out to her, and with the swiftness of love she ran into them, putting her hands to his face while he held her close and kissed her lips.

"You bet we'll fix that heathen devil before we go," he said. "You bet we will—SWEETHEART!"

XVIII

Wallie, suffering the outrage of one who sees his dinner growing cold, found Keith and Mary Josephine in the edge of the golden birch and implored them to come and eat. It was a marvel of a dinner. Over Mary Josephine's coffee and Keith's cigar they discussed their final plans. Keith made the big promise that he would "fix Shan Tung" in a hurry, perhaps that very afternoon. In the glow of Mary Josephine's proud eyes he felt no task too large for him, and he was eager to be at it. But when his cigar was half done, Mary Josephine came around and perched herself on the arm of his chair, and began running her fingers through his hair. All desire to go after Shan Tung left him. He would have remained there forever. Twice she bent down and touched his forehead lightly with her lips. Again his arm was round her soft little waist, and his heart was pumping like a thing overworked. It was Mary Josephine, finally, who sent him on his mission, but not before she stood on tiptoe, her hands on his shoulders, giving him her mouth to kiss.

An army at his back could not have strengthened Keith with a vaster determination than that kiss. There would be no more quibbling. His mind was made up definitely on the point. And his first move was to head straight for the Kirkstone house on the hill.

He did not get as far as the door this time. He caught a vision of Miriam Kirkstone in the shrubbery, bareheaded, her hair glowing radiantly in the sun. It occurred to him suddenly that it was her hair that roused the venom in him when he thought of her as the property of Shan Tung. If it had been black or even brown, the thought might not have emphasized itself so unpleasantly in his mind. But that vivid gold cried out against the crime, even against the girl herself. She saw him almost in the instant his eyes fell upon her, and came forward quickly to meet him. There was an eagerness in her face that told him his coming relieved her of a terrific suspense.

"I'm sorry I wasn't at the Shack when you came, Miss Kirkstone," he said, taking for a moment the hand she offered him. "I fancy you were up there to see me about Shan Tung."

He sent the shot bluntly, straight home. In the tone of his voice there was no apology. He saw her grow cold, her eyes fixed on him staringly, as though she not only heard his words but saw what was in his mind.

"Wasn't that it, Miss Kirkstone?"

She nodded affirmatively, but her lips did not move.

"Shan Tung," he repeated. "Miss Kirkstone, what is the trouble? Why don't you confide in someone, in McDowell, in me, in—"

He was going to say "your brother," but the suddenness with which she caught his arm cut the words short.

"Shan Tung has been to see him—McDowell?" she questioned excitedly. "He has been there today? And he told him—" She stopped, breathing quickly, her fingers tightening on his arm.

"I don't know what passed between them," said Keith. "But McDowell was tremendously worked up about you. So am I. We might as well be frank, Miss Kirkstone. There's something rotten in Denmark when two people like you and Shan Tung mix up. And you are mixed; you can't deny it. You have been to see Shan Tung late at night. He was in the house with you the first night I saw you. More than that—HE IS IN YOUR HOUSE NOW!"

She shrank back as if he had struck at her. "No, no, no," she cried. "He isn't there. I tell you, he isn't!"

"How am I to believe you?" demanded Keith. "You have not told the truth to McDowell. You are fighting to cover up the truth. And we know it is because of Shan Tung. WHY? I am here to fight for you, to help you. And McDowell, too. That is why we must know. Miss Kirkstone, do you love the Chinaman?"

He knew the words were an insult. He had guessed their effect. As if struck there suddenly by a painter's brush, two vivid spots appeared in the girl's pale cheeks. She shrank back from him another step. Her eyes blazed. Slowly, without turning their flame from his face, she pointed to the edge of the shrubbery a few feet from where they were standing. He looked. Twisted and partly coiled on the mold, where it had been clubbed to death, was a little green grass snake.

"I hate him—like that!" she said.

His eyes came back to her. "Then for some reason known only to you and Shan Tung you have sold or are intending to sell yourself to him!"

It was not a question. It was an accusation. He saw the flush of anger fading out of her cheeks. Her body relaxed, her head dropped, and slowly she nodded in confirmation.

"Yes, I am going to sell myself to him."

The astounding confession held him mute for a space. In the interval it was the girl who became self-possessed. What she said next amazed him still more.

"I have confessed so much because I am positive that you will not betray me. And I went up to the Shack to find you, because I want you to help me find a story to tell McDowell. You said you would help me. Will you?"

He still did not speak, and she went on.

"I am accepting that promise as granted, too. McDowell mistrusts, but he must not know. You must help me there. You must help me for two or three weeks, At the end of that time something may happen. He must be made to have faith in me again. Do you understand?"

"Partly," said Keith. "You ask me to do this blindly, without knowing why I am doing it, without any explanation whatever on your part except that for some unknown and mysterious price you are going to sell yourself to Shan Tung. You want me to cover and abet this monstrous deal by hoodwinking the man whose suspicions threaten its consummation. If there was not in my own mind a suspicion that you are insane, I should say your proposition is as ludicrous as it is impossible. Having that suspicion, it is a bit tragic. Also it is impossible. It is necessary for you first to tell me why you are going to sell yourself to Shan Tung."

Her face was coldly white and calm again. But her hands trembled. He saw her try to hide them, and pitied her.

"Then I won't trouble you any more, for that, too, is impossible," she said. "May I trust you to keep in confidence what I have told you? Perhaps I have had too much faith in you for a reason which has no reason, because you were with John Keith. John Keith was the one other man who might have helped me."

"And why John Keith? How could he have helped you?"

She shook her head. "If I told you that, I should be answering the question which is impossible."

He saw himself facing a checkmate. To plead, to argue with her, he knew would profit him nothing. A new thought came to him, swift and imperative. The end would justify the means. He clenched his hands. He forced into his face a look that was black and vengeful. And he turned it on her.

"Listen to me," he cried. "You are playing a game, and so am I. Possibly we are selfish, both of us, looking each to his own interests with no thought of the other. Will you help me, if I help you?"

Again he pitied her as he saw with what eager swiftness she caught at his bait.

"Yes," she nodded, catching her breath. "Yes, I will help you."

His face grew blacker. He raised his clenched hands so she could see them, and advanced a step toward her.

"Then tell me this—would you care if something happened to Shan Tung? Would you care if he died, if he was killed, if—"

Her breath was coming faster and faster. Again the red spots blazed in her cheeks.

"WOULD YOU CARE?" he demanded.

"No—no—I wouldn't care. He deserves to die."

"Then tell me where Shan Tung is. For my game is with him. And I believe it is a bigger game than your game, for it is a game of life and death. That is why I am interested in your affair. It is because I am selfish, because I have my own score to settle, and because you can help me. I shall ask you no more questions about yourself. And I shall keep your secret and help you with McDowell if you will keep mine and help me. First, where is Shan Tung?"

She hesitated for barely an instant. "He has gone out of town. He will be away for ten days."

"But he bought no ticket; no one saw him leave by train."

"No, he walked up the river. An auto was waiting for him. He will pass through tonight on the eastbound train on his way to Winnipeg."

"Will you tell me why he is going to Winnipeg?"

"No, I cannot."

He shrugged his shoulders. "It is scarcely necessary to ask. I can guess. It is to see your brother."

Again he knew he had struck home.

And yet she said, "No, it is not to see my brother."

He held out his hand to her. "Miss Kirkstone, I am going to keep my promise. I am going to help you with McDowell. Of course I demand my price. Will you swear on your word of honor to let me know the moment Shan Tung returns?"

"I will let you know."

Their hands clasped. Looking into her eyes, Keith saw what told him his was not the greatest cross to bear. Miriam Kirkstone also was fighting for her life, and as he turned to leave her, he said:

"While there is life there is hope. In settling my score with Shan Tung I believe that I shall also settle yours. It is a strong hunch, Miss Kirkstone, and it's holding me tight. Ten days, Shan Tung, and then—"

He left her, smiling. Miriam Kirkstone watched him go, her slim hands clutched at her breast, her eyes aglow with a new thought, a new hope; and as he heard the gate slam behind him, a sobbing cry rose in her throat, and she reached out her hands as if to call him back, for something was telling her that through this man lay the way to her salvation.

And her lips were moaning softly, "Ten days—ten days—and then—what?"

XIX

In those ten days all the wonders of June came up out of the south. Life pulsed with a new and vibrant force. The crimson fire-flowers, first of wild blooms to come after snow and frost, splashed the green spaces with red. The forests took on new colors, the blue of the sky grew nearer, and in men's veins the blood ran with new vigor and anticipations. To Keith they were all this and more. Four years along the rim of the Arctic had made it possible for him to drink to the full the glory of early summer along the Saskatchewan. And to Mary Josephine it was all new. Never had she seen a summer like this that was dawning, that most wonderful of all the summers in the world, which comes in June along the southern edge of the Northland.

Keith had played his promised part. It was not difficult for him to wipe away the worst of McDowell's suspicions regarding Miss Kirkstone, for McDowell was eager to believe. When Keith told him that Miriam was on the verge of a nervous breakdown simply because of certain trouble into which Shan Tung had inveigled her brother, and that everything would be straightened out the moment Shan Tung returned from Winnipeg, the iron man seized his hands in a sudden burst of relief and gratitude.

"But why didn't she confide in me, Conniston?" he complained. "Why didn't she confide in me?" The anxiety in his voice, its note of disappointment, were almost boyish.

Keith was prepared. "Because—"

He hesitated, as if projecting the thing in his mind. "McDowell, I'm in a delicate position. You must understand without forcing me to say too much. You are the last man in the world Miss Kirkstone wants to know about her trouble until she has triumphed, and it is over. Delicacy, perhaps; a woman's desire to keep something she is ashamed of from the one man she looks up to above all other men—to keep it away from him until she has cleared herself so that there is no suspicion. McDowell, if I were you, I'd be proud of her for that."

McDowell turned away, and for a space Keith saw the muscles in the back of his neck twitching.

"Derwent, maybe you've guessed, maybe you understand," he said after a moment with his face still turned to the window. "Of course she will never know. I'm too Old, old enough to be her father. But I've got the right to watch over her, and if any man ever injures her—"

His fists grew knotted, and softly Keith said behind him:

"You'd possibly do what John Keith did to the man who wronged his father. And because the Law is not always omniscient, it is also possible that Shan Tung may have to answer in some such way. Until then, until she comes to you of her own free will and with gladness in her eyes tells you her own secret and why she kept it from you—until she does that, I say, it is your part to treat her as if you had seen nothing, guessed nothing, suspected nothing. Do that, McDowell, and leave the rest to me."

He went out, leaving the iron man still with his face to the window.

With Mary Josephine there was no subterfuge. His mind was still centered in his own happiness. He could not wipe out of his brain the conviction that if he waited for Shan Tung he was waiting just so long under the sword of Damocles, with a hair between him and doom. He hoped that Miriam Kirkstone's refusal to confide in him and her reluctance to furnish him with the smallest facts in the matter would turn Mary Josephine's sympathy into a feeling of indifference if not of actual resentment. He was disappointed. Mary Josephine insisted on having Miss Kirkstone over for dinner the next day, and from that hour something grew between the two girls which Keith knew he was powerless to overcome. Thereafter he bowed his head to fate. He must wait for Shan Tung.

"If it wasn't for your promise not to fall in love, I'd be afraid," Mary Josephine confided to him that night, perched on the arm of his big chair. "At times I was afraid today, Derry. She's lovely. And you like pretty hair—and hers—is wonderful!"

"I don't remember," said Keith quietly, "that I promised you I wouldn't fall in love. I'm desperately in love, and with you, Mary Josephine. And as for Miss Kirkstone's lovely hair—I wouldn't trade one of yours for all she has on her head."

At that, with a riotous little laugh of joy, Mary Josephine swiftly unbound her hair and let it smother about his face and shoulders. "Sometimes I have a terribly funny thought, Derry," she whispered. "If we hadn't always been sweethearts, back there at home, and if you hadn't always liked my hair, and kissed me, and told me I was pretty, I'd almost think you weren't my brother!"

Keith laughed and was glad that her hair covered his face. During those wonderful first days of the summer they were inseparable, except when matters of business took Keith away. During these times he prepared for eventualities. The Keith properties in Prince Albert, he estimated, were worth at least a hundred thousand dollars, and he learned from McDowell that they would soon go through a process of law before being turned over to his fortunate inheritors. Before that time, however, he knew that his own fate would be sealed one way or the other, and now that he had Mary Josephine to look after, he made a will, leaving everything to her, and signing himself John Keith. This will he carried in an envelope pinned inside his shirt. As Derwent Conniston he collected one thousand two hundred and sixty dollars for three and a half years back wage in the Service. Two hundred and sixty of this he kept in his own pocket. The remaining thousand he counted out in new hundred-dollar bills under Mary Josephine's eyes, sealed the bills in another envelope, and gave the envelope to her.

"It's safer with you than with me," he excused himself. "Fasten it inside your dress. It's our grub-stake into the mountains."

Mary Josephine accepted the treasure with the repressed delight of one upon whose fair shoulders had been placed a tremendous responsibility.

There were days of both joy and pain for Keith. For even in the fullest hours of his happiness there was a thing eating at his heart, a thing that was eating deeper and deeper until at times it was like a destroying flame within him. One night he dreamed; he dreamed that Conniston came to his bedside and wakened him, and that after wakening him he taunted him in ghoulish glee and told him that in bequeathing him a sister he had given unto him forever and forever the curse of the daughters of Achelous. And Keith, waking in the dark hour of night, knew in his despair that it was so. For all time, even though he won this fight he was fighting, Mary Josephine would be the unattainable. A sister—and he loved her with the love of a man!

It was the next day after the dream that they wandered again into the grove that sheltered Keith's old home, and again they entered it and went through the cold and empty rooms. In one of these rooms he sought among the titles of dusty rows of books until he came to one and opened it. And there he found what had been in the corner of his mind when the sun rose to give him courage after the night of his dream. The daughters of Achelous lost in the end. Ulysses had tricked them. Ulysses had won. And in this day and age it was up to him, John Keith, to win, and win he would!

Always he felt this mastering certainty of the future when alone with Mary Josephine in the open day. With her at his side, her hand in his, and his arm about her waist, he told himself that all life was a lie—that there was no earth, no sun, no song or gladness in all the world, if that world held no hope for him. It was there. It was beyond the rim of forest. It was beyond the yellow plains, beyond the farthest timber of the farthest prairie, beyond the foothills; in the heart of the mountains was its abiding place. As he had dreamed of those mountains in boyhood and youth, so now he dreamed his dreams over again with Mary Josephine. For her he painted his pictures of them, as they wandered mile after mile up the shore of the Saskatchewan—the little world they would make all for themselves, how they would live, what they would do, the mysteries they would seek out, the triumphs they would achieve, the glory of that world—just for two. And Mary Josephine planned and dreamed with him.

In a week they lived what might have been encompassed in a year. So it seemed to Keith, who had known her only so long. With Mary Josephine the view-point was different. There had been a long separation, a separation filled with a heartbreak which she would never forget, but it had not served to weaken the bonds between her and this loved one, who, she thought, had always been her own. To her their comradeship was more complete now than it ever had been, even back in the old days, for they were alone in a land that was strange to her, and one was all that the world held for the other. So her possessorship of Keith was a thing which—again in the dark and brooding hours of night—sometimes made him writhe in an agony of shame. Hers was a shameless love, a love which had not even the lover's reason for embarrassment, a love unreserved and open as the day. It was her trick, nights, to nestle herself in the big armchair with him, and it was her fun to smother his face in her hair and tumble it about him, piling it over his mouth and nose until she made him plead for air. Again she would fit herself comfortably in the hollow of his arm and sit the evening out with her head on his shoulder, while they planned their future, and twice in that week she fell asleep there. Each morning she greeted him with a kiss, and each night she came to him to be kissed, and when it was her pleasure she kissed him—or made him kiss her—when they were on their long walks. It was bitter-sweet to Keith, and more frequently came the hours of crushing desolation for him, those hours in the still, dark night when his hypocrisy and his crime stood out stark and hideous in his troubled brain.

As this thing grew in him, a black and foreboding thunderstorm on the horizon of his dreams, an impulse which he did not resist dragged him more and more frequently down to the old home, and Mary Josephine was always with him. They let no one know of these visits. And they talked about John Keith, and in Mary Josephine's eyes he saw more than once a soft and starry glow of understanding. She loved the memory of this man because he, her brother, had loved him. And after these hours came the nights when truth, smiling at him, flung aside its mask and stood a grinning specter, and he measured to the depths the falseness of his triumph. His comfort was the thought that she knew. Whatever happened, she would know what John Keith had been. For he, John Keith, had told her. So much of the truth had he lived.

He fought against the new strain that was descending upon him slowly and steadily as the days passed. He could not but see the new light that had grown in Miriam Kirkstone's eyes. At times it was more than a dawn of hope. It was almost certainty. She had faith in him, faith in his promise to her, in his power to fight, his strength to win. Her growing friendship with Mary Josephine accentuated this, inspiring her at times almost to a point of conviction, for Mary Josephine's confidence in him was a passion. Even McDowell, primarily a fighter of his own battles, cautious and suspicious, had faith in him while he waited for Shan Tung. It was this blind belief in him that depressed him more than all else, for he knew that victory for himself must be based more or less on deceit and treachery. For the first time he heard Miriam laugh with Mary Josephine; he saw the gold and the brown head together out in the sun; he saw her face shining with a light that he had never seen there before, and then, when he came upon them, their faces were turned to him, and his heart bled even as he smiled and held out his hands to Mary Josephine. They trusted him, and he was a liar, a hypocrite, a Pharisee.

On the ninth day he had finished supper with Mary Josephine when the telephone rang. He rose to answer it. It was Miriam Kirkstone.

"He has returned," she said.

That was all. The words were in a choking voice. He answered and hung up the receiver. He knew a change had come into his face when he turned to Mary Josephine. He steeled himself to a composure that drew a questioning tenseness into her face. Gently he stroked her soft hair, explaining that Shan Tung had returned and that he was going to see him. In his bedroom he strapped his Service automatic under his coat.

At the door, ready to go, he paused. Mary Josephine came to him and put her hands to his shoulders. A strange unrest was in her eyes, a question which she did not ask.

Something whispered to him that it was the last time. Whatever happened now, tonight must leave him clean. His arms went around her, he drew her close against his breast, and for a space he held her there, looking into her eyes.

"You love me?" he asked softly.

"More than anything else in the world," she whispered.

"Kiss me, Mary Josephine."

Her lips pressed to his.

He released her from his arms, slowly, lingeringly.

After that she stood in the lighted doorway, watching him, until he disappeared in the gloom of the slope. She called good-by, and he answered her. The door closed.

And he went down into the valley, a hand of foreboding gripping at his heart.

XX

With a face out of which all color had fled, and eyes filled with the ghosts of a new horror, Miriam Kirkstone stood before Keith in the big room in the house on the hill.

"He was here—ten minutes," she said, and her voice was as if she was forcing it out of a part of her that was dead and cold. It was lifeless, emotionless, a living voice and yet strange with the chill of death. "In those ten minutes he told me—that! If you fail—"

It was her throat that held him, fascinated him. White, slim, beautiful—her heart seemed pulsing there. And he could see that heart choke back the words she was about to speak.

"If I fail—" he repeated the words slowly after her, watching that white, beating throat.

"There is only the one thing left for me to do. You—you—understand?"

"Yes, I understand. Therefore I shall not fail."

He backed away from her toward the door, and still he could not take his eyes from the white throat with its beating heart. "I shall not fail," he repeated. "And when the telephone rings, you will be here—to answer?"

"Yes, here," she replied huskily.

He went out. Under his feet the gravelly path ran through a flood of moonlight. Over him the sky was agleam with stars. It was a white night, one of those wonderful gold-white nights in the land of the Saskatchewan. Under that sky the world was alive. The little city lay in a golden glimmer of lights. Out of it rose a murmur, a rippling stream of sound, the voice of its life, softened by the little valley between. Into it Keith descended. He passed men and women, laughing, talking, gay. He heard music. The main street was a moving throng. On a corner the Salvation Army, a young woman, a young man, a crippled boy, two young girls, and an old man, were singing "Nearer, My God, to Thee." Opposite the Board of Trade building on the edge of the river a street medicine-fakir had drawn a crowd to his wagon. To the beat of the Salvation Army's tambourine rose the thrum of a made-up negro's banjo.

Through these things Keith passed, his eyes open, his ears listening, but he passed swiftly. What he saw and what he heard pressed upon him with the chilling thrill of that last swan-song, the swan-song of Ecla, of Kobat, of Ty, who had heard their doom chanted from the mountain-tops. It was the city rising up about his cars in rejoicing and triumph. And it put in his heart a cold, impassive anger. He sensed an impending doom, and yet he was not afraid. He was no longer chained by dreams, no more restrained by self. Before his eyes, beating, beating, beating, he saw that tremulous heart in Miriam Kirkstone's soft, white throat.

He came to Shan Tung's. Beyond the softly curtained windows it was a yellow glare of light. He entered and met the flow of life, the murmur of voices and laughter, the tinkle of glasses, the scent of cigarette smoke, and the fainter perfume of incense. And where he had seen him last, as though he had not moved since that hour nine days ago, still with his cigarette, still sphinx-like, narrow-eyed, watchful, stood Li King.

Keith walked straight to him. And this time, as he approached, Li King greeted him with a quick and subtle smile. He nipped his cigarette to the tiled floor. He was bowing, gracious. Tonight he was not stupid.

"I have come to see Shan Tung," said Keith.

He had half expected to be refused, in which event he was prepared to use his prerogative as an officer of the law to gain his point. But Li King did not hesitate. He was almost eager. And Keith knew that Shan Tung was expecting him.

They passed behind one of the screens and then behind another, until it seemed to Keith their way was a sinuous twisting among screens. They paused before a panel in the wall, and Li King pressed the black throat of a long-legged, swan-necked bird with huge wings and the panel opened and swung toward them. It was dark inside, but Li King turned on a light. Through a narrow hallway ten feet in length he led the way, unlocked a second door, and held it open, smiling at Keith.

"Up there," he said.

A flight of steps led upward and as Keith began to mount them the door closed softly behind him. Li King accompanied him no further.

He mounted the steps, treading softly. At the top was another door, and this he opened as quietly as Li King had closed the one below him. Again the omnipresent screens, and then his eyes looked out upon a scene which made him pause in astonishment. It was a great room, a room fifty feet long by thirty in width, and never before had he beheld such luxury as it contained. His feet sank into velvet carpets, the walls were hung richly with the golds and browns and crimsons of priceless tapestries, and carven tables and divans of deep plush and oriental chairs filled the space before him. At the far end was a raised dais, and before this, illumined in candleglow, was a kneeling figure. He noticed then that there were many candles burning, that the room was lighted by candles, and that in their illumination the figure did not move. He caught the glint of armors standing up, warrior like, against the tapestries, and he wondered for a moment if the kneeling figure was a heathen god made of wood. It was then that he smelled the odor of frankincense; it crept subtly into his nostrils and his mouth, sweetened his breath, and made him cough.

At the far end, before the dais, the kneeling figure began to move. Its arms extended slowly, they swept backward, then out again, and three times the figure bowed itself and straightened, and with the movement came a low, human monotone. It was over quickly. Probably two full minutes had not passed since Keith had entered when the kneeling figure sprang to its feet with the quickness of a cat, faced about, and stood there, smiling and bowing and extending its hand.

"Good evening, John Keith!" It was Shan Tung. An oriental gown fell about him, draping him like a woman. It was a crimson gown, grotesquely ornamented with embroidered peacocks, and it flowed and swept about him in graceful undulations as he advanced, his footfalls making not the sound of a mouse on the velvet floors.

"Good evening, John Keith!" He was close, smiling, his eyes glowing, his hand still outstretched, friendliness in his voice and manner. And yet in that voice there was a purr, the purr of a cat watching its prey, and in his eyes a glow that was the soft rejoicing of a triumph.

Keith did not take the hand. He made as if he did not see it. He was looking into those glowing, confident eyes of the Chinaman. A Chinaman! Was it possible? Could a Chinaman possess that voice, whose very perfection shamed him?

Shan Tung seemed to read his thoughts. And what he found amused him, and he bowed again, still smiling. "I am Shan Tung," he said with the slightest inflection of irony. "Here—in my home—I am different. Do you not recognize me?"

He waved gracefully a hand toward a table on either side of which was a chair. He seated himself, not waiting for Keith. Keith sat down opposite him. Again he must have read what was in Keith's heart, the desire and the intent to kill, for suddenly he clapped his hands, not loudly, once—twice—

"You will join me in tea?" he asked.

Scarcely had he spoken when about them, on all sides of them it seemed to Keith, there was a rustle of life. He saw tapestries move. Before his eyes a panel became a door. There was a clicking, a stir as of gowns, soft footsteps, a movement in the air. Out of the panel doorway came a Chinaman with a cloth, napkins, and chinaware. Behind him followed a second with tea-urn and a bowl, and with the suddenness of an apparition, without sound or movement, a third was standing at Keith's side. And still there was rustling behind, still there was the whispering beat of life, and Keith knew that there were others. He did not flinch, but smiled back at Shan Tung. A minute, no more, and the soft-footed yellow men had performed their errands and were gone.

"Quick service," he acknowledged. "VERY quick service. Shan Tung! But I have my hand on something that is quicker!"

Suddenly Shan Tung leaned over the table. "John Keith, you are a fool if you came here with murder in your heart," he said. "Let us be friends. It is best. Let us be friends."

XXI

It was as if with a swiftness invisible to the eye a mask had dropped from Shan Tung's face. Keith, preparing to fight, urging himself on to the step which he believed he must take, was amazed. Shan Tung was earnest. There was more than earnestness in his eyes, an anxiety, a frankly revealed hope that Keith would meet him halfway. But he did not offer his hand again. He seemed to sense, in that instant, the vast gulf between yellow and white. He felt Keith's contempt, the spurning contumely that was in the other's mind. Under the pallid texture of his skin there began to burn a slow and growing flush.

"Wait!" he said softly. In his flowing gown he seemed to glide to a carven desk near at hand. He was back in a moment with a roll of parchment in his hand. He sat down again and met Keith's eyes squarely and in silence for a moment.

"We are both MEN, John Keith." His voice was soft and calm. His tapering fingers with their carefully manicured nails fondled the roll of parchment, and then unrolled it, and held it so the other could read.

It was a university diploma. Keith stared. A strange name was scrolled upon it, Kao Lung, Prince of Shantung. His mind leaped to the truth. He looked at the other.

The man he had known as Shan Tung met his eyes with a quiet, strange smile, a smile in which there was pride, a flash of sovereignty, of a thing greater than skins that were white. "I am Prince Kao," he said. "That is my diploma. I am a graduate of Yale."

Keith's effort to speak was merely a grunt. He could find no words. And Kao, rolling up the parchment and forgetting the urn of tea that was growing cold, leaned a little over the table again. And then it was, deep in his narrowed, smoldering eyes, that Keith saw a devil, a living, burning thing of passion, Kao's soul itself. And Kao's voice was quiet, deadly.

"I recognized you in McDowell's office," he said. "I saw, first, that you were not Derwent Conniston. And then it was easy, so easy. Perhaps you killed Conniston. I am not asking, for I hated Conniston. Some day I should have killed him, if he had come back. John Keith, from that first time we met, you were a dead man. Why didn't I turn you over to the hangman? Why did I warn you in such a way that I knew you would come to see me? Why did I save your life which was in the hollow of my hand? Can you guess?"

"Partly," replied Keith. "But go on. I am waiting." Not for an instant had it enter his mind to deny that he was John Keith. Denial was folly, a waste of time, and just now he felt that nothing in the world was more precious to him than time.

Kao's quick mind, scheming and treacherous though it was, caught his view-point, and he nodded appreciatively. "Good, John Keith. It is easily guessed. Your life is mine. I can save it. I can destroy it. And you, in turn, can be of service to me. You help me, and I save you. It is a profitable arrangement. And we both are happy, for you keep Derwent Conniston's sister—and I—I get my golden-headed goddess, Miriam Kirkstone!"

"That much I have guessed," said Keith. "Go on!" For a moment Kao seemed to hesitate, to study the cold, gray passiveness of the other's face. "You love Derwent Conniston's sister," he continued in a voice still lower and softer. "And I—I love my golden-headed goddess. See! Up there on the dais I have her picture and a tress of her golden hair, and I worship them."

Colder and grayer was Keith's face as he saw the slumbering passion burn fiercer in Kao's eyes. It turned him sick. It was a terrible thing which could not be called love. It was a madness. But Kao, the man himself, was not mad. He was a monster. And while the eyes burned like two devils, his voice was still soft and low.

"I know what you are thinking; I see what you are seeing," he said. "You are thinking yellow, and you are seeing yellow. My skin! My birthright! My—" He smiled, and his voice was almost caressing.

"John Keith, in Pe-Chi-Li is the great city of Pekin, and Pe-Chi-Li is the greatest province in all China. And second only to that is the province of Shantung, which borders Pe-Chi-Li, the home of our Emperors for more centuries than you have years. And for so many generations that we cannot remember my forefathers have been rulers of Shantung. My grandfather was a Mandarin with the insignia of the Eighth Order, and my father was Ninth and highest of all Orders, with his palace at Tsi-Nan, on the Yellow Sea. And I, Prince Kao, eldest of his sons, came to America to learn American law and American ways. And I learned them, John Keith. I returned, and with my knowledge I undermined a government. For a time I was in power, and then this thing you call the god of luck turned against me, and I fled for my life. But the blood is still here—" he put his hand softly to his breast, "—the blood of a hundred generations of rulers. I tell you this because you dare not betray me, you dare not tell them who I am, though even that truth could not harm me. I prefer to be known as Shan Tung. Only you—and Miriam Kirkstone—have heard as much."

Keith's blood was like fire, but his voice was cold as ice. "GO ON!"

This time there could be no mistake. That cold gray of his passionless face, the steely glitter in his eyes, were read correctly by Kao. His eyes narrowed. For the first time a dull flame leaped into his colorless cheeks.

"Ah, I told you this because I thought we would work together, friends," he cried. "But it is not so. You, like my golden-headed goddess, hate me! You hate me because of my yellow skin. You say to yourself that I have a yellow heart. And she hates me, and she says that—but she is mine, MINE!" He sprang suddenly to his feet and swept about him with his flowing arms. "See what I have prepared for her! It is here she will come, here she will live until I take her away. There, on that dais, she will give up her soul and her beautiful body to me—and you cannot help it, she cannot help it, all the world cannot help it—AND SHE IS COMING TO ME TONIGHT!"

"TONIGHT!" gasped John Keith.

He, too, leaped to his feet. His face was ghastly. And Kao, in his silken gown, was sweeping his arms about him.

"See! The candles are lighted for her. They are waiting. And tonight, when the town is asleep, she will come. AND IT IS YOU WHO WILL MAKE HER COME, JOHN KEITH!"

Facing the devils in Kao's eyes, within striking distance of a creature who was no longer a man but a monster, Keith marveled at the coolness that held him back.

"Yes, it is you who will at last give her soul and her beautiful body to me," he repeated. "Come. I will show you how—and why!"

He glided toward the dais. His hand touched a panel. It opened and in the opening he turned about and waited for Keith.

"Come!" he said.

Keith, drawing a deep breath, his soul ready for the shock, his body ready for action, followed him.

XXII

Into a narrow corridor, through a second door that seemed made of padded wool, and then into a dimly lighted room John Keith followed Kao, the Chinaman. Out of this room there was no other exit; it was almost square, its ceiling was low, its walls darkly somber, and that life was there Keith knew by the heaviness of cigarette smoke in the air. For a moment his eyes did not discern the physical evidence of that life. And then, staring at him out of the yellow glow, he saw a face. It was a haunting, terrible face, a face heavy and deeply lined by sagging flesh and with eyes sunken and staring. They were more than staring. They greeted Keith like living coals. Under the face was a human form, a big, fat, sagging form that leaned outward from its seat in a chair.

Kao, bowing, sweeping his flowing raiment with his arms, said, "John Keith, allow me to introduce you to Peter Kirkstone."

For the first time amazement, shock, came to Keith's lips in an audible cry. He advanced a step. Yes, in that pitiable wreck of a man he recognized Peter Kirkstone, the fat creature who had stood under the picture of the Madonna that fateful night, Miriam Kirkstone's brother!

And as he stood, speechless, Kao said: "Peter Kirkstone, you know why I have brought this man to you tonight. You know that he is not Derwent Conniston. You know that he is John Keith, the murderer of your father. Is it not so?"

The thick lips moved. The voice was husky—"Yes."

"He does not believe. So I have brought him that he may listen to you. Peter Kirkstone, is it your desire that your sister, Miriam, give herself to me, Prince Kao, tonight?"

Again the thick lips moved. This time Keith saw the effort. He shuddered. He knew these questions and answers had been prepared. A doomed man was speaking.

And the voice came, choking, "Yes."

"WHY?"

The terrible face of Peter Kirkstone seemed to contort. He looked at Kao. And Kao's eyes were shining in that dull room like the eyes of a snake.

"Because—it will save my life."

"And why will it save your life?"

Again that pause, again the sickly, choking effort. "Because—I HAVE KILLED A MAN."

Bowing, smiling, rustling, Kao turned to the door. "That is all, Peter Kirkstone. Good night. John Keith, will you follow me?"

Dumbly Keith followed through the dark corridor, into the big room mellow with candle-glow, back to the table with its mocking tea-urn and chinaware. He felt a thing like clammy sweat on his back. He sat down. And Kao sat opposite him again.

"That is the reason, John Keith. Peter Kirkstone, her brother, is a murderer, a cold-blooded murderer. And only Miriam Kirkstone and your humble servant, Prince Kao, know his secret. And to buy my secret, to save his life, the golden-headed goddess is almost ready to give herself to me—almost, John Keith. She will decide tonight, when you go to her. She will come. Yes, she will come tonight. I do not fear. I have prepared for her the candles, the bridal dais, the nuptial supper. Oh, she will come. For if she does not, if she fails, with tomorrow's dawn Peter Kirkstone and John Keith both go to the hangman!"

Keith, in spite of the horror that had come over him, felt no excitement. The whole situation was clear to him now, and there was nothing to be gained by argument, no possibility of evasion. Kao held the winning hand, the hand that put him back to the wall in the face of impossible alternatives. These alternatives flashed upon him swiftly. There were two and only two—flight, and alone, without Mary Josephine; and betrayal of Miriam Kirkstone. Just how Kao schemed that he should accomplish that betrayal, he could not guess.

His voice, like his face, was cold and strange when it answered the Chinaman; it lacked passion; there was no emphasis, no inflection that gave to one word more than to another. And Keith, listening to his own voice, knew what it meant. He was cold inside, cold as ice, and his eyes were on the dais, the sacrificial altar that Kao had prepared, waiting in the candleglow. On the floor of that dais was a great splash of dull-gold altar cloth, and it made him think of Miriam Kirkstone's unbound and disheveled hair strewn in its outraged glory over the thing Kao had prepared for her.

"I see. It is a trade, Kao. You are offering me my life in return for Miriam Kirkstone."

"More than that, John Keith. Mine is the small price. And yet it is great to me, for it gives me the golden goddess. But is she more to me than Derwent Conniston's sister may be to you? Yes, I am giving you her, and I am giving you your life, and I am giving Peter Kirkstone his life—all for ONE."

"For one," repeated Keith.

"Yes, for one."

"And I, John Keith, in some mysterious way unknown to me at present, am to deliver Miriam Kirkstone to you?"

"Yes."

"And yet, if I should kill you, now—where you sit—"

Kao shrugged his slim shoulders, and Keith heard that soft, gurgling laugh that McDowell had said was like the splutter of oil.

"I have arranged. It is all in writing. If anything should happen to me, there are messengers who would carry it swiftly. To harm me would be to seal your own doom. Besides, you would not leave here alive. I am not afraid."

"How am I to deliver Miriam Kirkstone to you?"

Kao leaned forward, his fingers interlacing eagerly. "Ah, NOW you have asked the question, John Keith! And we shall be friends, great friends, for you see with the eyes of wisdom. It will be easy, so easy that you will wonder at the cheapness of the task. Ten days ago Miriam Kirkstone was about to pay my price. And then you came. From that moment she saw you in McDowell's office, there was a sudden change. Why? I don't know. Perhaps because of that thing you call intuition but to which we give a greater name. Perhaps only because you were the man who had run down her father's murderer. I saw her that afternoon, before you went up at night. Ah, yes, I could see, I could understand the spark that had begun to grow in her, hope, a wild, impossible hope, and I prepared for it by leaving you my message. I went away. I knew that in a few days all that hope would be centered in you, that it would live and die in you, that in the end it would be your word that would bring her to me. And that word you must speak tonight. You must go to her, hope-broken. You must tell her that no power on earth can save her, and that Kao waits to make her a princess, that tomorrow will be too late, that TONIGHT must the bargain be closed. She will come. She will save her brother from the hangman, and you, in bringing her, will save John Keith and keep Derwent Conniston's sister. Is it not a great reward for the little I am asking?"

It was Keith who now smiled into the eyes of the Chinaman, but it was a smile that did not soften that gray and rock-like hardness that had settled in his face. "Kao, you are a devil. I suppose that is a compliment to your dirty ears. You're rotten to the core of the thing that beats in you like a heart; you're a yellow snake from the skin in. I came to see you because I thought there might be a way out of this mess. I had almost made up my mind to kill you. But I won't do that. There's a better way. In half an hour I'll be with McDowell, and I'll beat you out by telling him that I'm John Keith. And I'll tell him this story of Miriam Kirkstone from beginning to end. I'll tell him of that dais you've built for her—your sacrificial altar!—and tomorrow Prince Albert will rise to a man to drag you out of this hole and kill you as they would kill a rat. That is my answer, you slit-eyed, Yale-veneered yellow devil! I may die, and Peter Kirkstone may die, but you'll not get Miriam Kirkstone!"

He was on his feet when he finished, amazed at the calmness of his own voice, amazed that his hands were steady and his brain was cool in this hour of his sacrifice. And Kao was stunned. Before his eyes he saw a white man throwing away his life. Here, in the final play, was a master-stroke he had not foreseen. A moment before the victor, he was now the vanquished. About him he saw his world falling, his power gone, his own life suddenly hanging by a thread. In Keith's face he read the truth. This white man was not bluffing. He would go to McDowell. He would tell the truth. This man who had ventured so much for his own life and freedom would now sacrifice that life to save a girl, one girl! He could not understand, and yet he believed. For it was there before his eyes in that gray, passionless face that was as inexorable as the face of one of his own stone gods.

As he uttered the words that smashed all that Kao had planned for, Keith sensed rather than saw the swift change of emotion sweeping through the yellow-visaged Moloch staring up at him. For a space the oriental's evil eyes had widened, exposing wider rims of saffron white, betraying his amazement, the shock of Keith's unexpected revolt, and then the lids closed slowly, until only dark and menacing gleams of fire shot between them, and Keith thought of the eyes of a snake. Swift as the strike of a rattler Kao was on his feet, his gown thrown back, one clawing hand jerking a derringer from his silken belt. In the same breath he raised his voice in a sharp call.

Keith sprang back. The snake-like threat in the Chinaman's eyes had prepared him, and his Service automatic leaped from its holster with lightning swiftness. Yet that movement was no swifter than the response to Kao's cry. The panel shot open, the screens moved, tapestries billowed suddenly as if moved by the wind, and Kao's servants sprang forth and were at him like a pack of dogs. Keith had no time to judge their number, for his brain was centered in the race with Kao's derringer. He saw its silver mountings flash in the candle-glow, saw its spurt of smoke and fire. But its report was drowned in the roar of his automatic as it replied with a stream of lead and flame. He saw the derringer fall and Kao crumple up like a jackknife. His brain turned red as he swung his weapon on the others, and as he fired, he backed toward the door. Then something caught him from behind, twisting his head almost from his shoulders, and he went down.

He lost his automatic. Weight of bodies was upon him; yellow hands clutched for his throat; he felt hot breaths and heard throaty cries. A madness of horror possessed him, a horror that was like the blind madness of Laocoon struggling with his sons in the coils of the giant serpent. In these moments he was not fighting men. They were monsters, yellow, foul-smelling, unhuman, and he fought as Laocoon fought. As if it had been a cane, he snapped the bone of an arm whose hand was throttling him; he twisted back a head until it snapped between its shoulders; he struck and broke with a blind fury and a giant strength, until at last, torn and covered with blood, he leaped free and reached the door. As he opened it and sprang through, he had the visual impression that only two of his assailants were rising from the floor.

For the space of a second he hesitated in the little hallway. Down the stairs was light—and people. He knew that he was bleeding and his clothes were torn, and that flight in that direction was impossible. At the opposite end of the hall was a curtain which he judged must cover a window. With a swift movement he tore down this curtain and found that he was right. In another second he had crashed the window outward with his shoulder, and felt the cool air of the night in his face. The door behind him was still closed when he crawled out upon a narrow landing at the top of a flight of steps leading down into the alley. He paused long enough to convince himself that his enemies were making no effort to follow him, and as he went down the steps, he caught himself grimly chuckling. He had given them enough.

In the darkness of the alley he paused again. A cool breeze fanned his cheeks, and the effect of it was to free him of the horror that had gripped him in his fight with the yellow men. Again the calmness with which he had faced Kao possessed him. The Chinaman was dead. He was sure of that. And for him there was not a minute to lose.

After all, it was his fate. The game had been played, and he had lost. There was one thing left undone, one play Conniston would still make, if he were there. And he, too, would make it. It was no longer necessary for him to give himself up to McDowell, for Kao was dead, and Miriam Kirkstone was saved. It was still right and just for him to fight for his life. But Mary Josephine must know FROM HIM. It was the last square play he could make.

No one saw him as he made his way through alleys to the outskirts of the town. A quarter of an hour later he came up the slope to the Shack. It was lighted, and the curtains were raised to brighten his way up the hill. Mary Josephine was waiting for him.

Again there came over him the strange and deadly calmness with which he had met the tragedy of that night. He had tried to wipe the blood from his face, but it was still there when he entered and faced Mary Josephine. The wounds made by the razor-like nails of his assailants were bleeding; he was hatless, his hair was disheveled, and his throat and a part of his chest were bare where his clothes had been torn away. As Mary Josephine came toward him, her arms reaching out to him, her face dead white, he stretched out a restraining hand, and said,

"Please wait, Mary Josephine!"

Something stopped her—the strangeness of his voice, the terrible hardness of his face, gray and blood-stained, the something appalling and commanding in the way he had spoken. He passed her quickly on his way to the telephone. Her lips moved; she tried to speak; one of her hands went to her throat. He was calling Miriam Kirkstone's number! And now she saw that his hands, too, were bleeding. There came the murmur of a voice in the telephone. Someone answered. And then she heard him say,

"SHAN TUNG IS DEAD!"

That was all. He hung up the receiver and turned toward her. With a little cry she moved toward him.

"DERRY—DERRY—"

He evaded her and pointed to the big chair in front of the fireplace. "Sit down, Mary Josephine."

She obeyed him. Her face was whiter than he had thought a living face could be, And then, from the beginning to the end, he told her everything. Mary Josephine made no sound, and in the big chair she seemed to crumple smaller and smaller as he confessed the great lie to her, from the hour Conniston and he had traded identities in the little cabin on the Barren. Until he died he knew she would haunt him as he saw her there for the last time—her dead-white face, her great eyes, her voiceless lips, her two little hands clutched at her breast as she listened to the story of the great lie and his love for her.

Even when he had done, she did not move or speak. He went into his room, closed the door, and turned on the lights. Quickly he put into his pack what he needed. And when he was ready, he wrote on a piece of paper:

"A thousand times I repeat, 'I love you.' Forgive me if you can. If you cannot forgive, you may tell McDowell, and the Law will find me up at the place of our dreams—the river's end.

—John Keith."

This last message he left on the table for Mary Josephine.

For a moment he listened at the door. Outside there was no movement, no sound. Quietly, then, he raised the window through which Kao had come into his room.

A moment later he stood under the light of the brilliant stars. Faintly there came to him the sounds of the city, the sound of life, of gayety, of laughter and of happiness, rising to him now from out of the valley.

He faced the north. Down the side of the hill and over the valley lay the forests. And through the starlight he strode back to them once more, back to their cloisters and their heritage, the heritage of the hunted and the outcast.

XXIII

All through the starlit hours of that night John Keith trudged steadily into the Northwest. For a long time his direction took him through slashings, second-growth timber, and cleared lands; he followed rough roads and worn trails and passed cabins that were dark and without life in the silence of midnight. Twice a dog caught the stranger scent in the air and howled; once he heard a man's voice, far away, raised in a shout. Then the trails grew rougher. He came to a deep wide swamp. He remembered that swamp, and before he plunged into it, he struck a match to look at his compass and his watch. It took him two hours to make the other side. He was in the deep and uncut timber then, and a sense of relief swept over him.

The forest was again his only friend. He did not rest. His brain and his body demanded the action of steady progress, though it was not through fear of what lay behind him. Fear had ceased to be a stimulating part of him; it was even dead within him. It was as if his energy was engaged in fighting for a principle, and the principle was his life; he was following a duty, and this duty impelled him to make his greatest effort. He saw clearly what he had done and what was ahead of him. He was twice a killer of men now, and each time the killing had rid the earth of a snake. This last time it had been an exceedingly good job. Even McDowell would concede that, and Miriam Kirkstone, on her knees, would thank God for what he had done. But Canadian law did not split hairs like its big neighbor on the south. It wanted him at least for Kirkstone's killing if not for that of Kao, the Chinaman. No one, not even Mary Josephine, would ever fully realize what he had sacrificed for the daughter of the man who had ruined his father. For Mary Josephine would never understand how deeply he had loved her.

It surprised him to find how naturally he fell back into his old habit of discussing things with himself, and how completely and calmly he accepted the fact that his home-coming had been but a brief and wonderful interlude to his fugitivism. He did not know it at first, but this calmness was the calmness of a despair more fatal than the menace of the hangman.

"They won't catch me," he encouraged himself. "And she won't tell them where I'm going. No, she won't do that." He found himself repeating that thought over and over again. Mary Josephine would not betray him. He repeated it, not as a conviction, but to fight back and hold down another thought that persisted in forcing itself upon him. And this thing, that at times was like a voice within him, cried out in its moments of life, "She hates you—and she WILL tell where you are going!"

With each hour it was harder for him to keep that voice down; it persisted, it grew stronger; in its intervals of triumph it rose over and submerged all other thoughts in him. It was not his fear of her betrayal that stabbed him; it was the underlying motive of it, the hatred that would inspire it. He tried not to vision her as he had seen her last, in the big chair, crushed, shamed, outraged—seeing in him no longer the beloved brother, but an impostor, a criminal, a man whom she might suspect of killing that brother for his name and his place in life. But the thing forced itself on him. It was reasonable, and it was justice.

"But she won't do it," he told himself. "She won't do it."

This was his fight, and its winning meant more to him than freedom. It was Mary Josephine who would live with him now, and not Conniston. It was her spirit that would abide with him, her voice he would hear in the whispers of the night, her face he would see in the glow of his lonely fires, and she must remain with him always as the Mary Josephine he had known. So he crushed back the whispering voice, beat it down with his hands clenched at his side, fought it through the hours of that night with the desperation of one who fights for a thing greater than life.

Toward dawn the stars began to fade out of the sky. He had been tireless, and he was tireless now. He felt no exhaustion. Through the gray gloom that came before day he went on, and the first glow of sun found him still traveling. Prince Albert and the Saskatchewan were thirty miles to the south and east of him.

He stopped at last on the edge of a little lake and unburdened himself of his pack for the first time. He was glad that the premonition of just such a sudden flight as this had urged him to fill his emergency grub-sack yesterday morning. "Won't do any harm for us to be prepared," he had laughed jokingly to Mary Josephine, and Mary Josephine herself had made him double the portion of bacon because she was fond of it. It was hard for him to slice that bacon without a lump rising in his throat. Pork and love! He wanted to laugh, and he wanted to cry, and between the two it was a queer, half-choked sound that came to his lips. He ate a good breakfast, rested for a couple of hours, and went on. At a more leisurely pace he traveled through most of the day, and at night he camped. In the ten days following his flight from Prince Albert he kept utterly out of sight. He avoided trappers' shacks and trails and occasional Indians. He rid himself of his beard and shaved himself every other day. Mary Josephine had never cared much for the beard. It prickled. She had wanted him smooth-faced, and now he was that. He looked better, too. But the most striking resemblance to Derwent Conniston was gone. At the end of the ten days he was at Turtle Lake, fifty miles east of Fort Pitt. He believed that he could show himself openly now, and on the tenth day bartered with some Indians for fresh supplies. Then he struck south of Fort Pitt, crossed the Saskatchewan, and hit between the Blackfoot Hills and the Vermillion River into the Buffalo Coulee country. In the open country he came upon occasional ranches, and at one of these he purchased a pack-horse. At Buffalo Lake he bought his supplies for the mountains, including fifty steel traps, crossed the upper branch of the Canadian Pacific at night, and the next day saw in the far distance the purple haze of the Rockies.

It was six weeks after the night in Kao's place that he struck the Saskatchewan again above the Brazeau. He did not hurry now. Just ahead of him slumbered the mountains; very close was the place of his dreams. But he was no longer impelled by the mighty lure of the years that were gone. Day by day something had worn away that lure, as the ceaseless grind of water wears away rock, and for two weeks he wandered slowly and without purpose in the green valleys that lay under the snow-tipped peaks of the ranges. He was gripped in the agony of an unutterable loneliness, which fell upon and scourged him like a disease. It was a deeper and more bitter thing than a yearning for companionship. He might have found that. Twice he was near camps. Three times he saw outfits coming out, and purposely drew away from them. He had no desire to meet men, no desire to talk or to be troubled by talking. Day And night his body and his soul cried out for Mary Josephine, and in his despair he cursed those who had taken her away from him. It was a crisis which was bound to come, and in his aloneness he fought it out. Day after day he fought it, until his face and his heart bore the scars of it. It was as if a being on whom he had set all his worship had died, only it was worse than death. Dead, Mary Josephine would still have been his inspiration; in a way she would have belonged to him. But living, hating him as she must, his dreams of her were a sacrilege and his love for her like the cut of a sword. In the end he was like a man who had triumphed over a malady that would always leave its marks upon him. In the beginning of the third week he knew that he had conquered, just as he had triumphed in a similar way over death and despair in the north. He would go into the mountains, as he had planned. He would build his cabin. And if the Law came to get him, it was possible that again he would fight.

On the second day of this third week he saw advancing toward him a solitary horseman. The stranger was possibly a mile away when he discovered him, and he was coming straight down the flat of the valley. That he was not accompanied by a pack-horse surprised Keith, for he was bound out of the mountains and not in. Then it occurred to him that he might be a prospector whose supplies were exhausted, and that he was easing his journey by using his pack as a mount. Whoever and whatever he was, Keith was not in any humor to meet him, and without attempting to conceal himself he swung away from the river, as if to climb the slope of the mountain on his right. No sooner had he clearly signified the new direction he was taking, than the stranger deliberately altered his course in a way to cut him off. Keith was irritated. Climbing up a narrow terrace of shale, he headed straight up the slope, as if his intention were to reach the higher terraces of the mountain, and then he swung suddenly down into a coulee, where he was out of sight. Here he waited for ten minutes, then struck deliberately and openly back into the valley. He chuckled when he saw how cleverly his ruse had worked. The stranger was a quarter of a mile up the mountain and still climbing.

"Now what the devil is he taking all that trouble for?" Keith asked himself.

An instant later the stranger saw him again. For perhaps a minute he halted, and in that minute Keith fancied he was getting a round cursing. Then the stranger headed for him, and this time there was no escape, for the moment he struck the shelving slope of the valley, he prodded his horse into a canter, swiftly diminishing the distance between them. Keith unbuttoned the flap of his pistol holster and maneuvered so that he would be partly concealed by his pack when the horseman rode up. The persistence of the stranger suggested to him that Mary Josephine had lost no time in telling McDowell where the law would be most likely to find him.

Then he looked over the neck of his pack at the horseman, who was quite near, and was convinced that he was not an officer. He was still jogging at a canter and riding atrociously. One leg was napping as if it had lost its stirrup-hold; the rider's arms were pumping, and his hat was sailing behind at the end of a string.

"Whoa!" said Keith.

His heart stopped its action. He was staring at a big red beard and a huge, shaggy head. The horseman reined in, floundered from his saddle, and swayed forward as if seasick.

"Well, I'll be——"

"DUGGAN!"

"JOHNNY—JOHNNY KEITH!"

XXIV

For a matter of ten seconds neither of the two men moved. Keith was stunned. Andy Duggan's eyes were fairly popping out from under his bushy brows. And then unmistakably Keith caught the scent of bacon in the air.

"Andy—Andy Duggan," he choked. "You know me—you know Johnny Keith—you know me—you——"

Duggan answered with an inarticulate bellow and jumped at Keith as if to bear him to the ground. He hugged him, and Keith hugged, and then for a minute they stood pumping hands until their faces were red, and Duggan was growling over and over:

"An' you passed me there at McCoffin's Bend—an' I didn't know you, I didn't know you, I didn't know you! I thought you was that cussed Conniston! I did. I thought you was Conniston!" He stood back at last. "Johnny—Johnny Keith!"

"Andy, you blessed old devil!"

They pumped hands again, pounded shoulders until they were sore, and in Keith's face blazed once more the love of life.

Suddenly old Duggan grew rigid and sniffed the air. "I smell bacon!"

"It's in the pack, Andy. But for Heaven's sake don't notice the bacon until you explain how you happen to be here."

"Been waitin' for you," replied Duggan in an affectionate growl. "Knew you'd have to come down this valley to hit the Little Fork. Been waitin' six weeks."

Keith dug his fingers into Duggan's arm.

"How did you know I was coming HERE?" he demanded. "Who told you?"

"All come out in the wash, Johnny. Pretty mess. Chinaman dead. Johnny Keith, alias Conniston, alive an' living with Conniston's pretty sister. Johnny gone—skipped. No one knew where. I made guesses. Knew the girl would know if anyone did. I went to her, told her how you'n me had been pals, an' she give me the idee you was goin' up to the river's end. I resigned from the Betty M., that night. Told her, though, that she was a ninny if she thought you'd go up there. Made her believe the note was just a blind."

"My God," breathed Keith hopelessly, "I meant it."

"Sure you did, Johnny. I knew it. But I didn't dare let HER know it. If you could ha' seen that pretty mouth o' hern curlin' up as if she'd liked to have bit open your throat, an' her hands clenched, an' that murder in her eyes—Man, I lied to her then! I told her I was after you, an' that if she wouldn't put the police on you, I'd bring back your head to her, as they used to do in the old times. An' she bit. Yes, sir, she said to me, 'If you'll do that, I won't say a word to the police!' An' here I am, Johnny. An' if I keep my word with that little tiger, I've got to shoot you right now. Haw! Haw!"

Keith had turned his face away.

Duggan, pulling him about by the shoulders, opened his eyes wide in amazement.—"Johnny—"

"Maybe you don't understand, Andy," struggled Keith. "I'm sorry—she feels—like that."

For a moment Duggan was silent. Then he exploded with a sudden curse. "SORRY! What the devil you sorry for, Johnny? You treated her square, an' you left her almost all of Conniston's money. She ain't no kick comin', and she ain't no reason for feelin' like she does. Let 'er go to the devil, I say. She's pretty an' sweet an' all that—but when anybody wants to go clawin' your heart out, don't be fool enough to feel sorry about it. You lied to her, but what's that? There's bigger lies than yourn been told, Johnny, a whole sight bigger! Don't you go worryin'. I've been here waitin' six weeks, an' I've done a lot of thinkin', and all our plans are set an' hatched. An' I've got the nicest cabin all built and waitin' for us up the Little Fork. Here we are. Let's be joyful, son!" He laughed into Keith's tense, gray face. "Let's be joyful!"

Keith forced a grin. Duggan didn't know. He hadn't guessed what that "little tiger who would have liked to have bit open his throat" had been to him. The thick-headed old hero, loyal to the bottom of his soul, hadn't guessed. And it came to Keith then that he would never tell him. He would keep that secret. He would bury it in his burned-out soul, and he would be "joyful" if he could. Duggan's blazing, happy face, half buried in its great beard, was like the inspiration and cheer of a sun rising on a dark world. He was not alone. Duggan, the old Duggan of years ago, the Duggan who had planned and dreamed with him, his best friend, was with him now, and the light came back into his face as he looked toward the mountains. Off there, only a few miles distant, was the Little Fork, winding into the heart of the Rockies, seeking out its hidden valleys, its trailless canons, its hidden mysteries. Life lay ahead of him, life with its thrill and adventure, and at his side was the friend of all friends to seek it with him. He thrust out his hands.

"God bless you, Andy," he cried. "You're the gamest pal that ever lived!"

A moment later Duggan pointed to a clump of timber half a mile ahead. "It's past dinner-time," he said. "There's wood. If you've got any bacon aboard, I move we eat."

An hour later Andy was demonstrating that his appetite was as voracious as ever. Before describing more of his own activities, he insisted that Keith recite his adventures from the night "he killed that old skunk, Kirkstone."

It was two o'clock when they resumed their journey. An hour later they struck the Little Fork and until seven traveled up the stream. They were deep in the lap of the mountains when they camped for the night. After supper, smoking his pipe, Duggan stretched himself out comfortably with his back to a tree.

"Good thing you come along when you did, Johnny," he said. "I been waitin' in that valley ten days, an' the eats was about gone when you hove in sight. Meant to hike back to the cabin for supplies tomorrow or next day. Gawd, ain't this the life! An' we're goin' to find gold, Johnny, we're goin' to find it!"

"We've got all our lives to—to find it in," said Keith.

Duggan puffed out a huge cloud of smoke and heaved a great sigh of pleasure. Then he grunted and chuckled. "Lord, what a little firebrand that sister of Conniston's is!" he exclaimed. "Johnny, I bet if you'd walk in on her now, she'd kill you with her own hands. Don't see why she hates you so, just because you tried to save your life. Of course you must ha' lied like the devil. Couldn't help it. But a lie ain't nothin'. I've told some whoppers, an' no one ain't never wanted to kill me for it. I ain't afraid of McDowell. Everyone said the Chink was a good riddance. It's the girl. There won't be a minute all her life she ain't thinkin' of you, an' she won't be satisfied until she's got you. That is, she thinks she won't. But we'll fool the little devil, Johnny. We'll keep our eyes open—an' fool her!"

"Let's talk of pleasanter things," said Keith. "I've got fifty traps in the pack, Andy. You remember how we used to plan on trapping during the winter and hunting for gold during the summer?"

Duggan rubbed his hands until they made a rasping sound; he talked of lynx signs he had seen, and of marten and fox. He had panned "colors" at a dozen places along the Little Fork and was ready to make his affidavit that it was the same gold he had dredged at McCoffin's Bend.

"If we don't find it this fall, we'll be sittin' on the mother lode next summer," he declared, and from then until it was time to turn in he talked of nothing but the yellow treasure it had been his lifelong dream to find. At the last, when they had rolled in their blankets, he raised himself on his elbow for a moment and said to Keith:

"Johnny, don't you worry about that Conniston girl. I forgot to tell you I've took time by the forelock. Two weeks ago I wrote an' told her I'd learned you was hittin' into the Great Slave country, an' that I was about to hike after you. So go to sleep an' don't worry about that pesky little rattlesnake."

"I'm not worrying," said Keith.

Fifteen minutes later he heard Duggan snoring. Quietly he unwrapped his blanket and sat up. There were still burning embers in the fire, the night—like that first night of his flight—was a glory of stars, and the moon was rising. Their camp was in a small, meadowy pocket in the center of which was a shimmering little lake across which he could easily have thrown a stone. On the far side of this was the sheer wall of a mountain, and the top of this wall, thousands of feet up, caught the glow of the moon first. Without awakening his comrade, Keith walked to the lake. He watched the golden illumination as it fell swiftly lower over the face of the mountain. He could see it move like a great flood. And then, suddenly, his shadow shot out ahead of him, and he turned to find the moon itself glowing like a monstrous ball between the low shoulders of a mountain to the east. The world about him became all at once vividly and wildly beautiful. It was as if a curtain had lifted so swiftly the eye could not follow it. Every tree and shrub and rock stood out in a mellow spotlight; the lake was transformed to a pool of molten silver, and as far as he could see, where shoulders and ridges did not cut him out, the moonlight was playing on the mountains. In the air was a soft droning like low music, and from a distant crag came the rattle of loosened rocks. He fancied, for a moment, that Mary Josephine was standing at his side, and that together they were drinking in the wonder of this dream at last come true. Then a cry came to his lips, a broken, gasping man-cry which he could not keep back, and his heart was filled with anguish.

With all its beauty, all its splendor of quiet and peace, the night was a bitter one for Keith, the bitterest of his life. He had not believed the worst of Mary Josephine. He knew he had lost her and that she might despise him, but that she would actually hate him with the desire for a personal vengeance he had not believed. Was Duggan right? Was Mary Josephine unfair? And should he in self-defense fight to poison his own thoughts against her? His face set hard, and a joyless laugh fell from his lips. He knew that he was facing the inevitable. No matter what had happened, he must go on loving Mary Josephine.

All through that night he was awake. Half a dozen times he went to his blanket, but it was impossible for him to sleep. At four o'clock he built up the fire and at five roused Duggan. The old river-man sprang up with the enthusiasm of a boy. He came back from the lake with his beard and head dripping and his face glowing. All the mountains held no cheerier comrade than Duggan.

They were on the trail at six o'clock and hour after hour kept steadily up the Little Fork. The trail grew rougher, narrower, and more difficult to follow, and at intervals Duggan halted to make sure of the way. At one of these times he said to Keith:

"Las' night proved there ain't no danger from her, Johnny. I had a dream, an' dreams goes by contraries an' always have. What you dream never comes true. It's always the opposite. An' I dreamed that little she-devil come up on you when you was asleep, took a big bread-knife, an' cut your head plumb off! Yessir, I could see her holdin' up that head o' yourn, an' the blood was drippin', an' she was a-laughin'—"

"SHUT UP!" Keith fairly yelled the words. His eyes blazed. His face was dead white.

With a shrug of his huge shoulders and a sullen grunt Duggan went on.

An hour later the trail narrowed into a short canon, and this canon, to Keith's surprise, opened suddenly into a beautiful valley, a narrow oasis of green hugged in between the two ranges. Scarcely had they entered it, when Duggan raised his voice in a series of wild yells and began firing his rifle into the air.

"Home-coming," he explained to Keith, after he was done. "Cabin's just over that bulge. Be there in ten minutes."

In less than ten minutes Keith saw it, sheltered in the edge of a thick growth of cedar and spruce from which its timbers had been taken. It was a larger cabin than he had expected to see—twice, three times as large.

"How did you do it alone!" he exclaimed in admiration. "It's a wonder, Andy. Big enough for—for a whole family!"

"Half a dozen Indians happened along, an' I hired 'em," explained Duggan. "Thought I might as well make it big enough, Johnny, seein' I had plenty of help. Sometimes I snore pretty loud, an'—"

"There's smoke coming out of it," cried Keith.

"Kept one of the Indians," chuckled Duggan. "Fine cook, an' a sassy-lookin' little squaw she is, Johnny. Her husband died last winter, an' she jumped at the chance to stay, for her board an' five bucks a month. How's your Uncle Andy for a schemer, eh, Johnny?"

A dozen rods from the cabin was a creek. Duggan halted here to water his horse and nodded for Keith to go on.

"Take a look, Johnny; go ahead an' take a look! I'm sort of sot up over that cabin."

Keith handed his reins to Duggan and obeyed. The cabin door was open, and he entered. One look assured him that Duggan had good reason to be "sot up." The first big room reminded him of the Shack. Beyond that was another room in which he heard someone moving and the crackle of a fire in a stove. Outside Duggan was whistling. He broke off whistling to sing, and as Keith listened to the river-man's bellowing voice chanting the words of the song he had sung at McCoffin's Bend for twenty years, he grinned. And then he heard the humming of a voice in the kitchen. Even the squaw was happy.

And then—and then—

"GREAT GOD IN HEAVEN—"

In the doorway she stood, her arms reaching out to him, love, glory, triumph in her face—MARY JOSEPHINE!

He swayed; he groped out; something blinded him—tears—hot, blinding tears that choked him, that came with a sob in his throat. And then she was in his arms, and her arms were around him, and she was laughing and crying, and he heard her say: "Why—why didn't you come back—to me—that night? Why—why did you—go out—through the—window? I—I was waiting—and I—I'd have gone—with you—"

From the door behind them came Duggan's voice, chuckling, exultant, booming with triumph. "Johnny, didn't I tell you there was lots bigger lies than yourn? Didn't I? Eh?"

XXV

It was many minutes, after Keith's arms had closed around Mary Josephine, before he released her enough to hold her out and look at her. She was there, every bit of her, eyes glowing with a greater glory and her face wildly aflush with a thing that had never been there before; and suddenly, as he devoured her in that hungry look, she gave a little cry, and hugged herself to his breast, and hid her face there.

And he was whispering again and again, as though he could find no other word,

"Mary—Mary—Mary—"

Duggan drew away from the door. The two had paid no attention to his voice, and the old river-man was one continuous chuckle as he unpacked Keith's horse and attended to his own, hobbling them both and tying cow-bells to them. It was half an hour before he ventured up out of the grove along the creek and approached the cabin again. Even then he halted, fussing with a piece of harness, until he saw Mary Josephine in the door. The sun was shining on her. Her glorious hair was down, and behind her was Keith, so close that his shoulders were covered with it. Like a bird Mary Josephine sped to Duggan. Great red beard and all she hugged him, and on the flaming red of his bare cheek-bone she kissed him.

"Gosh," said Duggan, at a loss for something better to say. "Gosh—"

Then Keith had him by the hand. "Andy, you ripsnorting old liar, if you weren't old enough to be my father, I'd whale the daylights out of you!" he cried joyously. "I would, just because I love you so! You've made this day the—the—the—"

"—The most memorable of my life," helped Mary Josephine. "Is that it—John?"

Timidly, for the first time, her cheek against his shoulder, she spoke his name. And before Duggan's eyes Keith kissed her.

Hours later, in a world aglow with the light of stars and a radiant moon, Keith and Mary Josephine were alone out in the heart of their little valley. To Keith it was last night returned, only more wonderful. There was the same droning song in the still air, the low rippling of running water, the mysterious whisperings of the mountains. All about them were the guardian peaks of the snow-capped ranges, and under their feet was the soft lush of grass and the sweet scent of flowers. "Our valley of dreams," Mary Josephine had named it, an infinite happiness trembling in her voice. "Our beautiful valley of dreams—come true!" "And you would have come with me—that night?" asked Keith wonderingly. "That night—I ran away?"

"Yes. I didn't hear you go. And at last I went to your door and listened, and then I knocked, and after that I called to you, and when you didn't answer, I entered your room."

"Dear heaven!" breathed Keith. "After all that, you would have come away with me, covered with blood, a—a murderer, they say—a hunted man—"

"John, dear." She took one of his hands in both her own and held it tight. "John, dear, I've got something to tell you."

He was silent.

"I made Duggan promise not to tell you I was here when he found you, and I made him promise something else—to keep a secret I wanted to tell you myself. It was wonderful of him. I don't see how he did it."

She snuggled still closer to him, and held his hand a little tighter. "You see, John, there was a terrible time after you killed Shan Tung. Only a little while after you had gone, I saw the sky growing red. It was Shan Tung's place—afire. I was terrified, and my heart was broken, and I didn't move. I must have sat at the window a long time, when the door burst open suddenly and Miriam ran in, and behind her came McDowell. Oh, I never heard a man swear as McDowell swore when he found you had gone, and Miriam flung herself on the floor at my feet and buried her head in my lap.

"McDowell tramped up and down, and at last he turned to me as if he was going to eat me, and he fairly shouted, 'Do you know—THAT CURSED FOOL DIDN'T KILL JUDGE KIRKSTONE!'"

There was a pause in which Keith's brain reeled. And Mary Josephine went on, as quietly as though she were talking about that evening's sunset:

"Of course, I knew all along, from what you had told me about John Keith, that he wasn't what you would call a murderer. You see, John, I had learned to LOVE John Keith. It was the other thing that horrified me! In the fight, that night, Judge Kirkstone wasn't badly hurt, just stunned. Peter Kirkstone and his father were always quarreling. Peter wanted money, and his father wouldn't give it to him. It seems impossible,—what happened then. But it's true. After you were gone, PETER KIRKSTONE KILLED HIS FATHER THAT HE MIGHT INHERIT THE ESTATE! And then he laid the crime on you!"

"My God!" breathed Keith. "Mary—Mary Josephine—how do you know?"

"Peter Kirkstone was terribly burned in the fire. He died that night, and before he died he confessed. That was the power Shan Tung held over Miriam. He knew. And Miriam was to pay the price that would save her brother from the hangman."

"And that," whispered Keith, as if to himself, "was why she was so interested in John Keith."

He looked away into the shimmering distance of the night, and for a long time both were silent. A woman had found happiness. A man's soul had come out of darkness into light.

Kazan

Chapter I
The Miracle

Kazan lay mute and motionless, his gray nose between his forepaws, his eyes half closed. A rock could have appeared scarcely less lifeless than he; not a muscle twitched; not a hair moved; not an eyelid quivered. Yet every drop of the wild blood in his splendid body was racing in a ferment of excitement that Kazan had never before experienced; every nerve and fiber of his wonderful muscles was tense as steel wire. Quarter-strain wolf, three-quarters "husky," he had lived the four years of his life in the wilderness. He had felt the pangs of starvation. He knew what it meant to freeze. He had listened to the wailing winds of the long Arctic night over the barrens. He had heard the thunder of the torrent and the cataract, and had cowered under the mighty crash of the storm. His throat and sides were scarred by battle, and his eyes were red with the blister of the snows. He was called Kazan, the Wild Dog, because he was a giant among his kind and as fearless, even, as the men who drove him through the perils of a frozen world.

He had never known fear—until now. He had never felt in him before the desire to *run*—not even on that terrible day in the forest when he had fought and killed the big gray lynx. He did not know what it was that frightened him, but he knew that he was in another world, and that many things in it startled and alarmed him. It was his first glimpse of civilization. He wished that his master would come back into the strange room where he had left him. It was a room filled with hideous things. There were great human faces on the wall, but they did not move or speak, but stared at him in a way he had never seen people look before. He remembered having looked on a master who lay very quiet and very cold in the snow, and he had sat back on his haunches and wailed forth the death song; but these people on the walls looked alive, and yet seemed dead.

Suddenly Kazan lifted his ears a little. He heard steps, then low voices. One of them was his master's voice. But the other—it sent a little tremor through him! Once, so long ago that it must have been in his puppyhood days, he seemed to have had a dream of a laugh that was like the girl's laugh—a laugh that was all at once filled with a wonderful happiness, the thrill of a wonderful love, and a sweetness that made Kazan lift his head as they came in. He looked straight at them, his red eyes gleaming. At once he knew that she must be dear to his master, for his master's arm was about her. In the glow of the light he saw that her hair was very bright, and that there was the color of the crimson *bakneesh* vine in her face and the blue of the *bakneesh* flower in her shining eyes. Suddenly she saw him, and with a little cry darted toward him.

"Stop!" shouted the man. "He's dangerous! Kazan—"

She was on her knees beside him, all fluffy and sweet and beautiful, her eyes shining wonderfully, her hands about to touch him. Should he cringe back? Should he snap? Was she one of the things on the wall, and his enemy? Should he leap at her white throat? He saw the man running forward, pale as death. Then her hand fell upon his head and the touch sent a thrill through him that quivered in every nerve of his body. With both hands she turned up his head. Her face was very close, and he heard her say, almost sobbingly:

"And you are Kazan—dear old Kazan, my Kazan, my hero dog—who brought him home to me when all the others had died! My Kazan—my hero!"

And then, miracle of miracles, her face was crushed down against him, and he felt her sweet warm touch.

In those moments Kazan did not move. He scarcely breathed. It seemed a long time before the girl lifted her face from him. And when she did, there were tears in her blue eyes, and the man was standing above them, his hands gripped tight, his jaws set.

"I never knew him to let any one touch him—with their naked hand," he said in a tense wondering voice. "Move back quietly, Isobel. Good heaven—look at that!"

Kazan whined softly, his bloodshot eyes on the girl's face. He wanted to feel her hand again; he wanted to touch her face. Would they beat him with a club, he wondered, if he *dared*! He meant no harm now. He would kill for her. He cringed toward her, inch by inch, his eyes never faltering. He heard what the man said—"Good heaven! Look at that!"—and he shuddered. But no blow fell to drive him back. His cold muzzle touched her filmy dress, and she looked at him, without moving, her wet eyes blazing like stars.

"See!" she whispered. "See!"

Half an inch more—an inch, two inches, and he gave his big gray body a hunch toward her. Now his muzzle traveled slowly upward—over her foot, to her lap, and at last touched the warm little hand that lay there. His eyes were still on her face: he saw a queer throbbing in her bare white throat, and then a trembling of her lips as she looked up at the man with a wonderful look. He, too, knelt down beside them, and put his arm about the girl again, and patted the dog on his head. Kazan did not like the man's touch. He mistrusted it, as nature had taught him to mistrust the touch of all men's hands, but he permitted it because he saw that it in some way pleased the girl.

"Kazan, old boy, you wouldn't hurt her, would you?" said his master softly. "We both love her, don't we, boy? Can't help it, can we? And she's ours, Kazan, all *ours*! She belongs to you and to me, and we're going to take care of her all our lives, and if we ever have to we'll fight for her like hell—won't we? Eh, Kazan, old boy?"

For a long time after they left him where he was lying on the rug, Kazan's eyes did not leave the girl. He watched and listened—and all the time there grew more and more in him the craving to creep up to them and touch the girl's hand, or her dress, or her foot. After a time his master said something, and with a little laugh the girl jumped up and ran to a big, square, shining thing that stood crosswise in a corner, and which had a row of white teeth longer than his own body. He had wondered what those teeth were for. The girl's fingers touched them now, and all the whispering of winds that he had ever heard, all the music of the waterfalls and the rapids and the trilling of birds in spring-time, could not equal the sounds they made. It was his first music. For a moment it startled and frightened him, and then he felt the fright pass away and a strange tingling in his body. He wanted to sit back on his haunches and howl, as he had howled at the billion stars in the skies on cold winter nights. But something kept him from doing that. It was the girl. Slowly he began slinking toward her. He felt the eyes of the man upon him, and stopped. Then a little more—inches at a time, with his throat and jaw straight out along the floor! He was half-way to her—half-way across the room—when the wonderful sounds grew very soft and very low.

"Go on!" he heard the man urge in a low quick voice. "Go on! Don't stop!"

The girl turned her head, saw Kazan cringing there on the floor, and continued to play. The man was still looking, but his eyes could not keep Kazan back now. He went nearer, still nearer, until at last his outreaching muzzle touched her dress where it lay piled on the floor. And then—he lay trembling, for she had begun to sing. He had heard a Cree woman crooning in front of her tepee; he had heard the wild chant of the caribou song—but he had never heard anything like this wonderful sweetness that fell from the lips of the girl. He forgot his master's presence now. Quietly, cringingly, so that she would not know, he lifted his head. He saw her looking at him; there was something in her wonderful eyes that gave him confidence, and he laid his head in her lap. For the second time he felt the touch of a woman's hand, and he closed his eyes with a long sighing breath. The music stopped. There came a little fluttering sound above him, like a laugh and a sob in one. He heard his master cough.

"I've always loved the old rascal—but I never thought he'd do that," he said; and his voice sounded queer to Kazan.

Chapter II
Into The North

Wonderful days followed for Kazan. He missed the forests and deep snows. He missed the daily strife of keeping his team-mates in trace, the yapping at his heels, the straight long pull over the open spaces and the barrens. He missed the "Koosh—koosh—Hoo-yah!" of the driver, the spiteful snap of his twenty-foot caribou-gut whip, and that yelping and straining behind him that told him he had his followers in line. But something had come to take the place of that which he missed. It was in the room, in the air all about him, even when the girl or his master was not near. Wherever she had been, he found the presence of that strange thing that took away his loneliness. It was the woman scent, and sometimes it made him whine softly when the girl herself was actually with him. He was not lonely, nights, when he should have been out howling at the stars. He was not lonely, because one night he prowled about until he found a certain door, and when the girl opened that door in the morning she found him curled up tight against it. She had reached down and hugged him, the thick smother of her long hair falling all over him in a delightful perfume; thereafter she placed a rug before the door for him to sleep on. All through the long nights he knew that she was just beyond the door, and he was content. Each day he thought less and less of the wild places, and more of her.

Then there came the beginning of the change. There was a strange hurry and excitement around him, and the girl paid less attention to him. He grew uneasy. He sniffed the change in the air, and he began to study his master's face. Then there came the morning, very early, when the babiche collar and the iron chain were fastened to him again. Not until he had followed his master out through the door and into the street did he begin to understand. They were sending him away! He sat suddenly back on his haunches and refused to budge.

"Come, Kazan," coaxed the man. "Come on, boy."

He hung back and showed his white fangs. He expected the lash of a whip or the blow of a club, but neither came. His master laughed and took him back to the house. When they left it again, the girl was with them and walked with her hand touching his head. It was she who persuaded him to leap up through a big dark hole into the still darker interior of a car, and it was she who lured him to the darkest corner of all, where his master fastened his chain. Then they went out, laughing like two children. For hours after that, Kazan lay still and tense, listening to the queer rumble of wheels under him. Several times those wheels stopped, and he heard voices outside. At last he was sure that he heard a familiar voice, and he strained at his chain and whined. The closed door slid back. A man with a lantern climbed in, followed by his master. He paid no attention to them, but glared out through the opening into the gloom of night. He almost broke loose when he leaped down upon the white snow, but when he saw no one there, he stood rigid, sniffing the air. Over him were the stars he had howled at all his life, and about him were the forests, black and silent, shutting them in like a wall. Vainly he sought for that one scent that was missing, and Thorpe heard the low note of grief in his shaggy throat. He took the lantern and held it above his head, at the same time loosening his hold on the leash. At that signal there came a voice from out of the night. It came from behind them, and Kazan whirled so suddenly that the loosely held chain slipped from the man's hand. He saw the glow of other lanterns. And then, once more, the voice—

"Kaa-aa-zan!"

He was off like a bolt. Thorpe laughed to himself as he followed.

"The old pirate!" he chuckled.

When he came to the lantern-lighted space back of the caboose, Thorpe found Kazan crouching down at a woman's feet. It was Thorpe's wife. She smiled triumphantly at him as he came up out of the gloom.

"You've won!" he laughed, not unhappily. "I'd have wagered my last dollar he wouldn't do that for any voice on earth. You've won! Kazan, you brute, I've lost you!"

His face suddenly sobered as Isobel stooped to pick up the end of the chain.

"He's yours, Issy," he added quickly, "but you must let me care for him until—we *know*. Give me the chain. I won't trust him even now. He's a wolf. I've seen him take an Indian's hand off at a single snap. I've seen him tear out another dog's jugular in one leap. He's an outlaw—a bad dog—in spite of the fact that he hung to me like a hero and brought me out alive. I can't trust him. Give me the chain—"

He did not finish. With the snarl of a wild beast Kazan had leaped to his feet. His lips drew up and bared his long fangs. His spine stiffened, and with a sudden cry of warning, Thorpe dropped a hand to the revolver at his belt.

Kazan paid no attention to him. Another form had approached out of the night, and stood now in the circle of illumination made by the lanterns. It was McCready, who was to accompany Thorpe and his young wife back to the Red River camp, where Thorpe was in charge of the building of the new Trans-continental. The man was straight, powerfully built and clean shaven. His jaw was so square that it was brutal, and there was a glow in his eyes that was almost like the passion in Kazan's as he looked at Isobel.

Her red and white stocking-cap had slipped free of her head and was hanging over her shoulder. The dull blaze of the lanterns shone in the warm glow of her hair. Her cheeks were flushed, and her eyes, suddenly turned to him, were as blue as the bluest *bakneesh* flower and glowed like diamonds. McCready shifted his gaze, and instantly her hand fell on Kazan's head. For the first time the dog did not seem to feel her touch. He still snarled at McCready, the rumbling menace in his throat growing deeper. Thorpe's wife tugged at the chain.

"Down, Kazan—down!" she commanded.

At the sound of her voice he relaxed.

"Down!" she repeated, and her free hand fell on his head again. He slunk to her feet. But his lips were still drawn back. Thorpe was watching him. He wondered at the deadly venom that shot from the wolfish eyes, and looked at McCready. The big guide had uncoiled his long dog-whip. A strange look had come into his face. He was staring hard at Kazan. Suddenly he leaned forward, with both hands on his knees, and for a tense moment or two he seemed to forget that Isobel Thorpe's wonderful blue eyes were looking at him.

"Hoo-koosh, Pedro—*charge*!"

That one word—*charge*—was taught only to the dogs in the service of the Northwest Mounted Police. Kazan did not move. McCready straightened, and quick as a shot sent the long lash of his whip curling out into the night with a crack like a pistol report.

"Charge, Pedro—*charge*!"

The rumble in Kazan's throat deepened to a snarling growl, but not a muscle of his body moved. McCready turned to Thorpe.

"I could have sworn that I knew that dog," he said. "If it's Pedro, he's *bad*!"

Thorpe was taking the chain. Only the girl saw the look that came for an instant into McCready's face. It made her shiver. A few minutes before, when the train had first stopped at Les Pas, she had offered her hand to this man and she had seen the same thing then. But even as she shuddered she recalled the many things her husband had told her of the forest people. She had grown to love them, to admire their big rough manhood and loyal hearts, before he had brought her among them; and suddenly she smiled at McCready, struggling to overcome that thrill of fear and dislike.

"He doesn't like you," she laughed at him softly. "Won't you make friends with him?"

She drew Kazan toward him, with Thorpe holding the end of the chain. McCready came to her side as she bent over the dog. His back was to Thorpe as he hunched down. Isobel's bowed head was within a foot of his face. He could see the glow in her cheek and the pouting curve of her mouth as she quieted the low rumbling in Kazan's throat. Thorpe stood ready to pull back on the chain, but for a moment McCready was between him and his wife, and he could not see McCready's face. The man's eyes were not on Kazan. He was staring at the girl.

"You're brave," he said. "I don't dare do that. He would take off my hand!"

He took the lantern from Thorpe and led the way to a narrow snow-path branching off, from the track. Hidden back in the thick spruce was the camp that Thorpe had left a fortnight before. There were two tents there now in place of the one that he and his guide had used. A big fire was burning in front of them. Close to the fire was a long sledge, and fastened to trees just within the outer circle of firelight Kazan saw the shadowy forms and gleaming eyes of his team-mates. He stood stiff and motionless while Thorpe fastened him to a sledge. Once more he was back in his forests—and in command. His mistress was laughing and clapping her hands delightedly in the excitement of the strange and wonderful life of which she had now become a part. Thorpe had thrown back the flap of their tent, and she was entering ahead of him. She did not look back. She spoke no word to him. He whined, and turned his red eyes on McCready.

In the tent Thorpe was saying:

"I'm sorry old Jackpine wouldn't go back with us, Issy. He drove me down, but for love or money I couldn't get him to return. He's a Mission Indian, and I'd give a month's salary to have you see him handle the dogs. I'm not sure about this man McCready. He's a queer chap, the Company's agent here tells me, and knows the woods like a book. But dogs don't like a stranger. Kazan isn't going to take to him worth a cent!"

Kazan heard the girl's voice, and stood rigid and motionless listening to it. He did not hear or see McCready when he came up stealthily behind him. The man's voice came as suddenly as a shot at his heels.

"*Pedro*!"

In an instant Kazan cringed as if touched by a lash.

"Got you that time—didn't I, you old devil!" whispered McCready, his face strangely pale in the firelight. "Changed your name, eh? But I *got* you—didn't I?"

Chapter III
McCready Pays The Debt

For a long time after he had uttered those words McCready sat in silence beside the fire. Only for a moment or two at a time did his eyes leave Kazan. After a little, when he was sure that Thorpe and Isobel had retired for the night, he went into his own tent and returned with a flask of whisky. During the next half-hour he drank frequently. Then he went over and sat on the end of the sledge, just beyond the reach of Kazan's chain.

"Got you, didn't I?" he repeated, the effect of the liquor beginning to show in the glitter of his eyes. "Wonder who changed your name, Pedro. And how the devil did *he* come by you? Ho, ho, if you could only talk—"

They heard Thorpe's voice inside the tent. It was followed by a low girlish peal of laughter, and McCready jerked himself erect. His face blazed suddenly red, and he rose to his feet, dropping the flask in his coat pocket. Walking around the fire, he tiptoed cautiously to the shadow of a tree close to the tent and stood there for many minutes listening. His eyes burned with a fiery madness when he returned to the sledge and Kazan. It was midnight before he went into his own tent.

In the warmth of the fire, Kazan's eyes slowly closed. He slumbered uneasily, and his brain was filled with troubled pictures. At times he was fighting, and his jaws snapped. At others he was straining at the end of his chain, with McCready or his mistress just out of reach. He felt the gentle touch of the girl's hand again and heard the wonderful sweetness of her voice as she sang to him and his master, and his body trembled and twitched with the thrills that had filled him that night. And then the picture changed. He was running at the head of a splendid team—six dogs of the Royal Northwest Mounted Police—and his master was calling him Pedro! The scene shifted. They were in camp. His master was young and smooth-faced and he helped from the sledge another man whose hands were fastened in front of him by curious black rings. Again it was later—and he was lying before a great fire. His master was sitting opposite him, with his back to a tent, and as he looked, there came out of the tent the man with the black rings—only now the rings were gone and his hands were free, and in one of them he carried a heavy club. He heard the terrible blow of the club as it fell on his master's head—and the sound of it aroused him from his restless sleep.

He sprang to his feet, his spine stiffening and a snarl in his throat. The fire had died down and the camp was in the darker gloom that precedes dawn. Through that gloom Kazan saw McCready. Again he was standing close to the tent of his mistress, and he knew now that this was the man who had worn the black iron rings, and that it was he who had beaten him with whip and club for many long days after he had killed his master. McCready heard the menace in his throat and came back quickly to the fire. He began to whistle and draw the half-burned logs together, and as the fire blazed up afresh he shouted to awaken Thorp and Isobel. In a few minutes Thorpe appeared at the tent-flap and his wife followed him out. Her loose hair rippled in billows of gold about her shoulders and she sat down on the sledge, close to Kazan, and began brushing it. McCready came up behind her and fumbled among the packages on the sledge. As if by accident one of his hands buried itself for an instant in the rich tresses that flowed down her back. She did not at first feel the caressing touch of his fingers, and Thorpe's back was toward them.

Only Kazan saw the stealthy movement of the hand, the fondling clutch of the fingers in her hair, and the mad passion burning in the eyes of the man. Quicker than a lynx, the dog had leaped the length of his chain across the sledge. McCready sprang back just in time, and as Kazan reached the end of his chain he was jerked back so that his body struck sidewise against the girl. Thorpe had turned in time to see the end of the leap. He believed that Kazan had sprung at Isobel, and in his horror no word or cry escaped his lips as he dragged her from where she had half fallen over the sledge. He saw that she was not hurt, and he reached for his revolver. It was in his holster in the tent. At his feet was McCready's whip, and in the passion of the moment he seized it and sprang upon Kazan. The dog crouched in the snow. He made no move to escape or to attack. Only once in his life could he remember having received a beating like that which Thorpe inflicted upon him now. But not a whimper or a growl escaped him.

And then, suddenly, his mistress ran forward and caught the whip poised above Thorpe's head.

"Not another blow!" she cried, and something in her voice held him from striking. McCready did not hear what she said then, but a strange look came into Thorpe's eyes, and without a word he followed his wife into their tent.

"Kazan did not leap at me," she whispered, and she was trembling with a sudden excitement. Her face was deathly white. "That man was behind me," she went on, clutching her husband by the arm. "I felt him touch me—and then Kazan sprang. He wouldn't bite *me*. It's the *man*! There's something—wrong—"

She was almost sobbing, and Thorpe drew her close in his arms.

"I hadn't thought before—but it's strange," he said. "Didn't McCready say something about knowing the dog? It's possible. Perhaps he's had Kazan before and abused him in a way that the dog has not forgotten. To-morrow I'll find out. But until I know—will you promise to keep away from Kazan?"

Isobel gave the promise. When they came out from the tent Kazan lifted his great head. The stinging lash had closed one of his eyes and his mouth was dripping blood. Isobel gave a low sob, but did not go near him. Half blinded, he knew that his mistress had stopped his punishment, and he whined softly, and wagged his thick tail in the snow.

Never had he felt so miserable as through the long hard hours of the day that followed, when he broke the trail for his team-mates into the North. One of his eyes was closed and filled with stinging fire, and his body was sore from the blows of the caribou lash. But it was not physical pain that gave the sullen droop to his head and robbed his body of that keen quick alertness of the lead-dog—the commander of his mates. It was his spirit. For the first time in his life, it was broken. McCready had beaten him—long ago; his master had beaten him; and during all this day their voices were fierce and vengeful in his ears. But it was his mistress who hurt him most. She held aloof from him, always beyond they reach of his leash; and when they stopped to rest, and again in camp, she looked at him with strange and wondering eyes, and did not speak. She, too, was ready to beat him. He believed that, and so slunk away from her and crouched on his belly in the snow. With him, a broken spirit meant a broken heart, and that night he lurked in one of the deepest shadows about the camp-fire and grieved alone. None knew that it was grief—unless it was the girl. She did not move toward him. She did not speak to him. But she watched him closely—and studied him hardest when he was looking at McCready.

Later, after Thorpe and his wife had gone into their tent, it began to snow, and the effect of the snow upon McCready puzzled Kazan. The man was restless, and he drank frequently from the flask that he had used the night before. In the firelight his face grew redder and redder, and Kazan could see the strange gleam of his teeth as he gazed at the tent in which his mistress was sleeping. Again and again he went close to that tent, and listened. Twice he heard movement. The last time, it was the sound of Thorpe's deep breathing. McCready hurried back to the fire and turned his face straight up to the sky. The snow was falling so thickly that when he lowered his face he blinked and wiped his eyes. Then he went out into the gloom and bent low over the trail they had made a few hours before. It was almost obliterated by the falling snow. Another hour and there would be no trail—nothing the next day to tell whoever might pass that they had come this way. By morning it would cover everything, even the fire, if he allowed it to die down. McCready drank again, out in the darkness. Low words of an insane joy burst from his lips. His head was hot with a drunken fire. His heart beat madly, but scarcely more furiously than did Kazan's when the dog saw that McCready was returning *with a club*! The club he placed on end against a tree. Then he took a lantern from the sledge and lighted it. He approached Thorpe's tent-flap, the lantern in his hand.

"Ho, Thorpe—Thorpe!" he called.

There was no answer. He could hear Thorpe breathing. He drew the flap aside a little, and raised his voice.

"Thorpe!"

Still there was no movement inside, and he untied the flap strings and thrust in his lantern. The light flashed on Isobel's golden head, and McCready stared at it, his eyes burning like red coals, until he saw that Thorpe was awakening. Quickly he dropped the flap and rustled it from the outside.

"Ho, Thorpe!—Thorpe!" he called again.

This time Thorpe replied.

"Hello, McCready—is that you?"

McCready drew the flap back a little, and spoke in a low voice.

"Yes. Can you come out a minute? Something's happening out in the woods. Don't wake up your wife!"

He drew back and waited. A minute later Thorpe came quietly out of the tent. McCready pointed into the thick spruce.

"I'll swear there's some one nosing around the camp," he said. "I'm certain that I saw a man out there a few minutes ago, when I went for a log. It's a good night for stealing dogs. Here— you take the lantern! If I wasn't clean fooled, we'll find a trail in the snow."

He gave Thorpe the lantern and picked up the heavy club. A growl rose in Kazan's throat, but he choked it back. He wanted to snarl forth his warning, to leap at the end of his leash, but he knew that if he did that, they would return and beat him. So he lay still, trembling and shivering, and whining softly. He watched them until they disappeared—and then waited— listened. At last he heard the crunch of snow. He was not surprised to see McCready come back alone. He had expected him to return alone. For he knew what a club meant!

McCready's face was terrible now. It was like a beast's. He was hatless. Kazan slunk deeper in his shadow at the low horrible laugh that fell from his lips—for the man still held the club. In a moment he dropped that, and approached the tent. He drew back the flap and peered in. Thorpe's wife was sleeping, and as quietly as a cat he entered and hung the lantern on a nail in the tent-pole. His movement did not awaken her, and for a few moments he stood there, staring—staring.

Outside, crouching in the deep shadow, Kazan tried to fathom the meaning of these strange things that were happening. Why had his master and McCready gone out into the forest? Why had not his master returned? It was his master, and not McCready, who belonged in that tent. Then why was McCready there? He watched McCready as he entered, and suddenly the dog was on his feet, his back tense and bristling, his limbs rigid. He saw McCready's huge shadow on the canvas, and a moment later there came a strange piercing cry. In the wild terror of that cry he recognized *her* voice—and he leaped toward the tent. The leash stopped him, choking the snarl in his throat. He saw the shadows struggling now, and there came cry after cry. She was calling to his master, and with his master's name she was calling *him*!

"Kazan—Kazan—"

He leaped again, and was thrown upon his back. A second and a third time he sprang the length of the leash into the night, and the babiche cord about his neck cut into his flesh like a knife. He stopped for an instant, gasping for breath. The shadows were still fighting. Now they were upright! Now they were crumpling down! With a fierce snarl he flung his whole weight once more at the end of the chain. There was a snap, as the thong about his neck gave way.

In half a dozen bounds Kazan made the tent and rushed under the flap. With a snarl he was at McCready's throat. The first snap of his powerful jaws was death, but he did not know that. He knew only that his mistress was there, and that he was fighting for her. There came one choking gasping cry that ended with a terrible sob; it was McCready. The man sank from his knees upon his back, and Kazan thrust his fangs deeper into his enemy's throat; he felt the warm blood.

The dog's mistress was calling to him now. She was pulling at his shaggy neck. But he would not loose his hold—not for a long time. When he did, his mistress looked down once upon the man and covered her face with her hands. Then she sank down upon the blankets. She was very still. Her face and hands were cold, and Kazan muzzled them tenderly. Her eyes were closed. He snuggled up close against her, with his ready jaws turned toward the dead man. Why was she so still, he wondered?

A long time passed, and then she moved. Her eyes opened. Her hand touched him.

Then he heard a step outside.

It was his master, and with that old thrill of fear—fear of the club—he went swiftly to the door. Yes, there was his master in the firelight—and in his hand he held the club. He was coming slowly, almost falling at each step, and his face was red with blood. But he had *the club*! He would beat him again—beat him terribly for hurting McCready; so Kazan slipped quietly under the tent-flap and stole off into the shadows. From out the gloom of the thick spruce he looked back, and a low whine of love and grief rose and died softly in his throat. They would beat him always now—after *that*. Even *she* would beat him. They would hunt him down, and beat him when they found him.

From out of the glow of the fire he turned his wolfish head to the depths of the forest. There were no clubs or stinging lashes out in that gloom. They would never find him there.

For another moment he wavered. And then, as silently as one of the wild creatures whose blood was partly his, he stole away into the blackness of the night.

Chapter IV
Free From Bonds

There was a low moaning of the wind in the spruce-tops as Kazan slunk off into the blackness and mystery of the forest. For hours he lay near the camp, his red and blistered eyes gazing steadily at the tent wherein the terrible thing had happened a little while before.

He knew now what death was. He could tell it farther than man. He could smell it in the air. And he knew that there was death all about him, and that he was the cause of it. He lay on his belly in the deep snow and shivered, and the three-quarters of him that was dog whined in a grief-stricken way, while the quarter that was wolf still revealed itself menacingly in his fangs, and in the vengeful glare of his eyes.

Three times the man—his master—came out of the tent, and shouted loudly, "Kazan—Kazan—Kazan!"

Three times the woman came with him. In the firelight Kazan could see her shining hair streaming about her, as he had seen it in the tent, when he had leaped up and killed the other man. In her blue eyes there was the same wild terror, and her face was white as the snow. And the second and third time, she too called, "Kazan—Kazan—Kazan!"—and all that part of him that was dog, and not wolf, trembled joyously at the sound of her voice, and he almost crept in to take his beating. But fear of the club was the greater, and he held back, hour after hour, until now it was silent again in the tent, and he could no longer see their shadows, and the fire was dying down.

Cautiously he crept out from the thick gloom, working his way on his belly toward the packed sledge, and what remained of the burned logs. Beyond that sledge, hidden in the darkness of the trees, was the body of the man he had killed, covered with a blanket. Thorpe, his master, had dragged it there.

He lay down, with his nose to the warm coals and his eyes leveled between his forepaws, straight at the closed tent-flap. He meant to keep awake, to watch, to be ready to slink off into the forest at the first movement there. But a warmth was rising from out of the gray ash of the fire-bed, and his eyes closed. Twice—three times—he fought himself back into watchfulness; but the last time his eyes came only half open, and closed heavily again.

And now, in his sleep, he whined softly, and the splendid muscles of his legs and shoulders twitched, and sudden shuddering ripples ran along his tawny spine. Thorpe, who was in the tent, if he had seen him, would have known that he was dreaming. And Thorpe's wife, whose golden head lay close against his breast, and who shuddered and trembled now and then even as Kazan was doing, would have known what he was dreaming about.

In his sleep he was leaping again at the end of his chain. His jaws snapped like castanets of steel,—and the sound awakened him, and he sprang to his feet, his spine as stiff as a brush, and his snarling fangs bared like ivory knives. He had awakened just in time. There was movement in the tent. His master was awake, and if he did not escape—

He sped swiftly into the thick spruce, and paused, flat and hidden, with only his head showing from behind a tree. He knew that his master would not spare him. Three times Thorpe had beaten him for snapping at McCready. The last time he would have shot him if the girl had not saved him. And now he had torn McCready's throat. He had taken the life from him, and his master would not spare him. Even the woman could not save him.

Kazan was sorry that his master had returned, dazed and bleeding, after he had torn McCready's jugular. Then he would have had her always. She would have loved him. She did love him. And he would have followed her, and fought for her always, and died for her when the time came. But Thorpe had come in from the forest again, and Kazan had slunk away quickly—for Thorpe meant to him what all men meant to him now: the club, the whip and the strange things that spat fire and death. And now—

Thorpe had come out from the tent. It was approaching dawn, and in his hand he held a rifle. A moment later the girl came out, and her hand caught the man's arm. They looked toward the thing covered by the blanket. Then she spoke to Thorpe and he suddenly straightened and threw back his head.

"H-o-o-o-o—Kazan—Kazan—Kazan!" he called.

A shiver ran through Kazan. The man was trying to inveigle him back. He had in his hand the thing that killed.

"Kazan—Kazan—Ka-a-a-a-zan!" he shouted again.

Kazan sneaked cautiously back from the tree. He knew that distance meant nothing to the cold thing of death that Thorpe held in his hand. He turned his head once, and whined softly, and for an instant a great longing filled his reddened eyes as he saw the last of the girl.

He knew, now, that he was leaving her forever, and there was an ache in his heart that had never been there before, a pain that was not of the club or whip, of cold or hunger, but which was greater than them all, and which filled him with a desire to throw back his head and cry out his loneliness to the gray emptiness of the sky.

Back in the camp the girl's voice quivered.

"He is gone."

The man's strong voice choked a little.

"Yes, he is gone. *He knew*—and I didn't. I'd give—a year of my life—if I hadn't whipped him yesterday and last night. He won't come back."

Isobel Thorpe's hand tightened on his arm.

"He will!" she cried. "He won't leave me. He loved me, if he was savage and terrible. And he knows that I love him. He'll come back—"

"Listen!"

From deep in the forest there came a long wailing howl, filled with a plaintive sadness. It was Kazan's farewell to the woman.

After that cry Kazan sat for a long time on his haunches, sniffing the new freedom of the air, and watching the deep black pits in the forest about him, as they faded away before dawn. 'Now and then, since the day the traders had first bought him and put him into sledge-traces away over on the Mackenzie, he had often thought of this freedom longingly, the wolf blood in him urging him to take it. But he had never quite dared. It thrilled him now. There were no clubs here, no whips, none of the man-beasts whom he had first learned to distrust, and then to hate. It was his misfortune—that quarter-strain of wolf; and the clubs, instead of subduing him, had added to the savagery that was born in him. Men had been his worst enemies. They had beaten him time and again until he was almost dead. They called him "bad," and stepped wide of him, and never missed the chance to snap a whip over his back. His body was covered with scars they had given him.

He had never felt kindness, or love, until the first night the woman had put her warm little hand on his head, and had snuggled her face close down to his, while Thorpe—her husband—had cried out in horror. He had almost buried his fangs in her white flesh, but in an instant her gentle touch, and her sweet voice, had sent through him that wonderful thrill that was his first knowledge of love. And now it was a man who was driving him from her, away from the hand that had never held a club or a whip, and he growled as he trotted deeper into the forest.

He came to the edge of a swamp as day broke. For a time he had been filled with a strange uneasiness, and light did not quite dispel it. At last he was free of men. He could detect nothing that reminded him of their hated presence in the air. But neither could he smell the presence of other dogs, of the sledge, the fire, of companionship and food, and so far back as he could remember they had always been a part of his life.

Here it was very quiet. The swamp lay in a hollow between two ridge-mountains, and the spruce and cedar grew low and thick—so thick that there was almost no snow under them, and day was like twilight. Two things he began to miss more than all others—food and company. Both the wolf and the dog that was in him demanded the first, and that part of him that was dog longed for the latter. To both desires the wolf blood that was strong in him rose responsively. It told him that somewhere in this silent world between the two ridges there was companionship, and that all he had to do to find it was to sit back on his haunches, and cry out his loneliness. More than once something trembled in his deep chest, rose in his throat, and ended there in a whine. It was the wolf howl, not yet quite born.

Food came more easily than voice. Toward midday he cornered a big white rabbit under a log, and killed it. The warm flesh and blood was better than frozen fish, or tallow and bran, and the feast he had gave him confidence. That afternoon he chased many rabbits, and killed two more. Until now, he had never known the delight of pursuing and killing at will, even though he did not eat all he killed.

But there was no fight in the rabbits. They died too easily. They were very sweet and tender to eat, when he was hungry, but the first thrill of killing them passed away after a time. He wanted something bigger. He no longer slunk along as if he were afraid, or as if he wanted to remain hidden. He held his head up. His back bristled. His tail swung free and bushy, like a wolf's. Every hair in his body quivered with the electric energy of life and action. He traveled north and west. It was the call of early days—the days away up on the Mackenzie. The Mackenzie was a thousand miles away.

He came upon many trails in the snow that day, and sniffed the scents left by the hoofs of moose and caribou, and the fur-padded feet of a lynx. He followed a fox, and the trail led him to a place shut in by tall spruce, where the snow was beaten down and reddened with blood. There was an owl's head, feathers, wings and entrails lying here, and he knew that there were other hunters abroad besides himself.

Toward evening he came upon tracks in the snow that were very much like his own. They were quite fresh, and there was a warm scent about them that made him whine, and filled him again with that desire to fall back upon his haunches and send forth the wolf-cry. This desire grew stronger in him as the shadows of night deepened in the forest. He had traveled all day, but he was not tired. There was something about night, now that there were no men near, that exhilarated him strangely. The wolf blood in him ran swifter and swifter. To-night it was clear. The sky was filled with stars. The moon rose. And at last he settled back in the snow and turned his head straight up to the spruce-tops, and the wolf came out of him in a long mournful cry which quivered through the still night for miles.

For a long time he sat and listened after that howl. He had found voice—a voice with a strange new note in it, and it gave him still greater confidence. He had expected an answer, but none came. He had traveled in the face of the wind, and as he howled, a bull moose crashed through the scrub timber ahead of him, his horns rattling against the trees like the tattoo of a clear birch club as he put distance between himself and that cry.

Twice Kazan howled before he went on, and he found joy in the practise of that new note. He came then to the foot of a rough ridge, and turned up out of the swamp to the top of it. The stars and the moon were nearer to him there, and on the other side of the ridge he looked down upon a great sweeping plain, with a frozen lake glistening in the moonlight, and a white river leading from it off into timber that was neither so thick nor so black as that in the swamp.

And then every muscle in his body grew tense, and his blood leaped. From far off in the plain there came a cry. It was *his* cry—the wolf-cry. His jaws snapped. His white fangs gleamed, and he growled deep in his throat. He wanted to reply, but some strange instinct urged him not to. That instinct of the wild was already becoming master of him. In the air, in the whispering of the spruce-tops, in the moon and the stars themselves, there breathed a spirit which told him that what he had heard was the wolf-cry, but that it was not the wolf *call*.

The other came an hour later, clear and distinct, that same wailing howl at the beginning— but ending in a staccato of quick sharp yelps that stirred his blood at once into a fiery excitement that it had never known before. The same instinct told him that this was the call— the hunt-cry. It urged him to come quickly. A few moments later it came again, and this time there was a reply from close down along the foot of the ridge, and another from so far away that Kazan could scarcely hear it. The hunt-pack was gathering for the night chase; but Kazan sat quiet and trembling.

He was not afraid, but he was not ready to go. The ridge seemed to split the world for him. Down there it was new, and strange, and without men. From the other side something seemed pulling him back, and suddenly he turned his head and gazed back through the moonlit space behind him, and whined. It was the dog-whine now. The woman was back there. He could hear her voice. He could feel the touch of her soft hand. He could see the laughter in her face and eyes, the laughter that had made him warm and happy. She was calling to him through the forests, and he was torn between desire to answer that call, and desire to go down into the plain. For he could also see many men waiting for him with clubs, and he could hear the cracking of whips, and feel the sting of their lashes.

For a long time he remained on the top of the ridge that divided his world. And then, at last, he turned and went down into the plain.

All that night he kept close to the hunt-pack, but never quite approached it. This was fortunate for him. He still bore the scent of traces, and of man. The pack would have torn him into pieces. The first instinct of the wild is that of self-preservation. It may have been this, a whisper back through the years of savage forebears, that made Kazan roll in the snow now and then where the feet of the pack had trod the thickest.

That night the pack killed a caribou on the edge of the lake, and feasted until nearly dawn. Kazan hung in the face of the wind. The smell of blood and of warm flesh tickled his nostrils, and his sharp ears could catch the cracking of bones. But the instinct was stronger than the temptation.

Not until broad day, when the pack had scattered far and wide over the plain, did he go boldly to the scene of the kill. He found nothing but an area of blood-reddened snow, covered with bones, entrails and torn bits of tough hide. But it was enough, and he rolled in it, and buried his nose in what was left, and remained all that day close to it, saturating himself with the scent of it.

That night, when the moon and the stars came out again, he sat back with fear and hesitation no longer in him, and announced himself to his new comrades of the great plain.

The pack hunted again that night, or else it was a new pack that started miles to the south, and came up with a doe caribou to the big frozen lake. The night was almost as clear as day, and from the edge of the forest Kazan first saw the caribou run out on the lake a third of a mile away. The pack was about a dozen strong, and had already split into the fatal horseshoe formation, the two leaders running almost abreast of the kill, and slowly closing in.

With a sharp yelp Kazan darted out into the moonlight. He was directly in the path of the fleeing doe, and bore down upon her with lightning speed. Two hundred yards away the doe saw him, and swerved to the right, and the leader on that side met her with open jaws. Kazan was in with the second leader, and leaped at the doe's soft throat. In a snarling mass the pack closed in from behind, and the doe went down, with Kazan half under her body, his fangs sunk deep in her jugular. She lay heavily on him, but he did not lose his hold. It was his first big kill. His blood ran like fire. He snarled between his clamped teeth.

Not until the last quiver had left the body over him did he pull himself out from under her chest and forelegs. He had killed a rabbit that day and was not hungry. So he sat back in the snow and waited, while the ravenous pack tore at the dead doe. After a little he came nearer, nosed in between two of them, and was nipped for his intrusion.

As Kazan drew back, still hesitating to mix with his wild brothers, a big gray form leaped out of the pack and drove straight for his throat. He had just time to throw his shoulder to the attack, and for a moment the two rolled over and over in the snow. They were up before the excitement of sudden battle had drawn the pack from the feast. Slowly they circled about each other, their white fangs bare, their yellowish backs bristling like brushes. The fatal ring of wolves drew about the fighters.

It was not new to Kazan. A dozen times he had sat in rings like this, waiting for the final moment. More than once he had fought for his life within the circle. It was the sledge-dog way of fighting. Unless man interrupted with a club or a whip it always ended in death. Only one fighter could come out alive. Sometimes both died. And there was no man here—only that fatal cordon of waiting white-fanged demons, ready to leap upon and tear to pieces the first of the fighters who was thrown upon his side or back. Kazan was a stranger, but he did not fear those that hemmed him in. The one great law of the pack would compel them to be fair.

He kept his eyes only on the big gray leader who had challenged him. Shoulder to shoulder they continued to circle. Where a few moments before there had been the snapping of jaws and the rending of flesh there was now silence. Soft-footed and soft-throated mongrel dogs from the South would have snarled and growled, but Kazan and the wolf were still, their ears laid forward instead of back, their tails free and bushy.

Suddenly the wolf struck in with the swiftness of lightning, and his jaws came together with the sharpness of steel striking steel. They missed by an inch. In that same instant Kazan darted in to the side, and like knives his teeth gashed the wolf's flank.

They circled again, their eyes growing redder, their lips drawn back until they seemed to have disappeared. And then Kazan leaped for that death-grip at the throat—and missed. It was only by an inch again, and the wolf came back, as he had done, and laid open Kazan's flank so that the blood ran down his leg and reddened the snow. The burn of that flank-wound told Kazan that his enemy was old in the game of fighting. He crouched low, his head straight out, and his throat close to the snow. It was a trick Kazan had learned in puppyhood—to shield his throat, and wait.

Twice the wolf circled about him, and Kazan pivoted slowly, his eyes half closed. A second time the wolf leaped, and Kazan threw up his terrible jaws, sure of that fatal grip just in front of the forelegs. His teeth snapped on empty air. With the nimbleness of a cat the wolf had gone completely over his back.

The trick had failed, and with a rumble of the dog-snarl in his throat, Kazan reached the wolf in a single bound. They met breast to breast. Their fangs clashed and with the whole weight of his body, Kazan flung himself against the wolf's shoulders, cleared his jaws, and struck again for the throat hold. It was another miss—by a hair's breadth—and before he could recover, the wolf's teeth were buried in the back of his neck.

For the first time in his life Kazan felt the terror and the pain of the death-grip, and with a mighty effort he flung his head a little forward and snapped blindly. His powerful jaws closed on the wolf's foreleg, close to the body. There was a cracking of bone and a crunching of flesh, and the circle of waiting wolves grew tense and alert. One or the other of the fighters was sure to go down before the holds were broken, and they but awaited that fatal fall as a signal to leap in to the death.

Only the thickness of hair and hide on the back of Kazan's neck, and the toughness of his muscles, saved him from that terrible fate of the vanquished. The wolf's teeth sank deep, but not deep enough to reach the vital spot, and suddenly Kazan put every ounce of strength in his limbs to the effort, and flung himself up bodily from under his antagonist. The grip on his neck relaxed, and with another rearing leap he tore himself free.

As swift as a whip-lash he whirled on the broken-legged leader of the pack and with the full rush and weight of his shoulders struck him fairly in the side. More deadly than the throat-grip had Kazan sometimes found the lunge when delivered at the right moment. It was deadly now. The big gray wolf lost his feet, rolled upon his back for an instant, and the pack rushed in, eager to rend the last of life from the leader whose power had ceased to exist.

From out of that gray, snarling, bloody-lipped mass, Kazan drew back, panting and bleeding. He was weak. There was a curious sickness in his head. He wanted to lie down in the snow. But the old and infallible instinct warned him not to betray that weakness. From out of the pack a slim, lithe, gray she-wolf came up to him, and lay down in the snow before him, and then rose swiftly and sniffed at his wounds.

She was young and strong and beautiful, but Kazan did not look at her. Where the fight had been he was looking, at what little remained of the old leader. The pack had returned to the feast. He heard again the cracking of bones and the rending of flesh, and something told him that hereafter all the wilderness would hear and recognize his voice, and that when he sat back on his haunches and called to the moon and the stars, those swift-footed hunters of the big plain would respond to it. He circled twice about the caribou and the pack, and then trotted off to the edge of the black spruce forest.

When he reached the shadows he looked back. Gray Wolf was following him. She was only a few yards behind. And now she came up to him, a little timidly, and she, too, looked back to the dark blotch of life out on the lake. And as she stood there close beside him, Kazan sniffed at something in the air that was not the scent of blood, nor the perfume of the balsam and spruce. It was a thing that seemed to come to him from the clear stars, the cloudless moon, the strange and beautiful quiet of the night itself. And its presence seemed to be a part of Gray Wolf.

He looked at her, and he found Gray Wolf's eyes alert and questioning. She was young—so young that she seemed scarcely to have passed out of puppyhood. Her body was strong and slim and beautifully shaped. In the moonlight the hair under her throat and along her back shone sleek and soft. She whined at the red staring light in Kazan's eyes, and it was not a puppy's whimper. Kazan moved toward her, and stood with his head over her back, facing the pack. He felt her trembling against his chest. He looked at the moon and the stars again, the mystery of Gray Wolf and of the night throbbing in his blood.

Not much of his life had been spent at the posts. Most of it had been on the trail—in the traces—and the spirit of the mating season had only stirred him from afar. But it was very near now. Gray Wolf lifted her head. Her soft muzzle touched the wound on his neck, and in the gentleness of that touch, in the low sound in her throat, Kazan felt and heard again that wonderful something that had come with the caress of the woman's hand and the sound of her voice.

He turned, whining, his back bristling, his head high and defiant of the wilderness which he faced. Gray Wolf trotted close at his side as they entered into the gloom of the forest.

Chapter V
The Fight In The Snow

They found shelter that night under thick balsam, and when they lay down on the soft carpet of needles which the snow had not covered, Gray Wolf snuggled her warm body close to Kazan and licked his wounds. The day broke with a velvety fall of snow, so white and thick that they could not see a dozen leaps ahead of them in the open. It was quite warm, and so still that the whole world seemed filled with only the flutter and whisper of the snowflakes. Through this day Kazan and Gray Wolf traveled side by side. Time and again he turned his head back to the ridge over which he had come, and Gray Wolf could not understand the strange note that trembled in his throat.

In the afternoon they returned to what was left of the caribou doe on the lake. In the edge of the forest Gray Wolf hung back. She did not yet know the meaning of poison-baits, deadfalls and traps, but the instinct of numberless generations was in her veins, and it told her there was danger in visiting a second time a thing that had grown cold in death.

Kazan had seen masters work about carcasses that the wolves had left. He had seen them conceal traps cleverly, and roll little capsules of strychnine in the fat of the entrails, and once he had put a foreleg in a trap, and had experienced its sting and pain and deadly grip. But he did not have Gray Wolf's fear. He urged her to accompany him to the white hummocks on the ice, and at last she went with him and sank back restlessly on her haunches, while he dug out the bones and pieces of flesh that the snow had kept from freezing. But she would not eat, and at last Kazan went and sat on his haunches at her side, and with her looked at what he had dug out from under the snow. He sniffed the air. He could not smell danger, but Gray Wolf told him that it might be there.

She told him many other things in the days and nights that followed. The third night Kazan himself gathered the hunt-pack and led in the chase. Three times that month, before the moon left the skies, he led the chase, and each time there was a kill. But as the snows began to grow softer under his feet he found a greater and greater companionship in Gray Wolf, and they hunted alone, living on the big white rabbits. In all the world he had loved but two things, the girl with the shining hair and the hands that had caressed him—and Gray Wolf.

He did not leave the big plain, and often He took his mate to the top of the ridge, and he would try to tell her what he had left back there. With the dark nights the call of the woman became so strong upon him that he was filled with a longing to go back, and take Gray Wolf with him.

Something happened very soon after that. They were crossing the open plain one day when up on the face of the ridge Kazan saw something that made his heart stand still. A man, with a dog-sledge and team, was coming down into their world. The wind had not warned them, and suddenly Kazan saw something glisten in the man's hands. He knew what it was. It was the thing that spat fire and thunder, and killed.

He gave his warning to Gray Wolf, and they were off like the wind, side by side. And then came the *sound*—and Kazan's hatred of men burst forth in a snarl as he leaped. There was a queer humming over their heads. The sound from behind came again, and this time Gray Wolf gave a yelp of pain, and rolled over and over in the snow. She was on her feet again in an instant, and Kazan dropped behind her, and ran there until they reached the shelter of the timber. Gray Wolf lay down, and began licking the wound in her shoulder. Kazan faced the ridge. The man was taking up their trail. He stopped where Gray Wolf had fallen, and examined the snow. Then he came on.

Kazan urged Gray Wolf to her feet, and they made for the thick swamp close to the lake. All that day they kept in the face of the wind, and when Gray Wolf lay down Kazan stole back over their trail, watching and sniffing the air.

For days after that Gray Wolf ran lame, and when once they came upon the remains of an old camp, Kazan's teeth were bared in snarling hatred of the man-scent that had been left behind. Growing in him there was a desire for vengeance—vengeance for his own hurts, and for Gray

Wolf's. He tried to nose out the man-trail under the cover of fresh snow, and Gray Wolf circled around him anxiously, and tried to lure him deeper into the forest. At last he followed her sullenly. There was a savage redness in his eyes.

Three days later the new moon came. And on the fifth night Kazan struck a trail. It was fresh—so fresh that he stopped as suddenly as though struck by a bullet when he ran upon it, and stood with every muscle in his body quivering, and his hair on end. It was a man-trail. There were the marks of the sledge, the dogs' feet, and the snow-shoeprints of his enemy.

Then he threw up his head to the stars, and from his throat there rolled out over the wide plains the hunt-cry—the wild and savage call for the pack. Never had he put the savagery in it that was there to-night. Again and again he sent forth that call, and then there came an answer and another and still another, until Gray Wolf herself sat back on her haunches and added her voice to Kazan's, and far out on the plain a white and haggard-faced man halted his exhausted dogs to listen, while a voice said faintly from the sledge:

"The wolves, father. Are they coming—after us?"

The man was silent. He was not young. The moon shone in his long white beard, and added grotesquely to the height of his tall gaunt figure. A girl had raised her head from a bearskin pillow on the sleigh. Her dark eyes were filled beautifully with the starlight. She was pale. Her hair fell in a thick shining braid over her shoulder, and she was hugging something tightly to her breast.

"They're on the trail of something—probably a deer," said the man, looking at the breech of his rifle. "Don't worry, Jo. We'll stop at the next bit of scrub and see if we can't find enough dry stuff for a fire.—Wee-ah-h-h-h, boys! Koosh—koosh—" and he snapped his whip over the backs of his team.

From the bundle at the girl's breast there came a small wailing cry. And far back in the plain there answered it the scattered voice of the pack.

At last Kazan was on the trail of vengeance. He ran slowly at first, with Gray Wolf close beside him, pausing every three or four hundred yards to send forth the cry. A gray leaping form joined them from behind. Another followed. Two came in from the side, and Kazan's solitary howl gave place to the wild tongue of the pack. Numbers grew, and with increasing number the pace became swifter. Four—six—seven—ten—fourteen, by the time the more open and wind-swept part of the plain was reached.

It was a strong pack, filled with old and fearless hunters. Gray Wolf was the youngest, and she kept close to Kazan's shoulders. She could see nothing of his red-shot eyes and dripping jaws, and would not have understood if she had seen. But she could *feel* and she was thrilled by the spirit of that strange and mysterious savagery that had made Kazan forget all things but hurt and death.

The pack made no sound. There was only the panting of breath and the soft fall of many feet. They ran swiftly and close. And always Kazan was a leap ahead, with Gray Wolf nosing his shoulder.

Never had he wanted to kill as he felt the desire in him to kill now. For the first time he had no fear of man, no fear of the club, of the whip, or of the thing that blazed forth fire and death. He ran more swiftly, in order to overtake them and give them battle sooner. All of the pent-up madness of four years of slavery and abuse at the hands of men broke loose in thin red streams of fire in his veins, and when at last he saw a moving blotch far out on the plain ahead of him, the cry that came out of his throat was one that Gray Wolf did not understand.

Three hundred yards beyond that moving blotch was the thin line of timber, and Kazan and his followers bore down swiftly. Half-way to the timber they were almost upon it, and suddenly it stopped and became a black and motionless shadow on the snow. From out of it there leaped that lightning tongue of flame that Kazan had always dreaded, and he heard the hissing song of the death-bee over his head. He did not mind it now. He yelped sharply, and the wolves raced in until four of them were neck-and-neck with him.

A second flash—and the death-bee drove from breast to tail of a huge gray fighter close to Gray Wolf. A third—a fourth—a fifth spurt of that fire from the black shadow, and Kazan himself felt a sudden swift passing of a red-hot thing along his shoulder, where the man's last bullet shaved off the hair and stung his flesh.

Three of the pack had gone down under the fire of the rifle, and half of the others were swinging to the right and the left. But Kazan drove straight ahead. Faithfully Gray Wolf followed him.

The sledge-dogs had been freed from their traces, and before he could reach the man, whom he saw with his rifle held like a club in his hands, Kazan was met by the fighting mass of them. He fought like a fiend, and there was the strength and the fierceness of two mates in the mad gnashing of Gray Wolf's fangs. Two of the wolves rushed in, and Kazan heard the terrific, back-breaking thud of the rifle. To him it was the *club*. He wanted to reach it. He wanted to reach the man who held it, and he freed himself from the fighting mass of the dogs and sprang to the sledge. For the first time he saw that there was something human on the sledge, and in an instant he was upon it. He buried his jaws deep. They sank in something soft and hairy, and he opened them for another lunge. And then he heard the voice! It was *her voice*! Every muscle in his body stood still. He became suddenly like flesh turned to lifeless stone.

Her voice! The bear rug was thrown back and what had been hidden under it he saw clearly now in the light of the moon and the stars. In him instinct worked more swiftly than human brain could have given birth to reason. It was not *she*. But the voice was the same, and the white girlish face so close to his own blood-reddened eyes held in it that same mystery that he had learned to love. And he saw now that which she was clutching to her breast, and there came from it a strange thrilling cry—and he knew that here on the sledge he had found not enmity and death, but that from which he had been driven away in the other world beyond the ridge.

In a flash he turned. He snapped at Gray Wolf's flank, and she dropped away with a startled yelp. It had all happened in a moment, but the man was almost down. Kazan leaped under his clubbed rifle and drove into the face of what was left of the pack. His fangs cut like knives. If he had fought like a demon against the dogs, he fought like ten demons now, and the man— bleeding and ready to fall—staggered back to the sledge, marveling at what was happening. For in Gray Wolf there was now the instinct of matehood, and seeing Kazan tearing and righting the pack she joined him in the struggle which she could not understand.

When it was over, Kazan and Gray Wolf were alone out on the plain. The pack had slunk away into the night, and the same moon and stars that had given to Kazan the first knowledge of his birthright told him now that no longer would those wild brothers of the plains respond to his call when he howled into the sky.

He was hurt. And Gray Wolf was hurt, but not so badly as Kazan. He was torn and bleeding. One of his legs was terribly bitten. After a time he saw a fire in the edge of the forest. The old call was strong upon him. He wanted to crawl in to it, and feel the girl's hand on his head, as he had felt that other hand in the world beyond the ridge. He would have gone—and would have urged Gray Wolf to go with him—but the man was there. He whined, and Gray Wolf thrust her warm muzzle against his neck. Something told them both that they were outcasts, that the plains, and the moon, and the stars were against them now, and they slunk into the shelter and the gloom of the forest.

Kazan could not go far. He could still smell the camp when he lay down. Gray Wolf snuggled close to him. Gently she soothed with her soft tongue Kazan's bleeding wounds. And Kazan, lifting his head, whined softly to the stars.

Chapter VI
Joan

On the edge of the cedar and spruce forest old Pierre Radisson built the fire. He was bleeding from a dozen wounds, where the fangs of the wolves had reached to his flesh, and he felt in his breast that old and terrible pain, of which no one knew the meaning but himself. He dragged in log after log, piled them on the fire until the flames leaped tip to the crisping needles of the limbs above, and heaped a supply close at hand for use later in the night.

From the sledge Joan watched him, still wild-eyed and fearful, still trembling. She was holding her baby close to her breast. Her long heavy hair smothered her shoulders and arms in a dark lustrous veil that glistened and rippled in the firelight when she moved. Her young face was scarcely a woman's to-night, though she was a mother. She looked like a child.

Old Pierre laughed as he threw down the last armful of fuel, and stood breathing hard.

"It was close, *ma cheri*!" he panted through his white beard. "We were nearer to death out there on the plain than we will ever be again, I hope. But we are comfortable now, and warm. Eh? You are no longer afraid?"

He sat down beside his daughter, and gently pulled back the soft fur that enveloped the bundle she held in her arms. He could see one pink cheek of baby Joan. The eyes of Joan, the mother, were like stars.

"It was the baby who saved us," she whispered. "The dogs were being torn to pieces by the wolves, and I saw them leaping upon you, when one of them sprang to the sledge. At first I thought it was one of the dogs. But it was a wolf. He tore once at us, and the bearskin saved us. He was almost at my throat when baby cried, and then he stood there, his red eyes a foot from us, and I could have sworn again that he was a dog. In an instant he turned, and was fighting the wolves. I saw him leap upon one that was almost at your throat."

"He *was* a dog," said old Pierre, holding out his hands to the warmth. "They often wander away from the posts, and join the wolves. I have had dogs do that. *Ma cheri*, a dog is a dog all his life. Kicks, abuse, even the wolves can not change him—for long. He was one of the pack. He came with them—to kill. But when he found *us*—"

"He fought for us," breathed the girl. She gave him the bundle, and stood up, straight and tall and slim in the firelight. "He fought for us—and he was terribly hurt," she said. "I saw him drag himself away. Father, if he is out there—dying—"

Pierre Radisson stood up. He coughed in a shuddering way, trying to stifle the sound under his beard. The fleck of crimson that came to his lips with the cough Joan did not see. She had seen nothing of it during the six days they had been traveling up from the edge of civilization. Because of that cough, and the stain that came with it, Pierre had made more than ordinary haste.

"I have been thinking of that," he said. "He was badly hurt, and I do not think he went far. Here—take little Joan and sit close to the fire until I come back."

The moon and the stars were brilliant in the sky when he went out in the plain. A short distance from the edge of the timber-line he stood for a moment upon the spot where the wolves had overtaken them an hour before. Not one of his four dogs had lived. The snow was red with their blood, and their bodies lay stiff where they had fallen under the pack. Pierre shuddered as he looked at them. If the wolves had not turned their first mad attack upon the dogs, what would have become of himself, Joan and the baby? He turned away, with another of those hollow coughs that brought the blood to his lips.

A few yards to one side he found in the snow the trail of the strange dog that had come with the wolves, and had turned against them in that moment when all seemed lost. It was not a clean running trail. It was more of a furrow in the snow, and Pierre Radisson followed it, expecting to find the dog dead at the end of it.

In the sheltered spot to which he had dragged himself in the edge of the forest Kazan lay for a long time after the fight, alert and watchful. He felt no very great pain. But he had lost the power to stand upon his legs. His flanks seemed paralyzed. Gray Wolf crouched close at his side, sniffing the air. They could smell the camp, and Kazan could detect the two things that were there—*man* and *woman*. He knew that the girl was there, where he could see the glow of the firelight through the spruce and the cedars. He wanted to go to her. He wanted to drag himself close in to the fire, and take Gray Wolf with him, and listen to her voice, and feel the touch of her hand. But the man was there, and to him man had always meant the club, the whip, pain, death.

Gray Wolf crouched close to his side, and whined softly as she urged Kazan to flee deeper with her into the forest. At last she understood that he could not move, and she ran nervously out into the plain, and back again, until her footprints were thick in the trail she made. The instincts of matehood were strong in her. It was she who first saw Pierre Radisson coming over their trail, and she ran swiftly back to Kazan and gave the warning.

Then Kazan caught the scent, and he saw the shadowy figure coming through the starlight. He tried to drag himself back, but he could move only by inches. The man came rapidly nearer. Kazan caught the glisten of the rifle in his hand. He heard his hollow cough, and the tread of his feet in the snow. Gray Wolf crouched shoulder to shoulder with him, trembling and showing her teeth. When Pierre had approached within fifty feet of them she slunk back into the deeper shadows of the spruce.

Kazan's fangs were bared menacingly when Pierre stopped and looked down at him. With an effort he dragged himself to his feet, but fell back into the snow again. The man leaned his rifle against a sapling and bent over him fearlessly. With a fierce growl Kazan snapped at his extended hands. To his surprise the man did not pick up a stick or a club. He held out his hand again—cautiously—and spoke in a voice new to Kazan. The dog snapped again, and growled.

The man persisted, talking to him all the time, and once his mittened hand touched Kazan's head, and escaped before the jaws could reach it. Again and again the man reached out his hand, and three times Kazan felt the touch of it, and there was neither threat nor hurt in it. At last Pierre turned away and went back over the trail.

When he was out of sight and hearing, Kazan whined, and the crest along his spine flattened. He looked wistfully toward the glow of the fire. The man had not hurt him, and the three-quarters of him that was dog wanted to follow.

Gray Wolf came back, and stood with stiffly planted forefeet at his side. She had never been this near to man before, except when the pack had overtaken the sledge out on the plain. She could not understand. Every instinct that was in her warned her that he was the most dangerous of all things, more to be feared than the strongest beasts, the storms, the floods, cold and starvation. And yet this man had not harmed her mate. She sniffed at Kazan's back and head, where the mittened hand had touched. Then she trotted back into the darkness again, for beyond the edge of the forest she once more saw moving life.

The man was returning, and with him was the girl. Her voice was soft and sweet, and there was about her the breath and sweetness of woman. The man stood prepared, but not threatening.

"Be careful, Joan," he warned.

She dropped on her knees in the snow, just out of reach.

"Come, boy—come!" she said gently. She held out her hand. Kazan's muscles twitched. He moved an inch—two inches toward her. There was the old light in her eyes and face now, the love and gentleness he had known once before, when another woman with shining hair and eyes had come into his life. "Come!" she whispered as she saw him move, and she bent a little, reached a little farther with her hand, and at last touched his head.

Pierre knelt beside her. He was proffering something, and Kazan smelled meat. But it was the girl's hand that made him tremble and shiver, and when she drew back, urging him to follow her, he dragged himself painfully a foot or two through the snow. Not until then did the girl see his mangled leg. In an instant she had forgotten all caution, and was down close at his side.

"He can't walk," she cried, a sudden tremble in her voice. "Look, *mon père!* Here is a terrible cut. We must carry him."

"I guessed that much," replied Radisson. "For that reason I brought the blanket. *Mon Dieu*, listen to that!"

From the darkness of the forest there came a low wailing cry.

Kazan lifted his head and a trembling whine answered in his throat. It was Gray Wolf calling to him.

It was a miracle that Pierre Radisson should put the blanket about Kazan, and carry him in to the camp, without scratch or bite. It was this miracle that he achieved, with Joan's arm resting on Kazan's shaggy neck as she held one end of the blanket. They laid him down close to the fire, and after a little it was the man again who brought warm water and washed away the blood from the torn leg, and then put something on it that was soft and warm and soothing, and finally bound a cloth about it.

All this Was strange and new to Kazan. Pierre's hand, as well as the girl's, stroked his head. It was the man who brought him a gruel of meal and tallow, and urged him to eat, while Joan sat with her chin in her two hands, looking at the dog, and talking to him. After this, when he was quite comfortable, and no longer afraid, he heard a strange small cry from the furry bundle on the sledge that brought his head up with a jerk.

Joan saw the movement, and heard the low answering whimper in his throat. She turned quickly to the bundle, talking and cooing to it as she took it in her arms, and then she pulled back the bearskin so that Kazan could see. He had never seen a baby before, and Joan held it out before him, so that he could look straight at it and see what a wonderful creature it was. Its little pink face stared steadily at Kazan. Its tiny fists reached out, and it made queer little sounds at him, and then suddenly it kicked and screamed with delight and laughed. At those sounds Kazan's whole body relaxed, and he dragged himself to the girl's feet.

"See, he likes the baby!" she cried. "*Mon père*, we must give him a name. What shall it be?"

"Wait till morning for that," replied the father. "It is late, Joan. Go into the tent, and sleep. We have no dogs now, and will travel slowly. So we must start early."

With her hand on the tent-flap, Joan, turned.

"He came with the wolves," she said. "Let us call him Wolf." With one arm she was holding the little Joan. The other she stretched out to Kazan. "Wolf! Wolf!" she called softly.

Kazan's eyes were on her. He knew that she was speaking to him, and he drew himself a foot toward her.

"He knows it already!" she cried. "Good night, *mon père*."

For a long time after she had gone into the tent, old Pierre Radisson sat on the edge of the sledge, facing the fire, with Kazan at his feet. Suddenly the silence was broken again by Gray Wolf's lonely howl deep in the forest. Kazan lifted his head and whined.

"She's calling for you, boy," said Pierre understandingly.

He coughed, and clutched a hand to his breast, where the pain seemed rending him.

"Frost-bitten lung," he said, speaking straight at Kazan. "Got it early in the winter, up at Fond du Lac. Hope we'll get home—in time—with the kids."

In the loneliness and emptiness of the big northern wilderness one falls into the habit of talking to one's self. But Kazan's head was alert, and his eyes watchful, so Pierre spoke to him.

"We've got to get them home, and there's only you and me to do it," he said, twisting his beard. Suddenly he clenched his fists.

His hollow racking cough convulsed him again.

"Home!" he panted, clutching his chest. "It's eighty miles straight north—to the Churchill—and I pray to God we'll get there—with the kids—before my lungs give out."

He rose to his feet, and staggered a little as he walked. There was a collar about Kazan's neck, and he chained him to the sledge. After that he dragged three or four small logs upon the fire, and went quietly into the tent where Joan and the baby were already asleep. Several times that night Kazan heard the distant voice of Gray Wolf calling for him, but something told him that he must not answer it now. Toward dawn Gray Wolf came close in to the camp, and for the first time Kazan replied to her.

His howl awakened the man. He came out of the tent, peered for a few moments up at the sky, built up the fire, and began to prepare breakfast. He patted Kazan on the head, and gave him a chunk of meat. Joan came out a few moments later, leaving the baby asleep in the tent. She ran up and kissed Pierre, and then dropped down on her knees beside Kazan, and talked to him almost as he had heard her talk to the baby. When she jumped up to help her father, Kazan followed her, and when Joan saw him standing firmly upon his legs she gave a cry of pleasure.

It was a strange journey that began into the North that day. Pierre Radisson emptied the sledge of everything but the tent, blankets, food and the furry nest for baby Joan. Then he harnessed himself in the traces and dragged the sledge over the snow. He coughed incessantly.

"It's a cough I've had half the winter," lied Pierre, careful that Joan saw no sign of blood on his lips or beard. "I'll keep in the cabin for a week when we get home."

Even Kazan, with that strange beast knowledge which man, unable to explain, calls instinct, knew that what he said was not the truth. Perhaps it was largely because he had heard other men cough like this, and that for generations his sledge-dog ancestors had heard men cough as Radisson coughed—and had learned what followed it.

More than once he had scented death in tepees and cabins, which he had not entered, and more than once he had sniffed at the mystery of death that was not quite present, but near—just as he had caught at a distance the subtle warning of storm and of fire. And that strange thing seemed to be very near to him now, as he followed at the end of his chain behind the sledge. It made him restless, and half a dozen times, when the sledge stopped, he sniffed at the bit of humanity buried in the bearskin. Each time that he did this Joan was quickly at his side, and twice she patted his scarred and grizzled head until every drop of blood in his body leaped riotously with a joy which his body did not reveal.

This day the chief thing that he came to understand was that the little creature on the sledge was very precious to the girl who stroked his head and talked to him, and that it was very helpless. He learned, too, that Joan was most delighted, and that her voice was softer and thrilled him more deeply, when he paid attention to that little, warm, living thing in the bearskin.

For a long time after they made camp Pierre Radisson sat beside the fire. To-night he did not smoke. He stared straight into the flames. When at last he rose to go into the tent with the girl and the baby, he bent over Kazan and examined his hurt.

"You've got to work in the traces to-morrow, boy," he said. "We must make the river by to-morrow night. If we don't—"

He did not finish. He was choking back one of those tearing coughs when the tent-flap dropped behind him. Kazan lay stiff and alert, his eyes filled with a strange anxiety. He did not like to see Radisson enter the tent, for stronger than ever there hung that oppressive mystery in the air about him, and it seemed to be a part of Pierre.

Three times that night he heard faithful Gray Wolf calling for him deep in the forest, and each time he answered her. Toward dawn she came in close to camp. Once he caught the scent of her when she circled around in the wind, and he tugged and whined at the end of his chain, hoping that she would come in and lie down at his side. But no sooner had Radisson moved in the tent than Gray Wolf was gone. The man's face was thinner, and his eyes were redder this morning. His cough was not so loud or so rending. It was like a wheeze, as if something had given way inside, and before the girl came out he clutched his hands often at his throat. Joan's face whitened when she saw him. Anxiety gave way to fear in her eyes. Pierre Radisson laughed when she flung her arms about him, and coughed to prove that what he said was true.

"You see the cough is not so bad, my Joan," he said. "It is breaking up. You can not have forgotten, *ma cheri*? It always leaves one red-eyed and weak."

It was a cold bleak dark day that followed, and through it Kazan and the man tugged at the fore of the sledge, with Joan following in the trail behind. Kazan's wound no longer hurt him. He pulled steadily with all his splendid strength, and the man never lashed him once, but patted him with his mittened hand on head and back. The day grew steadily darker and in the tops of the trees there was the low moaning of a storm.

Darkness and the coming of the storm did not drive Pierre Radisson into camp. "We must reach the river," he said to himself over and over again. "We must reach the river—we must reach the river——" And he steadily urged Kazan on to greater effort, while his own strength at the end of the traces grew less.

It had begun to storm when Pierre stopped to build a fire at noon. The snow fell straight down in a white deluge so thick that it hid the tree trunks fifty yards away. Pierre laughed when Joan shivered and snuggled close up to him with the baby in her arms. He waited only an hour, and then fastened Kazan in the traces again, and buckled the straps once more about his own waist. In the silent gloom that was almost night Pierre carried his compass in his hand, and at last, late in the afternoon, they came to a break in the timber-line, and ahead of them lay a plain, across which Radisson pointed an exultant hand.

"There's the river, Joan," he said, his voice faint and husky. "We can camp here now and wait for the storm to pass."

Under a thick clump of spruce he put up the tent, and then began gathering fire-wood. Joan helped him. As soon as they had boiled coffee and eaten a supper of meat and toasted biscuits, Joan went into the tent and dropped exhausted on her thick bed of balsam boughs, wrapping herself and the baby up close in the skins and blankets. To-night she had no word for Kazan. And Pierre was glad that she was too tired to sit beside the fire and talk. And yet—

Kazan's alert eyes saw Pierre start suddenly. He rose from his seat on the sledge and went to the tent. He drew back the flap and thrust in his head and shoulders.

"Asleep, Joan?" he asked.

"Almost, father. Won't you please come—soon?"

"After I smoke," he said. "Are you comfortable?"

"Yes, I'm so tired—and—sleepy—"

Pierre laughed softly. In the darkness he was gripping at his throat.

"We're almost home, Joan. That is our river out there—the Little Beaver. If I should run away and leave you to-night you could follow it right to our cabin. It's only forty miles. Do you hear?"

"Yes—I know—"

"Forty miles—straight down the river. You couldn't lose yourself, Joan. Only you'd have to be careful of air-holes in the ice."

"Won't you come to bed, father? You're tired—and almost sick."

"Yes—after I smoke," he repeated. "Joan, will you keep reminding me to-morrow of the air-holes? I might forget. You can always tell them, for the snow and the crust over them are whiter than that on the rest of the ice, and like a sponge. Will you remember—the airholes—"

"Yes-s-s-s—"

Pierre dropped the tent-flap and returned to the fire. He staggered as he walked.

"Good night, boy," he said. "Guess I'd better go in with the kids. Two days more—forty miles—two days—"

Kazan watched him as he entered the tent. He laid his weight against the end of his chain until the collar shut off his wind. His legs and back twitched. In that tent where Radisson had gone were Joan and the baby. He knew that Pierre would not hurt them, but he knew also that with Pierre Radisson something terrible and impending was hovering very near to them. He wanted the man outside—by the fire—where he could lie still, and watch him.

In the tent there was silence. Nearer to him than before came Gray Wolf's cry. Each night she was calling earlier, and coming closer to the camp. He wanted her very near to him to-night, but he did not even whine in response. He dared not break that strange silence in the tent. He lay still for a long time, tired and lame from the day's journey, but sleepless. The fire burned lower; the wind in the tree-tops died away; and the thick gray clouds rolled like a massive curtain from under the skies. The stars began to glow white and metallic, and from far in the North there came faintly a crisping moaning sound, like steel sleigh-runners running over frosty snow—the mysterious monotone of the Northern Lights. After that it grew steadily and swiftly colder.

To-night Gray Wolf did not compass herself by the direction of the wind. She followed like a sneaking shadow over the trail Pierre Radisson had made, and when Kazan heard her again, long after midnight, he lay with, his head erect, and his body rigid, save for a curious twitching of his muscles. There was a new note in Gray Wolf's voice, a wailing note in which there was more than the mate-call. It was The Message. And at the sound of it Kazan rose from out of his silence and his fear, and with his head turned straight up to the sky he howled as the wild dogs of the North howl before the tepees of masters who are newly dead.

Pierre Radisson was dead.

Chapter VII

It was dawn when the baby snuggled close to Joan's warm breast and awakened her with its cry of hunger. She opened her eyes, brushed back the thick hair from her face, and could see where the shadowy form of her father was lying at the other side of the tent. He was very quiet, and she was pleased that he was still sleeping. She knew that the day before he had been very near to exhaustion, and so for half an hour longer she lay quiet, cooing softly to the baby Joan. Then she arose cautiously, tucked the baby in the warm blankets and furs, put on her heavier garments, and went outside.

By this time it was broad day, and she breathed a sigh of relief when she saw that the storm had passed. It was bitterly cold. It seemed to her that she had never known it to be so cold in all her life. The fire was completely out. Kazan was huddled in a round ball, his nose tucked under his body. He raised his head, shivering, as Joan came out. With her heavily moccasined foot Joan scattered the ashes and charred sticks where the fire had been. There was not a spark left. In returning to the tent she stopped for a moment beside Kazan, and patted his shaggy head.

"Poor Wolf!" she said. "I wish I had given you one of the bearskins!"

She threw back the tent-flap and entered. For the first time she saw her father's face in the light—and outside, Kazan heard the terrible moaning cry that broke from her lips. No one could have looked at Pierre Radisson's face once—and not have understood.

After that one agonizing cry, Joan flung herself upon her father's breast, sobbing so softly that even Kazan's sharp ears heard no sound. She remained there in her grief until every vital energy of womanhood and motherhood in her girlish body was roused to action by the wailing cry of baby Joan. Then she sprang to her feet and ran out through the tent opening. Kazan tugged at the end of his chain to meet her, but she saw nothing of him now. The terror of the wilderness is greater than that of death, and in an instant it had fallen upon Joan. It was not because of fear for herself. It was the baby. The wailing cries from the tent pierced her like knife-thrusts.

And then, all at once, there came to her what old Pierre had said the night before—his words about the river, the air-holes, the home forty miles away. "*You couldn't lose yourself, Joan*" He had guessed what might happen.

She bundled the baby deep in the furs and returned to the fire-bed. Her one thought now was that they must have fire. She made a little pile of birch-bark, covered it with half-burned bits of wood, and went into the tent for the matches. Pierre Radisson carried them in a water-proof box in a pocket of his bearskin coat. She sobbed as she kneeled beside him again, and obtained the box. As the fire flared up she added other bits of wood, and then some of the larger pieces that Pierre had dragged into camp. The fire gave her courage. Forty miles—and the river led to their home! She must make that, with the baby and Wolf. For the first time she turned to him, and spoke his name as she put her hand on his head. After that she gave him a chunk of meat which she thawed out over the fire, and melted the snow for tea. She was not hungry, but she recalled how her father had made her eat four or five times a day, so she forced herself to make a breakfast of a biscuit, a shred of meat and as much hot tea as she could drink.

The terrible hour she dreaded followed that. She wrapped blankets closely about her father's body, and tied them with babiche cord. After that she piled all the furs and blankets that remained on the sledge close to the fire, and snuggled baby Joan deep down in them. Pulling down the tent was a task. The ropes were stiff and frozen, and when she had finished, one of her hands was bleeding. She piled the tent on the sledge, and then, half, covering her face, turned and looked back.

Pierre Radisson lay on his balsam bed, with nothing over him now but the gray sky and the spruce-tops. Kazan stood stiff-legged and sniffed the air. His spine bristled when Joan went back slowly and kneeled beside the blanket-wrapped object. When she returned to him her face was white and tense, and now there was a strange and terrible look in her eyes as she stared out across the barren. She put him in the traces, and fastened about her slender waist the strap that Pierre had used. Thus they struck out for the river, floundering knee-deep in the freshly fallen and drifted snow. Half-way Joan stumbled in a drift and fell, her loose hair flying in a shimmering veil over the snow. With a mighty pull Kazan was at her side, and his cold muzzle touched her face as she drew herself to her feet. For a moment Joan took his shaggy head between her two hands.

"Wolf!" she moaned. "Oh, Wolf!"

She went on, her breath coming pantingly now, even from her brief exertion. The snow was not so deep on the ice of the river. But a wind was rising. It came from the north and east, straight in her face, and Joan bowed her head as she pulled with Kazan. Half a mile down the river she stopped, and no longer could she repress the hopelessness that rose to her lips in a sobbing choking cry. Forty miles! She clutched her hands at her breast, and stood breathing like one who had been beaten, her back to the wind. The baby was quiet. Joan went back and peered down under the furs, and what she saw there spurred her on again almost fiercely. Twice she stumbled to her knees in the drifts during the next quarter of a mile.

After that there was a stretch of wind-swept ice, and Kazan pulled the sledge alone. Joan walked at his side. There was a pain in her chest. A thousand needles seemed pricking her face, and suddenly she remembered the thermometer. She exposed it for a time on the top of the tent. When she looked at it a few minutes later it was thirty degrees below zero. Forty miles! And her father had told her that she could make it—and could not lose herself! But she did not know that even her father would have been afraid to face the north that day, with the temperature at thirty below, and a moaning wind bringing the first warning of a blizzard.

The timber was far behind her now. Ahead there was nothing but the pitiless barren, and the timber beyond that was hidden by the gray gloom of the day. If there had been trees, Joan's heart would not have choked so with terror. But there was nothing—nothing but that gray ghostly gloom, with the rim of the sky touching the earth a mile away.

The snow grew heavy under her feet again. Always she was watching for those treacherous, frost-coated traps in the ice her father had spoken of. But she found now that all the ice and snow looked alike to her, and that there was a growing pain back of her eyes. It was the intense cold.

The river widened into a small lake, and here the wind struck her in the face with such force that her weight was taken from the strap, and Kazan dragged the sledge alone. A few inches of snow impeded her as much as a foot had done before. Little by little she dropped back. Kazan forged to her side, every ounce of his magnificent strength in the traces. By the time they were on the river channel again, Joan was at the back of the sledge, following in the trail made by Kazan. She was powerless to help him. She felt more and more the leaden weight of her legs. There was but one hope—and that was the forest. If they did not reach it soon, within half an hour, she would be able to go no farther. Over and over again she moaned a prayer for her baby as she struggled on. She fell in the snow-drifts. Kazan and the sledge became only a dark blotch to her. And then, all at once, she saw that they were leaving her. They were not more than twenty feet ahead of her—but the blotch seemed to be a vast distance away. Every bit of life and strength in her body was now bent upon reaching the sledge—and baby Joan.

It seemed an interminable time before she gained. With the sledge only six feet ahead of her she struggled for what seemed to her to be an hour before she could reach out and touch it. With a moan she flung herself forward, and fell upon it. She no longer heard the wailing of the storm. She no longer felt discomfort. With her face in the furs under which baby Joan was buried, there came to her with swiftness and joy a vision of warmth and home. And then the vision faded away, and was followed by deep night.

Kazan stopped in the trail. He came back then and sat down upon his haunches beside her, waiting for her to move and speak. But she was very still. He thrust his nose into her loose hair. A whine rose in his throat, and suddenly he raised his head and sniffed in the face of the wind. Something came to him with that wind. He muzzled Joan again, but she did not stir. Then he went forward, and stood in his traces, ready for the pull, and looked back at her. Still she did not move or speak, and Kazan's whine gave place to a sharp excited bark.

The strange thing in the wind came to him stronger for a moment. He began to pull. The sledge-runners had frozen to the snow, and it took every ounce of his strength to free them. Twice during the next five minutes he stopped and sniffed the air. The third time that he halted, in a drift of snow, he returned to Joan's side again, and whined to awaken her. Then he tugged again at the end of his traces, and foot by foot he dragged the sledge through the drift. Beyond the drift there was a stretch of clear ice, and here Kazan rested. During a lull in the wind the scent came to him stronger than before.

At the end of the clear ice was a narrow break in the shore, where a creek ran into the main stream. If Joan had been conscious she would have urged him straight ahead. But Kazan turned into the break, and for ten minutes he struggled through the snow without a rest, whining more and more frequently, until at last the whine broke into a joyous bark. Ahead of him, close to the creek, was a small cabin. Smoke was rising out of the chimney. It was the scent of smoke that had come to him in the wind. A hard level slope reached to the cabin door, and with the last strength that was in him Kazan dragged his burden up that. Then he settled himself back beside Joan, lifted his shaggy head to the dark sky and howled.

A moment later the door opened. A man came out. Kazan's reddened, snow-shot eyes followed him watchfully as he ran to the sledge. He heard his startled exclamation as he bent over Joan. In another lull of the wind there came from out of the mass of furs on the sledge the wailing, half-smothered voice of baby Joan.

A deep sigh of relief heaved up from Kazan's chest. He was exhausted. His strength was gone. His feet were torn and bleeding. But the voice of baby Joan filled him with a strange happiness, and he lay down in his traces, while the man carried Joan and the baby into the life and warmth of the cabin.

A few minutes later the man reappeared. He was not old, like Pierre Radisson. He came close to Kazan, and looked down at him.

"My God," he said. "And you did that—*alone!*"

He bent down fearlessly, unfastened him from the traces, and led him toward the cabin door. Kazan hesitated but once—almost on the threshold. He turned his head, swift and alert. From out of the moaning and wailing of the storm it seemed to him that for a moment he had heard the voice of Gray Wolf.

Then the cabin door closed behind him.

Back in a shadowy corner of the cabin he lay, while the man prepared something over a hot stove for Joan. It was a long time before Joan rose from the cot on which the man had placed her. After that Kazan heard her sobbing; and then the man made her eat, and for a time they talked. Then the stranger hung up a big blanket in front of the bunk, and sat down close to the stove. Quietly Kazan slipped along the wall, and crept under the bunk. For a long time he could hear the sobbing breath of the girl. Then all was still.

The next morning he slipped out through the door when the man opened it, and sped swiftly into the forest. Half a mile away he found the trail of Gray Wolf, and called to her. From the frozen river came her reply, and he went to her.

Vainly Gray Wolf tried to lure him back into their old haunts—away from the cabin and the scent of man. Late that morning the man harnessed his dogs, and from the fringe of the forest Kazan saw him tuck Joan and the baby among the furs on the sledge, as old Pierre had done. All that day he followed in the trail of the team, with Gray Wolf slinking behind him. They traveled until dark; and then, under the stars and the moon that had followed the storm, the man still urged on his team. It was deep in the night when they came to another cabin, and the man beat upon the door. A light, the opening of the door, the joyous welcome of a man's voice, Joan's sobbing cry—Kazan heard these from the shadows in which he was hidden, and then slipped back to Gray Wolf.

In the days and weeks that followed Joan's home-coming the lure of the cabin and of the woman's hand held Kazan. As he had tolerated Pierre, so now he tolerated the younger man who lived with Joan and the baby. He knew that the man was very dear to Joan, and that the baby was very dear to him, as it was to the girl. It was not until the third day that Joan succeeded in coaxing him into the cabin—and that was the day on which the man returned with the dead and frozen body of Pierre. It was Joan's husband who first found the name on the collar he wore, and they began calling him Kazan.

Half a mile away, at the summit of a huge mass of rock which the Indians called the Sun Rock, he and Gray Wolf had found a home; and from here they went down to their hunts on the plain, and often the girl's voice reached up to them, calling, "*Kazan! Kazan! Kazan!*"

Through all the long winter Kazan hovered thus between the lure of Joan and the cabin—and Gray Wolf.

Then came Spring—and the Great Change.

Chapter VIII
The Great Change

The rocks, the ridges and the valleys were taking on a warmer glow. The poplar buds were ready to burst. The scent of balsam and of spruce grew heavier in the air each day, and all through the wilderness, in plain and forest, there was the rippling murmur of the spring floods finding their way to Hudson's Bay. In that great bay there was the rumble and crash of the ice fields thundering down in the early break-up through the Roes Welcome—the doorway to the Arctic, and for that reason there still came with the April wind an occasional sharp breath of winter.

Kazan had sheltered himself against that wind. Not a breath of air stirred in the sunny spot the wolf-dog had chosen for himself. He was more comfortable than he had been at any time during the six months of terrible winter—and as he slept he dreamed.

Gray Wolf, his wild mate, lay near him, flat on her belly, her forepaws reaching out, her eyes and nostrils as keen and alert as the smell of man could make them. For there was that smell of man, as well as of balsam and spruce, in the warm spring air. She gazed anxiously and sometimes steadily, at Kazan as he slept. Her own gray spine stiffened when she saw the tawny hair along Kazan's back bristle at some dream vision. She whined softly as his upper lip snarled back, showing his long white fangs. But for the most part Kazan lay quiet, save for the muscular twitchings of legs, shoulders and muzzle, which always tell when a dog is dreaming;

and as he dreamed there came to the door of the cabin out on the plain a blue-eyed girl-woman, with a big brown braid over her shoulder, who called through the cup of her hands, "Kazan, Kazan, Kazan!"

The voice reached faintly to the top of the Sun Rock, and Gray Wolf flattened her ears. Kazan stirred, and in another instant he was awake and on his feet. He leaped to an outcropping ledge, sniffing the air and looking far out over the plain that lay below them.

Over the plain the woman's voice came to them again, and Kazan ran to the edge of the rock and whined. Gray Wolf stepped softly to his side and laid her muzzle on his shoulder. She had grown to know what the Voice meant. Day and night she feared it, more than she feared the scent or sound of man.

Since she had given up the pack and her old life for Kazan, the Voice had become Gray Wolf's greatest enemy, and she hated it. It took Kazan from her. And wherever it went, Kazan followed.

Night after night it robbed her of her mate, and left her to wander alone under the stars and the moon, keeping faithfully to her loneliness, and never once responding with her own tongue to the hunt-calls of her wild brothers and sisters in the forests and out on the plains. Usually she would snarl at the Voice, and sometimes nip Kazan lightly to show her displeasure. But to-day, as the Voice came a third time, she slunk back into the darkness of a fissure between two rocks, and Kazan saw only the fiery glow of her eyes.

Kazan ran nervously to the trail their feet had worn up to the top of the Sun Rock, and stood undecided. All day, and yesterday, he had been uneasy and disturbed. Whatever it was that stirred him seemed to be in the air, for he could not see it or hear it or scent it. But he could *feel* it. He went to the fissure and sniffed at Gray Wolf. Usually she whined coaxingly. But her response to-day was to draw back her lips until he could see her white fangs.

A fourth tune the Voice came to them faintly, and she snapped fiercely at some unseen thing in the darkness between the two rocks. Kazan went again to the trail, still hesitating. Then he began to go down. It was a narrow winding trail, worn only by the pads and claws of animals, for the Sun Rock was a huge crag that rose almost sheer up for a hundred feet above the tops of the spruce and balsam, its bald crest catching the first gleams of the sun in the morning and the last glow of it in the evening. Gray Wolf had first led Kazan to the security of the retreat at the top of the rock.

When he reached the bottom he no longer hesitated, but darted swiftly in the direction of the cabin. Because of that instinct of the wild that was still in him, he always approached the cabin with caution. He never gave warning, and for a moment Joan was startled when she looked up from her baby and saw Kazan's shaggy head and shoulders in the open door. The baby struggled and kicked in her delight, and held out her two hands with cooing cries to Kazan. Joan, too, held out a hand.

"Kazan!" she cried softly. "Come in, Kazan!"

Slowly the wild red light in Kazan's eyes softened. He put a forefoot on the sill, and stood there, while the girl urged him again. Suddenly his legs seemed to sink a little under him, his tail drooped and he slunk in with that doggish air of having committed a crime. The creatures he loved were in the cabin, but the cabin itself he hated. He hated all cabins, for they all breathed of the club and the whip and bondage. Like all sledge-dogs he preferred the open snow for a bed, and the spruce-tops for shelter.

Joan dropped her hand to his head, and at its touch there thrilled through him that strange joy that was his reward for leaving Gray Wolf and the wild. Slowly he raised his head until his black muzzle rested on her lap, and he closed his eyes while that wonderful little creature that mystified him so—the baby—prodded him with her tiny feet, and pulled his tawny hair. He loved these baby-maulings even more than the touch of Joan's hand.

Motionless, sphinx-like, undemonstrative in every muscle of his body, Kazan stood, scarcely breathing. More than once this lack of demonstration had urged Joan's husband to warn her. But the wolf that was in Kazan, his wild aloofness, even his mating with Gray Wolf had made her love him more. She understood, and had faith in him.

In the days of the last snow Kazan had proved himself. A neighboring trapper had run over with his team, and the baby Joan had toddled up to one of the big huskies. There was a fierce snap of jaws, a scream of horror from Joan, a shout from the men as they leaped toward the pack. But Kazan was ahead of them all. In a gray streak that traveled with the speed of a bullet he was at the big husky's throat. When they pulled him off, the husky was dead. Joan thought of that now, as the baby kicked and tousled Kazan's head.

"Good old Kazan," she cried softly, putting her face down close to him. "We're glad you came, Kazan, for we're going to be alone to-night—baby and I. Daddy's gone to the post, and you must care for us while he's away."

She tickled his nose with the end of her long shining braid. This always delighted the baby, for in spite of his stoicism Kazan had to sniff and sometimes to sneeze, and twig his ears. And it pleased him, too. He loved the sweet scent of Joan's hair.

"And you'd fight for us, if you had to, wouldn't you?" she went on. Then she rose quietly. "I must close the door," she said. "I don't want you to go away again to-day, Kazan. You must stay with us."

Kazan went off to his corner, and lay down. Just as there had been some strange thing at the top of the Sun Rock to disturb him that day, so now there was a mystery that disturbed him in the cabin. He sniffed the air, trying to fathom its secret. Whatever it was, it seemed to make his mistress different, too. And she was digging out all sorts of odds and ends of things about the cabin, and doing them up in packages. Late that night, before she went to bed, Joan came and snuggled her hand close down beside him for a few moments.

"We're going away," she whispered, and there was a curious tremble that was almost a sob in her voice. "We're going home, Kazan. We're going away down where his people live—where they have churches, and cities, and music, and all the beautiful things in the world. And we're going to take *you*, Kazan!"

Kazan didn't understand. But he was happy at having the woman so near to him, and talking to him. At these times he forgot Gray Wolf. The dog that was in him surged over his quarter-strain of wildness, and the woman and the baby alone filled his world. But after Joan had gone to her bed, and all was quiet in the cabin, his old uneasiness returned. He rose to his feet and moved stealthily about the cabin, sniffing at the walls, the door and the things his mistress had done into packages. A low whine rose in his throat. Joan, half asleep, heard it, and murmured: "Be quiet, Kazan. Go to sleep—go to sleep—"

Long after that, Kazan stood rigid in the center of the room, listening, trembling. And faintly he heard, far away, the wailing cry of, Gray Wolf. But to-night it was not the cry of loneliness. It sent a thrill through him. He ran to the door, and whined, but Joan was deep in slumber and did not hear him. Once more he heard the cry, and only once. Then the night grew still. He crouched down near the door.

Joan found him there, still watchful, still listening, when she awoke in the early morning. She came to open the door for him, and in a moment he was gone. His feet seemed scarcely to touch the earth as he sped in the direction of the Sun Rock. Across the plain he could see the cap of it already painted with a golden glow.

He came to the narrow winding trail, and wormed his way up it swiftly.

Gray Wolf was not at the top to greet him. But he could smell her, and the scent of that other thing was strong in the air. His muscles tightened; his legs grew tense. Deep down in his chest there began the low rumble of a growl. He knew now what that strange thing was that had haunted him, and made him uneasy. It was *life*. Something that lived and breathed had invaded the home which he and Gray Wolf had chosen. He bared his long fangs, and a snarl of defiance drew back his lips. Stiff-legged, prepared to spring, his neck and head reaching out, he approached the two rocks between which Gray Wolf had crept the night before. She was still there. And with her was *something else*. After a moment the tenseness left Kazan's body. His bristling crest drooped until it lay flat. His ears shot forward, and he put his head and shoulders between the two rocks, and whined softly. And Gray Wolf whined. Slowly Kazan backed out, and faced the rising sun. Then he lay down, so that his body shielded I the entrance to the chamber between the rocks.

Gray Wolf was a mother.

Chapter IX
The Tragedy On Sun Rock

All that day Kazan guarded the top of the Sun Rock. Fate, and the fear and brutality of masters, had heretofore kept him from fatherhood, and he was puzzled. Something told him now that he belonged to the Sun Rock, and not to the cabin. The call that came to him from over the plain was not so strong. At dusk Gray Wolf came out from her retreat, and slunk to his side, whimpering, and nipped gently at his shaggy neck. It was the old instinct of his fathers that made him respond by caressing Gray Wolf's face with his tongue. Then Gray Wolf's jaws opened, and she laughed in short panting breaths, as if she had been hard run. She was happy, and as they heard a little snuffling sound from between the rocks, Kazan wagged his tail, and Gray Wolf darted back to her young.

The babyish cry and its effect upon Gray Wolf taught Kazan his first lesson in fatherhood. Instinct again told him that Gray Wolf could not go down to the hunt with him now—that she must stay at the top of the Sun Rock. So when the moon rose he went down alone, and toward dawn returned with a big white rabbit between his jaws. It was the wild in him that made him do this, and Gray Wolf ate ravenously. Then he knew that each night hereafter he must hunt for Gray Wolf—and the little whimpering creatures hidden between the two rocks.

The next day, and still the next, he did not go to the cabin, though he heard the voices of both the man and the woman calling him. On the fifth he went down, and Joan and the baby were so glad that the woman hugged him, and the baby kicked and laughed and screamed at him, while the man stood by cautiously, watching their demonstrations with a gleam of disapprobation in his eyes.

"I'm afraid of him," he told Joan for the hundredth time. "That's the wolf-gleam in his eyes. He's of a treacherous breed. Sometimes I wish we'd never brought him home."

"If we hadn't—where would the baby—have gone?" Joan reminded him, a little catch in her voice.

"I had almost forgotten that," said her husband. "Kazan, you old devil, I guess I love you, too." He laid his hand caressingly on Kazan's head. "Wonder how he'll take to life down there?" he asked. "He has always been used to the forests. It'll seem mighty strange."

"And so—have I—always been used to the forests," whispered Joan. "I guess that's why I love Kazan—next to you and the baby. Kazan—dear old Kazan!"

This time Kazan felt and scented more of that mysterious change in the cabin. Joan and her husband talked incessantly of their plans when they were together; and when the man was away Joan talked to the baby, and to him. And each time that he came down to the cabin during the week that followed, he grew more and more restless, until at last the man noticed the change in him.

"I believe he knows," he said to Joan one evening. "I believe he knows we're preparing to leave." Then he added: "The river was rising again to-day. It will be another week before we can start, perhaps longer."

That same night the moon flooded the top of the Sun Rock with a golden light, and out into the glow of it came Gray Wolf, with her three little whelps toddling behind her. There was much about these soft little balls that tumbled about him and snuggled in his tawny coat that reminded Kazan of the baby. At times they made the same queer, soft little sounds, and they staggered about on their four little legs just as helplessly as baby Joan made her way about on two. He did not fondle them, as Gray Wolf did, but the touch of them, and their babyish whimperings, filled him with a kind of pleasure that he had never experienced before.

The moon was straight above them, and the night was almost as bright as day, when he went down again to hunt for Gray Wolf. At the foot of the rock a big white rabbit popped up ahead of him, and he gave chase. For half a mile he pursued, until the wolf instinct in him rose over the dog, and he gave up the futile race. A deer he might have overtaken, but small game the wolf must hunt as the fox hunts it, and he began to slip through the thickets slowly and as quietly as a shadow. He was a mile from the Sun Rock when two quick leaps put Gray Wolf's supper between his jaws. He trotted back slowly, dropping the big seven-pound snow-shoe hare now and then to rest.

When he came to the narrow trail that led to the top of the Sun Rock he stopped. In that trail was the warm scent of strange feet. The rabbit fell from his jaws. Every hair in his body was suddenly electrified into life. What he scented was not the scent of a rabbit, a marten or a porcupine. Fang and claw had climbed the path ahead of him. And then, coming faintly to him from the top of the rock, he heard sounds which sent him up with a terrible whining cry. When he reached the summit he saw in the white moonlight a scene that stopped him for a single moment. Close to the edge of the sheer fall to the rocks, fifty feet below, Gray Wolf was engaged in a death-struggle with a huge gray lynx. She was down—and under, and from her there came a sudden sharp terrible cry of pain.

Kazan flew across the rock. His attack was the swift silent assault of the wolf, combined with the greater courage, the fury and the strategy of the husky. Another husky would have died in that first attack. But the lynx was not a dog or a wolf. It was "Mow-lee, the swift," as the Sarcees had named it—the quickest creature in the wilderness. Kazan's inch-long fangs should have sunk deep in its jugular. But in a fractional part of a second the lynx had thrown itself back like a huge soft ball, and Kazan's teeth buried themselves in the flesh of its neck instead of the jugular. And Kazan was not now fighting the fangs of a wolf in the pack, or of another husky. He was fighting claws—claws that ripped like twenty razor-edged knives, and which even a jugular hold could not stop.

Once he had fought a lynx in a trap, and he had not forgotten the lesson the battle had taught him. He fought to pull the lynx *down*, instead of forcing it on its back, as he would have done with another dog or a wolf. He knew that when on its back the fierce cat was most dangerous. One rip of its powerful hindfeet could disembowel him.

Behind him he heard Gray Wolf sobbing and crying, and he knew that she was terribly hurt. He was filled with the rage and strength of two dogs, and his teeth met through the flesh and hide of the cat's throat. But the big lynx escaped death by half an inch. It would take a fresh grip to reach the jugular, and suddenly Kazan made the deadly lunge. There was an instant's freedom for the lynx, and in that moment it flung itself back, and Kazan gripped at its throat— *on top.*

The cat's claws ripped through his flesh, cutting open his side—a little too high to kill. Another stroke and they would have cut to his vitals. But they had struggled close to the edge of the rock wall, and suddenly, without a snarl or a cry, they rolled over. It was fifty or sixty feet to the rocks of the ledge below, and even as they pitched over and over in the fall, Kazan's teeth sank deeper. They struck with terrific force, Kazan uppermost. The shock sent him half a dozen feet from his enemy. He was up like a flash, dizzy, snarling, on the defensive. The lynx lay limp and motionless where it had fallen. Kazan came nearer, still prepared, and sniffed cautiously. Something told him that the fight was over. He turned and dragged himself slowly along the ledge to the trail, and returned to Gray Wolf.

Gray Wolf was no longer in the moonlight. Close to the two rocks lay the limp and lifeless little bodies of the three pups. The lynx had torn them to pieces. With a whine of grief Kazan approached the two boulders and thrust his head between them. Gray Wolf was there, crying to herself in that terrible sobbing way. He went in, and began to lick her bleeding shoulders and head. All the rest of that night she whimpered with pain. With dawn she dragged herself out to the lifeless little bodies on the rock.

And then Kazan saw the terrible work of the lynx. For Gray Wolf was blind—not for a day or a night, but blind for all time. A gloom that no sun could break had become her shroud. And perhaps again it was that instinct of animal creation, which often is more wonderful than man's reason, that told Kazan what had happened. For he knew now that she was helpless—more helpless than the little creatures that had gamboled in the moonlight a few hours before. He remained close beside her all that day.

Vainly that day did Joan call for Kazan. Her voice rose to the Sun Rock, and Gray Wolf's head snuggled closer to Kazan, and Kazan's ears dropped back, and he licked her wounds. Late in the afternoon Kazan left Gray Wolf long enough to run to the bottom of the trail and bring up the snow-shoe rabbit. Gray Wolf muzzled the fur and flesh, but would not eat. Still a little later Kazan urged her to follow him to the trail. He no longer wanted to stay at the top of the Sun Rock, and he no longer wanted Gray Wolf to stay there. Step by step he drew her down the winding path away from her dead puppies. She would move only when he was very near her—so near that she could touch his scarred flank with her nose.

They came at last to the point in the trail where they had to leap down a distance of three or four feet from the edge of a rock, and here Kazan saw how utterly helpless Gray Wolf had become. She whined, and crouched twenty times before she dared make the spring, and then she jumped stiff-legged, and fell in a heap at Kazan's feet. After this Kazan did not have to urge her so hard, for the fall impinged on her the fact that she was safe only when her muzzle touched her mate's flank. She followed him obediently when they reached the plain, trotting with her foreshoulder to his hip.

Kazan was heading for a thicket in the creek bottom half a mile away, and a dozen times in that short distance Gray Wolf stumbled and fell. And each time that she fell Kazan learned a little more of the limitations of blindness. Once he sprang off in pursuit of a rabbit, but he had not taken twenty leaps when he stopped and looked back. Gray Wolf had not moved an inch. She stood motionless, sniffing the air—waiting for him! For a full minute Kazan stood, also waiting. Then he returned to her. Ever after this he returned to the point where he had left Gray Wolf, knowing that he would find her there.

All that day they remained in the thicket. In the afternoon he visited the cabin. Joan and her husband were there, and both saw at once Kazan's torn side and his lacerated head and shoulders.

"Pretty near a finish fight for him," said the man, after he had examined him. "It was either a lynx or a bear. Another wolf could not do that."

For half an hour Joan worked over him, talking to him all the time, and fondling him with her soft hands. She bathed his wounds in warm water, and then covered them with a healing salve, and Kazan was filled again with that old restful desire to remain with her always, and never to go back into the forests. For an hour she let him lie on the edge of her dress, with his nose touching her foot, while she worked on baby things. Then she rose to prepare supper, and Kazan got up—a little wearily—and went to the door. Gray Wolf and the gloom of the night were calling him, and he answered that call with a slouch of his shoulders and a drooping head. Its old thrill was gone. He watched his chance, and went out through the door. The moon had risen when he rejoined Gray Wolf. She greeted his return with a low whine of joy, and muzzled him with her blind face. In her helplessness she looked happier than Kazan in all his strength.

From now on, during the days that followed, it was a last great fight between blind and faithful Gray Wolf and the woman. If Joan had known of what lay in the thicket, if she could once have seen the poor creature to whom Kazan was now all life—the sun, the stars, the moon, and food—she would have helped Gray Wolf. But as it was she tried to lure Kazan more and more to the cabin, and slowly she won.

At last the great day came, eight days after the fight on the Sun Rock. Kazan had taken Gray Wolf to a wooded point on the river two days before, and there he had left her the preceding night when he went to the cabin. This time a stout babiche thong was tied to the collar round his neck, and he was fastened to a staple in the log wall. Joan and her husband were up before it was light next day. The sun was just rising when they all went out, the man carrying the baby, and Joan leading him. Joan turned and locked the cabin door, and Kazan heard a sob in her throat as they followed the man down to the river. The big canoe was packed and waiting. Joan got in first, with the baby. Then, still holding the babiche thong, she drew Kazan up close to her, so that he lay with his weight against her.

The sun fell warmly on Kazan's back as they shoved off, and he closed his eyes, and rested his head on Joan's lap. Her hand fell softly on his shoulder. He heard again that sound which the man could not hear, the broken sob in her throat, as the canoe moved slowly down to the wooded point.

Joan waved her hand back at the cabin, just disappearing behind the trees.

"Good-by!" she cried sadly. "Good-by—" And then she buried her face close down to Kazan and the baby, and sobbed.

The man stopped paddling.

"You're not sorry—Joan?" he asked.

They were drifting past the point now, and the scent of Gray Wolf came to Kazan's nostrils, rousing him, and bringing a low whine from his throat.

"You're not sorry—we're going?" Joan shook her head.

"No," she replied. "Only I've—always lived here—in the forests—and they're—home!"

The point with its white finger of sand, was behind them now. And Kazan was standing rigid, facing it. The man called to him, and Joan lifted her head. She, too, saw the point, and suddenly the babiche leash slipped from her fingers, and a strange light leaped into her blue eyes as she saw what stood at the end of that white tip of sand. It was Gray Wolf. Her blind eyes were turned toward Kazan. At last Gray Wolf, the faithful, understood. Scent told her what her eyes could not see. Kazan and the man-smell were together. And they were going— going—going—

"Look!" whispered Joan.

The man turned. Gray Wolf's forefeet were in the water. And now, as the canoe drifted farther and farther away, she settled back on her haunches, raised her head to the sun which she could not see and gave her last long wailing cry for Kazan.

The canoe lurched. A tawny body shot through the air—and Kazan was gone.

The man reached forward for his rifle. Joan's hand stopped him. Her face was white.

"Let him go back to her! Let him go—let him go!" she cried. "It is his place—with her."

And Kazan reaching the shore, shook the water from his shaggy hair, and looked for the last time toward the woman. The canoe was drifting slowly around the first bend. A moment more and it had disappeared. Gray Wolf had won.

Chapter X
The Days Of Fire

From the night of the terrible fight with the big gray lynx on the top of the Sun Rock, Kazan remembered less and less vividly the old days when he had been a sledge-dog, and the leader of a pack. He would never quite forget them, and always there would stand out certain memories from among the rest, like fires cutting the blackness of night. But as man dates events from his birth, his marriage, his freedom from a bondage, or some foundation-step in his career, so all things seemed to Kazan to begin with two tragedies which had followed one fast upon the other after the birth of Gray Wolf's pups.

The first was the fight on the Sun Rock, when the big gray lynx had blinded his beautiful wolf mate for all time, and had torn her pups into pieces. He in turn had killed the lynx. But Gray Wolf was still blind. Vengeance had not been able to give her sight. She could no longer hunt with him, as they had hunted with the wild wolf-packs out on the plain, and in the dark forests. So at thought of that night he always snarled, and his lips curled back to reveal his inch-long fangs.

The other tragedy was the going of Joan, her baby and her husband. Something more infallible than reason told Kazan that they would not come back. Brightest of all the pictures that remained with him was that of the sunny morning when the woman and the baby he loved, and the man he endured because of them, had gone away in the canoe, and often he would go to the point, and gaze longingly down-stream, where he had leaped from the canoe to return to his blind mate.

So Kazan's life seemed now to be made up chiefly of three things: his hatred of everything that bore the scent or mark of the lynx, his grieving for Joan and the baby, and Gray Wolf. It was natural that the strongest passion in him should be his hatred of the lynx, for not only Gray Wolf's blindness and the death of the pups, but even the loss of the woman and the baby he laid to that fatal struggle on the Sun Rock. From that hour he became the deadliest enemy of the lynx tribe. Wherever he struck the scent of the big gray cat he was turned into a snarling demon, and his hatred grew day by day, as he became more completely a part of the wild.

He found that Gray Wolf was more necessary to him now than she had ever been since the day she had left the wolf-pack for him. He was three-quarters dog, and the dog-part of him demanded companionship. There was only Gray Wolf to give him that now. They were alone. Civilization was four hundred miles south of them. The nearest Hudson's Bay post was sixty miles to the west. Often, in the days of the woman and the baby, Gray Wolf had spent her nights alone out in the forest, waiting and calling for Kazan. Now it was Kazan who was lonely and uneasy when he was away from her side.

In her blindness Gray Wolf could no longer hunt with her mate. But gradually a new code of understanding grew up between them, and through her blindness they learned many things that they had not known before. By early summer Gray Wolf could travel with Kazan, if he did not move too swiftly. She ran at his flank, with her shoulder or muzzle touching him, and Kazan learned not to leap, but to trot. Very quickly he found that he must choose the easiest trails for Gray Wolf's feet. When they came to a space to be bridged by a leap, he would muzzle Gray Wolf and whine, and she would stand with ears alert—listening. Then Kazan would take the leap, and she understood the distance she had to cover. She always over-leaped, which was a good fault.

In another way, and one that was destined to serve them many times in the future, she became of greater help than ever to Kazan. Scent and hearing entirely took the place of sight. Each day developed these senses more and more, and at the same time there developed between them the dumb language whereby she could impress upon Kazan what she had discovered by scent or sound. It became a curious habit of Kazan's always to look at Gray Wolf when they stopped to listen, or to scent the air.

After the fight on the Sun Rock, Kazan had taken his blind mate to a thick clump of spruce and balsam in the river-bottom, where they remained until early summer. Every day for weeks Kazan went to the cabin where Joan and the baby—and the man—had been. For a long time he went hopefully, looking each day or night to see some sign of life there. But the door was never open. The boards and saplings at the windows always remained. Never a spiral of smoke rose from the clay chimney. Grass and vines began to grow in the path. And fainter and fainter grew that scent which Kazan could still find about it—the scent of man, of the woman, the baby.

One day he found a little baby moccasin under one of the closed windows. It was old, and worn out, and blackened by snow and rain, but he lay down beside it, and remained there for a long time, while the baby Joan—a thousand miles away—was playing with the strange toys of civilization. Then he returned to Gray Wolf among the spruce and balsam.

The cabin was the one place to which Gray Wolf would not follow him. At all other times she was at his side. Now that she had become accustomed to blindness, she even accompanied him on his hunts, until he struck game, and began the chase. Then she would wait for him. Kazan usually hunted the big snow-shoe rabbits. But one night he ran down and killed a young doe. The kill was too heavy to drag to Gray Wolf, so he returned to where she was waiting for him and guided her to the feast. In many ways they became more and more inseparable as the summer lengthened, until at last, through all the wilderness, their footprints were always two by two and never one by one.

Then came the great fire.

Gray Wolf caught the scent of it when it was still two days to the west. The sun that night went down in a lurid cloud. The moon, drifting into the west, became blood red. When it dropped behind the wilderness in this manner, the Indians called it the Bleeding Moon, and the air was filled with omens.

All the next day Gray Wolf was nervous, and toward noon Kazan caught in the air the warning that she had sensed many hours ahead of him. Steadily the scent grew stronger, and by the middle of the afternoon the sun was veiled by a film of smoke.

The flight of the wild things from the triangle of forest between the junctions of the Pipestone and Cree Rivers would have begun then, but the wind shifted. It was a fatal shift. The fire was raging from the west and south. Then the wind swept straight eastward, carrying the smoke with it, and during this breathing spell all the wild creatures in the triangle between the two rivers waited. This gave the fire time to sweep completely, across the base of the forest triangle, cutting off the last trails of escape.

Then the wind shifted again, and the fire swept north. The head of the triangle became a death-trap. All through the night the southern sky was filled with a lurid glow, and by morning the heat and smoke and ash were suffocating.

Panic-striken, Kazan searched vainly for a means of escape. Not for an instant did he leave Gray Wolf. It would have been easy for him to swim across either of the two streams, for he was three-quarters dog. But at the first touch of water on her paws, Gray Wolf drew back, shrinking. Like all her breed, she would face fire and death before water. Kazan urged. A dozen times he leaped in, and swam out into the stream. But Gray Wolf would come no farther than she could wade.

They could hear the distant murmuring roar of the fire now. Ahead of it came the wild things. Moose, caribou and deer plunged into the water of the streams and swam to the safety of the opposite side. Out upon a white finger of sand lumbered a big black bear with two cubs, and even the cubs took to the water, and swam across easily. Kazan watched them, and whined to Gray Wolf.

And then out upon that white finger of sand came other things that dreaded the water as Gray Wolf dreaded it: a big fat porcupine, a sleek little marten, a fisher-cat that sniffed the air and wailed like a child. Those things that could not or would not swim outnumbered the others three to one. Hundreds of little ermine scurried along the shore like rats, their squeaking little voices sounding incessantly; foxes ran swiftly along the banks, seeking a tree or a windfall that might bridge the water for them; the lynx snarled and faced the fire; and Gray Wolf's own tribe—the wolves—dared take no deeper step than she.

Dripping and panting, and half choked by heat and smoke, Kazan came to Gray Wolf's side. There was but one refuge left near them, and that was the sand-bar. It reached out for fifty feet into the stream. Quickly he led his blind mate toward it. As they came through the low bush to the river-bed, something stopped them both. To their nostrils had come the scent of a deadlier enemy than fire. A lynx had taken possession of the sand-bar, and was crouching at the end of it. Three porcupines had dragged themselves into the edge of the water, and lay there like balls, their quills alert and quivering. A fisher-cat was snarling at the lynx. And the lynx, with ears laid back, watched Kazan and Gray Wolf as they began the invasion of the sand-bar.

Faithful Gray Wolf was full of fight, and she sprang shoulder to shoulder with Kazan, her fangs bared. With an angry snap, Kazan drove her back, and she stood quivering and whining while he advanced. Light-footed, his pointed ears forward, no menace or threat in his attitude, he advanced. It was the deadly advance of the husky trained in battle, skilled in the art of killing. A man from civilization would have said that the dog was approaching the lynx with friendly intentions. But the lynx understood. It was the old feud of many generations—made deadlier now by Kazan's memory of that night at the top of the Sun Rock.

Instinct told the fisher-cat what was coming, and it crouched low and flat; the porcupines, scolding like little children at the presence of enemies and the thickening clouds of smoke, thrust their quills still more erect. The lynx lay on its belly, like a cat, its hindquarters twitching, and gathered for the spring. Kazan's feet seemed scarcely to touch the sand as he circled lightly around it. The lynx pivoted as he circled, and then it shot in a round snarling ball over the eight feet of space that separated them.

Kazan did not leap aside. He made no effort to escape the attack, but met it fairly with the full force of his shoulders, as sledge-dog meets sledge-dog. He was ten pounds heavier than the lynx, and for a moment the big loose-jointed cat with its twenty knife-like claws was thrown on its side. Like a flash Kazan took advantage of the moment, and drove for the back of the cat's neck.

In that same moment blind Gray Wolf leaped in with a snarling cry, and fighting under Kazan's belly, she fastened her jaws in one of the cat's hindlegs. The bone snapped. The lynx, twice outweighed, leaped backward, dragging both Kazan and Gray Wolf. It fell back down on one of the porcupines, and a hundred quills drove into its body. Another leap and it was free— fleeing into the face of the smoke. Kazan did not pursue. Gray Wolf came to his side and licked his neck, where fresh blood was crimsoning his tawny hide. The fisher-cat lay as if dead, watching them with fierce little black eyes. The porcupines continued to chatter, as if begging for mercy. And then a thick black suffocating pall of smoke drove low over the sand-bar and with it came air that was furnace-hot.

At the uttermost end of the sand-bar Kazan and Gray Wolf rolled themselves into balls and thrust their heads under their bodies. The fire was very near now. The roar of it was like that of a great cataract, with now and then a louder crash of falling trees. The air was filled with ash and burning sparks, and twice Kazan drew forth his head to snap at blazing embers that fell upon and seared him like hot irons.

Close along the edge of the stream grew thick green bush, and when the fire reached this, it burned more slowly, and the heat grew less. Still, it was a long time before Kazan and Gray Wolf could draw forth their heads and breathe more freely. Then they found that the finger of sand reaching out into the river had saved them. Everywhere in that triangle between the two rivers the world had turned black, and was hot underfoot.

The smoke cleared away. The wind changed again, and swung down cool and fresh from the west and north. The fisher-cat was the first to move cautiously back to the forests that had been, but the porcupines were still rolled into balls when Gray Wolf and Kazan left the sand-bar. They began to travel up-stream, and before night came, their feet were sore from hot ash and burning embers.

The moon was strange and foreboding that night, like a spatter of blood in the sky, and through the long silent hours there was not even the hoot of an owl to give a sign that life still existed where yesterday had been a paradise of wild things. Kazan knew that there was nothing to hunt, and they continued to travel all that night. With dawn they struck a narrow swamp along the edge of the stream. Here beavers had built a dam, and they were able to cross over into the green country on the opposite side. For another day and another night they traveled westward, and this brought them into the thick country of swamp and timber along the Waterfound.

And as Kazan and Gray Wolf came from the west, there came from the Hudson's Bay post to the east a slim dark-faced French half-breed by the name of Henri Loti, the most famous lynx hunter in all the Hudson's Bay country. He was prospecting for "signs," and he found them in abundance along the Waterfound. It was a game paradise, and the snow-shoe rabbit abounded in thousands. As a consequence, the lynxes were thick, and Henri built his trapping shack, and then returned to the post to wait until the first snows fell, when he would come back with his team, supplies and traps.

And up from the south, at this same time, there was slowly working his way by canoe and trail a young university zoologist who was gathering material for a book on *The Reasoning of the Wild*. His name was Paul Weyman, and he had made arrangements to spend a part of the winter with Henri Loti, the half-breed. He brought with him plenty of paper, a camera and the photograph of a girl. His only weapon was a pocket-knife.

And meanwhile Kazan and Gray Wolf found the home they were seeking in a thick swamp five or six miles from the cabin that Henri Loti had built.

Chapter XI
Always Two By Two

It was January when a guide from the post brought Paul Weyman to Henri Loti's cabin on the Waterfound. He was a man of thirty-two or three, full of the red-blooded life that made Henri like him at once. If this had not been the case, the first few days in the cabin might have been unpleasant, for Henri was in bad humor. He told Weyman about it their first night, as they were smoking pipes alongside the redly glowing box stove.

"It is damn strange," said Henri. "I have lost seven lynx in the traps, torn to pieces like they were no more than rabbits that the foxes had killed. No thing—not even bear—have ever tackled lynx in a trap before. It is the first time I ever see it. And they are torn up so bad they are not worth one half dollar at the post. Seven!—that is over two hundred dollar I have lost! There are two wolves who do it. Two—I know it by the tracks—always two—an'—never one. They follow my trap-line an' eat the rabbits I catch. They leave the fisher-cat, an' the mink, an' the ermine, an' the marten; but the lynx—*sacré* an' damn!—they jump on him an' pull the fur from him like you pull the wild cotton balls from the burn-bush! I have tried strychnine in deer fat, an' I have set traps and deadfalls, but I can not catch them. They will drive me out unless I get them, for I have taken only five good lynx, an' they have destroyed seven."

This roused Weyman. He was one of that growing number of thoughtful men who believe that man's egoism, as a race, blinds him to many of the more wonderful facts of creation. He had thrown down the gantlet, and with a logic that had gained him a nation-wide hearing, to those who believed that man was the only living creature who could reason, and that common sense and cleverness when displayed by any other breathing thing were merely instinct. The facts behind Henri's tale of woe struck him as important, and until midnight they talked about the two strange wolves.

"There is one big wolf an' one smaller," said Henri. "An' it is always the big wolf who goes in an' fights the lynx. I see that by the snow. While he's fighting, the smaller wolf makes many tracks in the snow just out of reach, an' then when the lynx is down, or dead, it jumps in an' helps tear it into pieces. All that I know by the snow. Only once have I seen where the smaller one went in an' fought with the other, an' then there was blood all about that was not lynx blood; I trailed the devils a mile by the dripping."

During the two weeks that followed, Weyman found much to add to the material of his book. Not a day passed that somewhere along Henri's trap-line they did not see the trails of the two wolves, and Weyman observed that—as Henri had told him—the footprints were always two by two, and never one by one. On the third day they came to a trap that had held a lynx, and at sight of what remained Henri cursed in both French and English until he was purple in the face. The lynx had been torn until its pelt was practically worthless.

Weyman saw where the smaller wolf had waited on its haunches, while its companion had killed the lynx. He did not tell Henri all he thought. But the days that followed convinced him more and more that he had found the most dramatic exemplification of his theory. Back of this mysterious tragedy of the trap-line there was a *reason*.

Why did the two wolves not destroy the fisher-cat, the ermine and the marten? Why was their feud with the lynx alone?

Weyman was strangely thrilled. He was a lover of wild things, and for that reason he never carried a gun. And when he saw Henri placing poison-baits for the two marauders, he shuddered, and when, day after day, he saw that these poison-baits were untouched, he rejoiced. Something in his own nature went out in sympathy to the heroic outlaw of the trap-line who never failed to give battle to the lynx. Nights in the cabin he wrote down his thoughts and discoveries of the day. One night he turned suddenly on Henri.

"Henri, doesn't it ever make you sorry to kill so many wild things?" he asked.

Henri stared and shook his head.

"I kill t'ousand an' t'ousand," he said. "I kill t'ousand more."

"And there are twenty thousand others just like you in this northern quarter of the continent—all killing, killing for hundreds of years back, and yet you can't kill out wild life. The war of Man and the Beast, you might call it. And, if you could return five hundred years from now, Henri, you'd still find wild life here. Nearly all the rest of the world is changing, but you can't change these almost impenetrable thousands of square miles of ridges and swamps and forests. The railroads won't come here, and I, for one, thank God for that. Take all the great prairies to the west, for instance. Why, the old buffalo trails are still there, plain as day—and yet, towns and cities are growing up everywhere. Did you ever hear of North Battleford?"

"Is she near Montreal or Quebec?" Henri asked.

Weyman smiled, and drew a photograph from his pocket. It was the picture of a girl.

"No. It's far to the west, in Saskatchewan. Seven years ago I used to go up there every year, to shoot prairie chickens, coyotes and elk. There wasn't any North Battleford then—just the glorious prairie, hundreds and hundreds of square miles of it. There was a single shack on the Saskatchewan River, where North Battleford now stands, and I used to stay there. In that shack there was a little girl, twelve years old. We used to go out hunting together—for I used to kill things in those days. And the little girl would cry sometimes when I killed, and I'd laugh at her.

"Then a railroad came, and then another, and they joined near the shack, and all at once a town sprang up. Seven years ago there was only the shack there, Henri. Two years ago there were eighteen hundred people. This year, when I came through, there were five thousand, and two years from now there'll be ten thousand.

"On the ground where that shack stood are three banks, with a capital of forty million dollars; you can see the glow of the electric lights of the city twenty miles away. It has a hundred-thousand dollar college, a high school, the provincial asylum, a fire department, two clubs, a board of trade, and it's going to have a street-car line within two years. Think of that—all where the coyotes howled a few years ago!

"People are coming in so fast that they can't keep a census. Five years from now there'll be a city of twenty thousand where the old shack stood. And the little girl in that shack, Henri—she's a young lady now, and her people are—well, rich. I don't care about that. The chief thing is that she is going to marry me in the spring. Because of her I stopped killing things when she was only sixteen. The last thing I killed was a prairie wolf, and it had young. Eileen kept the little puppy. She's got it now—tamed. That's why above all other wild things I love the wolves. And I hope these two leave your trap-line safe."

Henri was staring at him. Weyman gave him the picture. It was of a sweet-faced girl, with deep pure eyes, and there came a twitch at the corners of Henri's mouth as he looked at it.

"My Iowaka died t'ree year ago," he said. "She too loved the wild thing. But them wolf—damn! They drive me out if I can not kill them!" He put fresh fuel into the stove, and prepared for bed.

One day the big idea came to Henri.

Weyman was with him when they struck fresh signs of lynx. There was a great windfall ten or fifteen feet high, and in one place the logs had formed a sort of cavern, with almost solid walls on three sides. The snow was beaten down by tracks, and the fur of rabbit was scattered about. Henri was jubilant.

"We got heem—sure!" he said.

He built the bait-house, set a trap and looked about him shrewdly. Then he explained his scheme to Weyman. If the lynx was caught, and the two wolves came to destroy it, the fight would take place in that shelter under the windfall, and the marauders would have to pass through the opening. So Henri set five smaller traps, concealing them skilfully under leaves and moss and snow, and all were far enough away from the bait-house so that the trapped lynx could not spring them in his struggles.

"When they fight, wolf jump this way an' that—an' sure get in," said Henri. "He miss one, two, t'ree—but he sure get in trap somewhere."

That same morning a light snow fell, making the work more complete, for it covered up all footprints and buried the telltale scent of man. That night Kazan and Gray Wolf passed within a hundred feet of the windfall, and Gray Wolf's keen scent detected something strange and disquieting in the air. She informed Kazan by pressing her shoulder against his, and they swung off at right angles, keeping to windward of the trap-line.

For two days and three cold starlit nights nothing happened at the windfall. Henri understood, and explained to Weyman. The lynx was a hunter, like himself, and also had its hunt-line, which it covered about once a week. On the fifth night the lynx returned, went to the windfall, was lured straight to the bait, and the sharp-toothed steel trap closed relentlessly over its right hindfoot. Kazan and Gray Wolf were traveling a quarter of a mile deeper in the forest when they heard the clanking of the steel chain as the lynx fought; to free itself. Ten minutes later they stood in the door of the windfall cavern.

It was a white clear night, so filled with brilliant stars that Henri himself could have hunted by the light of them. The lynx had exhausted itself, and lay crouching on its belly as Kazan and Gray Wolf appeared. As usual, Gray Wolf held back while Kazan began the battle. In the first or second of these fights on the trap-line, Kazan would probably have been disemboweled or had his jugular vein cut open, had the fierce cats been free. They were more than his match in open fight, though the biggest of them fell ten pounds under his weight. Chance had saved him on the Sun Rock. Gray Wolf and the porcupine had both added to the defeat of the lynx on the sand-bar. And along Henri's hunting line it was the trap that was his ally. Even with his enemy thus shackled he took big chances. And he took bigger chances than ever with the lynx under the windfall.

The cat was an old warrior, six or seven years old. His claws were an inch and a quarter long, and curved like simitars. His forefeet and his left hindfoot were free, and as Kazan advanced, he drew back, so that the trap-chain was slack under his body. Here Kazan could not follow his old tactics of circling about his trapped foe, until it had become tangled in the chain, or had so shortened and twisted it that there was no chance for a leap. He had to attack face to face, and suddenly he lunged in. They met shoulder to shoulder. Kazan's fangs snapped at the other's throat, and missed. Before he could strike again, the lynx flung out its free hindfoot, and even Gray Wolf heard the ripping sound that it made. With a snarl Kazan was flung back, his shoulder torn to the bone.

Then it was that one of Henri's hidden traps saved him from a second attack—and death. Steel jaws snapped over one of his forefeet, and when he leaped, the chain stopped him. Once or twice before, blind Gray Wolf had leaped in, when she knew that Kazan was in great danger. For an instant she forgot her caution now, and as she heard Kazan's snarl of pain, she sprang in under the windfall. Five traps Henri had hidden in the space in front of the bait-house, and Gray Wolf's feet found two of these. She fell on her side, snapping and snarling. In his struggles Kazan sprung the remaining two traps. One of them missed. The fifth, and last, caught him by a hindfoot.

This was a little past midnight. From then until morning the earth and snow under the windfall were torn up by the struggles of the wolf, the dog and the lynx to regain their freedom. And when morning came, all three were exhausted, and lay on their sides, panting and with bleeding jaws, waiting for the coming of man—and death.

Henri and Weyman were out early. When they struck off the main line toward the windfall, Henri pointed to the tracks of Kazan and Gray Wolf, and his dark face lighted up with pleasure and excitement. When they reached the shelter under the mass of fallen timber, both stood speechless for a moment, astounded by what they saw. Even Henri had seen nothing like this before—two wolves and a lynx, all in traps, and almost within reach of one another's fangs. But surprise could not long delay the business of Henri's hunter's instinct. The wolves lay first in his path, and he was raising his rifle to put a steel-capped bullet through the base of Kazan's brain, when Weyman caught him eagerly by the arm. Weyman was staring. His fingers dug into Henri's flesh. His eyes had caught a glimpse of the steel-studded collar about Kazan's neck.

"Wait!" he cried. "It's not a wolf. It's a dog!"

Henri lowered his rifle, staring at the collar. Weyman's eyes shot to Gray Wolf. She was facing them, snarling, her white fangs bared to the foes she could not see. Her blind eyes were closed. Where there should have been eyes there was only hair, and an exclamation broke from Weyman's lips.

"Look!" he commanded of Henri. "What in the name of heaven—"

"One is dog—wild dog that has run to the wolves," said Henri. "And the other is—wolf."

"And *blind*!" gasped Weyman.

"*Oui*, blind, m'sieur," added Henri, falling partly into French in his amazement. He was raising his rifle again. Weyman seized it firmly.

"Don't kill them, Henri," he said. "Give them to me—alive. Figure up the value of the lynx they have destroyed, and add to that the wolf bounty, and I will pay. Alive, they are worth to me a great deal. My God, a dog—and a blind wolf—*mates*!"

He still held Henri's rifle, and Henri was staring at him, as if he did not yet quite understand.

Weyman continued speaking, his eyes and face blazing.

"A dog—and a blind wolf—*mates*!" he repeated. "It is wonderful, Henri. Down there, they will say I have gone beyond *reason*, when my book comes out. But I shall have proof. I shall take twenty photographs here, before you kill the lynx. I shall keep the dog and the wolf alive. And I shall pay you, Henri, a hundred dollars apiece for the two. May I have them?"

Henri nodded. He held his rifle in readiness, while Weyman unpacked his camera and got to work. Snarling fangs greeted the click of the camera-shutter—the fangs of wolf and lynx. But Kazan lay cringing, not through fear, but because he still recognized the mastery of man. And when he had finished with his pictures, Weyman approached almost within reach of him, and spoke even more kindly to him than the man who had lived back in the deserted cabin.

Henri shot the lynx, and when Kazan understood this, he tore at the end of his trap-chains and snarled at the writhing body of his forest enemy. By means of a pole and a babiche noose, Kazan was brought out from under the windfall and taken to Henri's cabin. The two men then returned with a thick sack and more babiche, and blind Gray Wolf, still fettered by the traps, was made prisoner. All the rest of that day Weyman and Henri worked to build a stout cage of saplings, and when it was finished, the two prisoners were placed in it.

Before the dog was put in with Gray Wolf, Weyman closely examined the worn and tooth-marked collar about his neck.

On the brass plate he found engraved the one word, "Kazan," and with a strange thrill made note of it in his diary.

After this Weyman often remained at the cabin when Henri went out on the trap-line. After the second day he dared to put his hand between the sapling bars and touch Kazan, and the next day Kazan accepted a piece of raw moose meat from his hand. But at his approach, Gray Wolf would always hide under the pile of balsam in the corner of their prison. The instinct of generations and perhaps of centuries had taught her that man was her deadliest enemy. And yet, this man did not hurt her, and Kazan was not afraid of him. She was frightened at first; then puzzled, and a growing curiosity followed that. Occasionally, after the third day, she would thrust her blind face out of the balsam and sniff the air when Weyman was at the cage, making friends with Kazan. But she would not eat. Weyman noted that, and each day he tempted her with the choicest morsels of deer and moose fat. Five days—six—seven passed, and she had not taken a mouthful. Weyman could count her ribs.

"She die," Henri told him on the seventh night. "She starve before she eat in that cage. She want the forest, the wild kill, the fresh blood. She two—t'ree year old—too old to make civilize."

Henri went to bed at the usual hour, but Weyman was troubled, and sat up late. He wrote a long letter to the sweet-faced girl at North Battleford, and then he turned out the light, and painted visions of her in the red glow of the fire. He saw her again for that first time when he camped in the little shack where the fifth city of Saskatchewan now stood—with her blue eyes, the big shining braid, and the fresh glow of the prairies in her cheeks. She had hated him—yes, actually hated him, because he loved to kill. He laughed softly as he thought of that. She had changed him—wonderfully.

He rose, opened the door, softly, and went out. Instinctively his eyes turned westward. The sky was a blaze of stars. In their light he could see the cage, and he stood, watching and listening. A sound came to him. It was Gray Wolf gnawing at the sapling bars of her prison. A moment later there came a low sobbing whine, and he knew that it was Kazan crying for his freedom.

Leaning against the side of the cabin was an ax. Weyman seized it, and his lips smiled silently. He was thrilled by a strange happiness, and a thousand miles away in that city on the Saskatchewan he could feel another spirit rejoicing with him. He moved toward the cage. A dozen blows, and two of the sapling bars were knocked out. Then Weyman drew back. Gray Wolf found the opening first, and she slipped out into the starlight like a shadow. But she did not flee. Out in the open space she waited for Kazan, and for a moment the two stood there, looking at the cabin. Then they set off into freedom, Gray Wolf's shoulder at Kazan's flank.

Weyman breathed deeply.

"Two by two—always two by two, until death finds one of them," he whispered.

Chapter XII
The Red Death

Kazan and Gray Wolf wandered northward into the Fond du Lac country, and were there when Jacques, a Hudson Bay Company's runner, came up to the post from the south with the first authentic news of the dread plague—the smallpox. For weeks there had been rumors on all sides. And rumor grew into rumor. From the east, the south and the west they multiplied, until on all sides the Paul Reveres of the wilderness were carrying word that *La Mort Rouge*—the Red Death—was at their heels, and the chill of a great fear swept like a shivering wind from the edge of civilization to the bay. Nineteen years before these same rumors had come up from the south, and the Red Terror had followed. The horror of it still remained with the forest people, for a thousand unmarked graves, shunned like a pestilence, and scattered from the lower waters of James Bay to the lake country of the Athabasca, gave evidence of the toll it demanded.

Now and then in their wanderings Kazan and Gray Wolf had come upon the little mounds that covered the dead. Instinct—something that was infinitely beyond the comprehension of man—made them *feel* the presence of death about them, perhaps smell it in the air. Gray Wolf's wild blood and her blindness gave her an immense advantage over Kazan when it came to detecting those mysteries of the air and the earth which the eyes were not made to see. Each day that had followed that terrible moonlit night on the Sun Rock, when the lynx had blinded her, had added to the infallibility of her two chief senses—hearing and scent. And it was she who discovered the presence of the plague first, just as she had scented the great forest fire hours before Kazan had found it in the air.

Kazan had lured her back to a trap-line. The trail they found was old. It had not been traveled for many days. In a trap they found a rabbit, but it had been dead a long time. In another there was the carcass of a fox, torn into bits by the owls. Most of the traps were sprung. Others were covered with snow. Kazan, with his three-quarters strain of dog, ran over the trail from trap to trap, intent only on something alive—meat to devour. Gray Wolf, in her blindness, scented *death*. It shivered in the tree-tops above her. She found it in every trap-house they came to—death—*man death*. It grew stronger and stronger, and she whined, and nipped Kazan's flank. And Kazan went on. Gray Wolf followed him to the edge of the clearing in which Loti's cabin stood, and then she sat back on her haunches, raised her blind face to the gray sky, and gave a long and wailing cry. In that moment the bristles began to stand up along Kazan's spine. Once, long ago, he had howled before the tepee of a master who was newly dead, and he settled back on his haunches, and gave the death-cry with Gray Wolf. He, too, scented it now. Death was in the cabin, and over the cabin there stood a sapling pole, and at the end of the pole there fluttered a strip of red cotton rag—the warning flag of the plague from Athabasca to the bay. This man, like a hundred other heroes of the North, had run up the warning before he laid himself down to die. And that same night, in the cold light of the moon, Kazan and Gray Wolf swung northward into the country of the Fond du Lac.

There preceded them a messenger from the post on Reindeer Lake, who was passing up the warning that had come from Nelson House and the country to the southeast.

"There's smallpox on the Nelson," the messenger informed Williams, at Fond du Lac, "and it has struck the Crees on Wollaston Lake. God only knows what it is doing to the Bay Indians, but we hear it is wiping out the Chippewas between the Albany and the Churchill." He left the same day with his winded dogs. "I'm off to carry word to the Reveillon people to the west," he explained.

Three days later, word came from Churchill that all of the company's servants and his majesty's subjects west of the bay should prepare themselves for the coming of the Red Terror. Williams' thin face turned as white as the paper he held, as he read the words of the Churchill factor.

"It means dig graves," he said. "That's the only preparation we can make."

He read the paper aloud to the men at Fond du Lac, and every available man was detailed to spread the warning throughout the post's territory. There was a quick harnessing of dogs, and on each sledge that went out was a roll of red cotton cloth—rolls that were ominous of death, lurid signals of pestilence and horror, whose touch sent shuddering chills through the men who were about to scatter them among the forest people. Kazan and Gray Wolf struck the trail of one of these sledges on the Gray Beaver, and followed it for half a mile. The next day, farther to the west, they struck another, and on the fourth day still a third. The last trail was fresh, and Gray Wolf drew back from it as if stung, her fangs snarling. On the wind there came to them the pungent odor of smoke. They cut at right angles to the trail, Gray Wolf leaping clear of the marks in the snow, and climbed to the cap of a ridge. To windward of them, and down in the plain, a cabin was burning. A team of huskies and a man were disappearing in the spruce forest. Deep down in his throat Kazan gave a rumbling whine. Gray Wolf stood as rigid as a rock. In the cabin a plague-dead man was burning. It was the law of the North. And the mystery of the funeral pyre came again to Kazan and Gray Wolf. This time they did not howl, but slunk down into the farther plain, and did not stop that day until they had buried themselves deep in a dry and sheltered swamp ten miles to the north.

After this they followed the days and weeks which marked the winter of nineteen hundred and ten as one of the most terrible in all the history of the Northland—a single month in which wild life as well as human hung in the balance, and when cold, starvation and plague wrote a chapter in the lives of the forest people which will not be forgotten for generations to come.

In the swamp Kazan and Gray Wolf found a home under a windfall. It was a small comfortable nest, shut in entirely from the snow and wind. Gray Wolf took possession of it immediately. She flattened herself out on her belly, and panted to show Kazan her contentment and satisfaction. Nature again kept Kazan close at her side. A vision came to him, unreal and dream-like, of that wonderful night under the stars—ages and ages ago, it seemed—when he had fought the leader of the wolf-pack, and young Gray Wolf had crept to his side after his victory and had given herself to him for mate. But this mating season there was no running after the doe or the caribou, or mingling with the wild pack. They lived chiefly on rabbit and spruce partridge, because of Gray Wolf's blindness. Kazan could hunt those alone. The hair had now grown over Gray Wolf's sightless eyes. She had ceased to grieve, to rub her eyes with her paws, to whine for the sunlight, the golden moon and the stars. Slowly she began to forget that she had ever seen those things. She could now run more swiftly at Kazan's flank. Scent and hearing had become wonderfully keen. She could wind a caribou two miles distant, and the presence of man she could pick up at an even greater distance. On a still night she had heard the splash of a trout half a mile away. And as these two things—scent and hearing—became more and more developed in her, those same senses became less active in Kazan.

He began to depend upon Gray Wolf. She would point out the hiding-place of a partridge fifty yards from their trail. In their hunts she became the leader—until game was found. And as Kazan learned to trust to her in the hunt, so he began just as instinctively to heed her warnings. If Gray Wolf reasoned, it was to the effect that without Kazan she would die. She had tried hard now and then to catch a partridge, or a rabbit, but she had always failed. Kazan meant life to her. And—if she reasoned—it was to make herself indispensable to her mate. Blindness had made her different than she would otherwise have been. Again nature promised motherhood to her. But she did not—as she would have done in the open, and with sight—hold more and more aloof from Kazan as the days passed. It was her habit, spring, summer and winter, to snuggle close to Kazan and lie with her beautiful head resting on his neck or back. If Kazan snarled at her she did not snap back, but slunk down as though struck a blow. With her warm tongue she would lick away the ice that froze to the long hair between Kazan's toes. For days after he had run a sliver in his paw she nursed his foot. Blindness had made Kazan absolutely necessary to her existence—and now, in a different way, she became more and more necessary to Kazan. They were happy in their swamp home. There was plenty of small game about them, and it was warm under the windfall. Rarely did they go beyond the limits of the swamp to hunt. Out on the more distant plains and the barren ridges they occasionally heard the cry of the wolf-pack on the trail of meat, but it no longer thrilled them with a desire to join in the chase.

One day they struck farther than usual to the west. They left the swamp, crossed a plain over which a fire had swept the preceding year, climbed a ridge, and descended into a second plain. At the bottom Gray Wolf stopped and sniffed the air. At these times Kazan always watched her, waiting eagerly and nervously if the scent was too faint for him to catch. But to-day he caught the edge of it, and he knew why Gray Wolf's ears flattened, and her hindquarters drooped. The scent of game would have made her rigid and alert. But it was not the game smell. It was human, and Gray Wolf slunk behind Kazan and whined. For several minutes they stood without moving or making a sound, and then Kazan led the way on. Less than three hundred yards away they came to a thick clump of scrub spruce, and almost ran into a snow-smothered tepee. It was abandoned. Life and fire had not been there for a long time. But from the tepee had come the man-smell. With legs rigid and his spine quivering Kazan approached the opening to the tepee. He looked in. In the middle of the tepee, lying on the charred embers of a fire, lay a ragged blanket—and in the blanket was wrapped the body of a little Indian child. Kazan could see the tiny moccasined feet. But so long had death been there that he could scarcely smell the presence of it. He drew back, and saw Gray Wolf cautiously nosing about a long and peculiarly shaped hummock in the snow. She had traveled about it three times, but never approaching nearer than a man could have reached with a rifle barrel. At the end of her third circle she sat down on her haunches, and Kazan went close to the hummock and sniffed. Under that bulge in the snow, as well as in the tepee, there was death. They slunk away, their ears flattened and their tails drooping until they trailed the snow, and did not stop until they reached their swamp home. Even there Gray Wolf still sniffed the horror of the plague, and her muscles twitched and shivered as she lay close at Kazan's side.

That night the big white moon had around its edge a crimson rim. It meant cold—intense cold. Always the plague came in the days of greatest cold—the lower the temperature the more terrible its havoc. It grew steadily colder that night, and the increased chill penetrated to the heart of the windfall, and drew Kazan and Gray Wolf closer together. With dawn, which came at about eight o'clock, Kazan and his blind mate sallied forth into the day. It was fifty degrees below zero. About them the trees cracked with reports like pistol-shots. In the thickest spruce the partridges were humped into round balls of feathers. The snow-shoe rabbits had burrowed deep under the snow or to the heart of the heaviest windfalls. Kazan and Gray Wolf found few fresh trails, and after an hour of fruitless hunting they returned to their lair. Kazan, dog-like, had buried the half of a rabbit two or three days before, and they dug this out of the snow and ate the frozen flesh.

All that day it grew colder—steadily colder. The night that followed was cloudless, with a white moon and brilliant stars. The temperature had fallen another ten degrees, and nothing was moving. Traps were never sprung on such nights, for even the furred things—the mink, and the ermine, and the lynx—lay snug in the holes and the nests they had found for themselves. An increasing hunger was not strong enough to drive Kazan and Gray Wolf from their windfall. The next day there was no break in the terrible cold, and toward noon Kazan set out on a hunt for meat, leaving Gray Wolf in the windfall. Being three-quarters dog, food was more necessary to Kazan than to his mate. Nature has fitted the wolf-breed for famine, and in ordinary temperature Gray Wolf could have lived for a fortnight without food. At sixty degrees below zero she could exist a week, perhaps ten days. Only thirty hours had passed since they had devoured the last of the frozen rabbit, and she was quite satisfied to remain in their snug retreat.

But Kazan was hungry. He began to hunt in the face of the wind, traveling toward the burned plain. He nosed about every windfall that he came to, and investigated the thickets. A thin shot-like snow had fallen, and in this—from the windfall to the burn—he found but a single trail, and that was the trail of an ermine. Under a windfall he caught the warm scent of a rabbit, but the rabbit was as safe from him there as were the partridges in the trees, and after an hour of futile digging and gnawing he gave up his effort to reach it. For three hours he had hunted when he returned to Gray Wolf. He was exhausted. While Gray Wolf, with the instinct of the wild, had saved her own strength and energy, Kazan had been burning up his reserve forces, and was hungrier than ever.

The moon rose clear and brilliant in the sky again that night, and Kazan set out once more on the hunt. He urged Gray Wolf to accompany him, whining for her outside the windfall—returning for her twice—but Gray Wolf laid her ears aslant and refused to move. The temperature had now fallen to sixty-five or seventy degrees below zero, and with it there came from the north an increasing wind, making the night one in which human life could not have existed for an hour. By midnight Kazan was back under the windfall. The wind grew stronger. It began to wail in mournful dirges over the swamp, and then it burst in fierce shrieking volleys, with intervals of quiet between. These were the first warnings from the great barrens that lay between the last lines of timber and the Arctic. With morning the storm burst in all its fury from out of the north, and Gray Wolf and Kazan lay close together and shivered as they listened to the roar of it over the windfall. Once Kazan thrust his head and shoulders out from the shelter of the fallen trees, but the storm drove him back. Everything that possessed life had sought shelter, according to its way and instinct. The furred creatures like the mink and the ermine were safest, for during the warmer hunting days they were of the kind that cached meat. The wolves and the foxes had sought out the windfalls, and the rocks. Winged things, with the exception of the owls, who were a tenth part body and nine-tenths feathers, burrowed under snow-drifts or found shelter in thick spruce. To the hoofed and horned animals the storm meant greatest havoc. The deer, the caribou and the moose could not crawl under windfalls or creep between rocks. The best they could do was to lie down in the lee of a drift, and allow themselves to be covered deep with the protecting snow. Even then they could not keep their shelter long, for they had to *eat*. For eighteen hours out of the twenty-four the moose had to feed to keep himself alive during the winter. His big stomach demanded quantity, and it took him most of his time to nibble from the tops of bushes the two or three bushels he needed a day. The caribou required almost as much—the deer least of the three.

And the storm kept up that day, and the next, and still a third—three days and three nights—and the third day and night there came with it a stinging, shot-like snow that fell two feet deep on the level, and in drifts of eight and ten. It was the "heavy snow" of the Indians—the snow that lay like lead on the earth, and under which partridges and rabbits were smothered in thousands.

On the fourth day after the beginning of the storm Kazan and Gray Wolf issued forth from the windfall. There was no longer a wind—no more falling snow. The whole world lay under a blanket of unbroken white, and it was intensely cold.

The plague had worked its havoc with men. Now had come the days of famine and death for the wild things.

<h1 style="text-align:center">Chapter XIII</h1>
<h2 style="text-align:center">The Trail Of Hunger</h2>

Kazan and Gray Wolf had been a hundred and forty hours without food. To Gray Wolf this meant acute discomfort, a growing weakness. To Kazan it was starvation. Six days and six nights of fasting had drawn in their ribs and put deep hollows in front of their hindquarters. Kazan's eyes were red, and they narrowed to slits as he looked forth into the day. Gray Wolf followed him this time when he went out on the hard snow. Eagerly and hopefully they began the hunt in the bitter cold. They swung around the edge of the windfall, where there had always been rabbits. There were no tracks now, and no scent. They continued in a horseshoe circle through the swamp, and the only scent they caught was that of a snow-owl perched up in a spruce. They came to the burn and turned back, hunting the opposite side of the swamp. On this side there was a ridge. They climbed the ridge, and from the cap of it looked out over a world that was barren of life. Ceaselessly Gray Wolf sniffed the air, but she gave no signal to Kazan. On the top of the ridge Kazan stood panting. His endurance was gone. On their return through the swamp he stumbled over an obstacle which he tried to clear with a jump. Hungrier and weaker, they returned to the windfall. The night that followed was clear, and brilliant with stars. They hunted the swamp again. Nothing was moving—save one other creature, and that was a fox. Instinct told them that it was futile to follow him.

It was then that the old thought of the cabin returned to Kazan. Two things the cabin had always meant to him—warmth and food. And far beyond the ridge was the cabin, where he and Gray Wolf had howled at the scent of death. He did not think of man—or of that mystery which he had howled at. He thought only of the cabin, and the cabin had always meant food. He set off in a straight line for the ridge, and Gray Wolf followed. They crossed the ridge and the burn beyond, and entered the edge of a second swamp. Kazan was hunting listlessly now. His head hung low. His bushy tail dragged in the snow. He was intent on the cabin—only the cabin. It was his last hope. But Gray Wolf was still alert, taking in the wind, and lifting her head whenever Kazan stopped to snuffle his chilled nose in the snow. At last it came—the scent! Kazan had moved on, but he stopped when he found that Gray Wolf was not following. All the strength that was in his starved body revealed itself in a sudden rigid tenseness as he looked at his mate. Her forefeet were planted firmly to the east; her slim gray head was reaching out for the scent; her body trembled.

Then—suddenly—they heard a sound, and with a whining cry Kazan set out in its direction, with Gray Wolf at his flank. The scent grew stronger and stronger in Gray Wolf's nostrils, and soon it came to Kazan. It was not the scent of a rabbit or a partridge. It was big game. They approached cautiously, keeping full in the wind. The swamp grew thicker, the spruce more dense, and now—from a hundred yards ahead of them—there came a crashing of locked and battling horns. Ten seconds more they climbed over a snowdrift, and Kazan stopped and dropped flat on his belly. Gray Wolf crouched close at his side, her blind eyes turned to what she could smell but could not see.

Fifty yards from them a number of moose had gathered for shelter in the thick spruce. They had eaten clear a space an acre in extent. The trees were cropped bare as high as they could reach, and the snow was beaten hard under their feet. There were six animals in the acre, two of them bulls—and these bulls were fighting, while three cows and a yearling were huddled in a group watching the mighty duel. Just before the storm a young bull, sleek, three-quarters grown, and with the small compact antlers of a four-year-old, had led the three cows and the yearling to this sheltered spot among the spruce. Until last night he had been master of the herd. During the night the older bull had invaded his dominion. The invader was four times as old as the young bull. He was half again as heavy. His huge palmate horns, knotted and irregular—but massive—spoke of age. A warrior of a hundred fights, he had not hesitated to give battle in his effort to rob the younger bull of his home and family. Three times they had fought since dawn, and the hard-trodden snow was red with blood. The smell of it came to Kazan's and Gray Wolf's nostrils. Kazan sniffed hungrily. Queer sounds rolled up and down in Gray Wolf's throat, and she licked her jaws.

For a moment the two fighters drew a few yards apart, and stood with lowered heads. The old bull had not yet won victory. The younger bull represented youth and endurance; in the older bull those things were pitted against craft, greater weight, maturer strength—and a head and horns that were like a battering ram. But in that great hulk of the older bull there was one other thing—age. His huge sides were panting. His nostrils were as wide as bells. Then, as if some invisible spirit of the arena had given the signal, the animals came together again. The crash of their horns could have been heard half a mile away, and under twelve hundred pounds of flesh and bone the younger bull went plunging back upon his haunches. Then was when youth displayed itself. In an instant he was up, and locking horns with his adversary. Twenty times he had done this, and each attack had seemed filled with increasing strength. And now, as if realizing that the last moments of the last fight had come, he twisted the old bull's neck and fought as he had never fought before. Kazan and Gray Wolf both heard the sharp crack that followed—as if a dry stick had been stepped upon and broken. It was February, and the hoofed animals were already beginning to shed their horns—especially the older bulls, whose palmate growths drop first. This fact gave victory to the younger bull in the blood-stained arena a few yards from Gray Wolf and Kazan. From its socket in the old bull's skull one of his huge antlers broke with that sharp snapping sound, and in another moment four inches of stiletto-like horn buried itself back of his foreleg. In an instant all hope and courage left him, and he swung backward yard by yard, with the younger bull prodding his neck and shoulders until blood dripped from him in little streams. At the edge of the clearing he flung himself free and crashed off into the forest.

The younger bull did not pursue. He tossed his head, and stood for a few moments with heaving sides and dilated nostrils, facing in the direction his vanquished foe had taken. Then he turned, and trotted back to the still motionless cows and yearling.

Kazan and Gray Wolf were quivering. Gray Wolf slunk back from the edge of the clearing, and Kazan followed. No longer were they interested in the cows and the young bull. From that clearing they had seen meat driven forth—meat that was beaten in fight, and bleeding. Every instinct of the wild pack returned to Gray Wolf now—and in Kazan the mad desire to taste the blood he smelled. Swiftly they turned toward the blood-stained trail of the old bull, and when they came to it they found it spattered red. Kazan's jaws dripped as the hot scent drove the blood like veins of fire through his weakened body. His eyes were reddened by starvation, and in them there was a light now that they had never known even in the days of the wolf-pack.

He set off swiftly, almost forgetful of Gray Wolf. But his mate no longer required his flank for guidance. With her nose close to the trail she ran—ran as she had run in the long and thrilling hunts before blindness came. Half a mile from the spruce thicket they came upon the old bull. He had sought shelter behind a clump of balsam, and he stood over a growing pool of blood in the snow. He was still breathing hard. His massive head, grotesque now with its one antler, was drooping. Flecks of blood dropped from his distended nostrils. Even then, with the old bull weakened by starvation, exhaustion and loss of blood, a wolf-pack would have hung back before attacking. Where they would have hesitated, Kazan leaped in with a snarling cry. For an instant his fangs sunk into the thick hide of the bull's throat. Then he was flung back—twenty feet. Hunger gnawing at his vitals robbed him of all caution, and he sprang to the attack again—full at the bull's front—while Gray Wolf crept up unseen behind, seeking in her blindness the vulnerable part which nature had not taught Kazan to find.

This time Kazan was caught fairly on the broad palmate leaf of the bull's antler, and he was flung back again, half stunned. In that same moment Gray Wolf's long white teeth cut like knives through one of the bull's rope-like hamstrings. For thirty seconds she kept the hold, while the bull plunged wildly in his efforts to trample her underfoot. Kazan was quick to learn, still quicker to be guided by Gray Wolf, and he leaped in again, snapping for a hold on the bulging cord just above the knee. He missed, and as he lunged forward on his shoulders Gray Wolf was flung off. But she had accomplished her purpose. Beaten in open battle with one of his kind, and now attacked by a still deadlier foe, the old bull began to retreat. As he went, one hip sank under him at every step. The tendon of his left leg was bitten half through.

Without being able to see, Gray Wolf seemed to realize what had happened. Again she was the pack-wolf—with all the old wolf strategy. Twice flung back by the old bull's horn, Kazan knew better than to attack openly again. Gray Wolf trotted after the bull, but he remained behind for a moment to lick up hungrily mouthfuls of the blood-soaked snow. Then he followed, and ran close against Gray Wolf's side, fifty yards behind the bull. There was more blood in the trail now—a thin red ribbon of it. Fifteen minutes later the bull stopped again, and faced about, his great head lowered. His eyes were red. There was a droop to his neck and shoulders that spoke no longer of the unconquerable fighting spirit that had been a part of him for nearly a score of years. No longer was he lord of the wilderness about him; no longer was there defiance in the poise of his splendid head, or the flash of eager fire in his bloodshot eyes. His breath came with a gasping sound that was growing more and more distinct. A hunter would have known what it meant. The stiletto-point of the younger bull's antler had gone home, and the old bull's lungs were failing him. More than once Gray Wolf had heard that sound in the early days of her hunting with the pack, and she understood. Slowly she began to circle about the wounded monarch at a distance of about twenty yards. Kazan kept at her side.

Once—twice—twenty times they made that slow circle, and with each turn they made the old bull turned, and his breath grew heavier and his head drooped lower. Noon came, and was followed by the more intense cold of the last half of the day. Twenty circles became a hundred—two hundred—and more. Under Gray Wolf's and Kazan's feet the snow grew hard in the path they made. Under the old bull's widespread hoofs the snow was no longer white— but red. A thousand times before this unseen tragedy of the wilderness had been enacted. It was an epoch of that life where life itself means the survival of the fittest, where to live means to kill, and to die means to perpetuate life. At last, in that steady and deadly circling of Gray Wolf and Kazan, there came a time when the old bull did not turn—then a second, a third and a fourth time, and Gray Wolf seemed to know. With Kazan she drew back from the hard-beaten trail, and they flattened themselves on their bellies under a dwarf spruce—and waited. For many minutes the bull stood motionless, his hamstrung quarter sinking lower and lower. And then with a deep blood-choked gasp he sank down.

For a long time Kazan and Gray Wolf did not move, and when at last they returned to the beaten trail the bull's heavy head was resting on the snow. Again they began to circle, and now the circle narrowed foot by foot, until only ten yards—then nine—then eight—separated them from their prey. The bull attempted to rise, and failed. Gray Wolf heard the effort. She heard him sink back and suddenly she leaped in swiftly and silently from behind. Her sharp fangs buried themselves in the bull's nostrils, and with the first instinct of the husky, Kazan sprang for a throat hold. This time he was not flung off. It was Gray Wolf's terrible hold that gave him time to tear through the half-inch hide, and to bury his teeth deeper and deeper, until at last they reached the jugular. A gush of warm blood spurted into his face. But he did not let go. Just as he had held to the jugular of his first buck on that moonlight night a long time ago, so he held to the old bull now. It was Gray Wolf who unclamped his jaws. She drew back, sniffing the air, listening. Then, slowly, she raised her head, and through the frozen and starving wilderness there went her wailing triumphant cry—the call to meat.

For them the days of famine had passed.

Chapter XIV
The Right Of Fang

After the fight Kazan lay down exhausted in the blood-stained snow, while faithful Gray Wolf, still filled with the endurance of her wild wolf breed, tore fiercely at the thick skin on the bull's neck to lay open the red flesh. When she had done this she did not eat, but ran to Kazan's side and whined softly as she muzzled him with her nose. After that they feasted, crouching side by side at the bull's neck and tearing at the warm sweet flesh.

The last pale light of the northern day was fading swiftly into night when they drew back, gorged until there were no longer hollows in their sides. The faint wind died away. The clouds that had hung in the sky during the day drifted eastward, and the moon shone brilliant and clear. For an hour the night continued to grow lighter. To the brilliance of the moon and the stars there was added now the pale fires of the aurora borealis, shivering and flashing over the Pole.

Its hissing crackling monotone, like the creaking of steel sledge-runners on frost-filled snow, came faintly to the ears of Kazan and Gray Wolf.

As yet they had not gone a hundred yards from the dead bull, and at the first sound of that strange mystery in the northern skies they stopped and listened to it, alert and suspicious. Then they laid their ears aslant and trotted slowly back to the meat they had killed. Instinct told them that it was theirs only by right of fang. They had fought to kill it. And it was in the law of the wild that they would have to fight to keep it. In good hunting days they would have gone on and wandered under the moon and the stars. But long days and nights of starvation had taught them something different now.

On that clear and stormless night following the days of plague and famine, a hundred thousand hungry creatures came out from their retreats to hunt for food. For eighteen hundred miles east and west and a thousand miles north and south, slim gaunt-bellied creatures hunted under the moon and the stars. Something told Kazan and Gray Wolf that this hunt was on, and never for an instant did they cease their vigilance. At last they lay down at the edge of the spruce thicket, and waited. Gray Wolf muzzled Kazan gently with her blind face. The uneasy whine in her throat was a warning to him. Then she sniffed the air, and listened—sniffed and listened.

Suddenly every muscle in their bodies grew rigid. Something living had passed near them, something that they could not see or hear, and scarcely scent. It came again, as mysterious as a shadow, and then out of the air there floated down as silently as a huge snowflake a great white owl. Kazan saw the hungry winged creature settle on the bull's shoulder. Like a flash he was out from his cover, Gray Wolf a yard behind him. With an angry snarl he lunged at the white robber, and his jaws snapped on empty air. His leap carried him clean over the bull. He turned, but the owl was gone.

Nearly all of his old strength had returned to him now. He trotted about the bull, the hair along his spine bristling like a brush, his eyes wide and menacing. He snarled at the still air. His jaws clicked, and he sat back on his haunches and faced the blood-stained trail that the moose had left before he died. Again that instinct as infallible as reason told him that danger would come from there.

Like a red ribbon the trail ran back through the wilderness. The little swift-moving ermine were everywhere this night, looking like white rats as they dodged about in the moonlight. They were first to find the trail, and with all the ferocity of their blood-eating nature followed it with quick exciting leaps. A fox caught the scent of it a quarter of a mile to windward, and came nearer. From out of a deep windfall a beady-eyed, thin-bellied fisher-cat came forth, and stopped with his feet in the crimson ribbon.

It was the fisher-cat that brought Kazan out; from under his cover of spruce again. In the moonlight there was a sharp quick fight, a snarling and scratching, a cat-like yowl of pain, and the fisher forgot his hunger in flight. Kazan returned to Gray Wolf with a lacerated and bleeding nose. Gray Wolf licked it sympathetically, while Kazan stood rigid and listening.

The fox swung swiftly away with the wind, warned by the sounds of conflict. He was not a fighter, but a murderer who killed from behind, and a little later he leaped upon an owl and tore it into bits for the half-pound of flesh within the mass of feathers.

But nothing could drive back those little white outlaws of the wilderness—the ermine. They would have stolen between the feet of man to get at the warm flesh and blood of the freshly killed bull. Kazan hunted them savagely. They were too quick for him, more like elusive flashes in the moonlight than things of life. They burrowed under the old bull's body and fed while he raved and filled his mouth with snow. Gray Wolf sat placidly on her haunches. The little ermine did not trouble her, and after a time Kazan realized this, and flung himself down beside her, panting and exhausted.

For a long time after that the night was almost unbroken by sound. Once in the far distance there came the cry of a wolf, and now and then, to punctuate the deathly silence, the snow owl hooted in blood-curdling protest from his home in the spruce-tops. The moon was straight above the old bull when Gray Wolf scented the first real danger. Instantly she gave the warning to Kazan and faced the bloody trail, her lithe body quivering, her fangs gleaming in the starlight, a snarling whine in her throat. Only in the face of their deadliest enemy, the lynx—the terrible fighter who had blinded her long ago in that battle on the Sun Rock!—did she give such warning as this to Kazan. He sprang ahead of her, ready for battle even before he caught the scent of the gray beautiful creature of death stealing over the trail.

Then came the interruption. From a mile away there burst forth a single fierce long-drawn howl.

After all, that was the cry of the true master of the wilderness—the wolf. It was the cry of hunger. It was the cry that sent men's blood running more swiftly through their veins, that brought the moose and the deer to their feet shivering in every limb—the cry that wailed like a note of death through swamp and forest and over the snow-smothered ridges until its faintest echoes reached for miles into the starlit night.

There was silence, and in that awesome stillness Kazan and Gray Wolf stood shoulder to shoulder facing the cry, and in response to that cry there worked within them a strange and mystic change, for what they had heard was not a warning or a menace but the call of Brotherhood. Away off there—beyond the lynx and the fox and the fisher-cat, were the creatures of their kind, the wild-wolf pack, to which the right to all flesh and blood was common—in which existed that savage socialism of the wilderness, the Brotherhood of the Wolf. And Gray Wolf, setting back on her haunches, sent forth the response to that cry—a wailing triumphant note that told her hungry brethren there was feasting at the end of the trail.

And the lynx, between those two cries, sneaked off into the wide and moonlit spaces of the forest.

Chapter XV
A Fight Under The Stars

On their haunches Kazan and Gray Wolf waited. Five minutes passed, ten—fifteen—and Gray Wolf became uneasy. No response had followed her call. Again she howled, with Kazan quivering and listening beside her, and again there followed that dead stillness of the night. This was not the way of the pack. She knew that it had not gone beyond the reach of her voice and its silence puzzled her. And then in a flash it came to them both that the pack, or the single wolf whose cry they had heard, was very near them. The scent was warm. A few moments later Kazan saw a moving object in the moonlight. It was followed by another, and still another, until there were five slouching in a half-circle about them, seventy yards away. Then they laid themselves flat in the snow and were motionless.

A snarl turned Kazan's eyes to Gray Wolf. His blind mate had drawn back. Her white fangs gleamed menacingly in the starlight. Her ears were flat. Kazan was puzzled. Why was she signaling danger to him when it was the wolf, and not the lynx, out there in the snow? And why did the wolves not come in and feast? Slowly he moved toward them, and Gray Wolf called to him with her whine. He paid no attention to her, but went on, stepping lightly, his head high in the air, his spine bristling.

In the scent of the strangers, Kazan was catching something now that was strangely familiar. It drew him toward them more swiftly and when at last he stopped twenty yards from where the little group lay flattened in the snow, his thick brush waved slightly. One of the animals sprang up and approached. The others followed and in another moment Kazan was in the midst of them, smelling and smelled, and wagging his tail. They were dogs, and not wolves.

In some lonely cabin in the wilderness their master had died, and they had taken to the forests. They still bore signs of the sledge-traces. About their necks were moose-hide collars. The hair was worn short at their flanks, and one still dragged after him three feet of corded babiche trace. Their eyes gleamed red and hungry in the glow of the moon and the stars. They were thin, and gaunt and starved, and Kazan suddenly turned and trotted ahead of them to the side of the dead bull. Then he fell back and sat proudly on his haunches beside Gray Wolf, listening to the snapping of jaws and the rending of flesh as the starved pack feasted.

Gray Wolf slunk closer to Kazan. She muzzled his neck and Kazan gave her a swift dog-like caress of his tongue, assuring her that all was well. She flattened herself in the snow when the dogs had finished and came up in their dog way to sniff at her, and make closer acquaintance with Kazan. Kazan towered over her, guarding her. One huge red-eyed dog who still dragged the bit of babiche trace muzzled Gray Wolf's soft neck for a fraction of a second too long, and Kazan uttered a savage snarl of warning. The dog drew back, and for a moment their fangs gleamed over Gray Wolf's blind face. It was the Challenge of the Breed.

The big husky was the leader of the pack, and if one of the other dogs had snarled at him, as Kazan snarled he would have leaped at his throat. But in Kazan, standing fierce and half wild over Gray Wolf, he recognized none of the serfdom of the sledge-dogs. It was master facing master; in Kazan it was more than that for he was Gray Wolf's mate. In an instant more he would have leaped over her body to have fought for her, more than for the right of leadership. But the big husky turned away sullenly, growling, still snarling, and vented his rage by nipping fiercely at the flank of one of his sledge-mates.

Gray Wolf understood what had happened, though she could not see. She shrank closer to Kazan. She knew that the moon and the stars had looked down on that thing that always meant death—the challenge to the right of mate. With her luring coyness, whining and softly muzzling his shoulder and neck, she tried to draw Kazan away from the pad-beaten circle in which the bull lay. Kazan's answer was an ominous rolling of smothered thunder deep down in his throat. He lay down beside her, licked her blind face swiftly, and faced the stranger dogs.

The moon sank lower and lower and at last dropped behind the western forests. The stars grew paler. One by one they faded from the sky and after a time there followed the cold gray dawn of the North. In that dawn the big husky leader rose from the hole he had made in the snow and returned to the bull. Kazan, alert, was on his feet in an instant and stood also close to the bull. The two circled ominously, their heads lowered, their crests bristling. The husky drew away, and Kazan crouched at the bull's neck and began tearing at the frozen flesh. He was not hungry. But in this way he showed his right to the flesh, his defiance of the right of the big husky.

For a few seconds he forgot Gray Wolf. The husky had slipped back like a shadow and now he stood again over Gray Wolf, sniffing her neck and body. Then he whined. In that whine were the passion, the invitation, the demand of the Wild. So quickly that the eye could scarcely follow her movement faithful Gray Wolf sank her gleaming fangs in the husky's shoulder.

A gray streak—nothing more tangible than a streak of gray, silent and terrible, shot through the dawn-gloom. It was Kazan. He came without a snarl, without a cry, and in a moment he and the husky were in the throes of terrific battle.

The four other huskies ran in quickly and stood waiting a dozen paces from the combatants. Gray Wolf lay crouched on her belly. The giant husky and the quarter-strain wolf-dog were not fighting like sledge-dog or wolf. For a few moments rage and hatred made them fight like mongrels. Both had holds. Now one was down, and now the other, and so swiftly did they change their positions that the four waiting sledge-dogs were puzzled and stood motionless. Under other conditions they would have leaped upon the first of the fighters to be thrown upon his back and torn him to pieces. That was the way of the wolf and the wolf-dog. But now they stood back, hesitating and fearful.

The big husky had never been beaten in battle. Great Dane ancestors had given him a huge bulk and a jaw that could crush an ordinary dog's head. But in Kazan he was meeting not only the dog and the wolf, but all that was best in the two. And Kazan had the advantage of a few hours of rest and a full stomach. More than that, he was fighting for Gray Wolf. His fangs had sunk deep in the husky's shoulder, and the husky's long teeth met through the hide and flesh of his neck. An inch deeper, and they would have pierced his jugular. Kazan knew this, as he crunched his enemy's shoulder-bone, and every instant—even in their fiercest struggling—he was guarding against a second and more successful lunge of those powerful jaws.

At last the lunge came, and quicker than the wolf itself Kazan freed himself and leaped back. His chest dripped blood, but he did not feel the hurt. They began slowly to circle, and now the watching sledge-dogs drew a step or two nearer, and their jaws drooled nervously and their red eyes glared as they waited for the fatal moment. Their eyes were on the big husky. He became the pivot of Kazan's wider circle now, and he limped as he turned. His shoulder was broken. His ears were flattened as he watched Kazan.

Kazan's ears were erect, and his feet touched the snow lightly. All his fighting cleverness and all his caution had returned to him. The blind rage of a few moments was gone and he fought now as he had fought his deadliest enemy, the long-clawed lynx. Five times he circled around the husky, and then like a shot he was in, sending his whole weight against the husky's shoulder, with the momentum of a ten-foot leap behind it. This time he did not try for a hold, but slashed at the husky's jaws. It was the deadliest of all attacks when that merciless tribunal of death stood waiting for the first fall of the vanquished. The huge dog was thrown from his feet. For a fatal moment he rolled upon his side and in the moment his four sledge-mates were upon him. All of their hatred of the weeks and months in which the long-fanged leader had bullied them in the traces was concentrated upon him now and he was literally torn into pieces.

Kazan pranced to Gray Wolf's side and with a joyful whine she laid her head over his neck. Twice he had fought the Fight of Death for her. Twice he had won. And in her blindness Gray Wolf's soul—if soul she had—rose in exultation to the cold gray sky, and her breast panted against Kazan's shoulder as she listened to the crunching of fangs in the flesh and bone of the foe her lord and master had overthrown.

Chapter XVI
The Call

Followed days of feasting on the frozen flesh of the old bull. In vain Gray Wolf tried to lure Kazan off into the forests and the swamps. Day by day the temperature rose. There was hunting now. And Gray Wolf wanted to be alone—with Kazan. But with Kazan, as with most men, leadership and power roused new sensations. And he was the leader of the dog-pack, as he had once been a leader among the wolves. Not only Gray Wolf followed at his flank now, but the four huskies trailed behind him. Once more he was experiencing that triumph and strange thrill that he had almost forgotten and only Gray Wolf, in that eternal night of her blindness, felt with dread foreboding the danger into which his newly achieved czarship might lead him.

For three days and three nights they remained in the neighborhood of the dead moose, ready to defend it against others, and yet each day and each night growing less vigilant in their guard. Then came the fourth night, on which they killed a young doe. Kazan led in that chase and for the first time, in the excitement of having the pack at his back, he left his blind mate behind. When they came to the kill he was the first to leap at its soft throat. And not until he had begun to tear at the doe's flesh did the others dare to eat. He was master. He could send them back with a snarl. At the gleam of his fangs they crouched quivering on their bellies in the snow.

Kazan's blood was fomented with brute exultation, and the excitement and fascination that came in the possession of new power took the place of Gray Wolf each day a little more. She came in half an hour after the kill, and there was no longer the lithesome alertness to her slender legs, or gladness in the tilt of her ears or the poise of her head. She did not eat much of the doe. Her blind face was turned always in Kazan's direction. Wherever he moved she followed with her unseeing eyes, as if expecting each moment his old signal to her—that low throat-note that had called to her so often when they were alone in the wilderness.

In Kazan, as leader of the pack, there was working a curious change. If his mates had been wolves it would not have been difficult for Gray Wolf to have lured him away. But Kazan was among his own kind. He was a dog. And they were dogs. Fires that had burned down and ceased to warm him flamed up in him anew. In his life with Gray Wolf one thing had oppressed him as it could not oppress her, and that thing was loneliness. Nature had created him of that kind which requires companionship—not of one but of many. It had given him birth that he might listen to and obey the commands of the voice of man. He had grown to hate men, but of the dogs—his kind—he was a part. He had been happy with Gray Wolf, happier than he had ever been in the companionship of men and his blood-brothers. But he had been a long time separated from the life that had once been his and the call of blood made him for a time forget. And only Gray Wolf, with that wonderful super-instinct which nature was giving her in place of her lost sight, foresaw the end to which it was leading him.

Each day the temperature continued to rise until when the sun was warmest the snow began to thaw a little. This was two weeks after the fight near the bull. Gradually the pack had swung eastward, until it was now fifty miles east and twenty miles south of the old home under the windfall. More than ever Gray Wolf began to long for their old nest under the fallen trees. Again with those first promises of spring in sunshine and air, there was coming also for the second time in her life the promise of approaching motherhood.

But her efforts to draw Kazan back were unavailing, and in spite of her protest he wandered each day a little farther east and south at the head of his pack.

Instinct impelled the four huskies to move in that direction. They had not yet been long enough a part of the wild to forget the necessity of man and in that direction there was man. In that direction, and not far from them now, was the Hudson Bay Company's post to which they and their dead master owed their allegiance. Kazan did not know this, but one day something happened to bring back visions and desires that widened still more the gulf between him and Gray Wolf.

They had come to the cap of a ridge when something stopped them. It was a man's voice crying shrilly that word of long ago that had so often stirred the blood in Kazan's own veins—"*m'hoosh! m'hoosh! m'hoosh!*"—and from the ridge they looked down upon the open space of the plain, where a team of six dogs was trotting ahead of a sledge, with a man running behind them, urging them on at every other step with that cry of "*m'hoosh! m'hoosh! m'hoosh!*"

Trembling and undecided, the four huskies and the wolf-dog stood on the ridge with Gray Wolf cringing behind them. Not until man and dogs and sledge had disappeared did they move, and then they trotted down to the trail and sniffed at it whiningly and excitedly. For a mile or two they followed it, Kazan and his mates going fearlessly in the trail. Gray Wolf hung back, traveling twenty yards to the right of them, with the hot man-scent driving the blood feverishly through her brain. Only her love for Kazan—and the faith she still had in him—kept her that near.

At the edge of a swamp Kazan halted and turned away from the trail. With the desire that was growing in him there was still that old suspicion which nothing could quite wipe out—the suspicion that was an inheritance of his quarter-strain of wolf. Gray Wolf whined joyfully when he turned into the forest, and drew so close to him that her shoulder rubbed against Kazan's as they traveled side by side.

The "slush" snows followed fast after this. And the "slush" snows meant spring—and the emptying of the wilderness of human life. Kazan and his mates soon began to scent the presence and the movement of this life. They were now within thirty miles of the post. For a hundred miles on all sides of them the trappers were moving in with their late winter's catch of furs. From east and west, south and north, all trails led to the post. The pack was caught in the mesh of them. For a week not a day passed that they did not cross a fresh trail, and sometimes two or three.

Gray Wolf was haunted by constant fear. In her blindness she knew that they were surrounded by the menace of men. To Kazan what was coming to pass had more and more ceased to fill him with fear and caution. Three times that week he heard the shouts of men— and once he heard a white man's laughter and the barking of dogs as their master tossed them their daily feed of fish. In the air he caught the pungent scent of camp-fires and one night, in the far distance, he heard a wild snatch of song, followed by the yelping and barking of a dog-pack.

Slowly and surely the lure of man drew him nearer to the post—a mile to-night, two miles to-morrow, but always nearer. And Gray Wolf, fighting her losing fight to the end, sensed in the danger-filled air the nearness of that hour when he would respond to the final call and she would be left alone.

These were days of activity and excitement at the fur company's post, the days of accounting, of profit and of pleasure;—the days when the wilderness poured in its treasure of fur, to be sent a little later to London and Paris and the capitals of Europe. And this year there was more than the usual interest in the foregathering of the forest people. The plague had wrought its terrible havoc, and not until the fur-hunters had come to answer to the spring roll-call would it be known accurately who had lived and who had died.

The Chippewans and half-breeds from the south began to arrive first, with their teams of mongrel curs, picked up along the borders of civilization. Close after them came the hunters from the western barren lands, bringing with them loads of white fox and caribou skins, and an army of big-footed, long-legged Mackenzie hounds that pulled like horses and wailed like whipped puppies when the huskies and Eskimo dogs set upon them. Packs of fierce Labrador dogs, never vanquished except by death, came from close to Hudson's Bay. Team after team of little yellow and gray Eskimo dogs, as quick with their fangs as were their black and swift-running masters with their hands and feet, met the much larger and dark-colored Malemutes from the Athabasca. Enemies of all these packs of fierce huskies trailed in from all sides, fighting, snapping and snarling, with the lust of killing deep born in them from their wolf progenitors.

There was no cessation in the battle of the fangs. It began with the first brute arrivals. It continued from dawn through the day and around the camp-fires at night. There was never an end to the strife between the dogs, and between the men and the dogs. The snow was trailed and stained with blood and the scent of it added greater fierceness to the wolf-breeds.

Half a dozen battles were fought to the death each day and night. Those that died were chiefly the south-bred curs—mixtures of mastiff, Great Dane, and sheep-dog—and the fatally slow Mackenzie hounds. About the post rose the smoke of a hundred camp-fires, and about these fires gathered the women and the children of the hunters. When the snow was no longer fit for sledging, Williams, the factor, noted that there were many who had not come, and the accounts of these he later scratched out of his ledgers knowing that they were victims of the plague.

At last came the night of the Big Carnival, For weeks and months women and children and men had been looking forward to this. In scores of forest cabins, in smoke-blackened tepees, and even in the frozen homes of the little Eskimos, anticipation of this wild night of pleasure had given an added zest to life. It was the Big Circus—the good time given twice each year by the company to its people.

This year, to offset the memory of plague and death, the factor had put forth unusual exertions. His hunters had killed four fat caribou. In the clearing there were great piles of dry logs, and in the center of all there rose eight ten-foot tree-butts crotched at the top; and from crotch to crotch there rested a stout sapling stripped of bark, and on each sapling was spitted the carcass of a caribou, to be roasted whole by the heat of the fire beneath. The fires were lighted at dusk, and Williams himself started the first of those wild songs of the Northland— the song of the caribou, as the flames leaped up into the dark night.

"Oh, ze cariboo-oo-oo, ze cariboo-oo-oo,
He roas' on high,
Jes' under ze sky.
air-holes beeg white cariboo-oo-oo!"

"Now!" he yelled. "Now—all together!" And carried away by his enthusiasm, the forest people awakened from their silence of months, and the song burst forth in a savage frenzy that reached to the skies.

Two miles to the south and west that first thunder of human voice reached the ears of Kazan and Gray Wolf and the masterless huskies. And with the voices of men they heard now the excited howlings of dogs. The huskies faced the direction of the sounds, moving restlessly and whining. For a few moments Kazan stood as though carven of rock. Then he turned his head, and his first look was to Gray Wolf. She had slunk back a dozen feet and lay crouched under the thick cover of a balsam shrub. Her body, legs and neck were flattened in the snow. She made no sound, but her lips were drawn back and her teeth shone white.

Kazan trotted back to her, sniffed at her blind face and whined. Gray Wolf still did not move. He returned to the dogs and his jaws opened and closed with a snap. Still more clearly came the wild voice of the carnival, and no longer to be held back by Kazan's leadership, the four huskies dropped their heads and slunk like shadows in its direction. Kazan hesitated, urging Gray Wolf. But not a muscle of Gray Wolf's body moved. She would have followed him in face of fire but not in face of man. Not a sound escaped her ears. She heard the quick fall of Kazan's feet as he left her. In another moment she knew that he was gone. Then—and not until then—did she lift her head, and from her soft throat there broke a whimpering cry.

It was her last call to Kazan. But stronger than that there was running through Kazan's excited blood the call of man and of dog. The huskies were far in advance of him now and for a few moments he raced madly to overtake them. Then he slowed down until he was trotting, and a hundred yards farther on he stopped. Less than a mile away he could see where the flames of the great fires were reddening the sky. He gazed back to see if Gray Wolf was following and then went on until he struck an open and hard traveled trail. It was beaten with the footprints of men and dogs, and over it two of the caribou had been dragged a day or two before.

At last he came to the thinned out strip of timber that surrounded the clearing and the flare of the flames was in his eyes. The bedlam of sound that came to him now was like fire in his brain. He heard the song and the laughter of men, the shrill cries of women and children, the barking and snarling and fighting of a hundred dogs. He wanted to rush out and join them, to become again a part of what he had once been. Yard by yard he sneaked through the thin timber until he reached the edge of the clearing. There he stood in the shadow of a spruce and looked out upon life as he had once lived it, trembling, wistful and yet hesitating in that final moment.

A hundred yards away was the savage circle of men and dogs and fire. His nostrils were filled with the rich aroma of the roasting caribou, and as he crouched down, still with that wolfish caution that Gray Wolf had taught him, men with long poles brought the huge carcasses crashing down upon the melting snow about the fires. In one great rush the horde of wild revelers crowded in with bared knives, and a snarling mass of dogs closed in behind them. In another moment he had forgotten Gray Wolf, had forgotten all that man and the wild had taught him, and like a gray streak was across the open.

The dogs were surging back when he reached them, with half a dozen of the factor's men lashing them in the faces with long caribou-gut whips. The sting of a lash fell in a fierce cut over an Eskimo dog's shoulder, and in snapping at the lash his fangs struck Kazan's rump. With lightning swiftness Kazan returned the cut, and in an instant the jaws of the dogs had met. In another instant they were down and Kazan had the Eskimo dog by the throat.

With shouts the men rushed in. Again and again their whips cut like knives through the air. Their blows fell on Kazan, who was uppermost, and as he felt the burning pain of the scourging whips there flooded through him all at once the fierce memory of the days of old— the days of the Club and the Lash. He snarled. Slowly he loosened his hold of the Eskimo dog's throat. And then, out of the mêlée of dogs and men, there sprang another man—*with a club*! It fell on Kazan's back and the force of it sent him flat into the snow. It was raised again. Behind the club there was a face—a brutal, fire-reddened face. It was such a face that had driven Kazan into the wild, and as the club fell again he evaded the full weight of its blow and his fangs gleamed like ivory knives. A third time the club was raised, and this time Kazan met it in mid-air, and his teeth ripped the length of the man's forearm.

"Good God!" shrieked the man in pain, and Kazan caught the gleam of a rifle barrel as he sped toward the forest. A shot followed. Something like a red-hot coal ran the length of Kazan's hip, and deep in the forest he stopped to lick at the burning furrow where the bullet had gone just deep enough to take the skin and hair from his flesh.

Gray Wolf was still waiting under the balsam shrub when Kazan returned to her. Joyously she sprang forth to meet him. Once more the man had sent back the old Kazan to her. He muzzled her neck and face, and stood for a few moments with his head resting across her back, listening to the distant sound.

Then, with ears laid flat, he set out straight into the north and west. And now Gray Wolf ran shoulder to shoulder with him like the Gray Wolf of the days before the dog-pack came; for that wonderful thing that lay beyond the realm of reason told her that once more she was comrade and mate, and that their trail that night was leading to their old home under the windfall.

Chapter XVII
His Son

It happened that Kazan was to remember three things above all others. He could never quite forget his old days in the traces, though they were growing more shadowy and indistinct in his memory as the summers and the winters passed. Like a dream there came to him a memory of the time he had gone down to Civilization. Like dreams were the visions that rose before him now and then of the face of the First Woman, and of the faces of masters who—to him—had lived ages ago. And never would he quite forget the Fire, and his fights with man and beast, and his long chases in the moonlight. But two things were always with him as if they had been but yesterday, rising clear and unforgetable above all others, like the two stars in the North that never lost their brilliance. One was Woman. The other was the terrible fight of that night on the top of the Sun Rock, when the lynx had blinded forever his wild mate, Gray Wolf. Certain events remain indelibly fixed in the minds of men; and so, in a not very different way, they remain in the minds of beasts. It takes neither brain nor reason to measure the depths of sorrow or of happiness. And Kazan in his unreasoning way knew that contentment and peace, a full stomach, and caresses and kind words instead of blows had come to him through Woman, and that comradeship in the wilderness—faith, loyalty and devotion—were a part of Gray Wolf. The third unforgetable thing was about to occur in the home they had found for themselves under the swamp windfall during the days of cold and famine.

They had left the swamp over a month before when it was smothered deep in snow. On the day they returned to it the sun was shining warmly in the first glorious days of spring warmth. Everywhere, big and small, there were the rushing torrents of melting snows and the crackle of crumbling ice, the dying cries of thawing rock and earth and tree, and each night for many nights past the cold pale glow of the aurora borealis had crept farther and farther toward the Pole in fading glory. So early as this the poplar buds had begun to swell and the air was filled with the sweet odor of balsam, spruce and cedar. Where there had been famine and death and stillness six weeks before, Kazan and Gray Wolf now stood at the edge of the swamp and breathed the earthy smells of spring, and listened to the sounds of life. Over their heads a pair of newly-mated moose-birds fluttered and scolded at them. A big jay sat pluming himself in the sunshine. Farther in they heard the crack of a stick broken under a heavy hoof. From the ridge behind them they caught the raw scent of a mother bear, busy pulling down the tender poplar buds for her six-weeks-old cubs, born while she was still deep in her winter sleep.

In the warmth of the sun and the sweetness of the air there breathed to Gray Wolf the mystery of matehood and of motherhood. She whined softly and rubbed her blind face against Kazan. For days, in her way, she tried to tell him. More than ever she wanted to curl herself up in that warm dry nest under the windfall. She had no desire to hunt. The crack of the dry stick under a cloven hoof and the warm scent of the she-bear and her cubs roused none of the old instincts in her. She wanted to curl herself up in the old windfall—and wait. And she tried hard to make Kazan understand her desire.

Now that the snow was gone they found that a narrow creek lay between them and the knoll on which the windfall was situated. Gray Wolf picked up her ears at the tumult of the little torrent. Since the day of the Fire, when Kazan and she had saved themselves on the sand-bar, she had ceased to have the inherent wolf horror of water. She followed fearlessly, even eagerly, behind Kazan as he sought a place where they could ford the rushing little stream. On the other side Kazan could see the big windfall. Gray Wolf could *smell* it and she whined joyously, with her blind face turned toward it. A hundred yards up the stream a big cedar had fallen over it and Kazan began to cross. For a moment Gray Wolf hesitated, and then followed. Side by side they trotted to the windfall. With their heads and shoulders in the dark opening to their nest they scented the air long and cautiously. Then they entered. Kazan heard Gray Wolf as she flung herself down on the dry floor of the snug cavern. She was panting, not from exhaustion, but because she was filled with a sensation of contentment and happiness. In the darkness Kazan's own jaws fell apart. He, too, was glad to get back to their old home. He went to Gray Wolf and, panting still harder, she licked his face. It had but one meaning. And Kazan understood.

For a moment he lay down beside her, listening, and eyeing the opening to their nest. Then he began to sniff about the log walls. He was close to the opening when a sudden fresh scent came to him, and he grew rigid, and his bristles stood up. The scent was followed by a whimpering, babyish chatter. A porcupine entered the opening and proceeded to advance in its foolish fashion, still chattering in that babyish way that has made its life inviolable at the hands of man. Kazan had heard that sound before, and like all other beasts had learned to ignore the presence of the innocuous creature that made it. But just now he did not stop to consider that what he saw was a porcupine and that at his first snarl the good-humored little creature would waddle away as fast as it could, still chattering baby talk to itself. His first reasoning was that it was a live thing invading the home to which Gray Wolf and he had just returned. A day later, or perhaps an hour later, he would have driven it back with a growl. Now he leaped upon it.

A wild chattering, intermingled with pig-like squeaks, and then a rising staccato of howls followed the attack. Gray Wolf sprang to the opening. The porcupine was rolled up in a thousand-spiked ball a dozen feet away, and she could hear Kazan tearing about in the throes of the direst agony that can befall a beast of the forests. His face and nose were a mat of quills. For a few moments he rolled and dug in the wet mold and earth, pawing madly at the things that pierced his flesh. Then he set off like all dogs will who have come into contact with the friendly porcupine, and raced again and again around the windfall, howling at every jump. Gray Wolf took the matter coolly. It is possible that at times there are moments of humor in the lives of animals. If so, she saw this one. She scented the porcupine and she knew that Kazan was full of quills. As there was nothing to do and nothing to fight she sat back on her haunches and waited, pricking up her ears every time Kazan passed her in his mad circuit around the windfall. At his fourth or fifth heat the porcupine smoothed itself down a little, and continuing the interrupted thread of its chatter waddled to a near-by poplar, climbed it and began to gnaw the tender bark from a limb.

At last Kazan halted before Gray Wolf. The first agony of a hundred little needles piercing his flesh had deadened into a steady burning pain. Gray Wolf went over to him and investigated him cautiously. With her teeth she seized the ends of two or three of the quills and pulled them out. Kazan was very much dog now. He gave a yelp, and whimpered as Gray Wolf jerked out a second bunch of quills. Then he flattened himself on his belly, stretched out his forelegs, closed his eyes, and without any other sound except an occasional yelp of pain allowed Gray Wolf to go on with the operation. Fortunately he had escaped getting any of the quills in his mouth and tongue. But his nose and jaws were soon red with blood. For an hour Gray Wolf kept faithfully at her task and by the end of that time had succeeded in pulling out most of the quills. A few still remained, too short and too deeply inbedded for her to extract with her teeth.

After this Kazan went down to the creek and buried his burning muzzle in the cold water. This gave him some relief, but only for a short time. The quills that remained worked their way deeper and deeper into his flesh, like living things. Nose and lips began to swell. Blood and saliva dripped from his mouth and his eyes grew red. Two hours after Gray Wolf had retired to her nest under the windfall a quill had completely pierced his lip and began to prick his tongue. In desperation Kazan chewed viciously upon a piece of wood. This broke and crumpled the quill, and destroyed its power to do further harm. Nature had told him the one thing to do to save himself. Most of that day he spent in gnawing at wood and crunching mouthfuls of earth and mold between his jaws. In this way the barb-toothed points of the quills were dulled and broken as they came through. At dusk he crawled under the windfall, and Gray Wolf gently licked his muzzle with her soft cool tongue. Frequently during the night Kazan went to the creek and found relief in its ice-cold water.

The next day he had what the forest people call "porcupine mumps." His face was swollen until Gray Wolf would have laughed if she had been human, and not blind. His chops bulged like cushions. His eyes were mere slits. When he went out into the day he blinked, for he could see scarcely better than his sightless mate. But the pain was mostly gone. The night that followed he began to think of hunting, and the next morning before it was yet dawn he brought a rabbit into their den. A few hours later he would have brought a spruce partridge to Gray Wolf, but just as he was about to spring upon his feathered prey the soft chatter of a porcupine a few yards away brought him to a sudden stop. Few things could make Kazan drop his tail. But that inane and incoherent prattle of the little spiked beast sent him off at double-quick with his tail between his legs. As man abhors and evades the creeping serpent, so Kazan would hereafter evade this little creature of the forests that never in animal history has been known to lose its good-humor or pick a quarrel.

Two weeks of lengthening days, of increasing warmth, of sunshine and hunting, followed Kazan's adventure with the porcupine. The last of the snow went rapidly. Out of the earth began to spring tips of green. The *bakneesh* vine glistened redder each day, the poplar buds began to split, and in the sunniest spots, between the rocks of the ridges the little white snow-flowers began to give a final proof that spring had come. For the first of those two weeks Gray Wolf hunted frequently with Kazan. They did not go far. The swamp was alive with small game and each day or night they killed fresh meat. After the first week Gray Wolf hunted less. Then came the soft and balmy night, glorious in the radiance of a full spring moon when she refused to leave the windfall. Kazan did not urge her. Instinct made him understand, and he did not go far from the windfall that night in his hunt. When he returned he brought a rabbit.

Came then the night when from the darkest corner of the windfall Gray Wolf warned him back with a low snarl. He stood in the opening, a rabbit between his jaws. He took no offense at the snarl, but stood for a moment, gazing into the gloom where Gray Wolf had hidden herself. Then he dropped the rabbit and lay down squarely in the opening. After a little he rose restlessly and went outside. But he did not leave the windfall. It was day when he reentered. He sniffed, as he had sniffed once before a long time ago, between the boulders at the top of the Sun Rock. That which was in the air was no longer a mystery to him. He came nearer and Gray Wolf did not snarl. She whined coaxingly as he touched her. Then his muzzle found something else. It was soft and warm and made a queer little sniffling sound. There was a responsive whine in his throat, and in the darkness came the quick soft caress of Gray Wolf's tongue. Kazan returned to the sunshine and stretched himself out before the door of the windfall. His jaws dropped open, for he was filled with a strange contentment.

Chapter XVIII
The Education Of Ba-Ree

Robbed once of the joys of parenthood by the murder on the Sun Rock, both Gray Wolf and Kazan were different from what they would have been had the big gray lynx not come into their lives at that time. As if it were but yesterday they remembered the moonlit night when the lynx brought blindness to Gray Wolf and destroyed her young, and when Kazan had avenged himself and his mate in his terrible fight to the death with their enemy. And now, with that soft little handful of life snuggling close up against her, Gray Wolf saw through her blind eyes the tragic picture of that night more vividly than ever and she quivered at every sound, ready to leap in the face of an unseen foe, to rend all flesh that was not the flesh of Kazan. And ceaselessly, the slightest sound bringing him to his feet, Kazan watched and guarded. He mistrusted the moving shadows. The snapping of a twig drew back his upper lip. His fangs gleamed menacingly when the soft air brought a strange scent. In him, too, the memory of the Sun Rock, the death of their first young and the blinding of Gray Wolf, had given birth to a new instinct. Not for an instant was he off his guard. As surely as one expects the sun to rise so did he expect that sooner or later their deadly enemy would creep on them from out of the forest. In another hour such as this the lynx had brought death. The lynx had brought blindness. And so day and night he waited and watched for the lynx to come again. And woe unto any other creature of flesh and blood that dared approach the windfall in these first days of Gray Wolf's motherhood!

But peace had spread its wings of sunshine and plenty over the swamp. There were no intruders, unless the noisy whisky-jacks, the big-eyed moose-birds, the chattering bush sparrows, and the wood-mice and ermine could be called such. After the first day or two Kazan went more frequently into the windfall, and though more than once he nosed searchingly about Gray Wolf he could find only the one little pup. A little farther west the Dog-Ribs would have called the pup Ba-ree for two reasons—because he had no brothers or sisters, and because he was a mixture of dog and wolf. He was a sleek and lively little fellow from the beginning, for there was no division of mother strength and attention. He developed with the true swiftness of the wolf-whelp, and not with the slowness of the dog-pup.

For three days he was satisfied to cuddle close against his mother, feeding when he was hungry, sleeping a great deal and preened and laundered almost constantly by Gray Wolf's affectionate tongue. From the fourth day he grew busier and more inquisitive with every hour. He found his mother's blind face, with tremendous effort he tumbled over her paws, and once he lost himself completely and sniffled for help when he rolled fifteen or eighteen inches away from her. It was not long after this that he began to recognize Kazan as a part of his mother, and he was scarcely more than a week old when he rolled himself up contentedly between Kazan's forelegs and went to sleep. Kazan was puzzled. Then with a deep sigh Gray Wolf laid her head across one of her mate's forelegs, with her nose touching her runaway baby, and seemed vastly contented. For half an hour Kazan did not move.

When he was ten days old Ba-ree discovered there was great sport in tussling with a bit of rabbit fur. It was a little later when he made his second exciting discovery—light and sunshine. The sun had now reached a point where in the middle of the afternoon a bright gleam of it found its way through an overhead opening in the windfall. At first Ba-ree would only stare at the golden streak. Then came the time when he tried to play with it as he played with the rabbit fur. Each day thereafter he went a little nearer the opening through which Kazan passed from the windfall into the big world outside. Finally came the time when he reached the opening and crouched there, blinking and frightened at what he saw, and now Gray Wolf no longer tried to hold him back but went out into the sunshine and tried to call him to her. It was three days before his weak eyes had grown strong enough to permit his following her, and very quickly after that Ba-ree learned to love the sun, the warm air, and the sweetness of life, and to dread the darkness of the closed-in den where he had been born.

That this world was not altogether so nice as it at first appeared he was very soon to learn. At the darkening signs of an approaching storm one day Gray Wolf tried to lure him back under the windfall. It was her first warning to Ba-ree and he did not understand. Where Gray Wolf failed, nature came to teach a first lesson. Ba-ree was caught in a sudden deluge of rain. It flattened him out in pure terror and he was drenched and half drowned before Gray Wolf caught him between her jaws and carried him into shelter. One by one after this the first strange experiences of life came to him, and one by one his instincts received their birth. Greatest for him of the days to follow was that on which his inquisitive nose touched the raw flesh of a freshly killed and bleeding rabbit. It was his first taste of blood. It was sweet. It filled him with a strange excitement and thereafter he knew what it meant when Kazan brought in something between his jaws. He soon began to battle with sticks in place of the soft fur and his teeth grew as hard and as sharp as little needles.

The Great Mystery was bared to him at last when Kazan brought in between his jaws, a big rabbit that was still alive but so badly crushed that it could not run when dropped to the ground. Ba-ree had learned to know what rabbits and partridges meant—the sweet warm blood that he loved better even than he had ever loved his mother's milk. But they had come to him dead. He had never seen one of the monsters alive. And now the rabbit that Kazan dropped to the ground, kicking and struggling with a broken back, sent Ba-ree back appalled. For a few moments he wonderingly watched the dying throes of Kazan's prey. Both Kazan and Gray Wolf seemed to understand that this was to be Ba-ree's first lesson in his education as a slaying and flesh-eating creature, and they stood close over the rabbit, making no effort to end its struggles. Half a dozen times Gray Wolf sniffed at the rabbit and then turned her blind face toward Ba-ree. After the third or fourth time Kazan stretched himself out on his belly a few feet away and watched the proceedings attentively. Each time that Gray Wolf lowered her head to muzzle the rabbit Ba-ree's little ears shot up expectantly. When he saw that nothing happened and that his mother was not hurt he came a little nearer. Soon he could reach out, stiff-legged and cautious, and touch the furry thing that was not yet dead.

In a last spasmodic convulsion the big rabbit doubled up its rear legs and gave a kick that sent Ba-ree sprawling back, yelping in terror. He regained his feet and then, for the first time, anger and the desire to retaliate took possession of him. The kick had completed his first education. He came back with less caution, but stiffer-legged, and a moment later had dug his tiny teeth in the rabbit's neck. He could feel the throb of life in the soft body, the muscles of the dying rabbit twitched convulsively under him, and he hung with his teeth until there was no longer a tremor of life in his first kill. Gray Wolf was delighted. She caressed Ba-ree with her tongue, and even Kazan condescended to sniff approvingly of his son when he returned to the rabbit. And never before had warm sweet blood tasted so good to Ba-ree as it did to-day.

Swiftly Ba-ree developed from a blood-tasting into a flesh-eating animal. One by one the mysteries of life were unfolded to him—the mating-night chortle of the gray owl, the crash of a falling tree, the roll of thunder, the rush of running water, the scream of a fisher-cat, the mooing of the cow moose, and the distant call of his tribe. But chief of all these mysteries that were already becoming a part of his instinct was the mystery of scent. One day he wandered fifty yards away from the windfall and his little nose touched the warm scent of a rabbit. Instantly, without reasoning or further process of education, he knew that to get at the sweet flesh and blood which he loved he must follow the scent. He wriggled slowly along the trail until he came to a big log, over which the rabbit had vaulted in a long leap, and from this log he turned back. Each day after this he went on adventures of his own. At first he was like an explorer without a compass in a vast and unknown world. Each day he encountered something new, always wonderful, frequently terrifying. But his terrors grew less and less and his confidence correspondingly greater. As he found that none of the things he feared did him any harm he became more and more bold in his investigations. And his appearance was changing, as well as his view of things. His round roly-poly body was taking a different form. He became lithe and quick. The yellow of his coat darkened, and there was a whitish-gray streak along his back like that along Kazan's. He had his mother's under-throat and her beautiful grace of head. Otherwise he was a true son of Kazan. His limbs gave signs of future strength and massiveness. He was broad across the chest. His eyes were wide apart, with a little red in the lower corners. The forest people know what to expect of husky pups who early develop that drop of red. It is a warning that they are born of the wild and that their mothers, or fathers, are of the savage hunt-packs. In Ba-ree that tinge of red was so pronounced that it could mean but one thing. While he was almost half dog, the wild had claimed him forever.

Not until the day of his first real battle with a living creature did Ba-ree come fully into his inheritance. He had gone farther than usual from the windfall—fully a hundred yards. Here he found a new wonder. It was the creek. He had heard it before and he had looked down on it from afar—from a distance of fifty yards at least. But to-day he ventured going to the edge of it, and there he stood for a long time, with the water rippling and singing at his feet, gazing across it into the new world that he saw. Then he moved cautiously along the stream. He had not gone a dozen steps when there was a furious fluttering close to him, and one of the fierce big-eyed jays of the Northland was directly in his path. It could not fly. One of its wings dragged, probably broken in a struggle with some one of the smaller preying beasts. But for an instant it was a most startling and defiant bit of life to Ba-ree.

Then the grayish crest along his back stiffened and he advanced. The wounded jay remained motionless until Ba-ree was within three feet of it. In short quick hops it began to retreat. Instantly Ba-ree's indecision had flown to the four winds. With one sharp excited yelp he flew at the defiant bird. For a few moments there was a thrilling race, and Ba-ree's sharp little teeth buried themselves in the jay's feathers. Swift as a flash the bird's beak began to strike. The jay was the king of the smaller birds. In nesting season it killed the brush sparrows, the mild-eyed moose-birds, and the tree-sappers. Again and again it struck Ba-ree with its powerful beak, but the son of Kazan had now reached the age of battle and the pain of the blows only made his own teeth sink deeper. At last he found the flesh; and a puppyish snarl rose in his throat. Fortunately he had gained a hold under the wing and after the first dozen blows the jay's resistance grew weaker. Five minutes later Ba-ree loosened his teeth and drew back a step to look at the crumpled and motionless creature before him. The jay was dead. He had won his first battle. And with victory came the wonderful dawning of that greatest instinct of all, which told him that no longer was he a drone in the marvelous mechanism of wilderness life—but a part of it from this time forth. *For he had killed.*

Half an hour later Gray Wolf came down over his trail. The jay was torn into bits. Its feathers were scattered about and Ba-ree's little nose was bloody. Ba-ree was lying in triumph beside his victim. Swiftly Gray Wolf understood and caressed him joyously. When they returned to the windfall Ba-ree carried in his jaws what was left of the jay.

From that hour of his first kill hunting became the chief passion of Ba-ree's life. When he was not sleeping in the sun, or under the windfall at night, he was seeking life that he could destroy. He slaughtered an entire family of wood-mice. Moose-birds were at first the easiest for him to stalk, and he killed three. Then he encountered an ermine and the fierce little white outlaw of the forests gave him his first defeat. Defeat cooled his ardor for a few days, but taught him the great lesson that there were other fanged and flesh-eating animals besides himself and that nature had so schemed things that fang must not prey upon fang—*for food.* Many things had been born in him. Instinctively he shunned the porcupine without experiencing the torture of its quills. He came face to face with a fisher-cat one day, a fortnight after his fight with the ermine. Both were seeking food, and as there was no food between them to fight over, each went his own way.

Farther and farther Ba-ree ventured from the windfall, always following the creek. Sometimes he was gone for hours. At first Gray Wolf was restless when he was away, but she seldom went with him and after a time her restlessness left her. Nature was working swiftly. It was Kazan who was restless now. Moonlight nights had come and the wanderlust was growing more and more insistent in his veins. And Gray Wolf, too, was filled with the strange longing to roam at large out into the big world.

Came then the afternoon when Ba-ree went on his longest hunt. Half a mile away he killed his first rabbit. He remained beside it until dusk. The moon rose, big and golden, flooding the forests and plains and ridges with a light almost like that of day. It was a glorious night. And Ba-ree found the moon, and left his kill. And the direction in which he traveled *was away from the windfall.*

All that night Gray Wolf watched and waited. And when at last the moon was sinking into the south and west she settled back on her haunches, turned her blind face to the sky and sent forth her first howl since the day Ba-ree was born. Nature had come into her own. Far away Ba-ree heard, but he did not answer. A new world was his. He had said good-by to the windfall—and home.

Chapter XIX
The Usurpers

It was that glorious season between spring and summer, when the northern nights were brilliant with moon and stars, that Kazan and Gray Wolf set up the valley between the two ridges on a long hunt. It was the beginning of that *wanderlust* which always comes to the furred and padded creatures of the wilderness immediately after the young-born of early spring have left their mothers to find their own way in the big world. They struck west from their winter home under the windfall in the swamp. They hunted mostly at night and behind them they left a trail marked by the partly eaten carcasses of rabbits and partridges. It was the season of slaughter and not of hunger. Ten miles west of the swamp they killed a fawn. This, too, they left after a single meal. Their appetites became satiated with warm flesh and blood. They grew sleek and fat and each day they basked longer in the warm sunshine. They had few rivals. The lynxes were in the heavier timber to the south. There were no wolves. Fisher-cat, marten and mink were numerous along the creek, but these were neither swift-hunting nor long-fanged. One day they came upon an old otter. He was a giant of his kind, turning a whitish gray with the approach of summer. Kazan, grown fat and lazy, watched him idly. Blind Gray Wolf sniffed at the fishy smell of him in the air. To them he was no more than a floating stick, a creature out of their element, along with the fish, and they continued on their way not knowing that this uncanny creature with the coal-like flappers was soon to become their ally in one of the strange and deadly feuds of the wilderness, which are as sanguinary to animal life as the deadliest feuds of men are to human life.

The day following their meeting with the otter Gray Wolf and Kazan continued three miles farther westward, still following the stream. Here they encountered the interruption to their progress which turned them over the northward ridge. The obstacle was a huge beaver dam. The dam was two hundred yards in width and flooded a mile of swamp and timber above it. Neither Gray Wolf nor Kazan was deeply interested in beavers. They also moved out of their element, along with the fish and the otter and swift-winged birds.

So they turned into the north, not knowing that nature had already schemed that they four—the dog, wolf, otter and beaver—should soon be engaged in one of those merciless struggles of the wild which keep animal life down to the survival of the fittest, and whose tragic histories are kept secret under the stars and the moon and the winds that tell no tales.

For many years no man had come into this valley between the two ridges to molest the beaver. If a Sarcee trapper had followed down the nameless creek and had caught the patriarch and chief of the colony, he would at once have judged him to be very old and his Indian tongue would have given him a name. He would have called him Broken Tooth, because one of the four long teeth with which he felled trees and built dams was broken off. Six years before Broken Tooth had led a few beavers of his own age down the stream, and they had built their first small dam and their first lodge. The following April Broken Tooth's mate had four little baby beavers, and each of the other mothers in the colony increased the population by two or three or four. At the end of the fourth year this first generation of children, had they followed the usual law of nature, would have mated and left the colony to build a dam and lodges of their own. They mated, but did not emigrate.

The next year the second generation of children, now four years old, mated but did not leave, so that in this early summer of the sixth year the colony was very much like a great city that had been long besieged by an enemy. It numbered fifteen lodges and over a hundred beavers, not counting the fourth babies which had been born during March and April. The dam had been lengthened until it was fully two hundred yards in length. Water had been made to flood large areas of birch and poplar and tangled swamps of tender willow and elder. Even with this food was growing scarce and the lodges were overcrowded. This was because beavers are almost human in their love for home. Broken Tooth's lodge was fully nine feet long by seven wide inside, and there were now living in it children and grandchildren to the number of twenty-seven. For this reason Broken Tooth was preparing to break the precedent of his tribe. When Kazan and Gray Wolf sniffed carelessly at the strong scents of the beaver city, Broken Tooth was marshaling his family, and two of his sons and their families, for the exodus.

As yet Broken Tooth was the recognized leader in the colony. No other beaver had grown to his size and strength. His thick body was fully three feet long. He weighed at least sixty pounds. His tail was fourteen inches in length and five in width, and on a still night he could strike the water a blow that could be heard a quarter of a mile away. His webbed hindfeet were twice as large as his mate's and he was easily the swiftest swimmer in the colony.

Following the afternoon when Gray Wolf and Kazan struck into the north came the clear still night when Broken Tooth climbed to the top of the dam, shook himself, and looked down to see that his army was behind him. The starlit water of the big pond rippled and flashed with the movement of many bodies. A few of the older beavers clambered up after Broken Tooth and the old patriarch plunged down into the narrow stream on the other side of the dam. Now the shining silken bodies of the emigrants followed him in the starlight. In ones and twos and threes they climbed over the dam and with them went a dozen children born three months before. Easily and swiftly they began the journey down-stream, the youngsters swimming furiously to keep up with their parents. In all they numbered forty. Broken Tooth swam well in the lead, with his older workers and battlers behind him. In the rear followed mothers and children.

All of that night the journey continued. The otter, their deadliest enemy—deadlier even than man—hid himself in a thick clump of willows as they passed. Nature, which sometimes sees beyond the vision of man, had made him the enemy of these creatures that were passing his hiding-place in the night. A fish-feeder, he was born to be a conserver as well as a destroyer of the creatures on which he fed. Perhaps nature told him that too many beaver dams stopped the run of spawning fish and that where there were many beavers there were always few fish. Maybe he reasoned as to why fish-hunting was poor and he went hungry. So, unable to cope singly with whole tribes of his enemies, he worked to destroy their dams. How this, in turn, destroyed the beavers will be seen in the feud in which nature had already schemed that he should play a part with Kazan and Gray Wolf.

A dozen times during this night Broken Tooth halted to investigate the food supplies along the banks. But in the two or three places where he found plenty of the bark on which they lived it would have been difficult to have constructed a dam. His wonderful engineering instincts rose even above food instincts. And when each time he moved onward, no beaver questioned his judgment by remaining behind. In the early dawn they crossed the burn and came to the edge of the swamp domain of Kazan and Gray Wolf. By right of discovery and possession that swamp belonged to the dog and the wolf. In every part of it they had left their mark of ownership. But Broken Tooth was a creature of the water and the scent of his tribe was not keen. He led on, traveling more slowly when they entered the timber. Just below the windfall home of Kazan and Gray Wolf he halted, and clambering ashore balanced himself upright on his webbed hindfeet and broad four-pound tail. Here he had found ideal conditions. A dam could be constructed easily across the narrow stream, and the water could be made to flood a big supply of poplar, birch, willow and alder. Also the place was sheltered by heavy timber, so that the winters would be warm. Broken Tooth quickly gave his followers to understand that this was to be their new home. On both sides of the stream they swarmed into the near-by timber. The babies began at once to nibble hungrily at the tender bark of willow and alder. The older ones, every one of them now a working engineer, investigated excitedly, breakfasting by nibbling off a mouthful of bark now and then.

That day the work of home-building began. Broken Tooth himself selected a big birch that leaned over the stream, and began the work of cutting through the ten-inch butt with his three long teeth. Though the old patriarch had lost one tooth, the three that remained had not deteriorated with age. The outer edge of them was formed of the hardest enamel; the inner side was of soft ivory. They were like the finest steel chisels, the enamel never wearing away and the softer ivory replacing itself year by year as it was consumed. Sitting on his hindlegs, with his forepaws resting against the tree and with his heavy tail giving him a firm balance, Broken Tooth began gnawing a narrow ring entirely around the tree. He worked tirelessly for several hours, and when at last he stopped to rest another workman took up the task. Meanwhile a dozen beavers were hard at work cutting timber. Long before Broken Tooth's tree was ready to fall across the stream, a smaller poplar crashed into the water. The cutting on the big birch was in the shape of an hour-glass. In twenty hours it fell straight across the creek. While the beaver prefers to do most of his work at night he is a day-laborer as well, and Broken Tooth gave his tribe but little rest during the days that followed. With almost human intelligence the little engineers kept at their task. Smaller trees were felled, and these were cut into four or five foot lengths. One by one these lengths were rolled to the stream, the beavers pushing them with their heads and forepaws, and by means of brush and small limbs they were fastened securely against the birch. When the framework was completed the wonderful cement construction was begun. In this the beavers were the masters of men. Dynamite was the only force that could hereafter break up what they were building now. Under their cup-like chins the beavers brought from the banks a mixture of mud and fine twigs, carrying from half a pound to a pound at a load and began filling up the framework with it. Their task seemed tremendous, and yet Broken Tooth's engineers could carry a ton of this mud and twig mixture during a day and night. In three days the water was beginning to back, until it rose about the butts of a dozen or more trees and was flooding a small area of brush. This made work easier. From now on materials could be cut in the water and easily floated. While a part of the beaver colony was taking advantage of the water, others were felling trees end to end with the birch, laying the working frame of a dam a hundred feet in width.

They had nearly accomplished this work when one morning Kazan and Gray Wolf returned to the swamp.

Chapter XX
A Feud In The Wilderness

A soft wind blowing from the south and east brought the scent of the invaders to Gray Wolf's nose when they were still half a mile away. She gave the warning to Kazan and he, too, found the strange scent in the air. It grew stronger as they advanced. When two hundred yards from the windfall they heard the sudden crash of a falling tree, and stopped. For a full minute they stood tense and listening. Then the silence was broken by a squeaking cry, followed by a splash. Gray Wolf's alert ears fell back and she turned her blind face understandingly toward Kazan. They trotted ahead slowly, approaching the windfall from behind. Not until they had reached the top of the knoll on which it was situated did Kazan begin to see the wonderful change that had taken place during their absence. Astounded, they stood while he stared. There was no longer a little creek below them. Where it had been was a pond that reached almost to the foot of the knoll. It was fully a hundred feet in width and the backwater had flooded the trees and bush for five or six times that distance toward the burn. They had come up quietly and Broken Tooth's dull-scented workers were unaware of their presence. Not fifty feet away Broken Tooth himself was gnawing at the butt of a tree. An equal distance to the right of him four or five of the baby beavers were at play building a miniature dam of mud and tiny twigs. On the opposite side of the pond was a steep bank six or seven feet high, and here a few of the older children—two years old, but still not workmen—were having great fun climbing the bank and using it as a toboggan-slide. It was their splashing that Kazan and Gray Wolf had heard. In a dozen different places the older beavers were at work.

A few weeks before Kazan had looked upon a similar scene when he had returned into the north from Broken Tooth's old home. It had not interested him then. But a quick and thrilling change swept through him now. The beavers had ceased to be mere water animals, uneatable and with an odor that displeased him. They were invaders—and enemies. His fangs bared silently. His crest stiffened like the hair of a brush, and the muscles of his forelegs and shoulders stood out like whipcords. Not a sound came from him as he rushed down upon Broken Tooth. The old beaver was oblivious of danger until Kazan was within twenty feet of him. Naturally slow of movement on land, he stood for an instant stupefied. Then he swung down from the tree as Kazan leaped upon him. Over and over they rolled to the edge of the bank, carried on by the dog's momentum. In another moment the thick heavy body of the beaver had slipped like oil from under Kazan and Broken Tooth was safe in his element, two holes bitten clean through his fleshy tail. Baffled in his effort to get a death-hold on Broken Tooth, Kazan swung like a flash to the right. The young beavers had not moved. Astonished and frightened at what they had seen, they stood as if stupefied. Not until they saw Kazan tearing toward them did they awaken to action. Three of them reached the water. The fourth and fifth—baby beavers not more than three months old—were too late. With a single snap of his jaw Kazan broke the hack of one. The other he pinned down by the throat and shook as a terrier shakes a rat. When Gray Wolf trotted down to him both of the little beavers were dead. She sniffed at their soft little bodies and whined. Perhaps the baby creatures reminded her of runaway Ba-ree, her own baby, for there was a note of longing in her whine as she nosed them. It was the mother whine.

But if Gray Wolf had visions of her own Kazan understood nothing of them. He had killed two of the creatures that had dared to invade their home. To the little beavers he had been as merciless as the gray lynx that had murdered Gray Wolf's first children on the top of the Sun Rock. Now that he had sunk his teeth into the flesh of his enemies his blood was filled with a frenzied desire to kill. He raved along the edge of the pond, snarling at the uneasy water under which Broken Tooth had disappeared. All of the beavers had taken refuge in the pond, and its surface was heaving with the passing of many bodies beneath. Kazan came to the end of the dam. This was new. Instinctively he knew that it was the work of Broken Tooth and his tribe and for a few moments he tore fiercely at the matted sticks and limbs. Suddenly there was an upheaval of water close to the dam, fifty feet out from the bank, and Broken Tooth's big gray head appeared. For a tense half minute Broken Tooth and Kazan measured each other at that distance. Then Broken Tooth drew his wet shining body out of the water to the top of the dam, and squatted flat, facing Kazan. The old patriarch was alone. Not another beaver had shown himself.

The surface of the pond had now become quiet. Vainly Kazan tried to discover a footing that would allow him to reach the watchful invader. But between the solid wall of the dam and the bank there was a tangled framework through which the water rushed with some violence. Three times Kazan fought to work his way through that tangle, and three times his efforts ended in sudden plunges into the water. All this time Broken Tooth did not move. When at last Kazan gave up the attack the old engineer slipped over the edge of the dam and disappeared under the water. He had learned that Kazan, like the lynx, could not fight water and he spread the news among the members of his colony.

Gray Wolf and Kazan returned to the windfall and lay down in the warm sun. Half an hour later Broken Tooth drew himself out on the opposite shore of the pond. He was followed by other beavers. Across the water they resumed their work as if nothing had happened. The tree-cutters returned to their trees. Half a dozen worked in the water, carrying loads of cement and twigs. The middle of the pond was their dead-line. Across this not one of them passed. A dozen times during the hour that followed one of the beavers swam up to the dead-line, and rested there, looking at the shining little bodies of the babies that Kazan had killed. Perhaps it was the mother, and perhaps some finer instinct unknown to Kazan told this to Gray Wolf. For Gray Wolf went down twice to sniff at the dead bodies, and each time—without seeing—she went when the mother beaver had come to the dead-line.

The first fierce animus had worn itself from Kazan's blood, and he now watched the beavers closely. He had learned that they were not fighters. They were many to one and yet they ran from him like a lot of rabbits. Broken Tooth had not even struck at him, and slowly it grew upon him that these invading creatures that used both the water and land would have to be hunted as he stalked the rabbit and the partridge. Early in the afternoon he slipped off into the bush, followed by Gray Wolf. He had often begun the stalking of a rabbit by moving *away* from it and he employed this wolf trick now with the beavers. Beyond the windfall he turned and began trotting up the creek, with the wind. For a quarter of a mile the creek was deeper than it had ever been. One of their old fording places was completely submerged, and at last Kazan plunged in and swam across, leaving Gray Wolf to wait for him on the windfall side of the stream.

Alone he made his way quickly in the direction of the dam, traveling two hundred yards back from the creek. Twenty yards below the dam a dense thicket of alder and willow grew close to the creek and Kazan took advantage of this. He approached within a leap or two of the dam without being seen and crouched close to the ground, ready to spring forth when the opportunity came. Most of the beavers were now working in the water. The four or five still on shore were close to the water and some distance up-stream. After a wait of several minutes Kazan was almost on the point of staking everything on a wild rush upon his enemies when a movement on the dam attracted his attention. Half-way out two or three beavers were at work strengthening the central structure with cement. Swift as a flash Kazan darted from his cover to the shelter behind the dam. Here the water was very shallow, the main portion of the stream finding a passage close to the opposite shore. Nowhere did it reach to his belly as he waded out. He was completely hidden from the beavers, and the wind was in his favor. The noise of running water drowned what little sound he made. Soon he heard the beaver workmen over him. The branches of the fallen birch gave him a footing, and he clambered up.

A moment later his head and shoulders appeared above the top of the dam. Scarce an arm's length away Broken Tooth was forcing into place a three-foot length of poplar as big around as a man's arm. He was so busy that he did not hear or see Kazan. Another beaver gave the warning as he plunged into the pond. Broken Tooth looked up, and his eyes met Kazan's bared fangs. There was no time to turn. He threw himself back, but it was a moment too late. Kazan was upon him. His long fangs sank deep into Broken Tooth's neck. But the old beaver had thrown himself enough back to make Kazan lose his footing. At the same moment his chisel-like teeth got a firm hold of the loose skin at Kazan's throat. Thus clinched, with Kazan's long teeth buried almost to the beaver's jugular, they plunged down into the deep water of the pond.

Broken Tooth weighed sixty pounds. The instant he struck the water he was in his element, and holding tenaciously to the grip he had obtained on Kazan's neck he sank like a chunk of iron. Kazan was pulled completely under. The water rushed into his mouth, his ears, eyes and nose. He was blinded, and his senses were a roaring tumult. But instead of struggling to free himself he held his breath and buried his teeth deeper. They touched the soft bottom and for a moment floundered in the mud. Then Kazan loosened his hold. He was fighting for his own life now—and not for Broken Tooth's. With all of the strength of his powerful limbs he struggled to break loose—to rise to the surface, to fresh air, to life. He clamped his jaws shut, knowing that to breathe was to die. On land he could have freed himself from Broken Tooth's hold without an effort. But under water the old beaver's grip was more deadly than would have been the fangs of a lynx ashore. There was a sudden swirl of water as a second beaver circled close about the struggling pair. Had he closed in with Broken Tooth, Kazan's struggles would quickly have ceased.

But nature had not foreseen the day when Broken Tooth would be fighting with fang. The old patriarch had no particular reason now for holding Kazan down. He was not vengeful. He did not thirst for blood or death. Finding that he was free, and that this strange enemy that had twice leaped upon him could do him no harm, he loosed his hold. It was not a moment too soon for Kazan. He was struggling weakly when he rose to the surface of the water. Three-quarters drowned, he succeeded in raising his forepaws over a slender branch that projected from the dam. This gave him time to fill his lungs with air, and to cough forth the water that had almost ended his existence. For ten minutes he clung to the branch before he dared attempt the short swim ashore. When he reached the bank he dragged himself up weakly. All the strength was gone from his body. His limbs shook. His jaws hung loose. He was beaten—completely beaten. And a creature without a fang had worsted him. He felt the abasement of it. Drenched and slinking, he went to the windfall, lay down in the sun, and waited for Gray Wolf.

Days followed in which Kazan's desire to destroy his beaver enemies became the consuming passion of his life. Each day the dam became more formidable. Cement work in the water was carried on by the beavers swiftly and safely. The water in the pond rose higher each twenty-four hours, and the pond grew steadily wider. The water had now been turned into the depression that encircled the windfall, and in another week or two, if the beavers continued their work, Kazan's and Gray Wolf's home would be nothing more than a small island in the center of a wide area of submerged swamp.

Kazan hunted only for food now, and not for pleasure. Ceaselessly he watched his opportunity to leap upon incautious members of Broken Tooth's tribe. The third day after the struggle under the water he killed a big beaver that approached too close to the willow thicket. The fifth day two of the young beavers wandered into the flooded depression back of the windfall and Kazan caught them in shallow water and tore them into pieces. After these successful assaults the beavers began to work mostly at night. This was to Kazan's advantage, for he was a night-hunter. On each of two consecutive nights he killed a beaver. Counting the young, he had killed seven when the otter came.

Never had Broken Tooth been placed between two deadlier or more ferocious enemies than the two that now assailed him. On shore Kazan was his master because of his swiftness, keener scent, and fighting trickery. In the water the otter was a still greater menace. He was swifter than the fish that he caught for food. His teeth were like steel needles. He was so sleek and slippery that it would have been impossible for them to hold him with their chisel-like teeth could they have caught him. The otter, like the beaver, possessed no hunger for blood. Yet in all the Northland he was the greatest destroyer of their kind—an even greater destroyer than man. He came and passed like a plague, and it was in the coldest days of winter that greatest destruction came with him. In those days he did not assault the beavers in their snug houses. He did what man could do only with dynamite—made an embrasure through their dam. Swiftly the water would fall, the surface ice would crash down, and the beaver houses would be left out of water. Then followed death for the beavers—starvation and cold. With the protecting water gone from about their houses, the drained pond a chaotic mass of broken ice, and the temperature forty or fifty degrees below zero, they would die within a few hours. For the beaver, with his thick coat of fur, can stand less cold than man. Through all the long winter the water about his home is as necessary to him as fire to a child.

But it was summer now and Broken Tooth and his colony had no very great fear of the otter. It would cost them some labor to repair the damage he did, but there was plenty of food and it was warm. For two days the otter frisked about the dam and the deep water of the pond. Kazan took him for a beaver, and tried vainly to stalk him. The otter regarded Kazan suspiciously and kept well out of his way. Neither knew that the other was an ally. Meanwhile the beavers continued their work with greater caution. The water in the pond had now risen to a point where the engineers had begun the construction of three lodges. On the third day the destructive instinct of the otter began its work. He began to examine the dam, close down to the foundation. It was not long before he found a weak spot to begin work on, and with his sharp teeth and small bullet-like head he commenced his drilling operations. Inch by inch he worked his way through the dam, burrowing and gnawing over and under the timbers, and always through the cement. The round hole he made was fully seven inches in diameter. In six hours he had cut it through the five-foot base of the dam.

A torrent of water began to rush from the pond as if forced out by a hydraulic pump. Kazan and Gray Wolf were hiding in the willows on the south side of the pond when this happened. They heard the roar of the stream tearing through the embrasure and Kazan saw the otter crawl up to the top of the dam and shake himself like a huge water-rat. Within thirty minutes the water in the pond had fallen perceptibly, and the force of the water pouring through the hole was constantly increasing the outlet. In another half hour the foundations of the three lodges, which had been laid in about ten inches of water, stood on mud. Not until Broken Tooth discovered that the water was receding from the houses did he take alarm. He was thrown into a panic, and very soon every beaver in the colony tearing excitedly about the pond. They swam swiftly from shore to shore, paying no attention to the dead-line now. Broken Tooth and the older workmen made for the dam, and with a snarling cry the otter plunged down among them and out like a flash for the creek above the pond. Swiftly the water continued to fall and as it fell the excitement of the beavers increased. They forgot Kazan and Gray Wolf.

Several of the younger members of the colony drew themselves ashore on the windfall side of the pond, and whining softly Kazan was about to slip back through the willows when one of the older beavers waddled up through the deepening mud close on his ambush. In two leaps Kazan was upon him, with Gray Wolf a leap behind him. The short fierce struggle in the mud was seen by the other beavers and they crossed swiftly to the opposite side of the pond. The water had receded to a half of its greatest width before Broken Tooth and his workmen discovered the breach in the wall of the dam. The work of repair was begun at once. For this work sticks and brush of considerable size were necessary, and to reach this material the beavers were compelled to drag their heavy bodies through the ten or fifteen yards of soft mud left by the falling water. Peril of fang no longer kept them back. Instinct told them that they were fighting for their existence—that if the embrasure were not filled up and the water kept in the pond they would very soon be completely exposed to their enemies. It was a day of slaughter for Gray Wolf and Kazan. They killed two more beavers in the mud close to the willows. Then they crossed the creek below the dam and cut off three beavers in the depression behind the windfall. There was no escape for these three. They were torn into pieces. Farther up the creek Kazan caught a young beaver and killed it.

Late in the afternoon the slaughter ended. Broken Tooth and his courageous engineers had at last repaired the breach, and the water in the pond began to rise.

Half a mile up the creek the big otter was squatted on a log basking in the last glow of the setting sun. To-morrow he would go and do over again his work of destruction. That was his method. For him it was play.

But that strange and unseen arbiter of the forests called O-ee-ki, "the Spirit," by those who speak the wild tongue, looked down at last with mercy upon Broken Tooth and his death-stricken tribe. For in that last glow of sunset Kazan and Gray Wolf slipped stealthily up the creek—to find the otter basking half asleep on the log.

The day's work, a full stomach, and the pool of warm sunlight in which he lay had all combined to make the otter sleepy. He was as motionless as the log on which he had stretched himself. He was big and gray and old. For ten years he had lived to prove his cunning superior to that of man. Vainly traps had been set for him. Wily trappers had built narrow sluice-ways of rock and tree in small streams for him, but the old otter had foiled their cunning and escaped the steel jaws waiting at the lower end of each sluice. The trail he left in soft mud told of his size. A few trappers had seen him. His soft pelt would long ago have found its way to London, Paris or Berlin had it not been for his cunning. He was fit for a princess, a duke or an emperor. For ten years he had lived and escaped the demands of the rich.

But this was summer. No trapper would have killed him now, for his pelt was worthless. Nature and instinct both told him this. At this season he did not dread man, for there was no man to dread. So he lay asleep on the log, oblivious to everything but the comfort of sleep and the warmth of the sun.

Soft-footed, searching still for signs of the furry enemies who had invaded their domain, Kazan slipped along the creek. Gray Wolf ran close at his shoulder. They made no sound, and the wind was in their favor—bringing scents toward them. It brought the otter smell. To Kazan and Gray Wolf it was the scent of a water animal, rank and fishy, and they took it for the beaver. They advanced still more cautiously. Then Kazan saw the big otter asleep on the log and he gave the warning to Gray Wolf. She stopped, standing with her head thrown up, while Kazan made his stealthy advance. The otter stirred uneasily. It was growing dusk. The golden pool of sunlight had faded away. Back in the darkening timber an owl greeted night with its first-low call. The otter breathed deeply. His whiskered muzzle twitched. He was awakening—stirring—when Kazan leaped upon him. Face to face, in fair fight, the old otter could have given a good account of himself. But there was no chance now. The wild itself had for the first time in his life become his deadliest enemy. It was not man now—but O-ee-ki, "the Spirit," that had laid its hand upon him. And from the Spirit there was no escape. Kazan's fangs sank into his soft jugular. Perhaps he died without knowing what it was that had leaped upon him. For he died—quickly, and Kazan and Gray Wolf went on their way, hunting still for enemies to slaughter, and not knowing that in the otter they had killed the one ally who would have driven the beavers from their swamp home.

The days that followed grew more and more hopeless for Kazan and Gray Wolf. With the otter gone Broken Tooth and his tribe held the winning hand. Each day the water backed a little farther into the depression surrounding the windfall. By the middle of July only a narrow strip of land connected the windfall hummock with the dry land of the swamp. In deep water the beavers now worked unmolested. Inch by inch the water rose, until there came the day when it began to overflow the connecting strip. For the last time Kazan and Gray Wolf passed from their windfall home and traveled up the stream between the two ridges. The creek held a new meaning for them now and as they traveled they sniffed its odors and listened to its sounds with an interest they had never known before. It was an interest mingled a little with fear, for something in the manner in which the beavers had beaten them reminded Kazan and Gray Wolf of *man*. And that night, when in the radiance of the big white moon they came within scent of the beaver colony that Broken Tooth had left, they turned quickly northward into the plains. Thus had brave old Broken Tooth taught them to respect the flesh and blood and handiwork of his tribe.

Chapter XXI
A Shot On The Sand-Bar

July and August of 1911 were months of great fires in the Northland. The swamp home of Kazan and Gray Wolf, and the green valley between the two ridges, had escaped the seas of devastating flame; but now, as they set forth on their wandering adventures again, it was not long before their padded feet came in contact with the seared and blackened desolation that had followed so closely after the plague and starvation of the preceding winter. In his humiliation and defeat, after being driven from his swamp home by the beavers, Kazan led his blind mate first into the south. Twenty miles beyond the ridge they struck the fire-killed forests. Winds from Hudson's Bay had driven the flames in an unbroken sea into the west, and they had left not a vestige of life or a patch of green. Blind Gray Wolf could not see the blackened world, but she *sensed* it. It recalled to her memory of that other fire, after the battle on the Sun Rock; and all of her wonderful instincts, sharpened and developed by her blindness, told her that to the north—and not south—lay the hunting-grounds they were seeking. The strain of dog that was in Kazan still pulled him south. It was not because he sought man, for to man he had now become as deadly an enemy as Gray Wolf herself. It was simply dog instinct to travel southward; in the face of fire it was wolf instinct to travel northward. At the end of the third day Gray Wolf won. They recrossed the little valley between the two ridges, and swung north and west into the Athabasca country, striking a course that would ultimately bring them to the headwaters of the McFarlane River.

Late in the preceding autumn a prospector had come up to Fort Smith, on the Slave River, with a pickle bottle filled with gold dust and nuggets. He had made the find on the McFarlane. The first mails had taken the news to the outside world, and by midwinter the earliest members of a treasure-hunting horde were rushing into the country by snow-shoe and dog-sledge. Other finds came thick and fast. The McFarlane was rich in free gold, and miners by the score staked out their claims along it and began work. Latecomers swung to new fields farther north and east, and to Fort Smith came rumors of "finds" richer than those of the Yukon. A score of men at first—then a hundred, five hundred, a thousand—rushed into the new country. Most of these were from the prairie countries to the south, and from the placer beds of the Saskatchewan and the Frazer. From the far North, traveling by way of the Mackenzie and the Liard, came a smaller number of seasoned prospectors and adventurers from the Yukon—men who knew what it meant to starve and freeze and die by inches.

One of these late comers was Sandy McTrigger. There were several reasons why Sandy had left the Yukon. He was "in bad" with the police who patrolled the country west of Dawson, and he was "broke." In spite of these facts he was one of the best prospectors that had ever followed the shores of the Klondike. He had made discoveries running up to a million or two, and had promptly lost them through gambling and drink. He had no conscience, and little fear. Brutality was the chief thing written in his face. His undershot jaw, his wide eyes, low forehead and grizzly mop of red hair proclaimed him at once as a man not to be trusted beyond one's own vision or the reach of a bullet. It was suspected that he had killed a couple of men, and robbed others, but as yet the police had failed to get anything "on" him. But along with this bad side of him, Sandy McTrigger possessed a coolness and a courage which even his worst enemies could not but admire, and also certain mental depths which his unpleasant features did not proclaim.

Inside of six months Red Gold City had sprung up on the McFarlane, a hundred and fifty miles from Fort Smith, and Fort Smith was five hundred miles from civilization. When Sandy came he looked over the crude collection of shacks, gambling houses and saloons in the new town, and made up his mind that the time was not ripe for any of his "inside" schemes just yet. He gambled a little, and won sufficient to buy himself grub and half an outfit. A feature of this outfit was an old muzzle-loading rifle. Sandy, who always carried the latest Savage on the market, laughed at it. But it was the best his finances would allow of. He started south—up the McFarlane. Beyond a certain point on the river prospectors had found no gold. Sandy pushed confidently *beyond* this point. Not until he was in new country did he begin his search. Slowly he worked his way up a small tributary whose headwaters were fifty or sixty miles to the south and east. Here and there he found fairly good placer gold. He might have panned six or eight dollars' worth a day. With this much he was disgusted. Week after week he continued to work his way up-stream, and the farther he went the poorer his pans became. At last only occasionally did he find colors. After such disgusting weeks as these Sandy was dangerous— when in the company of others. Alone he was harmless.

"Wolves," he grunted. "Wish I could 'a' shot at 'em with that old minute-gun back there. Gawd—listen to that! And in broad daylight, too!"

One afternoon he ran his canoe ashore on a white strip of sand. This was at a bend, where the stream had widened, and gave promise of at least a few colors. He had bent down close to the edge of the water when something caught his attention on the wet sand. What he saw were the footprints of animals. Two had come down to drink. They had stood side by side. And the footprints were fresh—made not more than an hour or two before. A gleam of interest shot into Sandy's eyes. He looked behind him, and up and down the stream.

"Wolves," he grunted. "Wish I could 'a' shot at 'em with that old minute-gun back there. Gawd—listen to that! And in broad daylight, too!"

He jumped to his feet, staring off into the bush.

A quarter of a mile away Gray Wolf had caught the dreaded scent of man in the wind, and was giving voice to her warning. It was a long wailing howl, and not until its last echoes had died away did Sandy McTrigger move. Then he returned to the canoe, took out his old gun, put a fresh cap on the nipple and disappeared quickly over the edge of the bank.

For a week Kazan and Gray Wolf had been wandering about the headwaters of the McFarlane and this was the first time since the preceding winter that Gray Wolf had caught the scent of man in the air. When the wind brought the danger-signal to her she was alone. Two or three minutes before the scent came to her Kazan had left her side in swift pursuit of a snow-shoe rabbit, and she lay flat on her belly under a bush, waiting for him. In these moments when she was alone Gray Wolf was constantly sniffing the air. Blindness had developed her scent and hearing until they were next to infallible. First she had heard the rattle of Sandy McTrigger's paddle against the side of his canoe a quarter of a mile away. Scent had followed swiftly. Five minutes after her warning howl Kazan stood at her side, his head flung up, his jaws open and panting. Sandy had hunted Arctic foxes, and he was using the Eskimo tactics now, swinging in a half-circle until he should come up in the face of the wind. Kazan caught a single whiff of the man-tainted air and his spine grew stiff. But blind Gray Wolf was keener than the little red-eyed fox of the North. Her pointed nose slowly followed Sandy's progress. She heard a dry stick crack under his feet three hundred yards away. She caught the metallic click of his gun-barrel as it struck a birch sapling. The moment she lost Sandy in the wind she whined and rubbed herself against Kazan and trotted a few steps to the southwest.

At times such as this Kazan seldom refused to take guidance from her. They trotted away side by side and by the time Sandy was creeping up snake-like with the wind in his face, Kazan was peering from the fringe of river brush down upon the canoe on the white strip of sand. When Sandy returned, after an hour of futile stalking, two fresh tracks led straight down to the canoe. He looked at them in amazement and then a sinister grin wrinkled his ugly face. He chuckled as he went to his kit and dug out a small rubber bag. From this he drew a tightly corked bottle, filled with gelatine capsules. In each little capsule were five grains of strychnine. There were dark hints that once upon a time Sandy McTrigger had tried one of these capsules by dropping it in a cup of coffee and giving it to a man, but the police had never proved it. He was expert in the use of poison. Probably he had killed a thousand foxes in his time, and he chuckled again as he counted out a dozen of the capsules and thought how easy it would be to get this inquisitive pair of wolves. Two or three days before he had killed a caribou, and each of the capsules he now rolled up in a little ball of deer fat, doing the work with short sticks in place of his fingers, so that there would be no man-smell clinging to the death-baits. Before sundown Sandy set out at right-angles over the plain, planting the baits. Most of them he hung to low bushes. Others he dropped in worn rabbit and caribou trails. Then he returned to the creek and cooked his supper.

Then next morning he was up early, and off to the poison baits. The first bait was untouched. The second was as he had planted it. The third was gone. A thrill shot through Sandy as he looked about him. Somewhere within a radius of two or three hundred yards he would find his game. Then his glance fell to the ground under the bush where he had hung the poison capsule and an oath broke from his lips. The bait had not been eaten. The caribou fat lay scattered under the bush and still imbedded in the largest portion of it was the little white capsule—unbroken. It was Sandy's first experience with a wild creature whose instincts were sharpened by blindness, and he was puzzled. He had never known this to happen before. If a fox or a wolf could be lured to the point of touching a bait, it followed that the bait was eaten. Sandy went on to the fourth and the fifth baits. They were untouched. The sixth was torn to pieces, like the third. In this instance the capsule was broken and the white powder scattered. Two more poison baits Sandy found pulled down in this manner. He knew that Kazan and Gray Wolf had done the work, for he found the marks of their feet in a dozen different places. The accumulated bad humor of weeks of futile labor found vent in his disappointment and anger. At last he had found something tangible to curse. The failure of his poison baits he accepted as a sort of climax to his general bad luck. Everything was against him, he believed, and he made up his mind to return to Red Gold City. Early in the afternoon he launched his canoe and drifted down-stream with the current. He was content to let the current do all of the work to-day, and he used his paddle just enough to keep his slender craft head on. He leaned back comfortably and smoked his pipe, with the old rifle between his knees. The wind was in his face and he kept a sharp watch for game.

It was late in the afternoon when Kazan and Gray Wolf came out on a sand-bar five or six miles down-stream. Kazan was lapping up the cool water when Sandy drifted quietly around a bend a hundred yards above them. If the wind had been right, or if Sandy had been using his paddle, Gray Wolf would have detected danger. It was the metallic click-click of the old-fashioned lock of Sandy's rifle that awakened her to a sense of peril. Instantly she was thrilled by the nearness of it. Kazan heard the sound and stopped drinking to face it. In that moment Sandy pressed the trigger. A belch of smoke, a roar of gunpowder, and Kazan felt a red-hot stream of fire pass with the swiftness of a lightning-flash through his brain. He stumbled back, his legs gave way under him, and he crumpled down in a limp heap. Gray Wolf darted like a streak off into the bush. Blind, she had not seen Kazan wilt down upon the white sand. Not until she was a quarter of a mile away from the terrifying thunder of the white man's rifle did she stop and wait for him.

Sandy McTrigger grounded his canoe on the sand-bar with an exultant yell.

"Got you, you old devil, didn't I?" he cried. "I'd 'a' got the other, too, if I'd 'a' had something besides this damned old relic!"

He turned Kazan's head over with the butt of his gun, and the leer of satisfaction in his face gave place to a sudden look of amazement. For the first time he saw the collar about Kazan's neck.

"My Gawd, it ain't a wolf," he gasped. "It's a dog, Sandy McTrigger—*a dog!*"

Chapter XXII
Sandy'S Method

McTrigger dropped on his knees in the sand. The look of exultation was gone from his face. He twisted the collar about the dog's limp neck until he came to the worn plate, on which he could make out the faintly engraved letters *K-a-z-a-n*. He spelled the letters out one by one, and the look in his face was of one who still disbelieved what he had seen and heard.

"A dog!" he exclaimed again. "A dog, Sandy McTrigger an' a—a beauty!"

He rose to his feet and looked down on his victim. A pool of blood lay in the white sand at the end of Kazan's nose. After a moment Sandy bent over to see where his bullet had struck. His inspection filled him with a new and greater interest. The heavy ball from the muzzle-loader had struck Kazan fairly on top of the head. It was a glancing blow that had not even broken the skull, and like a flash Sandy understood the quivering and twitching of Kazan's shoulders and legs. He had thought that they were the last muscular throes of death. But Kazan was not dying. He was only stunned, and would be on his feet again in a few minutes. Sandy was a connoisseur of dogs—of dogs that had worn sledge traces. He had lived among them two-thirds of his life. He could tell their age, their value, and a part of their history at a glance. In the snow he could tell the trail of a Mackenzie hound from that of a Malemute, and the track of an Eskimo dog from that of a Yukon husky. He looked at Kazan's feet. They were wolf feet, and he chuckled. Kazan was part wild. He was big and powerful, and Sandy thought of the coming winter, and of the high prices that dogs would bring at Red Gold City. He went to the canoe and returned with a roll of stout moose-hide babiche. Then he sat down cross-legged in front of Kazan and began making a muzzle. He did this by plaiting babiche thongs in the same manner that one does in making the web of a snow-shoe. In ten minutes he had the muzzle over Kazan's nose and fastened securely about his neck. To the dog's collar he then fastened a ten-foot rope of babiche. After that he sat back and waited for Kazan to come to life.

When Kazan first lifted his head he could not see. There was a red film before his eyes. But this passed away swiftly and he saw the man. His first instinct was to rise to his feet. Three times he fell back before he could stand up. Sandy was squatted six feet from him, holding the end of the babiche, and grinning. Kazan's fangs gleamed back. He growled, and the crest along his spine rose menacingly. Sandy jumped to his feet.

"Guess I know what you're figgering on," he said. "I've had *your* kind before. The dam' wolves have turned you bad, an' you'll need a whole lot of club before you're right again. Now, look here."

Sandy had taken the precaution of bringing a thick club along with the babiche. He picked it up from where he had dropped it in the sand. Kazan's strength had fairly returned to him now. He was no longer dizzy. The mist had cleared away from his eyes. Before him he saw once more his old enemy, man—man and the club. All of the wild ferocity of his nature was roused in an instant. Without reasoning he knew that Gray Wolf was gone, and that this man was accountable for her going. He knew that this man had also brought him his own hurt, and what he ascribed to the man he also attributed to the club. In his newer undertaking of things, born of freedom and Gray Wolf, Man and Club were one and inseparable. With a snarl he leaped at Sandy. The man was not expecting a direct assault, and before he could raise his club or spring aside Kazan had landed full on his chest. The muzzle about Kazan's jaws saved him. Fangs that would have torn his throat open snapped harmlessly. Under the weight of the dog's body he fell back, as if struck down by a catapult.

As quick as a cat he was on his feet again, with the end of the babiche twisted several times about his hand. Kazan leaped again, and this time he was met by a furious swing of the club. It smashed against his shoulder, and sent him down in the sand. Before he could recover Sandy was upon him, with all the fury of a man gone mad. He shortened the babiche by twisting it again and again about his hand, and the club rose and fell with the skill and strength of one long accustomed to its use. The first blows served only to add to Kazan's hatred of man, and the ferocity and fearlessness of his attacks. Again and again he leaped in, and each time the club fell upon him with a force that threatened to break his bones. There was a tense hard look about Sandy's cruel mouth. He had never known a dog like this before, and he was a bit nervous, even with Kazan muzzled. Three times Kazan's fangs would have sunk deep in his flesh had it not been for the babiche. And if the thongs about his jaws should slip, or break—.

Sandy followed up the thought with a smashing blow that landed on Kazan's head, and once more the old battler fell limp upon the sand. McTrigger's breath was coming in quick gasps. He was almost winded. Not until the club slipped from his hand did he realize how desperate the fight had been. Before Kazan recovered from the blow that had stunned him Sandy examined the muzzle and strengthened it by adding another babiche thong. Then he dragged Kazan to a log that high water had thrown up on the shore a few yards away and made the end of the babiche rope fast to a dead snag. After that he pulled his canoe higher up on the sand, and began to prepare camp for the night.

For some minutes after Kazan's stunned senses had become normal he lay motionless, watching Sandy McTrigger. Every bone in his body gave him pain. His jaws were sore and bleeding. His upper lip was smashed where the club had fallen. One eye was almost closed. Several times Sandy came near, much pleased at what he regarded as the good results of the beating. Each time he brought the club. The third time he prodded Kazan with it, and the dog snarled and snapped savagely at the end of it. That was what Sandy wanted—it was an old trick of the dog-slaver. Instantly he was using the club again, until with a whining cry Kazan slunk under the protection of the snag to which he was fastened. He could scarcely drag himself. His right forepaw was smashed. His hindquarters sank under him. For a time after this second beating he could not have escaped had he been free.

Sandy was in unusually good humor.

"I'll take the devil out of you all right," he told Kazan for the twentieth time. "There's nothin' like beatin's to make dogs an' wimmin live up to the mark. A month from now you'll be worth two hundred dollars or I'll skin you alive!"

Three or four times before dusk Sandy worked to rouse Kazan's animosity. But there was no longer any desire left in Kazan to fight. His two terrific beatings, and the crushing blow of the bullet against his skull, had made him sick. He lay with his head between his forepaws, his eyes closed, and did not see McTrigger. He paid no attention to the meat that was thrown under his nose. He did not know when the last of the sun sank behind the western forests, or when the darkness came. But at last something roused him from his stupor. To his dazed and sickened brain it came like a call from out of the far past, and he raised his head and listened. Out on the sand McTrigger had built a fire, and the man stood in the red glow of it now, facing the dark shadows beyond the shoreline. He, too, was listening. What had roused Kazan came again now—the lost mourning cry of Gray Wolf far out on the plain.

With a whine Kazan was on his feet, tugging at the babiche. Sandy snatched up his club, and leaped toward him.

"Down, you brute!" he commanded.

In the firelight the club rose and fell with ferocious quickness. When McTrigger returned to the fire he was breathing hard again. He tossed his club beside the blankets he had spread out for a bed. It was a different looking club now. It was covered with blood and hair.

"Guess that'll take the spirit out of him," he chuckled. "It'll do that—or kill 'im!"

Several times that night Kazan heard Gray Wolf's call. He whined softly in response, fearing the club. He watched the fire until the last embers of it died out, and then cautiously dragged himself from under the snag. Two or three times he tried to stand on his feet, but fell back each time. His legs were not broken, but the pain of standing on them was excruciating. He was hot and feverish. All that night he had craved a drink of water. When Sandy crawled out from between his blankets in the early dawn he gave him both meat and water. Kazan drank the water, but would not touch the meat. Sandy regarded the change in him with satisfaction. By the time the sun was up he had finished his breakfast and was ready to leave. He approached Kazan fearlessly now, without the club. Untying the babiche he dragged the dog to the canoe. Kazan slunk in the sand while his captor fastened the end of the hide rope to the stern of the canoe. Sandy grinned. What was about to happen would be fun for him. In the Yukon he had learned how to take the spirit out of dogs.

He pushed off, bow foremost. Bracing himself with his paddle he then began to pull Kazan toward the water. In a few moments Kazan stood with his forefeet planted in the damp sand at the edge of the stream. For a brief interval Sandy allowed the babiche to fall slack. Then with a sudden powerful pull he jerked Kazan out into the water. Instantly he sent the canoe into midstream, swung it quickly down with the current, and began to paddle enough to keep the babiche taut about his victim's neck. In spite of his sickness and injuries Kazan was now compelled to swim to keep his head above water. In the wash of the canoe, and with Sandy's strokes growing steadily stronger, his position became each moment one of increasing torture. At times his shaggy head was pulled completely under water. At others Sandy would wait until he had drifted alongside, and then thrust him under with the end of his paddle. He grew weaker. At the end of a half-mile he was drowning. Not until then did Sandy pull him alongside and drag him into the canoe. The dog fell limp and gasping in the bottom. Brutal though Sandy's methods had been, they had worked his purpose. In Kazan there was no longer a desire to fight. He no longer struggled for freedom. He knew that this man was his master, and for the time his spirit was gone. All he desired now was to be allowed to lie in the bottom of the canoe, out of reach of the club, and safe from the water. The club lay between him and the man. The end of it was within a foot or two of his nose, and what he smelled was his own blood.

For five days and five nights the journey down-stream continued, and McTrigger's process of civilizing Kazan was continued in three more beatings with the club, and another resort to the water torture. On the morning of the sixth day they reached Red Gold City, and McTrigger put up his tent close to the river. Somewhere he obtained a chain for Kazan, and after fastening the dog securely back of the tent he cut off the babiche muzzle.

"You can't put on meat in a muzzle," he told his prisoner. "An' I want you to git strong—an' fierce as hell. I've got an idee. It's an idee you can lick your weight in wildcats. We'll pull off a stunt pretty soon that'll fill our pockets with dust. I've done it afore, and we can do it *here*. Wolf an' dog—s'elp me Gawd but it'll be a drawin' card!"

Twice a day after this he brought fresh raw meat to Kazan. Quickly Kazan's spirit and courage returned to him. The soreness left his limbs. His battered jaws healed. And after the fourth day each time that Sandy came with meat he greeted him with the challenge of his snarling fangs. McTrigger did not beat him now. He gave him no fish, no tallow and meal— nothing but raw meat. He traveled five miles up the river to bring in the fresh entrail of a caribou that had been killed. One day Sandy brought another man with him and when the stranger came a step too near Kazan made a sudden swift lunge at him. The man jumped back with a startled oath.

"He'll do," he growled. "He's lighter by ten or fifteen pounds than the Dane, but he's got the teeth, an' the quickness, an' he'll give a good show before he goes under."

"I'll make you a bet of twenty-five per cent. of my share that he don't go under," offered Sandy.

"Done!" said the other. "How long before he'll be ready?"

Sandy thought a moment.

"Another week," he said. "He won't have his weight before then. A week from to-day, we'll say. Next Tuesday night. Does that suit you, Harker?"

Harker nodded.

"Next Tuesday night," he agreed. Then he added, "I'll make it a *half* of my share that the Dane kills your wolf-dog."

Sandy took a long look at Kazan.

"I'll just take you on that," he said. Then, as he shook Harker's hand, "I don't believe there's a dog between here and the Yukon that can kill the wolf!"

Chapter XXIII
Professor McGill

Red Gold City was ripe for a night of relaxation. There had been some gambling, a few fights and enough liquor to create excitement now and then, but the presence of the mounted police had served to keep things unusually tame compared with events a few hundred miles farther north, in the Dawson country. The entertainment proposed by Sandy McTrigger and Jan Harker met with excited favor. The news spread for twenty miles about Red Gold City and there had never been greater excitement in the town than on the afternoon and night of the big fight. This was largely because Kazan and the huge Dane had been placed on exhibition, each dog in a specially made cage of his own, and a fever of betting began. Three hundred men, each of whom was paying five dollars to see the battle, viewed the gladiators through the bars of their cages. Harker's dog was a combination of Great Dane and mastiff, born in the North, and bred to the traces. Betting favored him by the odds of two to one. Occasionally it ran three to one. At these odds there was plenty of Kazan money. Those who were risking their money on him were the older wilderness men—men who had spent their lives among dogs, and who knew what the red glint in Kazan's eyes meant. An old Kootenay miner spoke low in another's ear:

"I'd bet on 'im even. I'd give odds if I had to. He'll fight all around the Dane. The Dane won't have no method."

"But he's got the weight," said the other dubiously. "Look at his jaws, an' his shoulders—"

"An' his big feet, an' his soft throat, an' the clumsy thickness of his belly," interrupted the Kootenay man. "For Gawd's sake, man, take my word for it, an' don't put your money on the Dane!"

Others thrust themselves between them. At first Kazan had snarled at all these faces about him. But now he lay back against the boarded side of the cage and eyed them sullenly from between his forepaws.

The fight was to be pulled off in Barker's place, a combination of saloon and cafe. The benches and tables had been cleared out and in the center of the one big room a cage ten feet square rested on a platform three and a half feet from the floor. Seats for the three hundred spectators were drawn closely around this. Suspended just above the open top of the cage were two big oil lamps with glass reflectors.

It was eight o'clock when Harker, McTrigger and two other men bore Kazan to the arena by means of the wooden bars that projected from the bottom of his cage. The big Dane was already in the fighting cage. He stood blinking his eyes in the brilliant light of the reflecting lamps. He pricked up his ears when he saw Kazan. Kazan did not show his fangs. Neither revealed the expected animosity. It was the first they had seen of each other, and a murmur of disappointment swept the ranks of the three hundred men. The Dane remained as motionless as a rock when Kazan was prodded from his own cage into the fighting cage. He did not leap or snarl. He regarded Kazan with a dubious questioning poise to his splendid head, and then looked again to the expectant and excited faces of the waiting men. For a few moments Kazan stood stiff-legged, facing the Dane. Then his shoulders dropped, and he, too, coolly faced the crowd that had expected a fight to the death. A laugh of derision swept through the closely seated rows. Catcalls, jeering taunts flung at McTrigger and Harker, and angry voices demanding their money back mingled with a tumult of growing discontent. Sandy's face was red with mortification and rage. The blue veins in Barker's forehead had swollen twice their normal size. He shook his fist in the face of the crowd, and shouted:

"Wait! Give 'em a chance, you dam' fools!"

At his words every voice was stilled. Kazan had turned. He was facing the huge Dane. And the Dane had turned his eyes to Kazan. Cautiously, prepared for a lunge or a sidestep, Kazan advanced a little. The Dane's shoulders bristled. He, too, advanced upon Kazan. Four feet apart they stood rigid. One could have heard a whisper in the room now. Sandy and Harker, standing close to the cage, scarcely breathed. Splendid in every limb and muscle, warriors of a hundred fights, and fearless to the point of death, the two half-wolf victims of man stood facing each other. None could see the questioning look in their brute eyes. None knew that in this thrilling

125

moment the unseen hand of the wonderful Spirit God of the wilderness hovered between them, and that one of its miracles was descending upon them. It was *understanding*. Meeting in the open—rivals in the traces—they would have been rolling in the throes of terrific battle. But *here* came that mute appeal of brotherhood. In the final moment, when only a step separated them, and when men expected to see the first mad lunge, the splendid Dane slowly raised his head and looked over Kazan's back through the glare of the lights. Harker trembled, and under his breath he cursed. The Dane's throat was open to Kazan. But between the beasts had passed the voiceless pledge of peace. Kazan did not leap. He turned. And shoulder to shoulder—splendid in their contempt of man—they stood and looked through the bars of their prison into the one of human faces.

A roar burst from the crowd—a roar of anger, of demand, of threat. In his rage Harker drew a revolver and leveled it at the Dane. Above the tumult of the crowd a single voice stopped him.

"Hold!" it demanded. "Hold—in the name of the law!"

For a moment there was silence. Every face turned in the direction of the voice. Two men stood on chairs behind the last row. One was Sergeant Brokaw, of the Royal Northwest Mounted. It was he who had spoken. He was holding up a hand, commanding silence and attention. On the chair beside him stood another man. He was thin, with drooping shoulders, and a pale smooth face—a little man, whose physique and hollow cheeks told nothing of the years he had spent close up along the raw edge of the Arctic. It was he who spoke now, while the sergeant held up his hand. His voice was low and quiet:

"I'll give the owners five hundred dollars for those dogs," he said.

Every man in the room heard the offer. Harker looked at Sandy. For an instant their heads were close together.

"They won't fight, and they'll make good team-mates," the little man went on. "I'll give the owners five hundred dollars."

Harker raised a hand.

"Make it six," he said. "Make it six and they're yours."

The little man hesitated. Then he nodded.

"I'll give you six hundred," he agreed.

Murmurs of discontent rose throughout the crowd. Harker climbed to the edge of the platform.

"We ain't to blame because they wouldn't fight," he shouted, "but if there's any of you small enough to want your money back you can git it as you go out. The dogs laid down on us, that's all. We ain't to blame."

The little man was edging his way between the chairs, accompanied by the sergeant of police. With his pale face close to the sapling bars of the cage he looked at Kazan and the big Dane.

"I guess we'll be good friends," he said, and he spoke so low that only the dogs heard his voice. "It's a big price, but we'll charge it to the Smithsonian, lads. I'm going to need a couple of four-footed friends of your moral caliber."

And no one knew why Kazan and the Dane drew nearer to the little scientist's side of the cage as he pulled out a big roll of bills and counted out six hundred dollars for Harker and Sandy McTrigger.

Chapter XXIV
Alone In Darkness

Never had the terror and loneliness of blindness fallen upon Gray Wolf as in the days that followed the shooting of Kazan and his capture by Sandy McTrigger. For hours after the shot she crouched in the bush back from the river, waiting for him to come to her. She had faith that he would come, as he had come a thousand times before, and she lay close on her belly, sniffing the air, and whining when it brought no scent of her mate. Day and night were alike an endless chaos of darkness to her now, but she knew when the sun went down. She sensed the first deepening shadows of evening, and she knew that the stars were out, and that the river lay in moonlight. It was a night to roam, and after a time she moved restlessly about in a small circle on the plain, and sent out her first inquiring call for Kazan. Up from the river came the pungent odor of smoke, and instinctively she knew that it was this smoke, and the nearness of man, that was keeping Kazan from her. But she went no nearer than that first circle made by her padded feet. Blindness had taught her to wait. Since the day of the battle on the Sun Rock, when the lynx had destroyed her eyes, Kazan had never failed her. Three times she called for him in the early night. Then she made herself a nest under a *banskian* shrub, and waited until dawn.

Just how she knew when night blotted out the last glow of the sun, so without seeing she knew when day came. Not until she felt the warmth of the sun on her back did her anxiety overcome her caution. Slowly she moved toward the river, sniffing the air and whining. There was no longer the smell of smoke in the air, and she could not catch the scent of man. She followed her own trail back to the sand-bar, and in the fringe of thick bush overhanging the white shore of the stream she stopped and listened. After a little she scrambled down and went straight to the spot where she and Kazan were drinking when the shot came. And there her nose struck the sand still wet and thick with Kazan's blood. She knew it was the blood of her mate, for the scent of him was all about her in the sand, mingled with the man-smell of Sandy McTrigger. She sniffed the trail of his body to the edge of the stream, where Sandy had dragged him to the canoe. She found the fallen tree to which he had been tied. And then she came upon one of the two clubs that Sandy had used to beat wounded Kazan into submissiveness. It was covered with blood and hair, and all at once Gray Wolf lay back on her haunches and turned her blind face to the sky, and there rose from her throat a cry for Kazan that drifted for miles on the wings of the south wind. Never had Gray Wolf given quite that cry before. It was not the "call" that comes with the moonlit nights, and neither was it the hunt-cry, nor the she-wolf's yearning for matehood. It carried with it the lament of death. And after that one cry Gray Wolf slunk back to the fringe of bush over the river, and lay with her face turned to the stream.

A strange terror fell upon her. She had grown accustomed to darkness, but never before had she been *alone* in that darkness. Always there had been the guardianship of Kazan's presence. She heard the clucking sound of a spruce hen in the bush a few yards away, and now that sound came to her as if from out of another world. A ground-mouse rustled through the grass close to her forepaws, and she snapped at it, and closed her teeth on a rock. The muscles of her shoulders twitched tremulously and she shivered as if stricken by intense cold. She was terrified by the darkness that shut out the world from her, and she pawed at her closed eyes, as if she might open them to light. Early in the afternoon she wandered back on the plain. It was different. It frightened her, and soon she returned to the beach, and snuggled down under the tree where Kazan had lain. She was not so frightened here. The smell of Kazan was strong about her. For an hour she lay motionless, with her head resting on the club clotted with his hair and blood. Night found her still there. And when the moon and the stars came out she crawled back into the pit in the white sand that Kazan's body had made under the tree.

With dawn she went down to the edge of the stream to drink. She could not see that the day was almost as dark as night, and that the gray-black sky was a chaos of slumbering storm. But she could smell the presence of it in the thick air, and could *feel* the forked flashes of lightning that rolled up with the dense pall from the south and west. The distant rumbling of thunder grew louder, and she huddled herself again under the tree. For hours the storm crashed over her, and the rain fell in a deluge. When it had finished she slunk out from her shelter like a thing beaten. Vainly she sought for one last scent of Kazan. The club was washed clean. Again the sand was white where Kazan's blood had reddened it. Even under the tree there was no sign of him left.

Until now only the terror of being alone in the pit of darkness that enveloped her had oppressed Gray Wolf. With afternoon came hunger. It was this hunger that drew her from the sand-bar, and she wandered back into the plain. A dozen times she scented game, and each time it evaded her. Even a ground-mouse that she cornered under a root, and dug out with her paws, escaped her fangs.

Thirty-six hours before this Kazan and Gray Wolf had left a half of their last kill a mile of two farther back on the plain. The kill was one of the big barren rabbits, and Gray Wolf turned in its direction. She did not require sight to find it. In her was developed to its finest point that sixth sense of the animal kingdom, the sense of orientation, and as straight as a pigeon might have winged its flight she cut through the bush to the spot where they had cached the rabbit. A white fox had been there ahead of her, and she found only scattered bits of hair and fur. What the fox had left the moose-birds and bush-jays had carried away. Hungrily Gray Wolf turned back to the river.

That night she slept again where Kazan had lain, and three times she called for him without answer. A heavy dew fell, and it drenched the last vestige of her mate's scent out of the sand. But still through the day that followed, and the day that followed that, blind Gray Wolf clung to the narrow rim of white sand. On the fourth day her hunger reached a point where she gnawed the bark from willow bushes. It was on this day that she made a discovery. She was drinking, when her sensitive nose touched something in the water's edge that was smooth, and bore a faint odor of flesh. It was one of the big northern river clams. She pawed it ashore, sniffing at the hard shell. Then she crunched it between her teeth. She had never tasted sweeter meat than that which she found inside, and she began hunting for other clams. She found many of them, and ate until she was no longer hungry. For three days more she remained on the bar.

127

And then, one night, the call came to her. It set her quivering with a strange new excitement—something that may have been a new hope, and in the moonlight she trotted nervously up and down the shining strip of sand, facing now the north, and now the south, and then the east and the west—her head flung up, listening, as if in the soft wind of the night she was trying to locate the whispering lure of a wonderful voice. And whatever it was that came to her came from out of the south and east. Off there—across the barren, far beyond the outer edge of the northern timber-line—was *home*. And off there, in her brute way, she reasoned that she must find Kazan. The call did not come from their old windfall home in the swamp. It came from beyond that, and in a flashing vision there rose through her blindness a picture of the towering Sun Rock, of the winding trail that led to it, and the cabin on the plain. It was there that blindness had come to her. It was there that day had ended, and eternal night had begun. And it was there that she had mothered her first-born. Nature had registered these things so that they could never be wiped out of her memory, and when the call came it was from the sunlit world where she had last known light and life and had last seen the moon and the stars in the blue night of the skies.

And to that call she responded, leaving the river and its food behind her—straight out into the face of darkness and starvation, no longer fearing death or the emptiness of the world she could not see; for ahead of her, two hundred miles away, she could see the Sun Rock, the winding trail, the nest of her first-born between the two big rocks—*and Kazan*!

Chapter XXV
The Last Of McTrigger

Sixty miles farther north Kazan lay at the end of his fine steel chain, watching little Professor McGill mixing a pail of tallow and bran. A dozen yards from him lay the big Dane, his huge jaws drooling in anticipation of the unusual feast which McGill was preparing. He showed signs of pleasure when McGill approached him with a quart of the mixture, and he gulped it between his huge jaws. The little man with the cold blue eyes and the gray-blond hair stroked his back without fear. His attitude was different when he turned to Kazan. His movements were filled with caution, and yet his eyes and his lips were smiling, and he gave the wolf-dog no evidence of his fear, if it could be called fear.

The little professor, who was up in the north country for the Smithsonian Institution, had spent a third of his life among dogs. He loved them, and understood them. He had written a number of magazine articles on dog intellect that had attracted wide attention among naturalists. It was largely because he loved dogs, and understood them more than most men, that he had bought Kazan and the big Dane on the night when Sandy McTrigger and his partner had tried to get them to fight to the death in the Red Gold City saloon. The refusal of the two splendid beasts to kill each other for the pleasure of the three hundred men who had assembled to witness the fight delighted him. He had already planned a paper on the incident. Sandy had told him the story of Kazan's capture, and of his wild mate, Gray Wolf, and the professor had asked him a thousand questions. But each day Kazan puzzled him more. No amount of kindness on his part could bring a responsive gleam in Kazan's eyes. Not once did Kazan signify a willingness to become friends. And yet he did not snarl at McGill, or snap at his hands when they came within reach. Quite frequently Sandy McTrigger came over to the little cabin where McGill was staying, and three times Kazan leaped at the end of his chain to get at him, and his white fangs gleamed as long as Sandy was in sight. Alone with McGill he became quiet. Something told him that McGill had come as a friend that night when he and the big Dane stood shoulder to shoulder in the cage that had been built for a slaughter pen. Away down in his brute heart he held McGill apart from other men. He had no desire to harm him. He tolerated him, but showed none of the growing affection of the huge Dane. It was this fact that puzzled McGill. He had never before known a dog that he could not make love him.

To-day he placed the tallow and bran before Kazan, and the smile in his face gave way to a look of perplexity. Kazan's lips had drawn suddenly back. A fierce snarl rolled deep in his throat. The hair along his spine stood up. His muscles twitched. Instinctively the professor turned. Sandy McTrigger had come up quietly behind him. His brutal face wore a grin as he looked at Kazan.

"It's a fool job—tryin' to make friends with *him*," he said. Then he added, with a sudden interested gleam in his eyes, "When you startin'?"

"With first frost," replied McGill. "It ought to come soon. I'm going to join Sergeant Conroy and his party at Fond du Lac by the first of October."

"And you're going up to Fond du Lac—alone?" queried Sandy. "Why don't you take a man?"

The little professor laughed softly.

"Why?" he asked. "I've been through the Athabasca waterways a dozen times, and know the trail as well as I know Broadway. Besides, I like to be alone. And the work isn't too hard, with the currents all flowing to the north and east."

Sandy was looking at the Dane, with his back to McGill. An exultant gleam shot for an instant into his eyes.

"You're taking the dogs?"

"Yes."

Sandy lighted his pipe, and spoke like one strangely curious.

"Must cost a heap to take these trips o' yourn, don't it?"

"My last cost about seven thousand dollars. This will cost five," said McGill.

"Gawd!" breathed Sandy. "An' you carry all that along with you! Ain't you afraid—something might happen—?"

The little professor was looking the other way now. The carelessness in his face and manner changed. His blue eyes grew a shade darker. A hard smile which Sandy did not see hovered about his lips for an instant. Then he turned, laughing.

"I'm a very light sleeper," he said. "A footstep at night rouses me. Even a man's breathing awakes me, when I make up my mind that I must be on my guard. And, besides"—he drew from his pocket a blue-steeled Savage automatic—"I know how to use *this*." He pointed to a knot in the wall of the cabin. "Observe," he said. Five times he fired at twenty paces, and when Sandy went up to look at the knot he gave a gasp. There was one jagged hole where the knot had been.

"Pretty good," he grinned. "Most men couldn't do better'n that with a rifle."

When Sandy left, McGill followed him with a suspicious gleam in his eyes, and a curious smile on his lips. Then he turned to Kazan.

"Guess you've got him figgered out about right, old man," he laughed softly. "I don't blame you very much for wanting to get him by the throat. Perhaps—"

He shoved his hands deep in his pockets, and went into the cabin. Kazan dropped his head between his forepaws, and lay still, with wide-open eyes. It was late afternoon, early in September, and each night brought now the first chill breaths of autumn. Kazan watched the last glow of the sun as it faded out of the southern skies. Darkness always followed swiftly after that, and with darkness came more fiercely his wild longing for freedom. Night after night he had gnawed at his steel chain. Night after night he had watched the stars, and the moon, and had listened for Gray Wolf's call, while the big Dane lay sleeping. To-night it was colder than usual, and the keen tang of the wind that came fresh from the west stirred him strangely. It set his blood afire with what the Indians call the Frost Hunger. Lethargic summer was gone and the days and nights of hunting were at hand. He wanted to leap out into freedom and run until he was exhausted, with Gray Wolf at his side. He knew that Gray Wolf was off there—where the stars hung low in the clear sky, and that she was waiting. He strained at the end of his chain, and whined. All that night he was restless—more restless than he had been at any time before. Once, in the far distance, he heard a cry that he thought was the cry of Gray Wolf, and his answer roused McGill from deep sleep. It was dawn, and the little professor dressed himself and came out of the cabin. With satisfaction he noted the exhilarating snap in the air. He wet his fingers and held them above his head, chuckling when he found the wind had swung into the north. He went to Kazan, and talked to him. Among other things he said, "This'll put the black flies to sleep, Kazan. A day or two more of it and we'll start."

Five days later McGill led first the Dane, and then Kazan, to a packed canoe. Sandy McTrigger saw them off, and Kazan watched for a chance to leap at him. Sandy kept his distance, and McGill watched the two with a thought that set the blood running swiftly behind the mask of his careless smile. They had slipped a mile down-stream when he leaned over and laid a fearless hand on Kazan's head. Something in the touch of that hand, and in the professor's voice, kept Kazan from a desire to snap at him. He tolerated the friendship with expressionless eyes and a motionless body.

"I was beginning to fear I wouldn't have much sleep, old boy," chuckled McGill ambiguously, "but I guess I can take a nap now and then with *you* along!"

He made camp that night fifteen miles up the lake shore. The big Dane he fastened to a sapling twenty yards from his small silk tent, but Kazan's chain he made fast to the butt of a stunted birch that held down the tent-flap. Before he went into the tent for the night McGill pulled out his automatic and examined it with care.

For three days the journey continued without a mishap along the shore of Lake Athabasca. On the fourth night McGill pitched his tent in a clump of *banskian* pine a hundred yards back from the water. All that day the wind had come steadily from behind them, and for at least a half of the day the professor had been watching Kazan closely. From the west there had now and then come a scent that stirred him uneasily. Since noon he had sniffed that wind. Twice McGill had heard him growling deep in his throat, and once, when the scent had come stronger than usual, he had bared his fangs, and the bristles stood up along his spine. For an hour after striking camp the little professor did not build a fire, but sat looking up the shore of the lake through his hunting glass. It was dusk when he returned to where he had put up his tent and chained the dogs. For a few moments he stood unobserved, looking at the wolf-dog. Kazan was still uneasy. He lay *facing* the west. McGill made note of this, for the big Dane lay behind Kazan—to the east. Under ordinary conditions Kazan would have faced him. He was sure now that there was something in the west wind. A little shiver ran up his back as he thought of what it might be.

Behind a rock he built a very small fire, and prepared supper. After this he went into the tent, and when he came out he carried a blanket under his arm. He chuckled as he stood for a moment over Kazan.

"We're not going to sleep in there to-night, old hoy," he said. "I don't like what you've found in the west wind. It may he a—*thunder-storm!*" He laughed at his joke, and buried himself in a clump of stunted *banskians* thirty paces from the tent. Here he rolled himself in his blanket, and went to sleep.

It was a quiet starlit night, and hours afterward Kazan dropped his nose between his forepaws and drowsed. It was the snap of a twig that roused him. The sound did not awaken the sluggish Dane but instantly Kazan's head was alert, his keen nostrils sniffing the air. What he had smelled all day was heavy about him now. He lay still and quivering. Slowly, from out of the *banskians* behind the tent, there came a figure. It was not the little professor. It approached cautiously, with lowered head and hunched shoulders, and the starlight revealed the murderous face of Sandy McTrigger. Kazan crouched low. He laid his head flat between his forepaws. His long fangs gleamed. But he made no sound that betrayed his concealment under a thick *banskian* shrub. Step by step Sandy approached, and at last he reached the flap of the tent. He did not carry a club or a whip in his hand now. In the place of either of those was the glitter of steel. At the door to the tent he paused, and peered in, his back to Kazan.

Silently, swiftly—the wolf now in every movement, Kazan came to his feet. He forgot the chain that held him. Ten feet away stood the enemy he hated above all others he had ever known. Every ounce of strength in his splendid body gathered itself for the spring. And then he leaped. This time the chain did not pull him back, almost neck-broken. Age and the elements had weakened the leather collar he had worn since the days of his slavery in the traces, and it gave way with a snap. Sandy turned, and in a second leap Kazan's fangs sank into the flesh of his arm. With a startled cry the man fell, and as they rolled over on the ground the big Dane's deep voice rolled out in thunderous alarm as he tugged at his leash. In the fall Kazan's hold was broken. In an instant he was on his feet, ready for another attack. And then the change came. He was *free*. The collar was gone from his neck. The forest, the stars, the whispering wind were all about him. *Here* were men, and off there was—Gray Wolf! His ears dropped, and he turned swiftly, and slipped like a shadow back into the glorious freedom of his world.

A hundred yards away something stopped him for an instant. It was not the big Dane's voice, but the sharp *crack—crack—crack*, of the little professor's automatic. And above that sound there rose the voice of Sandy McTrigger in a weird and terrible cry.

Chapter XXVI
An Empty World

Mile after mile Kazan went on. For a time he was oppressed by the shivering note of death that had come to him in Sandy McTrigger's cry, and he slipped through the *banskians* like a shadow, his ears flattened, his tail trailing, his hindquarters betraying that curious slinking quality of the wolf and dog stealing away from danger. Then he came out upon a plain, and the stillness, the billion stars in the clear vault of the sky, and the keen air that carried with it a breath of the Arctic barrens made him alert and questioning. He faced the direction of the wind. Somewhere off there, far to the south and west, was Gray Wolf. For the first time in many weeks he sat back on his haunches and gave the deep and vibrant call that echoed weirdly for miles about him. Back in the *banskians* the big Dane heard it, and whined. From over the still body of Sandy McTrigger the little professor looked up with a white tense face, and listened for a second cry. But instinct told Kazan that to that first call there would be no answer, and now he struck out swiftly, galloping mile after mile, as a dog follows the trail of its master home. He did not turn hack to the lake, nor was his direction toward Red Gold City. As straight as he might have followed a road blazed by the hand of man he cut across the forty miles of plain and swamp and forest and rocky ridge that lay between him and the McFarlane. All that night he did not call again for Gray Wolf. With him reasoning was a process brought about by habit—by precedent—and as Gray Wolf had waited for him many times before he knew that she would be waiting for him now near the sand-bar.

By dawn he had reached the river, within three miles of the sand-bar. Scarcely was the sun up when he stood on the white strip of sand where he and Gray Wolf had come down to drink. Expectantly and confidently he looked about him for Gray Wolf, whining softly, and wagging his tail. He began to search for her scent, but rains had washed even her footprints from the clean sand. All that day he searched for her along the river and out on the plain. He went to where they had killed their last rabbit. He sniffed at the bushes where the poison baits had hung. Again and again he sat back on his haunches and sent out his mating cry to her. And slowly, as he did these things, nature was working in him that miracle of the wild which the Crees have named the "spirit call." As it had worked in Gray Wolf, so now it stirred the blood of Kazan. With the going of the sun, and the sweeping about him of shadowy night, he turned more and more to the south and east. His whole world was made up of the trails over which he had hunted. Beyond those places he did not know that there was such a thing as existence. And in that world, small in his understanding of things, was Gray Wolf. He could not miss her. That world, in his comprehension of it, ran from the McFarlane in a narrow trail through the forests and over the plains to the little valley from which the beavers had driven them. If Gray Wolf was not here—she was there, and tirelessly he resumed his quest of her.

Not until the stars were fading out of the sky again, and gray day was giving place to night, did exhaustion and hunger stop him. He killed a rabbit, and for hours after he had feasted he lay close to his kill, and slept. Then he went on.

The fourth night he came to the little valley between the two ridges, and under the stars, more brilliant now in the chill clearness of the early autumn nights, he followed the creek down into their old swamp home. It was broad day when he reached the edge of the great beaver pond that now completely surrounded the windfall under which Gray-Wolf's second-born had come into the world. Broken Tooth and the other beavers had wrought a big change in what had once been his home and Gray Wolf's, and for many minutes Kazan stood silent and motionless at the edge of the pond, sniffing the air heavy with the unpleasant odor of the usurpers. Until now his spirit had remained unbroken. Footsore, with thinned sides and gaunt head, he circled slowly through the swamp. All that day he searched. And his crest lay flat now, and there was a hunted look in the droop of his shoulders and in the shifting look of his eyes. Gray Wolf was gone.

Slowly nature was impinging that fact upon him. She had passed out of his world and out of his life, and he was filled with a loneliness and a grief so great that the forest seemed strange, and the stillness of the wild a thing that now oppressed and frightened him. Once more the dog in him was mastering the wolf. With Gray Wolf he had possessed the world of freedom. Without her, that world was so big and strange and empty that it appalled him. Late in the afternoon he came upon a little pile of crushed clamshells on the shore of the stream. He sniffed at them—turned away—went back, and sniffed again. It was where Gray Wolf had made a last feast in the swamp before continuing south. But the scent she had left behind was not strong enough to tell Kazan, and for a second time he turned away. That night he slunk under a log, and cried himself to sleep. Deep in the night he grieved in his uneasy slumber, like a child. And day after day, and night after night, Kazan remained a slinking creature of the big swamp, mourning for the one creature that had brought him out of chaos into light, who had filled his world for him, and who, in going from him, had taken from this world even the things that Gray Wolf had lost in her blindness.

Chapter XXVII
The Call Of Sun Rock

In the golden glow of the autumn sun there came up the stream overlooked by the Sun Rock one day a man, a woman and a child in a canoe. Civilization had done for lovely Joan what it had done for many another wild flower transplanted from the depths of the wilderness. Her cheeks were thin. Her blue eyes had lost their luster. She coughed, and when she coughed the man looked at her with love and fear in his eyes. But now, slowly, the man had begun to see the transformation, and on the day their canoe pointed up the stream and into the wonderful valley that had been their home before the call of the distant city came to them, he noted the flush gathering once more in her cheeks, the fuller redness of her lips, and the gathering glow of happiness and content in her eyes. He laughed softly as he saw these things, and he blessed the forests. In the canoe she had leaned back, with her head almost against his shoulder, and he stopped paddling to draw her to him, and run his fingers through the soft golden masses of her hair.

"You are happy again, Joan," he laughed joyously. "The doctors were right. You are a part of the forests."

"Yes, I am happy," she whispered, and suddenly there came a little thrill into her voice, and she pointed to a white finger of sand running out into the stream. "Do you remember—years and years ago, it seems—that Kazan left us here? *She* was on the sand over there, calling to him. Do you remember?" There was a little tremble about her mouth, and she added, "I wonder—where they—have gone."

The cabin was as they had left it. Only the crimson *bakneesh* had grown up about it, and shrubs and tall grass had sprung up near its walls. Once more it took on life, and day by day the color came deeper into Joan's cheeks, and her voice was filled with its old wild sweetness of song. Joan's husband cleared the trails over his old trap-lines, and Joan and the little Joan, who romped and talked now, transformed the cabin into *home*. One night the man returned to the cabin late, and when he came in there was a glow of excitement in Joan's blue eyes, and a tremble in her voice when she greeted him.

"Did you hear it?" she asked. "Did you hear—*the call?*"

He nodded, stroking her soft hair.

"I was a mile back in the creek swamp," he said. "I heard it!"

Joan's hands clutched his arms.

"It wasn't Kazan," she said. "I would recognize *his* voice. But it seemed to me it was like the other—the call that came that morning from the sand-bar, his *mate?*"

The man was thinking. Joan's fingers tightened. She was breathing a little quickly.

"Will you promise me this?" she asked, "Will you promise me that you will never hunt or trap for wolves?"

"I had thought of that," he replied. "I thought of it—after I heard the call. Yes, I will promise."

Joan's arms stole up about his neck.

"We loved Kazan," she whispered. "And you might kill him—or *her!*"

Suddenly she stopped. Both listened. The door was a little ajar, and to them there came again the wailing mate-call of the wolf. Joan ran to the door. Her husband followed. Together they stood silent, and with tense breath Joan pointed over the starlit plain.

"Listen! Listen!" she commanded. "It's her cry, *and it came from the Sun Rock!*"

She ran out into the night, forgetting that the man was close behind her now, forgetting that little Joan was alone in her bed. And to them, from miles and miles across the plain, there came a wailing cry in answer—a cry that seemed a part of the wind, and that thrilled Joan until her breath broke in a strange sob.

Farther out on the plain she went and then stopped, with the golden glow of the autumn moon and the stars shimmering in her hair and eyes. It was many minutes before the cry came again, and then it was so near that Joan put her hands to her mouth, and her cry rang out over the plain as in the days of old.

"*Kazan! Kazan! Kazan!*"

At the top of the Sun Rock, Gray Wolf—gaunt and thinned by starvation—heard the woman's cry, and the call that was in her throat died away in a whine. And to the north a swiftly moving shadow stopped for a moment, and stood like a thing of rock under the starlight. It was Kazan. A strange fire leaped through his body. Every fiber of his brute understanding was afire with the knowledge that here was *home*. It was here, long ago, that he had lived, and loved, and fought—and all at once the dreams that had grown faded and indistinct in his memory came back to him as real living things. For, coming to him faintly over the plain, *he heard Joan's voice!*

In the starlight Joan stood, tense and white, when from out of the pale mists of the moon-glow he came to her, cringing on his belly, panting and wind-run, and with a strange whining note in his throat. And as Joan went to him, her arms reaching out, her lips sobbing his name over and over again, the man stood and looked down upon them with the wonder of a new and greater understanding in his face. He had no fear of the wolf-dog now. And as Joan's arms hugged Kazan's great shaggy head up to her he heard the whining gasping joy of the beast and the sobbing whispering voice of the girl, and with tensely gripped hands he faced the Sun Rock.

"My Gawd," he breathed. "I believe—it's so—"

As if in response to the thought in his mind, there came once more across the plain Gray Wolf's mate-seeking cry of grief and of loneliness. Swiftly as though struck by a lash Kazan was on his feet—oblivious of Joan's touch, of her voice, of the presence of the man. In another instant he was gone, and Joan flung herself against her husband's breast, and almost fiercely took his face between her two hands.

"*Now* do you believe?" she cried pantingly. "*Now* do you believe in the God of my world—the God I have lived with, the God that gives souls to the wild things, the God that—that has brought—us, all—together—once more—*home*!"

His arms closed gently about her.

"I believe, my Joan," he whispered.

"And you understand—now—what it means, 'Thou shalt not kill'?"

"Except that it brings us life—yes, I understand," he replied.

Her warm soft hands stroked his face. Her blue eyes, filled with the glory of the stars, looked up into his.

"Kazan and *she*—you and I—and the baby! Are you sorry—that we came back?" she asked.

So close he drew her against his breast that she did not hear the words he whispered in the soft warmth of her hair. And after that, for many hours, they sat in the starlight in front of the cabin door. But they did not hear again that lonely cry from the Sun Rock. Joan and her husband understood.

"He'll visit us again to-morrow," the man said at last. "Come, Joan, let us go to bed."

Together they entered the cabin.

And that night, side by side, Kazan and Gray Wolf hunted again in the moonlit plain.

The Grizzly King

CHAPTER ONE

With the silence and immobility of a great reddish-tinted rock, Thor stood for many minutes looking out over his domain. He could not see far, for, like all grizzlies, his eyes were small and far apart, and his vision was bad. At a distance of a third or a half a mile he could make out a goat or a mountain sheep, but beyond that his world was a vast sun-filled or night-darkened mystery through which he ranged mostly by the guidance of sound and smell.

It was the sense of smell that held him still and motionless now. Up out of the valley a scent had come to his nostrils that he had never smelled before. It was something that did not belong there, and it stirred him strangely. Vainly his slow-working brute mind struggled to comprehend it. It was not caribou, for he had killed many caribou; it was not goat; it was not sheep; and it was not the smell of the fat and lazy whistlers sunning themselves on the rocks, for he had eaten hundreds of whistlers. It was a scent that did not enrage him, and neither did it frighten him. He was curious, and yet he did not go down to seek it out. Caution held him back.

If Thor could have seen distinctly for a mile, or two miles, his eyes would have discovered even less than the wind brought to him from down the valley. He stood at the edge of a little plain, with the valley an eighth of a mile below him, and the break over which he had come that afternoon an eighth of a mile above him. The plain was very much like a cup, perhaps an acre in extent, in the green slope of the mountain. It was covered with rich, soft grass and June flowers, mountain violets and patches of forget-me-nots, and wild asters and hyacinths, and in the centre of it was a fifty-foot spatter of soft mud which Thor visited frequently when his feet became rock-sore.

To the east and the west and the north of him spread out the wonderful panorama of the Canadian Rockies, softened in the golden sunshine of a June afternoon.

From up and down the valley, from the breaks between the peaks, and from the little gullies cleft in shale and rock that crept up to the snow-lines came a soft and droning murmur. It was the music of running water. That music was always in the air, for the rivers, the creeks, and the tiny streams gushing down from the snow that lay eternally up near the clouds were never still.

There were sweet perfumes as well as music in the air. June and July—the last of spring and the first of summer in the northern mountains—were commingling. The earth was bursting with green; the early flowers were turning the sunny slopes into coloured splashes of red and white and purple, and everything that had life was singing—the fat whistlers on their rocks, the pompous little gophers on their mounds, the big bumblebees that buzzed from flower to flower, the hawks in the valley, and the eagles over the peaks. Even Thor was singing in his way, for as he had paddled through the soft mud a few minutes before he had rumbled curiously deep down in his great chest. It was not a growl or a roar or a snarl; it was the noise he made when he was contented. It was his song.

And now, for some mysterious reason, there had suddenly come a change in this wonderful day for him. Motionless he still sniffed the wind. It puzzled him. It disquieted him without alarming him. To the new and strange smell that was in the air he was as keenly sensitive as a child's tongue to the first sharp touch of a drop of brandy. And then, at last, a low and sullen growl came like a distant roll of thunder from out of his chest. He was overlord of these domains, and slowly his brain told him that there should be no smell which he could not comprehend, and of which he was not the master.

Thor reared up slowly, until the whole nine feet of him rested on his haunches, and he sat like a trained dog, with his great forefeet, heavy with mud, drooping in front of his chest. For ten years he had lived in these mountains and never had he smelled that smell. He defied it. He waited for it, while it came stronger and nearer. He did not hide himself. Clean-cut and unafraid, he stood up.

He was a monster in size, and his new June coat shone a golden brown in the sun. His forearms were almost as large as a man's body; the three largest of his five knifelike claws were five and a half inches long; in the mud his feet had left tracks that were fifteen inches from tip to tip. He was fat, and sleek, and powerful. His eyes, no larger than hickory nuts, were eight inches apart. His two upper fangs, sharp as stiletto points, were as long as a man's thumb, and between his great jaws he could crush the neck of a caribou.

Thor's life had been free of the presence of man, and he was not ugly. Like most grizzlies, he did not kill for the pleasure of killing. Out of a herd he would take one caribou, and he would eat that caribou to the marrow in the last bone. He was a peaceful king. He had one law: "Let me alone!" he said, and the voice of that law was in his attitude as he sat on his haunches sniffing the strange smell.

In his massive strength, in his aloneness and his supremacy, the great bear was like the mountains, unrivalled in the valleys as they were in the skies. With the mountains, he had come down out of the ages. He was part of them. The history of his race had begun and was dying among them, and they were alike in many ways. Until this day he could not remember when anything had come to question his might and his right—except those of his own kind. With such rivals he had fought fairly and more than once to the death. He was ready to fight again, if it came to a question of sovereignty over the ranges which he claimed as his own. Until he was beaten he was dominator, arbiter, and despot, if he chose to be. He was dynast of the rich valleys and the green slopes, and liege lord of all living things about him. He had won and kept these things openly, without strategy or treachery. He was hated and he was feared, but he was without hatred or fear of his own—and he was honest. Therefore he waited openly for the strange thing that was coming to him from down the valley.

As he sat on his haunches, questioning the air with his keen brown nose, something within him was reaching back into dim and bygone generations. Never before had he caught the taint that was in his nostrils, yet now that it came to him it did not seem altogether new. He could not place it. He could not picture it. Yet he knew that it was a menace and a threat.

For ten minutes he sat like a carven thing on his haunches. Then the wind shifted, and the scent grew less and less, until it was gone altogether.

Thor's flat ears lifted a little. He turned his huge head slowly so that his eyes took in the green slope and the tiny plain. He easily forgot the smell now that the air was clear and sweet again. He dropped on his four feet, and resumed his gopher-hunting.

There was something of humour in his hunt. Thor weighed a thousand pounds; a mountain gopher is six inches long and weighs six ounces. Yet Thor would dig energetically for an hour, and rejoice at the end by swallowing the fat little gopher like a pill; it was his *bonne bouche*, the luscious tidbit in the quest of which he spent a third of his spring and summer digging.

He found a hole located to his satisfaction and began throwing out the earth like a huge dog after a rat. He was on the crest of the slope. Once or twice during the next half-hour he lifted his head, but he was no longer disturbed by the strange smell that had come to him with the wind.

CHAPTER TWO

A mile down the valley Jim Langdon stopped his horse where the spruce and balsam timber thinned out at the mouth of a coulee, looked ahead of him for a breathless moment or two, and then with an audible gasp of pleasure swung his right leg over so that his knee crooked restfully about the horn of his saddle, and waited.

Two or three hundred yards behind him, still buried in the timber, Otto was having trouble with Dishpan, a contumacious pack-mare. Langdon grinned happily as he listened to the other's vociferations, which threatened Dishpan with every known form of torture and punishment, from instant disembowelment to the more merciful end of losing her brain through the medium of a club. He grinned because Otto's vocabulary descriptive of terrible things always impending over the heads of his sleek and utterly heedless pack-horses was one of his chief joys. He knew that if Dishpan should elect to turn somersaults while diamond-hitched under her pack, big, good-natured Bruce Otto would do nothing more than make the welkin ring with his terrible, blood-curdling protest.

One after another the six horses of their outfit appeared out of the timber, and last of all rode the mountain man. He was gathered like a partly released spring in his saddle, an attitude born of years in the mountains, and because of a certain difficulty he had in distributing gracefully his six-foot-two-inch length of flesh and bone astride a mountain cayuse.

Upon his appearance Langdon dismounted, and turned his eyes again up the valley. The stubbly blond beard on his face did not conceal the deep tan painted there by weeks of exposure in the mountains; he had opened his shirt at the throat, exposing a neck darkened by sun and wind; his eyes were of a keen, searching blue-gray, and they quested the country ahead of him now with the joyous intentness of the hunter and the adventurer.

Langdon was thirty-five. A part of his life he spent in the wild places; the other part he spent in writing about the things he found there. His companion was five years his junior in age, but had the better of him by six inches in length of anatomy, if those additional inches could be called an advantage. Bruce thought they were not. "The devil of it is I ain't done growin' yet!" he often explained.

He rode up now and unlimbered himself. Langdon pointed ahead.

"Did you ever see anything to beat that?" he asked.

"Fine country," agreed Bruce. "Mighty good place to camp, too, Jim. There ought to be caribou in this range, an' bear. We need some fresh meat. Gimme a match, will you?"

It had come to be a habit with them to light both their pipes with one match when possible. They performed this ceremony now while viewing the situation. As he puffed the first luxurious cloud of smoke from his bulldog, Langdon nodded toward the timber from which they had just come.

"Fine place for our tepee," he said. "Dry wood, running water, and the first good balsam we've struck in a week for our beds. We can hobble the horses in that little open plain we crossed a quarter of a mile back. I saw plenty of buffalo grass and a lot of wild timothy."

He looked at his watch.

"It's only three o'clock. We might go on. But—what do you say? Shall we stick for a day or two, and see what this country looks like?"

"Looks good to me," said Bruce.

He sat down as he spoke, with his back to a rock, and over his knee he levelled a long brass telescope. From his saddle Langdon unslung a binocular glass imported from Paris. The telescope was a relic of the Civil War. Together, their shoulders touching as they steadied themselves against the rock, they studied the rolling slopes and the green sides of the mountains ahead of them.

They were in the Big Game country, and what Langdon called the Unknown. So far as he and Bruce Otto could discover, no other white man had ever preceded them. It was a country shut in by tremendous ranges, through which it had taken them twenty days of sweating toil to make a hundred miles.

That afternoon they had crossed the summit of the Great Divide that split the skies north and south, and through their glasses they were looking now upon the first green slopes and wonderful peaks of the Firepan Mountains. To the northward—and they had been travelling north—was the Skeena River; on the west and south were the Babine range and waterways; eastward, over the Divide, was the Driftwood, and still farther eastward the Ominica range and the tributaries of the Finley. They had started from civilization on the tenth day of May and this was the thirtieth of June.

As Langdon looked through his glasses he believed that at last they had reached the bourne of their desires. For nearly two months they had worked to get beyond the trails of men, and they had succeeded. There were no hunters here. There were no prospectors. The valley ahead of them was filled with golden promise, and as he sought out the first of its mystery and its wonder his heart was filled with the deep and satisfying joy which only men like Langdon can fully understand. To his friend and comrade, Bruce Otto, with whom he had gone five times into the North country, all mountains and all valleys were very much alike; he was born among them, he had lived among them all his life, and he would probably die among them.

It was Bruce who gave him a sudden sharp nudge with his elbow.

"I see the heads of three caribou crossing a dip about a mile and a half up the valley," he said, without taking his eyes from the telescope.

"And I see a Nanny and her kid on the black shale of that first mountain to the right," replied Langdon. "And, by George, there's a Sky Pilot looking down on her from a crag a thousand feet above the shale! He's got a beard a foot long. Bruce, I'll bet we've struck a regular Garden of Eden!"

"Looks it," vouchsafed Bruce, coiling up his long legs to get a better rest for his telescope. "If this ain't a sheep an' bear country, I've made the worst guess I ever made in my life."

For five minutes they looked, without a word passing between them. Behind them their horses were nibbling hungrily in the thick, rich grass. The sound of the many waters in the mountains droned in their ears, and the valley seemed sleeping in a sea of sunshine. Langdon could think of nothing more comparable than that—slumber. The valley was like a great, comfortable, happy cat, and the sounds they heard, all commingling in that pleasing drone, was its drowsy purring. He was focussing his glass a little more closely on the goat standing watchfully on its crag, when Otto spoke again.

"I see a grizzly as big as a house!" he announced quietly.

Bruce seldom allowed his equanimity to be disturbed, except by the pack-horses. Thrilling news like this he always introduced as unconcernedly as though speaking of a bunch of violets.

Langdon sat up with a jerk.

"Where?" he demanded.

He leaned over to get the range of the other's telescope, every nerve in his body suddenly aquiver.

"See that slope on the second shoulder, just beyond the ravine over there?" said Bruce, with one eye closed and the other still glued to the telescope. "He's halfway up, digging out a gopher."

Langdon focussed his glass on the slope, and a moment later an excited gasp came from him.

"See 'im?" asked Bruce.

"The glass has pulled him within four feet of my nose," replied Langdon. "Bruce, that's the biggest grizzly in the Rocky Mountains!"

"If he ain't, he's his twin brother," chuckled the packer, without moving a muscle. "He beats your eight-footer by a dozen inches, Jimmy! An'"—he paused at this psychological moment to pull a plug of black MacDonald from his pocket and bite off a mouthful, without taking the telescope from his eye—"an' the wind is in our favour an' he's as busy as a flea!" he finished.

Otto unwound himself and rose to his feet, and Langdon jumped up briskly. In such situations as this there was a mutual understanding between them which made words unnecessary. They led the eight horses back into the edge of the timber and tied them there, took their rifles from the leather holsters, and each was careful to put a sixth cartridge in the chamber of his weapon. Then for a matter of two minutes they both studied the slope and its approaches with their naked eyes.

"We can slip up the ravine," suggested Langdon.

Bruce nodded.

"I reckon it's a three-hundred-yard shot from there," he said. "It's the best we can do. He'd get our wind if we went below 'im. If it was a couple o' hours earlier—"

"We'd climb over the mountain and come down on him from *above*!" exclaimed Langdon, laughing.

"Bruce, you're the most senseless idiot on the face of the globe when it comes to climbing mountains! You'd climb over Hardesty or Geikie to shoot a goat from above, even though you could get him from the valley without any work at all. I'm glad it isn't morning. We can get that bear from the ravine!"

"Mebbe," said Bruce, and they started.

They walked openly over the green, flower-carpeted meadows ahead of them. Until they came within at least half a mile of the grizzly there was no danger of him seeing them. The wind had shifted, and was almost in their faces. Their swift walk changed to a dog-trot, and they swung in nearer to the slope, so that for fifteen minutes a huge knoll concealed the grizzly. In another ten minutes they came to the ravine, a narrow, rock-littered and precipitous gully worn in the mountainside by centuries of spring floods gushing down from the snow-peaks above. Here they made cautious observation.

The big grizzly was perhaps six hundred yards up the slope, and pretty close to three hundred yards from the nearest point reached by the gully.

Bruce spoke in a whisper now.

"You go up an' do the stalkin', Jimmy," he said. "That bear's goin' to do one of two things if you miss or only wound 'im—one o' three, mebbe: he's going to investigate *you*, or he's going up over the break, or he's comin' down in the valley—this way. We can't keep 'im from goin' over the break, an' if he tackles you—just summerset it down the gully. You can beat 'im out. He's most apt to come this way if you don't get 'im, so I'll wait here. Good luck to you, Jimmy!"

With this he went out and crouched behind a rock, where he could keep an eye on the grizzly, and Langdon began to climb quietly up the boulder-strewn gully.

CHAPTER THREE

Of all the living creatures in this sleeping valley, Thor was the busiest. He was a bear with individuality, you might say. Like some people, he went to bed very early; he began to get sleepy in October, and turned in for his long nap in November. He slept until April, and usually was a week or ten days behind other bears in waking. He was a sound sleeper, and when awake he was very wide awake. During April and May he permitted himself to doze considerably in the warmth of sunny rocks, but from the beginning of June until the middle of September he closed his eyes in real sleep just about four hours out of every twelve.

He was very busy as Langdon began his cautious climb up the gully. He had succeeded in getting his gopher, a fat, aldermanic old patriarch who had disappeared in one crunch and a gulp, and he was now absorbed in finishing off his day's feast with an occasional fat, white grub and a few sour ants captured from under stones which he turned over with his paw.

In his search after these delicacies Thor used his right paw in turning over the rocks. Ninety-nine out of every hundred bears—probably a hundred and ninety-nine out of every two hundred—are left-handed; Thor was right-handed. This gave him an advantage in fighting, in fishing, and in stalking meat, for a grizzly's right arm is longer than his left—so much longer that if he lost his sixth sense of orientation he would be constantly travelling in a circle.

In his quest Thor was headed for the gully. His huge head hung close to the ground. At short distances his vision was microscopic in its keenness; his olfactory nerves were so sensitive that he could catch one of the big rock-ants with his eyes shut.

He would choose the flat rocks mostly. His huge right paw, with its long claws, was as clever as a human hand. The stone lifted, a sniff or two, a lick of his hot, flat tongue, and he ambled on to the next.

He took this work with tremendous seriousness, much like an elephant hunting for peanuts hidden in a bale of hay. He saw no humour in the operation. As a matter of fact, Nature had not intended there should be any humour about it. Thor's time was more or less valueless, and during the course of a summer he absorbed in his system a good many hundred thousand sour ants, sweet grubs, and juicy insects of various kinds, not to mention a host of gophers and still tinier rock-rabbits. These small things all added to the huge rolls of fat which it was necessary for him to store up for that "absorptive consumption" which kept him alive during his long winter sleep. This was why Nature had made his little greenish-brown eyes twin microscopes, infallible at distances of a few feet, and almost worthless at a thousand yards.

As he was about to turn over a fresh stone Thor paused in his operations. For a full minute he stood nearly motionless. Then his head swung slowly, his nose close to the ground. Very faintly he had caught an exceedingly pleasing odour. It was so faint that he was afraid of losing it if he moved. So he stood until he was sure of himself, then he swung his huge shoulders around and descended two yards down the slope, swinging his head slowly from right to left, and sniffing. The scent grew stronger. Another two yards down the slope he found it very strong under a rock. It was a big rock, and weighed probably two hundred pounds. Thor dragged it aside with his one right hand as if it were no more than a pebble.

Instantly there was a wild and protesting chatter, and a tiny striped rock-rabbit, very much like a chipmunk, darted away just as Thor's left hand came down with a smash that would have broken the neck of a caribou.

It was not the scent of the rock-rabbit, but the savour of what the rock-rabbit had stored under the stone that had attracted Thor. And this booty still remained—a half-pint of ground-nuts piled carefully in a little hollow lined with moss. They were not really nuts. They were more like diminutive potatoes, about the size of cherries, and very much like potatoes in appearance. They were starchy and sweet, and fattening. Thor enjoyed them immensely, rumbling in that curious satisfied way deep down in his chest as he feasted. And then he resumed his quest.

He did not hear Langdon as the hunter came nearer and nearer up the broken gully. He did not smell him, for the wind was fatally wrong. He had forgotten the noxious man-smell that had disturbed and irritated him an hour before. He was quite happy; he was good-humoured; he was fat and sleek. An irritable, cross-grained, and quarrelsome bear is always thin. The true hunter knows him as soon as he sets eyes on him. He is like the rogue elephant.

Thor continued his food-seeking, edging still closer to the gully. He was within a hundred and fifty yards of it when a sound suddenly brought him alert. Langdon, in his effort to creep up the steep side of the gully for a shot, had accidentally loosened a rock. It went crashing down the ravine, starting other stones that followed in a noisy clatter. At the foot of the coulee, six hundred yards down, Bruce swore softly under his breath. He saw Thor sit up. At that distance he was going to shoot if the bear made for the break.

For thirty seconds Thor sat on his haunches. Then he started for the ravine, ambling slowly and deliberately. Langdon, panting and inwardly cursing at his ill luck, struggled to make the last ten feet to the edge of the slope. He heard Bruce yell, but he could not make out the warning. Hands and feet he dug fiercely into shale and rock as he fought to make those last three or four yards as quickly as possible.

He was almost to the top when he paused for a moment and turned his eyes upward. His heart went into his throat, and he started. For ten seconds he could not move. Directly over him was a monster head and a huge hulk of shoulder. Thor was looking down on him, his jaws agape, his finger-long fangs snarling, his eyes burning with a greenish-red fire.

In that moment Thor saw his first of man. His great lungs were filled with the hot smell of him, and suddenly he turned away from that smell as if from a plague. With his rifle half under him Langdon had had no opportunity to shoot. Wildly he clambered up the remaining few feet. The shale and stones slipped and slid under him. It was a matter of sixty seconds before he pulled himself over the top.

Thor was a hundred yards away, speeding in a rolling, ball-like motion toward the break. From the foot of the coulee came the sharp crack of Otto's rifle. Langdon squatted quickly, raising his left knee for a rest, and at a hundred and fifty yards began firing.

Sometimes it happens that an hour—a minute—changes the destiny of man; and the ten seconds which followed swiftly after that first shot from the foot of the coulee changed Thor. He had got his fill of the man-smell. He had seen man. And now he *felt* him.

It was as if one of the lightning flashes he had often seen splitting the dark skies had descended upon him and had entered his flesh like a red-hot knife; and with that first burning agony of pain came the strange, echoing roar of the rifles. He had turned up the slope when the bullet struck him in the fore-shoulder, mushrooming its deadly soft point against his tough hide, and tearing a hole through his flesh—but without touching the bone. He was two hundred yards from the ravine when it hit; he was nearer three hundred when the stinging fire seared him again, this time in his flank.

Neither shot had staggered his huge bulk, twenty such shots would not have killed him. But the second stopped him, and he turned with a roar of rage that was like the bellowing of a mad bull—a snarling, thunderous cry of wrath that could have been heard a quarter of a mile down the valley.

Bruce heard it as he fired his sixth unavailing shot at seven hundred yards. Langdon was reloading. For fifteen seconds Thor offered himself openly, roaring his defiance, challenging the enemy he could no longer see; and then at Langdon's seventh shot, a whiplash of fire raked his back, and in strange dread of this lightning which he could not fight, Thor continued up over the break. He heard other rifle shots, which were like a new kind of thunder. But he was not hit again. Painfully he began the descent into the next valley.

Thor knew that he was hurt, but he could not comprehend that hurt. Once in the descent he paused for a few moments, and a little pool of blood dripped upon the ground under his foreleg. He sniffed at it suspiciously and wonderingly.

He swung eastward, and a little later he caught a fresh taint of the man-smell in the air. The wind was bringing it to him now, and in spite of the fact that he wanted to lie down and nurse his wound he ambled on a little faster, for he had learned one thing that he would never forget: the man-smell and his hurt had come together.

He reached the bottoms, and buried himself in the thick timber; and then, crossing this timber, he came to a creek. Perhaps a hundred times he had travelled up and down this creek. It was the main trail that led from one half of his range to the other.

Instinctively he always took this trail when he was hurt or when he was sick, and also when he was ready to den up for the winter. There was one chief reason for this: he was born in the almost impenetrable fastnesses at the head of the creek, and his cubhood had been spent amid its brambles of wild currants and soap berries and its rich red ground carpets of kinnikinic. It was home. In it he was alone. It was the one part of his domain that he held inviolate from all other bears. He tolerated other bears—blacks and grizzlies—on the wider and sunnier slopes of his range just so long as they moved on when he approached. They might seek food there, and nap in the sun-pools, and live in quiet and peace if they did not defy his suzerainty.

Thor did not drive other bears from his range, except when it was necessary to demonstrate again that he was High Mogul. This happened occasionally, and there was a fight. And always after a fight Thor came into this valley and went up the creek to cure his wounds.

He made his way more slowly than usual to-day. There was a terrible pain in his fore-shoulder. Now and then it hurt him so that his leg doubled up, and he stumbled. Several times he waded shoulder-deep into pools and let the cold water run over his wounds. Gradually they stopped bleeding. But the pain grew worse.

Thor's best friend in such an emergency was a clay wallow. This was the second reason why he always took this trail when he was sick or hurt. It led to the clay wallow. And the clay wallow was his doctor.

The sun was setting before he reached the wallow. His jaws hung open a little. His great head drooped lower. He had lost a great deal of blood. He was tired, and his shoulder hurt him so badly that he wanted to tear with his teeth at the strange fire that was consuming it.

The clay wallow was twenty or thirty feet in diameter, and hollowed into a little shallow pool in the centre. It was a soft, cool, golden-coloured clay, and Thor waded into it to his armpits. Then he rolled over gently on his wounded side. The clay touched his hurt like a cooling salve. It sealed the cut, and Thor gave a great heaving gasp of relief. For a long time he lay in that soft bed of clay. The sun went down, darkness came, and the wonderful stars filled the sky. And still Thor lay there, nursing that first hurt of man.

CHAPTER FOUR

In the edge of the balsam and spruce Langdon and Otto sat smoking their pipes after supper, with the glowing embers of a fire at their feet. The night air in these higher altitudes of the mountains had grown chilly, and Bruce rose long enough to throw a fresh armful of dry spruce on the coals. Then he stretched out his long form again, with his head and shoulders bolstered comfortably against the butt of a tree, and for the fiftieth time he chuckled.

"Chuckle an' be blasted," growled Langdon. "I tell you I hit him twice, Bruce—twice anyway; and I was at a devilish disadvantage!"

"'Specially when 'e was lookin' down an' grinnin' in your face," retorted Bruce, who had enjoyed hugely his comrade's ill luck. "Jimmy, at that distance you should a'most ha' killed 'im with a rock!"

"My gun was under me," explained Langdon for the twentieth time.

"W'ich ain't just the proper place for a gun to be when yo'r hunting a grizzly," reminded Bruce.

"The gully was confoundedly steep. I had to dig in with both feet and my fingers. If it had been any steeper I would have used my teeth."

Langdon sat up, knocked the ash out of the bowl of his pipe, and reloaded it with fresh tobacco.

"Bruce, that's the biggest grizzly in the Rocky Mountains!"

"He'd 'a' made a fine rug in your den, Jimmy—if yo'r gun hadn't 'appened to 'ave been under you."

"And I'm going to have him in my den before I finish," declared Langdon. "I've made up my mind. We'll make a permanent camp here. I'm going to get that grizzly if it takes all summer. I'd rather have him than any other ten bears in the Firepan Range. He was a nine-footer if an inch. His head was as big as a bushel basket, and the hair on his shoulders was four inches long. I don't know that I'm sorry I didn't kill him. He's hit, and he'll surely fight say. There'll be a lot of fun in getting him."

"There will that," agreed Bruce, "'specially if you meet 'im again during the next week or so, while he's still sore from the bullets. Better not have the gun under you then, Jimmy!"

"What do you say to making this a permanent camp?"

"Couldn't be better. Plenty of fresh meat, good grazing, and fine water." After a moment he added: "He was hit pretty hard. He was bleedin' bad at the summit."

In the firelight Langdon began cleaning his rifle.

"You think he may clear out—leave the country?"

Bruce emitted a grunt of disgust.

"Clear out? *Run away*? Mebbe he would if he was a black. But he's a grizzly, and the boss of this country. He may fight shy of this valley for a while, but you can bet he ain't goin' to emigrate. The harder you hit a grizzly the madder he gets, an' if you keep on hittin' 'im he keeps on gettin' madder, until he drops dead. If you want that bear bad enough we can surely get him."

"I do," Langdon reiterated with emphasis. "He'll smash record measurements or I miss my guess. I want him, and I want him bad, Bruce. Do you think we'll be able to trail him in the morning?"

Bruce shook his head.

"It won't be a matter of trailing," he said. "It's just simply *hunt*. After a grizzly has been hit he keeps movin'. He won't go out of his range, an' neither is he going to show himself on the open slopes like that up there. Metoosin ought to be along with the dogs inside of three or four days, an' when we get that bunch of Airedales in action, there'll be some fun."

Langdon sighted at the fire through the polished barrel of his rifle, and said doubtfully:

"I've been having my doubts about Metoosin for a week back. We've come through some mighty rough country."

"That old Indian could follow our trail if we travelled on rock," declared Bruce confidently. "He'll be here inside o' three days, barring the dogs don't run their fool heads into too many porcupines. An' when they come"—he rose and stretched his gaunt frame—"we'll have the biggest time we ever had in our lives. I'm just guessin' these mount'ins are so full o' bear that them ten dogs will all be massacreed within a week. Want to bet?"

Langdon closed his rifle with a snap.

"I only want one bear," he said, ignoring the challenge, "and I have an idea we'll get him to-morrow. You're the bear specialist of the outfit, Bruce, but I think he was too hard hit to travel far."

They had made two beds of soft balsam boughs near the fire, and Langdon now followed his companion's example, and began spreading his blankets. It had been a hard day, and within five minutes after stretching himself out he was asleep.

He was still asleep when Bruce rolled out from under his blanket at dawn. Without rousing Langdon the young packer slipped on his boots and waded back a quarter of a mile through the heavy dew to round up the horses. When he returned he brought Dishpan and their saddle-horses with him. By that time Langdon was up, and starting a fire.

Langdon frequently reminded himself that such mornings as this had made him disappoint the doctors and rob the grave. Just eight years ago this June he had come into the North for the first time, thin-chested and with a bad lung. "You can go if you insist, young man," one of the doctors had told him, "but you're going to your own funeral." And now he had a five-inch expansion and was as tough as a knot. The first rose-tints of the sun were creeping over the mountain-tops; the air was filled with the sweetness of flowers, and dew, and growing things, and his lungs drew in deep breaths of oxygen laden with the tonic and perfume of balsam.

He was more demonstrative than his companion in the joyousness of this wild life. It made him want to shout, and sing, and whistle. He restrained himself this morning. The thrill of the hunt was in his blood.

While Otto saddled the horses Langdon made the bannock. He had become an expert at what he called "wild-bread" baking, and his method possessed the double efficiency of saving both waste and time.

He opened one of the heavy canvas flour sacks, made a hollow in the flour with his two doubled fists, partly filled this hollow with a pint of water and half a cupful of caribou grease, added a tablespoonful of baking powder and a three-finger pinch of salt, and began to mix. Inside of five minutes he had the bannock loaves in the big tin reflector, and half an hour later the sheep steaks were fried, the potatoes done, and the bannock baked to a golden brown.

The sun was just showing its face in the east when they trailed out of camp. They rode across the valley, but walked up the slope, the horses following obediently in their footsteps.

It was not difficult to pick up Thor's trail. Where he had paused to snarl back defiance at his enemies there was a big red spatter on the ground; from this point to the summit they followed a crimson thread of blood. Three times in descending into the other valley they found where Thor had stopped, and each time they saw where a pool of blood had soaked into the earth or run over the rock.

They passed through the timber and came to the creek, and here, in a strip of firm black sand, Thor's footprints brought them to a pause. Bruce stared. An exclamation of amazement came from Langdon, and without a word having passed between them he drew out his pocket-tape and knelt beside one of the tracks.

"Fifteen and a quarter inches!" he gasped.

"Measure another," said Bruce.

"Fifteen and—a half!"

Bruce looked up the gorge.

"The biggest I ever see was fourteen an' a half," he said, and there was a touch of awe in his voice. "He was shot up the Athabasca an' he's stood as the biggest grizzly ever killed in British Columbia. Jimmy, *this one beats 'im*!"

They went on, and measured the tracks again at the edge of the first pool where Thor had bathed his wounds. There was almost no variation in the measurements. Only occasionally after this did they find spots of blood. It was ten o'clock when they came to the clay wallow and saw where Thor had made his bed in it.

"He was pretty sick," said Bruce in a low voice. "He was here most all night."

Moved by the same impulse and the same thought, they looked ahead of them. Half a mile farther on the mountains closed in until the gorge between them was dark and sunless.

"He was pretty sick," repeated Bruce, still looking ahead. "Mebbe we'd better tie the horses an' go on alone. It's possible—he's in there."

They tied the horses to scrub cedars, and relieved Dishpan of her pack.

Then, with their rifles in readiness, and eyes and ears alert, they went on cautiously into the silence and gloom of the gorge.

CHAPTER FIVE

Thor had gone up the gorge at daybreak. He was stiff when he rose from the clay wallow, but a good deal of the burning and pain had gone from his wound. It still hurt him, but not as it had hurt him the preceding evening. His discomfort was not all in his shoulder, and it was not in any one place in particular. He was *sick*, and had he been human he would have been in bed with a thermometer under his tongue and a doctor holding his pulse. He walked up the gorge slowly and laggingly. An indefatigable seeker of food, he no longer thought of food. He was not hungry, and he did not want to eat.

With his hot tongue he lapped frequently at the cool water of the creek, and even more frequently he turned half about, and sniffed the wind. He knew that the man-smell and the strange thunder and the still more inexplicable lightning lay behind him. All night he had been on guard, and he was cautious now.

For a particular hurt Thor knew of no particular remedy. He was not a botanist in the finer sense of the word, but in creating him the Spirit of the Wild had ordained that he should be his own physician. As a cat seeks catnip, so Thor sought certain things when he was not feeling well. All bitterness is not quinine, but certainly bitter things were Thor's remedies, and as he made his way up the gorge his nose hung close to the ground, and he sniffed in the low copses and thick bush-tangles he passed.

He came to a small green spot covered with kinnikinic, a ground plant two inches high which bore red berries as big as a small pea. They were not red now, but green; bitter as gall, and contained an astringent tonic called uvaursi. Thor ate them.

After that he found soap berries growing on bushes that looked very much like currant bushes. The fruit was already larger than currants, and turning pink. Indians ate these berries when they had fever, and Thor gathered half a pint before he went on. They, too, were bitter.

He nosed the trees, and found at last what he wanted. It was a jackpine, and at several places within his reach the fresh pitch was oozing. A bear seldom passes a bleeding jackpine. It is his chief tonic, and Thor licked the fresh pitch with his tongue. In this way he absorbed not only turpentine, but also, in a roundabout sort of way, a whole pharmacopoeia of medicines made from this particular element.

By the time he arrived at the end of the gorge Thor's stomach was a fairly well-stocked drug emporium. Among other things he had eaten perhaps half a quart of spruce and balsam needles. When a dog is sick he eats grass; when a bear is sick he eats pine or balsam needles if he can get them. Also he pads his stomach and intestines with them in the last hour before denning himself away for the winter.

The sun was not yet up when Thor came to the end of the gorge, and stood for a few moments at the mouth of a low cave that reached back into the wall of the mountain. How far his memory went back it would be impossible to say; but in the whole world, as he knew it, this cave was home. It was not more than four feet high, and twice as wide, but it was many times as deep and was carpeted with a soft white floor of sand. In some past age a little stream had trickled out of this cavern, and the far end of it made a comfortable bedroom for a sleeping bear when the temperature was fifty degrees below zero.

Ten years before Thor's mother had gone in there to sleep through the winter, and when she waddled out to get her first glimpse of spring three little cubs waddled with her. Thor was one of them. He was still half blind, for it is five weeks after a grizzly cub is born before he can see; and there was not much hair on his body, for a grizzly cub is born as naked as a human baby. His eyes open and his hair begins to grow at just about the same time. Since then Thor had denned eight times in that cavern home.

He wanted to go in now. He wanted to lie down in the far end of it and wait until he felt better. For perhaps two or three minutes he hesitated, sniffing yearningly at the door to his cave, and then feeling the wind from down the gorge. Something told him that he should go on.

To the westward there was a sloping ascent up out of the gorge to the summit, and Thor climbed this. The sun was well up when he reached the top, and for a little while he rested again and looked down on the other half of his domain.

Even more wonderful was this valley than the one into which Bruce and Langdon had ridden a few hours before. From range to range it was a good two miles in width, and in the opposite directions it stretched away in a great rolling panorama of gold and green and black. From where Thor stood it was like an immense park. Green slopes reached almost to the summits of the mountains, and to a point halfway up these slopes—the last timber-line—clumps of spruce and balsam trees were scattered over the green as if set there by the hands of men. Some of these timber-patches were no larger than the decorative clumps in a city park, and others covered acres and tens of acres; and at the foot of the slopes on either side, like decorative fringes, were thin and unbroken lines of forest. Between these two lines of forest lay the open valley of soft and undulating meadow, dotted with its purplish bosks of buffalo willow and mountain sage, its green coppices of wild-rose and thorn, and its clumps of trees. In the hollow of the valley ran a stream.

Thor descended about four hundred yards from where he stood, and then turned northward along the green slope, so that he was travelling from patch to patch of the parklike timber, a hundred and fifty or two hundred yards above the fringe of forest. To this height, midway between the meadows in the valley and the first shale and bare rock of the peaks, he came most frequently on his small game hunts.

Like fat woodchucks the whistlers were already beginning to sun themselves on their rocks. Their long, soft, elusive whistlings, pleasant to hear above the drone of mountain waters, filled the air with a musical cadence. Now and then one would whistle shrilly and warningly close at hand, and then flatten himself out on his rock as the big bear passed, and for a few moments no whistling would break upon the gentle purring of the valley.

But Thor was giving no thought to the hunt this morning. Twice he encountered porcupines, the sweetest of all morsels to him, and passed them unnoticed; the warm, *sleeping* smell of a caribou came hot and fresh from a thicket, but he did not approach the thicket to investigate; out of a coulee, narrow and dark, like a black ditch, he caught the scent of a badger. For two hours he travelled steadily northward along the half-crest of the slopes before he struck down through the timber to the stream.

The clay adhering to his wound was beginning to harden, and again he waded shoulder-deep into a pool, and stood there for several minutes. The water washed most of the clay away. For another two hours he followed the creek, drinking frequently. Then came the *sapoos oowin*— six hours after he had left the clay wallow. The kinnikinic berries, the soap berries, the jackpine pitch, the spruce and balsam needles, and the water he had drunk, all mixed in his stomach in one big compelling dose, brought it about—and Thor felt tremendously better, so much better that for the first time he turned and growled back in the direction of his enemies. His shoulder still hurt him, but his sickness was gone.

For many minutes after the *sapoos oowin* he stood without moving, and many times he growled. The snarling rumble deep in his chest had a new meaning now. Until last night and to-day he had not known a real hatred. He had fought other bears, but the fighting rage was not hate. It came quickly, and passed away quickly; it left no growing ugliness; he licked the wounds of a clawed enemy, and was quite frequently happy while he nursed them. But this new thing that was born in him was different.

With an unforgetable and ferocious hatred he hated the thing that had hurt him. He hated the man-smell; he hated the strange, white-faced thing he had seen clinging to the side of the gorge; and his hatred included everything associated with them. It was a hatred born of instinct and roused sharply from its long slumber by experience.

Without ever having seen or smelled man before, he knew that man was his deadliest enemy, and to be feared more than all the wild things in the mountains. He would fight the biggest grizzly. He would turn on the fiercest pack of wolves. He would brave flood and fire without flinching. But before man he must flee! He must hide! He must constantly guard himself in the peaks and on the plains with eyes and ears and nose!

Why he sensed this, why he understood all at once that a creature had come into his world, a pigmy in size, yet more to be dreaded than any foe he had ever known, was a miracle which nature alone could explain. It was a hearkening back in the age-dimmed mental fabric of Thor's race to the earliest days of man—man, first of all, with the club; man with the spear hardened in fire; man with the flint-tipped arrow; man with the trap and the deadfall, and, lastly, man with the gun. Through all the ages man had been his one and only master. Nature had impressed it upon him—had been impressing it upon him through a hundred or a thousand or ten thousand generations.

And now for the first time in his life that dormant part of his instinct leaped into warning wakefulness, and he understood. He hated man, and hereafter he would hate everything that bore the man-smell. And with this hate there was also born in him for the first time *fear*. Had man never pushed Thor and his kind to the death the world would not have known him as Ursus Horribilis the Terrible.

Thor still followed the creek, nosing along slowly and lumberingly, but very steadily; his head and neck bent low, his huge rear quarters rising and falling in that rolling motion peculiar to all bears, and especially so of the grizzly. His long claws *click-click-clicked* on the stones; he crunched heavily in the gravel; in soft sand he left enormous footprints.

That part of the valley which he was now entering held a particular significance for Thor, and he began to loiter, pausing often to sniff the air on all sides of him. He was not a monogamist, but for many mating seasons past he had come to find his *Iskwao* in this wonderful sweep of meadow and plain between the two ranges. He could always expect her in July, waiting for him or seeking him with that strange savage longing of motherhood in her breast. She was a splendid grizzly who came from the western ranges when the spirit of mating days called; big, and strong, and of a beautiful golden-brown colour, so that the children of Thor and his *Iskwao* were the finest young grizzlies in all the mountains. The mother took them back with her unborn, and they opened their eyes and lived and fought in the valleys and on the slopes far to the west. If in later years Thor ever chased his own children out of his hunting grounds, or whipped them in a fight, Nature kindly blinded him to the fact. He was like most grouchy old bachelors: he did not like small folk. He tolerated a little cub as a cross-grained old woman-hater might have tolerated a pink baby; but he wasn't as cruel as Punch, for he had never killed a cub. He had cuffed them soundly whenever they had dared to come within reach of him, but always with the flat, soft palm of his paw, and with just enough force behind it to send them keeling over and over like little round fluffy balls.

This was Thor's only expression of displeasure when a strange mother-bear invaded his range with her cubs. In other ways he was quite chivalrous. He would not drive the mother-bear and her cubs away, and he would not fight with her, no matter how shrewish or unpleasant she was. Even if he found them eating at one of his kills, he would do nothing more than give the cubs a sound cuffing.

All this is somewhat necessary to show with what sudden and violent agitation Thor caught a certain warm, close smell as he came around the end of a mass of huge boulders. He stopped, turned his head, and swore in his low, growling way. Six feet away from him, grovelling flat in a patch of white sand, wriggling and shaking for all the world like a half-frightened puppy that had not yet made up its mind whether it had met a friend or an enemy, was a lone bear cub. It was not more than three months old—altogether too young to be away from its mother; and it had a sharp little tan face and a white spot on its baby breast which marked it as a member of the black bear family, and not a grizzly.

The cub was trying as hard as it could to say, "I am lost, strayed, or stolen; I'm hungry, and I've got a porcupine quill in my foot," but in spite of that, with another ominous growl, Thor began to look about the rocks for the mother. She was not in sight, and neither could he smell her, two facts which turned his great head again toward the cub.

Muskwa—an Indian would have called the cub that—had crawled a foot or two nearer on his little belly. He greeted Thor's second inspection with a genial wriggling which carried him forward another half foot, and a low warning rumbled in Thor's chest. "Don't come any nearer," it said plainly enough, "or I'll keel you over!"

Muskwa understood. He lay as if dead, his nose and paws and belly flat on the sand, and Thor looked about him again. When his eyes returned to Muskwa, the cub was within three feet of him, squirming flat in the sand and whimpering softly. Thor lifted his right paw four inches from the ground. "Another inch and I'll give you a welt!" he growled.

Muskwa wriggled and trembled; he licked his lips with his tiny red tongue, half in fear and half pleading for mercy, and in spite of Thor's lifted paw he wormed his way another six inches nearer.

There was a sort of rattle instead of a growl in Thor's throat. His heavy hand fell to the sand. A third time he looked about and sniffed the air; he growled again. Any crusty old bachelor would have understood that growl. "Now where the devil is the kid's mother!" it said.

Something happened then. Muskwa had crept close to Thor's wounded leg. He rose up, and his nose caught the scent of the raw wound. Gently his tongue touched it. It was like velvet— that tongue. It was wonderfully pleasant to feel, and Thor stood there for many moments, making neither movement nor sound while the cub licked his wound. Then he lowered his great head. He sniffed the soft little ball of friendship that had come to him. Muskwa whined in a motherless way. Thor growled, but more softly now. It was no longer a threat. The heat of his great tongue fell once on the cub's face.

"Come on!" he said, and resumed his journey into the north.

And close at his heels followed the motherless little tan-faced cub.

CHAPTER SIX

The creek which Thor was following was a tributary of the Babine, and he was headed pretty nearly straight for the Skeena. As he was travelling upstream the country was becoming higher and rougher. He had come perhaps seven or eight miles from the summit of the divide when he found Muskwa. From this point the slopes began to assume a different aspect. They were cut up by dark, narrow gullies, and broken by enormous masses of rocks, jagged cuffs, and steep slides of shale. The creek became noisier and more difficult to follow.

Thor was now entering one of his strongholds: a region which contained a thousand hiding-places, if he had wanted to hide; a wild, uptorn country where it was not difficult for him to kill big game, and where he was certain that the man-smell would not follow him.

For half an hour after leaving the mass of rocks where he had encountered Muskwa, Thor lumbered on as if utterly oblivious of the fact that the cub was following. But he could hear him and smell him.

Muskwa was having a hard time of it. His fat little body and his fat little legs were unaccustomed to this sort of journeying, but he was a game youngster, and only twice did he whimper in that half-hour—once he toppled off a rock into the edge of the creek, and again when he came down too hard on the porcupine quill in his foot.

At last Thor abandoned the creek and turned up a deep ravine, which he followed until he came to a dip, or plateau-like plain, halfway up a broad slope. Here he found a rock on the sunny side of a grassy knoll, and stopped. It may be that little Muskwa's babyish friendship, the caress of his soft little red tongue at just the psychological moment, and his perseverance in following Thor had all combined to touch a responsive chord in the other's big brute heart, for after nosing about restlessly for a few moments Thor stretched himself out beside the rock. Not until then did the utterly exhausted little tan-faced cub lie down, but when he did lie down he was so dead tired that he was sound asleep in three minutes.

Twice again during the early part of the afternoon the *sapoos oowin* worked on Thor, and he began to feel hungry. It was not the sort of hunger to be appeased by ants and grubs, or even gophers and whistlers. It may be, too, that he guessed how nearly starved little Muskwa was. The cub had not once opened his eyes, and he still lay in his warm pool of sunshine when Thor made up his mind to go on.

It was about three o'clock, a particularly quiet and drowsy part of a late June or early July day in a northern mountain valley. The whistlers had piped until they were tired, and lay squat out in the sunshine on their rocks; the eagles soared so high above the peaks that they were mere dots; the hawks, with meat-filled crops, had disappeared into the timber; goat and sheep were lying down far up toward the sky-line, and if there were any grazing animals near they were well fed and napping.

The mountain hunter knew that this was the hour when he should scan the green slopes and the open places between the clumps of timber for bears, and especially for flesh-eating bears.

It was Thor's chief prospecting hour. Instinct told him that when all other creatures were well fed and napping he could move more openly and with less fear of detection. He could find his game, and watch it. Occasionally he would kill a goat or a sheep or a caribou in broad daylight, for over short distances he could run faster than either a goat or a sheep, and as fast as a caribou. But chiefly he killed at sunset or in the darkness of early evening.

Thor rose from beside the rock with a prodigious whoof that roused Muskwa. The cub got up, blinked at Thor and then at the sun, and shook himself until he fell down.

Thor eyed the black and tan mite a bit sourly. After the *sapoos oowin* he was craving red, juicy flesh, just as a very hungry man yearns for a thick porterhouse instead of lady fingers or mayonnaise salad—flesh and plenty of it; and how he could hunt down and kill a caribou with that half-starved but very much interested cub at his heels puzzled him.

Muskwa himself seemed to understand and answer the question. He ran a dozen yards ahead of Thor, then stopped and looked back impudently, his little ears perked forward, and with the look in his face of a small boy proving to his father that he is perfectly qualified to go on his first rabbit hunt.

With another *whoof* Thor started along the slope in a spurt that brought him up to Muskwa immediately, and with a sudden sweep of his right paw he sent the cub rolling a dozen feet behind him, a manner of speech that said plainly enough, "That's where you belong if you're going hunting with me!"

Then Thor lumbered slowly on, eyes and ears and nostrils keyed for the hunt. He descended until he was not more than a hundred yards above the creek, and he no longer sought out the easiest trail, but the rough and broken places. He travelled slowly and in a zigzag fashion, stealing cautiously around great masses of boulders, sniffing up each coulee that he came to, and investigating the timber clumps and windfalls.

At one time he would be so high up that he was close to the bare shale, and again so low down that he walked in the sand and gravel of the creek. He caught many scents in the wind, but none that held or deeply interested him. Once, up near the shale, he smelled goat; but he never went above the shale for meat. Twice he smelled sheep, and late in the afternoon he saw a big ram looking down on him from a precipitous crag a hundred feet above.

Lower down his nose touched the trails of porcupines, and often his head hung over the footprints of caribou as he sniffed the air ahead.

There were other bears in the valley, too. Mostly these had travelled along the creek-bottom, showing they were blacks or cinnamons. Once Thor struck the scent of another grizzly, and he rumbled ill-humouredly.

Not once in the two hours after they left the sunrock did Thor pay any apparent attention to Muskwa, who was growing hungrier and weaker as the day lengthened. No boy that ever lived was gamer than the little tan-faced cub. In the rough places he stumbled and fell frequently; up places that Thor could make in a single step he had to fight desperately to make his way; three times Thor waded through the creek and Muskwa half drowned himself in following; he was battered and bruised and wet and his foot hurt him—but he followed. Sometimes he was close to Thor, and at others he had to run to catch up. The sun was setting when Thor at last found game, and Muskwa was almost dead.

He did not know why Thor flattened his huge bulk suddenly alongside a rock at the edge of a rough meadow, from which they could look down into a small hollow. He wanted to whimper, but he was afraid. And if he had ever wanted his mother at any time in his short life he wanted her now. He could not understand why she had left him among the rocks and had never come back; that tragedy Langdon and Bruce were to discover a little later. And he could not understand why she did not come to him now. This was just about his nursing hour before going to sleep for the night, for he was a March cub, and, according to the most approved mother-bear regulations, should have had milk for another month.

He was what Metoosin, the Indian, would have called *munookow*—that is, he was very soft. Being a bear, his birth had not been like that of other animals. His mother, like all mother-bears in a cold country, had brought him into life a long time before she had finished her winter nap in her den. He had come while she was asleep. For a month or six weeks after that, while he was still blind and naked, she had given him milk, while she herself neither ate nor drank nor saw the light of day. At the end of those six weeks she had gone forth with him from her den to seek the first mouthful of sustenance for herself. Not more than another six weeks had passed since then, and Muskwa weighed about twenty pounds—that is, he had weighed twenty pounds, but he was emptier now than he had ever been in his life, and probably weighed a little less.

Three hundred yards below Thor was a clump of balsams, a small thick patch that grew close to the edge of the miniature lake whose water crept around the farther end of the hollow. In that clump there was a caribou—perhaps two or three. Thor knew that as surely as though he saw them. The *wenipow*, or "lying down," smell of hoofed game was as different from the *nechisoo*, or "grazing smell," to Thor as day from night. One hung elusively in the air, like the faint and shifting breath of a passing woman's scented dress and hair; the other came hot and heavy, close to the earth, like the odour of a broken bottle of perfume.

Even Muskwa now caught the scent as he crept up close behind the big grizzly and lay down.

For fully ten minutes Thor did not move. His eyes took in the hollow, the edge of the lake, and the approach to the timber, and his nose gauged the wind as accurately as the pointing of a compass. The reason he remained quiet was that he was almost on the danger-line. In other words, the mountains and the sudden dip had formed a "split wind" in the hollow, and had Thor appeared fifty yards above where he now crouched, the keen-scented caribou would have got full wind of him.

With his little ears cocked forward and a new gleam of understanding in his eyes, Muskwa now looked upon his first lesson in game-stalking. Crouched so low that he seemed to be travelling on his belly, Thor moved slowly and noiselessly toward the creek, the huge ruff just forward of his shoulders standing out like the stiffened spine of a dog's back. Muskwa followed. For fully a hundred yards Thor continued his detour, and three times in that hundred yards he paused to sniff in the direction of the timber. At last he was satisfied. The wind was full in his face, and it was rich with promise.

He began to advance, in a slinking, rolling, rock-shouldered motion, taking shorter steps now, and with every muscle in his great body ready for action. Within two minutes he reached the edge of the balsams, and there he paused again. The crackling of underbrush came distinctly. The caribou were up, but they were not alarmed. They were going forth to drink and graze.

Thor moved again, parallel to the sound. This brought him quickly to the edge of the timber, and there he stood, concealed by foliage, but with the lake and the short stretch of meadow in view. A big bull caribou came out first. His horns were half grown, and in velvet. A two-year-old followed, round and sleek and glistening like brown velvet in the sunset. For two minutes the bull stood alert, eyes, ears, and nostrils seeking for danger-signals; at his heels the younger animal nibbled less suspiciously at the grass. Then lowering his head until his antlers swept back over his shoulders the old bull started slowly toward the lake for his evening drink. The two-year-old followed—and Thor came out softly from his hiding-place.

For a single moment he seemed to gather himself—and then he started. Fifty feet separated him from the caribou. He had covered half that distance like a huge rolling ball when the animals heard him. They were off like arrows sprung from the bow. But they were too late. It would have taken a swift horse to beat Thor and he had already gained momentum.

Like the wind he bore down on the flank of the two-year-old, swung a little to one side, and then without any apparent effort—still like a huge ball—he bounded in and upward, and the short race was done.

His huge right arm swung over the two-year-old's shoulder, and as they went down his left paw gripped the caribou's muzzle like a huge human hand. Thor fell under, as he always planned to fall. He did not hug his victim to death. Just once he doubled up one of his hind legs, and when it went back the five knives it carried disembowelled the caribou. They not only disembowelled him, but twisted and broke his ribs as though they were of wood. Then Thor got up, looked around, and shook himself with a rumbling growl which might have been either a growl of triumph or an invitation for Muskwa to come to the feast.

If it was an invitation, the little tan-faced cab did not wait for a second. For the first time he smelled and tasted the warm blood of meat. And this smell and taste had come at the psychological moment in his life, just as it had come in Thor's life years before. All grizzlies are not killers of big game. In fact, very few of them are. Most of them are chiefly vegetarians, with a meat diet of smaller animals, such as gophers, whistling marmots, and porcupines. Now and then chance makes of a grizzly a hunter of caribou, goat, sheep, deer, and even moose. Such was Thor. And such, in days to come, would Muskwa be, even though he was a black and not of the family Ursus Horribilis Ord.

For an hour the two feasted, not in the ravenous way of hungry dogs, but in the slow and satisfying manner of gourmets. Muskwa, flat on his little paunch, and almost between Thor's huge forearms, lapped up the blood and snarled like a kitten as he ground tender flesh between his tiny teeth. Thor, as in all his food-seeking, hunted first for the tidbits, though the *sapoos oovin* had made him as empty as a room without furniture. He pulled out the thin leafs of fat from about the kidneys and bowels, and munched at yard-long strings of it, his eyes half closed.

The last of the sun faded away from the mountains, and darkness followed swiftly after the twilight. It was dark when they finished, and little Muskwa was as wide as he was long.

Thor was the greatest of nature's conservators. With him nothing went to waste that was good to eat, and at the present moment if the old bull caribou had deliberately walked within his reach Thor in all probability would not have killed him. He had food, and his business was to store that food where it would be safe.

He went back to the balsam thicket, but the gorged cub now made no effort to follow him. He was vastly contented, and something told him that Thor would not leave the meat. Ten minutes later Thor verified his judgment by returning. In his huge jaws he caught the caribou at the back of the neck. Then he swung himself partly sidewise and began dragging the carcass toward the timber as a dog might have dragged a ten-pound slab of bacon.

The young bull probably weighed four hundred pounds. Had he weighed eight hundred, or even a thousand, Thor would still have dragged him—but had the carcass weighed that much he would have turned straight around and *backed* with his load.

In the edge of the balsams Thor had already found a hollow in the ground. He thrust the carcass into this hollow, and while Muskwa watched with a great and growing interest, he proceeded to cover it over with dry needles, sticks, a rotting tree butt, and a log. He did not rear himself up and leave his "mark" on a tree as a warning to other bears. He simply nosed round for a bit, and then went out of the timber.

Muskwa followed him now, and he had some trouble in properly navigating himself under the handicap of his added weight. The stars were beginning to fill the sky, and under these stars Thor struck straight up a steep and rugged slope that led to the mountain-tops. Up and up he went, higher than Muskwa had ever been. They crossed a patch of snow. And then they came to a place where it seemed as if a volcano had disrupted the bowels of a mountain. Man could hardly have travelled where Thor led Muskwa.

At last he stopped. He was on a narrow ledge, with a perpendicular wall of rock at his back. Under him fell away the chaos of torn-up rock and shale. Far below the valley lay a black and bottomless pit.

Thor lay down, and for the first time since his hurt in the other valley he stretched out his head between his great arms, and heaved a deep and restful sigh. Muskwa crept up close to him, so close that he was warmed by Thor's body; and together they slept the deep and peaceful sleep of full stomachs, while over them the stars grew brighter, and the moon came up to flood the peaks and the valley in a golden splendour.

CHAPTER SEVEN

Langdon and Bruce crossed the summit into the westward valley in the afternoon of the day Thor left the clay wallow. It was two o'clock when Bruce turned back for the three horses, leaving Langdon on a high ridge to scour the surrounding country through his glasses. For two hours after the packer returned with the outfit they followed slowly along the creek above which the grizzly had travelled, and when they camped for the night they were still two or three miles from the spot where Thor came upon Muskwa. They had not yet found his tracks in the sand of the creek bottom. Yet Bruce was confident. He knew that Thor had been following the crests of the slopes.

"If you go back out of this country an' write about bears, don't make a fool o' yo'rself like most of the writin' fellows, Jimmy," he said, as they sat back to smoke their pipes after supper. "Two years ago I took a natcherlist out for a month, an' he was so tickled he said 'e'd send me a bunch o' books about bears an' wild things. He did! I read 'em. I laughed at first, an' then I got mad an' made a fire of 'em. Bears is cur'ous. There's a mighty lot of interestin' things to say about 'em without making a fool o' yo'rself. There sure is!"

Langdon nodded.

"One has to hunt and kill and hunt and kill for years before he discovers the real pleasure in big game stalking," he said slowly, looking into the fire. "And when he comes down to that real pleasure, the part of it that absorbs him heart and soul, he finds that after all the big thrill isn't in killing, but in letting live. I want this grizzly, and I'm going to have him. I won't leave the mountains until I kill him. But, on the other hand, we could have killed two other bears to-day, and I didn't take a shot. I'm learning the game, Bruce—I'm beginning to taste the real pleasure of hunting. And when one hunts in the right way one learns facts. You needn't worry. I'm going to put only facts in what I write."

Suddenly he turned and looked at Bruce.

"What were some of the 'fool things' you read in those books?" he asked.

Bruce blew out a cloud of smoke reflectively.

"What made me maddest," he said, "was what those writer fellows said about bears havin' 'marks.' Good Lord, accordin' to what they said all a bear has to do is stretch 'imself up, put a mark on a tree, and that country is his'n until a bigger bear comes along an' licks 'im. In one book I remember where a grizzly rolled a log up under a tree so he could stand on it an' put his mark above another grizzly's mark. Think of that!

"No bear makes a mark that means anything. I've seen grizzlies bite hunks out o' trees an' scratch 'em just as a cat might, an' in the summer when they get itchy an' begin to lose their hair they stand up an' rub against trees. They rub because they itch an' not because they're leavin' their cards for other bears. Caribou an' moose an' deer do the same thing to get the velvet off their horns.

"Them same writers think every grizzly has his own range, an' they don't—not by a long shot they don't! I've seen eight full-grown grizzlies feedin' on the same slide! You remember, two years ago, we shot four grizzlies in a little valley that wasn't a mile long. Now an' then there's a boss among grizzlies, like this fellow we're after, but even he ain't got his range alone. I'll bet there's twenty other bears in these two valleys! An' that natcherlist I had two years ago couldn't tell a grizzly's track from a black bear's track, an so 'elp me if he knew what a cinnamon was!"

He took his pipe from his mouth and spat truculently into the fire, and Langdon knew that other things were coming. His richest hours were those when the usually silent Bruce fell into these moods.

"A cinnamon!" he growled. "Think of that, Jimmy—he thought there were such a thing as a cinnamon bear! An' when I told him there wasn't, an' that the cinnamon bear you read about is a black or a grizzly of a cinnamon colour, he laughed at me—an' there I was born an' brung up among bears! His eyes fair popped when I told him about the colour o' bears, an' he thought I was feedin' him rope. I figgered afterward mebby that was why he sent me the books. He wanted to show me he was right.

"Jimmy, there ain't anything on earth that's got more colours than a bear! I've seen black bears as white as snow, an' I've seen grizzlies almost as black as a black bear. I've seen cinnamon black bears an' I've seen cinnamon grizzlies, an' I've seen browns an' golds an' almost-yellows of both kinds. They're as different in colour as they are in their natchurs an' way of eatin'.

"I figger most natcherlists go out an' get acquainted with one grizzly, an' then they write up all grizzlies accordin' to that one. That ain't fair to the grizzlies, darned if it is! There wasn't one of them books that didn't say the grizzly wasn't the fiercest, man-eatingest cuss alive. He ain't—unless you corner 'im. He's as cur'ous as a kid, an' he's good-natured if you don't bother 'im. Most of 'em are vegetarians, but some of 'em ain't. I've seen grizzlies pull down goat an' sheep an' caribou, an' I've seen other grizzlies feed on the same slides with them animals an' never make a move toward them. They're cur'ous, Jimmy. There's lots you can say about 'em without makin' a fool o' yourself!"

Bruce beat the ash out of his pipe as an emphasis to his final remark. As he reloaded with fresh tobacco, Langdon said:

"You can make up your mind this big fellow we are after is a game-killer, Bruce."

"You can't tell," replied Bruce. "Size don't always tell. I knew a grizzly once that wasn't much bigger'n a dog, an' he was a game-killer. Hundreds of animals are winter-killed in these mount'ins every year, an' when spring comes the bears eat the carcasses; but old flesh don't make game-killers. Sometimes it's born in a grizzly to be a killer, an' sometimes he becomes a killer by chance. If he kills once, he'll kill again.

"Once I was on the side of a mount'in an' saw a goat walk straight into the face of a grizzly. The bear wasn't going to make a move, but the goat was so scared it ran plump into the old fellow, and he killed it. He acted mighty surprised for ten minutes afterward, an' he sniffed an' nosed around the warm carcass for half an hour before he tore it open. That was his first taste of what you might call live game. I didn't kill him, an' I'm sure from that day on he was a big-game hunter."

"I should think size would have something to do with it," argued Langdon. "It seems to me that a bear which eats flesh would be bigger and stronger than if he was a vegetarian."

"That's one o' the cur'ous things you want to write about," replied Bruce, with one of his odd chuckles. "Why is it a bear gets so fat he can hardly walk along in September when he don't feed on much else but berries an' ants an' grubs? Would you get fat on wild currants?

"An' why does he grow so fast during the four or five months he's denned up an' dead to the world without a mouthful to eat or drink?

"Why is it that for a month, an' sometimes two months, the mother gives her cubs milk while she's still what you might call asleep? Her nap ain't much more'n two-thirds over when the cubs are born.

"And why ain't them cubs bigger'n they are? That natcherlist laughed until I thought he'd split when I told him a grizzly bear cub wasn't much bigger'n a house-cat kitten when born!"

"He was one of the few fools who aren't willing to learn—and yet you cannot blame him altogether," said Langdon. "Four or five years ago I wouldn't have believed it, Bruce. I couldn't actually believe it until we dug out those cubs up the Athabasca—one weighed eleven ounces and the other nine. You remember?"

"An' they were a week old, Jimmy. An' the mother weighed eight hundred pounds."

For a few moments they both puffed silently on their pipes.

"Almost—inconceivable," said Langdon then. "And yet it's true. And it isn't a freak of nature, Bruce—it's simply a result of Nature's far-sightedness. If the cubs were as large comparatively as a house-cat's kittens the mother-bear could not sustain them during those weeks when she eats and drinks nothing herself. There seems to be just one flaw in this scheme: an ordinary black bear is only about half as large as a grizzly, yet a black bear cub when born is much larger than a grizzly cub. Now why the devil that should be—"

Bruce interrupted his friend with a good-natured laugh.

"That's easy—easy, Jimmy!" he exclaimed. "Do you remember last year when we picked strawberries in the valley an' threw snowballs two hours later up on the mountain? Higher you climb the colder it gets, don't it? Right now—first day of July—you'd half freeze up on some of those peaks! A grizzly dens high, Jimmy, and a black bear dens low. When the snow is four feet deep up where the grizzly dens, the black bear can still feed in the deep valleys an' thick timber. He goes to bed mebby a week or two weeks later than the grizzly, an' he gets up in the spring a week or two weeks earlier; he's fatter when he dens up an' he ain't so poor when he comes out—an' so the mother's got more strength to give to her cubs. It looks that way to me."

"You've hit the nail on the head as sure as you're a year old!" cried Langdon enthusiastically. "Bruce, I never thought of that!"

"There's a good many things you don't think about until you run across 'em," said the mountaineer. "It's what you said a while ago—such things are what makes huntin' a fine sport when you've learned huntin' ain't always killin'—but lettin' live. One day I lay seven hours on a mountain-top watchin' a band o' sheep at play, an' I had more fun than if I'd killed the whole bunch."

Bruce rose to his feet and stretched himself, an after-supper operation that always preceded his announcement that he was going to turn in.

"Fine day to-morrow," he said, yawning. "Look how white the snow is on the peaks."

"Bruce—"

"What?"

"How heavy is this bear we're after?"

"Twelve hundred pounds—mebby a little more. I didn't have the pleasure of lookin' at him so close as you did, Jimmy. If I had we'd been dryin' his skin now!"

"And he's in his prime?"

"Between eight and twelve years old, I'd say, by the way he went up the slope. An old bear don't roll so easy."

"You've run across some pretty old bears, Bruce?"

"So old some of 'em needed crutches," said Bruce, unlacing his boots. "I've shot bears so old they'd lost their teeth."

"How old?"

"Thirty—thirty-five—mebby forty years. Good-night, Jimmy!"

"Good-night, Bruce!"

Langdon was awakened some time hours later by a deluge of rain that brought him out of his blankets with a yell to Bruce. They had not put up their tepee, and a moment later he heard Bruce anathematizing their idiocy. The night was as black as a cavern, except when it was broken by lurid flashes of lightning, and the mountains rolled and rumbled with deep thunder. Disentangling himself from his drenched blanket, Langdon stood up. A glare of lightning revealed Bruce sitting in his blankets, his hair dripping down over his long, lean face, and at sight of him Langdon laughed outright.

"Fine day to-morrow," he taunted, repeating Bruce's words of a few hours before. "Look how white the snow is on the peaks!"

Whatever Bruce said was drowned in a crash of thunder.

Langdon waited for another lightning flash and then dove for the shelter of a thick balsam. Under this he crouched for five or ten minutes, when the rain stopped as suddenly as it had begun. The thunder rolled southward, and the lightning went with it. In the darkness he heard Bruce fumbling somewhere near. Then a match was lighted, and he saw his comrade looking at his watch.

"Pretty near three o'clock," he said. "Nice shower, wasn't it?"

"I rather expected it," replied Langdon carelessly. "You know, Bruce, whenever the snow on the peaks is so white—"

"Shut up—an' let's get a fire! Good thing we had sense enough to cover our grub with the blankets. Are yo' wet?"

Langdon was wringing the water from his hair. He felt like a drowned rat.

"No. I was under a thick balsam, and prepared for it. When you called my attention to the whiteness of the snow on the peaks I knew—"

"Forget the snow," growled Bruce, and Langdon could hear him breaking off dry pitch-filled twigs under a spruce.

He went to help him, and five minutes later they had a fire going. The light illumined their faces, and each saw that the other was not unhappy. Bruce was grinning under his sodden hair.

"I was dead asleep when it came," he explained. "An' I thought I'd fallen in a lake. I woke up tryin' to swim."

An early July rain at three o'clock in the morning in the northern British Columbia mountains is not as warm as it might be, and for the greater part of an hour Langdon and Bruce continued to gather fuel and dry their blankets and clothing. It was five o'clock before they had breakfast, and a little after six when they started with their two saddles and single pack up the valley. Bruce had the satisfaction of reminding Langdon that his prediction had come true for a glorious day followed the thunder shower.

Under them the meadows were dripping. The valley purred louder with the music of the swollen streamlets. From the mountain-tops a half of last night's snow was gone, and to Langdon the flowers seemed taller and more beautiful. The air that drifted through the valley was laden with the sweetness and freshness of the morning, and over and through it all the sun shone in a warm and golden sea.

They headed up the creek-bottom, bending over from their saddles to look at every strip of sand they passed for tracks. They had not gone a quarter of a mile when Bruce gave a sudden exclamation, and stopped. He pointed to a round patch of sand in which Thor had left one of his huge footprints. Langdon dismounted and measured it.

"It's he!" he cried, and there was a thrill of excitement in his voice. "Hadn't we better go on without the horses, Bruce?"

The mountaineer shook his head. But before he voiced an opinion he got down from his horse and scanned the sides of the mountains ahead of them through his long telescope. Langdon used his double-barrelled hunting glass. They discovered nothing.

"He's still in the creek-bottom, an' he's probably three or four miles ahead," said Bruce. "We'll ride on a couple o' miles an' find a place good for the horses. The grass an' bushes will be dry then."

It was easy to follow Thor's course after this, for he had hung close to the creek. Within three or four hundred yards of the great mass of boulders where the grizzly had come upon the tan-faced cub was a small copse of spruce in the heart of a grassy dip, and here the hunters stripped and hobbled their horses. Twenty minutes later they had come up cautiously to the soft carpet of sand where Thor and Muskwa had become acquainted. The heavy rain had obliterated the cub's tiny footprints, but the sand was cut up by the grizzly's tracks. The packer's teeth gleamed as he looked at Langdon.

"He ain't very far," he whispered. "Shouldn't wonder if he spent the night pretty close an' he's mooshing on just ahead of us."

He wet a finger and held it above his head to get the wind. He nodded significantly.

"We'd better get up on the slopes," he said.

They made their way around the end of the boulders, holding their guns in readiness, and headed for a small coulee that promised an easy ascent of the first slope. At the mouth of this both paused again. Its bottom was covered with sand, and in this sand were the tracks of another bear. Bruce dropped on his knees.

"It's another grizzly," said Langdon.

"No, it ain't; it's a black," said Bruce. "Jimmy, can't I ever knock into yo'r head the difference between a black an' a grizzly track? This is the hind foot, an' the heel is round. If it was a grizzly it would be pointed. An' it's too broad an' clubby f'r a grizzly, an' the claws are too long f'r the length of the foot. It's a black as plain as the nose on yo'r face!"

"And going our way," said Langdon. "Come on!" Two hundred yards up the coulee the bear had climbed out on the slope. Langdon and Bruce followed. In the thick grass and hard shale of the first crest of the slope the tracks were quickly lost, but the hunters were not much interested in these tracks now. From the height at which they were travelling they had a splendid view below them.

Not once did Bruce take his eyes from the creek bottom. He knew that it was down there they would find the grizzly, and he was interested in nothing else just at present. Langdon, on the other hand, was interested in everything that might be living or moving about them; every mass of rock and thicket of thorn held possibilities for him, and his eyes were questing the higher ridges and the peaks as well as their immediate trail. It was because of this that he saw something which made him suddenly grip his companion's arm and pull him down beside him on the ground.

"Look!" he whispered, stretching out an arm.

From his kneeling posture Bruce stared. His eyes fairly popped in amazement. Not more than thirty feet above them was a big rock shaped like a dry-goods box, and protruding from behind the farther side of this rock was the rear half of a bear. It was a black bear, its glossy coat shining in the sunlight. For a full half minute Bruce continued to stare. Then he grinned.

"Asleep—dead asleep! Jimmy—you want to see some fun?"

He put down his gun and drew out his long hunting knife. He chuckled softly as he felt of its keen point.

"If you never saw a bear run yo'r goin' to see one run now, Jimmy! You stay here!"

He began crawling slowly and quietly up the slope toward the rock, while Langdon held his breath in anticipation of what was about to happen. Twice Bruce looked back, and he was grinning broadly. There was undoubtedly going to be a very much astonished bear racing for the tops of the Rocky Mountains in another moment or two, and between this thought and the picture of Bruce's long lank figure snaking its way upward foot by foot the humour of the situation fell upon Langdon. Finally Bruce reached the rock. The long knife-blade gleamed in the sun; then it shot forward and a half inch of steel buried itself in the bear's rump. What followed in the next thirty seconds Langdon would never forget. The bear made no movement. Bruce jabbed again. Still there was no movement, and at the second thrust Bruce remained as motionless as the rock against which he was crouching, and his mouth was wide open as he stared down at Langdon.

"Now what the devil do you think of that?" he said, and rose slowly to his feet. "He ain't asleep—he's dead!"

Langdon ran up to him, and they went around the end of the rock. Bruce still held the knife in his hand and there was an odd expression in his face—a look that put troubled furrows between his eyes as he stood for a moment without speaking.

"I never see anything like that before," he said, slowly slipping his knife in its sheath. "It's a she-bear, an' she had cubs—pretty young cubs, too, from the looks o' her.'

"She was after a whistler, and undermined the rock," added Langdon. "Crushed to death, eh, Bruce?"

Bruce nodded.

"I never see anything like it before," he repeated. "I've wondered why they didn't get killed by diggin' under the rocks—but I never see it. Wonder where the cubs are? Poor little devils!"

He was on his knees examining the dead mother's teats.

"She didn't have more'n two—mebby one," he said, rising. "About three months old."

"And they'll starve?"

"If there was only one he probably will. The little cuss had so much milk he didn't have to forage for himself. Cubs is a good deal like babies—you can wean 'em early or you can ha'f grow 'em on pap. An' this is what comes of runnin' off an' leavin' your babies alone," moralized Bruce. "If you ever git married, Jimmy, don't you let yo'r wife do it. Sometimes th' babies burn up or break their necks!"

Again he turned along the crest of the slope, his eyes once more searching the valley, and Langdon followed a step behind him, wondering what had become of the cub.

And Muskwa, still slumbering on the rock-ledge with Thor, was dreaming of the mother who lay crushed under the rock on the slope, and as he dreamed he whimpered softly.

CHAPTER EIGHT

The ledge where Thor and Muskwa lay caught the first gleams of the morning sun, and as the sun rose higher the ledge grew warmer and warmer, and Thor, when he awoke, merely stretched himself and made no effort to rise. After his wounds and the *sapoos oowin* and the feast in the valley he was feeling tremendously fine and comfortable, and he was in no very great haste to leave this golden pool of sunlight. For a long time he looked steadily and curiously at Muskwa. In the chill of the night the little cub had snuggled up close between the warmth of Thor's huge forearms, and still lay there, whimpering in his babyish way as he dreamed.

After a time Thor did something that he had never been guilty of before—he sniffed gently at the soft little ball between his paws, and just once his big flat red tongue touched the cub's face; and Muskwa, perhaps still dreaming of his mother, snuggled closer. As little white children have won the hearts of savages who were about to slay them, so Muskwa had come strangely into the life of Thor.

The big grizzly was still puzzled. Not only was he struggling against an unaccountable dislike of all cubs in general, but also against the firmly established habits of ten years of aloneness. Yet he was beginning to comprehend that there was something very pleasant and companionable in the nearness of Muskwa. With the coming of man a new emotion had entered into his being—perhaps only the spark of an emotion. Until one has enemies, and faces dangers, one cannot fully appreciate friendship—and it may be that Thor, who now confronted real enemies and a real danger for the first time, was beginning to understand what friendship meant. Also it was drawing near to his mating season, and about Muskwa was the scent of his mother. And so as Muskwa continued to bask and dream in the sunshine, there was a growing content in Thor.

He looked down into the valley, shimmering in the wet of the night's rain, and he saw nothing to rouse discontent; he sniffed the air, and it was filled with the unpolluted sweetness of growing grass, of flowers, and balsam, and water fresh from the clouds.

Thor began to lick his wound, and it was this movement that roused Muskwa. The cub lifted his head. He blinked at the sun for a moment—then rubbed his face sleepily with his tiny paw and stood up. Like all youngsters, he was ready for another day, in spite of the hardships and toil of the preceding one.

While Thor still lay restfully looking down into the valley, Muskwa began investigating the crevices in the rock wall, and tumbled about among the boulders on the ledge.

From the valley Thor turned his eyes to the cub. There was curiosity in his attitude as he watched Muskwa's antics and queer tumblings among the rocks. Then he rose cumbrously and shook himself.

For at least five minutes he stood looking down into the valley, and sniffing the wind, as motionless as though carven out of rock. And Muskwa, perking up his little ears, came and stood beside him, his sharp little eyes peering from Thor off into sunlit space, and then back to Thor again, as if wondering what was about to happen next.

The big grizzly answered the question. He turned along the rock shelf and began descending into the valley. Muskwa tagged behind, just as he had followed the day before. The cub felt twice as big and fully twice as strong as yesterday, and he no longer was obsessed by that uncomfortable yearning for his mother's milk. Thor had graduated him quickly, and he was a meat-eater. And he knew they were returning to where they had feasted last night.

They had descended half the distance of the slope when the wind brought something to Thor. A deep-chested growl rolled out of him as he stopped for a moment, the thick ruff about his neck bristling ominously. The scent he had caught came from the direction of his cache, and it was an odour which he was not in a humour to tolerate in this particular locality. Strongly he smelled the presence of another bear. This would not have excited him under ordinary conditions, and it would not have excited him now had the presence been that of a female bear. But the scent was that of a he-bear, and it drifted strongly up a rock-cut ravine that ran straight down toward the balsam patch in which he had hidden the caribou.

Thor stopped to ask himself no questions. Growling under his breath, he began to descend so swiftly that Muskwa had great difficulty in keeping up with him. Not until they came to the edge of the plain that overlooked the lake and the balsams did they stop. Muskwa's little jaws hung open as he panted. Then his ears pricked forward, he stared, and suddenly every muscle in his small body became rigid.

Seventy-five yards below them their cache was being outraged. The robber was a huge black bear. He was a splendid outlaw. He was, perhaps, three hundred pounds lighter than Thor, but he stood almost as high, and in the sunlight his coat shone with the velvety gloss of sable—the biggest and boldest bear that had entered Thor's domain in many a day. He had pulled the caribou carcass from its hiding-place and was eating as Thor and Muskwa looked down on him.

After a moment Muskwa peered up questioningly at Thor. "What are we going to do?" he seemed to ask. "He's got our dinner!"

Slowly and very deliberately Thor began picking his way down those last seventy-five yards. He seemed to be in no hurry bow.

When he reached the edge of the meadow, perhaps thirty or forty yards from the big invader, he stopped again. There was nothing particularly ugly in his attitude, but the ruff about his shoulders was bigger than Muskwa had ever seen it before.

The black looked up from his feast, and for a full half minute they eyed each other. In a slow, pendulum-like motion the grizzly's huge head swung from side to side; the black was as motionless as a sphinx.

Four or five feet from Thor stood Muskwa. In a small-boyish sort of way he knew that something was going to happen soon, and in that same small-boyish way he was ready to put his stub of a tail between his legs and flee with Thor, or advance and fight with him. His eyes were curiously attracted by that pendulum-like swing of Thor's head. All nature understood that swing. Man had learned to understand it. "Look out when a grizzly rolls his head!" is the first commandment of the bear-hunter in the mountains.

The big black understood, and like other bears in Thor's domain, he should have slunk a little backward, turned about and made his exit. Thor gave him ample time. But the black was a new bear in the valley—and he was not only that: he was a powerful bear, and unwhipped; and he had overlorded a range of his own. He stood his ground.

The first growl of menace that passed between the two came from the black.

Again Thor advanced, slowly and deliberately—straight for the robber. Muskwa followed halfway and then stopped and squatted himself on his belly. Ten feet from the carcass Thor paused again; and now his huge head swung more swiftly back and forth, and a low rumbling thunder came from between his half-open jaws. The black's ivory fangs snarled; Muskwa whined.

Again Thor advanced, a foot at a time, and now his gaping jaws almost touched the ground, and his huge body was hunched low.

When no more than the length of a yardstick separated them there came a pause. For perhaps thirty seconds they were like two angry men, each trying to strike terror to the other's heart by the steadiness of his look.

Muskwa shook as if with the ague, and whined—softly and steadily he whined, and the whine reached Thor's ears. What happened after that began so quickly that Muskwa was struck dumb with terror, and he lay flattened out on the earth as motionless as a stone.

With that grinding, snarling grizzly roar, which is unlike any other animal cry in the world, Thor flung himself at the black. The black reared a little—just enough to fling himself backward easily as they came together breast to breast. He rolled upon his back, but Thor was too old a fighter to be caught by that first vicious ripping stroke of the black's hind foot, and he buried his four long flesh-rending teeth to the bone of his enemy's shoulder. At the same time he struck a terrific cutting stroke with his left paw.

Thor was a digger, and his claws were dulled; the black was not a digger, but a tree-climber, and his claws were like knives. And like knives they buried themselves in Thor's wounded shoulder, and the blood spurted forth afresh.

With a roar that seemed to set the earth trembling, the huge grizzly lunged backward and reared himself to his full nine feet. He had given the black warning. Even after their first tussle his enemy might have retreated and he would not have pursued. Now it was a fight to the death! The black had done more than ravage his cache. He had opened the man-wound!

A minute before Thor had been fighting for law and right—without great animosity or serious desire to kill. Now, however, he was terrible. His mouth was open, and it was eight inches from jaw to jaw; his lips were drawn up until his white teeth and his red gums were bared; muscles stood out like cords on his nostrils, and between his eyes was a furrow like the cleft made by an axe in the trunk of a pine. His eyes shone with the glare of red garnets, their greenish-black pupils almost obliterated by the ferocious fire that was in them. Man, facing Thor in this moment, would have known that only one would come out alive.

Thor was not a "stand-up" fighter. For perhaps six or seven seconds he remained erect, but as the black advanced a step he dropped quickly to all fours.

The black met him halfway, and after this—for many minutes—Muskwa hugged closer and closer to the earth while with gleaming eyes he watched the battle. It was such a fight as only the jungles and the mountains see, and the roar of it drifted up and down the valley.

Like human creatures the two giant beasts used their powerful forearms while with fangs and hind feet they ripped and tore. For two minutes they were in a close and deadly embrace, both rolling on the ground, now one under and then the other. The black clawed ferociously; Thor used chiefly his teeth and his terrible right hind foot. With his forearms he made no effort to rend the black, but used them to hold and throw his enemy. He was fighting to get *under*, as he had flung himself under the caribou he had disembowelled.

Again and again Thor buried his long fangs in the other's flesh; but in fang-fighting the black was even quicker than he, and his right shoulder was being literally torn to pieces when their jaws met in midair. Muskwa heard the clash of them; he heard the grind of teeth on teeth, the sickening crunch of bone.

Then suddenly the black was flung upon his side as though his neck had been broken, and Thor was at his throat. Still the black fought, his gaping and bleeding jaws powerless now as the grizzly closed his own huge jaws on the jugular.

Muskwa stood up. He was shivering still, but with a new and strange emotion. This was not play, as he and his mother had played. For the first time he was looking upon *battle*, and the thrill of it sent the blood hot and fast through his little body. With a faint, puppyish snarl he darted in. His teeth sank futilely into the thick hair and tough hide of the black's rump. He pulled and he snarled; he braced himself with his forefeet and tugged at his mouthful of hair, filled with a blind and unaccountable rage.

The black twisted himself upon his back, and one of his hind feet raked Thor from chest to vent. That stroke would have disembowelled a caribou or a deer; it left a red, open, bleeding wound three feet long on Thor.

Before it could be repeated, the grizzly swung himself sidewise, and the second blow caught Muskwa. The flat of the black's foot struck him, and for twenty feet he was sent like a stone out of a sling-shot. He was not cut, but he was stunned.

In that same moment Thor released his hold on his enemy's throat, and swung two or three feet to one side. He was dripping blood. The black's shoulders, chest, and neck were saturated with it; huge chunks had been torn from his body. He made an effort to rise, and Thor was on him again.

This time Thor got his deadliest of all holds. His great jaws clamped in a death-grip over the upper part of the black's nose. One terrific grinding crunch, and the fight was over. The black could not have lived after that. But this fact Thor did not know. It was now easy for him to rip with those knifelike claws on his hind feet. He continued to maul and tear for ten minutes after the black was dead.

When Thor finally quit the scene of battle was terrible to look upon. The ground was torn up and red; it was covered with great strips of black hide and pieces of flesh; and the black, on the under side, was torn open from end to end.

Two miles away, tense and white and scarcely breathing as they looked through their glasses, Langdon and Bruce crouched beside a rock on the mountainside. At that distance they had witnessed the terrific spectacle, but they could not see the cub. As Thor stood panting and bleeding over his lifeless enemy, Langdon lowered his glass.

"My God!" he breathed.

Bruce sprang to his feet.

"Come on!" he cried. "The black's dead! If we hustle we can get our grizzly!"

And down in the meadow Muskwa ran to Thor with a bit of warm black hide in his mouth, and Thor lowered his great bleeding head, and just once his red tongue shot out and caressed Muskwa's face. For the little tan-faced cub had proved himself; and it may be that Thor had seen and understood.

CHAPTER NINE

Neither Thor nor Muskwa went near the caribou meat after the big fight. Thor was in no condition to eat, and Muskwa was so filled with excitement and trembling that he could not swallow a mouthful. He continued to worry a strip of black hide, snarling and growling in his puny way, as though finishing what the other had begun.

For many minutes the grizzly stood with his big head drooping, and the blood gathered in splashes under him. He was facing down the valley. There was almost no wind—so little that it was scarcely possible to tell from which direction it came. Eddies of it were caught in the coulees, and higher up about the shoulders and peaks it blew stronger. Now and then one of these higher movements of air would sweep gently downward and flow through the valley for a few moments in a great noiseless breath that barely stirred the tops of the balsams and spruce.

One of these mountain-breaths came as Thor faced the east. And with it, faint and terrible, came the *man-smell!*

Thor roused himself with a sudden growl from the lethargy into which he had momentarily allowed himself to sink. His relaxed muscles hardened. He raised his head and sniffed the wind.

Muskwa ceased his futile fight with the bit of hide and also sniffed the air. It was warm with the man-scent, for Langdon and Bruce were running and sweating, and the odour of man-sweat drifts heavy and far. It filled Thor with a fresh rage. For a second time it came when he was hurt and bleeding. He had already associated the man-smell with hurt, and now it was doubly impressed upon him. He turned his head and snarled at the mutilated body of the big black. Then he snarled menacingly in the face of the wind. He was in no humour to run away. In these moments, if Bruce and Langdon had appeared over the rise, Thor would have charged with that deadly ferocity which lead can scarcely stop, and which has given to his kind their terrible name.

But the breath of air passed, and there followed a peaceful calm. The valley was filled with the purr of running water; from their rocks the whistlers called forth their soft notes; up on the green plain the ptarmigan were fluting, and rising in white-winged flocks. These things soothed Thor, as a woman's gentle hand quiets an angry man. For five minutes he continued to rumble and growl as he tried vainly to catch the scent again; but the rumbling and growling grew steadily less, and finally he turned and walked slowly toward the coulee down which he and Muskwa had come a little while before. Muskwa followed.

The coulee, or ravine, hid them from the valley as they ascended. Its bottom was covered with rock and shale. The wounds Thor had received in the fight, unlike bullet wounds, had stopped bleeding after the first few minutes, and he left no telltale red spots behind. The ravine took them to the first chaotic upheaval of rock halfway up the mountain, and here they were still more lost to view from below.

They stopped and drank at a pool formed by the melting snow on the peaks, and then went on. Thor did not stop when they reached the ledge on which they had slept the previous night.

And this time Muskwa was not tired when they reached the ledge. Two days had made a big change in the little tan-faced cub. He was not so round and puffy. And he was stronger—a great deal stronger; he was becoming hardened, and under Thor's strenuous tutelage he was swiftly graduating from cubhood to young bearhood.

It was evident that Thor had followed this ledge at some previous time. He knew where he was going. It continued up and up, and finally seemed to end in the face of a precipitous wall of rock. Thor's trail led him directly to a great crevice, hardly wider than his body, and through this he went, emerging at the edge of the wildest and roughest slide of rock that Muskwa had ever seen. It looked like a huge quarry, and it broke through the timber far below them, and reached almost to the top of the mountain above.

For Muskwa to make his way over the thousand pitfalls of that chaotic upheaval was an impossibility, and as Thor began to climb over the first rocks the cub stopped and whined. It was the first time he had given up, and when he saw that Thor gave no attention to his whine, terror seized upon him and he cried for help as loudly as he could while he hunted frantically for a path up through the rocks.

Utterly oblivious of Muskwa's predicament, Thor continued until he was fully thirty yards away. Then he stopped, faced about deliberately, and waited.

This gave Muskwa courage, and he scratched and clawed and even used his chin and teeth in his efforts to follow. It took him ten minutes to reach Thor, and he was completely winded. Then, all at once, his terror vanished. For Thor stood on a white, narrow path that was as solid as a floor.

The path was perhaps eighteen inches wide. It was unusual—and mysterious-looking, and strangely out of place where it was. It looked as though an army of workmen had come along with hammers and had broken up tons of sandstone and slate, and then filled in between the boulders with rubble, making a smooth and narrow road that in places was ground to the fineness of powder and the hardness of cement. But instead of hammers, the hoofs of a hundred or perhaps a thousand generations of mountain sheep had made the trail. It was the sheep-path over the range. The first band of bighorn may have blazed the way before Columbus discovered America; surely it had taken a great many years for hoofs to make that smooth road among the rocks.

Thor used the path as one of his highways from valley to valley, and there were other creatures of the mountains who used it as well as he, and more frequently. As he stood waiting for Muskwa to get his wind they both heard an odd chuckling sound approaching them from above. Forty or fifty feet up the slide the path twisted and descended a little depression behind a huge boulder, and out from behind this boulder came a big porcupine.

There is a law throughout the North that a man shall not kill a porcupine. He is the "lost man's friend," for the wandering and starving prospector or hunter can nearly always find a porcupine, if nothing else; and a child can kill him. He is the humourist of the wilderness—the happiest, the best-natured, and altogether the mildest-mannered beast that ever drew breath. He talks and chatters and chuckles incessantly, and when he travels he walks like a huge animated pincushion; he is oblivious of everything about him as though asleep.

As this particular "porky" advanced upon Muskwa and Thor, he was communing happily with himself, the chuckling notes he made sounding very much like a baby's cooing. He was enormously fat, and as he waddled slowly along his side and tail quills clicked on the stones. His eyes were on the path at his feet. He was deeply absorbed in nothing at all, and he was within five feet of Thor before he saw the grizzly. Then, in a wink, he humped himself into a ball. For a few seconds he scolded vociferously. After that he was as silent as a sphinx, his little red eyes watching the big bear.

Thor did not want to kill him, but the path was narrow, and he was ready to go on. He advanced a foot or two, and Porky turned his back toward Thor and made ready to deliver a swipe with his powerful tail. In that tail were several hundred quills. As Thor had more than once come into contact with porcupine quills, he hesitated.

Muskwa was looking on curiously. He still had his lesson to learn, for the quill he had once picked up in his foot had been a loose quill. But since the porcupine seemed to puzzle Thor, the cub turned and made ready to go back along the slide if it became necessary. Thor advanced another foot, and with a sudden *chuck, chuck, chuck*—the most vicious sound he was capable of making—Porky advanced backward and his broad, thick tail whipped through the air with a force that would have driven quills a quarter of an inch into the butt of a tree. Having missed, he humped himself again, and Thor stepped out on the boulder and circled around him. There he waited for Muskwa.

Porky was immensely satisfied with his triumph. He unlimbered himself; his quills settled a bit; and he advanced toward Muskwa, at the same time resuming his good-natured chuckling.

Instinctively the cub hugged the edge of the path, and in doing so slipped over the edge. By the time he had scrambled up again Porky was four or five feet beyond him and totally absorbed in his travel.

The adventure of the sheep-trail was not yet quite over, for scarcely had Porky maneuvered himself to safety when around the edge of the big boulder above appeared a badger, hot on the fresh and luscious scent of his favourite dinner, a porcupine. This worthless outlaw of the mountains was three times as large as Muskwa, and every ounce of him was fighting muscle and bone and claw and sharp teeth. He had a white mark on his nose and forehead; his legs were short and thick; his tail was bushy, and the claws on his front feet were almost as long as a bear's. Thor greeted him with an immediate growl of warning, and the badger scooted back up the trail in fear of his life.

Meanwhile Porky lumbered slowly along in quest of new feeding-grounds, talking and singing to himself, forgetting entirely what had happened a minute or two before, and unconscious of the fact that Thor had saved him from a death as certain as though he had fallen over a thousand-foot precipice.

For nearly a mile Thor and Muskwa followed the Bighorn Highway before its winding course brought them at last to the very top of the range. They were fully three-quarters of a mile above the creek-bottom, and so narrow in places was the crest of the mountain along which the sheep-trail led that they could look down into both valleys.

To Muskwa it was all a greenish golden haze below him; the depths seemed illimitable; the forest along the stream was only a black streak, and the parklike clumps of balsams and cedars on the farther slopes looked like very small bosks of thorn or buffalo willow.

Up here the wind was blowing, too. It whipped him with a strange fierceness, and half a dozen times he felt the mysterious and very unpleasant chill of snow under his feet. Twice a great bird swooped near him. It was the biggest bird he had ever seen—an eagle. The second time it came so near that he heard the *beat* of it, and saw its great, fierce head and lowering talons.

Thor whirled toward the eagle and growled. If Muskwa had been alone, the cub would have gone sailing off in those murderous talons. As it was, the third time the eagle circled it was down the slope from them. It was after other game. The scent of the game came to Thor and Muskwa, and they stopped.

Perhaps a hundred yards below them was a shelving slide of soft shale, and on this shale, basking in the warm sun after their morning's feed lower down, was a band of sheep. There were twenty or thirty of them, mostly ewes and their lambs. Three huge old rams were lying on a patch of snow farther to the east.

With his six-foot wings spread out like twin fans, the eagle continued to circle. He was as silent as a feather floating with the wind. The ewes and even the old bighorns were unconscious of his presence over them. Most of the lambs were lying close to their mothers, but two or three of a livelier turn of mind were wandering over the shale and occasionally hopping about in playful frolic.

The eagle's fierce eyes were upon these youngsters. Suddenly he drifted farther away—a full rifle-shot distance straight in the face of the wind; then he swung gracefully, and came back with the wind. And as he came, his wings apparently motionless, he gathered greater and greater speed, and shot like a rocket straight for the lambs. He seemed to have come and gone like a great shadow, and just one plaintive, agonized bleat marked his passing-and two little lambs were left where there had been three.

There was instant commotion on the slide. The ewes began to run back and forth and bleat excitedly. The three rams sprang up and stood like rocks, their huge battlemented heads held high as they scanned the depths below them and the peaks above for new danger.

One of them saw Thor, and the deep, grating bleat of warning that rattled out of his throat a hunter could have heard a mile away. As he gave his danger signal he started down the slide, and in another moment an avalanche of hoofs was clattering down the steep shale slope, loosening small stones and boulders that went tumbling and crashing down the mountain with a din that steadily increased as they set others in motion on the way. This was all mighty interesting to Muskwa, and he would have stood for a long time looking down for other things to happen if Thor had not led him on.

After a time the Bighorn Highway began to descend into the valley from the upper end of which Thor had been driven by Langdon's first shots. They were now six or eight miles north of the timber in which the hunters had made their permanent camp, and headed for the lower tributaries of the Skeena.

Another hour of travel, and the bare shale and gray crags were above them again, and they were on the green slopes. After the rocks, and the cold winds, and the terrible glare he had seen in the eagle's eyes, the warm and lovely valley into which they were descending lower and lower was a paradise to Muskwa.

It was evident that Thor had something in his mind. He was not rambling now. He cut off the ends and the bulges of the slopes. With his head hunched low he travelled steadily northward, and a compass could not have marked out a straighter line for the lower waters of the Skeena. He was tremendously businesslike, and Muskwa, tagging bravely along behind, wondered if he were never going to stop; if there could be anything in the whole wide world finer for a big grizzly and a little tan-faced cub than these wonderful sunlit slopes which Thor seemed in such great haste to leave.

CHAPTER TEN

If it had not been for Langdon, this day of the fight between the two bears would have held still greater excitement and another and deadlier peril for Thor and Muskwa. Three minutes after the hunters had arrived breathless and sweating upon the scene of the sanguinary conflict Bruce was ready and anxious to continue the pursuit of Thor. He knew the big grizzly could not be far away; he was certain that Thor had gone up the mountain. He found signs of the grizzly's feet in the gravel of the coulee at just about the time Thor and the tan-faced cub struck the Bighorn Highway.

His arguments failed to move Langdon. Stirred to the depth of his soul by what he had seen, and what he saw about him now, the hunter-naturalist refused to leave the blood-stained and torn-up arena in which the grizzly and the black had fought their duel.

"If I knew that I was not going to fire a single shot, I would travel five thousand miles to see this," he said. "It's worth thinking about, and looking over, Bruce. The grizzly won't spoil. This will—in a few hours. If there's a story here we can dig out I want it."

Again and again Langdon went over the battlefield, noting the ripped-up ground, the big spots of dark-red stain, the strips of flayed skin, and the terrible wounds on the body of the dead black. For half an hour Bruce paid less attention to these things than he did to the carcass of the caribou. At the end of that time he called Langdon to the edge of the clump of balsams.

"You wanted the story," he said, "an' I've got it for you, Jimmy."

He entered the balsams and Langdon followed him. A few steps under the cover Bruce halted and pointed to the hollow in which Thor had cached his meat. The hollow was stained with blood.

"You was right in your guess, Jimmy," he said. "Our grizzly is a meat-eater. Last night he killed a caribou out there in the meadow. I know it was the grizzly that killed 'im an' not the black, because the tracks along the edge of the timber are grizzly tracks. Come on. I'll show you where 'e jumped the caribou!"

He led the way back into the meadow, and pointed out where Thor had dragged down the young bull. There were bits of flesh and a great deal of stain where he and Muskwa had feasted.

"He hid the carcass in the balsams after he had filled himself," went on Bruce. "This morning the black came along, smelled the meat, an' robbed the cache. Then back come the grizzly after his morning feed, an' that's what happened! There's yo'r story, Jimmy."

"And—he may come back again?" asked Langdon.

"Not on your life, he won't!" cried Bruce. "He wouldn't touch that carcass ag'in if he was starving. Just now this place is like poison to him."

After that Bruce left Langdon to meditate alone on the field of battle while he began trailing Thor. In the shade of the balsams Langdon wrote for a steady hour, frequently rising to establish new facts or verify others already discovered. Meanwhile the mountaineer made his way foot by foot up the coulee. Thor had left no blood, but where others would have seen nothing Bruce detected the signs of his passing. When he returned to where Langdon was completing his notes, his face wore a look of satisfaction.

"He went over the mount'in," he said briefly.

It was noon before they climbed over the volcanic quarry of rock and followed the Bighorn Highway to the point where Thor and Muskwa had watched the eagle and the sheep. They ate their lunch here, and scanned the valley through their glasses. Bruce was silent for a long time. Then he lowered his telescope, and turned to Langdon.

"I guess I've got his range pretty well figgered out," he said. "He runs these two valleys, an' we've got our camp too far south. See that timber down there? That's where our camp should be. What do you say to goin' back over the divide with our horses an' moving up here?"

"And leave our grizzly until to-morrow?"

Bruce nodded.

"We can't go after 'im and leave our horses tied up in the creek-bottom back there."

Langdon boxed his glasses and rose to his feet. Suddenly he grew rigid.

"What was that?"

"I didn't hear anything," said Bruce.

For a moment they stood side by side, listening. A gust of wind whistled about their ears. It died away.

"Hear it!" whispered Langdon, and his voice was filled with a sudden excitement.

"The dogs!" cried Bruce.

"Yes, the dogs!"

They leaned forward, their ears turned to the south, and faintly there came to them the distant, thrilling tongue of the Airedales!

Metoosin had come, and he was seeking them in the valley!

CHAPTER ELEVEN

Thor was on what the Indians call a *pimootao*. His brute mind had all at once added two and two together, and while perhaps he did not make four of it, his mental arithmetic was accurate enough to convince him that straight north was the road to travel.

By the time Langdon and Bruce had reached the summit of the Bighorn Highway, and were listening to the distant tongueing of the dogs, little Muskwa was in abject despair. Following Thor had been like a game of tag with never a moment's rest.

An hour after they left the sheep trail they came to the rise in the valley where the waters separated. From this point one creek flowed southward into the Tacla Lake country and the other northward into the Babine, which was a tributary of the Skeena. They descended very quickly into a much lower country, and for the first time Muskwa encountered marshland, and travelled at times through grass so rank and thick that he could not see but could only hear Thor forging on ahead of him.

The stream grew wider and deeper, and in places they skirted the edges of dark, quiet pools that Muskwa thought must have been of immeasurable depth. These pools gave Muskwa his first breathing-spells. Now and then Thor would stop and sniff over the edge of them. He was hunting for something, and yet he never seemed to find it; and each time that he started on afresh Muskwa was so much nearer to the end of his endurance.

They were fully seven miles north of the point from which Bruce and Langdon were scanning the valley through their glasses when they came to a lake. It was a dark and unfriendly looking lake to Muskwa, who had never seen anything but sunlit pools in the dips. The forest grew close down to its shore. In places it was almost black. Queer birds squawked in the thick reeds. It was heavy with a strange odour—a fragrance of something that made the cub lick his little chops, and filled him with hunger.

For a minute or two Thor stood sniffing this scent that filled the air. It was the smell of fish.

Slowly the big grizzly began picking his way along the edge of the lake. He soon came to the mouth of a small creek. It was not more than twenty feet wide, but it was dark and quiet and deep, like the lake itself. For a hundred yards Thor made his way up this creek, until he came to where a number of trees had fallen across it, forming a jam. Close to this jam the water was covered with a green scum. Thor knew what lay under that scum, and very quietly he crept out on the logs.

Midway in the stream he paused, and with his right paw gently brushed back the scum so that an open pool of clear water lay directly under him.

Muskwa's bright little eyes watched him from the shore. He knew that Thor was after something to eat, but how he was going to get it out of that pool of water puzzled and interested him in spite of his weariness.

Thor stretched himself out on his belly, his head and right paw well over the jam. He now put his paw a foot into the water and held it there very quietly. He could see clearly to the bottom of the stream. For a few moments he saw only this bottom, a few sticks, and the protruding end of a limb. Then a long slim shadow moved slowly under him—a fifteen-inch trout. It was too deep for him, and Thor did not make an excited plunge.

Patiently he waited, and very soon this patience was rewarded. A beautiful red-spotted trout floated out from under the scum, and so suddenly that Muskwa gave a yelp of terror, Thor's huge paw sent a shower of water a dozen feet into the air, and the fish landed with a thump within three feet of the cub. Instantly Muskwa was upon it. His sharp teeth dug into it as it flopped and struggled.

Thor rose on the logs, but when he saw that Muskwa had taken possession of the fish, he resumed his former position. Muskwa was just finishing his first real kill when a second spout of water shot upward and another trout pirouetted shoreward through the air. This time Thor followed quickly, for he was hungry.

It was a glorious feast they had that early afternoon beside the shaded creek. Five times Thor knocked fish out from under the scum, but for the life of him Muskwa could not eat more than his first trout.

For several hours after their dinner they lay in a cool, hidden spot close to the log-jam. Muskwa did not sleep soundly. He was beginning to understand that life was now largely a matter of personal responsibility with him, and his ears had begun to attune themselves to sound. Whenever Thor moved or heaved a deep sigh, Muskwa knew it. After that day's Marathon with the grizzly he was filled with uneasiness—a fear that he might lose his big friend and food-killer, and he was determined that the parent he had adopted should have no opportunity of slipping away from him unheard and unseen. But Thor had no intention of deserting his little comrade. In fact, he was becoming quite fond of Muskwa.

It was not alone his hunger for fish or fear of his enemies that was bringing Thor into the lower country of the Babine waterways. For a week past there had been in him a steadily growing unrest, and it had reached its climax in these last two or three days of battle and flight. He was filled with a strange and unsatisfied yearning, and as Muskwa napped in his little bed among the bushes Thor's ears were keenly alert for certain sounds and his nose frequently sniffed the air. He wanted a mate. It was *puskoowepesim*—the "moulting moon"—and always in this moon, or the end of the "egg-laying moon," which was June, he hunted for the female that came to him from the western ranges. He was almost entirely a creature of habit, and always he made this particular detour, entering the other valley again far down toward the Babine. He never failed to feed on fish along the way, and the more fish he ate the stronger was the odour of him. It is barely possible Thor had discovered that this perfume of golden-spotted trout made him more attractive to his lady-love. Anyway, he ate fish, and he smelled abundantly.

Thor rose and stretched himself two hours before sunset, and he knocked three more fish out of the water. Muskwa ate the head of one and Thor finished the rest. Then they continued their pilgrimage.

It was a new world that Muskwa entered now. In it there were none of the old familiar sounds. The purring drone of the upper valley was gone. There were no whistlers, and no ptarmigan, and no fat little gophers running about. The water of the lake lay still, and dark, and deep, with black and sunless pools hiding themselves under the roots of trees, so close did the forest cling to it. There were no rocks to climb over, but dank, soft logs, thick windfalls, and litters of brush. The air was different, too. It was very still. Under their feet at times was a wonderful carpet of soft moss in which Thor sank nearly to his armpits. And the forest was filled with a strange gloom and many mysterious shadows, and there hung heavily in it the pungent smells of decaying vegetation.

Thor did not travel so swiftly here. The silence and the gloom and the oppressively scented air seemed to rouse his caution. He stepped quietly; frequently he stopped and looked about him, and listened; he smelled at the edges of pools hidden under the roots; every new sound brought him to a stop, his head hung low and his ears alert.

Several times Muskwa saw shadowy things floating through the gloom. They were the big gray owls that turned snow white in winter. And once, when it was almost dark, they came upon a pop-eyed, loose-jointed, fierce-looking creature in the trail who scurried away like a ball at sight of Thor. It was a lynx.

It was not yet quite dark when Thor came out very quietly into a clearing, and Muskwa found himself first on the shore of a creek, and then close to a big pond. The air was full of the breath and warmth of a new kind of life. It was not fish, and yet it seemed to come from the pond, in the centre of which were three or four circular masses that looked like great brush-heaps plastered with a coating of mud.

Whenever he came into this end of the valley Thor always paid a visit to the beaver colony, and occasionally he helped himself to a fat young beaver for supper or breakfast. This evening he was not hungry, and he was in a hurry. In spite of these two facts he stood for some minutes in the shadows near the pond.

The beavers had already begun their night's work. Muskwa soon understood the significance of the shimmering streaks that ran swiftly over the surface of the water. At the end of each streak was always a dark, flat head, and now he saw that most of these streaks began at the farther edge of the pond and made directly for a long, low barrier that shut in the water a hundred yards to the east.

This particular barrier was strange to Thor, and with his maturer knowledge of beaver ways he knew that his engineering friends—whom he ate only occasionally—were broadening their domain by building a new dam. As they watched, two fat workmen shoved a four-foot length of log into the pond with a big splash, and one of them began piloting it toward the scene of building operations, while his companion returned to other work. A little later there was a crash in the timber on the opposite side of the pond, where another workman had succeeded in felling a tree. Then Thor made his way toward the dam.

Almost instantly there was a terrific crack out in the middle of the pond, followed by a tremendous splash. An old beaver had seen Thor and with the flat side of his broad tail had given the surface of the water a warning slap that cut the still air like a rifle-shot. All at once there were splashings and divings in every direction, and a moment later the pond was ruffled and heaving as a score of interrupted workers dove excitedly under the surface to the safety of their brush-ribbed and mud-plastered strongholds, and Muskwa was so absorbed in the general excitement that he almost forgot to follow Thor.

He overtook the grizzly at the dam. For a few moments Thor inspected the new work, and then tested it with his weight. It was solid, and over this bridge ready built for them they crossed to the higher ground on the opposite side. A few hundred yards farther on Thor struck a fairly well-beaten caribou trail which in the course of half an hour led them around the end of the lake to the outlet stream flowing north.

Every minute Muskwa was hoping that Thor would stop. His afternoon's nap had not taken the lameness out of his legs nor the soreness from the tender pads of his feet. He had had enough, and more than enough, of travel, and could he have regulated the world according to his own wishes he would not have walked another mile for a whole month. Mere walking would not have been so bad, but to keep up with Thor's ambling gait he was compelled to trot, like a stubby four-year-old child hanging desperately to the thumb of a big and fast-walking man. Muskwa had not even a thumb to hang to. The bottoms of his feet were like boils; his tender nose was raw from contact with brush and the knife-edged marsh grass, and his little back felt all caved in. Still he hung on desperately, until the creek-bottom was again sand and gravel, and travelling was easier.

The stars were up now, millions of them, clear and brilliant; and it was quite evident that Thor had set his mind on an "all-night hike," a *kuppatipsk pimootao* as a Cree tracker would have called it. Just how it would have ended for Muskwa is a matter of conjecture had not the spirits of thunder and rain and lightning put their heads together to give him a rest.

For perhaps an hour the stars were undimmed, and Thor kept on like a heathen without a soul, while Muskwa limped on all four feet. Then a low rumbling gathered in the west. It grew louder and louder, and approached swiftly—straight from the warm Pacific. Thor grew uneasy, and sniffed in the face of it. Livid streaks began to criss-cross a huge pall of black that was closing in on them like a vast curtain. The stars began to go out. A moaning wind came. And then the rain.

Thor had found a huge rock that shelved inward, like a lean-to, and he crept back under this with Muskwa before the deluge descended. For many minutes it was more like a flood than a rain. It seemed as though a part of the Pacific Ocean had been scooped up and dropped on them, and in half an hour the creek was a swollen torrent.

The lightning and the crash of thunder terrified Muskwa. Now he could see Thor in great blinding flashes of fire, and the next instant it was as black as pitch; the tops of the mountains seemed falling down into the valley; the earth trembled and shook—and he snuggled closer and closer to Thor until at last he lay between his two forearms, half buried in the long hair of the big grizzly's shaggy chest. Thor himself was not much concerned in these noisy convulsions of nature, except to keep himself dry. When he took a bath he wanted the sun to be shining and a nice warm rock close at hand on which to stretch himself.

For a long time after its first fierce outbreak the rain continued to fall in a gentle shower. Muskwa liked this, and under the sheltering rock, snuggled against Thor, he felt very comfortable and easily fell asleep. Through long hours Thor kept his vigil alone, drowsing now and then, but kept from sound slumber by the restlessness that was in him.

It stopped raining soon after midnight, but it was very dark, the stream was flooding over its bars, and Thor remained under the rock. Muskwa had a splendid sleep.

Day had come when Thor's stirring roused Muskwa. He followed the grizzly out into the open, feeling tremendously better than last night, though his feet were still sore and his body was stiff.

Thor began to follow the creek again. Along this stream there were low flats and many small bayous where grew luxuriantly the tender grass and roots, and especially the slim long-stemmed lilies on which Thor was fond of feeding. But for a thousand-pound grizzly to fill up on such vegetarian dainties as these consumed many hours, if not one's whole time, and Thor considered that he had no time to lose. Thor was a most ardent lover when he loved at all, which was only a few days out of the year; and during these days he twisted his mode of living around so that while the spirit possessed him he no longer existed for the sole purpose of eating and growing fat. For a short time he put aside his habit of living to eat, and ate to live; and poor Muskwa was almost famished before another dinner was forthcoming.

But at last, early in the afternoon, Thor came to a pool which he could not pass. It was not a dozen feet in width, and it was alive with trout. The fish had not been able to reach the lake above, and they had waited too long after the flood-season to descend into the deeper waters of the Babine and the Skeena. They had taken refuge in this pool, which was now about to become a death-trap.

At one end the water was two feet deep; at the other end only a few inches. After pondering over this fact for a few moments, the grizzly waded openly into the deepest part, and from the bank above Muskwa saw the shimmering trout darting into the shallower water. Thor advanced slowly, and now, when he stood in less than eight inches of water, the panic-stricken fish one after another tried to escape back into the deeper part of the pool.

Again and again Thor's big right paw swept up great showers of water. The first inundation knocked Muskwa off his feet. But with it came a two-pound trout which the cub quickly dragged out of range and began eating. So agitated became the pool because of the mighty strokes of Thor's paw that the trout completely lost their heads, and no sooner did they reach one end than they turned about and darted for the other. They kept this up until the grizzly had thrown fully a dozen of their number ashore.

So absorbed was Muskwa in his fish, and Thor in his fishing, that neither had noticed a visitor. Both saw him at about the same time, and for fully thirty seconds they stood and stared, Thor in his pool and the cub over his fish, utter amazement robbing them of the power of movement. The visitor was another grizzly, and as coolly as though he had done the fishing himself he began eating the fish which Thor had thrown out! A worse insult or a deadlier challenge could not have been known in the land of Beardom. Even Muskwa sensed that fact. He looked expectantly at Thor. There was going to be another fight, and he licked his little chops in anticipation.

Thor came up out of the pool slowly. On the bank he paused. The grizzlies gazed at each other, the newcomer crunching a fish as he looked. Neither growled. Muskwa perceived no signs of enmity, and then to his increased astonishment Thor began eating a fish within three feet of the interloper!

Perhaps man is the finest of all God's creations, but when it comes to his respect for old age he is no better, and sometimes not as good, as a grizzly bear; for Thor would not rob an old bear, he would not fight an old bear, and he would not drive an old bear from his own meat— which is more than can be said of some humans. And the visitor was an old bear, and a sick bear as well. He stood almost as high as Thor, but he was so old that he was only half as broad across the chest, and his neck and head were grotesquely thin. The Indians have a name for him. *Kuyas Wapusk* they call him—the bear so old he is about to die. They let him go unharmed; other bears tolerate him and let him eat their meat if he chances along; the white man kills him.

This old bear was famished. His claws were gone; his hair was thin, and in some places his skin was naked, and he had barely more than red, hard gums to chew with. If he lived until autumn he would den up—for the last time. Perhaps death would come even sooner than that. If so, *Kuyas Wapusk* would know in time, and he would crawl off into some hidden cave or deep crevice in the rocks to breathe his last. For in all the Rocky Mountains, so far as Bruce or Langdon knew, there was not a man who had found the bones or body of a grizzly that had died a natural death!

And big, hunted Thor, torn by wound and pursued by man, seemed to understand that this would be the last real feast on earth for *Kuyas Wapusk*—too old to fish for himself, too old to hunt, too old even to dig out the tender lily roots; and so he let him eat until the last fish was gone, and then went on, with Muskwa tagging at his heels.

For still another two hours Thor led Muskwa on that tiresome jaunt into the north. They had travelled a good twenty miles since leaving the Bighorn Highway, and to the little tan-faced cub those twenty miles were like a journey around the world. Ordinarily he would not have gone that far away from his birthplace until his second year, and very possibly his third.

Not once in this hike down the valley had Thor wasted time on the mountain slopes. He had picked out the easiest trails along the creek. Three or four miles below the pool where they had left the old bear he suddenly changed this procedure by swinging due westward, and a little later they were once more climbing a mountain. They went up a long green slide for a quarter of a mile, and luckily for Muskwa's legs this brought them to the smooth plainlike floor of a break which took them without much more effort out on the slopes of the other valley. This was the valley in which Thor had killed the black bear twenty miles to the southward.

From the moment Thor looked out over the northern limits of his range a change took possession of him. All at once he lost his eagerness to hurry. For fifteen minutes he stood looking down into the valley, sniffing the air. He descended slowly, and when he reached the green meadows and the creek-bottom he *mooshed* along straight in the face of the wind, which was coming from the south and west. It did not bring him the scent he wanted—the smell of his mate. Yet an instinct that was more infallible than reason told him that she was near, or should be near. He did not take accident or sickness or the possibility of hunters having killed her into consideration. This was where he had always started in to hunt for her, and sooner or later he had found her. He knew her smell. And he crossed and recrossed the bottoms so that it could not escape him.

When Thor was love-sick he was more or less like a man: that is to say, he was an idiot. The importance of all other things dwindled into nothingness. His habits, which were as fixed as the stars at other times, took a complete vacation. He even forgot hunger, and the whistlers and gophers were quite safe. He was tireless. He rambled during the night as well as the day in quest of his lady-love.

It was quite natural that in these exciting hours he should forget Muskwa almost entirely. At least ten times before sunset he crossed and recrossed the creek, and the disgusted and almost ready-to-quit cub waded and swam and floundered after him until he was nearly drowned. The tenth or dozenth time Thor forded the stream Muskwa revolted and followed along on his own side. It was not long before the grizzly returned.

It was soon after this, just as the sun was setting, that the unexpected happened. What little wind there was suddenly swung straight into the east, and from the western slopes half a mile away it brought a scent that held Thor motionless in his tracks for perhaps half a minute, and then set him off on that ambling run which is the ungainliest gait of all four-footed creatures.

Muskwa rolled after him like a ball, pegging away for dear life, but losing ground at every jump. In that half-mile stretch he would have lost Thor altogether if the grizzly had not stopped near the bottom of the first slope to take fresh reckonings. When he started up the slope Muskwa could see him, and with a yelping cry for him to wait a minute set after him again.

Two or three hundred yards up the mountainside the slope shelved downward into a hollow, or dip, and nosing about in this dip, questing the air as Thor had quested it, was the beautiful she-grizzly from over the range. With her was one of her last year's cubs. Thor was within fifty yards of her when he came over the crest. He stopped. He looked at her. And Iskwao, "the female," looked at him.

Then followed true bear courtship. All haste, all eagerness, all desire for his mate seemed to have left Thor; and if Iskwao had been eager and yearning she was profoundly indifferent now. For two or three minutes Thor stood looking casually about, and this gave Muskwa time to come up and perch himself beside him, expecting another fight.

As though Thor was a thousand miles or so from her thoughts, Iskwao turned over a flat rock and began hunting for grubs and ants, and not to be outdone in this stoic unconcern Thor pulled up a bunch of grass and swallowed it. Iskwao moved a step or two, and Thor moved a step or two, and as if purely by accident their steps were toward each other.

Muskwa was puzzled. The older cub was puzzled. They sat on their haunches like two dogs, one three times as big as the other, and wondered what was going to happen.

It took Thor and Iskwao five minutes to arrive within five feet of each other, and then very decorously they smelled noses.

The year-old cub joined the family circle. He was of just the right age to have an exceedingly long name, for the Indians called him Pipoonaskoos—"the yearling." He came boldly up to Thor and his mother. For a moment Thor did not seem to notice him. Then his long right arm shot out in a sudden swinging upper-cut that lifted Pipoonaskoos clean off the ground and sent him spinning two-thirds of the distance up to Muskwa.

The mother paid no attention to this elimination of her offspring, and still lovingly smelled noses with Thor. Muskwa, however, thought this was the preliminary of another tremendous fight, and with a yelp of defiance he darted down the slope and set upon Pipoonaskoos with all his might.

Pipoonaskoos was "mother's boy." That is, he was one of those cubs who persist in following their mothers through a second season, instead of striking out for themselves. He had nursed until he was five months old; his parent had continued to hunt tidbits for him; he was fat, and sleek, and soft; he was, in fact, a "Willie" of the mountains.

On the other hand, a few days had put a lot of real mettle into Muskwa, and though he was only a third as large as Pipoonaskoos, and his feet were sore, and his back ached, he landed on the other cub like a shot out of a gun.

Still dazed by the blow of Thor's paw, Pipoonaskoos gave a yelping call to his mother for help at this sudden onslaught. He had never been in a fight, and he rolled over on his back and side, kicking and scratching and yelping as Muskwa's needle-like teeth sank again and again into his tender hide.

Luckily Muskwa got him once by the nose, and bit deep, and if there was any sand at all in Willie Pipoonaskoos this took it out of him, and while Muskwa held on for dear life he let out a steady stream of yelps, informing his mother that he was being murdered. To these cries Iskwao paid no attention at all, but continued to smell noses with Thor.

Finally freeing his bleeding nose, Pipoonaskoos shook Muskwa off by sheer force of superior weight and took to flight on a dead run. Muskwa pegged valiantly after him. Twice they made the circle of the basin, and in spite of his shorter legs, Muskwa was a close second in the race when Pipoonaskoos, turning an affrighted glance sidewise for an instant, hit against a rock and went sprawling. In another moment Muskwa was at him again, and he would have continued biting and snarling until there was no more strength left in him had he not happened to see Thor and Iskwao disappearing slowly over the edge of the slope toward the valley.

Almost immediately Muskwa forgot fighting. He was amazed to find that Thor, instead of tearing up the other bear, was walking off with her. Pipoonaskoos also pulled himself together and looked. Then Muskwa looked at Pipoonaskoos, and Pipoonaskoos looked at Muskwa. The tan-faced cub licked his chops just once, as if torn between the prospective delight of mauling Pipoonaskoos and the more imperative duty of following Thor. The other gave him no choice. With a whimpering yelp he set off after his mother.

Exciting times followed for the two cubs. All that night Thor and Iskwao kept by themselves in the buffalo willow thickets and the balsams of the creek-bottom. Early in the evening Pipoonaskoos sneaked up to his mother again, and Thor lifted him into the middle of the creek. The second visual proof of Thor's displeasure impinged upon Muskwa the fact that the older bears were not in a mood to tolerate the companionship of cubs, and the result was a wary and suspicious truce between him and Pipoonaskoos.

All the next day Thor and Iskwao kept to themselves. Early in the morning Muskwa began adventuring about a little in quest of food. He liked tender grass, but it was not very filling. Several times he saw Pipoonaskoos digging in the soft bottom close to the creek, and finally he drove the other cub away from a partly digged hole and investigated for himself. After a little more excavating he pulled out a white, bulbous, tender root that he thought was the sweetest and nicest thing he had ever eaten, not even excepting fish. It was the one *bonne bouche* of all the good things he would eventually learn to eat—the spring beauty. One other thing alone was at all comparable with it, and that was the dog-tooth violet. Spring beauties were growing about him abundantly, and he continued to dig until his feet were grievously tender. But he had the satisfaction of being comfortably fed.

Thor was again responsible for a fight between Muskwa and Pipoonaskoos. Late in the afternoon the older bears were lying down side by side in a thicket when, without any apparent reason at all, Thor opened his huge jaws and emitted a low, steady, growling roar that sounded very much like the sound he had made when tearing the life out of the big black. Iskwao raised her head and joined him in the tumult, both of them perfectly good-natured and quite happy during the operation. Why mating bears indulge in this blood-curdling duet is a mystery which only the bears themselves can explain. It lasts for about a minute, and during this particular minute Muskwa, who lay outside the thicket, thought that surely the glorious hour had come when Thor was beating up the parent of Pipoonaskoos. And instantly he looked for Pipoonaskoos.

Unfortunately the Willie-bear came sneaking round the edge of the brush just then, and Muskwa gave him no chance to ask questions. He shot at him in a black streak and

Pipoonaskoos bowled over like a fat baby. For several minutes they bit and dug and clawed, most of the biting and digging and clawing being done by Muskwa, while Pipoonaskoos devoted his time and energy to yelping.

Finally the larger cub got away and again took to flight. Muskwa pursued him, into the brush and out, down to the creek and back, halfway up the slope and down again, until he was so tired he had to drop on his belly for a rest.

At this juncture Thor emerged from the thicket. He was alone. For the first time since last night he seemed to notice Muskwa. Then he sniffed the wind up the valley and down the valley, and after that turned and walked straight toward the distant slopes down which they had come the preceding afternoon. Muskwa was both pleased and perplexed. He wanted to go into the thicket and snarl and pull at the hide of the dead bear that must be in there, and he also wanted to finish Pipoonaskoos. After a moment or two of hesitation he ran after Thor and again followed close at his heels.

After a little Iskwao came from the thicket and nosed the wind as Thor had felt it. Then she turned in the opposite direction, and with Pipoonaskoos close behind her, went up the slope and continued slowly and steadily in the face of the setting sun.

So ended Thor's love-making and Muskwa's first fighting; and together they trailed eastward again, to face the most terrible peril that had ever come into the mountains for four-footed beast-a peril that was merciless, a peril from which there was no escape, a peril that was fraught with death.

CHAPTER THIRTEEN

The first night after leaving Iskwao and Pipoonaskoos the big grizzly and the tan-faced cub wandered without sleep under the brilliant stars. Thor did not hunt for meat. He climbed a steep slope, then went down the shale side of a dip, and in a small basin hidden at the foot of a mountain came to a soft green meadow where the dog-tooth violet, with its slender stem, its two lily-like leaves, its single cluster of five-petalled flowers, and its luscious, bulbous root grew in great profusion. And here all through the night he dug and ate.

Muskwa, who had filled himself on spring beauty roots, was not hungry, and as the day had been a restful one for him, outside of his fighting, he found this night filled with its brilliant stars quite enjoyable. The moon came up about ten o'clock, and it was the biggest, and the reddest, and the most beautiful moon Muskwa had seen in his short life. It rolled up over the peaks like a forest fire, and filled all the Rocky Mountains with a wonderful glow. The basin, in which there were perhaps ten acres of meadow, was lighted up almost like day. The little lake at the foot of the mountain glimmered softly, and the tiny stream that fed it from the melting snows a thousand feet above shot down in glistening cascades that caught the moonlight like rivulets of dull polished diamonds.

About the meadow were scattered little clumps of bushes and a few balsams and spruce, as if set there for ornamental purposes; and on one side there was a narrow, verdure-covered slide that sloped upward for a third of a mile, and at the top of which, unseen by Muskwa and Thor, a band of sheep were sleeping.

Muskwa wandered about, always near Thor, investigating the clumps of bushes, the dark shadows of the balsams and spruce, and the edge of the lake. Here he found a plashet of soft mud which was a great solace to his sore feet. Twenty times during the night he waded in the mud.

Even when the dawn came Thor seemed to be in no great haste to leave the basin. Until the sun was well up he continued to wander about the meadow and the edge of the lake, digging up occasional roots, and eating tender grass. This did not displease Muskwa, who made his breakfast of the dog-tooth violet bulbs. The one matter that puzzled him was why Thor did not go into the lake and throw out trout, for he yet had to learn that all water did not contain fish. At last he went fishing for himself, and succeeded in getting a black hard-shelled water beetle that nipped his nose with a pair of needle-like pincers and brought a yelp from him.

It was perhaps ten o'clock, and the sun-filled basin was like a warm oven to a thick-coated bear, when Thor searched up among the rocks near the waterfall until he found a place that was as cool as an old-fashioned cellar. It was a miniature cavern. All about it the slate and sandstone was of a dark and clammy wet from a hundred little trickles of snow water that ran down from the peaks.

It was just the sort of a place Thor loved on a July day, but to Muskwa it was dark and gloomy and not a thousandth part as pleasant as the sun. So after an hour or two he left Thor in his frigidarium and began to investigate the treacherous ledges.

For a few minutes all went well—then he stepped on a green-tinted slope of slate over which a very shallow dribble of water was running. The water had been running over it in just that way for some centuries, and the shelving slate was worn as smooth as the surface of a polished pearl, and it was as slippery as a greased pole. Muskwa's feet went out from under him so quickly that he hardly knew what had happened. The next moment he was on his way to the lake a hundred feet below. He rolled over and over. He plashed into shallow pools. He bounced over miniature waterfalls like a rubber ball. The wind was knocked out of him. He was blinded and dazed by water and shock, and he gathered fresh speed with every yard he made. He had succeeded in letting out half a dozen terrified yelps at the start, and these roused Thor.

Where the water from the peaks fell into the lake there was a precipitous drop of ten feet, and over this Muskwa shot with a momentum that carried him twice as far out into the pond. He hit with a big splash, and disappeared. Down and down he went, where everything was black and cold and suffocating; then the life-preserver with which nature had endowed him in the form of his fat brought him to the surface. He began to paddle with all four feet. It was his first swim, and when he finally dragged himself ashore he was limp and exhausted.

While he still lay panting and very much frightened, Thor came down from the rocks. Muskwa's mother had given him a sound cuffing when he got the porcupine quill in his foot. She had cuffed him for every accident he had had, because she believed that cuffing was good medicine. Education is largely cuffed into a bear cub, and she would have given him a fine cuffing now. But Thor only smelled of him, saw that he was all right, and began to dig up a dog-tooth violet.

He had not finished the violet when suddenly he stopped. For a half-minute he stood like a statue. Muskwa jumped and shook himself. Then he listened. A sound came to both of them. In one slow, graceful movement the grizzly reared himself to his full height. He faced the north, his ears thrust forward, the sensitive muscles of his nostrils twitching. He could smell nothing, but he *heard*!

Over the slopes which they had climbed there had come to him faintly a sound that was new to him, a sound that had never before been a part of his life. It was the barking of dogs.

For two minutes Thor sat on his haunches without moving a muscle of his great body except those twitching thews in his nose.

Deep down in this cup under the mountain it was difficult even for sound to reach him. Quickly he swung down on all fours and made for the green slope to the southward, at the top of which the band of sheep had slept during the preceding night. Muskwa hurried after.

A hundred yards up the slope Thor stopped and turned. Again he reared himself. Now Muskwa also faced to the north. A sudden downward drift of the wind brought the barking of the dogs to them clearly.

Less than half a mile away Langdon's pack of trained Airedales were hot on the scent. Their baying was filled with the fierce excitement which told Bruce and Langdon, a quarter of a mile behind them, that they were close upon their prey.

And even more than it thrilled them did the tongueing of the dogs thrill Thor. Again it was instinct that told him a new enemy had come into his world. He was not afraid. But that instinct urged him to retreat, and he went higher until he came to a part of the mountain that was rough and broken, where once more he halted.

This time he waited. Whatever the menace was it was drawing nearer with the swiftness of the wind. He could hear it coming up the slope that sheltered the basin from the valley.

The crest of that slope was just about on a level with Thor's eyes, and as he looked the leader of the pack came up over the edge of it and stood for a moment outlined against the sky. The others followed quickly, and for perhaps thirty seconds they stood rigid on the cap of the hill, looking down into the basin at their feet and sniffing the heavy scent with which it was filled.

During those thirty seconds Thor watched his enemies without moving, while in his deep chest there gathered slowly a low and terrible growl. Not until the pack swept down into the cup of the mountain, giving full tongue again, did he continue his retreat. But it was not flight. He was not afraid. He was going on—because to go on was his business. He was not seeking trouble; he had no desire even to defend his possession of the meadow and the little lake under the mountain. There were other meadows and other lakes, and he was not naturally a lover of fighting. But he was ready to fight.

He continued to rumble ominously, and in him there was burning a slow and sullen anger. He buried himself among the rocks; he followed a ledge with Muskwa slinking close at his heels; he climbed over a huge scarp of rock, and twisted among boulders half as big as houses.

But not once did he go where Muskwa could not easily follow. Once, when he drew himself from a ledge to a projecting seam of sandstone higher up, and found that Muskwa could not climb it, he came down and went another way.

The baying of the dogs was now deep down in the basin. Then it began to rise swiftly, as if on wings, and Thor knew that the pack was coming up the green slide. He stopped again, and this time the wind brought their scent to him full and strong.

It was a scent that tightened every muscle in his great body and set strange fires burning in him like raging furnaces. With the dogs came also the *man-smell!*

He travelled upward a little faster now, and the fierce and joyous yelping of the dogs seemed scarcely a hundred yards away when he entered a small open space in the wild upheaval of rock. On the mountainside was a wall that rose perpendicularly. Twenty feet on the other side was a sheer fall of a hundred feet, and the way ahead was closed with the exception of a trail scarcely wider than Thor's body by a huge crag of rock that had fallen from the shoulder of the mountain. The big grizzly led Muskwa close up to this crag and the break that opened through it, and then turned suddenly back, so that Muskwa was behind him. In the face of the peril that was almost upon them a mother-bear would have driven Muskwa into the safety of a crevice in the rock wall. Thor did not do this. He fronted the danger that was coming, and reared himself up on his hind quarters.

Twenty feet away the trail he had followed swung sharply around a projecting bulge in the perpendicular wall, and with eyes that were now red and terrible Thor watched the trap he had set.

The pack was coming full tongue. Fifty yards beyond the bulge the dogs were running shoulder to shoulder, and a moment later the first of them rushed into the arena which Thor had chosen for himself. The bulk of the horde followed so closely that the first dogs were flung under him as they strove frantically to stop themselves in time.

With a roar Thor launched himself among them. His great right arm swept out and inward, and it seemed to Muskwa that he had gathered a half of the pack under his huge body. With a single crunch of his jaws he broke the back of the foremost hunter. From a second he tore the head so that the windpipe trailed out like a red rope.

He rolled himself forward, and before the remaining dogs could recover from their panic he had caught one a blow that sent him flying over the edge of the precipice to the rocks a hundred feet below. It had all happened in half a minute, and in that half-minute the remaining nine dogs had scattered.

But Langdon's Airedales were fighters. To the last dog they had come of fighting stock, and Bruce and Metoosin had trained them until they could be hung up by their ears without whimpering. The tragic fate of three of their number frightened them no more than their own pursuit had frightened Thor.

Swift as lightning they circled about the grizzly, spreading themselves on their forefeet, ready to spring aside or backward to avoid sudden rushes, and giving voice now to that quick, fierce yapping which tells hunters their quarry is at bay. This was their business—to harass and torment, to retard flight, to stop their prey again and again until their masters came to finish the kill. It was a quite fair and thrilling sport for the bear and the dogs. The man who comes up with the rifle ends it in murder.

But if the dogs had their tricks, Thor also had his. After three or four vain rushes, in which the Airedales eluded him by their superior quickness, he backed slowly toward the huge rock beside which Muskwa was crouching, and as he retreated the dogs advanced.

Their increased barking and Thor's evident inability to drive them away or tear them to pieces terrified Muskwa more than ever. Suddenly he turned tail and darted into a crevice in the rock behind him.

Thor continued to back until his great hips touched the stone. Then he swung his head side wise and looked for the cub. Not a hair of Muskwa was to be seen. Twice Thor turned his head. After that, seeing that Muskwa was gone, he continued to retreat until he blocked the narrow passage that was his back door to safety.

The dogs were now barking like mad. They were drooling at their mouths, their wiry crests stood up like brushes, and their snarling fangs were bared to their red gums.

Nearer and nearer they came to him, challenging him to stay, to rush them, to catch them if he could—and in their excitement they put ten yards of open space behind them. Thor measured this space, as he had measured the distance between him and the young bull caribou a few days before. And then, without so much as a snarl of warning, he darted out upon his enemies with a suddenness that sent them flying wildly for their lives.

Thor did not stop. He kept on. Where the rock wall bulged out the trail narrowed to five feet, and he had measured this fact as well as the distance. He caught the last dog, and drove it down under his paw. As it was torn to pieces the Airedale emitted piercing cries of agony that reached Bruce and Langdon as they hurried panting and wind-broken up the slide that led from the basin.

Thor dropped on his belly in the narrowed trail, and as the pack broke loose with fresh voice he continued to tear at his victim until the rock was smeared with blood and hair and entrails. Then he rose to his feet and looked again for Muskwa. The cub was curled up in a shivering ball two feet in the crevice. It may be that Thor thought he had gone on up the mountain, for he lost no time now in retreating from the scene of battle. He had caught the wind again. Bruce and Langdon were sweating, and their smell came to him strongly.

For ten minutes Thor paid no attention to the eight dogs yapping at his heels, except to pause now and then and swing his head about. As he continued in his retreat the Airedales became bolder, until finally one of them sprang ahead of the rest and buried his fangs in the grizzly's leg.

This accomplished what barking had failed to do. With another roar Thor turned and pursued the pack headlong for fifty yards over the back-trail, and five precious minutes were lost before he continued upward toward the shoulder of the mountain.

Had the wind been in another direction the pack would have triumphed, but each time that Langdon and Bruce gained ground the wind warned Thor by bringing to him the warm odour of their bodies. And the grizzly was careful to keep that wind from the right quarter. He could have gained the top of the mountain more easily and quickly by quartering the face of it on a back-trail, but this would have thrown the wind too far under him. As long as he held the wind he was safe, unless the hunters made an effort to checkmate his method of escape by detouring and cutting him off.

It took him half an hour to reach the topmost ridge of rock, from which point he would have to break cover and reveal himself as he made the last two or three hundred yards up the shale side of the mountain to the backbone of the range.

When Thor made this break he put on a sudden spurt of speed that left the dogs thirty or forty yards behind him. For two or three minutes he was clearly outlined on the face of the mountain, and during the last minute of those three he was splendidly profiled against a carpet of pure-white snow, without a shrub or a rock to conceal him from the eyes below.

Bruce and Langdon saw him at five hundred yards, and began firing. Close over his head Thor heard the curious ripping wail of the first bullet, and an instant later came the crack of the rifle.

A second shot sent up a spurt of snow five yards ahead of him. He swung sharply to the right. This put him broadside to the marksmen. Thor heard a third shot—and that was all.

While the reports were still echoing among the crags and peaks something struck Thor a terrific blow on the flat of his skull, five inches back of his right ear. It was as if a club had descended upon him from out of the sky. He went down like a log.

It was a glancing shot. It scarcely drew blood, but for a moment it stunned the grizzly, as a man is dazed by a blow on the end of the chin.

Before he could rise from where he had fallen the dogs were upon him, tearing at his throat and neck and body. With a roar Thor sprang to his feet and shook them off. He struck out savagely, and Langdon and Bruce could hear his bellowing as they stood with fingers on the triggers of their rifles waiting for the dogs to draw away far enough to give them the final shots.

Yard by yard Thor worked his way upward, snarling at the frantic pack, defying the man-smell, the strange thunder, the burning lightning—even death itself, and five hundred yards below Langdon cursed despairingly as the dogs hung so close he could not fire.

Up to the very sky-line the blood-thirsting pack shielded Thor. He disappeared over the summit. The dogs followed. And after that their baying came fainter and fainter as the big grizzly led them swiftly away from the menace of man in a long and thrilling race from which more than one was doomed not to return.

CHAPTER FOURTEEN

In his hiding-place Muskwa heard the last sounds of the battle on the ledge. The crevice was a V-shaped crack in the rock, and he had wedged himself as far back in this as he could. He saw Thor pass the opening of his refuge after he had killed the fourth dog; he heard the click, click, click of his claws as he retreated up the trail; and at last he knew that the grizzly was gone, and that the enemy had followed him.

Still he was afraid to come out. These strange pursuers that had come up out of the valley had filled him with a deadly terror. Pipoonaskoos had not made him afraid. Even the big black bear that Thor killed had not terrified him as these red-lipped, white-fanged strangers had frightened him. So he remained in his crevice, crowded as far back as he could get, like a wad shoved in a gun-barrel.

He could still hear the tongueing of the dogs when other and nearer sounds alarmed him. Langdon and Bruce came rushing around the bulge in the mountain wall, and at sight of the dead dogs they stopped. Langdon cried out in horror.

He was not more than twenty feet from Muskwa. For the first time the cub heard human voices; for the first time the sweaty odour of men filled his nostrils, and he scarcely breathed in his new fear. Then one of the hunters stood directly in front of the crack in which he was hidden, and he saw his first man. A moment later the men, too, were gone.

Later Muskwa heard the shots. After that the barking of the dogs grew more and more distant until finally he could not hear them at all. It was about three o'clock—the siesta hour in the mountains, and it was very quiet.

For a long time Muskwa did not move. He listened. And he heard nothing. Another fear was growing in him now—the fear of losing Thor. With every breath he drew he was hoping that Thor would return. For an hour he remained wedged in the rock. Then he heard a *cheep, cheep, cheep*, and a tiny striped rock-rabbit came out on the ledge where Muskwa could see him and began cautiously investigating one of the slain Airedales. This gave Muskwa courage. He pricked up his ears a bit. He whimpered softly, as if beseeching recognition and friendship of the one tiny creature that was near him in this dreadful hour of loneliness and fear.

Inch by inch he crawled out of his hiding-place. At last his little round, furry head was out, and he looked about him. The trail was clear, and he advanced toward the rock-rabbit. With a shrill chatter the striped mite darted for its own stronghold, and Muskwa was alone again.

For a few moments he stood undecided, sniffing the air that was heavy with the scent of blood, of man, and of Thor; then he turned up the mountain.

He knew Thor had gone in that direction, and if little Muskwa possessed a mind and a soul they were filled with but one desire now—to overtake his big friend and protector. Even fear of dogs and men, unknown quantities in his life until to-day, was now overshadowed by the fear that he had lost Thor.

He did not need eyes to follow the trail. It was warm under his nose, and he started in the zigzag ascent of the mountain as fast as he could go. There were places where progress was difficult for his short legs, but he kept on valiantly and hopefully, encouraged by Thor's fresh scent.

It took him a good hour to reach the beginning of the naked shale that reached up to the belt of snow and the sky-line, and it was four o'clock when he started up those last three hundred yards between him and the mountain-top. Up there he believed he would find Thor. But he was afraid, and he continued to whimper softly to himself as he dug his little claws bravely into the shale.

Muskwa did not look up to the crest of the peak again after he had started. To have done that it would have been necessary for him to stop and turn sidewise, for the ascent was steep. And so, when Muskwa was halfway to the top, it happened that he did not see Langdon and Bruce as they came over the sky-line; and he could not smell them, for the wind was blowing up instead of down. Oblivious of their presence he came to the snow-belt. Joyously he smelled of Thor's huge footprints, and followed them. And above him Bruce and Langdon waited, crouched low, their guns on the ground, and each with his thick flannel shirt stripped off and held ready in his hands. When Muskwa was less than twenty yards from them they came tearing down upon him like an avalanche.

Not until Bruce was upon him did Muskwa recover himself sufficiently to move. He saw and realized danger in the last fifth of a second, and as Bruce flung himself forward, his shirt outspread like a net, Muskwa darted to one side. Sprawling on his face, Bruce gathered up a shirtful of snow and clutched it to his breast, believing for a moment that he had the cub, and at this same instant Langdon made a drive that entangled him with his friend's long legs and sent him turning somersaults down the snow-slide.

Muskwa bolted down the mountain as fast as his short legs could carry him. In another second Bruce was after him, and Langdon joined in ten feet behind.

Suddenly Muskwa made a sharp turn, and the momentum with which Bruce was coming carried him thirty or forty feet below him, where the lanky mountaineer stopped himself only by doubling up like a jack-knife and digging toes, hands, elbows, and even his shoulders in the soft shale.

Langdon had switched, and was hot after Muskwa. He flung himself face downward, shirt outspread, just as the cub made another turn, and when he rose to his feet his face was scratched and he spat half a handful of dirt and shale out of his mouth.

Unfortunately for Muskwa his second turn brought him straight down to Bruce, and before he could turn again he was enveloped in sudden darkness and suffocation, and over him there rang out a fiendish and triumphant yell.

"I got 'im!" shouted Bruce.

Inside the shirt Muskwa scratched and bit and snarled, and Bruce was having his hands full when Langdon ran down with the second shirt. Very shortly Muskwa was trussed up like a papoose. His legs and his body were swathed so tightly that he could not move them. His head was not covered. It was the only part of him that showed, and the only part of him that he could move, and it looked so round and frightened and funny that for a minute or two Langdon and Bruce forgot their disappointments and losses of the day and laughed.

Then Langdon sat down on one side of Muskwa, and Bruce on the other, and they filled and lighted their pipes. Muskwa could not even kick an objection.

"A couple of husky hunters we are," said Langdon then. "Come out for a grizzly and end up with that!"

He looked at the cub. Muskwa was eying him so earnestly that Langdon sat in mute wonder for a moment, and then slowly took his pipe from his mouth and stretched out a hand.

"Cubby, cubby, nice cubby," he cajoled softly.

Muskwa's tiny ears were perked forward. His bright eyes were like glass. Bruce, unobserved by Langdon, was grinning expectantly.

"Cubby won't bite—no—no—nice little cubby—we won't hurt cubby—"

The next instant a wild yell startled the mountain-tops as Muskwa's needle-like teeth sank into one of Langdon's fingers. Bruce's howls of joy would have frightened game a mile away.

"You little devil!" gasped Langdon, and then, as he sucked his wounded finger, he laughed with Bruce. "He's a sport—a dead game sport," he added. "We'll call him Spitfire, Bruce. By George, I've wanted a cub like that ever since I first came into the mountains. I'm going to take him home with me! Ain't he a funny looking little cuss?"

Muskwa shifted his head, the only part of him that was not as stiffly immovable as a mummy, and scrutinized Bruce. Langdon rose to his feet and looked back to the sky-line. His face was set and hard.

"Four dogs!" he said, as if speaking to himself. "Three down below—and one up there!" He was silent for a moment, and then said: "I can't understand it, Bruce. They've cornered fifty bears for us, and until to-day we've never lost a dog."

Bruce was looping a buckskin thong about Muskwa's middle, making of it a sort of handle by which he could carry the cub as he would have conveyed a pail of water or a slab of bacon. He stood up, and Muskwa dangled at the end of his string.

"We've run up against a killer," he said. "An' a meat-killin' grizzly is the worst animal on the face of the earth when it comes to a fight or a hunt. The dogs'll never hold 'im, Jimmy, an' if it don't get dark pretty soon there won't none of the bunch come back. They'll quit at dark—if there's any left. The old fellow's got our wind, an' you can bet he knows what knocked him down up there on the snow. He's hikin'—an' hikin' fast. When we see 'im ag'in it'll be twenty miles from here."

Langdon went up for the guns. When he returned Bruce led the way down the mountain, carrying Muskwa by the buckskin thong. For a few moments they paused on the blood-stained ledge of rock where Thor had wreaked his vengeance upon his tormentors. Langdon bent over the dog the grizzly had decapitated.

"This is Biscuits," he said. "And we always thought she was the one coward of the bunch. The other two are Jane and Tober; old Fritz is up on the summit. Three of the best dogs we had, Bruce!"

Bruce was looking over the ledge. He pointed downward.

"There's another—pitched clean off the face o' the mount'in!" he gasped. "Jimmy, that's five!"

Langdon's fists were clenched tightly as he stared over the edge of the precipice. A choking sound came from his throat. Bruce understood its meaning. From where they stood they could see a black patch on the upturned breast of the dog a hundred feet under them. Only one of the pack was marked like that. It was Langdon's favourite. He had made her a camp pet.

"It's Dixie," he said. For the first time he felt a surge of anger sweep through him, and his face was white as he turned back to the trail. "I've got more than one reason for getting that grizzly now, Bruce," he added. "Wild horses can't tear me away from these mountains until I kill him. I'll stick until winter if I have to. I swear I'm going to kill him—if he doesn't run away."

"He won't do that," said Bruce tersely, as he once more swung down the trail with Muskwa.

Until now Muskwa had been stunned into submissiveness by what must have appeared to him to be an utterly hopeless situation. He had strained every muscle in his body to move a leg or a paw, but he was swathed as tightly as Rameses had ever been. But now, however, it slowly dawned upon him that as he dangled back and forth his face frequently brushed his enemy's leg, and he still had the use of his teeth. He watched his opportunity, and this came when Bruce took a long step down from a rock, thus allowing Muskwa's body to rest for the fraction of a second on the surface of the stone from which he was descending.

Quicker than a wink Muskwa took a bite. It was a good deep bite, and if Langdon's howl had stirred the silences a mile away the yell which now came from Bruce beat him by at least a half. It was the wildest, most blood-curdling sound Muskwa had ever heard, even more terrible than the barking of the dogs, and it frightened him so that he released his hold at once.

Then, again, he was amazed. These queer bipeds made no effort to retaliate. The one he had bitten hopped up and down on one foot in a most unaccountable manner for a minute or so, while the other sat down on a boulder and rocked back and forth, with his hands on his stomach, and made a queer, uproarious noise with his mouth wide open. Then the other stopped his hopping and also made that queer noise.

It was anything but laughter to Muskwa. But it impinged upon him the truth of one of two things: either these grotesque looking monsters did not dare to fight him, or they were very peaceful and had no intention of harming him. But they were more cautious thereafter, and as soon as they reached the valley they carried him between them, strung on a rifle-barrel.

It was almost dark when they approached a clump of balsams red with the glow of a fire. It was Muskwa's first fire. Also he saw his first horses, terrific looking monsters even larger than Thor.

A third man—Metoosin, the Indian—came out to meet the hunters, and into this creature's hands Muskwa found himself transferred. He was laid on his side with the glare of the fire in his eyes, and while one of his captors held him by both ears, and so tightly that it hurt, another fastened a hobble-strap around his neck for a collar. A heavy halter rope was then tied to the ring on this strap, and the end of the rope was fastened to a tree.

During these operations Muskwa snarled and snapped as much as he could. In another half-minute he was free of the shirts, and as he staggered on four wobbly legs, from which all power of flight had temporarily gone, he bared his tiny fangs and snarled as fiercely as he could.

To his further amazement this had no effect upon his strange company at all, except that the three of them—even the Indian—opened their mouths and joined in that loud and incomprehensible din, to which one of them had given voice when he sank his teeth into his captor's leg on the mountainside. It was all tremendously puzzling to Muskwa.

CHAPTER FIFTEEN

Greatly to Muskwa's relief the three men soon turned away from him and began to busy themselves about the fire. This gave him a chance to escape, and he pulled and tugged at the end of the rope until he nearly choked himself to death. Finally he gave up in despair, and crumpling himself up against the foot of the balsam he began to watch the camp.

He was not more than thirty feet from the fire. Bruce was washing his hands in a canvas basin. Langdon was mopping his face with a towel. Close to the fire Metoosin was kneeling, and from the big black skittle he was holding over the coals came the hissing and sputtering of fat caribou steaks, and about the pleasantest smell that had ever come Muskwa's way. The air all about him was heavy with the aroma of good things.

When Langdon had finished drying his face he opened a can of something. It was sweetened condensed milk. He poured the white fluid into a basin, and came with it toward Muskwa. The cub had unsuccessfully attempted flight on the ground until his neck was sore; now he climbed the tree. He went up so quickly that Langdon was astonished, and he snarled and spat at the man as the basin of milk was placed where he would almost fall into it when he came down.

Muskwa remained at the end of his rope up the tree, and for a long time the hunters paid no more attention to him. He could see them eating and he could hear them talking as they planned a new campaign against Thor.

"We've got to trick him after what happened to-day," declared Bruce. "No more tracking 'im after this, Jimmy. We can track until doomsday an' he'll always know where we are." He paused for a moment and listened. "Funny the dogs don't come," he said. "I wonder——"

He looked at Langdon.

"Impossible!" exclaimed the latter, as he read the significance of his companion's look. "Bruce, you don't mean to say that bear might kill them all!"

"I've hunted a good many grizzlies," replied the mountaineer quietly, "but I ain't never hunted a trickier one than this. Jimmy, he trapped them dogs on the ledge, an' he tricked the dog he killed up on the peak. He's liable to get 'em all into a corner, an' if that happens——"

He shrugged his shoulders suggestively.

Again Langdon listened.

"If there were any alive at dark they should be here pretty soon," he said. "I'm sorry, now—sorry we didn't leave the dogs at home."

Bruce laughed a little grimly.

"Fortunes o' war, Jimmy," he said. "You don't go hunting grizzlies with a pack of lapdogs, an' you've got to expect to lose some of them sooner or later. We've tackled the wrong bear, that's all. He's beat us."

"Beat us?"

"I mean he's beat us in a square game, an' we dealt a raw hand at that in using dogs at all. Do you want that bear bad enough to go after him my way?"

Langdon nodded.

"What's your scheme?"

"You've got to drop pretty idees when you go grizzly hunting," began Bruce. "And especially when you run up against a 'killer.' There won't be any hour between now an' denning-up time that this grizzly doesn't get the wind from all directions. How? He'll make detours. I'll bet if there was snow on the ground you'd find him back-tracking two miles out of every six, so he can get the wind of anything that's following him. An' he'll travel mostly nights, layin' high up in the rocks an' shale during the day. If you want any more shootin', there's just two things to do, an' the best of them two things is to move on and find other bears."

"Which I won't do, Bruce. What's your scheme for getting this one?"

Bruce was silent for several moments before he replied.

"We've got his range mapped out to a mile," he said then. "It begins up at the first break we crossed, an' it ends down here where we came into this valley. It's about twenty-five miles up an' down. He don't touch the mount'ins west of this valley nor the mount'ins east of the other valleys an' he's dead certain to keep on makin' circles so long as we're after him. He's hikin' southward now on the other side of the range.

"We'll lay here for a few days an' not move. Then we'll start Metoosin through the valley over there with the dogs, if there's any left, and we'll start south through this valley at the same time. One of us will keep to the slopes an' the other to the bottom, an' we'll travel slow. Get the idee?

"That grizzly won't leave his country, an' Metoosin is pretty near bound to drive him around to us. We'll let him do the open hunting an' we'll skulk. The bear can't get past us both without giving one of us shooting."

"It sounds good," agreed Langdon. "And I've got a lame knee that I'm not unwilling to nurse for a few days."

Scarcely were the words out of Langdon's mouth when a sudden rattle of hobble-chains and the startled snort of a grazing horse out in the meadow brought them both to their feet.

"Utim!" whispered Metoosin, his dark face aglow in the firelight.

"You're right—the dogs," said Bruce, and he whistled softly.

They heard a movement in the brush near them, and a moment later two of the dogs came into the firelight. They slunk in, half on their bellies, and as they prostrated themselves at the hunters' feet a third and a fourth joined them.

They were not like the pack that had gone out that morning. There were deep hollows in their sides; their wiry crests were flat; they were hard run, and they knew that they were beaten. Their aggressiveness was gone, and they had the appearance of whipped curs.

A fifth came in out of the night. He was limping, and dragging a torn foreleg. The head and throat of one of the others was red with blood. They all lay flat on their bellies, as if expecting condemnation.

"We have failed," their attitude said; "we are beaten, and this is all of us that are left."

Mutely Bruce and Langdon stared at them. They listened—waited. No other came. And then they looked at each other.

"Two more of them gone," said Langdon.

Bruce turned to a pile of panniers and canvases and pulled out the dog-leashes. Up in his tree Muskwa was all atremble. Within a few yards of him he saw again the white-fanged horde that had chased Thor and had driven him into the rock-crevice. Of the men he was no longer greatly afraid. They had attempted him no harm, and he had ceased to quake and snarl when one of them passed near. But the dogs were monsters. They had given battle to Thor. They must have beaten him, for Thor had run away.

The tree to which Muskwa was fastened was not much more than a sapling, and he lay in the saddle of a crotch five feet from the ground when Metoosin led one of the dogs past him. The Airedale saw him and made a sudden spring that tore the leash from the Indian's hand. His leap carried him almost up to Muskwa. He was about to make another spring when Langdon rushed forward with a fierce cry, caught the dog by his collar, and with the end of the leash gave him a sound beating. Then he led him away.

This act puzzled Muskwa more than ever. The man had saved him. He had beaten the monster with the red mouth and the white fangs, and all of those monsters were now being taken away at the end of ropes.

When Langdon returned he stopped close to Muskwa's tree and talked to him. Muskwa allowed Langdon's hand to approach within six inches of him, and did not snap at it. Then a strange and sudden thrill shot through him. While his head was turned a little Langdon had boldly put his hand on his furry back. And in the touch there was not hurt! His mother had never put her paw on him as gently as that!

Half a dozen times in the next ten minutes Langdon touched him. For the first three or four times Muskwa bared his two rows of shining teeth, but he made no sound. Gradually he ceased even to bare his teeth.

Langdon left him then, and in a few moments he returned with a chunk of raw caribou meat. He held this close to Muskwa's nose. Muskwa could smell it, but he backed away from it, and at last Langdon placed it beside the basin at the foot of the tree and returned to where Bruce was smoking.

"Inside of two days he'll be eating out of my hand," he said.

It was not long before the camp became very quiet. Langdon, Bruce, and the Indian rolled themselves in their blankets and were soon asleep. The fire burned lower and lower. Soon there was only a single smouldering log. An owl hooted a little deeper in the timber. The drone of the valley and the mountains filled the peaceful night. The stars grew brighter. Far away Muskwa heard the rumbling of a boulder rolling down the side of a mountain.

There was nothing to fear now. Everything was still and asleep but himself, and very cautiously he began to back down the tree. He reached the foot of it, loosed his hold, and half fell into the basin of condensed milk, a part of it slopping up over his face. Involuntarily he shot out his tongue and licked his chops, and the sweet, sticky stuff that it gathered filled him with a sudden and entirely unexpected pleasure. For a quarter of an hour he licked himself. And then, as if the secret of this delightful ambrosia had just dawned upon him, his bright little eyes fixed themselves covetously upon the tin basin. He approached it with commendable strategy and caution, circling first on one side of it and then on the other, every muscle in his body prepared for a quick spring backward if it should make a jump for him. At last his nose touched the thick, luscious feast in the basin, and he did not raise his head again until the last drop of it was gone.

The condensed milk was the one biggest factor in the civilizing of Muskwa. It was the missing link that connected certain things in his lively little mind. He knew that the same hand that had touched him so gently had also placed this strange and wonderful feast at the foot of his tree, and that same hand had also offered him meat. He did not eat the meat, but he licked the interior of the basin until it shone like a mirror in the starlight.

In spite of the milk, he was still filled with a desire to escape, though his efforts were not as frantic and unreasoning as they had been. Experience had taught him that it was futile to jump and tug at the end of his leash, and now he fell to chewing at the rope. Had he gnawed in one place he would probably have won freedom before morning, but when his jaws became tired he rested, and when he resumed his work it was usually at a fresh place in the rope. By midnight his gums were sore, and he gave up his exertions entirely.

Humped close to the tree, ready to climb up it at the first sign of danger, the cub waited for morning. Not a wink did he sleep. Even though he was less afraid than he had been, he was terribly lonesome. He missed Thor, and he whimpered so softly that the men a few yards away could not have heard him had they been awake. If Pipoonaskoos had come into the camp then he would have welcomed him joyfully.

Morning came, and Metoosin was the first out of his blankets. He built a fire, and this roused Bruce and Langdon. The latter, after he had dressed himself, paid a visit to Muskwa, and when he found the basin licked clean he showed his pleasure by calling the others' attention to what had happened.

Muskwa had climbed to his crotch in the tree, and again he tolerated the stroking touch of Langdon's hand. Then Langdon brought forth another can from a cowhide pannier and opened it directly under Muskwa, so that he could see the creamy white fluid as it was turned into the basin. He held the basin up to Muskwa, so close that the milk touched the cub's nose, and for the life of him Muskwa could not keep his tongue in his mouth. Inside of five minutes he was eating from the basin in Langdon's hand! But when Bruce came up to watch the proceedings the cub bared all his teeth and snarled.

"Bears make better pets than dogs," affirmed Bruce a little later, when they were eating breakfast. "He'll be following you around like a puppy in a few days, Jimmy."

"I'm getting fond of the little cuss already," replied Langdon. "What was that you were telling me about Jameson's bears, Bruce?"

"Jameson lived up in the Kootenay country," said Bruce. "Reg'lar hermit, I guess you'd call him. Came out of the mountains only twice a year to get grub. He made pets of grizzlies. For years he had one as big as this fellow we're chasing. He got 'im when a cub, an 'when I saw him he weighed a thousand pounds an' followed Jameson wherever he went like a dog. Even went on his hunts with him, an 'they slept beside the same campfire. Jameson loved bears, an' he'd never kill one."

Langdon was silent. After a moment he said: "And I'm beginning to love them, Bruce. I don't know just why, but there's something about bears that makes you love them. I'm not going to shoot many more—perhaps none after we get this dog-killer we're after. I almost believe he will be my last bear." Suddenly he clenched his hands, and added angrily: "And to think there isn't a province in the Dominion or a state south of the Border that has a 'closed season' for bear! It's an outrage, Bruce. They're classed with vermin, and can be exterminated at all seasons. They can even be dug out of their dens with their young—and—so help me Heaven!—I've helped to dig them out! We're beasts, Bruce. Sometimes I almost think it's a crime for a man to carry a gun. And yet—I go on killing."

"It's in our blood," laughed Bruce, unmoved. "Did you ever know a man, Jimmy, that didn't like to see things die? Wouldn't every mother's soul of 'em go to a hanging if they had the chance? Won't they crowd like buzzards round a dead horse to get a look at a man crushed to a pulp under a rock or a locomotive engine? Why, Jimmie, if there weren't no law to be afraid of, we humans'd be killing one another for the fun of it! We would. It's born in us to want to kill."

"And we take it all out on brute creation," mused Langdon. "After all, we can't have much sympathy for ourselves if a generation or two of us are killed in war, can we? Mebby you're right, Bruce. Inasmuch as we can't kill our neighbours legally whenever we have the inclination, it's possible the Chief Arbiter of things sends us a war now and then to relieve us temporarily of our blood-thirstiness. Hello, what in thunder is the cub up to now?"

Muskwa had fallen the wrong way out of his crotch and was dangling like the victim at the end of a hangman's rope. Langdon ran to him, caught him boldly in his bare hands, lifted him up over the limb and placed him on the ground. Muskwa did not snap at him or even growl.

Bruce and Metoosin were away from camp all of that day, spying over the range to the westward, and Langdon was left to doctor a knee which he had battered against a rock the previous day. He spent most of his time in company with Muskwa. He opened a can of their griddle-cake syrup and by noon he had the cub following him about the tree and straining to reach the dish which he held temptingly just out of reach. Then he would sit down, and Muskwa would climb half over his lap to reach the syrup.

At his present age Muskwa's affection and confidence were easily won. A baby black bear is very much like a human baby: he likes milk, he loves sweet things, and he wants to cuddle up close to any living thing that is good to him. He is the most lovable creature on four legs— round and soft and fluffy, and so funny that he is sure to keep every one about him in good humour. More than once that day Langdon laughed until the tears came, and especially when Muskwa made determined efforts to climb up his leg to reach the dish of syrup.

As for Muskwa, he had gone syrup mad. He could not remember that his mother had ever given him anything like it, and Thor had produced nothing better than fish.

Late in the afternoon Langdon untied Muskwa's rope and led him for a stroll down toward the creek. He carried the syrup dish and every few yards he would pause and let the cub have a taste of its contents. After half an hour of this manoeuvring he dropped his end of the leash entirely, and walked campward. And Muskwa followed! It was a triumph, and in Langdon's veins there pulsed a pleasurable thrill which his life in the open had never brought to him before.

It was late when Metoosin returned, and he was quite surprised that Bruce had not shown up. Darkness came, and they built up the fire. They were finishing supper an hour later when Bruce came in, carrying something swung over his shoulders. He tossed it close to where Muskwa was hidden behind his tree.

"A skin like velvet, and some meat for the dogs," he said. "I shot it with my pistol."

He sat down and began eating. After a little Muskwa cautiously approached the carcass that lay doubled up three or four feet from him. He smelled of it, and a curious thrill shot through him. Then he whimpered softly as he muzzled the soft fur, still warm with life. And for a time after that he was very still.

For the thing that Bruce had brought into camp and flung at the foot of his tree was the dead body of little Pipoonaskoos!

CHAPTER SIXTEEN

That night the big loneliness returned to Muskwa. Bruce and Metoosin were so tired after their hard climb over the range that they went to bed early, and Langdon followed them, leaving Pipoonaskoos where Bruce had first thrown him.

Scarcely a move had Muskwa made after the discovery that had set his heart beating a little faster. He did not know what death was, or what it meant, and as Pipoonaskoos was so warm and soft he was sure that he would move after a little. He had no inclination to fight him now.

Again it grew very, very still, and the stars filled the sky, and the fire burned low. But Pipoonaskoos did not move. Gently at first, Muskwa began nosing him and pulling at his silken hair, and as he did this he whimpered softly, as if saying, "I don't want to fight you any more, Pipoonaskoos! Wake up, and let's be friends!"

But still Pipoonaskoos did not stir, and at last Muskwa gave up all hope of waking him. And still whimpering to his fat little enemy of the green meadow how sorry he was that he had chased him, he snuggled close up to Pipoonaskoos and in time went to sleep.

Langdon was first up in the morning, and when he came over to see how Muskwa had fared during the night he suddenly stopped, and for a full minute he stood without moving, and then a low, strange cry broke from his lips. For Muskwa and Pipoonaskoos were snuggled as closely as they could have snuggled had both been living, and in some way Muskwa had arranged it so that one of the dead cub's little paws was embracing him.

Quietly Langdon returned to where Bruce was sleeping, and in a minute or two Bruce returned with him, rubbing his eyes. And then he, too, stared, and the men looked at each other.

"Dog meat," breathed Langdon. "You brought it home for dog meat, Bruce!"

Bruce did not answer, Langdon said nothing more, and neither talked very much for a full hour after that. During that hour Metoosin came and dragged Pipoonaskoos away, and instead of being skinned and fed to the dogs he was put into a hole down in the creek-bottom and covered with sand and stones. That much, at least, Bruce and Langdon did for Pipoonaskoos.

This day Metoosin and Bruce again went over the range. The mountaineer had brought back with him bits of quartz in which were unmistakable signs of gold, and they returned with an outfit for panning.

Langdon continued his education of Muskwa. Several times he took the cub near the dogs, and when they snarled and strained at the ends of their leashes he whipped them, until with quick understanding they gripped the fact that Muskwa, although a bear, must not be harmed.

In the afternoon of this second day he freed the cub entirely from the rope, and he had no difficulty in recapturing it when he wanted to tie it up again. The third and fourth days Bruce and the Indian explored the valley west of the range and convinced themselves finally that the "colours" they found were only a part of the flood-drifts, and would not lead to fortune.

On this fourth night, which happened to be thick with clouds, and chilly, Langdon experimented by taking Muskwa to bed with him. He expected trouble. But Muskwa was as quiet as a kitten, and once he found a proper nest for himself he scarcely made a move until morning. A part of the night Langdon slept with one of his hands resting on the cub's soft, warm body.

According to Bruce it was now time to continue the hunt for Thor, but a change for the worse in Langdon's knee broke in upon their plans. It was impossible for Langdon to walk more than a quarter of a mile at a time, and the position he was compelled to take in the saddle caused him so much pain that to prosecute the hunt even on horseback was out of the question.

"A few more days won't hurt any," consoled Bruce. "If we give the old fellow a longer rest he may get a bit careless."

The three days that followed were not without profit and pleasure for Langdon. Muskwa was teaching him more than he had ever known about bears, and especially bear cubs, and he made notes voluminously.

The dogs were now confined to a clump of trees fully three hundred yards from the camp, and gradually the cub was given his freedom. He made no effort to run away, and he soon discovered that Bruce and Metoosin were also his friends. But Langdon was the only one he would follow.

On the morning of the eighth day after their pursuit of Thor, Bruce and Metoosin rode over into the eastward valley with the dogs. Metoosin was to have a day's start, and Bruce planned to return to camp that afternoon so that he and Langdon could begin their hunt up the valley the next day.

It was a glorious morning. A cool breeze came from the north and west, and about nine o'clock Langdon fastened Muskwa to his tree, saddled a horse, and rode down the valley. He had no intention of hunting. It was a joy merely to ride and breathe in the face of that wind and gaze upon the wonders of the mountains.

He travelled northward for three or four miles, until he came to a broad, low slope that broke through the range to the westward. A desire seized upon him to look over into the other valley, and as his knee was giving him no trouble he cut a zigzag course upward that in half an hour brought him almost to the top.

Here he came to a short, steep slide that compelled him to dismount and continue on foot. At the summit he found himself on a level sweep of meadow, shut in on each side of him by the bare rock walls of the split mountains, and a quarter of a mile ahead he could see where the meadow broke suddenly into the slope that shelved downward into the valley he was seeking.

Halfway over this quarter of a mile of meadow there was a dip into which he could not see, and as he came to the edge of this he flung himself suddenly upon his face and for a minute or two lay as motionless as a rock. Then he slowly raised his head.

A hundred yards from him, gathered about a small water-hole in the hollow, was a herd of goats. There were thirty or more, most of them Nannies with young kids. Langdon could make out only two Billies in the lot. For half an hour he lay still and watched them. Then one of the Nannies struck out with her two kids for the side of the mountain; another followed, and seeing that the whole band was about to move, Langdon rose quickly to his feet and ran as fast as he could toward them.

For a moment Nannies, Billies, and little kids were paralyzed by his sudden appearance. They faced half about and stood as if without the power of flight until he had covered half the distance between t hem. Then their wits seemed to return all at once, and they broke in a wild panic for the side of the nearest mountain. Their hoofs soon began to clatter on boulder and shale, and for another half-hour Langdon heard the hollow booming of the rocks loosened by their feet high up among the crags and peaks. At the end of that time they were infinitesimal white dots on the sky-line.

He went on, and a few minutes later looked down into the other valley. Southward this valley was shut out from his vision by a huge shoulder of rock. It was not very high, and he began to climb it. He had almost reached the top when his toe caught in a piece of slate, and in falling he brought his rifle down with tremendous force on a boulder.

He was not hurt, except for a slight twinge in his lame knee. But his gun was a wreck. The stock was shattered close to the breech and a twist of his hand broke it off entirely.

As he carried two extra rifles in his outfit the mishap did not disturb Langdon as much as it might otherwise have done, and he continued to climb over the rocks until he came to what appeared to be a broad, smooth ledge leading around the sandstone spur of the mountain. A hundred feet farther on he found that the ledge ended in a perpendicular wall of rock. From this point, however, he had a splendid view of the broad sweep of country between the two ranges to the south. He sat down, pulled out his pipe, and prepared to enjoy the magnificent panorama under him while he was getting his wind.

Through his glasses he could see for miles, and what he looked upon was an unhunted country. Scarcely half a mile away a band of caribou was filing slowly across the bottom toward the green slopes to the west. He caught the glint of many ptarmigan wings in the sunlight below. After a time, fully two miles away, he saw sheep grazing on a thinly verdured slide.

He wondered how many valleys there were like this in the vast reaches of the Canadian mountains that stretched three hundred miles from sea to prairie and a thousand miles north and south. Hundreds, even thousands, he told himself, and each wonderful valley a world complete within itself; a world filled with its own life, its own lakes and streams and forests, its own joys and its own tragedies.

Here in this valley into which he gazed was the same soft droning and the same warm sunshine that had filled all the other valleys; and yet here, also, was a different life. Other bears ranged the slopes that he could see dimly with his naked eyes far to the west and north. It was a new domain, filled with other promise and other mystery, and he forgot time and hunger as he sat lost in the enchantment of it.

It seemed to Langdon that these hundreds or thousands of valleys would never grow old for him; that he could wander on for all time, passing from one into another, and that each would possess its own charm, its own secrets to be solved, its own life to be learned. To him they were largely inscrutable; they were cryptic, as enigmatical as life itself, hiding their treasures as they droned through the centuries, giving birth to multitudes of the living, demanding in return other multitudes of the dead. As he looked off through the sunlit space he wondered what the story of this valley would be, and how many volumes it would fill, if the valley itself could tell it.

First of all, he knew, it would whisper of the creation of a world; it would tell of oceans torn and twisted and thrown aside—of those first strange eons of time when there was no night, but all was day; when weird and tremendous monsters stalked where he now saw the caribou drinking at the creek, and when huge winged creatures half bird and half beast swept the sky where he now saw an eagle soaring.

And then it would tell of The Change—of that terrific hour when the earth tilted on its axis, and night came, and a tropical world was turned into a frigid one, and new kinds of life were born to fill it.

It must have been long after that, thought Langdon, that the first bear came to replace the mammoth, the mastodon, and the monstrous beasts that had been their company. And that first bear was the forefather of the grizzly he and Bruce were setting forth to kill the next day!

So engrossed was Langdon in his thoughts that he did not hear a sound behind him. And then something roused him.

It was as if one of the monsters he had been picturing in his imagination had let out a great breath close to him. He turned slowly, and the next moment his heart seemed to stop its beating; his blood seemed to grow cold and lifeless in his veins.

Barring the ledge not more than fifteen feet from him, his great jaws agape, his head moving slowly from side to side as he regarded his trapped enemy, stood Thor, the King of the Mountains!

And in that space of a second or two Langdon's hands involuntarily gripped at his broken rifle, and he decided that he was doomed!

CHAPTER SEVENTEEN

A broken, choking breath—a stifled sound that was scarcely a cry—was all that came from Langdon's lips as he saw the monstrous grizzly looking at him. In the ten seconds that followed he lived hours.

His first thought was that he was powerless—utterly powerless. He could not even run, for the rock wall was behind him; he could not fling himself valleyward, for there was a sheer fall of a hundred feet on that side. He was face to face with death, a death as terrible as that which had overtaken the dogs.

And yet in these last moments Langdon did not lose himself in terror. He noted even the redness in the avenging grizzly's eyes. He saw the naked scat along his back where one of his bullets had plowed; he saw the bare spot where another of his bullets had torn its way through Thor's fore-shoulder. And he believed, as he observed these things, that Thor had deliberately trailed him, that the bear had followed him along the ledge and had cornered him here that he might repay in full measure what had been inflicted upon him.

Thor advanced—just one step; and then in that slow, graceful movement, reared himself to full height. Langdon, even then, thought that he was magnificent. On his part, the man did not move; he looked steadily up at Thor, and he had made up his mind what to do when the great beast lunged forward. He would fling himself over the edge. Down below there was one chance in a thousand for life. There might be a ledge or a projecting spur to catch him.

And Thor!

Suddenly—unexpectedly—he had come upon man! This was the creature that had hunted him, this was the creature that had hurt him—and it was so near that he could reach out with his paw and crush it! And how weak, and white, and shrinking it looked now! Where was its strange thunder? Where was its burning lightning? Why did it make no sound?

Even a dog would have done more than this creature, for the dog would have shown its fangs; it would have snarled, it would have fought. But this thing that was man did nothing. And a great, slow doubt swept through Thor's massive head. Was it really this shrinking, harmless, terrified thing that had hurt him? He smelled the man-smell. It was thick. And yet this time there came with it no hurt.

And then, slowly again, Thor came down to all fours. Steadily he looked at the man.

Had Langdon moved then he would have died. But Thor was not, like man, a murderer. For another half-minute he waited for a hurt, for some sign of menace. Neither came, and he was puzzled. His nose swept the ground, and Langdon saw the dust rise where the grizzly's hot breath stirred it. And after that, for another long and terrible thirty seconds, the bear and the man looked at each other.

Then very slowly—and doubtfully—Thor half turned. He growled. His lips drew partly back. Yet he saw no reason to fight, for that shrinking, white-faced pigmy crouching on the rock made no movement to offer him battle. He saw that he could not go on, for the ledge was blocked by the mountain wall. Had there been a trail the story might have been different for Langdon. As it was, Thor disappeared slowly in the direction from which he had come, his great head hung low, his long claws click, click, clicking like ivory castanets as he went.

Not until then did it seem to Langdon that he breathed again, and that his heart resumed its beating. He gave a great sobbing gasp. He rose to his feet, and his legs seemed weak. He waited—one minute, two, three; and then he stole cautiously to the twist in the ledge around which Thor had gone.

The rocks were clear, and he began to retrace his own steps toward the meadowy break, watching and listening, and still clutching the broken parts of his rifle. When he came to the edge of the plain he dropped down behind a huge boulder.

Three hundred yards away Thor was ambling slowly over the crest of the dip toward the eastward valley. Not until the bear reappeared on the farther ridge of the hollow, and then vanished again, did Langdon follow.

When he reached the slope on which he had hobbled his horse Thor was no longer in sight. The horse was where he had left it. Not until he was in the saddle did Langdon feel that he was completely safe. Then he laughed, a nervous, broken, joyous sort of laugh, and as he scanned the valley he filled his pipe with fresh tobacco.

"You great big god of a bear!" he whispered, and every fibre in him was trembling in a wonderful excitement as he found voice for the first time. "You—you monster with a heart bigger than man!" And then he added, under his breath, as if not conscious that he was speaking: "If I'd cornered you like that I'd have killed you! And you! You cornered me, and let me live!"

He rode toward camp, and as he went he knew that this day had given the final touch to the big change that had been working in him. He had met the King of the Mountains; he had stood face to face with death, and in the last moment the four-footed thing he had hunted and maimed had been merciful. He believed that Bruce would not understand; that Bruce could not understand; but unto himself the day and the hour had brought its meaning in a way that he would not forget so long as he lived, and he knew that hereafter and for all time he would not again hunt the life of Thor, or the lives of any of his kind.

Langdon reached the camp and prepared himself some dinner, and as he ate this, with Muskwa for company, he made new plans for the days and weeks that were to follow. He would send Bruce back to overtake Metoosin the next day, and they would no longer hunt the big grizzly. They would go on to the Skeena and possibly even up to the edge of the Yukon, and then swing eastward into the caribou country some time early in September, hitting back toward civilization on the prairie side of the Rockies. He would take Muskwa with them. Back in the land of men and cities they would be great friends. It did not occur to him just then what this would mean for Muskwa.

It was two o'clock, and he was still dreaming of new and unknown trails into the North when a sound came to rouse and disturb him. For a few minutes he paid no attention to it, for it seemed to be only a part of the droning murmur of the valley. But slowly and steadily it rose above this, and at last he got up from where he was lying with his back to a tree and walked out from the timber, where he could hear more plainly.

Muskwa followed him, and when Langdon stopped the tan-faced cub also stopped. His little ears shot out inquisitively. He turned his head to the north. From that direction the sound was coming.

In another moment Langdon had recognized it, and yet even then he told himself that his ears must be playing him false. It could not be the barking of dogs! By this time Bruce and Metoosin were far to the south with the pack; at least Metoosin should be, and Bruce was on his return to the camp! Quickly the sound grew more distinct, and at last he knew that he could not be mistaken. The dogs were coming up the valley. Something had turned Bruce and Metoosin northward instead of into the south. And the pack was giving tongue—that fierce, heated baying which told him they were again on the fresh spoor of game. A sudden thrill shot through him. There could be but one living thing in the length and breadth of the valley that Bruce would set the dogs after, and that was the big grizzly!

For a few moments longer Langdon stood and listened. Then he hurried back to camp, tied Muskwa to his tree, armed himself with another rifle, and resaddled his horse. Five minutes later he was riding swiftly in the direction of the range where a short time before Thor had given him his life.

CHAPTER EIGHTEEN

Thor heard the dogs when they were a mile away. There were two reasons why he was even less in a mood to run from them now than a few days before. Of the dogs alone he had no more fear than if they had been so many badgers, or so many whistlers piping at him from the rocks. He had found them all mouth and little fang, and easy to kill. It was what followed close after them that disturbed him. But to-day he had stood face to face with the thing that had brought the strange scent into his valleys, and it had not offered to hurt him, and he had refused to kill it. Besides, he was again seeking Iskwao, the she-bear, and man is not the only animal that will risk his life for love.

After killing his last dog at dusk of that fatal day when they had pursued him over the mountain Thor had done just what Bruce thought that he would do, and instead of continuing southward had made a wider detour toward the north, and the third night after the fight and the loss of Muskwa he found Iskwao again. In the twilight of that same evening Pipoonaskoos had died, and Thor had heard the sharp cracking of Bruce's automatic. All that night and the next day and the night that followed he spent with Iskwao, and then he left her once more. A third time he was seeking her when he found Langdon in the trap on the ledge, and he had not yet got wind of her when he first heard the baying of the dogs on his trail.

He was travelling southward, which brought him nearer the hunters' camp. He was keeping to the high slopes where there were little dips and meadows, broken by patches of shale, deep coulees, and occasionally wild upheavals of rock. He was keeping the wind straight ahead so that he would not fail to catch the smell of Iskwao when he came near her, and with the baying of the dogs he caught no scent of the pursuing beasts, or of the two men who were riding behind them.

At another time he would have played his favourite trick of detouring so that the danger would be ahead of him, with the wind in his favour. Caution had now become secondary to his desire to find his mate. The dogs were less than half a mile away when he stopped suddenly, sniffed the air for a moment, and then went on swiftly until he was halted by a narrow ravine.

Up that ravine Iskwao was coming from a dip lower down the mountain, and she was running. The yelping of the pack was fierce and close when Thor scrambled down in time to meet her as she rushed upward. Iskwao paused for a single moment, smelled noses with Thor, and then went on, her ears laid back flat and sullen and her throat filled with growling menace.

Thor followed her, and he also growled. He knew that his mate was fleeing from the dogs, and again that deadly and slowly increasing wrath swept through him as he climbed after her higher up the mountain.

In such an hour as this Thor was at his worst. He was a fighter when pursued as the dogs had pursued him a week before—but he was a demon, terrible and without mercy, when danger threatened his mate.

He fell farther and farther behind Iskwao, and twice lie turned, his fangs gleaming under drawn lips, and his defiance rolling back upon his enemies in low thunder.

When he came up out of the coulee he was in the shadow of the peak, and Iskwao had already disappeared in her skyward scramble. Where she had gone was a wild chaos of rock-slide and the piled-up débris of fallen and shattered masses of sandstone crag. The sky-line was not more than three hundred yards above him. He looked up. Iskwao was among the rocks, and here was the place to fight. The dogs were close upon him now. They were coming up the last stretch of the coulee, baying loudly. Thor turned about, and waited for them.

Half a mile to the south, looking through his glasses, Langdon saw Thor, and at almost the same instant the dogs appeared over the edge of the coulee. He had ridden halfway up the mountain; from that point he had climbed higher, and was following a well-beaten sheep trail at about the same altitude as Thor. From where he stood the valley lay under his glasses for miles. He did not have far to look to discover Bruce and the Indian. They were dismounting at the foot of the coulee, and as he gazed they ran quickly into it and disappeared.

Again Langdon swung back to Thor. The dogs were holding him now, and he knew there was no chance of the grizzly killing them in that open space. Then he saw movement among the rocks higher up, and a low cry of understanding broke from his lips as he made out Iskwao climbing steadily toward the ragged peak. He knew that this second bear was a female. The big grizzly—her mate—had stopped to fight. And there was no hope for him if the dogs succeeded in holding him for a matter of ten or fifteen minutes. Bruce and Metoosin would appear in that time over the rim of the coulee at a range of less than a hundred yards!

Langdon thrust his binoculars in their case and started at a run along the sheep trail. For two hundred yards his progress was easy, and then the patch broke into a thousand individual tracks on a slope of soft and slippery shale, and it took him five minutes to make the next fifty yards.

The trail hardened again. He ran on pantingly, and for another five minutes the shoulder of a ridge hid Thor and the dogs from him. When he came over that ridge and ran fifty yards, down the farther side of it, he stopped short. Further progress was barred by a steep ravine. He was five hundred yards from where Thor stood with his back to the rocks and his huge head to the pack.

Even as he looked, struggling to get breath enough to shout, Langdon expected to see Bruce and Metoosin appear out of the coulee. It flashed upon him then that even if he could make them hear it would be impossible for them to understand him. Bruce would not guess that he wanted to spare the beast they had been hunting for almost two weeks.

Thor had rushed the dogs a full twenty yards toward the coulee when Langdon dropped quickly behind a rock. There was only one way of saving him now, if he was not too late. The pack had retreated a few yards down the slope, and he aimed at the pack. One thought only filled his brain—he must sacrifice his dogs or let Thor die. And that day Thor had given him his life!

There was no hesitation as he pressed the trigger. It was a long shot, and the first bullet threw up a cloud of dust fifty feet short of the Airedales. He fired again, and missed. The third time his rifle cracked there answered it a sharp yelp of pain which Laagdon himself did not hear. One of the dogs rolled over and over down the slope.

The reports of the shots alone had not stirred Thor, but now when he saw one of his enemies crumple up and go rolling down the mountain he turned slowly toward the safety of the rocks. A fourth and then a fifth shot followed, and at the fifth the yelping dogs dropped back toward the coulee, one of them limping with a shattered fore-foot.

Langdon sprang upon the boulder over which he had rested his gun, and his eyes caught the sky-line. Iskwao had just reached the top. She paused for a moment and looked down. Then she disappeared.

Thor was now hidden among the boulders and broken masses of sandstone, following her trail. Within two minutes after the grizzly disappeared Bruce and Metoosin scrambled up over the edge of the coulee. From where they stood even the sky-line was within fairly good shooting distance, and Langdon suddenly began shouting excitedly, waving his arms, and pointing downward.

Bruce and Metoosin were caught by his ruse, in spite of the fact that the dogs were again giving fierce tongue close to the rocks among which Thor had gone. They believed that from where he stood Langdon could see the progress of the bear, and that it was running toward the valley. Not until they were another hundred yards down the slope did they stop and look back at Langdon to get further directions. From his rock Langdon was pointing to the sky-line.

Thor was just going over. He paused for a moment, as Iskwao had stopped, and took one last look at man.

And Langdon, as he saw the last of him, waved his hat and shouted, "Good luck to you, old man—good luck!"

CHAPTER NINETEEN

That night Langdon and Bruce made their new plans, while Metoosin sat aloof, smoking in stolid silence, and gazing now and then at Langdon as if he could not yet bring himself to the point of believing what had happened that afternoon. Thereafter through many moons Metoosin would never forget to relate to his children and his grandchildren and his friends of the tepee tribes how he had once hunted with a white man who had shot his own dogs to save the life of a grizzly bear. Langdon was no longer the same old Langdon to him, and after this hunt Metoosin knew that he would never hunt with him again. For Langdon was *keskwao* now. Something had gone wrong in his head. The Great Spirit had taken away his heart and had given it to a grizzly bear, and over his pipe Metoosin watched him cautiously. This suspicion was confirmed when he saw Bruce and Langdon making a cage out of a cowhide pannier and realized that the cub was to accompany them on their long journey. There was no doubt in his mind now. Langdon was "queer," and to an Indian that sort of queerness boded no good to man.

The next morning at sunrise the outfit was ready for its long trail into the northland. Bruce and Langdon led the way up the slope and over the divide into the valley where they had first encountered Thor, the train filing picturesquely behind them, with Metoosin bringing up the rear. In his cowhide pannier rode Muskwa.

Langdon was satisfied and happy.

"It was the best hunt of my life," he said to Bruce. "I'll never be sorry we let him live."

"You're the doctor," said Bruce rather irreverently. "If I had my way about it his hide would be back there on Dishpan. Almost any tourist down on the line of rail would jump for it at a hundred dollars."

"He's worth several thousand to me alive," replied Langdon, with which enigmatic retort he dropped behind to see how Muskwa was riding.

The cub was rolling and pitching about in his pannier like a raw amateur in a howdab on an elephant's back, and after contemplating him for a few moments Langdon caught up with Bruce again.

Half a dozen times during the next two or three hours he visited Muskwa, and each time that he returned to Bruce he was quieter, as if debating something with himself.

It was nine o'clock when they came to what was undoubtedly the end of Thor's valley. A mountain rose up squarely in the face of it, and the stream they were following swung sharply to the westward into a narrow canyon. On the east rose a green and undulating slope up which the horses could easily travel, and which would take the outfit into a new valley in the direction of the Driftwood. This course Bruce decided to pursue.

Halfway up the slope they stopped to give the horses a breathing spell. In his cowhide prison Muskwa whimpered pleadingly. Langdon heard, but he seemed to pay no attention. He was looking steadily back into the valley. It was glorious in the morning sun. He could see the peaks under which lay the cool, dark lake in which Thor had fished; for miles the slopes were like green velvet and there came to him as he looked the last droning music of Thor's world. It struck him in a curious way as a sort of anthem, a hymnal rejoicing that he was going, and that he was leaving things as they were before he came. And yet, *was* he leaving things as they had been? Did his ears not catch in that music of the mountains something of sadness, of grief, of plaintive prayer?

And again, close to him, Muskwa whimpered softly.

Then Langdon turned to Bruce.

"It's settled," he said, and his words had a decisive ring in them. "I've been trying to make up my mind all the morning, and it's made up now. You and Metoosin go on when the horses get their wind. I'm going to ride down there a mile or so and free the cub where he'll find his way back home!"

He did not wait for arguments or remarks, and Bruce made none. He took Muskwa in his arms and rode back into the south.

A mile up the valley Langdon came to a wide, open meadow dotted with clumps of spruce and willows and sweet with the perfume of flowers. Here he dismounted, and for ten minutes sat on the ground with Muskwa. From his pocket he drew forth a small paper bag and fed the cub its last sugar. A thick lump grew in his throat as Muskwa's soft little nose muzzled the palm of his hand, and when at last he jumped up and sprang into his saddle there was a mist in his eyes. He tried to laugh. Perhaps he was weak. But he loved Muskwa, and he knew that he was leaving more than a human friend in this mountain valley.

"Good-bye, old fellow," he said, and his voice was choking. "Good-bye, little Spitfire! Mebby some day I'll come back and see you, and you'll be a big, fierce bear—but I won't shoot—never—never—"

He rode fast into the north. Three hundred yards away he turned his head and looked back. Muskwa was following, but losing ground. Langdon waved his hand.

"Good-bye!" he called through the lump in his throat. "Good-bye!"

Half an hour later he looked down from the top of the slope through his glasses. He saw Muskwa, a black dot. The cub had stopped, and was waiting confidently for him to return.

And trying to laugh again, but failing dismally, Langdon rode over the divide and out of Muskwa's life.

CHAPTER TWENTY

For a good half-mile Muskwa followed over the trail of Langdon. He ran at first; then he walked; finally he stopped entirely and sat down like a dog, facing the distant slope. Had Langdon been afoot he would not have halted until he was tired. But the cub had not liked his pannier prison. He had been tremendously jostled and bounced about, and twice the horse that carried him had shaken himself, and those shakings had been like earthquakes to Muskwa. He knew that the cage as well as Langdon was ahead of him. He sat for a time and whimpered wistfully, but he went no farther. He was sure that the friend he had grown to love would return after a little. He always came back. He had never failed him. So he began to hunt about for a spring beauty or a dog-tooth violet, and for some time he was careful not to stray very far away from where the outfit had passed.

All that day the cub remained in the flower-strewn meadows under the slope; it was very pleasant in the sunshine, and he found more than one patch of the bulbous roots he liked. He dug, and he filled himself, and he took a nap in the afternoon; but when the sun began to go down and the heavy shadows of the mountain darkened the valley he began to grow afraid.

He was still a very small baby of a cub, and only that one dreadful night after his mother had died had he spent entirely alone. Thor had replaced mother, and Langdon had taken the place of Thor, so that until now he had never felt the loneliness and emptiness of darkness. He crawled under a clump of thorn close to the trail, and continued to wait, and listen, and sniff expectantly. The stars came out clear and brilliant, but to-night their lure was not strong enough to call him forth. Not until dawn did he steal out cautiously from his shelter of thorn.

The sun gave him courage and confidence again and he began wandering back through the valley, the scent of the horse-trail growing fainter and fainter until at last it disappeared entirely. That day Muskwa ate some grass and a few dog-tooth violet roots, and when the second night came he was abreast of the slope over which the outfit had come from the valley in which were Thor and Iskwao. He was tired and hungry, and he was utterly lost.

That night he slept in the end of a hollow log. The next day he went on, and for many days and many nights after that he was alone in the big valley. He passed close to the pool where Thor and he had met the old bear, and he nosed hungrily among the fishbones; he skirted the edge of the dark, deep lake; he saw the shadowy things fluttering in the gloom of the forest again; he passed over the beaver dam, and he slept for two nights close to the log-jam from which he had watched Thor throw out their first fish. He was almost forgetting Langdon now, and was thinking more and more about Thor and his mother. He wanted them. He wanted them more than he had ever wanted the companionship of man, for Muskwa was fast becoming a creature of the wild again.

It was the beginning of August before the cub came to the break in the valley and climbed up the slope where Thor had first heard the thunder and had first felt the sting of the white men's guns. In these two weeks Muskwa had grown rapidly, in spite of the fact that he often went to bed on an empty stomach; and he was no longer afraid of the dark. Through the deep, sunless canyon above the clay wallow he went, and as there was only one way out he came at last to the summit of the break over which Thor had gone, and over which Langdon and Bruce had followed in close pursuit. And the other valley—his home—lay under Muskwa.

Of course he did not recognize it. He saw and smelled in it nothing that was familiar. But it was such a beautiful valley, and so abundantly filled with plenty and sunshine, that he did not hurry through it. He found whole gardens of spring beauties and dog-tooth violets. And on the third day he made his first real kill. He almost stumbled over a baby whistler no larger than a red squirrel, and before the little creature could escape he was upon it. It made him a splendid feast.

It was fully a week before he passed along the creek-bottom close under the slope where his mother had died. If he had been travelling along the crest of the slope he would have found her bones, picked clean by the wild things. It was another week before he came to the little meadow where Thor had killed the bull caribou and the big black bear.

And now Muskwa knew that he was home!

For two days he did not travel two hundred yards from the scene of feast and battle, and night and day he was on the watch for Thor. Then he had to seek farther for food, but each afternoon when the mountains began to throw out long shadows he would return to the clump of trees in which they had made the cache that the black bear robber had despoiled.

One day he went farther than usual in his quest for roots. He was a good half-mile from the place he had made home, and he was sniffing about the end of a rock when a great shadow fell suddenly upon him. He looked up, and for a full half-minute he stood transfixed, his heart pounding and jumping as it had never pounded and jumped before in his life. Within five feet of him stood Thor! The big grizzly was as motionless as he, looking at him steadily. And then Muskwa gave a puppy-like whine of joy and ran forward. Thor lowered his huge head, and for another half-minute they stood without moving, with Thor's nose buried in the hair on Muskwa's back. After that Thor went up the slope as if the cub had never been lost at all, and Muskwa followed him happily.

Many days of wonderful travel and of glorious feasting came after this, and Thor led Muskwa into a thousand new places in the two valleys and the mountains between. There were great fishing days, and there was another caribou killed over the range, and Muskwa grew fatter and fatter and heavier and heavier until by the middle of September he was as large as a good-sized dog.

Then came the berries, and Thor knew where they all grew low down in the valleys—first the wild red raspberries, then the soap berries, and after those the delicious black currants which grew in the cool depths of the forests and were almost as large as cherries and nearly as sweet as the sugar which Langdon had fed Muskwa. Muskwa liked the black currants best of all. They grew in thick, rich clusters; there were no leaves on the bushes that were loaded with them, and he could pick and eat a quart in five minutes.

But at last the time came when there were no berries. This was in October. The nights were very cold, and for whole days at a time the sun would not shine, and the skies were dark and heavy with clouds. On the peaks the snow was growing deeper and deeper, and it never thawed now up near the sky-line. Snow fell in the valley, too—at first just enough to make a white carpet that chilled Muskwa's feet, but it quickly disappeared. Raw winds began to come out of the north, and in place of the droning music of the valley in summertime there were now shrill wailings and screechings at night, and the trees made mournful sounds.

To Muskwa the whole world seemed changing. He wondered in these chill and dark days why Thor kept to the windswept slopes when he might have found shelter in the bottoms. And Thor, if he explained to him at all, told him that winter was very near, and that these slopes were their last feeding grounds. In the valleys the berries were gone; grass and roots alone were no longer nourishing enough for their bodies; they could no longer waste time in seeking ants and grubs; the fish were in deep water. It was the season when the caribou were keen-scented as foxes and swift as the wind. Only along the slopes lay the dinners they were sure of— famine-day dinners of whistlers and gophers. Thor dug for them now, and in this digging Muskwa helped as much as he could. More than once they turned out wagonloads of earth to get at the cozy winter sleeping quarters of a whistler family, and sometimes they dug for hours to capture three or four little gophers no larger than red squirrels, but lusciously fat.

Thus they lived through the last days of October into November. And now the snow and the cold winds and the fierce blizzards from the north came in earnest, and the ponds and lakes began to freeze over. Still Thor hung to the slopes, and Muskwa shivered with the cold at night and wondered if the sun was never going to shine again.

One day about the middle of November Thor stopped in the very act of digging out a family of whistlers, went straight down into the valley, and struck southward in a most businesslike way. They were ten miles from the clay-wallow canyon when they started, but so lively was the pace set by the big grizzly that they reached it before dark that same afternoon.

For two days after this Thor seemed to have no object in life at all. There was nothing in the canyon to eat, and he wandered about among the rocks, smelling and listening and deporting himself generally in a fashion that was altogether mystifying to Muskwa. In the afternoon of the second day Thor stopped in a dump of jackpines under which the ground was strewn with fallen needles. He began to eat these needles. They did not look good to Muskwa, but something told the cub that he should do as Thor was doing; so he licked them up and swallowed them, not knowing that it was nature's last preparation for his long sleep.

It was four o'clock when they came to the mouth of the deep cavern in which Thor was born, and here again Thor paused, sniffing up and down the wind, and waiting for nothing in particular.

It was growing dark. A wailing storm hung over the canyon. Biting winds swept down from the peaks, and the sky was black and full of snow.

For a minute the grizzly stood with his head and shoulders in the cavern door. Then he entered. Muskwa followed. Deep back they went through a pitch-black gloom, and it grew warmer and warmer, and the wailing of the wind died away until it was only a murmur.

It took Thor at least half an hour to arrange himself just as he wanted to sleep. Then Muskwa curled up beside him. The cub was very warm and very comfortable.

That night the storm raged, and the snow fell deep. It came up the canyon in clouds, and it drifted down through the canyon roof in still thicker clouds, and all the world was buried deep. When morning came there was no cavern door, there were no rocks, and no black and purple of tree and shrub. All was white and still, and there was no longer the droning music in the valley.

Deep back in the cavern Muskwa moved restlessly. Thor heaved a deep sigh. After that long and soundly they slept. And it may be that they dreamed.

THE VALLEY OF SILENT MEN

"You are going up from among a people who have many gods to a people who have but one," said Ransom quietly, looking across at the other. "It would be better for you if you turned back. I've spent four years in the Government service, mostly north of Fifty-three, and I know what I'm talking about. I've read all of your books carefully, and I tell you now—go back. If you strike up into the Bay country, as you say you're going to, every dream of socialism you ever had will be shattered, and you will laugh at your own books. Go back!"

Roscoe's fine young face lighted up with a laugh at his old college chum's seriousness.

"You're mistaken, Ranny," he said. "I'm not a socialist but a sociologist. There's a distinction, isn't there? I don't believe that my series of books will be at all complete without a study of socialism as it exists in its crudest form, and as it must exist up here in the North. My material for this last book will show what tremendous progress the civilization of two centuries on this continent has made over the lowest and wildest forms of human brotherhood. That's my idea, Ranny. I'm an optimist. I believe that every invention we make, that every step we take in the advancement of science, of mental and physical uplift, brings us just so much nearer to the Nirvana of universal love. This trip of mine among your wild people of the North will give me a good picture of what civilization has gained."

"What it has lost, you will say a little later," replied Ransom. "See here, Roscoe—has it ever occurred to you that brotherly love, as you call it—the real thing—ended when civilization began? Has it ever occurred to you that somewhere away back in the darkest ages your socialistic Nirvana may have existed, and that you sociologists might still find traces of it, if you would? Has the idea ever come to you that there has been a time when the world has been better than it is to-day, and better than it ever will be again? Will you, as a student of life, concede that the savage can teach you a lesson? Will any of your kind? No, for you are self-appointed civilizers, working according to a certain code."

Ransom's weather-tanned face had taken on a deeper flush, and there was a questioning look in Roscoe's eyes, as though he were striving to look through a veil of clouds to a picture just beyond his vision.

"If most of us believed as you believe," he said at last, "civilization would end. We would progress no farther."

"And this civilization," said Ransom, "can there not be too much of it? Was it any worse for God's first men to set forth and slay twenty thousand other men, than it is for civilization's sweat-shops to slay twenty thousand men, women, and children each year in the making of your cigars and the things you wear? Civilization means the uplifting of man, doesn't it, and when it ceases to uplift when it kills, robs, and disrupts in the name of progress; when the dollar-fight for commercial and industrial supremacy kills more people in a day than God's first people killed in a year; when not only people, but nations, are sparring for throat-grips, can we call it civilization any longer? This talk may all be bally rot, Roscoe. Ninety-nine out of every hundred people will think that it is. There are very few these days who stoop to the thought that the human soul is the greatest of all creations, and that it is the development of the soul, and not of engines and flying machines and warships, that measures progress as God meant progress to be. I am saying this because I want you to be honest when you go up among the savages, as you call them. You may find up there the last chapter in life, as it was largely intended that life should be in the beginning of things. And I want you to understand it, because in your books you possess a power which should be well directed. When I received your last letter I hunted up the best man I knew as guide and companion for you—old Rameses, down at the Mission.

He is called Rameses because he looks like the old boy himself. You said you wanted to learn Cree, and he'll teach it to you. He will teach you a lot of other things, and when you look at him, especially at night beside the campfire, you will find something in his face which will recall what I have said, and make you think of the first people."

Roscoe, at thirty-two, had not lost his boy's enthusiasm in life, in spite of the fact that he had studied too deeply, and had seen too much, and had begun fighting for existence while still in bare feet. From the beginning it seemed as though some grim monster of fate had hovered about him, making his path as rough as it could, and striking him down whenever the opportunity came. His own tremendous energy and ambition had carried him to the top.

He worked himself through college, and became a success in his way. But at no time could he remember real happiness. It had almost come to him, he thought, a year before—in the form of a girl; but this promise had passed like the others because, of a sudden, he found that she had shattered the most precious of all his ideals. So he picked himself up, and, encouraged by his virile optimism, began looking forward again. Bad luck had so worked its hand in the moulding of him that he had come to live chiefly in anticipation, and though this bad luck had played battledore and shuttlecock with him, the things which he anticipated were pleasant and beautiful. He believed that the human race was growing better, and that each year was bringing his ideals just so much nearer to realization. More than once he had told himself that he was living two or three centuries too soon. Ransom, his old college chum, had been the first to suggest that he was living some thousands of years too late.

He thought of this a great deal during the first pleasant weeks of the autumn, which he and old Rameses spent up in the Lac la Ronge and Reindeer Lake country. During this time he devoted himself almost entirely to the study of Cree under Rameses' tutelage, and the more he learned of it the more he saw the truth of what Ransom had told him once upon a time, that the Cree language was the most beautiful in the world. At the upper end of the Reindeer they spent a week at a Cree village, and one day Roscoe stood unobserved and listened to the conversation of three young Cree women, who were weaving reed baskets. They talked so quickly that he could understand but little of what they said, but their low, soft voices were like music. He had learned French in Paris, and had heard Italian in Rome, but never in his life had he heard words or voices so beautiful as those which fell from the red, full lips of the Cree girls. He thought more seriously than ever of what Ransom had said about the first people, and the beginning of things.

Late in October they swung westward through the Sissipuk and Burntwood water ways to Nelson House, and at this point Rameses returned homeward. Roscoe struck north, with two new guides, and on the eighteenth of November the first of the two great storms which made the year of 1907 one of the most tragic in the history of the far Northern people overtook them on Split Lake, thirty miles from a Hudson's Bay post. It was two weeks later before they reached this post, and here Roscoe was given the first of several warnings.

"This has been the worst autumn we've had for years," said the factor to him. "The Indians haven't caught half enough fish to carry them through, and this storm has ruined the early-snow hunting in which they usually get enough meat to last them until spring. We're stinting ourselves on our own supplies now, and farther north the Company will soon be on famine rations if the cold doesn't let up—and it won't. They won't want an extra mouth up there, so you'd better turn back. It's going to be a starvation winter."

But Roscoe, knowing as little as the rest of man-kind of the terrible famines of the northern people, which keep an area one-half as large as the whole of Europe down to a population of thirty thousand, went on. A famine, he argued, would give him greater opportunity for study.

Two weeks later he was at York Factory, and from there he continued to Fort Churchill, farther up on Hudson's Bay. By the time he reached this point, early in January, the famine of those few terrible weeks during which more than fifteen hundred people died of starvation had begun. From the Barren Lands to the edge of the southern watershed the earth lay under from four to six feet of snow, and from the middle of December until late in February the temperature did not rise above thirty degrees below zero, and remained for the most of the time between fifty and sixty. From all points in the wilderness reports of starvation came to the Company's posts. Traplines could not be followed because of the intense cold. Moose, caribou, and even the furred animals had buried themselves under the snow. Indians and halfbreeds dragged themselves into the posts. Twice Roscoe saw mothers who brought dead babies in their arms. One day a white trapper came in with his dogs and sledge, and on the sledge, wrapped in a bear skin, was his wife, who had died fifty miles back in the forest.

Late in January there came a sudden rise in the temperature, and Roscoe prepared to take advantage of the change to strike south and westward again, toward Nelson House. Dogs could not be had for love or money, so on the first of February he set out on snowshoes with an

Indian guide and two weeks' supply of provisions. The fifth night, in the wild, Barren country west of the Etawney, his Indian failed to keep up the fire, and when Roscoe investigated he found him half dead with a strange sickness. Roscoe thought of smallpox, the terrible plague that usually follows northern famine, and a shiver ran through him. He made the Indian's balsam shelter snow and wind proof, cut wood, and waited. The temperature fell again, and the cold became intense. Each day the provisions grew less, and at last the time came when Roscoe knew that he was standing face to face with the Great Peril. He went farther and farther from camp in his search for game. But there was no life. Even the brush sparrows and snow hawks were gone. Once the thought came to him that he might take what food was left, and accept the little chance that remained of saving himself. But the idea never got further than a first thought. He kept to his post, and each day spent half an hour in writing. On the twelfth day the Indian died. It was a terrible day, the beginning of the second great storm of that winter. There was food for another twenty-four hours, and Roscoe packed it, together with his blankets and a little tinware. He wondered if the Indian had died of a contagious disease. Anyway, he made up his mind to put out the warning for others if they came that way, and over the dead Indian's balsam shelter he planted a sapling, and at the end of the sapling he fastened a strip of red cotton cloth—the plague-signal of the North.

Then he struck out through the deep snows and the twisting storm, knowing that there was no more than one chance in a thousand ahead of him, and that his one chance was to keep the wind at his back.

This was the beginning of the wonderful experience which Roscoe Cummins afterward described in his book "The First People and the Valley of Silent Men." He prepared another manuscript which for personal reasons was never published, the story of a dark-eyed girl of the First People—but this is to come. It has to do with the last tragic weeks of this winter of 1907, in which it was a toss-up between all things of flesh and blood in the Northland to see which would win—life or death—and in which a pair of dark eyes and a voice from the First People turned a sociologist into a possible Member of Parliament.

At the end of his first day's struggle Roscoe built himself a camp in a bit of scrub timber, which was not much more than brush. If he had been an older hand he would have observed that this bit of timber, and every tree and bush that he had passed since noon, was stripped and dead on the side that faced the north. It was a sign of the Great Barrens, and of the fierce storms that swept over them, destroying even the life of the trees. He cooked and ate his last food the following day, and went on. The small timber turned to scrub, and the scrub, in time, to vast snow wastes over which the storm swept mercilessly. All this day he looked for game, for a flutter of bird life; he chewed bark, and in the afternoon got a mouthful of Fox-bite, which made his throat swell until he could scarcely breathe. At night he made tea, but had nothing to eat. His hunger was acute and painful. It was torture the next day—the third—for the process of starvation is a rapid one in this country where only the fittest survive on four meals a day. He camped, built a small bush fire at night, and slept. He almost failed to rouse himself on the morning that followed, and when he staggered to his feet and felt the cutting sting of the storm still in his face, and heard the swishing wail of it over the Barren, he knew that at last the moment had come when he was standing face to face with the Almighty.

For some strange reason he was not frightened at the situation. He found that even over the level spaces he could scarcely drag his snow shoes, but this had ceased to alarm him as he had been alarmed at first. He went on, hour after hour, weaker and weaker. Within himself there was still life which reasoned that if death were to come it could not come in a better way. It at least promised to be painless—even pleasant. The sharp, stinging pains of hunger, like little electrical knives piercing him, were gone; he no longer experienced a sensation of intense cold; he almost felt that he could lie down in the drifted snow and sleep peacefully. He knew what it would be—a sleep without end—with the arctic foxes to pick his bones, and so he resisted the temptation and forced himself onward. The storm still swept straight west from Hudson's Bay, bringing with it endless volleys of snow, round and hard as fine shot; snow that had at first seemed to pierce his flesh, and which swished past his feet, as if trying to trip him, and tossed itself in windrows and mountains in his path. If he could only find timber—shelter! That was what he worked for now. When he had last looked at his watch it was nine o'clock in the morning; now it was late in the afternoon. It might as well have been night. The storm had long since half blinded him. He could not see a dozen paces ahead. But the little life in him still reasoned bravely. It was a heroic spark of life, a fighting spark, and hard to put out. It told him that when he came to shelter be would at least *feel* it, and that he must fight until the last. And all this time, for ages and ages it seemed to him, he kept mumbling over and over again Ransom's words:

"Go back—Go back—Go back——"

They rang in his brain. He tried to keep step with their monotone. The storm could not drown them. They were meaningless words to him now, but they kept him company. Also, his rifle was meaningless, but he clung to it. The pack on his back held no significance and no weight for him. He might have travelled a mile or ten miles an hour and he would not have sensed the difference. Most men would have buried themselves in the snow, and died in comfort, dreaming the pleasant dreams which come as a sort of recompense to the unfortunate who die of starvation and cold. But the fighting spark commanded Roscoe to die upon his feet, if he died at all. It was this spark which brought him at last to a bit of timber thick enough to give him shelter from wind and snow. It burned a little more warmly then. It flared up, and gave him new vision. And, for the first time, he realized that it must be night. For a light was burning ahead of him, and all else was gloom. His first thought was that it was a campfire, miles and miles away. Then it drew nearer—until he knew that it was a light in a cabin window. He dragged himself toward it, and when he came to the door he tried to shout. But no sound fell from his swollen lips. It seemed an hour before he could twist his feet out of his snowshoes. Then he groped for a latch, pressed against the door, and plunged in.

What he saw was like a picture suddenly revealed for an instant by a flashlight. In the cabin there were four men. Two sat at a table, directly in front of him. One held a dice box poised in the air, and had turned a rough, bearded face toward him. The other was a younger man, and in this moment of lapsing consciousness it struck Roscoe as strange that he should be clutching a can of beans between his hands. A third man stared from where he had been looking down upon the dice-play of the other two. As Roscoe came in he was in the act of lowering a half-filled bottle from his lips. The fourth man sat on the edge of a bunk, with a face so white and thin that he might have been taken for a corpse if it had not been for a dark glare in his sunken eyes. Roscoe smelled the odor of whisky; he smelled food. He saw no sign of welcome in the faces turned toward him, but he advanced upon them, mumbling incoherently. And then the spark—the fighting spark in him—gave out, and he crumpled down on the floor. He heard a voice, which came to him—as if from a great distance, and which said, "Who the h—l is this?" And then, after what seemed to be a long time, he heard another voice say, "Pitch him back into the snow."

After that he lost consciousness.

A long time before he awoke he knew that he was not in the snow, and that hot stuff was running down his throat. When he opened his eyes there was no longer a light burning in the cabin. It was day. He felt strangely comfortable, but there was something in the cabin that stirred him from his rest. It was the odour of frying bacon. He raised himself upon his elbow, prepared to thank his deliverers, and to eat. All of his hunger had come back. The joy of life, of anticipation, shone in his thin face as he pulled himself up. Another face—the bearded face—red-eyed, almost animal-like in its fierce questioning, bent over him.

"Where's your grub, pardner?"

The question was like a stab. Roscoe did not hear his own voice as he explained.

"Got none!" The bearded man's voice was like a bellow as he turned upon the others.

"He's got no grub!"

"We'll divvy up, Jack," came a weak voice. It was from the thin, white-faced man who had sat corpse-like on the edge of his bunk the night before.

"Divvy h—l!" growled the bearded man. "It's up to you—you and Scotty. You're to blame!" You're to blame!

The words struck upon Roscoe's ears with a chill of horror. He recalled the voice that had suggested throwing him back into the snow. Starvation was in the cabin. He had fallen among animals instead of men, and his body grew cold with a chill that was more horrible than that of the snow and the wind. He saw the thin-faced man who had spoken for him sitting again on the edge of his bunk. Mutely he looked to the others to see which was Scotty. He was the young man who had clutched the can of beans. It was he who was frying bacon over the sheet iron stove.

"We'll divvy—Henry and I," he said. "I told you that last night." He looked over at Roscoe. "Glad you're better," he greeted. "You see—you've struck us at a bad time. We're on our last legs for grub. Our two Indians went out to hunt a week ago and never came back. They're dead—or gone, and we're as good as dead if the storm doesn't let up pretty soon. You can have some of our grub—Henry's and mine."

It was a cold invitation, lacking warmth or sympathy, and Roscoe felt that even this man wished that he had died before he reached the cabin. But the man was human; he at least had not cast his voice with those who had wanted to throw him back into the snow, and Roscoe tried to voice his gratitude, and at the same time to hide his hunger. He saw that there were three thin slices of bacon in the frying pan, and it struck him that it would be bad taste to reveal a starvation appetite in the face of such famine. He came up, limping, and stood on the other side of the stove from Scotty.

"You saved my life," he said, holding out a hand. "Will you shake?"

Scotty shook hands limply.

"It's h—l," he said in a low voice. "We'd have had beans this morning if I hadn't shook dice with him last night." He nodded toward the bearded man, who was cutting open the top of a can. "He won!"

"My God!" began Roscoe.

He didn't finish. Scotty turned the meat, and added:

"He won a square meal off me yesterday—a quarter of a pound of bacon. Day before that he won Henry's last can of beans. He's got his share under his blanket over there, and swears he'll shoot any one who goes to monkeying with his bed—so you'd better fight shy of it. Thompson—he isn't up yet—chose the whisky for *his* share, so you'd better fight shy of him, too. Henry and I'll divvy up with you."

"Thanks," said Roscoe, the one word choking him.

Henry came from his bunk, bent and wobbling. He looked like a dying man, and for the first time Roscoe saw that his hair was gray. He was a little man, and his thin hands shook as he held them out over the stove, and nodded at Roscoe. The bearded man had opened his can, and approached the stove with a pan of water, coming in beside Roscoe without noticing him. He brought with him a foul odour of stale tobacco smoke and whisky. After he had put his water over the fire he turned to one of the bunks and with half a dozen coarse epithets roused Thompson, who sat up stupidly, still half drunk. Henry had gone to a small table, and Scotty followed him with the bacon. But Roscoe did not move. He forgot his hunger. His pulse was beating quickly. Sensations filled him which he had never known or imagined before. He had known tragedy; he had investigated to what he had supposed to be the depths of human vileness—but this that he was experiencing now stunned him. Was it possible that these were people of his own kind? Had a madness of some sort driven all human instincts from them? He saw Thompson's red eyes fastened upon him, and he turned his face to escape their questioning, stupid leer. The bearded man was turning out the can of beans he had won from Scotty. Beyond the bearded man the door creaked, and Roscoe heard the wail of the storm. It came to him now as a friendly sort of sound.

"Better draw up, pardner," he heard Scotty say. "Here's your share."

One of the thin slices of bacon and a hard biscuit were waiting for him on a tin plate. He ate as ravenously as Henry and Scotty, and drank a cup of hot tea. In two minutes the meal was over. It was terribly inadequate. The few mouthfuls of food stirred up all his craving, and he found it impossible to keep his eyes from the bearded man and his beans. The bearded man, whom Scotty called Croker, was the only one who seemed well fed, and his horror increased when Henry bent over and said to him in a low whisper: "He didn't get my beans fair. I had three aces and a pair of deuces, an' he took it on three fives and two sixes. When I objected he called me a liar an' hit me. Them's my beans, or Scotty's!" There was something almost like murder in the little man's red eyes.

Roscoe remained silent. He did not care to talk, or question. No one had asked him who he was or whence he came, and he felt no inclination to know more of the men he had fallen among. Croker finished, wiped his mouth with his hand, and looked across at Roscoe.

"How about going out with me to get some wood?" he demanded.

"I'm ready," replied Roscoe.

For the first time he took notice of himself. He was lame, and sickeningly weak, but apparently sound in other ways. The intense cold had not frozen his ears or feet. He put on his heavy moccasins, his thick coat and fur cap, and Croker pointed to his rifle.

"Better take that along," he said. "Can't tell what you might see."

Roscoe picked it up and the pack which lay beside it. He did not catch the ugly leer which the bearded man turned upon Thompson. But Henry did, and his little eyes grew smaller and blacker. On snowshoes the two men went out into the storm, Croker carrying an axe. He led the way through the bit of thin timber, and across a wide open over which the storm swept so fiercely that their trail was covered behind them as they travelled. Roscoe figured that they had gone a quarter of a mile when they came to another clump of trees, and Croker gave him the axe.

"You can cut down some of this," he said. "It's better burning than that back there. I'm going on for a dry log that I know of. You wait until I come back."

Roscoe set to work upon a spruce, but he could scarcely strike out a chip. After a little he was compelled to drop his axe, and lean against the tree, exhausted. At intervals he resumed his cutting. It was half an hour before the small tree fell. Then he waited for Croker. Behind him his trail was already obliterated. After a little he raised his voice and called for Croker. There was no reply. The wind moaned above him in the spruce tops. It made a noise like the wash of the sea out on the open Barren. He shouted again. And again. The truth dawned upon him slowly—but it came. Croker had brought him out purposely—to lose him. He was saving the bacon and the cold biscuits back in the cabin. Roscoe's hands clenched tightly, and then they relaxed. At last he had found what he was after—his book! It would be a terrible book, if he carried out the idea that flashed upon him now in the wailing and twisting of the storm. And then he laughed, for it occurred to him quickly that the idea would die—with himself. He might find the cabin, but he would not make the effort. Once more he would fight alone and for himself. The Spark returned to him, loyally. He buttoned himself up closely, saw that his snowshoes were securely fastened, and struck out once more with his back to the storm. He was at least a trifle better off for meeting with the flesh and blood of his kind.

The clump of timber thinned out, and Roscoe struck out boldly into the low bush. As he went, he wondered what would happen in the cabin. He believed that Henry, of the four, would not pull through alive, and that Croker would come out best. It was not until the following summer that he learned the facts of Henry's madness, and of the terrible manner in which he avenged himself on Croker by sticking a knife under the latter's ribs.

For the first time in his life Roscoe found himself in a position to measure accurately the amount of energy contained in a slice of bacon and a cold biscuit. It was not much. Long before noon his old weakness was upon him again. He found even greater difficulty in dragging his feet over the snow, and it seemed now as though all ambition had left him, and that even the fighting spark was becoming disheartened. He made up his mind to go on until the arctic gloom of night began mingling with the storm; then he would stop, build a fire, and go to sleep in its warmth. He would never wake up, and there would be no sensation of discomfort in his dying.

During the afternoon he passed out of the scrub into a rougher country. His progress was slower, but more comfortable, for at times he found himself protected from the wind. A gloom darker and more sombre than that of the storm was falling about him when he came to what appeared to be the end of the Barren. The earth dropped away from under his feet, and far below him, in a ravine shut out from wind and storm, he saw the black tops of thick spruce. What life was left in him leaped joyously, and he began to scramble downward. His eyes were no longer fit to judge distance or chance, and he slipped. He slipped a dozen times in the first five minutes, and then there came the time when he did not make a recovery, but plunged down the side of the mountain like a rock. He stopped with a terrific jar, and for the first time during the fall he wanted to cry out with pain. But the voice that he heard did not come from his own lips. It was another voice—and then two, three, many of them. His dazed eyes caught glimpses of dark objects floundering in the deep snow about him, and just beyond these objects were four or five tall mounds of snow, like tents, arranged in a circle. A number of times that winter Roscoe had seen mounds of snow like these, and he knew what they meant. He had fallen into an Indian village. He tried to call out the words of greeting that Rameses had taught him, but he had no tongue. Then the floundering figures caught him up, and he was carried to the circle of snow-mounds. The last that he knew was that warmth was entering his lungs, and that once again there came to him the low, sweet music of a Cree girl's voice.

It was a face that he first saw after that, a face that seemed to come to him slowly from out of night, approaching nearer and nearer until he knew that it was a girl's face, with great, dark, shining eyes whose lustre suffused him with warmth and a strange happiness. It was a face of wonderful beauty, he thought—of a wild sort of beauty, yet with something so gentle in the shining eyes that he sighed restfully. In these first moments of his returning consciousness the whimsical thought came to him that he was dying, and the face was a part of a pleasant dream. If that were not so he had fallen at last among friends. His eyes opened wider, he moved, and the face drew back. Movement stimulated returning life, and reason rehabilitated itself in great bounds. In a dozen flashes he went over all that had happened up to the point where he had fallen down the mountain and into the Cree camp. Straight above him he saw a funnel-like peak through which there drifted a blue film of smoke. He was in a wigwam. It was warm and exceedingly comfortable. Wondering if he was hurt, he moved. The movement drew a sharp exclamation of pain from him. It was the first real sound he had made, and in an instant the face was over him again. He saw it plainly this time, with its dark eyes and oval cheeks framed between two great braids of black hair. A hand touched his brow cool and gentle, and a sweet voice soothed him in half a dozen musical words. The girl was a Cree.

At the sound of her voice an Indian woman came up beside her, looked down at Roscoe for a moment, and then went to the door of the wigwam, speaking in a low voice to some one who was outside. When she returned a man followed in after her. He was old and bent, and his face was thin. His cheek-bones shone, so tightly was the skin drawn over them. And behind him came a younger man, as straight as a tree, with strong shoulders, and a head set like a piece of bronze sculpture. Roscoe thought of Ransom and of his words about old Rameses:

"You will find something in his face which will recall what I have said, and make you think of the First People."

The second man carried in his hand a frozen fish, which he gave to the woman. And as he gave it to her he spoke words in Cree which Roscoe understood.

"It is the last fish."

For a moment some terrible hand gripped at Roscoe's heart and stopped its beating. He saw the woman take the fish and cut it into two equal parts with a knife, and one of these parts he saw her drop into a pot of boiling water which hung over the stone fireplace built under the vent in the wall. The girl went up and stood beside the older woman, with her back turned to him. He opened his eyes wide, and stared. The girl was tall and slender, as lithely and as beautifully formed as one of the northern lilies that thrust their slender stems from between the mountain rocks. Her two heavy braids fell down her back almost to her knees. And this girl, the woman, the two men *were dividing with him their last fish*!

He made an effort and sat up. The younger man came to him, and put a bear skin at his back. He had picked up some of the patois of half-blood French and English.

"You seek," he said, "you hurt—you hungr'. You have eat soon."

He motioned with his hand to the boiling pot. There was not a ficker of animation in his splendid face. There was something godlike in his immobility, something that was awesome in the way he moved and breathed. His voice, too, it seemed to Roscoe, was filled with the old, old mystery of the beginning of things, of history that was long dead and lost for all time. And it came upon Roscoe now, like a flood of rare knowledge descending from a mysterious source, that he had at last discovered the key to new life, and that through the blindness of reason, through starvation and death, fate had led him to the Great Truth that was dying with the last sons of the First People. For the half of the last fish was brought to him, and he ate; and when the knowledge that he was eating life away from these people choked him, and he thrust a part of it back, the girl herself urged him to continue, and he finished, with her dark, glorious eyes fixed upon him and sending warm floods through his veins. And after that the men bolstered him up with the bear skin, and the two went out again into the storm. The woman sat hunched before the fire, and after a little the girl joined her and piled fresh fagots on the blaze. Then she sat beside her, with her chin resting in the little brown palms of her hands, the fire lighting up a half profile of her face and painting rich colour in her deep-black hair.

For a long time there was silence, and Roscoe lay as if he were asleep. It was not an ordinary silence, the silence of a still room, or of emptiness—but a silence that throbbed and palpitated with an unheard life, a silence which was thrilling because it spoke a language which Roscoe was just beginning to understand. The fire grew redder, and the cone-shaped vacancy at the top of the tepee grew duskier, so Roscoe knew that night was falling outside. Far above he could hear the storm wailing over the top of the mountain. Redder and redder grew the birch flame that lighted up the profile of the girl's face. Once she turned, so that he caught the lustrous darkness of her eyes upon him. He could not hear the breath of the two in front of the fire. He heard no sound outside except that of the wind and the trees, and all grew as dark as it was silent in the snow-covered tepee, except in front of the fire. And then, as he lay with wide-open eyes, it seemed to Roscoe as though the stillness was broken by a sob that was scarcely more than a sigh, and he saw the girl's head droop a little lower in her hands, and fancied that a shuddering tremor ran through her slender shoulders. The fire burned low, and she reached out for more fagots. Then she rose slowly, and turned toward him. She could not see his face in the gloom, but the deep breathing which he feigned drew her to him, and through his half-closed eyes he could see her face bending over him, until one of her heavy braids slipped over her shoulder and fell upon his breast. After a moment she sat down silently beside him, and he felt her fingers brush gently through his tangled hair. Something in their light, soft touch thrilled him, and he moved his hand in the darkness until it came in contact with the big, soft braid that still lay where it had fallen across him. He was on the point of speaking, but the fingers left his hair and stroked as gentle as velvet over his storm-beaten face. She believed that he was asleep, and a warm flood of shame swept through him at the thought of his hypocrisy. The birch flared up suddenly, and he saw the glisten of her hair, the glow of her eyes, and the startled change that came into them when she saw that his own eyes were wide open, and looking up at her. Before she could move he had caught her hand, and was holding it tighter to his face—against his lips. The birch bark died as suddenly as it had flared up; he heard her breathing quickly, he saw her great eyes melt away like lustrous stars into the returning gloom, and a wild, irresistible impulse moved him. He raised his free hand to the dark head, and drew it down to him, holding it against his feverish face while he whispered Rameses's prayer of thankfulness in Cree:

"The spirits bless you forever, *Meeani*."

The nearness of her, the touch of her heavy hair, the caress of her breath stirred him still more deeply with the strange, new emotion that was born in him, and in the darkness he found and kissed a pair of lips, soft and warm.

The woman stirred before the fire. The girl drew back, her breath coming almost sobbingly. And then the thought of what he had done rushed in a flood of horror upon Roscoe. These wild people had saved his life; they had given him to eat of their last fish; they were nursing him back from the very threshold of death—and he had already repaid them by offering to the Cree maiden next to the greatest insult that could come to her people. He remembered what Rameses had told him—that the Cree girl's first kiss was her betrothal kiss; that it was the white garment of her purity, the pledge of her fealty forever. He lifted himself upon his elbow, but the girl had run to the door. Voices came from outside, and the two men reëntered the tepee. He understood enough of what was said to learn that the camp had been holding council, and that two men were about to make an effort to reach the nearest post. Each tepee was to furnish these two men a bit of food to keep them alive on their terrible hazard, and the woman brought forth the half of a fish. She cut it into quarters, and with one of the pieces the elder man went out again into the night. The younger man spoke to the girl. He called her Oachi, and to Roscoe's astonishment spoke in French.

"If they do not come back, or if we do not find meat in seven days," he said, "we will die."

Roscoe made an effort to rise, and the effort sent a rush of fire into his head. He turned dizzy, and fell back with a groan. In an instant the girl was at his side—ahead of the man. Her hands were at his face, her eyes glowing again. He felt that he was falling into a deep sleep. But the eyes did not leave him. They were wonderful eyes, glorious eyes! He dreamed of them in the strange sleep that came to him, and they grew more and more beautiful, shining with a light which thrilled him even in his unconsciousness. After a time there came a black, more natural sort of night to him. He awoke from it refreshed. It was day. The tepee was filled with light, and for the first time he looked about him. He was alone. A fire burned low among the stones; over it simmered a pot. The earth floor of the tepee was covered with deer and caribou skins, and opposite him there was another bunk. He drew himself painfully to a sitting posture and found that it was his shoulder and hip that hurt him. He rose to his feet, and stood balancing himself feebly when the door to the tepee was drawn back and Oachi entered. At sight of him, standing up from his bed, she made a quick movement to draw back, but Roscoe reached out his hands with a low cry of pleasure.

"Oachi," he cried softly. "Come in!" He spoke in French, and Oachi's face lighted up like sunlight. "I am better," he said. "I am well. I want to thank you—and the others." He made a step toward her, and the strength of his left leg gave way. He would have fallen if she had not darted to him so quickly that she made a prop for him, and her eyes looked up into his whitened face, big and frightened and filled with pain.

"Oo-ee-ee," she said in Cree, her red lips rounded as she saw him flinch, and that one word, a song in a word; came to him like a flute note.

"It hurts—a little," he said. He dropped back on his bunk, and Oachi sank upon the skins at his feet, looking up at him steadily with her wonderful, pure eyes, her mouth still rounded, little wrinkles of tense anxiety drawn in her forehead. Roscoe laughed.

For a few moments his soul was filled with a strange gladness. He reached out his hand and stroked it over her shining hair, and a radiance such as he had never seen leapt into her eyes. "You—talk—French?" he asked slowly.

She nodded.

"Then tell me this—you are hungry—starving?"

She nodded again, and made a cup of her two small hands. "No meat. This little—so much—flour—" Her throat trembled and her voice fluttered. But even as she measured out their starvation her face was looking at him joyously. And then she added, with the gladness of a child, "*Feesh*, for you," and pointed to the simmering pot.

"For *ME*!" Roscoe looked at the pot, and then back at her.

"Oachi," he said gently, "go tell your father that I am ready to talk with him. Ask him to come—now."

She looked at him for a moment as though she did not quite understand what he had said, and he repeated the words. Even as he was speaking he marvelled at the fairness of her skin, which shone with a pink flush, and at the softness and beauty of her hair. What he saw impelled him to ask, as she made to rise:

"Your father—your mother—is French. Is that so, Oachi?" The girl nodded again, with the soft little Cree throat note that meant yes. Then she slipped to her feet and ran out, and a little later there came into the tepee the man who had first loomed up in the dusky light like a god of the First People to Roscoe Cummins. His splendid face was a little more gaunt than the night before, and Roscoe knew that famine came hand in hand with him. He had seen starvation before, and he knew that it reddened the eyes and gave the lips a grayish pallor. These things, and more, he saw in Oachi's father. But Mukoki came in straight and erect, hiding his weakness under the pride of his race. Fighting down his pain Roscoe rose at sight of him and held out his hands.

"I want to thank you," he said, repeating the words he had spoken to Oachi. "You have saved my life. But I have eyes, and I can see. You gave me of your last fish. You have no meat. You have no flour. You are starving. What? I have asked you to come and tell me, so that I may know how it fares with your women and children. You will give me a council, and we will smoke." Roscoe dropped back on his bunk. He drew forth his pipe and filled it with tobacco. The Cree sat down mutely in the centre of the tepee. They smoked, passing the pipe back and forth without speaking. Once Roscoe loaded the pipe, and once the chief; and when the last puff of the last pipeful was taken the Indian reached over his hand, and Roscoe gripped it hard.

And then, while the storm still moaned far up over their heads, Roscoe Cummins listened to the old, old story of the First People—the story of starvation and of death. To him it was epic. It was terrible. But to the other it was the mere coming and going of a natural thing, of a thing that had existed for him and for his kind since life began, and he spoke of it quietly and without a gesture. There had been a camp of twenty-two, and there were now fifteen. Seven had died, four men, two women, and one child. Each day during the great storm the men had gone out on their futile search for game, and every few days one of them had failed to return. Thus four had died. The dogs were eaten. Corn and fish were gone; there remained but a little flour, and this was for the women and the children. The men had eaten nothing but bark and roots for five days. And there seemed to be no hope. It was death to stray far from the camp. That morning the two men had set out for the post, but Mukoki said calmly that they would never return. And then Roscoe spoke of Oachi, his daughter, and for the first time the iron lines of the chief's bronze face seemed to soften, and his head bent over a little, and his shoulders drooped. Not until then did Roscoe learn the depths of sorrow hidden behind the splendid strength of the starving man. Oachi's mother had been a French woman. Six months before she had died in this tepee, and Mukoki had buried his wife up on the face of the mountain, where the storm was moaning. After this Roscoe could not speak. He was choking. He loaded his pipe again, and sat down close to the chief, so that their knees and their shoulders touched, and thus, as taught him by old Rameses, he smoked with Oachi's father the pledge of eternal friendship, of brotherhood in life, of spirit communion in the Valley of Silent Men. After that Mukoki left him and he crawled back upon his bunk, weak and filled with pain, knowing that he was facing death with the others. He was not afraid, but was filled with a great thankfulness that, even at the price of starvation, fate had allowed him to touch at last the edge of the fabric of his dreams. All of that day he wrote, in the hours when he felt best. He filled page after page of the tablets which he carried in his pack, writing feverishly and with great haste, oppressed only by the fear that he would not be able to finish the message which he had for the people of that other world a thousand miles away. Three times during the morning Oachi came in and brought him the cooked fish and a biscuit which she had made for him out of flour and meal. And each time he said, "I am a man with the other men, Oachi. I would be a woman if I ate."

The third time Oachi knelt close down at his side, and when he refused the food again there came a strange light into her eyes, and she said, "If you starve—I starve!"

It was the first revelation to him. He put up his hands. They touched her face. Some potent spirit in him carried him across all gulfs. In that moment, thrilling, strange, he was heart and soul of the First People. In an instant he had drifted back a thousand years, beyond the memory of cities, of clubs, of all that went with civilization. A wild, half savage longing filled him. One of his hands slipped to her shining hair, and suddenly their faces lay close to each other, and he knew that in that moment love had come to him from the fount of glory itself.

Days followed—black days filled with the endless terrors of the storm. And yet they were days of a strange contentment which Roscoe had never felt before. Oachi and her father were with him a great deal in the tepee which they had given up to him. On the third day Roscoe noticed that Oachi's little hands were bruised and red and he found that the chief's daughter had gone out to dig down through ice and snow with the other women after roots. The camp lived entirely on roots now—wild flag and moose roots ground up and cooked in a batter. On this same day, late in the afternoon, there came a low wailing grief from one of the tepees, a moaning sound that pitched itself to the key of the storm until it seemed to be a part of it. A child had died, and the mother was mourning. That night another of the camp huntsmen failed to return at dusk.

The next day Roscoe was able to move about in his tepee without pain. Oachi and her father were with him when, for the first time, he got out his comb and military brushes and began grooming his touselled hair. Oachi watched him, and suddenly, seeing the wondering pleasure in her eyes, he held out the brushes to her. "You may have them, Oachi," he said, and the girl accepted them with a soft little cry of delight. To his amazement she began unbraiding her hair immediately, and then she stood up before him, hidden to her knees in her wonderful wealth of shining tresses, and Roscoe Cummins thought in this moment that he had never seen a woman more beautiful than the half Cree girl. When they had gone he still saw her, and the vision troubled him. They came in again at night, when the fire was sending red and yellow lights up and down the tepee walls, and the more he watched Oachi the stronger there grew within him something that seemed to gnaw and gripe with a dull sort of pain. Oachi was beautiful. He had never seen hair like her hair. He had never before seen eyes more beautiful. He had never heard a voice so low and sweet and filled with bird-like ripples of music. She was beautiful, and yet with her beauty there was a primitiveness, a gentle savagery, and an age-old story written in the fine lines of her face which made him uneasy with the thought of a thing that was almost tragedy. Oachi loved him. He could see that love in her eyes, in her movement; he could feel it in her presence, and the sweet song of it trembled in her voice when she spoke to him. Ordinarily a white man would have accepted this love; he would have rejoiced in it, and would have played with it for a time, as they have done with the loves of the women of Oachi's people since the beginning of white man's time. But Roscoe Cummins was of a different type. He was a man of ideals, and in Oachi's love he saw his ideal of love set apart from him by illimitable voids. This night, in the firelit tepee, there came to him like a painful stab the truth of Ransom's words. He had been born some thousands of years too late. He saw in Oachi love and life as they might have been for him; but beyond them he also saw, like a grim and threatening hand, a vision of cities, of toiling millions, of a great work just begun—a vision of life as it was intended that he should live it; and to shut it out from him he bowed his head in his two hands, overwhelmed by a new grief.

The chief sat with his face to the fire, smoking silently, and Oachi came to Roscoe's side, and touched hands timidly, like a little child. She seemed to him wondrously like a child when he lifted his head and looked down into her face. She smiled at him, questioning him, and he smiled his answer back, yet neither broke the silence with words. He heard only the soft little note in Oachi's throat that filled him with such an exquisite sensation, and he wondered what music would be if it could find expression through a voice like hers.

"Oachi," he asked softly, "why did you never sing?"

The girl looked at him in silence for a moment.

"We starve," she said. She swept her hand toward the door of the tepee. "We starve—die—there is no song."

He put his hand under her chin and lifted her face to him, as he might have done with a little child.

"I wish you would sing, Oachi," he said.

For a moment the girl's dark eyes glowed up at him. Then she drew back softly, and seated herself before the fire, with her back turned toward him, close beside her father. A strange quiet filled the tepee. Over their heads the wailing storm seemed to die for a moment; and then something rose in its place, so low and gentle at first that it seemed like a whisper, but growing in sweetness and volume until Roscoe Cummins sat erect, his eyes flashing, his hands clenched, looking at Oachi. The storm rose, and with it the song—a song that reached down into his soul, stirring him now with its gladness, now with a half savage pain; but always with a sweetness that engulfed for him all other things, until he was listening only to the voice. And then silence came again within the tepee. Over the mountain the wind burst more fiercely. The chief sat motionless. In Oachi's hair the firelight glistened with a dull radiance. There was quiet, and yet Roscoe still heard the voice. He knew that he would always hear it, that it would never die.

Not until long afterward did he know that Oachi had sung to him the great love song of the Crees.

That night and the next day, and the terrible night and day that followed, Roscoe fought with himself. He won—when alone—and lost when Oachi was with him. In some ways she knew intuitively that he loved to see her with her splendid hair down, and she would sit at his feet and brush it, while he tried to hide his admiration and smother the passion which sprang up in his breast when she was near. He knew, in these moments, that it was too late to kill the thing that was born in him—the craving of his heart and his soul for this girl of the First People who had laid her life at his feet and who was removed from him by barriers which he could never pass. On the afternoon of his seventh day in camp an Indian hunter ran in from the forest nearly crazed with joy. He had ventured farther away than the others, and had found a moose-yard. He had killed two of the animals. The days of famine were over. Oachi brought the first news to Roscoe. Her face was radiant with joy, her eyes burned like stars, and in her excitement she stretched out her arms to him as she cried out the wonderful news. Roscoe took her two hands.

"Is it true, Oachi?" he asked. "They have surely killed meat?"

"Yes—yes—yes," she cried. "They have killed meat—much meat—"

She stopped at the strange, hard look in Roscoe's eyes. He was looking overhead. If he had looked down, into the glory and love of her eyes, he would have swept her close in his arms, and the last fight would have been over then and there. Oachi went out, wondering at the coldness with which he had received the word of their deliverance, and little guessing that in that moment he had fought the greatest battle of his life. Each day after this called him back to the fight. His two broken ribs healed slowly. The storm passed. The sun followed it, and the March winds began bringing up warmth from the south. Days grew into weeks, and the snow was growing soft underfoot before he dared venture forth short distances from the camp alone. He tried often to make Oachi understand, but he always stopped short of what he meant to say; his hand would steal to her beautiful hair, and in Oachi's throat would sound the inimitable little note of happiness. Each day he was more and more handicapped. For in the joy of her great love Oachi became more beautiful and her voice still sweeter. By the time the snows began running down from the mountains and the poplar buds began to swell she was telling him the most sacred of all sacred things, and one day she told him of the wonderful world far to the west, painted by the glow of the setting sun, wherein lay the Valley of Silent Men.

"And that is Heaven—your Heaven," breathed Roscoe. He was almost well now, but he was sitting on the edge of his bunk, and Oachi knelt in the old place upon the deer skin at his feet. As he spoke he stroked her hair.

"Tell me," he said, "what sort of a place it is, Oachi."

"It is beautiful," spoke Oachi softly.

"Long, long ago the Great God came down among us and lived for a time; and He came at a time like that which has just passed, and He saw suffering, and hunger, and death. And when He saw what life was He made for us another world, and told us that it should be called the Valley of Silent Men; and that when we died we would go to this place, and that at last—when all of our race were gone—He would cause the earth to roll three times, and in the Valley of Silent Men all would awaken into life which would never know death, or sorrow, or pain again. And He says that those who love will awaken there—hand in hand."

"It is beautiful," said Roscoe. He felt himself trembling. Oachi's breath was against his hand. It was his last fight. He half reached out, as if to clasp her to him; but beyond her he still saw the other thing—the other world. He rose to his feet, not daring to look at her now. He loved her too much to sacrifice her. And it would be a sacrifice. He tried to speak firmly.

"Oachi," he said, "I am nearly well enough to travel now. I have spent pleasant weeks with you, weeks which I shall never forget. But it is time for me to go back to my people. They are expecting me. They are waiting for me, and wondering at my absence. I am as you would be if you were down there in a great city. So I must go. I must go to-morrow, or the next day, or soon after. Oachi—"

He still looked where he could not see her face. But he heard her move. He knew that slowly she was drawing away.

"Oachi—"

She was near the door now, and his eyes turned toward her. She was looking back, her slender shoulders bent over, her glorious hair rippling to her knees, as she had left it undone for him. In her eyes was love such as falls from the heavens. But her face was as white as a mask.

"Oachi!"

With a cry Roscoe reached out his arms. But Oachi was gone. At last the Cree girl understood.

Three days later there came in the passing of a single day and night the splendour of northern spring. The sun rose warm and golden. From the sides of the mountains and in the valleys water poured forth in rippling, singing floods. There bakneesh glowed on bared rocks. Moose-birds, and jays, and wood-thrushes flitted about the camp, and the air was filled with the fragrant smells of new life bursting from earth, and tree, and shrub. On this morning of the third day Roscoe strode forth from his tepee, with his pack upon his back. An Indian guide waited for him outside. He had smoked his last pipe with the chief, and now he went from tepee to tepee, in the fashion of the Crees, and drew a single puff from the pipe of each master, until there was but one tepee left, and in that was Oachi. With a white face he rubbed his hand over the deer-flap, and waited. Slowly it was drawn back, and Oachi came out. He had not seen her since the night he had driven her from him, and he had planned to say things in this last moment which he might have said then. But words stumbled on his lips. Oachi was changed. She seemed taller. Her beautiful eyes looked at him clearly and proudly. For the first time she was to him Oachi, the "Sun Child," a princess of the First People—the daughter of a Cree chief. He held out his hand, and the hand which Oachi gave to him was cold and lifeless. She smiled when he told her that he had come to say good-bye, and when she spoke to him her voice was as clear as the stream singing through the cañon. His own voice trembled. In spite of his mightiest effort a tightening fist seemed choking him.

"I am coming back—some day," he managed.

Oachi smiled, with the glory of the morning sun in her eyes and hair. She turned, still smiling, and pointed far to the west.

"And some day—the Valley of Silent Men will awaken," she said, and reëntered her father's tepee.

Out of the camp staggered Roscoe Cummins behind his Indian guide, a blinding heat in his eyes. Once or twice a gulping sob rose in his throat, and he clutched hard at his heart to beat himself into submission to the great law of life as it had been made for him.

An hour later the two came to a stream where there was a canoe. Because of rapids and the fierceness of the spring floods, portages were many, and progress slow during the whole of that day. They had made twenty miles when the sun began sinking in the west, and they struck camp. After their supper of meat the Cree rolled himself in his blanket and slept. But for long hours Roscoe sat beside their fire. Night dropped about him, a splendid night filled with sweet breaths and stars and a new moon, and with strange sounds which came to him now in a language which he was beginning to understand. From far away there floated faintly to his ears the lonely cry of a wolf, and it no longer made him shudder, but filled him with the mysterious longing of the cry itself. It was the mate-song of the beast of prey, sending up its message to the stars—crying out to all the wilderness for a response to its loneliness. Night birds twittered about him. A loon laughed in its mocking joy. An owl hooted down at him from the black top of a tall spruce. From out of starvation and death the wilderness had awakened. Its sounds spoke to him still of grief, of the suffering that would never know end; and yet there trembled in them a note of happiness and of content. Beside the campfire it came to him that in this world he had discovered two things—a suffering that he had never known, and a peace he had never known. And Oachi stood for them both. He thought of her until drowsiness drew a pale film over his eyes. The birch crackled more and more faintly in the fire and sounds died away. The stillness of sleep fell about him. Scarce had he fallen into slumber than his eyes seemed to open wide and wakeful, and out of the gloom beyond the smouldering fire he saw a human form slowly revealing itself, until there stood clearly within his vision a figure which he at first took to be that of Mukoki, the chief. But in another moment he saw that it was even taller than the tall chief, and that its eyes had searched him out. When he heard a voice, speaking in Cree the words which mean, "Whither goest thou?" he was startled to hear his own voice reply: "I am going back to my people."

He stared into vacancy, for at the sound of his voice the vision faded away; but there came a voice to him back through the night, which said: "And it is here that you have found that of which you have dreamed—Life, and the Valley of Silent Men!"

Roscoe was wide awake now. The voice and the vision had seemed so real to him that he looked about him tremblingly into the starlit gloom of the forest, as if not quite sure that he had been dreaming. Then he crawled into his balsam shelter, drew his blankets about him, and fell asleep.

The next day he had little to say to his Indian companion as they made their way downstream. At each dip of their paddles a deeper sickness seemed to enter into his heart. Life, after all, he tried to reason, was like a tailored garment. One might have an ideal, and if that ideal became a realization it would be found a misfit for one reason or another. So he told himself, in spite of fill the dreams which had urged him on in the fight for better things. There flooded upon him now the forceful truth of what Ransom had said. His work, as he had begun it, was at an end, his fabric of idealism had fallen into ruins. For he had found all that was ideal—love, faith, purity, and beauty—and he, Roscoe Cummins, the idealist, had repulsed them because they were not dressed in the tailored fashion of his kind. He told himself the truth with brutal directness. Before him he saw another work in his books, but of a different kind; and each hour that passed added to the conviction within him that at last that work would prove a failure. He went off alone into the forest when they camped, early in the afternoon, and thought of Oachi, who would mourn him until the end of time. And he—could he forget? What if he had yielded to temptation, and had taken Oachi with him? She would have come. He knew that. She would have sacrificed herself to him forever, would have gone with him into a life which she could not understand, and would never understand, satisfied to live in his love alone. The old, choking hand gripped at his heart, and yet with the pain of it there was still a rejoicing that he had not surrendered to the temptation, that he had been strong enough to save her.

The last light of the setting sun cast film-like webs of yellow and gold through the forest as he turned in the direction of camp. It was that hour in which a wonderful quiet falls upon the wilderness, the last minutes between night and day, when all wild life seems to shrink in suspensive waiting for the change. Seven months had taught Roscoe a quiet of his own. His moccasined feet made no sound. His head was bent, his shoulders had a tired droop, and his eyes searched for nothing in the mystery about him. His heart seemed weighted under a pressure that had taken all life from him, and close above him, in a balsam bough, a night bird twittered. In response to it a low cry burst from his lips, a cry of loneliness and of grief. In that moment he saw Oachi again at his feet; he heard the low, sweet note of love in her throat, so much like that of the bird over his head; he saw the soft lustre of her hair, the glory of her eyes, looking up at him from the half gloom of the tepee, telling him that they had found their god. It was all so near, so real for a moment, that he sprang erect, his fingers clutching handfuls of moss. He looked toward the camp, and he saw something move between the rock and the fire.

It was a wolf, he thought, or perhaps a lynx, and drawing his revolver he moved quickly and silently in its direction. The object had disappeared behind a little clump of balsam shrub within fifty paces of the camp, and as he drew nearer, until he was no more than ten paces away, he wondered why it did not break cover.

There were no trees, and it was quite light where the balsam grew. He approached, step by step. And then, suddenly, from almost under his hands, something darted away with a strange, human cry, turning upon him for a single instant a face that was as white as the white stars of early night—a face with great, glowing, half-mad eyes. It was Oachi. His pistol dropped to the ground. His heart stopped beating. No cry, no breath of sound, came from his paralyzed lips. And like a wild thing Oachi was fleeing from him into the darkening depths of the forest. Life leaped into his limbs, and he raced like mad after her, overtaking her with a panting, joyous cry. When she saw that she was caught the girl turned. Her hair had fallen, and swept about her shoulders and her body. She tried to speak, but only bursting sobs came from her breast. As she shrank from him, Roscoe saw that her clothing was in shreds, and that her thin moccasins were almost torn from her little feet. The truth held him for another moment stunned and speechless. Like a lightning flash there recurred to him her last words: "And some day—the Valley of Silent Men will awaken." He understood—now. She had followed him, fighting her way through swamp and forest along the river, hiding from him, and yet keeping him company so long as her little broken heart could urge her on. And then alone, with a last prayer for him— *she had planned to kill herself.* He trembled. Something wonderful happened with him, flooding his soul with day—with a joy that descended upon him as the Hand of the Messiah must have fallen upon the heads of the children of Samaria. With a great, glad cry he sprang toward Oachi and caught her in his arms, crushing her face to him, kissing her hair and her eyes and her mouth until at last with a strange, soft cry she put her arms up about his neck and sobbed like a little child upon his breast.

Back in the camp the Indian waited. The white stars grew red. In the forest the shadows deepened to the chaos of night. Once more there was sound, the pulse and beat of a life that moves in darkness. In the camp the Indian grew restless with the thought that Roscoe had wandered away until he was lost. So at last he fired his rifle.

Oachi started in Roscoe's arms.

"You should go back—alone," she whispered. The old, fluttering love-note was in her voice, sweeter than the sweetest music to Roscoe Cummins. He turned her face up, and held it between his two hands.

"If I go there," he said, pointing for a moment into the south, "I go *alone*. But if I go there—" and he pointed into the north—"I go *with you*. Oachi, my beloved, I am going with you." He drew her close again, and asked, almost in a whisper: "And when we awaken in the Valley of Silent Men, how shall it be, my Oachi?"

And with the sweet love-note, Oachi said in Cree:

"Hand in hand, my master."

Hand in hand they returned to the waiting Indian and the fire.

The Alaskan

CHAPTER I

Captain Rifle, gray and old in the Alaskan Steamship service, had not lost the spirit of his youth along with his years. Romance was not dead in him, and the fire which is built up of clean adventure and the association of strong men and a mighty country had not died out of his veins. He could still see the picturesque, feel the thrill of the unusual, and--at times--warm memories crowded upon him so closely that yesterday seemed today, and Alaska was young again, thrilling the world with her wild call to those who had courage to come and fight for her treasures, and live--or die.

Tonight, with the softly musical throb of his ship under his feet, and the yellow moon climbing up from behind the ramparts of the Alaskan mountains, something of loneliness seized upon him, and he said simply:

"That is Alaska."

The girl standing beside him at the rail did not turn, nor for a moment did she answer. He could see her profile clear-cut as a cameo in the almost vivid light, and in that light her eyes were wide and filled with a dusky fire, and her lips were parted a little, and her slim body was tense as she looked at the wonder of the moon silhouetting the cragged castles of the peaks, up where the soft, gray clouds lay like shimmering draperies.

Then she turned her face a little and nodded. "Yes, Alaska," she said, and the old captain fancied there was the slightest ripple of a tremor in her voice. "Your Alaska, Captain Rifle."

Out of the clearness of the night came to them a distant sound like the low moan of thunder. Twice before, Mary Standish had heard it, and now she asked: "What was that? Surely it can not be a storm, with the moon like that, and the stars so clear above!"

"It is ice breaking from the glaciers and falling into the sea. We are in the Wrangel Narrows, and very near the shore, Miss Standish. If it were day you could hear the birds singing. This is what we call the Inside Passage. I have always called it the water-wonderland of the world, and yet, if you will observe, I must be mistaken--for we are almost alone on this side of the ship. Is it not proof? If I were right, the men and women in there--dancing, playing cards, chattering-- would be crowding this rail. Can you imagine humans like that? But they can't see what I see, for I am a ridiculous old fool who remembers things. Ah, do you catch that in the air, Miss Standish--the perfume of flowers, of forests, of green things ashore? It is faint, but I catch it."

"And so do I."

She breathed in deeply of the sweet air, and turned then, so that she stood with her back to the rail, facing the flaming lights of the ship.

The mellow cadence of the music came to her, soft-stringed and sleepy; she could hear the shuffle of dancing feet. Laughter rippled with the rhythmic thrum of the ship, voices rose and fell beyond the lighted windows, and as the old captain looked at her, there was something in her face which he could not understand.

She had come aboard strangely at Seattle, alone and almost at the last minute--defying the necessity of making reservation where half a thousand others had been turned away--and chance had brought her under his eyes. In desperation she had appealed to him, and he had discovered a strange terror under the forced calm of her appearance. Since then he had fathered her with his attentions, watching closely with the wisdom of years. And more than once he had observed that questing, defiant poise of her head with which she was regarding the cabin windows now.

She had told him she was twenty-three and on her way to meet relatives in Nome. She had named certain people. And he had believed her. It was impossible not to believe her, and he admired her pluck in breaking all official regulations in coming aboard.

In many ways she was companionable and sweet. Yet out of his experience, he gathered the fact that she was under a tension. He knew that in some way she was making a fight, but, influenced by the wisdom of three and sixty years, he did not let her know he had guessed the truth.

He watched her closely now, without seeming to do so. She was very pretty in a quiet and unusual way. There was something irresistibly attractive about her, appealing to old memories which were painted clearly in his heart. She was girlishly slim. He had observed that her eyes were beautifully clear and gray in the sunlight, and her exquisitely smooth dark hair, neatly coiled and luxuriant crown of beauty, reminded him of puritanism in its simplicity. At times he doubted that she was twenty-three. If she had said nineteen or twenty he would have been better satisfied. She puzzled him and roused speculation in him. But it was a part of his business to see many things which others might not see--and hold his tongue.

"We are not quite alone," she was saying. "There are others," and she made a little gesture toward two figures farther up the rail.

"Old Donald Hardwick, of Skagway," he said. "And the other is Alan Holt."

"Oh, yes."

She was facing the mountains again, her eyes shining in the light of the moon. Gently her hand touched the old captain's arm. "Listen," she whispered.

"Another berg breaking away from Old Thunder. We are very near the shore, and there are glaciers all the way up."

"And that other sound, like low wind--on a night so still and calm! What is it?"

"You always hear that when very close to the big mountains, Miss Standish. It is made by the water of a thousand streams and rivulets rushing down to the sea. Wherever there is melting snow in the mountains, you hear that song."

"And this man, Alan Holt," she reminded him. "He is a part of these things?"

"Possibly more than any other man, Miss Standish. He was born in Alaska before Nome or Fairbanks or Dawson City were thought of. It was in Eighty-four, I think. Let me see, that would make him--"

"Thirty-eight," she said, so quickly that for a moment he was astonished.

Then he chuckled. "You are very good at figures."

He felt an almost imperceptible tightening of her fingers on his arm.

"This evening, just after dinner, old Donald found me sitting alone. He said he was lonely and wanted to talk with someone--like me. He almost frightened me, with his great, gray beard and shaggy hair. I thought of ghosts as we talked there in the dusk."

"Old Donald belongs to the days when the Chilkoot and the White Horse ate up men's lives, and a trail of living dead led from the Summit to Klondike, Miss Standish," said Captain Rifle. "You will meet many like him in Alaska. And they remember. You can see it in their faces--always the memory of those days that are gone."

She bowed her head a little, looking to the sea. "And Alan Holt? You know him well?"

"Few men know him well. He is a part of Alaska itself, and I have sometimes thought him more aloof than the mountains. But I know him. All northern Alaska knows Alan Holt. He has a reindeer range up beyond the Endicott Mountains and is always seeking the last frontier."

"He must be very brave."

"Alaska breeds heroic men, Miss Standish."

"And honorable men--men you can trust and believe in?"

"Yes."

"It is odd," she said, with a trembling little laugh that was like a bird-note in her throat. "I have never seen Alaska before, and yet something about these mountains makes me feel that I have known them a long time ago. I seem to feel they are welcoming me and that I am going home. Alan Holt is a fortunate man. I should like to be an Alaskan."

"And you are--"

"An American," she finished for him, a sudden, swift irony in her voice. "A poor product out of the melting-pot, Captain Rifle. I am going north--to learn."

"Only that, Miss Standish?"

His question, quietly spoken and without emphasis, demanded an answer. His kindly face, seamed by the suns and winds of many years at sea, was filled with honest anxiety as she turned to look straight into his eyes.

"I must press the question," he said. "As the captain of this ship, and as a father, it is my duty. Is there not something you would like to tell me--in confidence, if you will have it so?"

For an instant she hesitated, then slowly she shook her head. "There is nothing, Captain Rifle."

"And yet--you came aboard very strangely," he urged. "You will recall that it was most unusual--without reservation, without baggage--"

"You forget the hand-bag," she reminded him.

"Yes, but one does not start for northern Alaska with only a hand-bag scarcely large enough to contain a change of linen, Miss Standish."

"But I did, Captain Rifle."

"True. And I saw you fighting past the guards like a little wildcat. It was without precedent."

"I am sorry. But they were stupid and difficult to pass."

"Only by chance did I happen to see it all, my child. Otherwise the ship's regulations would have compelled me to send you ashore. You were frightened. You can not deny that. You were running away from something!"

He was amazed at the childish simplicity with which she answered him.

"Yes, I was running away--from something."

Her eyes were beautifully clear and unafraid, and yet again he sensed the thrill of the fight she was making.

"And you will not tell me why--or from what you were escaping?"

"I can not--tonight. I may do so before we reach Nome. But--it is possible--"

"What?"

"That I shall never reach Nome."

Suddenly she caught one of his hands in both her own. Her fingers clung to him, and with a little note of fierceness in her voice she hugged the hand to her breast. "I know just how good you have been to me," she cried. "I should like to tell you why I came aboard--like that. But I can not. Look! Look at those wonderful mountains!" With one free hand she pointed.

"Behind them and beyond them lie the romance and adventure and mystery of centuries, and for nearly thirty years you have been very near those things, Captain Rifle. No man will ever see again what you have seen or feel what you have felt, or forget what you have had to forget. I know it. And after all that, can't you--won't you--forget the strange manner in which I came aboard this ship? It is such a simple, little thing to put out of your mind, so trivial, so unimportant when you look back--and think. Please Captain Rifle--please!"

So quickly that he scarcely sensed the happening of it she pressed his hand to her lips. Their warm thrill came and went in an instant, leaving him speechless, his resolution gone.

"I love you because you have been so good to me," she whispered, and as suddenly as she had kissed his hand, she was gone, leaving him alone at the rail.

CHAPTER II

Alan Holt saw the slim figure of the girl silhouetted against the vivid light of the open doorway of the upper-deck salon. He was not watching her, nor did he look closely at the exceedingly attractive picture which she made as she paused there for an instant after leaving Captain Rifle. To him she was only one of the five hundred human atoms that went to make up the tremendously interesting life of one of the first ships of the season going north. Fate, through the suave agency of the purser, had brought him into a bit closer proximity to her than the others; that was all. For two days her seat in the dining-salon had been at the same table, not quite opposite him. As she had missed both breakfast hours, and he had skipped two luncheons, the requirements of neighborliness and of courtesy had not imposed more than a dozen words of speech upon them. This was very satisfactory to Alan. He was not talkative or communicative of his own free will. There was a certain cynicism back of his love of silence. He was a good listener and a first-rate analyst. Some people, he knew, were born to talk; and others, to trim the balance, were burdened with the necessity of holding their tongues. For him silence was not a burden.

In his cool and causal way he admired Mary Standish. She was very quiet, and he liked her because of that. He could not, of course, escape the beauty of her eyes or the shimmering luster of the long lashes that darkened them. But these were details which did not thrill him, but merely pleased him. And her hair pleased him possibly even more than her gray eyes, though he was not sufficiently concerned to discuss the matter with himself. But if he had pointed out any one thing, it would have been her hair--not so much the color of it as the care she evidently gave it, and the manner in which she dressed it. He noted that it was dark, with varying flashes of luster in it under the dinner lights. But what he approved of most of all were the smooth, silky coils in which she fastened it to her pretty head. It was an intense relief after looking on so many frowsy heads, bobbed and marcelled, during his six months' visit in the States. So he liked her, generally speaking, because there was not a thing about her that he might dislike.

He did not, of course, wonder what the girl might be thinking of him--with his quiet, stern face, his cold indifference, his rather Indian-like litheness, and the single patch of gray that streaked his thick, blond hair. His interest had not reached anywhere near that point.

Tonight it was probable that no woman in the world could have interested him, except as the always casual observer of humanity. Another and greater thing gripped him and had thrilled him since he first felt the throbbing pulse of the engines of the new steamship *Nome* under his feet at Seattle. He was going *home*. And home meant Alaska. It meant the mountains, the vast tundras, the immeasurable spaces into which civilization had not yet come with its clang and clamor. It meant friends, the stars he knew, his herds, everything he loved. Such was his reaction after six months of exile, six months of loneliness and desolation in cities which he had learned to hate.

"I'll not make the trip again--not for a whole winter--unless I'm sent at the point of a gun," he said to Captain Rifle, a few moments after Mary Standish had left the deck. "An Eskimo winter is long enough, but one in Seattle, Minneapolis, Chicago, and New York is longer--for me."

"I understand they had you up before the Committee on Ways and Means at Washington."

"Yes, along with Carl Lomen, of Nome. But Lomen was the real man. He has forty thousand head of reindeer in the Seward Peninsula, and they had to listen to him. We may get action."

"May!" Captain Rifle grunted his doubt. "Alaska has been waiting ten years for a new deck and a new deal. I doubt if you'll get anything. When politicians from Iowa and south Texas tell us what we can have and what we need north of Fifty-eight--why, what's the use? Alaska might as well shut up shop!"

"But she isn't going to do that," said Alan Holt, his face grimly set in the moonlight. "They've tried hard to get us, and they've made us shut up a lot of our doors. In 1910 we were thirty-six thousand whites in the Territory. Since then the politicians at Washington have driven out nine thousand, a quarter of the population. But those that are left are hard-boiled. We're not going to quit, Captain. A lot of us are Alaskans, and we are not afraid to fight."

"You mean--"

"That we'll have a square deal within another five years, or know the reason why. And another five years after that, we'll he shipping a million reindeer carcasses down into the States each year. Within twenty years we'll be shipping five million. Nice thought for the beef barons, eh? But rather fortunate, I think, for the hundred million Americans who are turning their grazing lands into farms and irrigation systems."

One of Alan Holt's hands was clenched at the rail. "Until I went down this winter, I didn't realize just how bad it was," he said, a note hard as iron in his voice. "Lomen is a diplomat, but I'm not. I want to fight when I see such things--fight with a gun. Because we happened to find gold up here, they think Alaska is an orange to be sucked as quickly as possible, and that when the sucking process is over, the skin will be worthless. That's modern, dollar-chasing Americanism for you!"

"And are you not an American, Mr. Holt?"

So soft and near was the voice that both men started. Then both turned and stared. Close behind them, her quiet, beautiful face flooded with the moon-glow, stood Mary Standish.

"You ask me a question, madam," said Alan Holt, bowing courteously. "No, I am not an American. I am an Alaskan."

The girl's lips were parted. Her eyes were very bright and clear. "Please pardon me for listening," she said. "I couldn't help it. I am an American. I love America. I think I love it more than anything else in the world--more than my religion, even. *America,* Mr. Holt. And America doesn't necessarily mean a great many of America's people. I love to think that I first came ashore in the *Mayflower.* That is why my name is Standish. And I just wanted to remind you that Alaska *is* America."

Alan Holt was a bit amazed. The girl's face was no longer placidly quiet. Her eyes were radiant. He sensed the repressed thrill in her voice, and he knew that in the light of day he would have seen fire in her cheeks. He smiled, and in that smile he could not quite keep back the cynicism of his thought.

"And what do you know about Alaska, Miss Standish?"

"Nothing," she said. "And yet I love it." She pointed to the mountains. "I wish I might have been born among them. You are fortunate. You should love America."

"Alaska, you mean!"

"No, America." There was a flashing challenge in her eyes. She was not speaking apologetically. Her meaning was direct.

The irony on Alan's lips died away. With a little laugh he bowed again. "If I am speaking to a daughter of Captain Miles Standish, who came over in the *Mayflower,* I stand reproved," he said. "You should be an authority on Americanism, if I am correct in surmising your relationship."

"You are correct," she replied with a proud, little tilt of her glossy head, "though I think that only lately have I come to an understanding of its significance--and its responsibility. I ask your pardon again for interrupting you. It was not premeditated. It just happened."

She did not wait for either of them to speak, but flashed the two a swift smile and passed down the promenade.

The music had ceased and the cabins at last were emptying themselves of life.

"A remarkable young woman," Alan remarked. "I imagine that the spirit of Captain Miles Standish may be a little proud of this particular olive-branch. A chip off the old block, you might say. One would almost suppose he had married Priscilla and this young lady was a definite though rather indirect result."

He had a curious way of laughing without any more visible manifestation of humor than spoken words. It was a quality in his voice which one could not miss, and at times, when ironically amused, it carried a sting which he did not altogether intend.

In another moment Mary Standish was forgotten, and he was asking the captain a question which was in his mind.

"The itinerary of this ship is rather confused, is it not?"

"Yes--rather," acknowledged Captain Rifle. "Hereafter she will ply directly between Seattle and Nome. But this time we're doing the Inside Passage to Juneau and Skagway and will make the Aleutian Passage via Cordova and Seward. A whim of the owners, which they haven't seen fit to explain to me. Possibly the Canadian junket aboard may have something to do with it. We're landing them at Skagway, where they make the Yukon by way of White Horse Pass. A pleasure trip for flabby people nowadays, Holt. I can remember--"

"So can I," nodded Alan Holt, looking at the mountains beyond which lay the dead-strewn trails of the gold stampede of a generation before. "I remember. And old Donald is dreaming of that hell of death back there. He was all choked up tonight. I wish he might forget."

"Men don't forget such women as Jane Hope," said the captain softly.

"You knew her?"

"Yes. She came up with her father on my ship. That was twenty-five years ago last autumn, Alan. A long time, isn't it? And when I look at Mary Standish and hear her voice--" He hesitated, as if betraying a secret, and then he added: "--I can't help thinking of the girl Donald Hardwick fought for and won in that death-hole at White Horse. It's too bad she had to die."

"She isn't dead," said Alan. The hardness was gone from his voice. "She isn't dead," he repeated. "That's the pity of it. She is as much a living thing to him today as she was twenty years ago."

After a moment the captain said, "She was talking with him early this evening, Alan."

"Miss Captain Miles Standish, you mean?"

"Yes. There seems to be something about her that amuses you."

Alan shrugged his shoulders. "Not at all. I think she is a most admirable young person. Will you have a cigar, Captain? I'm going to promenade a bit. It does me good to mix in with the sour-doughs."

The two lighted their cigars from a single match, and Alan went his way, while the captain turned in the direction of his cabin.

To Alan, on this particular night, the steamship *Nome* was more than a thing of wood and steel. It was a living, pulsating being, throbbing with the very heart-beat of Alaska. The purr of the mighty engines was a human intelligence crooning a song of joy. For him the crowded passenger list held a significance that was almost epic, and its names represented more than mere men and women. They were the vital fiber of the land he loved, its heart's blood, its very element--"giving in." He knew that with the throb of those engines romance, adventure, tragedy, and hope were on their way north--and with these things also arrogance and greed. On board were a hundred conflicting elements--some that had fought for Alaska, others that would make her, and others that would destroy.

He puffed at his cigar and walked alone, brushing sleeves with men and women whom he scarcely seemed to notice. But he was observant. He knew the tourists almost without looking at them. The spirit of the north had not yet seized upon them. They were voluble and rather excitedly enthusiastic in the face of beauty and awesomeness. The sour-doughs were tucked away here and there in shadowy nooks, watching in silence, or they walked the deck slowly and quietly, smoking their cigars or pipes, and seeing things beyond the mountains. Between these two, the newcomers and the old-timers, ran the gamut of all human thrill for Alan, the flesh-and-blood fiber of everything that went to make up life north of Fifty-four. And he could have gone from man to man and picked out those who belonged north of Fifty-eight.

Aft of the smoking-room he paused, tipping the ash of his cigar over the edge of the rail. A little group of three stood near him, and he recognized them as the young engineers, fresh from college, going up to work on the government railroad running from Seward to Tanana. One of them was talking, filled with the enthusiasm of his first adventure.

"I tell you," he said, "people don't know what they ought to know about Alaska. In school they teach us that it's an eternal icebox full of gold, and is headquarters for Santa Claus, because that's where reindeer come from. And grown-ups think about the same thing. Why"-- he drew in a deep breath--"it's nine times as large as the state of Washington, twelve times as big as the state of New York, and we bought it from Russia for less than two cents an acre. If you put it down on the face of the United States, the city of Juneau would be in St. Augustine, Florida, and Unalaska would be in Los Angeles. That's how big it is, and the geographical center of our country isn't Omaha or Sioux City, but exactly San Francisco, California."

"Good for you, sonny," came a quiet voice from beyond the group. "Your geography is correct. And you might add for the education of your people that Alaska is only thirty-seven miles from Bolshevik Siberia, and wireless messages are sent into Alaska by the Bolsheviks urging our people to rise against the Washington government. We've asked Washington for a few guns and a few men to guard Nome, but they laugh at us. Do you see a moral?"

From half-amused interest Alan jerked himself to alert tension. He caught a glimpse of the gaunt, old graybeard who had spoken, but did not know him. And as this man turned away, a shadowy hulk in the moonlight, the same deep, quiet voice came back very clearly:

"And if you ever care for Alaska, you might tell your government to hang a few such men as John Graham, sonny."

At the sound of that name Alan felt the blood in him run suddenly hot. Only one man on the face of the earth did he hate with undying hatred, and that man was John Graham. He would have followed, seeking the identity of the stranger whose words had temporarily stunned the young engineers, when he saw a slim figure standing between him and the light of the smoking-room windows. It was Mary Standish. He knew by her attitude that she had heard the words of the young engineer and the old graybeard, but she was looking at *him*. And he could not remember that he had ever seen quite that same look in a woman's face before. It was not fright. It was more an expression of horror which comes from thought and mental vision rather than physical things. Instantly it annoyed Alan Holt. This was the second time she had betrayed a too susceptible reaction in matters which did not concern her. So he said, speaking to the silent young men a few steps away:

"He was mistaken, gentlemen. John Graham should not be hung. That would be too merciful."

He resumed his way then, nodding at them as he passed. But he had scarcely gone out of their vision when quick footsteps pattered behind him, and the girl's hand touched his arm lightly.

"Mr. Holt, please--"

He stopped, sensing the fact that the soft pressure of her fingers was not altogether unpleasant. She hesitated, and when she spoke again, only her finger-tips touched his arm. She was looking shoreward, so that for a moment he could see only the lustrous richness of her smooth hair. Then she was meeting his eyes squarely, a flash of challenge in the gray depths of her own.

"I am alone on the ship," she said. "I have no friends here. I want to see things and ask questions. Will you ... help me a little?"

"You mean ... escort you?"

"Yes, if you will. I should feel more comfortable."

Nettled at first, the humor of the situation began to appeal to him, and he wondered at the intense seriousness of the girl. She did not smile. Her eyes were very steady and very businesslike, and at the same time very lovely.

"The way you put it, I don't see how I can refuse," he said. "As for the questions--probably Captain Rifle can answer them better than I."

"I don't like to trouble him," she replied. "He has much to think about. And you are alone."

"Yes, quite alone. And with very little to think about."

"You know what I mean, Mr. Holt. Possibly you can not understand me, or won't try. But I'm going into a new country, and I have a passionate desire to learn as much about that country as I can before I get there. I want to know about many things. For instance--"

"Yes."

"Why did you say what you did about John Graham? What did the other man mean when he said he should be hung?"

There was an intense directness in her question which for a moment astonished him. She had withdrawn her fingers from his arm, and her slim figure seemed possessed of a sudden throbbing suspense as she waited for an answer. They had turned a little, so that in the light of the moon the almost flowerlike whiteness of her face was clear to him. With her smooth, shining hair, the pallor of her face under its lustrous darkness, and the clearness of her eyes she held Alan speechless for a moment, while his brain struggled to seize upon and understand the something about her which made him interested in spite of himself. Then he smiled and there was a sudden glitter in his eyes.

"Did you ever see a dog fight?" he asked.

She hesitated, as if trying to remember, and shuddered slightly. "Once."

"What happened?"

"It was my dog--a little dog. His throat was torn--"

He nodded. "Exactly. And that is just what John Graham is doing to Alaska, Miss Standish. He's the dog--a monster. Imagine a man with a colossal financial power behind him, setting out to strip the wealth from a new land and enslave it to his own desires and political ambitions. That is what John Graham is doing from his money-throne down there in the States. It's the financial support he represents, curse him! Money--and a man without conscience. A man who would starve thousands or millions to achieve his ends. A man who, in every sense of the word, is a murderer--"

The sharpness of her cry stopped him. If possible, her face had gone whiter, and he saw her hands clutched suddenly at her breast. And the look in her eyes brought the old, cynical twist back to his lips.

"There, I've hurt your puritanism again, Miss Standish," he said, bowing a little. "In order to appeal to your finer sensibilities I suppose I must apologize for swearing and calling another man a murderer. Well, I do. And now--if you care to stroll about the ship--"

From a respectful distance the three young engineers watched Alan and Mary Standish as they walked forward.

"A corking pretty girl," said one of them, drawing a deep breath. "I never saw such hair and eyes--"

"I'm at the same table with them," interrupted another. "I'm second on her left, and she hasn't spoken three words to me. And that fellow she is with is like an icicle out of Labrador."

And Mary Standish was saying: "Do you know, Mr. Holt, I envy those young engineers. I wish I were a man."

"I wish you were," agreed Alan amiably.

Whereupon Mary Standish's pretty mouth lost its softness for an instant. But Alan did not observe this. He was enjoying his cigar and the sweet air.

CHAPTER III

Alan Holt was a man whom other men looked at twice. With women it was different. He was, in no solitary sense of the word, a woman's man. He admired them in an abstract way, and he was ready to fight for them, or die for them, at any time such a course became necessary. But his sentiment was entirely a matter of common sense. His chivalry was born and bred of the mountains and the open and had nothing in common with the insincere brand which develops in the softer and more luxurious laps of civilization. Years of aloneness had put their mark upon him. Men of the north, reading the lines, understood what they meant. But only now and then could a woman possibly understand. Yet if in any given moment a supreme physical crisis had come, women would have turned instinctively in their helplessness to such a man as Alan Holt.

He possessed a vein of humor which few had been privileged to discover. The mountains had taught him to laugh in silence. With him a chuckle meant as much as a riotous outburst of merriment from another, and he could enjoy greatly without any noticeable muscular disturbance of his face. And not always was his smile a reflection of humorous thought. There were times when it betrayed another kind of thought more forcefully than speech.

Because he understood fairly well and knew what he was, the present situation amused him. He could not but see what an error in judgment Miss Standish had made in selecting him, when compared with the intoxicating thrill she could easily have aroused by choosing one of the young engineers as a companion in her evening adventure. He chuckled. And Mary Standish, hearing the smothered note of amusement, gave to her head that swift little birdlike tilt which he had observed once before, in the presence of Captain Rifle. But she said nothing. As if challenged, she calmly took possession of his arm.

Halfway round the deck, Alan began to sense the fact that there was a decidedly pleasant flavor to the whole thing. The girl's hand did not merely touch his arm; it was snuggled there confidently, and she was necessarily so close to him that when he looked down, the glossy coils of her hair were within a few inches of his face. His nearness to her, together with the soft pressure of her hand on his arm, was a jolt to his stoicism.

"It's not half bad," he expressed himself frankly. "I really believe I am going to enjoy answering your questions, Miss Standish."

"Oh!" He felt the slim, little figure stiffen for an instant. "You thought--possibly--I might be dangerous?"

"A little. I don't understand women. Collectively I think they are God's most wonderful handiwork. Individually I don't care much about them. But you--"

She nodded approvingly. "That is very nice of you. But you needn't say I am different from the others. I am not. All women are alike."

"Possibly--except in the way they dress their hair."

"You like mine?"

"Very much."

He was amazed at the admission, so much so that he puffed out a huge cloud of smoke from his cigar in mental protest.

They had come to the smoking-room again. This was an innovation aboard the *Nome*. There was no other like it in the Alaskan service, with its luxurious space, its comfortable hospitality, and the observation parlor built at one end for those ladies who cared to sit with their husbands while they smoked their after-dinner cigars.

"If you want to hear about Alaska and see some of its human make-up, let's go in," he suggested. "I know; of no better place. Are you afraid of smoke?"

"No. If I were a man, I would smoke."

"Perhaps you do?"

"I do not. When I begin that, if you please, I shall bob my hair."

"Which would be a crime," he replied so earnestly that again he was surprised at himself.

Two or three ladies, with their escorts, were in the parlor when they entered. The huge main room, covering a third of the aft deck, was blue with smoke. A score of men were playing cards at round tables. Twice as many were gathered in groups, talking, while others walked aimlessly up and down the carpeted floor. Here and there were men who sat alone. A few were asleep, which made Alan look at his watch. Then he observed Mary Standish studying the innumerable bundles of neatly rolled blankets that lay about. One of them was at her feet. She touched it with her toe.

"What do they mean?" she asked.

"We are overloaded," he explained. "Alaskan steam-ships have no steerage passengers as we generally know them. It isn't poverty that rides steerage when you go north. You can always find a millionaire or two on the lower deck. When they get sleepy, most of the men you see in there will unroll blankets and sleep on the floor. Did you ever see an earl?"

He felt it his duty to make explanations now that he had brought her in, and directed her attention to the third table on their left. Three men were seated at this table.

"The man facing us, the one with a flabby face and pale mustache, is an earl--I forget his name," he said. "He doesn't look it, but he is a real sport. He is going up to shoot Kadiak bears, and sleeps on the floor. The group beyond them, at the fifth table, are Treadwell mining men, and that fellow you see slouched against the wall, half asleep, with whiskers nearly to his waist, is Stampede Smith, an old-time partner of George Carmack, who discovered gold on Bonanza Creek in Ninety-six. The thud of Carmack's spade, as it hit first pay, was the 'sound heard round the world,' Miss Standish. And the gentleman with crumpled whiskers was the second-best man at Bonanza, excepting Skookum Jim and Taglish Charlie, two Siwah Indians who were with Carmack when the strike was made. Also, if you care for the romantic, he was in love with Belinda Mulrooney, the most courageous woman who ever came into the north."

"Why was she courageous?"

"Because she came alone into a man's land, without a soul to fight for her, determined to make a fortune along with the others. And she did. As long as there is a Dawson sour-dough alive, he will remember Belinda Mulrooney."

"She proved what a woman could do, Mr. Holt."

"Yes, and a little later she proved how foolish a woman can be, Miss Standish. She became the richest woman in Dawson. Then came a man who posed as a count, Belinda married him, and they went to Paris. *Finis*, I think. Now, if she had married Stampede Smith over there, with his big whiskers--"

He did not finish. Half a dozen paces from them a man had risen from a table and was facing them. There was nothing unusual about him, except his boldness as he looked at Mary Standish. It was as if he knew her and was deliberately insulting her in a stare that was more than impudent in its directness. Then a sudden twist came to his lips; he shrugged his shoulders slightly and turned away.

Alan glanced swiftly at his companion. Her lips were compressed, and her cheeks were flaming hotly. Even then, as his own blood boiled, he could not but observe how beautiful anger made her.

"If you will pardon me a moment," he said quietly, "I shall demand an explanation."

Her hand linked itself quickly through his arm.

"Please don't," she entreated. "It is kind of you, and you are just the sort of man I should expect to resent a thing like that. But it would be absurd to notice it. Don't you think so?"

In spite of her effort to speak calmly, there was a tremble in her voice, and Alan was puzzled at the quickness with which the color went from her face, leaving it strangely white.

"I am at your service," he replied with a rather cold inclination of his head. "But if you were my sister, Miss Standish, I would not allow anything like that to go unchallenged."

He watched the stranger until he disappeared through a door out upon the deck.

"One of John Graham's men," he said. "A fellow named Rossland, going up to get a final grip on the salmon fishing, I understand. They'll choke the life out of it in another two years. Funny what this filthy stuff we call money can do, isn't it? Two winters ago I saw whole Indian villages starving, and women and little children dying by the score because of this John Graham's money. Over-fishing did it, you understand. If you could have seen some of those poor little devils, just skin and bones, crying for a rag to eat--"

Her hand clutched at his arm. "How could John Graham--do that?" she whispered.

He laughed unpleasantly. "When you have been a year in Alaska you won't ask that question, Miss Standish. *How*? Why, simply by glutting his canneries and taking from the streams the food supply which the natives have depended upon for generations. In other words, the money he handles represents the fish trust--and many other things. Please don't misunderstand me. Alaska needs capital for its development. Without it we will not only cease to progress; we will die. No territory on the face of the earth offers greater opportunities for capital than Alaska does today. Ten thousand fortunes are waiting to be made here by men who have money to invest.

"But John Graham does not represent the type we want. He is a despoiler, one of those whose only desire is to turn original resource into dollars as fast as he can, even though those operations make both land and water barren. You must remember until recently the government of Alaska as manipulated by Washington politicians was little better than that against which the American colonies rebelled in 1776. A hard thing for one to say about the country he loves, isn't it? And John Graham stands for the worst--he and the money which guarantees his power.

"As a matter of fact, big and legitimate capital is fighting shy of Alaska. Conditions are such, thanks to red-tapeism and bad politics, that capital, big and little, looks askance at Alaska and cannot be interested. Think of it, Miss Standish! There are thirty-eight separate bureaus at Washington operating on Alaska, five thousand miles away. Is it a wonder the patient is sick? And is it a wonder that a man like John Graham, dishonest and corrupt to the soul, has a fertile field to work in?

"But we are progressing. We are slowly coming out from under the shadow which has so long clouded Alaska's interests. There is now a growing concentration of authority and responsibility. Both the Department of the Interior and the Department of Agriculture now realize that Alaska is a mighty empire in itself, and with their help we are bound to go ahead in spite of all our handicaps. It is men like John Graham I fear. Some day--"

Suddenly he caught himself. "There--I'm talking politics, and I should entertain you with pleasanter and more interesting things," he apologized. "Shall we go to the lower decks?"

"Or the open air," she suggested. "I am afraid this smoke is upsetting me."

He could feel the change in her and did not attribute it entirely to the thickness of the air. Rossland's inexplicable rudeness had disturbed her more deeply than she had admitted, he believed.

"There are a number of Thlinkit Indians and a tame bear down in what we should ordinarily call the steerage. Would you like to see them?" he asked, when they were outside. "The Thlinkit girls are the prettiest Indian women in the world, and there are two among those below who are--well--unusually good-looking, the Captain says."

"And he has already made me acquainted with them," she laughed softly. "Kolo and Haidah are the girls. They are sweet, and I love them. I had breakfast with them this morning long before you were awake."

"The deuce you say! And that is why you were not at table? And the morning before--"

"You noticed my absence?" she asked demurely.

"It was difficult for me not to see an empty chair. On second thought, I think the young engineer called my attention to it by wondering if you were ill."

"Oh!"

"He is very much interested in you, Miss Standish. It amuses me to see him torture the corners of his eyes to look at you. I have thought it would be only charity and good-will to change seats with him."

"In which event, of course, your eyes would not suffer."

"Probably not."

"Have they ever suffered?"

"I think not."

"When looking at the Thlinkit girls, for instance?"

"I haven't seen them."

She gave her shoulders a little shrug.

"Ordinarily I would think you most uninteresting, Mr. Holt. As it is I think you unusual. And I rather like you for it. Would you mind taking me to my cabin? It is number sixteen, on this deck."

She walked with her fingers touching his arm again. "What is your room?" she asked.

"Twenty-seven, Miss Standish."

"This deck?"

"Yes."

Not until she had said good night, quietly and without offering him her hand, did the intimacy of her last questions strike him. He grunted and lighted a fresh cigar. A number of things occurred to him all at once, as he slowly made a final round or two of the deck. Then he went to his cabin and looked over papers which were going ashore at Juneau. These were memoranda giving an account of his appearance with Carl Lomen before the Ways and Means Committee at Washington.

It was nearly midnight when he had finished. He wondered if Mary Standish was asleep. He was a little irritated, and slightly amused, by the recurring insistency with which his mind turned to her. She was a clever girl, he admitted. He had asked her nothing about herself, and she had told him nothing, while he had been quite garrulous. He was a little ashamed when he recalled how he had unburdened his mind to a girl who could not possibly be interested in the political affairs of John Graham and Alaska. Well, it was not entirely his fault. She had fairly catapulted herself upon him, and he had been decent under the circumstances, he thought.

He put out his light and stood with his face at the open port-hole. Only the soft throbbing of the vessel as she made her way slowly through the last of the Narrows into Frederick Sound came to his ears. The ship, at last, was asleep. The moon was straight overhead, no longer silhouetting the mountains, and beyond its misty rim of light the world was dark. Out of this darkness, rising like a deeper shadow, Alan could make out faintly the huge mass of Kupreanof Island. And he wondered, knowing the perils of the Narrows in places scarcely wider than the length of the ship, why Captain Rifle had chosen this course instead of going around by Cape Decision. He could feel that the land was more distant now, but the *Nome* was still pushing ahead under slow bell, and he could smell the fresh odor of kelp, and breathe deeply of the scent of forests that came from both east and west.

Suddenly his ears became attentive to slowly approaching footsteps. They seemed to hesitate and then advanced; he heard a subdued voice, a man's voice--and in answer to it a woman's. Instinctively he drew a step back and stood unseen in the gloom. There was no longer a sound of voices. In silence they walked past his window, clearly revealed to him in the moonlight. One of the two was Mary Standish. The man was Rossland, who had stared at her so boldly in the smoking-room.

Amazement gripped Alan. He switched on his light and made his final arrangements for bed. He had no inclination to spy upon either Mary Standish or Graham's agent, but he possessed an inborn hatred of fraud and humbug, and what he had seen convinced him that Mary Standish knew more about Rossland than she had allowed him to believe. She had not lied to him. She had said nothing at all--except to restrain him from demanding an apology. Evidently she had taken advantage of him, but beyond that fact her affairs had nothing to do with his own business in life. Possibly she and Rossland had quarreled, and now they were making up. Quite probable, he thought. Silly of him to think over the matter at all.

So he put out his light again and went to bed. But he had no great desire to sleep. It was pleasant to lie there, flat on his back, with the soothing movement of the ship under him, listening to the musical thrum of it. And it was pleasant to think of the fact that he was going home. How infernally long those seven months had been, down in the States! And how he had missed everyone he had ever known--even his enemies!

He closed his eyes and visualized the home that was still thousands of miles away--the endless tundras, the blue and purple foothills of the Endicott Mountains, and "Alan's Range" at the beginning of them. Spring was breaking up there, and it was warm on the tundras and the southern slopes, and the pussy-willow buds were popping out of their coats like corn from a hopper.

He prayed God the months had been kind to his people--the people of the range. It was a long time to be away from them, when one loved them as he did. He was sure that Tautuk and Amuk Toolik, his two chief herdsmen, would care for things as well as himself. But much could happen in seven months. Nawadlook, the little beauty of his distant kingdom, was not looking well when he left. He was worried about her. The pneumonia of the previous winters had left its mark. And Keok, her rival in prettiness! He smiled in the darkness, wondering how

Tautuk's sometimes hopeless love affair had progressed. For Keok was a little heart-breaker and had long reveled in Tautuk's sufferings. An archangel of iniquity, Alan thought, as he grinned--but worth any man's risk of life, if he had but a drop of brown blood in him! As for his herds, they had undoubtedly fared well. Ten thousand head was something to be proud of--

Suddenly he drew in his breath and listened. Someone was at his door and had paused there. Twice he had heard footsteps outside, but each time they had passed. He sat up, and the springs of his berth made a sound under him. He heard movement then, a swift, running movement-- and he switched on his light. A moment later he opened the door. No one was there. The long corridor was empty. And then--a distance away--he heard the soft opening and closing of another door.

It was then that his eyes saw a white, crumpled object on the floor. He picked it up and reentered his room. It was a woman's handkerchief. And he had seen it before. He had admired the pretty laciness of it that evening in the smoking-room. Rather curious, he thought, that he should now find it at his door.

CHAPTER IV

For a few minutes after finding the handkerchief at his door, Alan experienced a feeling of mingled curiosity and disappointment--also a certain resentment. The suspicion that he was becoming involved in spite of himself was not altogether pleasant. The evening, up to a certain point, had been fairly entertaining. It was true he might have passed a pleasanter hour recalling old times with Stampede Smith, or discussing Kadiak bears with the English earl, or striking up an acquaintance with the unknown graybeard who had voiced an opinion about John Graham. But he was not regretting lost hours, nor was he holding Mary Standish accountable for them. It was, last of all, the handkerchief that momentarily upset him.

Why had she dropped it at his door? It was not a dangerous-looking affair, to be sure, with its filmy lace edging and ridiculous diminutiveness. As the question came to him, he was wondering how even as dainty a nose as that possessed by Mary Standish could be much comforted by it. But it was pretty. And, like Mary Standish, there was something exquisitely quiet and perfect about it, like the simplicity of her hair. He was not analyzing the matter. It was a thought that came to him almost unconsciously, as he tossed the annoying bit of fabric on the little table at the head of his berth. Undoubtedly the dropping of it had been entirely unpremeditated and accidental. At least he told himself so. And he also assured himself, with an involuntary shrug of his shoulders, that any woman or girl had the right to pass his door if she so desired, and that he was an idiot for thinking otherwise. The argument was only slightly adequate. But Alan was not interested in mysteries, especially when they had to do with woman--and such an absurdly inconsequential thing as a handkerchief.

A second time he went to bed. He fell asleep thinking about Keok and Nawadlook and the people of his range. From somewhere he had been given the priceless heritage of dreaming pleasantly, and Keok was very real, with her swift smile and mischievous face, and Nawadlook's big, soft eyes were brighter than when he had gone away. He saw Tautuk, gloomy as usual over the heartlessness of Keok. He was beating a tom-tom that gave out the peculiar sound of bells, and to this Amuk Toolik was dancing the Bear Dance, while Keok clapped her hands in exaggerated admiration. Even in his dreams Alan chuckled. He knew what was happening, and that out of the corners of her laughing eyes Keok was enjoying Tautuk's jealousy. Tautuk was so stupid he would never understand. That was the funny part of it. And he beat his drum savagely, scowling so that he almost shut his eyes, while Keok laughed outright.

It was then that Alan opened his eyes and heard the last of the ship's bells. It was still dark. He turned on the light and looked at his watch. Tautuk's drum had tolled eight bells, aboard the ship, and it was four o'clock in the morning.

Through the open port came the smell of sea and land, and with it a chill air which Alan drank in deeply as he stretched himself for a few minutes after awakening. The tang of it was like wine in his blood, and he got up quietly and dressed while he smoked the stub-end of a cigar he had laid aside at midnight. Not until he had finished dressing did he notice the handkerchief on the table. If its presence had suggested a significance a few hours before, he no longer disturbed himself by thinking about it. A bit of carelessness on the girl's part, that was all. He would return it. Mechanically he put the crumpled bit of cambric in his coat pocket before going on deck.

He had guessed that he would be alone. The promenade was deserted. Through the ghost-white mist of morning he saw the rows of empty chairs, and lights burning dully in the wheel-house. Asian monsoon and the drifting warmth of the Japan current had brought an early spring to the Alexander Archipelago, and May had stolen much of the flowering softness of June. But the dawns of these days were chilly and gray. Mists and fogs settled in the valleys, and like thin smoke rolled down the sides of the mountains to the sea, so that a ship traveling the inner waters felt its way like a child creeping in darkness.

Alan loved this idiosyncrasy of the Alaskan coast. The phantom mystery of it was stimulating, and in the peril of it was a challenging lure. He could feel the care with which the *Nome* was picking her way northward. Her engines were thrumming softly, and her movement was a slow and cautious glide, catlike and slightly trembling, as if every pound of steel in her were a living nerve widely alert. He knew Captain Rifle would not be asleep and that straining eyes were peering into the white gloom from the wheel-house. Somewhere west of them, hazardously near, must lie the rocks of Admiralty Island; eastward were the still more pitiless glacial sandstones and granites of the coast, with that deadly finger of sea-washed reef between, along the lip of which they must creep to Juneau. And Juneau could not be far ahead.

He leaned over the rail, puffing at the stub of his cigar. He was eager for his work. Juneau, Skagway, and Cordova meant nothing to him, except that they were Alaska. He yearned for the still farther north, the wide tundras, and the mighty achievement that lay ahead of him there. His blood sang to the surety of it now, and for that reason he was not sorry he had spent seven months of loneliness in the States. He had proved with his own eyes that the day was near when Alaska would come into her own. Gold! He laughed. Gold had its lure, its romance, its thrill, but what was all the gold the mountains might possess compared with this greater thing he was helping to build! It seemed to him the people he had met in the south had thought only of gold when they learned he was from Alaska. Always gold--that first, and then ice, snow, endless nights, desolate barrens, and craggy mountains frowning everlastingly upon a blasted land in which men fought against odds and only the fittest survived. It was gold that had been Alaska's doom. When people thought of it, they visioned nothing beyond the old stampede days, the Chilkoot, White Horse, Dawson, and Circle City. Romance and glamor and the tragedies of dead men clung to their ribs. But they were beginning to believe now. Their eyes were opening. Even the Government was waking up, after proving there was something besides graft in railroad building north of Mount St. Elias. Senators and Congressmen at Washington had listened to him seriously, and especially to Carl Lomen. And the beef barons, wisest of all, had tried to buy him off and had offered a fortune for Lomen's forty thousand head of reindeer in the Seward Peninsula! That was proof of the awakening. Absolute proof.

He lighted a fresh cigar, and his mind shot through the dissolving mist into the vast land ahead of him. Some Alaskans had cursed Theodore Roosevelt for putting what they called "the conservation shackles" on their country. But he, for one, did not. Roosevelt's far-sightedness had kept the body-snatchers at bay, and because he had foreseen what money-power and greed would do, Alaska was not entirely stripped today, but lay ready to serve with all her mighty resources the mother who had neglected her for a generation. But it was going to be a struggle, this opening up of a great land. It must be done resourcefully and with intelligence. Once the bars were down, Roosevelt's shadow-hand could not hold back such desecrating forces as John Graham and the syndicate he represented.

Thought of Graham was an unpleasant reminder, and his face grew hard in the sea-mist. Alaskans themselves must fight against the licensed plunderers. And it would be a hard fight. He had seen the pillaging work of these financial brigands in a dozen states during the past winter--states raped of their forests, their lakes and streams robbed and polluted, their resources hewn down to naked skeletons. He had been horrified and a little frightened when he looked over the desolation of Michigan, once the richest timber state in America. What if the Government at Washington made it possible for such a thing to happen in Alaska? Politics-- and money--were already fighting for just that thing.

He no longer heard the throb of the ship under his feet. It was *his* fight, and brain and muscle reacted to it almost as if it had been a physical thing. And his end of that fight he was determined to win, if it took every year of his life. He, with a few others, would prove to the world that the millions of acres of treeless tundras of the north were not the cast-off ends of the earth. They would populate them, and the so-called "barrens" would thunder to the innumerable hoofs of reindeer herds as the American plains had never thundered to the beat of cattle. He was not thinking of the treasure he would find at the end of this rainbow of success which he visioned. Money, simply as money, he hated. It was the achievement of the thing that gripped him; the passion to hew a trail through which his beloved land might come into its own, and the desire to see it achieve a final triumph by feeding a half of that America which had laughed at it and kicked it when it was down.

The tolling of the ship's bell roused him from the subconscious struggle into which he had allowed himself to be drawn. Ordinarily he had no sympathy with himself when he fell into one of these mental spasms, as he called them. Without knowing it, he was a little proud of a certain dispassionate tolerance which he possessed--a philosophical mastery of his emotions which at times was almost cold-blooded, and which made some people think he was a thing of stone instead of flesh and blood. His thrills he kept to himself. And a mildly disturbing sensation passed through him now, when he found that unconsciously his fingers had twined themselves about the little handkerchief in his pocket. He drew it out and made a sudden movement as if to toss it overboard. Then, with a grunt expressive of the absurdity of the thing, he replaced it in his pocket and began to walk slowly toward the bow of the ship.

He wondered, as he noted the lifting of the fog, what he would have been had he possessed a sister like Mary Standish. Or any family at all, for that matter--even an uncle or two who might have been interested in him. He remembered his father vividly, his mother a little less so, because his mother had died when he was six and his father when he was twenty. It was his father who stood out above everything else, like the mountains he loved. The father would remain with him always, inspiring him, urging him, encouraging him to live like a gentleman, fight like a man, and die at last unafraid. In that fashion the older Alan Holt had lived and died. But his mother, her face and voice scarcely remembered in the passing of many years, was more a hallowed memory to him than a thing of flesh and blood. And there had been no sisters or brothers. Often he had regretted this lack of brotherhood. But a sister.... He grunted his disapprobation of the thought. A sister would have meant enchainment to civilization. Cities, probably. Even the States. And slavery to a life he detested. He appreciated the immensity of his freedom. A Mary Standish, even though she were his sister, would be a catastrophe. He could not conceive of her, or any other woman like her, living with Keok and Nawadlook and the rest of his people in the heart of the tundras. And the tundras would always be his home, because his heart was there.

He had passed round the wheel-house and came suddenly upon an odd figure crumpled in a chair. It was Stampede Smith. In the clearer light that came with the dissolution of the sea-mist Alan saw that he was not asleep. He paused, unseen by the other. Stampede stretched himself, groaned, and stood up. He was a little man, and his fiercely bristling red whiskers, wet with dew, were luxuriant enough for a giant. His head of tawny hair, bristling like his whiskers, added to the piratical effect of him above the neck, but below that part of his anatomy there was little to strike fear into the hearts of humanity. Some people smiled when they looked at him. Others, not knowing their man, laughed outright. Whiskers could be funny. And they were undoubtedly funny on Stampede Smith. But Alan neither smiled nor laughed, for in his heart was something very near to the missing love of brotherhood for this little man who had written his name across so many pages of Alaskan history.

This morning, as Alan saw him, Stampede Smith was no longer the swiftest gunman between White Horse and Dawson City. He was a pathetic reminder of the old days when, single-handed, he had run down Soapy Smith and his gang--days when the going of Stampede Smith to new fields meant a stampede behind him, and when his name was mentioned in the same breath with those of George Carmack, and Alex McDonald, and Jerome Chute, and a hundred men like Curley Monroe and Joe Barret set their compasses by his. To Alan there was tragedy in his aloneness as he stood in the gray of the morning. Twenty times a millionaire, he knew that Stampede Smith was broke again.

"Good morning," he said so unexpectedly that the little man jerked himself round like the lash of a whip, a trick of the old gun days. "Why so much loneliness, Stampede?"

Stampede grinned wryly. He had humorous, blue eyes, buried like an Airedale's under brows which bristled even more fiercely than his whiskers. "I'm thinkin'," said he, "what a fool thing is money. Good mornin', Alan!"

He nodded and chuckled, and continued to chuckle in the face of the lifting fog, and Alan saw the old humor which had always been Stampede's last asset when in trouble. He drew nearer and stood beside him, so that their shoulders touched as they leaned over the rail.

"Alan," said Stampede, "it ain't often I have a big thought, but I've been having one all night. Ain't forgot Bonanza, have you?"

Alan shook his head. "As long as there is an Alaska, we won't forget Bonanza, Stampede."

"I took a million out of it, next to Carmack's Discovery--an' went busted afterward, didn't I?"

Alan nodded without speaking.

"But that wasn't a circumstance to Gold Run Creek, over the Divide," Stampede continued ruminatively. "Ain't forgot old Aleck McDonald, the Scotchman, have you, Alan? In the 'wash' of Ninety-eight we took up seventy sacks to bring our gold back in and we lacked thirty of doin' the job. Nine hundred thousand dollars in a single clean-up, and that was only the beginning. Well, I went busted again. And old Aleck went busted later on. But he had a pretty wife left. A girl from Seattle. I had to grub-stake."

He was silent for a moment, caressing his damp whiskers, as he noted the first rose-flush of the sun breaking through the mist between them and the unseen mountain tops.

"Five times after that I made strikes and went busted," he said a little proudly. "And I'm busted again!"

"I know it," sympathized Alan.

"They took every cent away from me down in Seattle an' Frisco," chuckled Stampede, rubbing his hands together cheerfully, "an' then bought me a ticket to Nome. Mighty fine of them, don't you think? Couldn't have been more decent. I knew that fellow Kopf had a heart. That's why I trusted him with my money. It wasn't his fault he lost it."

"Of course not," agreed Alan.

"And I'm sort of sorry I shot him up for it. I am, for a fact."

"You killed him?"

"Not quite. I clipped one ear off as a reminder, down in Chink Holleran's place. Mighty sorry. Didn't think then how decent it was of him to buy me a ticket to Nome. I just let go in the heat of the moment. He did me a favor in cleanin' me, Alan. He did, so help me! You don't realize how free an' easy an' beautiful everything is until you're busted."

Smiling, his odd face almost boyish behind its ambush of hair, he saw the grim look in Alan's eyes and about his jaws. He caught hold of the other's arm and shook it.

"Alan, I mean it!" he declared. "That's why I think money is a fool thing. It ain't *spendin'* money that makes me happy. It's *findin'* it--the gold in the mountains--that makes the blood run fast through my gizzard. After I've found it, I can't find any use for it in particular. I want to go broke. If I didn't, I'd get lazy and fat, an' some newfangled doctor would operate on me, and I'd die. They're doing a lot of that operatin' down in Frisco, Alan. One day I had a pain, and they wanted to cut out something from inside me. Think what can happen to a man when he's got money!"

"You mean all that, Stampede?"

"On my life, I do. I'm just aching for the open skies, Alan. The mountains. And the yellow stuff that's going to be my playmate till I die. Somebody'll grub-stake me in Nome."

"They won't," said Alan suddenly. "Not if I can help it. Stampede, I want you. I want you with me up under the Endicott Mountains. I've got ten thousand reindeer up there. It's No Man's Land, and we can do as we please in it. I'm not after gold. I want another sort of thing. But I've fancied the Endicott ranges are full of that yellow playmate of yours. It's a new country. You've never seen it. God only knows what you may find. Will you come?"

The humorous twinkle had gone out of Stampede's eyes. He was staring at Alan.

"Will I *come?* Alan, will a cub nurse its mother? Try me. Ask me. Say it all over ag'in."

The two men gripped hands. Smiling, Alan nodded to the east. The last of the fog was clearing swiftly. The tips of the cragged Alaskan ranges rose up against the blue of a cloudless sky, and the morning sun was flashing in rose and gold at their snowy peaks. Stampede also nodded. Speech was unnecessary. They both understood, and the thrill of the life they loved passed from one to the other in the grip of their hands.

CHAPTER V

Breakfast hour was half over when Alan went into the dining-room. There were only two empty chairs at his table. One was his own. The other belonged to Mary Standish. There was something almost aggressively suggestive in their simultaneous vacancy, it struck him at first. He nodded as he sat down, a flash of amusement in his eyes when he observed the look in the young engineer's face. It was both envious and accusing, and yet Alan was sure the young man was unconscious of betraying an emotion. The fact lent to the eating of his grapefruit an accompaniment of pleasing and amusing thought. He recalled the young man's name. It was Tucker. He was a clean-faced, athletic, likable-looking chap. And an idiot would have guessed the truth, Alan told himself. The young engineer was more than casually interested in Mary Standish; he was in love. It was not a discovery which Alan made. It was a decision, and as soon as possible he would remedy the unfortunate omission of a general introduction at their table by bringing the two together. Such an introduction would undoubtedly relieve him of a certain responsibility which had persisted in attaching itself to him.

So he tried to think. But in spite of his resolution he could not get the empty chair opposite him out of his mind. It refused to be obliterated, and when other chairs became vacant as their owners left the table, this one straight across from him continued to thrust itself upon him. Until this morning it had been like other empty chairs. Now it was persistently annoying, inasmuch as he had no desire to be so constantly reminded of last night, and the twelve o'clock tryst of Mary Standish with Graham's agent, Rossland.

He was the last at the table. Tucker, remaining until his final hope of seeing Mary Standish was gone, rose with two others. The first two had made their exit through the door leading from the dining salon when the young engineer paused. Alan, watching him, saw a sudden change in his face. In a moment it was explained. Mary Standish came in. She passed Tucker without appearing to notice him, and gave Alan a cool little nod as she seated herself at the table. She was very pale. He could see nothing of the flush of color that had been in her cheeks last night. As she bowed her head a little, arranging her dress, a pool of sunlight played in her hair, and Alan was staring at it when she raised her eyes. They were coolly beautiful, very direct, and without embarrassment. Something inside him challenged their loveliness. It seemed inconceivable that such eyes could play a part in fraud and deception, yet he was in possession of quite conclusive proof of it. If they had lowered themselves an instant, if they had in any way betrayed a shadow of regret, he would have found an apology. Instead of that, his fingers touched the handkerchief in his pocket.

"Did you sleep well, Miss Standish?" he asked politely.

"Not at all," she replied, so frankly that his conviction was a bit unsettled. "I tried to powder away the dark rings under my eyes, but I am afraid I have failed. Is that why you ask?"

He was holding the handkerchief in his hand. "This is the first morning I have seen you at breakfast. I accepted it for granted you must have slept well. Is this yours, Miss Standish?"

He watched her face as she took the crumpled bit of cambric from his fingers. In a moment she was smiling. The smile was not forced. It was the quick response to a feminine instinct of pleasure, and he was disappointed not to catch in her face a betrayal of embarrassment.

"It is my handkerchief, Mr. Holt. Where did you find it?"

"In front of my cabin door a little after midnight."

He was almost brutal in the definiteness of detail. He expected some kind of result. But there was none, except that the smile remained on her lips a moment longer, and there was a laughing flash back in the clear depths of her eyes. Her level glance was as innocent as a child's and as he looked at her, he thought of a child--a most beautiful child--and so utterly did he feel the discomfiture of his mental analysis of her that he rose to his feet with a frigid bow.

"I thank you, Mr. Holt," she said. "You can imagine my sense of obligation when I tell you I have only three handkerchiefs aboard the ship with me. And this is my favorite."

She busied herself with the breakfast card, and as Alan left, he heard her give the waiter an order for fruit and cereal. His blood was hot, but the flush of it did not show in his face. He felt the uncomfortable sensation of her eyes following him as he stalked through the door. He did not look back. Something was wrong with him, and he knew it. This chit of a girl with her smooth hair and clear eyes had thrown a grain of dust into the satisfactory mechanism of his normal self, and the grind of it was upsetting certain specific formulae which made up his life. He was a fool. He lighted a cigar and called himself names.

Someone brushed against him, jarring the hand that held the burning match. He looked up. It was Rossland. The man had a mere twist of a smile on his lips. In his eyes was a coolly appraising look as he nodded.

"Beg pardon." The words were condescending, carelessly flung at him over Rossland's shoulder. He might as well have said, "I'm sorry, Boy, but you must keep out of my way."

Alan smiled back and returned the nod. Once, in a spirit of sauciness, Keok had told him his eyes were like purring cats when he was in a humor to kill. They were like that now as they flashed their smile at Rossland. The sneering twist left Rossland's lips as he entered the dining-room.

A rather obvious prearrangement between Mary Standish and John Graham's agent, Alan thought. There were not half a dozen people left at the tables, and the scheme was that Rossland should be served tête-à-tête with Miss Standish, of course. That, apparently, was why she had greeted him with such cool civility. Her anxiety for him to leave the table before Rossland appeared upon the scene was evident, now that he understood the situation.

He puffed at his cigar. Rossland's interference had spoiled a perfect lighting of it, and he struck another match. This time he was successful, and he was about to extinguish the burning end when he hesitated and held it until the fire touched his flesh. Mary Standish was coming through the door. Amazed by the suddenness of her appearance, he made no movement except to drop the match. Her eyes were flaming, and two vivid spots burned in her cheeks. She saw him and gave the slightest inclination to her head as she passed. When she had gone, he could not resist looking into the salon. As he expected, Rossland was seated in a chair next to the one she had occupied, and was calmly engaged in looking over the breakfast card.

All this was rather interesting, Alan conceded, if one liked puzzles. Personally he had no desire to become an answerer of conundrums, and he was a little ashamed of the curiosity that had urged him to look in upon Rossland. At the same time he was mildly elated at the freezing reception which Miss Standish had evidently given to the dislikable individual who had jostled him in passing.

He went on deck. The sun was pouring in an iridescent splendor over the snowy peaks of the mountains, and it seemed as if he could almost reach out his arms and touch them. The *Nome* appeared to be drifting in the heart of a paradise of mountains. Eastward, very near, was the mainland; so close on the other hand that he could hear the shout of a man was Douglas Island, and ahead, reaching out like a silver-blue ribbon was Gastineau Channel. The mining towns of Treadwell and Douglas were in sight.

Someone nudged him, and he found Stampede Smith at his side.

"That's Bill Treadwell's place," he said. "Once the richest gold mines in Alaska. They're flooded now. I knew Bill when he was worrying about the price of a pair of boots. Had to buy a second-hand pair an' patched 'em himself. Then he struck it lucky, got four hundred dollars somewhere, and bought some claims over there from a man named French Pete. They called it Glory Hole. An' there was a time when there were nine hundred stamps at work. Take a look, Alan. It's worth it."

Somehow Stampede's voice and information lacked appeal. The decks were crowded with passengers as the ship picked her way into Juneau, and Alan wandered among them with a gathering sense of disillusionment pressing upon him. He knew that he was looking with more than casual interest for Mary Standish, and he was glad when Stampede bumped into an old acquaintance and permitted him to be alone. He was not pleased with the discovery, and yet he was compelled to acknowledge the truth of it. The grain of dust had become more than annoying. It did not wear away, as he had supposed it would, but was becoming an obsessive factor in his thoughts. And the half-desire it built up in him, while aggravatingly persistent, was less disturbing than before. The little drama in the dining-room had had its effect upon him in spite of himself. He liked fighters. And Mary Standish, intensely feminine in her quiet prettiness, had shown her mettle in those few moments when he had seen her flashing eyes and blazing cheeks after leaving Rossland. He began to look for Rossland, too. He was in a humor to meet him.

Not until Juneau hung before him in all its picturesque beauty, literally terraced against the green sweep of Mount Juneau, did he go down to the lower deck. The few passengers ready to leave the ship gathered near the gangway with their luggage. Alan was about to pass them when he suddenly stopped. A short distance from him, where he could see every person who disembarked, stood Rossland. There was something grimly unpleasant in his attitude as he fumbled his watch-fob and eyed the stair from above. His watchfulness sent an unexpected thrill through Alan. Like a shot his mind jumped to a conclusion. He stepped to Rossland's side and touched his arm.

"Watching for Miss Standish?" he asked.

"I am." There was no evasion in Rossland's words. They possessed the hard and definite quality of one who had an incontestable authority behind him.

"And if she goes ashore?"

"I am going too. Is it any affair of yours, Mr. Holt? Has she asked you to discuss the matter with me? If so--"

"No, Miss Standish hasn't done that."

"Then please attend to your own business. If you haven't enough to take up your time, I'll lend you some books. I have several in my cabin."

Without waiting for an answer Rossland coolly moved away. Alan did not follow. There was nothing for him to resent, nothing for him to imprecate but his own folly. Rossland's words were not an insult. They were truth. He had deliberately intruded in an affair which was undoubtedly of a highly private nature. Possibly it was a domestic tangle. He shuddered. A sense of humiliation swept over him, and he was glad that Rossland did not even look back at him. He tried to whistle as he climbed back to the main-deck; Rossland, even though he detested the man, had set him right. And he would lend him books, if he wanted to be amused! Egad, but the fellow had turned the trick nicely. And it was something to be remembered. He stiffened his shoulders and found old Donald Hardwick and Stampede Smith. He did not leave them until the *Nome* had landed her passengers and freight and was churning her way out of Gastineau Channel toward Skagway. Then he went to the smoking-room and remained there until luncheon hour.

Today Mary Standish was ahead of him at the table. She was seated with her back toward him as he entered, so she did not see him as he came up behind her, so near that his coat brushed her chair. He looked across at her and smiled as he seated himself. She returned the smile, but it seemed to him an apologetic little effort. She did not look well, and her presence at the table struck him as being a brave front to hide something from someone. Casually he looked over his left shoulder. Rossland was there, in his seat at the opposite side of the room. Indirect as his glance had been, Alan saw the girl understood the significance of it. She bowed her head a little, and her long lashes shaded her eyes for a moment. He wondered why he always looked at her hair first. It had a peculiarly pleasing effect on him. He had been observant enough to know that she had rearranged it since breakfast, and the smooth coils twisted in mysterious intricacy at the crown of her head were like softly glowing velvet. The ridiculous thought came to him that he would like to see them tumbling down about her. They must be even more beautiful when freed from their bondage.

The pallor of her face was unusual. Possibly it was the way the light fell upon her through the window. But when she looked across at him again, he caught for an instant the tiniest quiver about her mouth. He began telling her something about Skagway, quite carelessly, as if he had seen nothing which she might want to conceal. The light in her eyes changed, and it was almost a glow of gratitude he caught in them. He had broken a tension, relieved her of some unaccountable strain she was under. He noticed that her ordering of food was merely a pretense. She scarcely touched it, and yet he was sure no other person at the table had discovered the insincerity of her effort, not even Tucker, the enamored engineer. It was likely Tucker placed a delicate halo about her lack of appetite, accepting daintiness of that sort as an angelic virtue.

Only Alan, sitting opposite her, guessed the truth. She was making a splendid effort, but he felt that every nerve in her body was at the breaking-point. When she arose from her seat, he thrust back his own chair. At the same time he saw Rossland get up and advance rather hurriedly from the opposite side of the room. The girl passed through the door first, Rossland followed a dozen steps behind, and Alan came last, almost shoulder to shoulder with Tucker. It was amusing in a way, yet beyond the humor of it was something that drew a grim line about the corners of his mouth.

At the foot of the luxuriously carpeted stair leading from the dining salon to the main deck Miss Standish suddenly stopped and turned upon Rossland. For only an instant her eyes were leveled at him. Then they flashed past him, and with a swift movement she came toward Alan. A flush had leaped into her cheeks, but there was no excitement in her voice when she spoke. Yet it was distinct, and clearly heard by Rossland.

"I understand we are approaching Skagway, Mr. Holt," she said. "Will you take me on deck, and tell me about it?"

Graham's agent had paused at the foot of the stair and was slowly preparing to light a cigarette. Recalling his humiliation of a few hours before at Juneau, when the other had very clearly proved him a meddler, words refused to form quickly on Alan's lips. Before he was ready with an answer Mary Standish had confidently taken his arm. He could see the red flush deepening in her upturned face. She was amazingly unexpected, bewilderingly pretty, and as cool as ice except for the softly glowing fire in her cheeks. He saw Rossland staring with his cigarette half poised. It was instinctive for him to smile in the face of danger, and he smiled now, without speaking. The girl laughed softly. She gave his arm a gentle tug, and he found himself moving past Rossland, amazed but obedient, her eyes looking at him in a way that sent a gentle thrill through him.

At the head of the wide stair she whispered, with her lips close to his shoulder: "You are splendid! I thank you, Mr. Holt."

Her words, along with the decisive relaxing of her hand upon his arm, were like a dash of cold water in his face. Rossland could no longer see them, unless he had followed. The girl had played her part, and a second time he had accepted the role of a slow-witted fool. But the thought did not anger him. There was a remarkable element of humor about it for him, viewing himself in the matter, and Mary Standish heard him chuckling as they came out on deck.

Her fingers tightened resentfully upon his arm. "It isn't funny," she reproved. "It is tragic to be bored by a man like that."

He knew she was politely lying to anticipate the question he might ask, and he wondered what would happen if he embarrassed her by letting her know he had seen her alone with Rossland at midnight. He looked down at her, and she met his scrutiny unflinchingly. She even smiled at him, and her eyes, he thought, were the loveliest liars he had ever looked into. He felt the stir of an unusual sentiment--a sort of pride in her, and he made up his mind to say nothing about Rossland. He was still absurdly convinced that he had not the smallest interest in affairs which were not entirely his own. Mary Standish evidently believed he was blind, and he would make no effort to spoil her illusion. Such a course would undoubtedly be most satisfactory in the end.

Even now she seemed to have forgotten the incident at the foot of the stair. A softer light was in her eyes when they came to the bow of the ship, and Alan fancied he heard a strange little cry on her lips as she looked about her upon the paradise of Taiya Inlet. Straight ahead, like a lilac ribbon, ran the narrow waterway to Skagway's door, while on both sides rose high mountains, covered with green forests to the snowy crests that gleamed like white blankets near the clouds. In this melting season there came to them above the slow throb of the ship's engines the liquid music of innumerable cascades, and from a mountain that seemed to float almost directly over their heads fell a stream of water a sheer thousand feet to the sea, smoking and twisting in the sunshine like a living thing at play. And then a miracle happened which even Alan wondered at, for the ship seemed to stand still and the mountain to swing slowly, as if some unseen and mighty force were opening a guarded door, and green foothills with glistening white cottages floated into the picture, and Skagway, heart of romance, monument to brave men and thrilling deeds, drifted out slowly from its hiding-place. Alan turned to speak, but what he saw in the girl's face held him silent. Her lips were parted, and she was staring as if an unexpected thing had risen before her eyes, something that bewildered her and even startled her.

And then, as if speaking to herself and not to Alan Holt, she said in a tense whisper: "I have seen this place before. It was a long time ago. Maybe it was a hundred years or a thousand. But I have been here. I have lived under that mountain with the waterfall creeping down it--"

A tremor ran through her, and she remembered Alan. She looked up at him, and he was puzzled. A weirdly beautiful mystery lay in her eyes.

"I must go ashore here," she said. "I didn't know I would find it so soon. Please--"

With her hand touching his arm she turned. He was looking at her and saw the strange light fade swiftly out of her eyes. Following her glance he saw Rossland standing half a dozen paces behind them.

In another moment Mary Standish was facing the sea, and again her hand was resting confidently in the crook of Alan's arm. "Did you ever feel like killing a man, Mr. Holt?" she asked with an icy little laugh.

"Yes," he answered rather unexpectedly. "And some day, if the right opportunity comes, I am going to kill a certain man--the man who murdered my father."

She gave a little gasp of horror. "Your father--was--murdered--"

"Indirectly--yes. It wasn't done with knife or gun, Miss Standish. Money was the weapon. Somebody's money. And John Graham was the man who struck the blow. Some day, if there is justice, I shall kill him. And right now, if you will allow me to demand an explanation of this man Rossland--"

"*No.*" Her hand tightened on his arm. Then, slowly, she drew it away. "I don't want you to ask an explanation of him," she said. "If he should make it, you would hate me. Tell me about Skagway, Mr. Holt. That will be pleasanter."

CHAPTER VI

Not until early twilight came with the deep shadows of the western mountains, and the *Nome* was churning slowly back through the narrow water-trails to the open Pacific, did the significance of that afternoon fully impress itself upon Alan. For hours he had surrendered himself to an impulse which he could not understand, and which in ordinary moments he would not have excused. He had taken Mary Standish ashore. For two hours she had walked at his side, asking him questions and listening to him as no other had ever questioned him or listened to him before. He had shown her Skagway. Between the mountains he pictured the wind-racked cañon where Skagway grew from one tent to hundreds in a day, from hundreds to thousands in a week; he visioned for her the old days of romance, adventure, and death; he told her of Soapy Smith and his gang of outlaws, and side by side they stood over Soapy's sunken grave as the first somber shadows of the mountains grew upon them.

But among it all, and through it all, she had asked him about *himself.* And he had responded. Until now he did not realize how much he had confided in her. It seemed to him that the very soul of this slim and beautiful girl who had walked at his side had urged him on to the indiscretion of personal confidence. He had seemed to feel her heart beating with his own as he described his beloved land under the Endicott Mountains, with its vast tundras, his herds, and his people. There, he had told her, a new world was in the making, and the glow in her eyes and the thrilling something in her voice had urged him on until he forgot that Rossland was waiting at the ship's gangway to see when they returned. He had built up for her his castles in the air, and the miracle of it was that she had helped him to build them. He had described for her the change that was creeping slowly over Alaska, the replacement of mountain trails by stage and automobile highways, the building of railroads, the growth of cities where tents had stood a few years before. It was then, when he had pictured progress and civilization and the breaking down of nature's last barriers before science and invention, that he had seen a cloud of doubt in her gray eyes.

And now, as they stood on the deck of the *Nome* looking at the white peaks of the mountains dissolving into the lavender mist of twilight, doubt and perplexity were still deeper in her eyes, and she said:

"I would always love tents and old trails and nature's barriers. I envy Belinda Mulrooney, whom you told me about this afternoon. I hate cities and railroads and automobiles, and all that goes with them, and I am sorry to see those things come to Alaska. And I, too, hate this man--John Graham!"

Her words startled him.

"And I want you to tell me what he is doing--with his money--now." Her voice was cold, and one little hand, he noticed, was clenched at the edge of the rail.

"He has stripped Alaskan waters of fish resources which will never be replaced, Miss Standish. But that is not all. I believe I state the case well within fact when I say he has killed many women and little children by robbing the inland waters of the food supplies upon which the natives have subsisted for centuries. I know. I have seen them die."

It seemed to him that she swayed against him for an instant.

"And that--is all?"

He laughed grimly. "Possibly some people would think it enough, Miss Standish. But the tentacles of his power are reaching everywhere in Alaska. His agents swarm throughout the territory, and Soapy Smith was a gentleman outlaw compared with these men and their master. If men like John Graham are allowed to have their way, in ten years greed and graft will despoil what two hundred years of Rooseveltian conservation would not be able to replace."

She raised her head, and in the dusk her pale face looked up at the ghost-peaks of the mountains still visible through the thickening gloom of evening. "I am glad you told me about Belinda Mulrooney," she said. "I am beginning to understand, and it gives me courage to think of a woman like her. She could fight, couldn't she? She could make a man's fight?"

"Yes, and did make it."

"And she had no money to give her power. Her last dollar, you told me, she flung into the Yukon for luck."

"Yes, at Dawson. It was the one thing between her and hunger."

She raised her hand, and on it he saw gleaming faintly the single ring which she wore. Slowly she drew it from her finger.

"Then this, too, for luck--the luck of Mary Standish," she laughed softly, and flung the ring into the sea.

She faced him, as if expecting the necessity of defending what she had done. "It isn't melodrama," she said. "I mean it. And I believe in it. I want something of mine to lie at the bottom of the sea in this gateway to Skagway, just as Belinda Mulrooney wanted her dollar to rest forever at the bottom of the Yukon."

She gave him the hand from which she had taken the ring, and for a moment the warm thrill of it lay in his own. "Thank you for the wonderful afternoon you have given me, Mr. Holt. I shall never forget it. It is dinner time. I must say good night."

He followed her slim figure with his eyes until she disappeared. In returning to his cabin he almost bumped into Rossland. The incident was irritating. Neither of the men spoke or nodded, but Rossland met Alan's look squarely, his face rock-like in its repression of emotion. Alan's impression of the man was changing in spite of his prejudice. There was a growing something about him which commanded attention, a certainty of poise which could not be mistaken for sham. A scoundrel he might be, but a cool brain was at work inside his head--a brain not easily disturbed by unimportant things, he decided. He disliked the man. As an agent of John Graham Alan looked upon him as an enemy, and as an acquaintance of Mary Standish he was as much of a mystery as the girl herself. And only now, in his cabin, was Alan beginning to sense the presence of a real authority behind Rossland's attitude.

He was not curious. All his life he had lived too near the raw edge of practical things to dissipate in gossipy conjecture. He cared nothing about the relationship between Mary Standish and Rossland except as it involved himself, and the situation had become a trifle too delicate to please him. He could see no sport in an adventure of the kind it suggested, and the possibility that he had been misjudged by both Rossland and Mary Standish sent a flush of anger into his cheeks. He cared nothing for Rossland, except that he would like to wipe him out of existence with all other Graham agents. And he persisted in the conviction that he thought of the girl only in a most casual sort of way. He had made no effort to discover her history. He had not questioned her. At no time had he intimated a desire to intrude upon her personal affairs, and at no time had she offered information about herself, or an explanation of the singular espionage which Rossland had presumed to take upon himself. He grimaced as he reflected how dangerously near that hazard he had been--and he admired her for the splendid judgment she had shown in the matter. She had saved him the possible alternative of apologizing to Rossland or throwing him overboard!

There was a certain bellicose twist to his mind as he went down to the dining salon, an obstinate determination to hold himself aloof from any increasing intimacy with Mary Standish. No matter how pleasing his experience had been, he resented the idea of being commandeered at unexpected moments. Had Mary Standish read his thoughts, her bearing toward him during the dinner hour could not have been more satisfying. There was, in a way, something seductively provocative about it. She greeted him with the slightest inclination of her head and a cool little smile. Her attitude did not invite spoken words, either from him or from his neighbors, yet no one would have accused her of deliberate reserve.

Her demure unapproachableness was a growing revelation to him, and he found himself interested in spite of the new law of self-preservation he had set down for himself. He could not keep his eyes from stealing glimpses at her hair when her head was bowed a little. She had smoothed it tonight until it was like softest velvet, with rich glints in it, and the amazing thought came to him that it would be sweetly pleasant to touch with one's hand. The discovery was almost a shock. Keok and Nawadlook had beautiful hair, but he had never thought of it in this way. And he had never thought of Keok's pretty mouth as he was thinking of the girl's opposite him. He shifted uneasily and was glad Mary Standish did not look at him in these moments of mental unbalance.

When he left the table, the girl scarcely noticed his going. It was as if she had used him and then calmly shuttled him out of the way. He tried to laugh as he hunted up Stampede Smith. He found him, half an hour later, feeding a captive bear on the lower deck. It was odd, he thought, that a captive bear should be going north. Stampede explained. The animal was a pet and belonged to the Thlinkit Indians. There were seven, getting off at Cordova. Alan observed that the two girls watched him closely and whispered together. They were very pretty, with large, dark eyes and pink in their cheeks. One of the men did not look at him at all, but sat cross-legged on the deck, with his face turned away.

With Stampede he went to the smoking-room, and until a late hour they discussed the big range up under the Endicott Mountains, and Alan's plans for the future. Once, early in the evening, Alan went to his cabin to get maps and photographs. Stampede's eyes glistened as his mind seized upon the possibilities of the new adventure. It was a vast land. An unknown country. And Alan was its first pioneer. The old thrill ran in Stampede's blood, and its infectiousness caught Alan, so that he forgot Mary Standish, and all else but the miles that lay between them and the mighty tundras beyond the Seward Peninsula. It was midnight when Alan went to his cabin.

He was happy. Love of life swept in an irresistible surge through his body, and he breathed in deeply of the soft sea air that came in through his open port from the west. In Stampede Smith he had at last found the comradeship which he had missed, and the responsive note to the wild and half-savage desires always smoldering in his heart. He looked out at the stars and smiled up at them, and his soul was filled with an unspoken thankfulness that he was not born too late. Another generation and there would be no last frontier. Twenty-five years more and the world would lie utterly in the shackles of science and invention and what the human race called progress.

So God had been good to him. He was helping to write the last page in that history which would go down through the eons of time, written in the red blood of men who had cut the first trails into the unknown. After him, there would be no more frontiers. No more mysteries of unknown lands to solve. No more pioneering hazards to make. The earth would be tamed. And suddenly he thought of Mary Standish and of what she had said to him in the dusk of evening. Strange that it had been *her* thought, too--that she would always love tents and old trails and nature's barriers, and hated to see cities and railroads and automobiles come to Alaska. He shrugged his shoulders. Probably she had guessed what was in his own mind, for she was clever, very clever.

A tap at his door drew his eyes from the open watch in his hand. It was a quarter after twelve o'clock, an unusual hour for someone to be tapping at his door.

It was repeated--a bit hesitatingly, he thought. Then it came again, quick and decisive. Replacing his watch in his pocket, he opened the door.

It was Mary Standish who stood facing him.

He saw only her eyes at first, wide-open, strange, frightened eyes. And then he saw the pallor of her face as she came slowly in, without waiting for him to speak or give her permission to enter. And it was Mary Standish herself who closed the door, while he stared at her in stupid wonderment--and stood there with her back against it, straight and slim and deathly pale.

"May I come in?" she asked.

"My God, you're in!" gasped Alan. "*You're in.*"

CHAPTER VII

That it was past midnight, and Mary Standish had deliberately come to his room, entering it and closing the door without a word or a nod of invitation from him, seemed incredible to Alan. After his first explosion of astonishment he stood mute, while the girl looked at him steadily and her breath came a little quickly. But she was not excited. Even in his amazement he could see that. What he had thought was fright had gone out of her eyes. But he had never seen her so white, and never had she appeared quite so slim and childish-looking as while she stood there in these astounding moments with her back against the door.

The pallor of her face accentuated the rich darkness of her hair. Even her lips were pale. But she was not embarrassed. Her eyes were clear and unafraid now, and in the poise of her head and body was a sureness of purpose that staggered him. A feeling of anger, almost of personal resentment, began to possess him as he waited for her to speak. This, at last, was the cost of his courtesies to her, The advantage she was taking of him was an indignity and an outrage, and his mind flashed to the suspicion that Rossland was standing just outside the door.

In another moment he would have brushed her aside and opened it, but her quiet face held him. The tenseness was fading out of it. He saw her lips tremble, and then a miracle happened. In her wide-open, beautiful eyes tears were gathering. Even then she did not lower her glance or bury her face in her hands, but looked at him bravely while the tear-drops glistened like diamonds on her cheeks. He felt his heart give way. She read his thoughts, had guessed his suspicion, and he was wrong.

"You--you will have a seat, Miss Standish?" he asked lamely, inclining his head toward the cabin chair.

"No. Please let me stand." She drew in a deep breath. "It is late, Mr. Holt?"

"Rather an irregular hour for a visit such as this," he assured her. "Half an hour after midnight, to be exact. It must be very important business that has urged you to make such a hazard aboard ship, Miss Standish."

For a moment she did not answer him, and he saw the little heart-throb in her white throat.

"Would Belinda Mulrooney have considered this a very great hazard, Mr. Holt? In a matter of life and death, do you not think she would have come to your cabin at midnight--even aboard ship? And it is that with me--a matter of life and death. Less than an hour ago I came to that decision. I could not wait until morning. I had to see you tonight."

"And why me?" he asked. "Why not Rossland, or Captain Rifle, or some other? Is it because--"

He did not finish. He saw the shadow of something gather in her eyes, as if for an instant she had felt a stab of humiliation or of pain, but it was gone as quickly as it came. And very quietly, almost without emotion, she answered him.

"I know how you feel. I have tried to place myself in your position. It is all very irregular, as you say. But I am not ashamed. I have come to you as I would want anyone to come to me under similar circumstances, if I were a man. If watching you, thinking about you, making up my mind about you is taking an advantage--then I have been unfair, Mr. Holt. But I am not sorry. I trust you. I know you will believe me good until I am proved bad. I have come to ask you to help me. Would you make it possible for another human being to avert a great tragedy if you found it in your power to do so?"

He felt his sense of judgment wavering. Had he been coolly analyzing such a situation in the detached environment of the smoking-room, he would have called any man a fool who hesitated to open his cabin door and show his visitor out. But such a thought did not occur to him now. He was thinking of the handkerchief he had found the preceding midnight. Twice she had come to his cabin at a late hour.

"It would be my inclination to make such a thing possible," he said, answering her question. "Tragedy is a nasty thing."

She caught the hint of irony in his voice. If anything, it added to her calmness. He was to suffer no weeping entreaties, no feminine play of helplessness and beauty. Her pretty mouth was a little firmer and the tilt of her dainty chin a bit higher.

"Of course, I can't pay you," she said. "You are the sort of man who would resent an offer of payment for what I am about to ask you to do. But I must have help. If I don't have it, and quickly"--she shuddered slightly and tried to smile--"something very unpleasant will happen, Mr. Holt," she finished.

"If you will permit me to take you to Captain Rifle--"

"No. Captain Rifle would question me. He would demand explanations. You will understand when I tell you what I want. And I will do that if I may have your word of honor to hold in confidence what I tell you, whether you help me or not. Will you give me that pledge?"

"Yes, if such a pledge will relieve your mind, Miss Standish."

He was almost brutally incurious. As he reached for a cigar, he did not see the sudden movement she made, as if about to fly from his room, or the quicker throb that came in her throat. When he turned, a faint flush was gathering in her cheeks.

"I want to leave the ship," she said.

The simplicity of her desire held him silent.

"And I must leave it tonight, or tomorrow night--before we reach Cordova."

"Is that--your problem?" he demanded, astonished.

"No. I must leave it in such a way that the world will believe I am dead. I can not reach Cordova alive."

At last she struck home and he stared at her, wondering if she were insane. Her quiet, beautiful eyes met his own with unflinching steadiness. His brain all at once was crowded with questioning, but no word of it came to his lips.

"You can help me," he heard her saying in the same quiet, calm voice, softened so that one could not have heard it beyond the cabin door. "I haven't a plan. But I know you can arrange one--if you will. It must appear to be an accident. I must disappear, fall overboard, anything, just so the world will believe I am dead. It is necessary. And I can not tell you why. I can not. Oh, I *can not*."

A note of passion crept into her voice, but it was gone in an instant, leaving it cold and steady again. A second time she tried to smile. He could see courage, and a bit of defiance, shining in her eyes.

"I know what you are thinking, Mr. Holt. You are asking yourself if I am mad, if I am a criminal, what my reason can be, and why I haven't gone to Rossland, or Captain Rifle, or some one else. And the only answer I can make is that I have come to you because you are the only man in the world--in this hour--that I have faith in. Some day you will understand, if you help me. If you do not care to help me--"

She stopped, and he made a gesture.

"Yes, if I don't? What will happen then?"

"I shall be forced to the inevitable," she said. "It is rather unusual, isn't it, to be asking for one's life? But that is what I mean."

"I'm afraid--I don't quite understand."

"Isn't it clear, Mr. Holt? I don't like to appear spectacular, and I don't want you to think of me as theatrical--even now. I hate that sort of thing. You must simply believe me when I tell you it is impossible for me to reach Cordova alive. If you do not help me to disappear, help me to live--and at the same time give all others the impression that I am dead--then I must do the other thing. I must really die."

For a moment his eyes blazed angrily. He felt like taking her by the shoulders and shaking her, as he would have shaken the truth out of a child.

"You come to me with a silly threat like that, Miss Standish? A threat of suicide?"

"If you want to call it that--yes."

"And you expect me to believe you?"

"I had hoped you would."

She had his nerves going. There was no doubt of that. He half believed her and half disbelieved. If she had cried, if she had made the smallest effort to work upon his sentiment, he would have disbelieved utterly. But he was not blind to the fact that she was making a brave fight, even though a lie was behind it, and with a consciousness of pride that bewildered him.

She was not humiliating herself. Even when she saw the struggle going on within him she made no effort to turn the balance in her favor. She had stated the facts, as she claimed them to be. Now she waited. Her long lashes glistened a little. But her eyes were clear, and her hair glowed softly, so softly that he would never forget it, as she stood there with her back against the door, nor the strange desire that came to him--even then--to touch it with his hand.

He nipped off the end of his cigar and lighted a match. "It is Rossland," he said. "You're afraid of Rossland?"

"In a way, yes; in a large way, no. I would laugh at Rossland if it were not for the other."

The *other*! Why the deuce was she so provokingly ambiguous? And she had no intention of explaining. She simply waited for him to decide.

"What other?" he demanded.

"I can not tell you. I don't want you to hate me. And you would hate me if I told you the truth."

"Then you confess you are lying," he suggested brutally.

Even this did not stir her as he had expected it might. It did not anger her or shame her. But she raised a pale hand and a little handkerchief to her eyes, and he turned toward the open port, puffing at his cigar, knowing she was fighting to keep the tears back. And she succeeded.

"No, I am not lying. What I have told you is true. It is because I will not lie that I have not told you more. And I thank you for the time you have given me, Mr. Holt. That you have not driven me from your cabin is a kindness which I appreciate. I have made a mistake, that is all. I thought--"

"How could I bring about what you ask?" he interrupted.

"I don't know. You are a man. I believed you could plan a way, but I see now how foolish I have been. It is impossible." Her hand reached slowly for the knob of the door.

"Yes, you are foolish," he agreed, and his voice was softer. "Don't let such thoughts overcome you, Miss Standish. Go back to your cabin and get a night's sleep. Don't let Rossland worry you. If you want me to settle with that man--"

"Good night, Mr. Holt."

She was opening the door. And as she went out she turned a little and looked at him, and now she was smiling, and there were tears in her eyes.

"Good night."

"Good night."

The door closed behind her. He heard her retreating footsteps. In half a minute he would have called her back. But it was too late.

CHAPTER VIII

For half an hour Alan sat smoking his cigar. Mentally he was not at ease. Mary Standish had come to him like a soldier, and she had left him like a soldier. But in that last glimpse of her face he had caught for an instant something which she had not betrayed in his cabin--a stab of what he thought was pain in her tear-wet eyes as she smiled, a proud regret, possibly a shadow of humiliation at last--or it may have been a pity for him. He was not sure. But it was not despair. Not once had she whimpered in look or word, even when the tears were in her eyes, and the thought was beginning to impress itself upon him that it was he--and not Mary Standish--who had shown a yellow streak this night. A half shame fell upon him as he smoked. For it was clear he had not come up to her judgment of him, or else he was not so big a fool as she had hoped he might be. In his own mind, for a time, he was at a loss to decide.

It was possibly the first time he had ever deeply absorbed himself in the analysis of a woman. It was outside his business. But, born and bred of the open country, it was as natural for him to recognize courage as it was for him to breathe. And the girl's courage was unusual, now that he had time to think about it. It was this thought of her coolness and her calm refusal to impose her case upon him with greater warmth that comforted him after a little. A young and beautiful woman who was actually facing death would have urged her necessity with more enthusiasm, it seemed to him. Her threat, when he debated it intelligently, was merely thrown in, possibly on the spur of the moment, to give impetus to his decision. She had not meant it. The idea of a girl like Mary Standish committing suicide was stupendously impossible. Her quiet and wonderful eyes, her beauty and the exquisite care which she gave to herself emphasized the absurdity of such a supposition. She had come to him bravely. There was no doubt of that. She had merely exaggerated the importance of her visit.

Even after he had turned many things over in his mind to bolster up this conclusion, he was still not at ease. Against his will he recalled certain unpleasant things which had happened within his knowledge under sudden and unexpected stress of emotion. He tried to laugh the absurd stuff out of his thoughts and to the end that he might add a new color to his visionings he exchanged his half-burned cigar for a black-bowled pipe, which he filled and lighted. Then he began walking back and forth in his cabin, like a big animal in a small cage, until at last he stood with his head half out of the open port, looking at the clear stars and setting the perfume of his tobacco adrift with the soft sea wind.

He felt himself growing comforted. Reason seated itself within him again, with sentiment shuttled under his feet. If he had been a little harsh with Miss Standish tonight, he would make up for it by apologizing tomorrow. She would probably have recovered her balance by that time, and they would laugh over her excitement and their little adventure. That is, he would. "I'm not at all curious in the matter," some persistent voice kept telling him, "and I haven't any interest in knowing what irrational whim drove her to my cabin." But he smoked viciously and smiled grimly as the voice kept at him. He would have liked to obliterate Rossland from his mind. But Rossland persisted in bobbing up, and with him Mary Standish's words, "If I should make an explanation, you would hate me," or something to that effect. He couldn't remember exactly. And he didn't want to remember exactly, for it was none of his business.

In this humor, with half of his thoughts on one side of the fence and half on the other, he put out his light and went to bed. And he began thinking of the Range. That was pleasanter. For the tenth time he figured out how long it would be before the glacial-twisted ramparts of the Endicott Mountains rose up in first welcome to his home-coming. Carl Lomen, following on the next ship, would join him at Unalaska. They would go on to Nome together. After that he would spend a week or so in the Peninsula, then go up the Kobuk, across the big portage to the Koyukuk and the far headwaters of the north, and still farther--beyond the last trails of civilized men--to his herds and his people. And Stampede Smith would be with him. After a long winter of homesickness it was all a comforting inducement to sleep and pleasant dreams. But somewhere there was a wrong note in his anticipations tonight. Stampede Smith slipped away from him, and Rossland took his place. And Keok, laughing, changed into Mary Standish with tantalizing deviltry. It was like Keok, Alan thought drowsily--she was always tormenting someone.

He felt better in the morning. The sun was up, flooding the wall of his cabin, when he awoke, and under him he could feel the roll of the open sea. Eastward the Alaskan coast was a deep blue haze, but the white peaks of the St. Elias Range flung themselves high up against the sun-filled sky behind it, like snowy banners. The *Nome* was pounding ahead at full speed, and Alan's blood responded suddenly to the impelling thrill of her engines, beating like twin hearts with the mighty force that was speeding them on. This was business. It meant miles foaming away behind them and a swift biting off of space between him and Unalaska, midway of the Aleutians. He was sorry they were losing time by making the swing up the coast to Cordova. And with Cordova he thought of Mary Standish.

He dressed and shaved and went down to breakfast, still thinking of her. The thought of meeting her again was rather discomforting, now that the time of that possibility was actually at hand, for he dreaded moments of embarrassment even when he was not directly accountable for them. But Mary Standish saved him any qualms of conscience which he might have had because of his lack of chivalry the preceding night. She was at the table. And she was not at all disturbed when he seated himself opposite her. There was color in her cheeks, a fragile touch of that warm glow in the heart of the wild rose of the tundras. And it seemed to him there was a deeper, more beautiful light in her eyes than he had ever seen before.

She nodded, smiled at him, and resumed a conversation which she had evidently broken for a moment with a lady who sat next to her. It was the first time Alan had seen her interested in this way. He had no intention of listening, but something perverse and compelling overcame his will. He discovered the lady was going up to teach in a native school at Noorvik, on the Kobuk River, and that for many years she had taught in Dawson and knew well the story of Belinda Mulrooney. He gathered that Mary Standish had shown a great interest, for Miss Robson, the teacher, was offering to send her a photograph she possessed of Belinda Mulrooney; if Miss Standish would give her an address. The girl hesitated, then said she was not certain of her destination, but would write Miss Robson at Noorvik.

"You will surely keep your promise?" urged Miss Robson.

"Yes, I will keep my promise."

A sense of relief swept over Alan. The words were spoken so softly that he thought she had not wanted him to hear. It was evident that a few hours' sleep and the beauty of the morning had completely changed her mental attitude, and he no longer felt the suspicion of responsibility which had persisted in attaching itself to him. Only a fool, he assured himself, could possibly see a note of tragedy in her appearance now. Nor was she different at luncheon or at dinner. During the day he saw nothing of her, and he was growing conscious of the fact that she was purposely avoiding contact with him. This did not displease him. It allowed him to pick up the threads of other interests in a normal sort of way. He discussed Alaskan politics in the smoking-room, smoked his black pipe without fear of giving offense, and listened to the talk of the ship with a freedom of mind which he had not experienced since his first meeting with Miss Standish. Yet, as night drew on, and he walked his two-mile promenade about the deck, he felt gathering about him a peculiar impression of aloneness. Something was missing. He did not acknowledge to himself what it was until, as if to convict him, he saw Mary Standish come out of the door leading from her cabin passageway, and stand alone at the rail of the ship. For a moment he hesitated, then quietly he came up beside her.

"It has been a wonderful day, Miss Standish," he said, "and Cordova is only a few hours ahead of us."

She scarcely turned her face and continued to look off into the shrouding darkness of the sea. "Yes, a wonderful day, Mr. Holt," she repeated after him, "and Cordova is only a few hours ahead." Then, in the same soft, unemotional voice, she added: "I want to thank you for last night. You brought me to a great decision."

"I fear I did not help you."

It may have been fancy of the gathering dusk, that made him believe he caught a shuddering movement of her slim shoulders.

"I thought there were two ways," she said, "but you made me see there was only *one*." She emphasized that word. It seemed to come with a little tremble in her voice. "I was foolish. But please let us forget. I want to think of pleasanter things. I am about to make a great experiment, and it takes all my courage."

"You will win, Miss Standish," he said in a sure voice. "In whatever you undertake you will win. I know it. If this experiment you speak of is the adventure of coming to Alaska--seeking your fortune--finding your life here--it will be glorious. I can assure you of that."

She was quiet for a moment, and then said:

"The unknown has always held a fascination for me. When we were under the mountains in Skagway yesterday, I almost told you of an odd faith which I have. I believe I have lived before, a long time ago, when America was very young. At times the feeling is so strong that I must have faith in it. Possibly I am foolish. But when the mountain swung back, like a great door, and we saw Skagway, I knew that sometime--somewhere--I had seen a thing like that before. And I have had strange visions of it. Maybe it is a touch of madness in me. But it is that faith which gives me courage to go on with my experiment. That--and *you*!"

Suddenly she faced him, her eyes flaming.

"You--and your suspicions and your brutality," she went on, her voice trembling a little as she drew herself up straight and tense before him. "I wasn't going to tell you, Mr. Holt. But you have given me the opportunity, and it may do you good--after tomorrow. I came to you because I foolishly misjudged you. I thought you were different, like your mountains. I made a great gamble, and set you up on a pedestal as clean and unafraid and believing all things good until you found them bad--and I lost. I was terribly mistaken. Your first thoughts of me when I came to your cabin were suspicious. You were angry and afraid. Yes, *afraid*--fearful of something happening which you didn't want to happen. You thought, almost, that I was unclean. And you believed I was a liar, and told me so. It wasn't fair, Mr. Holt. It wasn't *fair*. There were things which I couldn't explain to you, but I told you Rossland knew. I didn't keep everything back. And I believed you were big enough to think that I was not dishonoring you with my--friendship, even though I came to your cabin. Oh, I had that much faith in myself--I didn't think I would be mistaken for something unclean and lying!"

"Good God!" he cried. "Listen to me--Miss Standish--"

She was gone, so suddenly that his movement to intercept her was futile, and she passed through the door before he could reach her. Again he called her name, but her footsteps were almost running up the passageway. He dropped back, his blood cold, his hands clenched in the darkness, and his face as white as the girl's had been. Her words had held him stunned and mute. He saw himself stripped naked, as she believed him to be, and the thing gripped him with a sort of horror. And she was wrong. He had followed what he believed to be good judgment and common sense. If, in doing that, he had been an accursed fool--

Determinedly he started for her cabin, his mind set upon correcting her malformed judgment of him. There was no light coming under her door. When he knocked, there was no answer from within. He waited, and tried again, listening for a sound of movement. And each moment he waited he was readjusting himself. He was half glad, in the end, that the door did not open. He believed Miss Standish was inside, and she would undoubtedly accept the reason for his coming without an apology in words.

He went to his cabin, and his mind became increasingly persistent in its disapproval of the wrong viewpoint she had taken of him. He was not comfortable, no matter how he looked at the thing. For her clear eyes, her smoothly glorious hair, and the pride and courage with which she had faced him remained with him overpoweringly. He could not get away from the vision of her as she had stood against the door with tears like diamonds on her cheeks. Somewhere he had missed fire. He knew it. Something had escaped him which he could not understand. And she was holding him accountable.

The talk of the smoking-room did not interest him tonight. His efforts to become a part of it were forced. A jazzy concert of piano and string music in the social hall annoyed him, and a little later he watched the dancing with such grimness that someone remarked about it. He saw Rossland whirling round the floor with a handsome, young blonde in his arms. The girl was looking up into his eyes, smiling, and her cheek lay unashamed against his shoulder, while

Rossland's face rested against her fluffy hair when they mingled closely with the other dancers. Alan turned away, an unpleasant thought of Rossland's association with Mary Standish in his mind. He strolled down into the steerage. The Thlinkit people had shut themselves in with a curtain of blankets, and from the stillness he judged they were asleep. The evening passed slowly for him after that, until at last he went to his cabin and tried to interest himself in a book. It was something he had anticipated reading, but after a little he wondered if the writing was stupid, or if it was himself. The thrill he had always experienced with this particular writer was missing. There was no inspiration. The words were dead. Even the tobacco in his pipe seemed to lack something, and he changed it for a cigar--and chose another book. The result was the same. His mind refused to function, and there was no comfort in his cigar.

He knew he was fighting against a new thing, even as he subconsciously lied to himself. And he was obstinately determined to win. It was a fight between himself and Mary Standish as she had stood against his door. Mary Standish--the slim beauty of her--her courage--a score of things that had never touched his life before. He undressed and put on his smoking-gown and slippers, repudiating the honesty of the emotions that were struggling for acknowledgment within him. He was a bit mad and entirely a fool, he told himself. But the assurance did him no good.

He went to bed, propped himself up against his pillows, and made another effort to read. He half-heartedly succeeded. At ten o'clock music and dancing ceased, and stillness fell over the ship. After that he found himself becoming more interested in the first book he had started to read. His old satisfaction slowly returned to him. He relighted his cigar and enjoyed it. Distantly he heard the ship's bells, eleven o'clock, and after that the half-hour and midnight. The printed pages were growing dim, and drowsily he marked his book, placed it on the table, and yawned. They must be nearing Cordova. He could feel the slackened speed of the *Nome* and the softer throb of her engines. Probably they had passed Cape St. Elias and were drawing inshore.

And then, sudden and thrilling, came a woman's scream. A piercing cry of terror, of agony-- and of something else that froze the blood in his veins as he sprang from his berth. Twice it came, the second time ending in a moaning wail and a man's husky shout. Feet ran swiftly past his window. He heard another shout and then a voice of command. He could not distinguish the words, but the ship herself seemed to respond. There came the sudden smoothness of dead engines, followed by the pounding shock of reverse and the clanging alarm of a bell calling boats' crews to quarters.

Alan faced his cabin door. He knew what had happened. Someone was overboard. And in this moment all life and strength were gone out of his body, for the pale face of Mary Standish seemed to rise for an instant before him, and in her quiet voice she was telling him again that *this was the other way*. His face went white as he caught up his smoking-gown, flung open his door, and ran down the dimly lighted corridor.

CHAPTER IX

The reversing of the engines had not stopped the momentum of the ship when Alan reached the open deck. She was fighting, but still swept slowly ahead against the force struggling to hold her back. He heard running feet, voices, and the rattle of davit blocks, and came up as the starboard boat aft began swinging over the smooth sea. Captain Rifle was ahead of him, half-dressed, and the second officer was giving swift commands. A dozen passengers had come from the smoking-room. There was only one woman. She stood a little back, partly supported in a man's arms, her face buried in her hands. Alan looked at the man, and he knew from his appearance that she was the woman who had screamed.

He heard the splash of the boat as it struck water, and the rattle of oars, but the sound seemed a long distance away. Only one thing came to him distinctly in the sudden sickness that gripped him, and that was the terrible sobbing of the woman. He went to them, and the deck seemed to sway under his feet. He was conscious of a crowd gathering about the empty davits, but he had eyes only for these two.

"Was it a man--or a woman?" he asked.

It did not seem to him it was his voice speaking. The words were forced from his lips. And the other man, with the woman's head crumpled against his shoulder, looked into a face as emotionless as stone.

"A woman," he replied. "This is my wife. We were sitting here when she climbed upon the rail and leaped in. My wife screamed when she saw her going."

The woman raised her head. She was still sobbing, with no tears in her eyes, but only horror. Her hands were clenched about her husband's arm. She struggled to speak and failed, and the man bowed his head to comfort her. And then Captain Rifle stood at their side. His face was haggard, and a glance told Alan that he knew.

"Who was it?" he demanded.

"This lady thinks it was Miss Standish."

Alan did not move or speak. Something seemed to have gone wrong for a moment in his head. He could not hear distinctly the excitement behind him, and before him things were a blur. The sensation came and passed swiftly, with no sign of it in the immobility of his pale face.

"Yes, the girl at your table. The pretty girl. I saw her clearly, and then--then--"

It was the woman. The captain broke in, as she caught herself with a choking breath:

"It is possible you are mistaken. I can not believe Miss Standish would do that. We shall soon know. Two boats are gone, and a third lowering." He was hurrying away, throwing the last words over his shoulder.

Alan made no movement to follow. His brain cleared itself of shock, and a strange calmness began to possess him. "You are quite sure it was the girl at my table?" he found himself saying. "Is it possible you might be mistaken?"

"No," said the woman. "She was so quiet and pretty that I have noticed her often. I saw her clearly in the starlight. And she saw me just before she climbed to the rail and jumped. I'm almost sure she smiled at me and was going to speak. And then--then--she was gone!"

"I didn't know until my wife screamed," added the man. "I was seated facing her at the time. I ran to the rail and could see nothing behind but the wash of the ship. I think she went down instantly."

Alan turned. He thrust himself silently through a crowd of excited and questioning people, but he did not hear their questions and scarcely sensed the presence of their voices. His desire to make great haste had left him, and he walked calmly and deliberately to the cabin where Mary Standish would be if the woman was mistaken, and it was not she who had leaped into the sea. He knocked at the door only once. Then he opened it. There was no cry of fear or protest from within, and he knew the room was empty before he turned on the electric light. He had known it from the beginning, from the moment he heard the woman's scream. Mary Standish was gone.

He looked at her bed. There was the depression made by her head in the pillow. A little handkerchief lay on the coverlet, crumpled and twisted. Her few possessions were arranged neatly on the reading table. Then he saw her shoes and her stockings, and a dress on the bed, and he picked up one of the shoes and held it in a cold, steady hand. It was a little shoe. His fingers closed about it until it crushed like paper.

He was holding it when he heard someone behind him, and he turned slowly to confront Captain Rifle. The little man's face was like gray wax. For a moment neither of them spoke. Captain Rifle looked at the shoe crumpled in Alan's hand.

"The boats got away quickly," he said in a husky voice. "We stopped inside the third-mile. If she can swim--there is a chance."

"She won't swim," replied Alan. "She didn't jump in for that. She is gone."

In a vague and detached sort of way he was surprised at the calmness of his own voice. Captain Rifle saw the veins standing out on his clenched hands and in his forehead. Through many years he had witnessed tragedy of one kind and another. It was not strange to him. But a look of wonderment shot into his eyes at Alan's words. It took only a few seconds to tell what had happened the preceding night, without going into details. The captain's hand was on Alan's arm when he finished, and the flesh under his fingers was rigid and hard as steel.

"We'll talk with Rossland after the boats return," he said.

He drew Alan from the room and closed the door.

Not until he had reentered his own cabin did Alan realize he still held the crushed shoe in his hand. He placed it on his bed and dressed. It took him only a few minutes. Then he went aft and found the captain. Half an hour later the first boat returned. Five minutes after that, a second came in. And then a third. Alan stood back, alone, while the passengers crowded the rail. He knew what to expect. And the murmur of it came to him--failure! It was like a sob rising softly out of the throats of many people. He drew away. He did not want to meet their eyes, or talk with them, or hear the things they would be saying. And as he went, a moan came to his lips, a strangled cry filled with an agony which told him he was breaking down. He dreaded that. It was the first law of his kind to stand up under blows, and he fought against the desire to reach out his arms to the sea and entreat Mary Standish to rise up out of it and forgive him.

He drove himself on like a mechanical thing. His white face was a mask through which burned no sign of his grief, and in his eyes was a deadly coldness. Heartless, the woman who had screamed might have said. And she would have been right. His heart was gone.

Two people were at Rossland's door when he came up. One was Captain Rifle, the other Marston, the ship's doctor. The captain was knocking when Alan joined them. He tried the door. It was locked.

"I can't rouse him," he said. "And I did not see him among the passengers."

"Nor did I," said Alan.

Captain Rifle fumbled with his master key.

"I think the circumstances permit," he explained. In a moment he looked up, puzzled. "The door is locked on the inside, and the key is in the lock."

He pounded with his fist on the panel. He continued to pound until his knuckles were red. There was still no response.

"Odd," he muttered.

"Very odd," agreed Alan.

His shoulder was against the door. He drew back and with a single crash sent it in. A pale light filtered into the room from a corridor lamp, and the men stared. Rossland was in bed. They could see his face dimly, upturned, as if staring at the ceiling. But even now he made no movement and spoke no word. Marston entered and turned on the light.

After that, for ten seconds, no man moved. Then Alan heard Captain Rifle close the door behind them, and from Marston's lips came a startled whisper:

"Good God!"

Rossland was not covered. He was undressed and flat on his back. His arms were stretched out, his head thrown back, his mouth agape. And the white sheet under him was red with blood. It had trickled over the edges and to the floor. His eyes were loosely closed. After the first shock Doctor Marston reacted swiftly. He bent over Rossland, and in that moment, when his back was toward them, Captain Rifle's eyes met Alan's. The same thought--and in another instant disbelief--flashed from one to the other.

Marston was speaking, professionally cool now. "A knife stab, close to the right lung, if not in it. And an ugly bruise over his eye. He is not dead. Let him lie as he is until I return with instruments and dressing."

"The door was locked on the inside," said Alan, as soon as the doctor was gone. "And the window is closed. It looks like--suicide. It is possible--there was an understanding between them--and Rossland chose this way instead of the sea?"

Captain Rifle was on his knees. He looked under the berth, peered into the corners, and pulled back the blanket and sheet. "There is no knife," he said stonily. And in a moment he added: "There are red stains on the window. It was not attempted suicide. It was--"

"Murder."

"Yes, if Rossland dies. It was done through the open window. Someone called Rossland to the window, struck him, and then closed the window. Or it is possible, if he were sitting or standing here, that a long-armed man might have reached him. It was a man, Alan. We've got to believe that. It was a *man*."

"Of course, a man," Alan nodded.

They could hear Marston returning, and he was not alone. Captain Rifle made a gesture toward the door. "Better go," he advised. "This is a ship's matter, and you won't want to be unnecessarily mixed up in it. Come to my cabin in half an hour. I shall want to see you."

The second officer and the purser were with Doctor Marston when Alan passed them, and he heard the door of Rossland's room close behind him. The ship was trembling under his feet again. They were moving away. He went to Mary Standish's cabin and deliberately gathered her belongings and put them in the small hand-bag with which she had come aboard. Without any effort at concealment he carried the bag to his room and packed his own dunnage. After that he hunted up Stampede Smith and explained to him that an unexpected change in his plans compelled them to stop at Cordova. He was five minutes late in his appointment with the captain.

Captain Rifle was seated at his desk when Alan entered his cabin. He nodded toward a chair.

"We'll reach Cordova inside of an hour," he said. "Doctor Marston says Rossland will live, but of course we can not hold the *Nome* in port until he is able to talk. He was struck through the window. I will make oath to that. Have you anything--in mind?"

"Only one thing," replied Alan, "a determination to go ashore as soon as I can. If it is possible, I shall recover her body and care for it. As for Rossland, it is not a matter of importance to me whether he lives or dies. Mary Standish had nothing to do with the assault upon him. It was merely coincident with her own act and nothing more. Will you tell me our location when she leaped into the sea."

He was fighting to retain his calmness, his resolution not to let Captain Rifle see clearly what the tragedy of her death had meant to him.

"We were seven miles off the Eyak River coast, a little south and west. If her body goes ashore, it will be on the island, or the mainland east of Eyak River. I am glad you are going to make an effort. There is a chance. And I hope you will find her."

Captain Rifle rose from his chair and walked nervously back and forth. "It's a bad blow for the ship--her first trip," he said. "But I'm not thinking of the *Nome*. I'm thinking of Mary Standish. My God, it is terrible! If it had been anyone else--*anyone*--" His words seemed to choke him, and he made a despairing gesture with his hands. "It is hard to believe--almost impossible to believe she would deliberately kill herself. Tell me again what happened in your cabin."

Crushing all emotion out of his voice, Alan repeated briefly certain details of the girl's visit. But a number of things which she had trusted to his confidence he did not betray. He did not dwell upon Rossland's influence or her fear of him. Captain Rifle saw his effort, and when he had finished, he gripped his hand, understanding in his eyes.

"You're not responsible--not so much as you believe," he said. "Don't take it too much to heart, Alan. But find her. Find her if you can, and let me know. You will do that--you will let me know?"

"Yes, I shall let you know."

"And Rossland. He is a man with many enemies. I am positive his assailant is still on board."

"Undoubtedly."

The captain hesitated. He did not look at Alan as he said: "There is nothing in Miss Standish's room. Even her bag is gone. I thought I saw things in there when I was with you. I thought I saw something in your hand. But I must have been mistaken. She probably flung everything into the sea--before she went."

"Such a thought is possible," agreed Alan evasively.

Captain Rifle drummed the top of his desk with his finger-tips. His face looked haggard and old in the shaded light of the cabin. "That's all, Alan. God knows I'd give this old life of mine to bring her back if I could. To me she was much like--someone--a long time dead. That's why I broke ship's regulations when she came aboard so strangely at Seattle, without reservation. I'm sorry now. I should have sent her ashore. But she is gone, and it is best that you and I keep to ourselves a little of what we guess. I hope you will find her, and if you do--"

"I shall send you word."

They shook hands, and Captain Rifle's fingers still held to Alan's as they went to the door and opened it. A swift change had come in the sky. The stars were gone, and a moaning whisper hovered over the darkened sea.

"A thunder-storm," said the captain.

His mastery was gone, his shoulders bent, and there was a tremulous note in his voice that compelled Alan to look straight out into darkness. And then he said,

"Rossland will be sent to the hospital in Cordova, if he lives."

Alan made no answer. The door closed softly behind him, and slowly he went through gloom to the rail of the ship, and stood there, with the whispered moaning of the sea coming to him out of a pit of darkness. A vast distance away he heard a low intonation of thunder.

He struggled to keep hold of himself as he returned to his cabin. Stampede Smith was waiting for him, his dunnage packed in an oilskin bag. Alan explained the unexpected change in his plans. Business in Cordova would make him miss a boat and would delay him at least a month in reaching the tundras. It was necessary for Stampede to go on to the range alone. He could make a quick trip by way of the Government railroad to Tanana. After that he would go to Allakakat, and thence still farther north into the Endicott country. It would be easy for a man like Stampede to find the range. He drew a map, gave him certain written instructions, money, and a final warning not to lose his head and take up gold-hunting on the way. While it was necessary for him to go ashore at once, he advised Stampede not to leave the ship until morning. And Stampede swore on oath he would not fail him.

Alan did not explain his own haste and was glad Captain Rifle had not questioned him too closely. He was not analyzing the reasonableness of his action. He only knew that every muscle in his body was aching for physical action and that he must have it immediately or break. The desire was a touch of madness in his blood, a thing which he was holding back by sheer force of will. He tried to shut out the vision of a pale face floating in the sea; he fought to keep a grip on the dispassionate calmness which was a part of him. But the ship itself was battering down his stoic resistance. In an hour--since he had heard the scream of the woman--

he had come to hate it. He wanted the feel of solid earth under his feet. He wanted, with all his soul, to reach that narrow strip of coast where Mary Standish was drifting in.

But even Stampede saw no sign of the fire that was consuming him. And not until Alan's feet touched land, and Cordova lay before him like a great hole in the mountains, did the strain give way within him. After he had left the wharf, he stood alone in the darkness, breathing deeply of the mountain smell and getting his bearings. It was more than darkness about him. An occasional light burning dimly here and there gave to it the appearance of a sea of ink threatening to inundate him. The storm had not broken, but it was close, and the air was filled with a creeping warning. The moaning of thunder was low, and yet very near, as if smothered by the hand of a mighty force preparing to take the earth unaware.

Through the pit of gloom Alan made his way. He was not lost. Three years ago he had walked a score of times to the cabin of old Olaf Ericksen, half a mile up the shore, and he knew Ericksen would still be there, where he had squatted for twenty years, and where he had sworn to stay until the sea itself was ready to claim him. So he felt his way instinctively, while a crash of thunder broke over his head. The forces of the night were unleashing. He could hear a gathering tumult in the mountains hidden beyond the wall of blackness, and there came a sudden glare of lightning that illumined his way. It helped him. He saw a white reach of sand ahead and quickened his steps. And out of the sea he heard more distinctly an increasing sound. It was as if he walked between two great armies that were setting earth and sea atremble as they advanced to deadly combat.

The lightning came again, and after it followed a discharge of thunder that gave to the ground under his feet a shuddering tremor. It rolled away, echo upon echo, through the mountains, like the booming of signal-guns, each more distant than the other. A cold breath of air struck Alan in the face, and something inside him rose up to meet the thrill of storm.

He had always loved the rolling echoes of thunder in the mountains and the fire of lightning among their peaks. On such a night, with the crash of the elements about his father's cabin and the roaring voices of the ranges filling the darkness with tumult, his mother had brought him into the world. Love of it was in his blood, a part of his soul, and there were times when he yearned for this "talk of the mountains" as others yearn for the coming of spring. He welcomed it now as his eyes sought through the darkness for a glimmer of the light that always burned from dusk until dawn in Olaf Ericksen's cabin.

He saw it at last, a yellow eye peering at him through a slit in an inky wall. A moment later the darker shadow of the cabin rose up in his face, and a flash of lightning showed him the door. In a moment of silence he could hear the patter of huge raindrops on the roof as he dropped his bags and began hammering with his fist to arouse the Swede. Then he flung open the unlocked door and entered, tossing his dunnage to the floor, and shouted the old greeting that Ericksen would not have forgotten, though nearly a quarter of a century had passed since he and Alan's father had tramped the mountains together.

He had turned up the wick of the oil lamp on the table when into the frame of an inner door came Ericksen himself, with his huge, bent shoulders, his massive head, his fierce eyes, and a great gray beard streaming over his naked chest. He stared for a moment, and Alan flung off his hat, and as the storm broke, beating upon the cabin in a mighty shock of thunder and wind and rain, a bellow of recognition came from Ericksen. They gripped hands.

The Swede's voice rose above wind and rain and the rattle of loose windows, and he was saying something about three years ago and rubbing the sleep from his eyes, when the strange look in Alan's face made him pause to hear other words than his own.

Five minutes later he opened a door looking out over the black sea, bracing his arm against it. The wind tore in, beating his whitening beard over his shoulders, and with it came a deluge of rain that drenched him as he stood there. He forced the door shut and faced Alan, a great, gray ghost of a man in the yellow glow of the oil lamp.

From then until dawn they waited. And in the first break of that dawn the long, black launch of Olaf, the Swede, nosed its way steadily out to sea.

CHAPTER X

The wind had died away, but the rain continued, torrential in its downpour, and the mountains grumbled with dying thunder. The town was blotted out, and fifty feet ahead of the hissing nose of the launch Alan could see only a gray wall. Water ran in streams from his rubber slicker, and Olaf's great beard was dripping like a wet rag. He was like a huge gargoyle at the wheel, and in the face of impenetrable gloom he opened speed until the *Norden* was shooting with the swiftness of a torpedo through the sea.

In Olaf's cabin Alan had listened to the folly of expecting to find Mary Standish. Between Eyak River and Katalla was a mainland of battered reefs and rocks and an archipelago of islands in which a pirate fleet might have found a hundred hiding-places. In his experience of twenty years Ericksen had never known of the finding of a body washed ashore, and he stated firmly his belief that the girl was at the bottom of the sea. But the impulse to go on grew no less in Alan. It quickened with the straining eagerness of the *Norden* as the slim craft leaped through the water.

Even the drone of thunder and the beat of rain urged him on. To him there was nothing absurd in the quest he was about to make. It was the least he could do, and the only honest thing he could do, he kept telling himself. And there was a chance that he would find her. All through his life had run that element of chance; usually it was against odds he had won, and there rode with him in the gray dawn a conviction he was going to win now--that he would find Mary Standish somewhere in the sea or along the coast between Eyak River and the first of the islands against which the shoreward current drifted. And when he found her--

He had not gone beyond that. But it pressed upon him now, and in moments it overcame him, and he saw her in a way which he was fighting to keep out of his mind. Death had given a vivid clearness to his mental pictures of her. A strip of white beach persisted in his mind, and waiting for him on this beach was the slim body of the girl, her pale face turned up to the morning sun, her long hair streaming over the sand. It was a vision that choked him, and he struggled to keep away from it. If he found her like that, he knew, at last, what he would do. It was the final crumbling away of something inside him, the breaking down of that other Alan Holt whose negative laws and self-imposed blindness had sent Mary Standish to her death.

Truth seemed to mock at him, flaying him for that invulnerable poise in which he had taken such an egotistical pride. For she had come to *him* in her hour of trouble, and there were five hundred others aboard the *Nome*. She had believed in him, had given him her friendship and her confidence, and at the last had placed her life in his hands. And when he had failed her, she had not gone to another. She had kept her word, proving to him she was not a liar and a fraud, and he knew at last the courage of womanhood and the truth of her words, "You will understand--tomorrow."

He kept the fight within himself. Olaf did not see it as the dawn lightened swiftly into the beginning of day. There was no change in the tense lines of his face and the grim resolution in his eyes. And Olaf did not press his folly upon him, but kept the *Norden* pointed seaward, adding still greater speed as the huge shadow of the headland loomed up in the direction of Hinchinbrook Island. With increasing day the rain subsided; it fell in a drizzle for a time and then stopped. Alan threw off his slicker and wiped the water from his eyes and hair. White mists began to rise, and through them shot faint rose-gleams of light. Olaf grunted approbation as he wrung water from his beard. The sun was breaking through over the mountain tops, and straight above, as the mist dissolved, was radiant blue sky.

The miracle of change came swiftly in the next half-hour. Storm had washed the air until it was like tonic; a salty perfume rose from the sea; and Olaf stood up and stretched himself and shook the wet from his body as he drank the sweetness into his lungs. Shoreward Alan saw the mountains taking form, and one after another they rose up like living things, their crests catching the fire of the sun. Dark inundations of forest took up the shimmering gleam, green slopes rolled out from behind veils of smoking vapor, and suddenly--in a final triumph of the sun--the Alaskan coast lay before him in all its glory.

The Swede made a great gesture of exultation with his free arm, grinning at his companion, pride and the joy of living in his bearded face. But in Alan's there was no change. Dully he sensed the wonder of day and of sunlight breaking over the mighty ranges to the sea, but something was missing. The soul of it was gone, and the old thrill was dead. He felt the tragedy of it, and his lips tightened even as he met the other's smile, for he no longer made an effort to blind himself to the truth.

Olaf began to guess deeply at that truth, now that he could see Alan's face in the pitiless light of the day, and after a little the thing lay naked in his mind. The quest was not a matter of duty, nor was it inspired by the captain of the *Nome*, as Alan had given him reason to believe. There was more than grimness in the other's face, and a strange sort of sickness lay in his eyes. A little later he observed the straining eagerness with which those eyes scanned the softly undulating surface of the sea.

At last he said, "If Captain Rifle was right, the girl went overboard *out there*," and he pointed. Alan stood up.

"But she wouldn't be there now," Olaf added.

In his heart he believed she was, straight down--at the bottom. He turned his boat shoreward. Creeping out from the shadow of the mountains was the white sand of the beach three or four miles away. A quarter of an hour later a spiral of smoke detached itself from the rocks and timber that came down close to the sea.

"That's McCormick's," he said.

Alan made no answer. Through Olaf's binoculars he picked out the Scotchman's cabin. It was Sandy McCormick, Olaf had assured him, who knew every eddy and drift in fifty miles of coast, and with his eyes shut could find Mary Standish if she came ashore. And it was Sandy who came down to greet them when Ericksen dropped his anchor in shallow water.

They leaped out, thigh-deep, and waded to the beach, and in the door of the cabin beyond Alan saw a woman looking down at them wonderingly. Sandy himself was young and ruddy-faced, more like a boy than a man. They shook hands. Then Alan told of the tragedy aboard the *Nome* and what his mission was. He made a great effort to speak calmly, and believed that he succeeded. Certainly there was no break of emotion in his cold, even voice, and at the same time no possibility of evading its deadly earnestness. McCormick, whose means of livelihood were frequently more unsubstantial than real, listened to the offer of pecuniary reward for his services with something like shock. Fifty dollars a day for his time, and an additional five thousand dollars if he found the girl's body.

To Alan the sums meant nothing. He was not measuring dollars, and if he had said ten thousand or twenty thousand, the detail of price would not have impressed him as important. He possessed as much money as that in the Nome banks, and a little more, and had the thing been practicable he would as willingly have offered his reindeer herds could they have guaranteed him the possession of what he sought. In Olaf's face McCormick caught a look which explained the situation a little. Alan Holt was not mad. He was as any other man might be who had lost the most precious thing in the world. And unconsciously, as he pledged his services in acceptance of the offer, he glanced in the direction of the little woman standing in the doorway of the cabin.

Alan met her. She was a quiet, sweet-looking girl-woman. She smiled gravely at Olaf, gave her hand to Alan, and her blue eyes dilated when she heard what had happened aboard the *Nome*. Alan left the three together and returned to the beach, while between the loading and the lighting of his pipe the Swede told what he had guessed--that this girl whose body would never be washed ashore was the beginning and the end of the world to Alan Holt.

For many miles they searched the beach that day, while Sandy McCormick skirmished among the islands south and eastward in a light shore-launch. He was, in a way, a Paul Revere spreading intelligence, and with Scotch canniness made a good bargain for himself. In a dozen cabins he left details of the drowning and offered a reward of five hundred dollars for the finding of the body, so that twenty men and boys and half as many women were seeking before nightfall.

"And remember," Sandy told each of them, "the chances are she'll wash ashore sometime between tomorrow and three days later, if she comes ashore at all."

In the dusk of that first day Alan found himself ten miles up the coast. He was alone, for Olaf Ericksen had gone in the opposite direction. It was a different Alan who watched the setting sun dipping into the western sea, with the golden slopes of the mountains reflecting its glory behind him. It was as if he had passed through a great sickness, and up from the earth of his own beloved land had crept slowly into his body and soul a new understanding of life. There was despair in his face, but it was a gentler thing now. The harsh lines of an obstinate will were gone from about his mouth, his eyes no longer concealed their grief, and there was something in his attitude of a man chastened by a consuming fire. He retraced his steps through deepening twilight, and with each mile of his questing return there grew in him that something which had come to him out of death, and which he knew would never leave him. And with this change the droning softness of the night itself seemed to whisper that the sea would not give up its dead.

Olaf and Sandy McCormick and Sandy's wife were in the cabin when he returned at midnight. He was exhausted. Seven months in the States had softened him, he explained. He did not inquire how successful the others had been. He knew. The woman's eyes told him, the almost mothering eagerness in them when he came through the door. She had coffee and food ready for him, and he forced himself to eat. Sandy gave a report of what he had done, and Olaf smoked his pipe and tried to speak cheerfully of the splendid weather that was coming tomorrow. Not one of them spoke of Mary Standish.

Alan felt the strain they were under and knew his presence was the cause of it, so he lighted his own pipe after eating and talked to Ellen McCormick about the splendor of the mountains back of Eyak River, and how fortunate she was to have her home in this little corner of paradise. He caught a flash of something unspoken in her eyes. It was a lonely place for a woman, alone, without children, and he spoke about children to Sandy, smiling. They should have children--a lot of them. Sandy blushed, and Olaf let out a boom of laughter. But the woman's face was unflushed and serious; only her eyes betrayed her, something wistful and appealing in them as she looked at Sandy.

"We're building a new cabin," he said, "and there's two rooms in it specially for kids."

There was pride in his voice as he made pretense to light a pipe that was already lighted, and pride in the look he gave his young wife. A moment later Ellen McCormick deftly covered with her apron something which lay on a little table near the door through which Alan had to pass to enter his sleeping-room. Olaf's eyes twinkled. But Alan did not see. Only he knew there should be children here, where there was surely love. It did not occur to him as being strange that he, Alan Holt, should think of such a matter at all.

The next morning the search was resumed. Sandy drew a crude map of certain hidden places up the east coast where drifts and cross-currents tossed the flotsam of the sea, and Alan set out for these shores with Olaf at the wheel of the *Norden*. It was sunset when they returned, and in the calm of a wonderful evening, with the comforting peace of the mountains smiling down at them, Olaf believed the time had come to speak what was in his mind. He spoke first of the weird tricks of the Alaskan waters, and of strange forces deep down under the surface which he had never had explained to him, and of how he had lost a cask once upon a time, and a week later had run upon it well upon its way to Japan. He emphasized the hide-and-seek playfulness of the undertows and the treachery of them.

Then he came bluntly to the point of the matter. It would be better if Mary Standish never did come ashore. It would be days--probably weeks--if it ever happened at all, and there would be nothing about her for Alan to recognize. Better a peaceful resting-place at the bottom of the sea. That was what he called it--"a peaceful resting-place"--and in his earnestness to soothe another's grief he blundered still more deeply into the horror of it all, describing certain details of what flesh and bone could and could not stand, until Alan felt like clubbing him beyond the power of speech. He was glad when he saw the McCormick cabin.

Sandy was waiting for them when they waded ashore. Something unusual was in his face, Alan thought, and for a moment his heart waited in suspense. But the Scotchman shook his head negatively and went close to Olaf Ericksen. Alan did not see the look that passed between them. He went to the cabin, and Ellen McCormick put a hand on his arm when he entered. It was an unusual thing for her to do. And there was a glow in her eyes which had not been there last night, and a flush in her cheeks, and a new, strange note in her voice when she spoke to him. It was almost exultation, something she was trying to keep back.

"You--you didn't find her?" she asked.

"No." His voice was tired and a little old. "Do you think I shall ever find her?"

"Not as you have expected," she answered quietly. "She will never come like that." She seemed to be making an effort. "You--you would give a great deal to have her back, Mr. Holt?"

Her question was childish in its absurdity, and she was like a child looking at him as she did in this moment. He forced a smile to his lips and nodded.

"Of course. Everything I possess."

"You--you--loved her--"

Her voice trembled. It was odd she should ask these questions. But the probing did not sting him; it was not a woman's curiosity that inspired them, and the comforting softness in her voice did him good. He had not realized before how much he wanted to answer that question, not only for himself, but for someone else--aloud.

"Yes, I did."

The confession almost startled him. It seemed an amazing confidence to be making under any circumstances, and especially upon such brief acquaintance. But he said no more, though in Ellen McCormick's face and eyes was a tremulous expectancy. He stepped into the little room which had been his sleeping place, and returned with his dunnage-sack. Out of this he took the bag in which were Mary Standish's belongings, and gave it to Sandy's wife. It was a matter of business now, and he tried to speak in a businesslike way.

"Her things are inside. I got them in her cabin. If you find her, after I am gone, you will need them. You understand, of course. And if you don't find her, keep them for me. I shall return some day." It seemed hard for him to give his simple instructions. He went on: "I don't think I shall stay any longer, but I will leave a certified check at Cordova, and it will be turned over to your husband when she is found. And if you do find her, you will look after her yourself, won't you, Mrs. McCormick?"

Ellen McCormick choked a little as she answered him, promising to do what he asked. He would always remember her as a sympathetic little thing, and half an hour later, after he had explained everything to Sandy, he wished her happiness when he took her hand in saying good-by. Her hand was trembling. He wondered at it and said something to Sandy about the priceless value of a happiness such as his, as they went down to the beach.

The velvety darkness of the sky was athrob with the heart-beat of stars, when the *Norden's* shimmering trail led once more out to sea. Alan looked up at them, and his mind groped strangely in the infinity that lay above him. He had never measured it before. Life had been too full. But now it seemed so vast, and his range in the tundras so far away, that a great loneliness seized upon him as he turned his eyes to look back at the dimly white shore-line dissolving swiftly in the gloom that lay beneath the mountains.

CHAPTER XI

That night, in Olaf's cabin, Alan put himself back on the old track again. He made no effort to minimize the tragedy that had come into his life, and he knew its effect upon him would never be wiped away, and that Mary Standish would always live in his thoughts, no matter what happened in the years to come. But he was not the sort to let any part of himself wither up and die because of a blow that had darkened his mental visions of things. His plans lay ahead of him, his old ambitions and his dreams of achievement. They seemed pulseless and dead now, but he knew it was because his own fire had temporarily burned out. And he realized the vital necessity of building it up again. So he first wrote a letter to Ellen McCormick, and in this placed a second letter--carefully sealed--which was not to be opened unless they found Mary Standish, and which contained something he had found impossible to put into words in Sandy's cabin. It was trivial and embarrassing when spoken to others, but it meant a great deal to him. Then he made the final arrangements for Olaf to carry him to Seward in the *Norden*, for Captain Rifle's ship was well on her way to Unalaska. Thought of Captain Rifle urged him to write another letter in which he told briefly the disappointing details of his search.

He was rather surprised the next morning to find he had entirely forgotten Rossland. While he was attending to his affairs at the bank, Olaf secured information that Rossland was resting comfortably in the hospital and had not one chance in ten of dying. It was not Alan's intention to see him. He wanted to hear nothing he might have to say about Mary Standish. To associate them in any way, as he thought of her now, was little short of sacrilege. He was conscious of the change in himself, for it was rather an amazing upsetting of the original Alan Holt. That person would have gone to Rossland with the deliberate and businesslike intention of sifting the matter to the bottom that he might disprove his own responsibility and set himself right in his own eyes. In self-defense he would have given Rossland an opportunity to break down with cold facts the disturbing something which his mind had unconsciously built up. But the new Alan revolted. He wanted to carry the thing away with him, he wanted it to live, and so it went with him, uncontaminated by any truths or lies which Rossland might have told him.

They left Cordova early in the afternoon, and at sunset that evening camped on the tip of a wooded island a mile or two from the mainland. Olaf knew the island and had chosen it for reasons of his own. It was primitive and alive with birds. Olaf loved the birds, and the cheer of their vesper song and bedtime twitter comforted Alan. He seized an ax, and for the first time in seven months his muscles responded to the swing of it. And Ericksen, old as his years in the way of the north, whistled loudly and rumbled a bit of crude song through his beard as he lighted a fire, knowing the medicine of the big open was getting its hold on Alan again. To Alan it was like coming to the edge of home once more. It seemed an age, an infinity, since he had heard the sputtering of bacon in an open skillet and the bubbling of coffee over a bed of coals with the mysterious darkness of the timber gathering in about him. He loaded his pipe after his chopping, and sat watching Olaf as he mothered the half-baked bannock loaf. It made him think of his father. A thousand times the two must have camped like this in the days when Alaska was new and there were no maps to tell them what lay beyond the next range.

Olaf felt resting upon him something of the responsibility of a doctor, and after supper he sat with his back to a tree and talked of the old days as if they were yesterday and the day before, with tomorrow always the pot of gold at the end of the rainbow which he had pursued for thirty years. He was sixty just a week ago this evening, he said, and he was beginning to doubt if he would remain on the beach at Cordova much longer. Siberia was dragging him--that forbidden world of adventure and mystery and monumental opportunity which lay only a few miles across the strait from the Seward Peninsula. In his enthusiasm he forgot Alan's tragedy. He cursed Cossack law and the prohibitory measures to keep Americans out. More gold was over there than had ever been dreamed of in Alaska; even the mountains and rivers were unnamed; and he was going if he lived another year or two--going to find his fortune or his end in the Stanovoi Mountains and among the Chukchi tribes. Twice he had tried it since his old comrade had died, and twice he had been driven out. The next time he would know how to go about it, and he invited Alan to go with him.

There was a thrill in this talk of a land so near, scarcely a night ride across the neck of Bering Sea, and yet as proscribed as the sacred plains of Tibet. It stirred old desires in Alan's blood, for he knew that of all frontiers the Siberian would be the last and the greatest, and that not only men, but nations, would play their part in the breaking of it. He saw the red gleam of firelight in Olaf's eyes.

"And if we don't go in first from *this side*, Alan, the yellow fellows will come out some day from *that,*" rumbled the old sour-dough, striking his pipe in the hollow of his hand. "And when they do, they won't come over to us in ones an' twos an' threes, but in millions. That's what the yellow fellows will do when they once get started, an' it's up to a few Alaska Jacks an' Tough-Nut Bills to get their feet planted first on the other side. Will you go?"

Alan shook his head. "Some day--but not now." The old flash was in his eyes and he was seeing the fight ahead of him again--the fight to do his bit in striking the shackles of misgovernment from Alaska and rousing the world to an understanding of the menace which hung over her like a smoldering cloud. "But you're right about the danger," he said. "It won't come from Japan to California. It will pour like a flood through Siberia and jump to Alaska in a night. It isn't the danger of the yellow man alone, Olaf. You've got to combine that with Bolshevism, the menace of blackest Russia. A disease which, if it crosses the little neck of water and gets hold of Alaska, will shake the American continent to bed-rock. It may be a generation from now, maybe a century, but it's coming sure as God makes light--if we let Alaska go down and out. And my way of preventing it is different from yours."

He stared into the fire, watching the embers flare up and die. "I'm not proud of the States," he went on, as if speaking to something which he saw in the flames. "I can't be, after the ruin their unintelligent propaganda and legislation have brought upon Alaska. But they're our salvation and conditions are improving. I concede we have factions in Alaska and we are not at all unanimous in what we want. It's going to be largely a matter of education. We can't take Alaska down to the States--we've got to bring them up to us. We must make a large part of a hundred and ten million Americans understand. We must bring a million of them up here before that danger-flood we speak of comes beyond the Gulf of Anadyr. It's God's own country we have north of Fifty-eight, Olaf. And we have ten times the wealth of California. We can care for a million people easily. But bad politics and bad judgment both here in Alaska and at Washington won't let them come. With coal enough under our feet to last a thousand years, we are buying fuel from the States. We've got billions in copper and oil, but can't touch them. We should have some of the world's greatest manufacturing plants, but we can not, because everything up here is locked away from us. I repeat that isn't conservation. If they had applied a little of it to the salmon industry--but they didn't. And the salmon are going, like the buffalo of the plains.

"The destruction of the salmon shows what will happen to us if the bars are let down all at once to the financial banditti. Understanding and common sense must guard the gates. The fight we must win is to bring about an honest and reasonable adjustment, Olaf. And that fight will take place right here--in Alaska--and not in Siberia. And if we don't win--"

He raised his eyes from the fire and smiled grimly into Olaf's bearded face.

"Then we can count on that thing coming across the neck of sea from the Gulf of Anadyr," he finished. "And if it ever does come, the people of the States will at last face the tragic realization of what Alaska could have meant to the nation."

The force of the old spirit surged uppermost in Alan again, and after that, for an hour or more, something lived for him in the glow of the fire which Olaf kept burning. It was the memory of Mary Standish, her quiet, beautiful eyes gazing at him, her pale face taking form in the lacy wisps of birch-smoke. His mind pictured her in the flame-glow as she had listened to him that day in Skagway, when he had told her of this fight that was ahead. And it pleased him to think she would have made this same fight for Alaska if she had lived. It was a thought which brought a painful thickening in his breath, for always these visions which Olaf could not see ended with Mary Standish as she had faced him in his cabin, her back against the door, her lips trembling, and her eyes softly radiant with tears in the broken pride of that last moment of her plea for life.

He could not have told how long he slept that night. Dreams came to him in his restless slumber, and always they awakened him, so that he was looking at the stars again and trying not to think. In spite of the grief in his soul they were pleasant dreams, as though some gentle force were at work in him subconsciously to wipe away the shadows of tragedy. Mary Standish was with him again, between the mountains at Skagway; she was at his side in the heart of the tundras, the sun in her shining hair and eyes, and all about them the wonder of wild roses and purple iris and white seas of sedge-cotton and yellow-eyed daisies, and birds singing in the gladness of summer. He heard the birds. And he heard the girl's voice, answering them in her happiness and turning that happiness from the radiance of her eyes upon him. When he awoke, it was with a little cry, as if someone had stabbed him; and Olaf was building a fire, and dawn was breaking in rose-gleams over the mountains.

CHAPTER XII

This first night and dawn in the heard of his wilderness, with the new import of life gleaming down at him from the mighty peaks of the Chugach and Kenai ranges, marked the beginning of that uplift which drew Alan out of the pit into which he had fallen. He understood, now, how it was that through many long years his father had worshiped the memory of a woman who had died, it seemed to him, an infinity ago. Unnumbered times he had seen the miracle of her presence in his father's eyes, and once, when they had stood overlooking a sun-filled valley back in the mountains, the elder Holt had said:

"Twenty-seven years ago the twelfth day of last month, mother went with me through this valley, Alan. Do you see the little bend in the creek, with the great rock in the sun? We rested there--before you were born!"

He had spoken of that day as if it had been but yesterday. And Alan recalled the strange happiness in his father's face as he had looked down upon something in the valley which no other but himself could see.

And it was happiness, the same strange, soul-aching happiness, that began to build itself a house close up against the grief in Alan's heart. It would never be a house quite empty. Never again would he be alone. He knew at last it was an undying part of him, as it had been a part of his father, clinging to him in sweet pain, encouraging him, pressing gently upon him the beginning of a great faith that somewhere beyond was a place to meet again. In the many days that followed, it grew in him, but in a way no man or woman could see. It was a secret about which he built a wall, setting it apart from that stoical placidity of his nature which some people called indifference. Olaf could see farther than others, because he had known Alan's father as a brother. It had always been that way with the elder Holt--straight, clean, deep-breathing, and with a smile on his lips in times of hurt. Olaf had seen him face death like that. He had seen him rise up with awesome courage from the beautiful form that had turned to clay under his eyes, and fight forth again into a world burned to ashes. Something of that look which he had seen in the eyes of the father he saw in Alan's, in these days when they nosed their way up the Alaskan coast together. Only to himself did Alan speak the name of Mary Standish, just as his father had kept Elizabeth Holt's name sacred in his own heart. Olaf, with mildly casual eyes and strong in the possession of memories, observed how much alike they were, but discretion held his tongue, and he said nothing to Alan of many things that ran in his mind.

He talked of Siberia--always of Siberia, and did not hurry on the way to Seward. Alan himself felt no great urge to make haste. The days were soft with the premature breath of summer. The nights were cold, and filled with stars. Day after day mountains hung about them like mighty castles whose battlements reached up into the cloud-draperies of the sky. They kept close to the mainland and among the islands, camping early each evening. Birds were coming northward by the thousand, and each night Olaf's camp-fire sent up the delicious aroma of flesh-pots and roasts. When at last they reached Seward, and the time came for Olaf to turn back, there was an odd blinking in the old Swede's eyes, and as a final comfort Alan told him again that the day would probably come when he would go to Siberia with him. After that, he watched the *Norden* until the little boat was lost in the distance of the sea.

Alone, Alan felt once more a greater desire to reach his own country. And he was fortunate. Two days after his arrival at Seward the steamer which carried mail and the necessities of life to the string of settlements reaching a thousand miles out into the Pacific left Resurrection Bay, and he was given passage. Thereafter the countless islands of the North Pacific drifted behind, while always northward were the gray cliffs of the Alaskan Peninsula, with the ramparted ranges beyond, glistening with glaciers, smoking with occasional volcanoes, and at times so high their snowy peaks were lost in the clouds. First touching the hatchery at Karluk and then the canneries at Uyak and Chignik, the mail boat visited the settlements on the Island of Unga, and thence covered swiftly the three hundred miles to Dutch Harbor and Unalaska. Again he was fortunate. Within a week he was berthed on a freighter, and on the twelfth day of June set foot in Nome.

His home-coming was unheralded, but the little, gray town, with its peculiar, black shadowings, its sea of stove-pipes, and its two solitary brick chimneys, brought a lump of joy into his throat as he watched its growing outlines from the small boat that brought him ashore. He could see one of the only two brick chimneys in northern Alaska gleaming in the sun; beyond it, fifty miles away, were the ragged peaks of the Saw-Tooth Range, looking as if one might walk to them in half an hour, and over all the world between seemed to hover a misty gloom. But it was where he had lived, where happiness and tragedy and unforgetable memories had come to him, and the welcoming of its frame buildings, its crooked streets, and what to others might have been ugliness, was a warm and thrilling thing. For here were his *people*. Here were the men and women who were guarding the northern door of the world, an epic place, filled with strong hearts, courage, and a love of country as inextinguishable as one's love of life. From this drab little place, shut out from all the world for half the year, young men and women went down to southern universities, to big cities, to the glamor and lure of "outside." But they always came back. Nome called them. Its loneliness in winter. Its gray gloom in springtime. Its glory in summer and autumn. It was the breeding-place of a new race of men, and they loved it as Alan loved it. To him the black wireless tower meant more than the Statue of Liberty, the three weather-beaten church spires more than the architectural colossi of New York and Washington. Beside one of the churches he had played as a boy. He had seen the steeples painted. He had helped make the crooked streets. And his mother had laughed and lived and died here, and his father's footprints had been in the white sands of the beach when tents dotted the shore like gulls.

When he stepped ashore, people stared at him and then greeted him. He was unexpected. And the surprise of his arrival added strength to the grip which men's hands gave him. He had not heard voices like theirs down in the States, with a gladness in them that was almost excitement. Small boys ran up to his side, and with white men came the Eskimo, grinning and shaking his hands. Word traveled swiftly that Alan Holt had come back from the States. Before the day was over, it was on its way to Shelton and Candle and Keewalik and Kotzebue Sound. Such was the beginning of his home-coming. But ahead of the news of his arrival Alan walked up Front Street, stopped at Bahlke's restaurant for a cup of coffee, and then dropped casually into Lomen's offices in the Tin Bank Building.

For a week Alan remained in Nome. Carl Lomen had arrived a few days before, and his brothers were "in" from the big ranges over on the Choris Peninsula. It had been a good winter and promised to be a tremendously successful summer. The Lomen herds would exceed forty thousand head, when the final figures were in. A hundred other herds were prospering, and the Eskimo and Lapps were full-cheeked and plump with good feeding and prosperity. A third of a million reindeer were on the hoof in Alaska, and the breeders were exultant. Pretty good, when compared with the fact that in 1902 there were less than five thousand! In another twenty years there would be ten million.

But with this prosperity of the present and still greater promise for the future Alan sensed the undercurrent of unrest and suspicion in Nome. After waiting and hoping through another long winter, with their best men fighting for Alaska's salvation at Washington, word was traveling from mouth to mouth, from settlement to settlement, and from range to range, that the Bureaucracy which misgoverned them from thousands of miles away was not lifting a hand to relieve them. Federal office-holders refused to surrender their deadly power, and their strangling methods were to continue. Coal, which should cost ten dollars a ton if dug from Alaskan mines, would continue to cost forty dollars; cold storage from Nome would continue to be fifty-two dollars a ton, when it should be twenty. Commercial brigandage was still given letters of marque. Bureaus were fighting among themselves for greater power, and in the turmoil Alaska was still chained like a starving man just outside the reach of all the milk and honey in a wonderful land. Pauperizing, degrading, actually killing, the political misrule that had already driven 25 per cent of Alaska's population from their homes was to continue indefinitely. A President of the United States had promised to visit the mighty land of the north and see with his own eyes. But would he come? There had been other promises, many of them, and promises had always been futile. But it was a hope that crept through Alaska, and upon this hope men whose courage never died began to build. Freedom was on its way, even if slowly. Justice must triumph ultimately, as it always triumphed. Rusty keys would at last be turned in the locks which had kept from Alaskans all the riches and resources of their country, and these men were determined to go on building against odds that they might be better prepared for that freedom of human endeavor when it came.

In these days, when the fires of achievement needed to be encouraged, and not smothered, neither Alan nor Carl Lomen emphasized the menace of gigantic financial interests like that controlled by John Graham--interests fighting to do away with the best friend Alaska ever had, the Biological Survey, and backing with all their power the ruinous legislation to put Alaska in the control of a group of five men that an aggrandizement even more deadly than a suffocating policy of conservation might be more easily accomplished. Instead, they spread the optimism of men possessed of inextinguishable faith. The blackest days were gone. Rifts were breaking in the clouds. Intelligence was creeping through, like rays of sunshine. The end of Alaska's serfdom was near at hand. So they preached, and knew they were preaching truth, for what remained of Alaska's men after years of hopelessness and distress were fighting men. And the women who had remained with them were the mothers and wives of a new nation in the making.

These mothers and wives Alan met during his week in Nome. He would have given his life if a few million people in the States could have known these women. Something would have happened then, and the sisterhood of half a continent--possessing the power of the ballot-- would have opened their arms to them. Men like John Graham would have gone out of existence; Alaska would have received her birthright. For these women were of the kind who greeted the sun each day, and the gloom of winter, with something greater than hope in their hearts. They, too, were builders. Fear of God and love of land lay deep in their souls, and side by side with their men-folk they went on in this epic struggle for the building of a nation at the top of the world.

Many times during this week Alan felt it in his heart to speak of Mary Standish. But in the end, not even to Carl Lomen did word of her escape his lips. The passing of each day had made her more intimately a part of him, and a secret part. He could not tell people about her. He even made evasions when questioned about his business and experiences at Cordova and up the coast. Curiously, she seemed nearer to him when he was away from other men and women. He remembered it had been that way with his father, who was always happiest when in the deep mountains or the unending tundras. And so Alan thrilled with an inner gladness when his business was finished and the day came for him to leave Nome.

Carl Lomen went with him as far as the big herd on Choris Peninsula. For one hundred miles, up to Shelton, they rode over a narrow-gauge, four-foot railway on a hand-car drawn by dogs. And it seemed to Alan, at times, as though Mary Standish were with him, riding in this strange way through a great wilderness. He could *see* her. That was the strange thing which began to possess him. There were moments when her eyes were shining softly upon him, her lips smiling, her presence so real he might have spoken to her if Lomen had not been at his side. He did not fight against these visionings. It pleased him to think of her going with him into the heart of Alaska, riding the picturesque "pup-mobile," losing herself in the mountains and in his tundras, with all the wonder and glory of a new world breaking upon her a little at a time, like the unfolding of a great mystery. For there was both wonder and glory in these countless miles running ahead and drifting behind, and the miracle of northward-sweeping life. The days were long. Night, as Mary Standish had always known night, was gone. On the twentieth of June there were twenty hours of day, with a dim and beautiful twilight between the hours of eleven and one. Sleep was no longer a matter of the rising and setting of the sun, but was regulated by the hands of the watch. A world frozen to the core for seven months was bursting open like a great flower.

From Shelton, Alan and his companion visited the eighty or ninety people at Candle, and thence continued down the Keewalik River to Keewalik, on Kotzebue Sound. A Lomen power-boat, run by Lapps, carried them to Choris Peninsula, where for a week Alan remained with Lomen and his huge herd of fifteen thousand reindeer. He was eager to go on, but tried to hide his impatience. Something was urging him, whipping him on to greater haste. For the first time in months he heard the crackling thunder of reindeer hoofs, and the music of it was like a wild call from his own herds hurrying him home. He was glad when the week-end came and his business was done. The power-boat took him to Kotzebue. It was night, as his watch went, when Paul Davidovich started up the delta of the Kobuk River with him in a lighterage company's boat. But there was no darkness. In the afternoon of the fourth day they came to the Redstone, two hundred miles above the mouth of the Kobuk as the river winds. They had supper together on the shore. After that Paul Davidovich turned back with the slow sweep of the current, waving his hand until he was out of sight.

Not until the sound of the Russian's motor-boat was lost in distance did Alan sense fully the immensity of the freedom that swept upon him. At last, after months that had seemed like so many years, he was *alone*. North and eastward stretched the unmarked trail which he knew so well, a hundred and fifty miles straight as a bird might fly, almost unmapped, unpeopled, right up to the doors of his range in the slopes of the Endicott Mountains. A little cry from his own lips gave him a start. It was as if he had called out aloud to Tautuk and Amuk Toolik, and to Keok and Nawadlook, telling them he was on his way home and would soon be there. Never had this hidden land which he had found for himself seemed so desirable as it did in this hour. There was something about it that was all-mothering, all-good, all-sweetly-comforting to that other thing which had become a part of him now. It was holding out its arms to him, understanding, welcoming, inspiring him to travel strongly and swiftly the space between. And he was ready to answer its call.

He looked at his watch. It was five o'clock in the afternoon. He had spent a long day with the Russian, but he felt no desire for rest or sleep. The musk-tang of the tundras, coming to him through the thin timber of the river-courses, worked like an intoxicant in his blood. It was the tundra he wanted, before he lay down upon his back with his face to the stars. He was eager to get away from timber and to feel the immeasurable space of the big country, the open country, about him. What fool had given to it the name of *Barren Lands*? What idiots people were to lie about it in that way on the maps! He strapped his pack over his shoulders and seized his rifle. Barren Lands!

He set out, walking like a man in a race. And long before the twilight hours of sleep they were sweeping out ahead of him in all their glory--the Barren Lands of the map-makers, *his* paradise. On a knoll he stood in the golden sun and looked about him. He set his pack down and stood with bared head, a whispering of cool wind in his hair. If Mary Standish could have lived to see *this*! He stretched out his arms, as if pointing for her eyes to follow, and her name was in his heart and whispering on his silent lips. Immeasurable the tundras reached ahead of him--rolling, sweeping, treeless, green and golden and a glory of flowers, athrill with a life no forest land had ever known. Under his feet was a crush of forget-me-nots and of white and purple violets, their sweet perfume filling his lungs as he breathed. Ahead of him lay a white sea of yellow-eyed daisies, with purple iris high as his knees in between, and as far as he could see, waving softly in the breeze, was the cotton-tufted sedge he loved. The pods were green. In a few days they would be opening, and the tundras would be white carpets.

He listened to the call of life. It was about him everywhere, a melody of bird-life subdued and sleepy even though the sun was still warmly aglow in the sky. A hundred times he had watched this miracle of bird instinct, the going-to-bed of feathered creatures in the weeks and months when there was no real night. He picked up his pack and went on. From a pool hidden in the lush grasses of a distant hollow came to him the twilight honking of nesting geese and the quacking content of wild ducks. He heard the reed-like, musical notes of a lone "organ-duck" and the plaintive cries of plover, and farther out, where the shadows seemed deepening against the rim of the horizon, rose the harsh, rolling notes of cranes and the raucous cries of the loons. And then, from a clump of willows near him, came the chirping twitter of a thrush whose throat was tired for the day, and the sweet, sleepy evening song of a robin. *Night!* Alan laughed softly, the pale flush of the sun in his face. *Bedtime!* He looked at his watch.

It was nine o'clock. Nine o'clock, and the flowers still answering to the glow of the sun! And the people down there--in the States--called it a frozen land, a hell of ice and snow at the end of the earth, a place of the survival of the fittest! Well, to just such extremes had stupidity and ignorance gone through all the years of history, even though men called themselves super-creatures of intelligence and knowledge. It was humorous. And it was tragic.

At last he came to a shining pool between two tufted ridges, and in this velvety hollow the twilight was gathering like a shadow in a cup. A little creek ran out of the pool, and here Alan gathered soft grass and spread out his blankets. A great stillness drew in about him, broken only by the old squaws and the loons. At eleven o'clock he could still see clearly the sleeping water-fowl on the surface of the pool. But the stars were appearing. It grew duskier, and the rose-tint of the sun faded into purple gloom as pale night drew near--four hours of rest that was neither darkness nor day. With a pillow of sedge and grass under his head he slept.

The song and cry of bird-life wakened him, and at dawn he bathed in the pool, with dozens of fluffy, new-born ducks dodging away from him among the grasses and reeds. That day, and the next, and the day after that he traveled steadily into the heart of the tundra country, swiftly and almost without rest. It seemed to him, at last, that he must be in that country where all the bird-life of the world was born, for wherever there was water, in the pools and little streams and the hollows between the ridges, the voice of it in the morning was a babel of sound. Out of the sweet breast of the earth he could feel the irresistible pulse of motherhood filling him with its strength and its courage, and whispering to him its everlasting message that because of the glory and need and faith of life had God created this land of twenty-hour day and four-hour twilight. In it, in these days of summer, was no abiding place for gloom; yet in his own heart, as he drew nearer to his home, was a place of darkness which its light could not quite enter.

The tundras had made Mary Standish more real to him. In the treeless spaces, in the vast reaches with only the sky shutting out his vision, she seemed to be walking nearer to him, almost with her hand in his. At times it was like a torture inflicted upon him for his folly, and when he visioned what might have been, and recalled too vividly that it was he who had stilled with death that living glory which dwelt with him in spirit now, a crying sob of which he was not ashamed came from his lips. For when he thought too deeply, he knew that Mary Standish would have lived if he had said other things to her that night aboard the ship. She had died, not for him, but *because* of him--because, in his failure to live up to what she believed she had found in him, he had broken down what must have been her last hope and her final faith. If he had been less blind, and God had given him the inspiration of a greater wisdom, she would have been walking with him now, laughing in the rose-tinted dawn, growing tired amid the flowers, sleeping under the clear stars--happy and unafraid, and looking to him for all things. At least so he dreamed, in his immeasurable loneliness.

He did not tolerate the thought that other forces might have called her even had she lived, and that she might not have been his to hold and to fight for. He did not question the possibility of shackles and chains that might have bound her, or other inclinations that might have led her. He claimed her, now that she was dead, and knew that living he would have possessed her. Nothing could have kept him from that. But she was gone. And for that he was accountable, and the fifth night he lay sleepless under the stars, and like a boy he cried for her with his face upon his arm, and when morning came, and he went on, never had the world seemed so vast and empty.

His face was gray and haggard, a face grown suddenly old, and he traveled slowly, for the desire to reach his people was dying within him. He could not laugh with Keok and Nawadlook, or give the old tundra call to Amuk Toolik and his people, who would be riotous in their happiness at his return. They loved him. He knew that. Their love had been a part of his life, and the knowledge that his response to this love would be at best a poor and broken thing filled him with dread. A strange sickness crept through his blood; it grew in his head, so that when noon came, he did not trouble himself to eat.

It was late in the afternoon when he saw far ahead of him the clump of cottonwoods near the warm springs, very near his home. Often he had come to these old cottonwoods, an oasis of timber lost in the great tundras, and he had built himself a little camp among them. He loved the place. It had seemed to him that now and then he must visit the forlorn trees to give them cheer and comradeship. His father's name was carved in the bole of the greatest of them all, and under it the date and day when the elder Holt had discovered them in a land where no man had gone before. And under his father's name was his mother's, and under that, his own. He had made of the place a sort of shrine, a green and sweet-flowered tabernacle of memories, and its bird-song and peace in summer and the weird aloneness of it in winter had played their parts in the making of his soul. Through many months he had anticipated this hour of his home-coming, when in the distance he would see the beckoning welcome of the old cottonwoods, with the rolling foothills and frosted peaks of the Endicott Mountains beyond. And now he was looking at the trees and the mountains, and something was lacking in the thrill of them. He came up from the west, between two willow ridges through which ran the little creek from the warm springs, and he was within a quarter of a mile of them when something stopped him in his tracks.

At first he thought the sound was the popping of guns, but in a moment he knew it could not be so, and the truth flashed suddenly upon him. This day was the Fourth of July, and someone in the cottonwoods was shooting firecrackers!

A smile softened his lips. He recalled Keok's mischievous habit of lighting a whole bunch at one time, for which apparent wastefulness Nawadlook never failed to scold her. They had prepared for his home-coming with a celebration, and Tautuk and Amuk Toolik had probably imported a supply of "bing-bangs" from Allakakat or Tanana. The oppressive weight inside him lifted, and the smile remained on his lips. And then as if commanded by a voice, his eyes turned to the dead cottonwood stub which had sentineled the little oasis of trees for many years. At the very crest of it, floating bravely in the breeze that came with the evening sun, was an American flag!

He laughed softly. These were the people who loved him, who thought of him, who wanted him back. His heart beat faster, stirred by the old happiness, and he drew himself quickly into a strip of willows that grew almost up to the cottonwoods. He would surprise them! He would walk suddenly in among them, unseen and unheard. That was the sort of thing that would amaze and delight them.

He came to the first of the trees and concealed himself carefully. He heard the popping of individual firecrackers and the louder bang of one of the "giants" that always made Nawadlook put her fingers in her pretty ears. He crept stealthily over a knoll, down through a hollow, and then up again to the opposite crest. It was as he had thought. He could see Keok a hundred yards away, standing on the trunk of a fallen tree, and as he looked, she tossed another bunch of sputtering crackers away from her. The others were probably circled about her, out of his sight, watching her performance. He continued cautiously, making his way so that he could come up behind a thick growth of bush unseen, within a dozen paces of them. At last he was as near as that to her, and Keok was still standing on the log with her back toward him.

It puzzled him that he could not see or hear the others. And something about Keok puzzled him, too. And then his heart gave a sudden throb and seemed to stop its beating. It was not Keok on the log. And it was not Nawadlook! He stood up and stepped out from his hiding-place. The slender figure of the girl on the log turned a little, and he saw the glint of golden sunshine in her hair. He called out.

"Keok!"

Was he mad? Had the sickness in his head turned his brain?

And then:

"Mary!" he called. "*Mary Standish*!"

She turned. And in that moment Alan Holt's face was the color of gray rock. It was the dead he had been thinking of, and it was the dead that had risen before him now. For it was Mary Standish who stood there on the old cottonwood log, shooting firecrackers in this evening of his home-coming.

CHAPTER XIII

After that one calling of her name Alan's voice was dead, and he made no movement. He could not disbelieve. It was not a mental illusion or a temporary upsetting of his sanity. It was truth. The shock of it was rending every nerve in his body, even as he stood as if carved out of wood. And then a strange relaxation swept over him. Some force seemed to pass out of his flesh, and his arms hung limp. She was there, *alive!* He could see the whiteness leave her face and a flush of color come into it, and he heard a little cry as she jumped down from the log and came toward him. It had all happened in a few seconds, but it seemed a long time to Alan.

He saw nothing about her or beyond her. It was as if she were floating up to him out of the cold mists of the sea. And she stopped only a step away from him, when she saw more clearly what was in his face. It must have been something that startled her. Vaguely he realized this and made an effort to recover himself.

"You almost frightened me," she said. "We have been expecting you and watching for you, and I was out there a few minutes ago looking back over the tundra. The sun was in my eyes, and I didn't see you."

It seemed incredible that he should be hearing her voice, the same voice, unexcited, sweet, and thrilling, speaking as if she had seen him yesterday and with a certain reserved gladness was welcoming him again today. It was impossible for him to realize in these moments the immeasurable distance that lay between their viewpoints. He was simply Alan Holt--she was the dead risen to life. Many times in his grief he had visualized what he would do if some miracle could bring her back to him like this; he had thought of taking her in his arms and never letting her go. But now that the miracle had come to pass, and she was within his reach, he stood without moving, trying only to speak.

"You--Mary Standish!" he said at last. "I thought--"

He did not finish. It was not himself speaking. It was another individual within him, a detached individual trying to explain his lack of physical expression. He wanted to cry out his gladness, to shout with joy, yet the directing soul of action in him was stricken. She touched his arm hesitatingly.

"I didn't think you would care," she said. "I thought you wouldn't mind--if I came up here."

Care! The word was like an explosion setting things loose in his brain, and the touch of her hand sent a sweep of fire through him. He heard himself cry out, a strange, unhuman sort of cry, as he swept her to his breast. He held her close, crushing kisses upon her mouth, his fingers buried in her hair, her slender body almost broken in his arms. She was alive--she had come back to him--and he forgot everything in these blind moments but that great truth which was sweeping over him in a glorious inundation. Then, suddenly, he found that she was fighting him, struggling to free herself and putting her hands against his face in her efforts. She was so close that he seemed to see nothing but her eyes, and in them he did not see what he had dreamed of finding--but horror. It was a stab that went into his heart, and his arms relaxed. She staggered back, trembling and swaying a little as she got her breath, her face very white.

He had hurt her. The hurt was in her eyes, in the way she looked at him, as if he had become a menace from which she would run if he had not taken the strength from her. As she stood there, her parted lips showing the red of his kisses, her shining hair almost undone, he held out his hands mutely.

"You think--I came here for *that?*" she panted.

"No," he said. "Forgive me. I am sorry."

It was not anger that he saw in her face. It was, instead, a mingling of shock and physical hurt; a measurement of him now, as she looked at him, which recalled her to him as she had stood that night with her back against his cabin door. Yet he was not trying to piece things together. Even subconsciously that was impossible, for all life in him was centered in the one stupendous thought that she was not dead, but living, and he did not wonder why. There was no question in his mind as to the manner in which she had been saved from the sea. He felt a weakness in his limbs; he wanted to laugh, to cry out, to give himself up to strange inclinations for a moment or two, like a woman. Such was the shock of his happiness. It crept in a living fluid through his flesh. She saw it in the swift change of the rock-like color in his face, and his quicker breathing, and was a little amazed, but Alan was too completely possessed by the one great thing to discover the astonishment growing in her eyes.

"You are alive," he said, giving voice again to the one thought pounding in his brain. "*Alive!*"

It seemed to him that word wanted to utter itself an impossible number of times. Then the truth that was partly dawning came entirely to the girl.

"Mr. Holt, you did not receive my letter at Nome?" she asked.

"Your letter? At Nome?" He repeated the words, shaking his head. "No."

"And all this time--you have been thinking--I was dead?"

He nodded, because the thickness in his throat made it the easier form of speech.

"I wrote you there," she said. "I wrote the letter before I jumped into the sea. It went to Nome with Captain Rifle's ship."

"I didn't get it."

"You didn't get it?" There was wonderment in her voice, and then, if he had observed it, understanding.

"Then you didn't mean that just now? You didn't intend to do it? It was because you had blamed yourself for my death, and it was a great relief to find me alive. That was it, wasn't it?"

Stupidly he nodded again. "Yes, it was a great relief."

"You see, I had faith in you even when you wouldn't help me," she went on. "So much faith that I trusted you with my secret in the letter I wrote. To all the world but you I am dead--to Rossland, Captain Rifle, everyone. In my letter I told you I had arranged with the young Thlinkit Indian. He smuggled the canoe over the side just before I leaped in, and picked me up. I am a good swimmer. Then he paddled me ashore while the boats were making their search."

In a moment she had placed a gulf between them again, on the other side of which she stood unattainable. It was inconceivable that only a few moments ago he had crushed her in his arms. The knowledge that he had done this thing, and that she was looking at him now as if it had never happened, filled him with a smothering sense of humiliation. She made it impossible for him to speak about it, even to apologize more fully.

"Now I am here," she was saying in a quiet, possessive sort of way. "I didn't think of coming when I jumped into the sea. I made up my mind afterward. I think it was because I met a little man with red whiskers whom you once pointed out to me in the smoking salon on the *Nome.* And so--I am your guest, Mr. Holt."

There was not the slightest suspicion of apology in her voice as she smoothed back her hair where he had crumpled it. It was as if she belonged here, and had always belonged here, and was giving him permission to enter her domain. Shock was beginning to pass away from him, and he could feel his feet upon the earth once more. His spirit-visions of her as she had walked hand in hand with him during the past weeks, her soft eyes filled with love, faded away before the reality of Mary Standish in flesh and blood, her quiet mastery of things, her almost omniscient unapproachableness. He reached out his hands, but there was a different light in his eyes, and she placed her own in them confidently.

"It was like a bolt of lightning," he said, his voice free at last and trembling. "Day and night I have been thinking of you, dreaming of you, and cursing myself because I believed I had killed you. And now I find you alive. And *here!*"

She was so near that the hands he clasped lay against her breast. But reason had returned to him, and he saw the folly of dreams.

"It is difficult to believe. Out there I thought I was sick. Perhaps I am. But if I am not sick, and you are really you, I am glad. If I wake up and find I have imagined it all, as I imagined so many of the other things--"

He laughed, freeing her hands and looking into eyes shining half out of tears at him. But he did not finish. She drew away from him, with a lingering of her finger-tips on his arm, and the little heart-beat in her throat revealed itself clearly again as on that night in his cabin.

"I have been thinking of you back there, every hour, every step," he said, making a gesture toward the tundras over which he had come. "Then I heard the firecrackers and saw the flag. It is almost as if I had created you!"

A quick answer was on her lips, but she stopped it.

"And when I found you here, and you didn't fade away like a ghost, I thought something was wrong with my head. Something must have been wrong, I guess, or I wouldn't have done *that.* You see, it puzzled me that a ghost should be setting off firecrackers--and I suppose that was the first impulse I had of making sure you were real."

A voice came from the edge of the cottonwoods beyond them. It was a clear, wild voice with a sweet trill in it. "*Maa-rie!*" it called. "*Maa-rie!*"

"Supper," nodded the girl. "You are just in time. And then we are going home in the twilight."

It made his heart thump, that casual way in which she spoke of his place as home. She went ahead of him, with the sun glinting in the soft coils of her hair, and he picked up his rifle and followed, eyes and soul filled only with the beauty of her slim figure--a glory of life where for a long time he had fashioned a spirit of the dead. They came into an open, soft with grass and strewn with flowers, and in this open a man was kneeling beside a fire no larger than his two hands, and at his side, watching him, stood a girl with two braids of black hair rippling down her back. It was Nawadlook who turned first and saw who it was with Mary Standish, and from his right came an odd little screech that only one person in the world could make, and that was Keok. She dropped the armful of sticks she had gathered for the fire and made straight for him, while Nawadlook, taller and less like a wild creature in the manner of her coming, was only a moment behind. And then he was shaking hands with Stampede, and Keok had slipped down among the flowers and was crying. That was like Keok. She always cried when he went away, and cried when he returned; and then, in another moment, it was Keok who was laughing first, and Alan noticed she no longer wore her hair in braids, as the quieter Nawadlook persisted in doing, but had it coiled about her head just as Mary Standish wore her own.

These details pressed themselves upon him in a vague and unreal sort of way. No one, not even Mary Standish, could understand how his mind and nerves were fighting to recover themselves. His senses were swimming back one by one to a vital point from which they had been swept by an unexpected sea, gripping rather incoherently at unimportant realities as they assembled themselves. In the edge of the tundra beyond the cottonwoods he noticed three saddle-deer grazing at the ends of ropes which were fastened to cotton-tufted nigger-heads. He drew off his pack as Mary Standish went to help Keok pick up the fallen sticks. Nawadlook was pulling a coffee-pot from the tiny fire. Stampede began to fill a pipe. He realized that because they had expected him, if not today then tomorrow or the next day or a day soon after that, no one had experienced shock but himself, and with a mighty effort he reached back and dragged the old Alan Holt into existence again. It was like bringing an intelligence out of darkness into light.

It was difficult for him--afterward--to remember just what happened during the next half-hour. The amazing thing was that Mary Standish sat opposite him, with the cloth on which Nawadlook had spread the supper things between them, and that she was the same clear-eyed, beautiful Mary Standish who had sat across the table from him in the dining-salon of the *Nome*.

Not until later, when he stood alone with Stampede Smith in the edge of the cottonwoods, and the three girls were riding deer back over the tundra in the direction of the Range, did the sea of questions which had been gathering begin to sweep upon him. It had been Keok's suggestion that she and Mary and Nawadlook ride on ahead, and he had noticed how quickly Mary Standish had caught at the idea. She had smiled at him as she left, and a little farther out had waved her hand at him, as Keok and Nawadlook both had done, but not another word had passed between them alone. And as they rode off in the warm glow of sunset Alan stood watching them, and would have stared without speech until they were out of sight, if Stampede's fingers had not gripped his arm.

"Now, go to it, Alan," he said. "I'm ready. Give me hell!"

CHAPTER XIV

It was thus, with a note of something inevitable in his voice, that Stampede brought Alan back solidly to earth. There was a practical and awakening inspiration in the manner of the little red-whiskered man's invitation.

"I've been a damn fool," he confessed. "And I'm waiting."

The word was like a key opening a door through which a flood of things began to rush in upon Alan. There were other fools, and evidently he had been one. His mind went back to the *Nome*. It seemed only a few hours ago--only yesterday--that the girl had so artfully deceived them all, and he had gone through hell because of that deception. The trickery had been simple, and exceedingly clever because of its simplicity; it must have taken a tremendous amount of courage, now that he clearly understood that at no time had she wanted to die.

"I wonder," he said, "why she did a thing like that?"

Stampede shook his head, misunderstanding what was in Alan's mind. "I couldn't keep her back, not unless I tied her to a tree." And he added, "The little witch even threatened to shoot me!"

A flash of exultant humor filled his eyes. "Begin, Alan. I'm waiting. Go the limit."

"For what?"

"For letting her ride over me, of course. For bringing her up. For not shufflin' her in the bush. You can't take it out of *her* hide, can you?"

He twisted his red whiskers, waiting for an answer. Alan was silent. Mary Standish was leading the way up out of a dip in the tundra a quarter of a mile away, with Nawadlook and Keok close behind her. They trotted up a low ridge and disappeared.

"It's none of my business," persisted Stampede, "but you didn't seem to expect her--"

"You're right," interrupted Alan, turning toward his pack. "I didn't expect her. I thought she was dead."

A low whistle escaped Stampede's lips. He opened his mouth to speak and closed it again. Alan observed him as he slipped the pack over his shoulders. Evidently his companion did not know Mary Standish was the girl who had jumped overboard from the *Nome*, and if she had kept her secret, it was not his business just now to explain, even though he guessed that Stampede's quick wits would readily jump at the truth. A light was beginning to dispel the little man's bewilderment as they started toward the Range. He had seen Mary Standish frequently aboard the *Nome*, a number of times he had observed her in Alan's company, and he knew of the hours they had spent together in Skagway. Therefore, if Alan had believed her dead when they went ashore at Cordova, a few hours after the supposed tragedy, it must have been she who jumped into the sea. He shrugged his shoulders in deprecation of his failure to discover this amazing fact in his association with Mary Standish.

"It beats the devil!" he exclaimed suddenly.

"It does," agreed Alan.

Cold, hard reason began to shoulder itself inevitably against the happiness that possessed him, and questions which he had found no interest in asking when aboard ship leaped upon him with compelling force. Why was it so tragically important to Mary Standish that the world should believe her dead? What was it that had driven her to appeal to him and afterward to jump into the sea? What was her mysterious association with Rossland, an agent of Alaska's deadliest enemy, John Graham--the one man upon whom he had sworn vengeance if opportunity ever came his way? Over him, clubbing other emotions with its insistence, rode a demand for explanations which it was impossible for him to make. Stampede saw the tense lines in his face and remained silent in the lengthening twilight, while Alan's mind struggled to bring coherence and reason out of a tidal wave of mystery and doubt. Why had she come to *his* cabin aboard the *Nome*? Why had she played him with such conspicuous intent against Rossland, and why--in the end--had she preceded him to his home in the tundras? It was this question which persisted, never for an instant swept aside by the others. She had not come because of love for him. In a brutal sort of way he had proved that, for when he had taken her in his arms, he had seen distress and fear and a flash of horror in her face. Another and more mysterious force had driven her.

The joy in him was a living flame even as this realization pressed upon him. He was like a man who had found life after a period of something that was worse than death, and with his happiness he felt himself twisted upon an upheaval of conflicting sensations and half convictions out of which, in spite of his effort to hold it back, suspicion began to creep like a shadow. But it was not the sort of suspicion to cool the thrill in his blood or frighten him, for he was quite ready to concede that Mary Standish was a fugitive, and that her flight from Seattle had been in the face of a desperate necessity. What had happened aboard ship was further proof, and her presence at his range a final one. Forces had driven her which it had been impossible for her to combat, and in desperation she had come to him for refuge. She had chosen him out of all the world to help her; she believed in him; she had faith that with him no harm could come, and his muscles tightened with sudden desire to fight for her.

In these moments he became conscious of the evening song of the tundras and the soft splendor of the miles reaching out ahead of them. He strained his eyes to catch another glimpse of the mounted figures when they came up out of hollows to the clough-tops, but the lacy veils of evening were drawing closer, and he looked in vain. Bird-song grew softer; sleepy cries rose from the grasses and pools; the fire of the sun itself died out, leaving its radiance in a mingling of vivid rose and mellow gold over the edge of the world. It was night and yet day, and Alan wondered what thoughts were in the heart of Mary Standish. What had driven her to the Range was of small importance compared with the thrilling fact that she was just ahead of him. The mystery of her would be explained tomorrow. He was sure of that. She would confide in him. Now that she had so utterly placed herself under his protection, she would tell him what she had not dared to disclose aboard the *Nome*. So he thought only of the silvery distance of twilight that separated them, and spoke at last to Stampede.

"I'm rather glad you brought her," he said.

"I didn't bring her," protested Stampede. "She *came*." He shrugged his shoulders with a grunt. "And furthermore I didn't manage it. She did that herself. She didn't come with me. I came with *her*."

He stopped and struck a match to light his pipe. Over the tiny flame he glared fiercely at Alan, but in his eyes was something that betrayed him. Alan saw it and felt a desire to laugh out of sheer happiness. His keen vision and sense of humor were returning.

"How did it happen?"

Stampede puffed loudly at his pipe, then took it from his mouth and drew in a deep breath.

"First I remember was the fourth night after we landed at Cordova. Couldn't get a train on the new line until then. Somewhere up near Chitina we came to a washout. It didn't rain. You couldn't call it that, Alan. It was the Pacific Ocean falling on us, with two or three other oceans backing it up. The stage came along, horses swimming, coach floating, driver half drowned in his seat. I was that hungry I got in for Chitina. There was one other climbed in after me, and I wondered what sort of fool he was. I said something about being starved or I'd have hung to the train. The other didn't answer. Then I began to swear. I did, Alan. I cursed terrible. Swore at the Government for building such a road, swore at the rain, an' I swore at myself for not bringin' along grub. I said my belly was as empty as a shot-off cartridge, and I said it good an' loud. I was mad. Then a big flash of lightning lit up the coach. Alan, it was *her* sittin' there with a box in her lap, facing me, drippin' wet, her eyes shining--and she was smiling at me! Yessir, *smiling*."

Stampede paused to let the shock sink in. He was not disappointed.

Alan stared at him in amazement. "The fourth night--after--" He caught himself. "Go on, Stampede!"

"I began hunting for the latch on the door, Alan. I was goin' to sneak out, drop in the mud, disappear before the lightnin' come again. But it caught me. An' there she was, undoing the box, and I heard her saying she had plenty of good stuff to eat. An' she called me Stampede, like she'd known me all her life, and with that coach rolling an' rocking and the thunder an' lightning an' rain piling up against each other like sin, she came over and sat down beside me and began to feed me. She did that, Alan--*fed* me. When the lightning fired up, I could see her eyes shining and her lips smilin' as if all that hell about us made her happy, and I thought she was plumb crazy. Before I knew it she was telling me how you pointed me out to her in the smoking-room, and how happy she was that I was goin' her way. *Her* way, mind you, Alan, not *mine*. And that's just the way she's kept me goin' up to the minute you hove in sight back there in the cottonwoods!"

He lighted his pipe again. "Alan, how the devil did she know I was hitting the trail for your place?"

"She didn't," replied Alan.

"But she did. She said that meeting with me in the coach was the happiest moment of her life, because *she* was on her way up to your range, and I'd be such jolly good company for her. 'Jolly good'--them were the words she used! When I asked her if you knew she was coming up, she said no, of course not, and that it was going to be a grand surprise. Said it was possible she'd buy your range, and she wanted to look it over before you arrived. An' it seems queer I can't remember anything more about the thunder and lightning between there and Chitina. When we took the train again, she began askin' a million questions about you and the Range and Alaska. Soak me if you want to, Alan--but everything I knew she got out of me between Chitina and Fairbanks, and she got it in such a sure-fire nice way that I'd have eat soap out of her hand if she'd offered it to me. Then, sort of sly and soft-like, she began asking questions about John Graham--and I woke up."

"John Graham!" Alan repeated the name.

"Yes, John Graham. And I had a lot to tell. After that I tried to get away from her. But she caught me just as I was sneakin' aboard a down-river boat, and cool as you please--with her hand on my arm--she said she wasn't quite ready to go yet, and would I please come and help her carry some stuff she was going to buy. Alan, it ain't a lie what I'm going to tell you! She led me up the street, telling me what a wonderful idea she had for surprisin' *you*. Said she knew you would return to the Range by the Fourth of July and we sure must have some fireworks. Said you was such a good American you'd be disappointed if you didn't have 'em. So she took me in a store an' bought it out. Asked the man what he'd take for everything in his joint that had powder in it. Five hundred dollars, that was what she paid. She pulled a silk something out of the front of her dress with a pad of hundred-dollar bills in it an inch think. Then she asked *me* to get them firecrackers 'n' wheels 'n' skyrockets 'n' balloons 'n' other stuff down to the boat, and she asked me just as if I was a sweet little boy who'd be tickled to death to do it!"

In the excitement of unburdening himself of a matter which he had borne in secret for many days, Stampede did not observe the effect of his words upon his companion. Incredulity shot into Alan's eyes, and the humorous lines about his mouth vanished when he saw clearly that Stampede was not drawing upon his imagination. Yet what he had told him seemed impossible. Mary Standish had come aboard the *Nome* a fugitive. All her possessions she had brought with her in a small hand-bag, and these things she had left in her cabin when she leaped into the sea. How, then, could she logically have had such a sum of money at Fairbanks as Stampede described? Was it possible the Thlinkit Indian had also become her agent in transporting the money ashore on the night she played her desperate game by making the world believe she had died? And was this money--possibly the manner in which she had secured it in Seattle--the cause of her flight and the clever scheme she had put into execution a little later?

He had been thinking crime, and his face grew hot at the sin of it. It was like thinking it of another woman, who was dead, and whose name was cut under his father's in the old cottonwood tree.

Stampede, having gained his wind, was saying: "You don't seem interested, Alan. But I'm going on, or I'll bust. I've got to tell you what happened, and then if you want to lead me out and shoot me, I won't say a word. I say, curse a firecracker anyway!"

"Go on," urged Alan. "I'm interested."

"I got 'em on the boat," continued Stampede viciously. "And she with me every minute, smiling in that angel way of hers, and not letting me out of her sight a flick of her eyelash, unless there was only one hole to go in an' come out at. And then she said she wanted to do a little shopping, which meant going into every shack in town and buyin' something, an' I did the lugging. At last she bought a gun, and when I asked her what she was goin' to do with it, she said, 'Stampede, that's for you,' an' when I went to thank her, she said: 'No, I don't mean it that way. I mean that if you try to run away from me again I'm going to fill you full of holes.' She said that! Threatened me. Then she bought me a new outfit from toe to summit--boots, pants, shirt, hat *and* a necktie! And I didn't say a word, not a word. She just led me in an' bought what she wanted and made me put 'em on."

Stampede drew in a mighty breath, and a fourth time wasted a match on his pipe. "I was getting used to it by the time we reached Tanana," he half groaned. "Then the hell of it begun. She hired six Indians to tote the luggage, and we set out over the trail for your place. 'You're goin' to have a rest, Stampede,' she says to me, smiling so cool and sweet like you wanted to eat her alive. 'All you've got to do is show us the way and carry the bums.' 'Carry the what?' I asks. 'The bums,' she says, an' then she explains that a bum is a thing filled with powder which makes a terrible racket when it goes off. So I took the bums, and the next day one of the Indians sprained a leg, and dropped out. He had the firecrackers, pretty near a hundred pounds, and we whacked up his load among us. I couldn't stand up straight when we camped. We had crooks in our backs every inch of the way to the Range. And *would* she let us cache some of that junk? Not on your life she wouldn't! And all the time while they was puffing an' panting them Indians was worshipin' her with their eyes. The last day, when we camped with the Range almost in sight, she drew 'em all up in a circle about her and gave 'em each a handful of money above their pay. 'That's because I love you,' she says, and then she begins asking them funny questions. Did they have wives and children? Were they ever hungry? Did they ever know about any of their people starving to death? And just *why* did they starve? And, Alan, so help me thunder if them Indians didn't talk! Never knew Indians tell so much. And in the end she asked them the funniest question of all, asked them if they'd heard of a man named John Graham. One of them had, and afterward I saw her talking a long time with him alone, and when she come back to me, her eyes were sort of burning up, and she didn't say good night when she went into her tent. That's all, Alan, except--"

"Except what, Stampede?" said Alan, his heart throbbing like a drum inside him.

Stampede took his time to answer, and Alan heard him chuckling and saw a flash of humor in the little man's eyes.

"Except that she's done with everyone on the Range just what she did with me between Chitina and here," he said. "Alan, if she wants to say the word, why, *you* ain't boss any more, that's all. She's been there ten days, and you won't know the place. It's all done up in flags, waiting for you. She an' Nawadlook and Keok are running everything but the deer. The kids would leave their mothers for her, and the men--" He chuckled again. "Why, the men even go to the Sunday school she's started! I went. Nawadlook sings."

For a moment he was silent. Then he said in a subdued voice, "Alan, you've been a big fool."

"I know it, Stampede."

"She's a--a flower, Alan. She's worth more than all the gold in the world. And you could have married her. I know it. But it's too late now. I'm warnin' you."

"I don't quite understand, Stampede. Why is it too late?"

"Because she likes me," declared Stampede a bit fiercely. "I'm after her myself, Alan. You can't butt in now."

"Great Scott!" gasped Alan. "You mean that Mary Standish--"

"I'm not talking about Mary Standish," said Stampede. "It's Nawadlook. If it wasn't for my whiskers--"

His words were broken by a sudden detonation which came out of the pale gloom ahead of them. It was like the explosion of a cannon a long distance away.

"One of them cussed bums," he explained. "That's why they hurried on ahead of us, Alan. *She* says this Fourth of July celebration is going to mean a lot for Alaska. Wonder what she means?"

"I wonder," said Alan.

CHAPTER XV

Half an hour more of the tundra and they came to what Alan had named Ghost Kloof, a deep and jagged scar in the face of the earth, running down from the foothills of the mountains. It was a sinister thing, and in the depths lay abysmal darkness as they descended a rocky path worn smooth by reindeer and caribou hoofs. At the bottom, a hundred feet below the twilight of the plains, Alan dropped on his knees beside a little spring that he groped for among the stones, and as he drank he could hear the weird whispering and gurgling of water up and down the kloof, choked and smothered in the moss of the rock walls and eternally dripping from the crevices. Then he saw Stampede's face in the glow of another match, and the little man's eyes were staring into the black chasm that reached for miles up into the mountains.

"Alan, you've been up this gorge?"

"It's a favorite runway for the lynx and big brown bears that kill our fawns," replied Alan. "I hunt alone, Stampede. The place is supposed to be haunted, you know. Ghost Kloof, I call it, and no Eskimo will enter it. The bones of dead men lie up there."

"Never prospected it?" persisted Stampede.

"Never."

Alan heard the other's grunt of disgust.

"You're reindeer-crazy," he grumbled. "There's gold in this canyon. Twice I've found it where there were dead men's bones. They bring me good luck."

"But these were Eskimos. They didn't come for gold."

"I know it. The Boss settled that for me. When she heard what was the matter with this place, she made me take her into it. Nerve? Say, I'm telling you there wasn't any of it left out of her when she was born!" He was silent for a moment, and then added: "When we came to that dripping, slimy rock with the big yellow skull layin' there like a poison toadstool, she didn't screech and pull back, but just gave a little gasp and stared at it hard, and her fingers pinched my arm until it hurt. It was a devilish-looking thing, yellow as a sick orange and soppy with the drip of the wet moss over it. I wanted to blow it to pieces, and I guess I would if she hadn't put a hand on my gun. An' with a funny little smile she says: 'Don't do it, Stampede. It makes me think of someone I know--and I wouldn't want you to shoot him.' Darned funny thing to say, wasn't it? Made her think of someone she knew! Now, who the devil could look like a rotten skull?"

Alan made no effort to reply, except to shrug his shoulders. They climbed up out of gloom into the light of the plain. Smoothness of the tundra was gone on this side of the crevasse. Ahead of them rolled up a low hill, and mountainward hills piled one upon another until they were lost in misty distance. From the crest of the ridge they looked out into a vast sweep of tundra which ran in among the out-guarding billows and hills of the Endicott Mountains in the form of a wide, semicircular bay. Beyond the next swell in the tundra lay the range, and scarcely had they reached this when Stampede drew his big gun from its holster. Twice he blazed in the air.

"Orders," he said a little sheepishly. "Orders, Alan!"

Scarcely were the words out of his mouth when a yell came to them from beyond the light-mists that hovered like floating lace over the tundra. It was joined by another, and still another, until there was such a sound that Alan knew Tautuk and Amuk Toolik and Topkok and Tatpan and all the others were splitting their throats in welcome, and with it very soon came a series of explosions that set the earth athrill under their feet.

"Bums!" growled Stampede. "She's got Chink lanterns hanging up all about, too. You should have seen her face, Alan, when she found there was sunlight all night up here on July Fourth!"

From the range a pale streak went sizzling into the air, mounting until it seemed to pause for a moment to look down upon the gray world, then burst into innumerable little balls of puffy smoke. Stampede blazed away with his forty-five, and Alan felt the thrill of it and emptied the magazine of his gun, the detonations of revolver and rifle drowning the chorus of sound that came from the range. A second rocket answered them. Two columns of flame leaped up from the earth as huge fires gained headway, and Alan could hear the shrill chorus of children's voices mingling with the vocal tumult of men. All the people of his range were there. They had come in from the timber-naked plateaux and high ranges where the herds were feeding, and from the outlying shacks of the tundras to greet him. Never had there been such a concentration of effort on the part of his people. And Mary Standish was behind it all! He knew he was fighting against odds when he tried to keep that fact from choking up his heart a little.

He had not heard what Stampede was saying--that he and Amuk Toolik and forty kids had labored a week gathering dry moss and timber fuel for the big fires. There were three of these fires now, and the tom-toms were booming their hollow notes over the tundra as Alan quickened his steps. Over a little knoll, and he was looking at the buildings of the range, wildly excited figures running about, women and children flinging moss on the fires, the tom-tom beaters squatted in a half-circle facing the direction from which he would come, and fifty Chinese lanterns swinging in the soft night-breeze.

He knew what they were expecting of him, for they were children, all of them. Even Tautuk and Amuk Toolik, his chief herdsmen, were children. Nawadlook and Keok were children. Strong and loyal and ready to die for him in any fight or stress, they were still children. He gave Stampede his rifle and hastened on, determined to keep his eyes from questing for Mary Standish in these first minutes of his return. He sounded the tundra call, and men, women, and little children came running to meet him. The drumming of the tom-toms ceased, and the beaters leaped to their feet. He was inundated. There was a shrill crackling of voice, laughter, children's squeals, a babel of delight. He gripped hands with both his own--hard, thick, brown hands of men; little, softer, brown hands of women; he lifted children up in his arms, slapped his palm affectionately against the men's shoulders, and talked, talked, talked, calling each by name without a slip of memory, though there were fifty around him counting the children. First, last, and always these were *his people*. The old pride swept over him, a compelling sense of power and possession. They loved him, crowding in about him like a great family, and he shook hands twice and three times with the same men and women, and lifted the same children from the arms of delighted mothers, and cried out greetings and familiarities with an abandon which a few minutes ago knowledge of Mary Standish's presence would have tempered. Then, suddenly, he saw her under the Chinese lanterns in front of his cabin. Sokwenna, so old that he hobbled double and looked like a witch, stood beside her. In a moment Sokwenna's head disappeared, and there came the booming of a tom-tom. As quickly as the crowd had gathered about him, it fell away. The beaters squatted themselves in their semicircle again. Fireworks began to go off. Dancers assembled. Rockets hissed through the air. Roman candles popped. From the open door of his cabin came the sound of a phonograph. It was aimed directly at him, the one thing intended for his understanding alone. It was playing "When Johnny Comes Marching Home."

Mary Standish had not moved. He saw her laughing at him, and she was alone. She was not the Mary Standish he had known aboard ship. Fear, the quiet pallor of her face, and the strain and repression which had seemed to be a part of her were gone. She was aflame with life, yet it was not with voice or action that she revealed herself. It was in her eyes, the flush of her cheeks and lips, the poise of her slim body as she waited for him. A thought flashed upon him that for a space she had forgotten herself and the shadow which had driven her to leap into the sea.

"It is splendid!" she said when he came up to her, and her voice trembled a little. "I didn't guess how badly they wanted you back. It must be a great happiness to have people think of you like that."

"And I thank you for your part," he replied. "Stampede has told me. It was quite a bit of trouble, wasn't it, with nothing more than the hope of Americanizing a pagan to inspire you?" He nodded at the half-dozen flags over his cabin. "They're rather pretty."

"It was no trouble. And I hope you don't mind. It has been great fun."

He tried to look casually out upon his people as he answered her. It seemed to him there was only one thing to say, and that it was a duty to speak what was in his mind calmly and without emotion.

"Yes, I do mind," he said. "I mind so much that I wouldn't trade what has happened for all the gold in these mountains. I'm sorry because of what happened back in the cottonwoods, but I wouldn't trade that, either. I'm glad you're alive. I'm glad you're here. But something is missing. You know what it is. You must tell me about yourself. It is the only fair thing for you to do now."

She touched his arm with her hand. "Let us wait for tomorrow. Please--let us wait."

"And then--tomorrow--"

"It is your right to question me and send me back if I am not welcome. But not tonight. All this is too fine--just you--and your people--and their happiness." He bent his head to catch her words, almost drowned by the hissing of a sky-rocket and the popping of firecrackers. She nodded toward the buildings beyond his cabin. "I am with Keok and Nawadlook. They have given me a home." And then swiftly she added, "I don't think you love your people more than I do, Alan Holt!"

Nawadlook was approaching, and with a lingering touch of her fingers on his arm she drew away from him. His face did not show his disappointment, nor did he make a movement to keep her with him.

"Your people are expecting things of you," she said. "A little later, if you ask me, I may dance with you to the music of the tom-toms."

He watched her as she went away with Nawadlook. She looked back at him and smiled, and there was something in her face which set his heart beating faster. She had been afraid aboard the ship, but she was not afraid of tomorrow. Thought of it and the questions he would ask did not frighten her, and a happiness which he had persistently held away from himself triumphed in a sudden, submerging flood. It was as if something in her eyes and voice had promised him that the dreams he had dreamed through weeks of torture and living death were coming true, and that possibly in her ride over the tundra that night she had come a little nearer to the truth of what those weeks had meant to him. Surely he would never quite be able to tell her. And what she said to him tomorrow would, in the end, make little difference. She was alive, and he could not let her go away from him again.

He joined the tom-tom beaters and the dancers. It rather amazed him to discover himself doing things which he had never done before. His nature was an aloof one, observing and sympathetic, but always more or less detached. At his people's dances it was his habit to stand on the side-line, smiling and nodding encouragement, but never taking a part. His habit of reserve fell from him now, and he seemed possessed of a new sense of freedom and a new desire to give physical expression to something within him. Stampede was dancing. He was kicking his feet and howling with the men, while the women dancers went through the muscular movements of arms and bodies. A chorus of voices invited Alan. They had always invited him. And tonight he accepted, and took his place between Stampede and Amuk Toolik and the tom-tom beaters almost burst their instruments in their excitement. Not until he dropped out, half breathless, did he see Mary Standish and Keok in the outer circle. Keok was frankly amazed. Mary Standish's eyes were shining, and she clapped her hands when she saw that he had observed her. He tried to laugh, and waved his hand, but he felt too foolish to go to her. And then the balloon went up, a big, six-foot balloon, and with all its fire made only a pale glow in the sky, and after another hour of hand-shaking, shoulder-clapping, and asking of questions about health and domestic matters, Alan went to his cabin.

He looked about the one big room that was his living-room, and it never had seemed quite so comforting as now. At first he thought it was as he had left it, for there was his desk where it should be, the big table in the middle of the room, the same pictures on the walls, his gun-rack filled with polished weapons, his pipes, the rugs on the floor--and then, one at a time, he began to observe things that were different. In place of dark shades there were soft curtains at his windows, and new covers on his table and the home-made couch in the corner. On his desk were two pictures in copper-colored frames, one of George Washington and the other of Abraham Lincoln, and behind them crisscrossed against the wall just over the top of the desk, were four tiny American flags. They recalled Alan's mind to the evening aboard the *Nome* when Mary Standish had challenged his assertion that he was an Alaskan and not an American. Only she would have thought of those two pictures and the little flags. There were flowers in his room, and she had placed them there. She must have picked fresh flowers each day and kept them waiting the hour of his coming, and she had thought of him in Tanana, where she had purchased the cloth for the curtains and the covers. He went into his bedroom and found new curtains at the window, a new coverlet on his bed, and a pair of red morocco slippers that he had never seen before. He took them up in his hands and laughed when he saw how she had misjudged the size of his feet.

In the living-room he sat down and lighted his pipe, observing that Keok's phonograph, which had been there earlier in the evening, was gone. Outside, the noise of the celebration died away, and the growing stillness drew him to the window from which he could see the cabin where lived Keok and Nawadlook with their foster-father, the old and shriveled Sokwenna. It was there Mary Standish had said she was staying. For a long time Alan watched it while the final sounds of the night drifted away into utter silence.

It was a knock at his door that turned him about at last, and in answer to his invitation Stampede came in. He nodded and sat down. Shiftingly his eyes traveled about the room.

"Been a fine night, Alan. Everybody glad to see you."

"They seemed to be. I'm happy to be home again."

"Mary Standish did a lot. She fixed up this room."

"I guessed as much," replied Alan. "Of course Keok and Nawadlook helped her."

"Not very much. She did it. Made the curtains. Put them pictures and flags there. Picked the flowers. Been nice an' thoughtful, hasn't she?"

"And somewhat unusual," added Alan.

"And she is pretty."

"Most decidedly so."

There was a puzzling look in Stampede's eyes. He twisted nervously in his chair and waited for words. Alan sat down opposite him.

"What's on your mind, Stampede?"

"Hell, mostly," shot back Stampede with sudden desperation. "I've come loaded down with a dirty job, and I've kept it back this long because I didn't want to spoil your fun tonight. I guess a man ought to keep to himself what he knows about a woman, but I'm thinking this is a little different. I hate to do it. I'd rather take the chance of a snake-bite. But you'd shoot me if you knew I was keeping it to myself."

"Keeping what to yourself?"

"The truth, Alan. It's up to me to tell you what I know about this young woman who calls herself Mary Standish."

CHAPTER XVI

The physical sign of strain in Stampede's face, and the stolid effort he was making to say something which it was difficult for him to put into words, did not excite Alan as he waited for his companion's promised disclosure. Instead of suspense he felt rather a sense of anticipation and relief. What he had passed through recently had burned out of him a certain demand upon human ethics which had been almost callous in its insistence, and while he believed that something very real and very stern in the way of necessity had driven Mary Standish north, he was now anxious to be given the privilege of gripping with any force of circumstance that had turned against her. He wanted to know the truth, yet he had dreaded the moment when the girl herself must tell it to him, and the fact that Stampede had in some way discovered this truth, and was about to make disclosure of it, was a tremendous lightening of the situation.

"Go on," he said at last. "What do you know about Mary Standish?"

Stampede leaned over the table, a gleam of distress in his eyes. "It's rotten. I know it. A man who backslides on a woman the way I'm goin' to oughta be shot, and if it was anything else--*anything*--I'd keep it to myself. But you've got to know. And you can't understand just how rotten it is, either; you haven't ridden in a coach with her during a storm that was blowing the Pacific outa bed, an' you haven't hit the trail with her all the way from Chitina to the Range as I did. If you'd done that, Alan, you'd feel like killing a man who said anything against her."

"I'm not inquiring into your personal affairs," reminded Alan. "It's your own business."

"That's the trouble," protested Stampede. "It's not my business. It's yours. If I'd guessed the truth before we hit the Range, everything would have been different. I'd have rid myself of her some way. But I didn't find out what she was until this evening, when I returned Keok's music machine to their cabin. I've been trying to make up my mind what to do ever since. If she was only making her get-away from the States, a pickpocket, a coiner, somebody's bunco pigeon chased by the police--almost anything--we could forgive her. Even if she'd shot up somebody--" He made a gesture of despair. "But she didn't. She's worse than that!"

He leaned a little nearer to Alan.

"She's one of John Graham's tools sent up here to sneak and spy on you," he finished desperately. "I'm sorry--but I've got the proof."

His hand crept over the top of the table; slowly the closed palm opened, and when he drew it back, a crumpled paper lay between them. "Found it on the floor when I took the phonograph back," he explained. "It was twisted up hard. Don't know why I unrolled it. Just chance."

He waited until Alan had read the few words on the bit of paper, watching closely the slight tensing of the other's face. After a moment Alan dropped the paper, rose to his feet, and went to the window. There was no longer a light in the cabin where Mary Standish had been accepted as a guest. Stampede, too, had risen from his seat. He saw the sudden and almost imperceptible shrug of Alan's shoulders.

It was Alan who spoke, after a half-mixture of silence. "Rather a missing link, isn't it? Adds up a number of things fairly well. And I'm grateful to you, Stampede. Almost--you didn't tell me."

"Almost," admitted Stampede.

"And I wouldn't have blamed you. She's that kind--the kind that makes you feel anything said against her is a lie. And I'm going to believe that paper is a lie--until tomorrow. Will you take a message to Tautuk and Amuk Toolik when you go out? I'm having breakfast at seven. Tell them to come to my cabin with their reports and records at eight. Later I'm going up into the foothills to look over the herds."

Stampede nodded. It was a good fight on Alan's part, and it was just the way he had expected him to take the matter. It made him rather ashamed of the weakness and uncertainty to which he had confessed. Of course they could do nothing with a woman; it wasn't a shooting business--yet. But there was a debatable future, if the gist of the note on the table ran true to their unspoken analysis of it. Promise of something like that was in Alan's eyes.

He opened the door. "I'll have Tautuk and Amuk Toolik here at eight. Good night, Alan!"

"Good night!"

Alan watched Stampede's figure until it had disappeared before he closed the door.

Now that he was alone, he no longer made an effort to restrain the anxiety which the prospector's unexpected revealment had aroused in him. The other's footsteps were scarcely gone when he again had the paper in his hand. It was clearly the lower part of a letter sheet of ordinary business size and had been carelessly torn from the larger part of the page, so that nothing more than the signature and half a dozen lines of writing in a man's heavy script remained.

What was left of the letter which Alan would have given much to have possessed, read as follows:

"*--If you work carefully and guard your real identity in securing facts and information, we should have the entire industry in our hands within a year.*"

Under these words was the strong and unmistakable signature of John Graham.

A score of times Alan had seen that signature, and the hatred he bore for its maker, and the desire for vengeance which had entwined itself like a fibrous plant through all his plans for the future, had made of it an unforgetable writing in his brain. Now that he held in his hand words written by his enemy, and the man who had been his father's enemy, all that he had kept away from Stampede's sharp eyes blazed in a sudden fury in his face. He dropped the paper as if it had been a thing unclean, and his hands clenched until his knuckles snapped in the stillness of the room, as he slowly faced the window through which a few moments ago he had looked in the direction of Mary Standish's cabin.

So John Graham was keeping his promise, the deadly promise he had made in the one hour of his father's triumph--that hour in which the elder Holt might have rid the earth of a serpent if his hands had not revolted in the last of those terrific minutes which he as a youth had witnessed. And Mary Standish was the instrument he had chosen to work his ends!

In these first minutes Alan could not find a doubt with which to fend the absoluteness of the convictions which were raging in his head, or still the tumult that was in his heart and blood. He made no pretense to deny the fact that John Graham must have written this letter to Mary Standish; inadvertently she had kept it, had finally attempted to destroy it, and Stampede, by chance, had discovered a small but convincing remnant of it. In a whirlwind of thought he pieced together things that had happened: her efforts to interest him from the beginning, the determination with which she had held to her purpose, her boldness in following him to the Range, and her apparent endeavor to work herself into his confidence--and with John Graham's signature staring at him from the table these things seemed conclusive and irrefutable evidence. The "industry" which Graham had referred to could mean only his own and Carl Lomen's, the reindeer industry which they had built up and were fighting to perpetuate, and which Graham and his beef-baron friends were combining to handicap and destroy. And in this game of destruction clever Mary Standish had come to play a part!

But why had she leaped into the sea?

It was as if a new voice had made itself heard in Alan's brain, a voice that rose insistently over a vast tumult of things, crying out against his arguments and demanding order and reason in place of the mad convictions that possessed him. If Mary Standish's mission was to pave the way for his ruin, and if she was John Graham's agent sent for that purpose, what reason could she have had for so dramatically attempting to give the world the impression that she had ended her life at sea? Surely such an act could in no way have been related with any plot which she might have had against him! In building up this structure of her defense he made no effort to sever her relationship with John Graham; that, he knew, was impossible. The note, her actions, and many of the things she had said were links inevitably associating her with his enemy, but these same things, now that they came pressing one upon another in his memory, gave to their collusion a new significance.

Was it conceivable that Mary Standish, instead of working for John Graham, was working *against* him? Could some conflict between them have been the reason for her flight aboard the *Nome*, and was it because she discovered Rossland there--John Graham's most trusted servant--that she formed her desperate scheme of leaping into the sea?

Between the two oppositions of his thought a sickening burden of what he knew to be true settled upon him. Mary Standish, even if she hated John Graham now, had at one time--and not very long ago--been an instrument of his trust; the letter he had written to her was positive proof of that. What it was that had caused a possible split between them and had inspired her flight from Seattle, and, later, her effort to bury a past under the fraud of a make-believe death, he might never learn, and just now he had no very great desire to look entirely into the whole truth of the matter. It was enough to know that of the past, and of the things that happened, she had been afraid, and it was in the desperation of this fear, with Graham's cleverest agent at her heels, that she had appealed to him in his cabin, and, failing to win him to her assistance, had taken the matter so dramatically into her own hands. And within that same hour a nearly successful attempt had been made upon Rossland's life. Of course the facts had shown that she could not have been directly responsible for his injury, but it was a haunting thing to remember as happening almost simultaneously with her disappearance into the sea.

He drew away from the window and, opening the door, went out into the night. Cool breaths of air gave a crinkly rattle to the swinging paper lanterns, and he could hear the soft whipping of the flags which Mary Standish had placed over his cabin. There was something comforting in the sound, a solace to the dishevelment of nerves he had suffered, a reminder of their day in Skagway when she had walked at his side with her hand resting warmly in his arm and her eyes and face filled with the inspiration of the mountains.

No matter what she was, or had been, there was something tenaciously admirable about her, a quality which had risen even above her feminine loveliness. She had proved herself not only clever; she was inspired by courage--a courage which he would have been compelled to respect even in a man like John Graham, and in this slim and fragile girl it appealed to him as a virtue to be laid up apart and aside from any of the motives which might be directing it. From the beginning it had been a bewildering part of her--a clean, swift, unhesitating courage that had leaped bounds where his own volition and judgment would have hung waveringly; that one courage in all the world--a woman's courage--which finds in the effort of its achievement no obstacle too high and no abyss too wide though death waits with outreaching arms on the other side. And, surely, where there had been all this, there must also have been some deeper and finer impulse than one of destruction, of physical gain, or of mere duty in the weaving of a human scheme.

The thought and the desire to believe brought words half aloud from Alan's lips, as he looked up again at the flags beating softly above his cabin. Mary Standish was not what Stampede's discovery had proclaimed her to be; there was some mistake, a monumental stupidity of reasoning on their part, and tomorrow would reveal the littleness and the injustice of their suspicions. He tried to force the conviction upon himself, and reentering the cabin he went to bed, still telling himself that a great lie had built itself up out of nothing, and that the God of all things was good to him because Mary Standish was alive, and not dead.

CHAPTER XVII

Alan slept soundly for several hours, but the long strain of the preceding day did not make him overreach the time he had set for himself, and he was up at six o'clock. Wegaruk had not forgotten her old habits, and a tub filled with cold water was waiting for him. He bathed, shaved himself, put on fresh clothes, and promptly at seven was at breakfast. The table at which he ordinarily sat alone was in a little room with double windows, through which, as he enjoyed his meals, he could see most of the habitations of the range. Unlike the average Eskimo dwellings they were neatly built of small timber brought down from the mountains, and were arranged in orderly fashion like the cottages of a village, strung out prettily on a single street. A sea of flowers lay in front of them, and at the end of the row, built on a little knoll that looked down into one of the watered hollows of the tundra, was Sokwenna's cabin. Because Sokwenna was the "old man" of the community and therefore the wisest--and because with him lived his foster-daughters, Keok and Nawadlook, the loveliest of Alan's tribal colony--Sokwenna's cabin was next to Alan's in size. And Alan, looking at it now and then as he ate his breakfast, saw a thin spiral of smoke rising from the chimney, but no other sign of life.

The sun was already up almost to its highest point, a little more than half-way between the horizon and the zenith, performing the apparent miracle of rising in the north and traveling east instead of west. Alan knew the men-folk of the village had departed hours ago for the distant herds. Always, when the reindeer drifted into the higher and cooler feeding-grounds of the foothills, there was this apparent abandonment, and after last night's celebration the women and children were not yet awake to the activities of the long day, where the rising and setting of the sun meant so little.

As he rose from the table, he glanced again toward Sokwenna's cabin. A solitary figure had climbed up out of the ravine and stood against the sun on the clough-top. Even at that distance, with the sun in his eyes, he knew it was Mary Standish.

He turned his back stoically to the window and lighted his pipe. For half an hour after that he sorted out his papers and range-books in preparation for the coming of Tautuk and Amuk Toolik, and when they arrived, the minute hand of his watch was at the hour of eight.

That the months of his absence had been prosperous ones he perceived by the smiling eagerness in the brown faces of his companions as they spread out the papers on which they had, in their own crude fashion, set down a record of the winter's happenings. Tautuk's voice, slow and very deliberate in its unfailing effort to master English without a slip, had in it a subdued note of satisfaction and triumph, while Amuk Toolik, who was quick and staccato in his manner of speech, using sentences seldom of greater length than three or four words, and who picked up slang and swear-words like a parrot, swelled with pride as he lighted his pipe, and then rubbed his hands with a rasping sound that always sent a chill up Alan's back.

"A ver' fine and prosper' year," said Tautuk in response to Alan's first question as to general conditions. "We bean ver' fortunate."

"One hell-good year," backed up Amuk Toolik with the quickness of a gun. "Plenty calf. Good hoof. Moss. Little wolf. Herds fat. This year--she peach!"

After this opening of the matter in hand Alan buried himself in the affairs of the range, and the old thrill, the glow which comes through achievement, and the pioneer's pride in marking a new frontier with the creative forces of success rose uppermost in him, and he forgot the passing of time. A hundred questions he had to ask, and the tongues of Tautuk and Amuk Toolik were crowded with the things they desired to tell him. Their voices filled the room with a paean of triumph. His herds had increased by a thousand head during the fawning months of April and May, and interbreeding of the Asiatic stock with wild, woodland caribou had produced a hundred calves of the super-animal whose flesh was bound to fill the markets of the States within a few years. Never had the moss been thicker under the winter snow; there had been no destructive fires; soft-hoof had escaped them; breeding records had been beaten, and dairying in the edge of the Arctic was no longer an experiment, but an established fact, for Tautuk now had seven deer giving a pint and a half of milk each twice a day, nearly as rich as the best of cream from cattle, and more than twenty that were delivering from a cupful to a pint at a milking. And to this Amuk Toolik added the amazing record of their running-deer, Kauk, the three-year-old, had drawn a sledge five miles over unbeaten snow in thirteen minutes and forty-seven seconds; Kauk and Olo, in team, had drawn the same sledge ten miles in twenty-six minutes and forty seconds, and one day he had driven the two ninety-eight miles in a mighty endurance test; and with Eno and Sutka, the first of their inter-breed with the wild woodland caribou, and heavier beasts, he had drawn a load of eight hundred pounds for three consecutive days at the rate of forty miles a day. From Fairbanks, Tanana, and the ranges of the Seward Peninsula agents of the swiftly spreading industry had offered as high as a hundred and ten dollars a head for breeding stock with the blood of the woodland caribou, and of these native and larger caribou of the tundras and forests seven young bulls and nine female calves had been captured and added to their own propagative forces.

For Alan this was triumph. He saw nothing of what it all meant in the way of ultimate personal fortune. It was the earth under his feet, the vast expanse of unpeopled waste traduced and scorned in the blindness of a hundred million people, which he saw fighting itself on the glory and reward of the conqueror through such achievement as this; a land betrayed rising at last out of the slime of political greed and ignorance; a giant irresistible in its awakening, that was destined in his lifetime to rock the destiny of a continent. It was Alaska rising up slowly but inexorably out of its eternity of sleep, mountain-sealed forces of a great land that was once the cradle of the earth coming into possession of life and power again; and his own feeble efforts in that long and fighting process of planting the seeds which meant its ultimate ascendancy possessed in themselves their own reward.

Long after Tautuk and Amuk Toolik had gone, his heart was filled with the song of success.

He was surprised at the swiftness with which time had gone, when he looked at his watch. It was almost dinner hour when he had finished with his papers and books and went outside. He heard Wegaruk's voice coming from the dark mouth of the underground icebox dug into the frozen subsoil of the tundra, and pausing at the glimmer of his old housekeeper's candle, he turned aside, descended the few steps, and entered quietly into the big, square chamber eight feet under the surface, where the earth had remained steadfastly frozen for some hundreds of thousands of years. Wegaruk had a habit of talking when alone, but Alan thought it odd that she should be explaining to herself that the tundra-soil, in spite of its almost tropical summer richness and luxuriance, never thawed deeper than three or four feet, below which point remained the icy cold placed there so long ago that "even the spirits did not know." He smiled when he heard Wegaruk measuring time and faith in terms of "spirits," which she had never quite given up for the missionaries, and was about to make his presence known when a voice interrupted him, so close at his side that the speaker, concealed in the shadow of the wall, could have reached out a hand and touched him.

"Good morning, Mr. Holt!"

It was Mary Standish, and he stared rather foolishly to make her out in the gloom.

"Good morning," he replied. "I was on my way to your place when Wegaruk's voice brought me here. You see, even this icebox seems like a friend after my experience in the States. Are you after a steak, Mammy?" he called.

Wegaruk's strong, squat figure turned as she answered him, and the light from her candle, glowing brightly in a split tomato can, fell clearly upon Mary Standish as the old woman waddled toward them. It was as if a spotlight had been thrown upon the girl suddenly out of a pit of darkness, and something about her, which was not her prettiness or the beauty that was in her eyes and hair, sent a sudden and unaccountable thrill through Alan. It remained with him when they drew back out of gloom and chill into sunshine and warmth, leaving Wegaruk to snuff her tomato-can lantern and follow with the steak, and it did not leave him when they walked over the tundra together toward Sokwenna's cabin. It was a puzzling thrill, stirring an emotion which it was impossible for him to subdue or explain; something which he knew he should understand but could not. And it seemed to him that knowledge of this mystery was in the girl's face, glowing in a gentle embarrassment, as she told him she had been expecting him, and that Keok and Nawadlook had given up the cabin to them, so that he might question her uninterrupted. But with this soft flush of her uneasiness, revealing itself in her eyes and cheeks, he saw neither fear nor hesitation.

In the "big room" of Sokwenna's cabin, which was patterned after his own, he sat down amid the color and delicate fragrance of masses of flowers, and the girl seated herself near him and waited for him to speak.

"You love flowers," he said lamely. "I want to thank you for the flowers you placed in my cabin. And the other things."

"Flowers are a habit with me," she replied, "and I have never seen such flowers as these. Flowers--and birds. I never dreamed that there were so many up here."

"Nor the world," he added. "It is ignorant of Alaska."

He was looking at her, trying to understand the inexplicable something about her. She knew what was in his mind, because the strangely thrilling emotion that possessed him could not keep its betrayal from his eyes. The color was fading slowly out of her cheeks; her lips grew a little tense, yet in her attitude of suspense and of waiting there was no longer a suspicion of embarrassment, no trace of fear, and no sign that a moment was at hand when her confidence was on the ebb. In this moment Alan did not think of John Graham. It seemed to him that she was like a child again, the child who had come to him in his cabin, and who had stood with her back against his cabin door, entreating him to achieve the impossible; an angel, almost, with her smooth, shining hair, her clear, beautiful eyes, her white throat which waited with its little heart-throb for him to beat down the fragile defense which now lay in the greater power of his own hands. The inequality of it, and the pitilessness of what had been in his mind to say and do, together with an inundating sense of his own brute mastery, swept over him, and in sudden desperation he reached out his hands toward her and cried:

"Mary Standish, in God's name tell me the truth. Tell me why you have come up here!"

"I have come," she said, looking at him steadily, "because I know that a man like you, when he loves a woman, will fight for her and protect her even though he may not possess her."

"But you didn't know that--not until--the cottonwoods!" he protested.

"Yes, I did. I knew it in Ellen McCormick's cabin."

She rose slowly before him, and he, too, rose to his feet, staring at her like a man who had been struck, while intelligence--a dawning reason--an understanding of the strange mystery of her that morning, sent the still greater thrill of its shock through him. He gave an exclamation of amazement.

"You were at Ellen McCormick's! She gave you--*that!*"

She nodded. "Yes, the dress you brought from the ship. Please don't scold me, Mr. Holt. Be a little kind with me when you have heard what I am going to tell you. I was in the cabin that last day, when you returned from searching for me in the sea. Mr. McCormick didn't know. But *she* did. I lied a little, just a little, so that she, being a woman, would promise not to tell you I was there. You see, I had lost a great deal of my faith, and my courage was about gone, and I was afraid of you."

"Afraid of me?"

"Yes, afraid of everybody. I was in the room behind Ellen McCormick when she asked you-- that question; and when you answered as you did, I was like stone. I was amazed and didn't believe, for I was certain that after what had happened on the ship you despised me, and only through a peculiar sense of honor were making the search for me. Not until two days later, when your letters came to Ellen McCormick, and we read them--"

"You opened both?"

"Of course. One was to be read immediately, the other when I was found--and I had found myself. Maybe it wasn't exactly fair, but you couldn't expect two women to resist a temptation like that. And--*I wanted to know.*"

She did not lower her eyes or turn her head aside as she made the confession. Her gaze met Alan's with beautiful steadiness.

"And then I believed. I knew, because of what you said in that letter, that you were the one man in all the world who would help me and give me a fighting chance if I came to you. But it has taken all my courage--and in the end you will drive me away--"

Again he looked upon the miracle of tears in wide-open, unfaltering eyes, tears which she did not brush away, but through which, in a moment, she smiled at him as no woman had ever smiled at him before. And with the tears there seemed to possess her a pride which lifted her above all confusion, a living spirit of will and courage and womanhood that broke away the dark clouds of suspicion and fear that had gathered in his mind. He tried to speak, and his lips were thick.

"You have come--because you know I love you, and you--"

"Because, from the beginning, it must have been a great faith in you that inspired me, Alan Holt."

"There must have been more than that," he persisted. "Some other reason."

"Two," she acknowledged, and now he noticed that with the dissolution of tears a flush of color was returning into her cheeks.

"And those--"

"One it is impossible for you to know; the other, if I tell you, will make you despise me. I am sure of that."

"It has to do with John Graham?"

She bowed her head. "Yes, with John Graham."

For the first time long lashes hid her eyes from him, and for a moment it seemed that her resolution was gone and she stood stricken by the import of the thing that lay behind his question; yet her cheeks flamed red instead of paling, and when she looked at him again, her eyes burned with a lustrous fire.

"John Graham," she repeated. "The man you hate and want to kill."

Slowly he turned toward the door. "I am leaving immediately after dinner to inspect the herds up in the foothills," he said. "And you--*are welcome here.*"

He caught the swift intake of her breath as he paused for an instant at the door, and saw the new light that leaped into her eyes.

"Thank you, Alan Holt," she cried softly, "*Oh, I thank you!*"

And then, suddenly, she stopped him with a little cry, as if at last something had broken away from her control. He faced her, and for a moment they stood in silence.

"I'm sorry--sorry I said to you what I did that night on the *Nome,*" she said. "I accused you of brutality, of unfairness, of--of even worse than that, and I want to take it all back. You are big and clean and splendid, for you would go away now, knowing I am poisoned by an association with the man who has injured you so terribly, *and you say I am welcome!* And I don't want you to go. You have made me *want* to tell you who I am, and why I have come to you, and I pray God you will think as kindly of me as you can when you have heard."

CHAPTER XVIII

It seemed to Alan that in an instant a sudden change had come over the world. There was silence in the cabin, except for the breath which came like a sob to the girl's lips as she turned to the window and looked out into the blaze of golden sunlight that filled the tundra. He heard Tautuk's voice, calling to Keok away over near the reindeer corral, and he heard clearly Keok's merry laughter as she answered him. A gray-cheeked thrush flew up to the roof of Sokwenna's cabin and began to sing. It was as if these things had come as a message to both of them, relieving a tension, and significant of the beauty and glory and undying hope of life. Mary Standish turned from the window with shining eyes.

"Every day the thrush comes and sings on our cabin roof," she said.

"It is--possibly--because you are here," he replied.

She regarded him seriously. "I have thought of that. You know, I have faith in a great many unbelievable things. I can think of nothing more beautiful than the spirit that lives in the heart of a bird. I am sure, if I were dying, I would like to have a bird singing near me. Hopelessness cannot be so deep that bird-song will not reach it."

He nodded, trying to answer in that way. He felt uncomfortable. She closed the door which he had left partly open, and made a little gesture for him to resume the chair which he had left a few moments before. She seated herself first and smiled at him wistfully, half regretfully, as she said:

"I have been very foolish. What I am going to tell you now I should have told you aboard the *Nome*. But I was afraid. Now I am not afraid, but ashamed, terribly ashamed, to let you know the truth. And yet I am not sorry it happened so, because otherwise I would not have come up here, and all this--your world, your people, and you--have meant a great deal to me. You will understand when I have made my confession."

"No, I don't want that," he protested almost roughly. "I don't want you to put it that way. If I can help you, and if you wish to tell me as a friend, that's different. I don't want a confession, which would imply that I have no faith in you."

"And you have faith in me?"

"Yes; so much that the sun will darken and bird-song never seem the same if I lose you again, as I thought I had lost you from the ship."

"Oh, *you mean that*!"

The words came from her in a strange, tense, little cry, and he seemed to see only her eyes as he looked at her face, pale as the petals of the tundra daises behind her. With the thrill of what he had dared to say tugging at his heart, he wondered why she was so white.

"You mean that," her lips repeated slowly, "after all that has happened--even after--that part of a letter--which Stampede brought to you last night--"

He was surprised. How had she discovered what he thought was a secret between himself and Stampede? His mind leaped to a conclusion, and she saw it written in his face.

"No, it wasn't Stampede," she said. "He didn't tell me. It--just happened. And after this letter--you still believe in me?"

"I must. I should be unhappy if I did not. And I am--most perversely hoping for happiness. I have told myself that what I saw over John Graham's signature was a lie."

"It wasn't that--quite. But it didn't refer to you, or to me. It was part of a letter written to Rossland. He sent me some books while I was on the ship, and inadvertently left a page of this letter in one of them as a marker. It was really quite unimportant, when one read the whole of it. The other half of the page is in the toe of the slipper which you did not return to Ellen McCormick. You know that is the conventional thing for a woman to do--to use paper for padding in a soft-toed slipper."

He wanted to shout; he wanted to throw up his arms and laugh as Tautuk and Amuk Toolik and a score of others had laughed to the beat of the tom-toms last night, not because he was amused, but out of sheer happiness. But Mary Standish's voice, continuing in its quiet and matter-of-fact way, held him speechless, though she could not fail to see the effect upon him of this simple explanation of the presence of Graham's letter.

"I was in Nawadlook's room when I saw Stampede pick up the wad of paper from the floor," she was saying. "I was looking at the slipper a few minutes before, regretting that you had left its mate in my cabin on the ship, and the paper must have dropped then. I saw Stampede read it, and the shock that came in his face. Then he placed it on the table and went out. I hurried to see what he had found and had scarcely read the few words when I heard him returning. I returned the paper where he had laid it, hid myself in Nawadlook's room, and saw Stampede when he carried it to you. I don't know why I allowed it to be done. I had no reason. Maybe it was just--intuition, and maybe it was because--just in that hour--I so hated myself that I wanted someone to flay me alive, and I thought that what Stampede had found would make you do it. And I deserve it! I deserve nothing better at your hands."

"But it isn't true," he protested. "The letter was to Rossland."

There was no responsive gladness in her eyes. "Better that it were true, and all that *is* true were false," she said in a quiet, hopeless voice. "I would almost give my life to be no more than what those words implied, dishonest, a spy, a criminal of a sort; almost any alternative would I accept in place of what I actually am. Do you begin to understand?"

"I am afraid--I can not." Even as he persisted in denial, the pain which had grown like velvety dew in her eyes clutched at his heart, and he felt dread of what lay behind it. "I understand--only--that I am glad you are here, more glad than yesterday, or this morning, or an hour ago."

She bowed her head, so that the bright light of day made a radiance of rich color in her hair, and he saw the sudden tremble of the shining lashes that lay against her cheeks; and then, quickly, she caught her breath, and her hands grew steady in her lap.

"Would you mind--if I asked you first--to tell me *your* story of John Graham?" she spoke softly. "I know it, a little, but I think it would make everything easier if I could hear it from you--now."

He stood up and looked down upon her where she sat, with the light playing in her hair; and then he moved to the window, and back, and she had not changed her position, but was waiting for him to speak. She raised her eyes, and the question her lips had formed was glowing in them as clearly as if she had voiced it again in words. A desire rose in him to speak to her as he had never spoken to another human being, and to reveal for her--and for her alone--the thing that had harbored itself in his soul for many years. Looking up at him, waiting, partial understanding softening her sweet face, a dusky glow in her eyes, she was so beautiful that he cried out softly and then laughed in a strange repressed sort of way as he half held out his arms toward her.

"I think I know how my father must have loved my mother," he said. "But I can't make you feel it. I can't hope for that. She died when I was so young that she remained only as a beautiful dream for me. But for my father she *never* died, and as I grew older she became more and more alive for me, so that in our journeys we would talk about her as if she were waiting for us back home and would welcome us when we returned. And never could my father remain away from the place where she was buried very long at a time. He called it *home*, that little cup at the foot of the mountain, with the waterfall singing in summer, and a paradise of birds and flowers keeping her company, and all the great, wild world she loved about her. There was the cabin, too; the little cabin where I was born, with its back to the big mountain, and filled with the handiwork of my mother as she had left it when she died. And my father too used to laugh and sing there--he had a clear voice that would roll half-way up the mountain; and as I grew older the miracle at times stirred me with a strange fear, so real to my father did my dead mother seem when he was home. But you look frightened, Miss Standish! Oh, it may seem weird and ghostly now, but it was *true*--so true that I have lain awake nights thinking of it and wishing that it had never been so!"

"Then you have wished a great sin," said the girl in a voice that seemed scarcely to whisper between her parted lips. "I hope someone will feel toward me--some day--like that."

"But it was this which brought the tragedy, the thing you have asked me to tell you about," he said, unclenching his hands slowly, and then tightening them again until the blood ebbed from their veins. "Interests were coming in; the tentacles of power and greed were reaching out, encroaching steadily a little nearer to our cup at the foot of the mountain. But my father did not dream of what might happen. It came in the spring of the year he took me on my first trip to the States, when I was eighteen. We were gone five months, and they were five months of hell for him. Day and night he grieved for my mother and the little home under the mountain. And when at last we came back--"

He turned again to the window, but he did not see the golden sun of the tundra or hear Tautuk calling from the corral.

"When we came back," he repeated in a cold, hard voice, "a construction camp of a hundred men had invaded my father's little paradise. The cabin was gone; a channel had been cut from the waterfall, and this channel ran where my mother's grave had been. They had treated it with that same desecration with which they have destroyed ten thousand Indian graves since then. Her bones were scattered in the sand and mud. And from the moment my father saw what had happened, never another sun rose in the heavens for him. His heart died, yet he went on living-- for a time."

Mary Standish had bowed her face in her hands. He saw the tremor of her slim shoulders; and when he came back, and she looked up at him, it was as if he beheld the pallid beauty of one of the white tundra flowers.

"And the man who committed that crime--was John Graham," she said, in the strangely passionless voice of one who knew what his answer would be.

"Yes, John Graham. He was there, representing big interests in the States. The foreman had objected to what happened; many of the men had protested; a few of them, who knew my father, had thrown up their work rather than be partners to that crime. But Graham had the legal power; they say he laughed as if he thought it a great joke that a cabin and a grave should be considered obstacles in his way. And he laughed when my father and I went to see him; yes, *laughed*, in that noiseless, oily, inside way of his, as you might think of a snake laughing.

"We found him among the men. My God, you don't know how I hated him!--Big, loose, powerful, dangling the watch-fob that hung over his vest, and looking at my father in that way as he told him what a fool he was to think a worthless grave should interfere with his work. I wanted to kill him, but my father put a hand on my shoulder, a quiet, steady hand, and said: 'It is my duty, Alan. *My duty.*'

"And then--it happened. My father was older, much older than Graham, but God put such strength in him that day as I had never seen before, and with his naked hands he would have killed the brute if I had not unlocked them with my own. Before all his men Graham became a mass of helpless pulp, and from the ground, with the last of the breath that was in him, he cursed my father, and he cursed me. He said that all the days of his life he would follow us, until we paid a thousand times for what we had done. And then my father dragged him as he would have dragged a rat to the edge of a piece of bush, and there he tore his clothes from him until the brute was naked; and in that nakedness he scourged him with whips until his arms were weak, and John Graham was unconscious and like a great hulk of raw beef. When it was over, we went into the mountains."

During the terrible recital Mary Standish had not looked away from him, and now her hands were clenched like his own, and her eyes and face were aflame, as if she wanted to leap up and strike at something unseen between them.

"And after that, Alan; after that--"

She did not know that she had spoken his name, and he, hearing it, scarcely understood.

"John Graham kept his promise," he answered grimly. "The influence and money behind him haunted us wherever we went. My father had been successful, but one after another the properties in which he was interested were made worthless. A successful mine in which he was most heavily interested was allowed to become abandoned. A hotel which he partly owned in Dawson was bankrupted. One after another things happened, and after each happening my father would receive a polite note of regret from Graham, written as if the word actually came from a friend. But my father cared little for money losses now. His heart was drying up and his life ebbing away for the little cabin and the grave that were gone from the foot of the mountain. It went on this way for three years, and then, one morning, my father was found on the beach at Nome, dead."

"*Dead!*"

Alan heard only the gasping breath in which the word came from Mary Standish, for he was facing the window, looking steadily away from her.

"Yes--murdered. I know it was the work of John Graham. He didn't do it personally, but it was *his money* that accomplished the end. Of course nothing ever came of it. I won't tell you how his influence and power have dogged me; how they destroyed the first herd of reindeer I had, and how they filled the newspapers with laughter and lies about me when I was down in the States last winter in an effort to make *your* people see a little something of the truth about Alaska. I am waiting. I know the day is coming when I shall have John Graham as my father had him under our mountain twenty years ago. He must be fifty now. But that won't save him when the time comes. No one will loosen my hands as I loosened my father's. And all Alaska will rejoice, for his power and his money have become twin monsters that are destroying Alaska just as he destroyed the life of my father. Unless he dies, and his money-power ends, he will make of this great land nothing more than a shell out of which he and his kind have taken all the meat. And the hour of deadliest danger is now upon us."

He looked at Mary Standish, and it was as if death had come to her where she sat. She seemed not to breathe, and her face was so white it frightened him. And then, slowly, she turned her eyes upon him, and never had he seen such living pools of torture and of horror. He was amazed at the quietness of her voice when she began to speak, and startled by the almost deadly coldness of it.

"I think you can understand--now--why I leaped into the sea, why I wanted the world to think I was dead, and why I have feared to tell you the truth," she said. "*I am John Graham's wife.*"

CHAPTER XIX

Alan's first thought was of the monstrous incongruity of the thing, the almost physical impossibility of a mésalliance of the sort Mary Standish had revealed to him. He saw her, young and beautiful, with face and eyes that from the beginning had made him feel all that was good and sweet in life, and behind her he saw the shadow-hulk of John Graham, the pitiless iron-man, without conscience and without soul, coarsened by power, fiendish in his iniquities, and old enough to be her father!

A slow smile twisted his lips, but he did not know he smiled. He pulled himself together without letting her see the physical part of the effort it was taking. And he tried to find something to say that would help clear her eyes of the agony that was in them.

"That--is a most unreasonable thing--to be true," he said.

It seemed to him his lips were making words out of wood, and that the words were fatuously inefficient compared with what he should have said, or acted, under the circumstances.

She nodded. "It is. But the world doesn't look at it in that way. Such things just happen."

She reached for a book which lay on the table where the tundra daisies were heaped. It was a book written around the early phases of pioneer life in Alaska, taken from his own library, a volume of statistical worth, dryly but carefully written--and she had been reading it. It struck him as a symbol of the fight she was making, of her courage, and of her desire to triumph in the face of tremendous odds that must have beset her. He still could not associate her completely with John Graham. Yet his face was cold and white.

Her hand trembled a little as she opened the book and took from it a newspaper clipping. She did not speak as she unfolded it and gave it to him.

At the top of two printed columns was the picture of a young and beautiful girl; in an oval, covering a small space over the girl's shoulder, was a picture of a man of fifty or so. Both were strangers to him. He read their names, and then the headlines. "A Hundred-Million-Dollar Love" was the caption, and after the word love was a dollar sign. Youth and age, beauty and the other thing, two great fortunes united. He caught the idea and looked at Mary Standish. It was impossible for him to think of her as Mary Graham.

"I tore that from a paper in Cordova," she said. "They have nothing to do with me. The girl lives in Texas. But don't you see something in her eyes? Can't you see it, even in the picture? She has on her wedding things. But it seemed to me--when I saw her face--that in her eyes were agony and despair and hopelessness, and that she was bravely trying to hide them from the world. It's just another proof, one of thousands, that such unreasonable things do happen."

He was beginning to feel a dull and painless sort of calm, the stoicism which came to possess him whenever he was confronted by the inevitable. He sat down, and with his head bowed over it took one of the limp, little hands that lay in Mary Standish's lap. The warmth had gone out of it. It was cold and lifeless. He caressed it gently and held it between his brown, muscular hands, staring at it, and yet seeing nothing in particular. It was only the ticking of Keok's clock that broke the silence for a time. Then he released the hand, and it dropped in the girl's lap again. She had been looking steadily at the streak of gray in his hair. And a light came into her eyes, a light which he did not see, and a little tremble of her lips, and an almost imperceptible inclination of her head toward him.

"I'm sorry I didn't know," he said. "I realize now how you must have felt back there in the cottonwoods."

"No, you don't realize--*you don't!*" she protested.

In an instant, it seemed to him, a vibrant, flaming life swept over her again. It was as if his words had touched fire to some secret thing, as if he had unlocked a door which grim hopelessness had closed. He was amazed at the swiftness with which color came into her cheeks.

"You don't understand, and I am determined that you *shall*," she went on. "I would die before I let you go away thinking what is now in your mind. You will despise me, but I would rather be hated for the truth than because of the horrible thing which you must believe if I remain silent." She forced a wan smile to her lips. "You know, Belinda Mulrooneys were very well in their day, but they don't fit in now, do they? If a woman makes a mistake and tries to remedy it in a fighting sort of way, as Belinda Mulrooney might have done back in the days when Alaska was young--"

She finished with a little gesture of despair.

"I have committed a great folly," she said, hesitating an instant in his silence. "I see very clearly now the course I should have taken. You will advise me that it is still not too late when you have heard what I am going to say. Your face is like--a rock."

"It is because your tragedy is mine," he said.

She turned her eyes from him. The color in her cheeks deepened. It was a vivid, feverish glow. "I was born rich, enormously, hatefully rich," she said in the low, unimpassioned voice of a confessional. "I don't remember father or mother. I lived always with my Grandfather Standish and my Uncle Peter Standish. Until I was thirteen I had my Uncle Peter, who was grandfather's brother, and lived with us. I worshiped Uncle Peter. He was a cripple. From young manhood he had lived in a wheel-chair, and he was nearly seventy-five when he died. As a baby that wheel-chair, and my rides in it with him about the great house in which we lived, were my delights. He was my father and mother, everything that was good and sweet in life. I remember thinking, as a child, that if God was as good as Uncle Peter, He was a wonderful God. It was Uncle Peter who told me, year after year, the old stories and legends of the Standishes. And he was always happy--always happy and glad and seeing nothing but sunshine though he hadn't stood on his feet for nearly sixty years. And my Uncle Peter died when I was thirteen, five days before my birthday came. I think he must have been to me what your father was to you."

He nodded. There was something that was not the hardness of rock in his face now, and John Graham seemed to have faded away.

"I was left, then, alone with my Grandfather Standish," she went on. "He didn't love me as my Uncle Peter loved me, and I don't think I loved him. But I was proud of him. I thought the whole world must have stood in awe of him, as I did. As I grew older I learned the world *was* afraid of him--bankers, presidents, even the strongest men in great financial interests; afraid of him, and of his partners, the Grahams, and of Sharpleigh, who my Uncle Peter had told me was the cleverest lawyer in the nation, and who had grown up in the business of the two families. My grandfather was sixty-eight when Uncle Peter died, so it was John Graham who was the actual working force behind the combined fortunes of the two families. Sometimes, as I now recall it, Uncle Peter was like a little child. I remember how he tried to make me understand just how big my grandfather's interests were by telling me that if two dollars were taken from every man, woman, and child in the United States, it would just about add up to what he and the Grahams possessed, and my Grandfather Standish's interests were three-quarters of the whole. I remember how a hunted look would come into my Uncle Peter's face at times when I asked him how all this money was used, and where it was. And he never answered me as I wanted to be answered, and I never understood. I didn't know *why* people feared my grandfather and John Graham. I didn't know of the stupendous power my grandfather's money had rolled up for them. I didn't know"--her voice sank to a shuddering whisper--"I didn't know how they were using it in Alaska, for instance. I didn't know it was feeding upon starvation and ruin and death. I don't think even Uncle Peter knew *that*."

She looked at Alan steadily, and her gray eyes seemed burning up with a slow fire.

"Why, even then, before Uncle Peter died, I had become one of the biggest factors in all their schemes. It was impossible for me to suspect that John Graham was *anticipating* a little girl of thirteen, and I didn't guess that my Grandfather Standish, so straight, so grandly white of beard and hair, so like a god of power when he stood among men, was even then planning that I should be given to him, so that a monumental combination of wealth might increase itself still more in that juggernaut of financial achievement for which he lived. And to bring about my sacrifice, to make sure it would not fail, they set Sharpleigh to the task, because Sharpleigh was sweet and good of face, and gentle like Uncle Peter, so that I loved him and had confidence in him, without a suspicion that under his white hair lay a brain which matched in cunning and mercilessness that of John Graham himself. And he did his work well, Alan."

A second time she had spoken his name, softly and without embarrassment. With her nervous fingers tying and untying the two corners of a little handkerchief in her lap, she went on, after a moment of silence in which the ticking of Keok's clock seemed tense and loud.

"When I was seventeen, Grandfather Standish died. I wish you could understand all that followed without my telling you: how I clung to Sharpleigh as a father, how I trusted him, and how cleverly and gently he educated me to the thought that it was right and just, and my greatest duty in life, to carry out the stipulation of my grandfather's will and marry John Graham. Otherwise, he told me--if that union was not brought about before I was twenty-two-- not a dollar of the great fortune would go to the house of Standish; and because he was clever enough to know that money alone would not urge me, he showed me a letter which he said my Uncle Peter had written, and which I was to read on my seventeenth birthday, and in that letter Uncle Peter urged me to live up to the Standish name and join in that union of the two great fortunes which he and Grandfather Standish had always planned. I didn't dream the letter was a forgery. And in the end they won--and I promised."

She sat with bowed head, crumpling the bit of cambric between her fingers. "Do you despise me?" she asked.

"No," he replied in a tense, unimpassioned voice. "I love you."

She tried to look at him calmly and bravely. In his face again lay the immobility of rock, and in his eyes a sullen, slumbering fire.

"I promised," she repeated quickly, as if regretting the impulse that had made her ask him the question. "But it was to be business, a cold, unsentimental business. I disliked John Graham. Yet I would marry him. In the eyes of the law I would be his wife; in the eyes of the world I would remain his wife--but never more than that. They agreed, and I in my ignorance believed.

"I didn't see the trap. I didn't see the wicked triumph in John Graham's heart. No power could have made me believe then that he wanted to possess only *me*; that he was horrible enough to want me even without love; that he was a great monster of a spider, and I the fly lured into his web. And the agony of it was that in all the years since Uncle Peter died I had dreamed strange and beautiful dreams. I lived in a make-believe world of my own, and I read, read, read; and the thought grew stronger and stronger in me that I had lived another life somewhere, and that I belonged back in the years when the world was clean, and there was love, and vast reaches of land wherein money and power were little guessed of, and where romance and the glory of manhood and womanhood rose above all other things. Oh, I wanted these things, and yet because others had molded me, and because of my misguided Standish sense of pride and honor, I was shackling myself to John Graham.

"In the last months preceding my twenty-second birthday I learned more of the man than I had ever known before; rumors came to me; I investigated a little, and I began to find the hatred, and the reason for it, which has come to me so conclusively here in Alaska. I almost knew, at the last, that he was a monster, but the world had been told I was to marry him, and Sharpleigh with his fatherly hypocrisy was behind me, and John Graham treated me so courteously and so coolly that I did not suspect the terrible things in his heart and mind--and I went on with the bargain. *I married him.*"

She drew a sudden, deep breath, as if she had passed through the ordeal of what she had most dreaded to say, and now, meeting the changeless expression of Alan's face with a fierce, little cry that leaped from her like a flash of gun-fire, she sprang to her feet and stood with her back crushed against the tundra flowers, her voice trembling as she continued, while he stood up and faced her.

"You needn't go on," he interrupted in a voice so low and terribly hard that she felt the menacing thrill of it. "You needn't. I will settle with John Graham, if God gives me the chance."

"You would have me stop *now*--before I have told you of the only shred of triumph to which I may lay claim!" she protested. "Oh, you may be sure that I realize the sickening folly and wickedness of it all, but I swear before my God that I didn't realize it then, until it was too late. To you, Alan, clean as the great mountains and plains that have been a part of you, I know how impossible this must seem--that I should marry a man I at first feared, then loathed, then came to hate with a deadly hatred; that I should sacrifice myself because I thought it was a duty; that I should be so weak, so ignorant, so like soft clay in the hands of those I trusted. Yet I tell you that at no time did I think or suspect that I was sacrificing *myself*; at no time, blind though you may call me, did I see a hint of that sickening danger into which I was voluntarily going. No, not even an hour before the wedding did I suspect that, for it had all been so coldly planned, like a great deal in finance--so carefully adjudged by us all as a business affair, that I felt no fear except that sickness of soul which comes of giving up one's life. And no hint of it came until the last of the few words were spoken which made us man and wife, and then I saw in John Graham's eyes something which I had never seen there before. And Sharpleigh--"

Her hands caught at her breast. Her gray eyes were pools of flame.

"I went to my room. I didn't lock my door, because never had it been necessary to do that. I didn't cry. No, I didn't cry. But something strange was happening to me which tears might have prevented. It seemed to me there were many walls to my room; I was faint; the windows seemed to appear and disappear, and in that sickness I reached my bed. Then I saw the door open, and John Graham came in, and closed the door behind him, and locked it. My room. He had come into *my room!* The unexpectedness of it--the horror--the insult roused me from my stupor. I sprang up to face him, and there he stood, within arm's reach of me, a look in his face which told me at last the truth which I had failed to suspect--or fear. His arms were reaching out--

"'You are my wife,' he said.

"Oh, I knew, then. '*You are my wife,*' he repeated. I wanted to scream, but I couldn't; and then--then--his arms reached me; I felt them crushing around me like the coils of a great snake; the poison of his lips was at my face--and I believed that I was lost, and that no power could save me in this hour from the man who had come to my room--the man who was my husband. I think it was Uncle Peter who gave me voice, who put the right words in my brain, who made me laugh--yes, laugh, and almost caress him with my hands. The change in me amazed him, stunned him, and he freed me--while I told him that in these first few hours of wifehood I wanted to be alone, and that he should come to me that evening, and that I would be waiting for him. And I smiled at him as I said these things, smiled while I wanted to kill him, and he went, a great, gloating, triumphant beast, believing that the obedience of wifehood was about to give him what he had expected to find through dishonor--and I was left alone.

"I thought of only one thing then--escape. I saw the truth. It swept over me, inundated me, roared in my ears. All that I had ever lived with Uncle Peter came back to me. This was not his world; it had never been--and it was not mine. It was, all at once, a world of monsters. I wanted never to face it again, never to look into the eyes of those I had known. And even as these thoughts and desires swept upon me, I was filling a traveling bag in a fever of madness, and Uncle Peter was at my side, urging me to hurry, telling me I had no minutes to lose, for the man who had left me was clever and might guess the truth that lay hid behind my smiles and cajolery.

"I stole out through the back of the house, and as I went I heard Sharpleigh's low laughter in the library. It was a new kind of laughter, and with it I heard John Graham's voice. I was thinking only of the sea--to get away on the sea. A taxi took me to my bank, and I drew money. I went to the wharves, intent only on boarding a ship, any ship, and it seemed to me that Uncle Peter was leading me; and we came to a great ship that was leaving for Alaska--and you know--what happened then--Alan Holt."

With a sob she bowed her face in her hands, but only an instant it was there, and when she looked at Alan again, there were no tears in her eyes, but a soft glory of pride and exultation.

"I am clean of John Graham," she cried. "*Clean!*"

He stood twisting his hands, twisting them in a helpless, futile sort of way, and it was he, and not the girl, who felt like bowing his head that the tears might come unseen. For her eyes were bright and shining and clear as stars.

"Do you despise me now?"

"I love you," he said again, and made no movement toward her.

"I am glad," she whispered, and she did not look at him, but at the sunlit plain which lay beyond the window.

"And Rossland was on the *Nome*, and saw you, and sent word back to Graham," he said, fighting to keep himself from going nearer to her.

She nodded. "Yes; and so I came to you, and failing there, I leaped into the sea, for I wanted them to think I was dead."

"And Rossland was hurt."

"Yes. Strangely. I heard of it in Cordova. Men like Rossland frequently come to unexpected ends."

He went to the door which she had closed, and opened it, and stood looking toward the blue billows of the foothills with the white crests of the mountains behind them. She came, after a moment, and stood beside him.

"I understand," she said softly, and her hand lay in a gentle touch upon his arm. "You are trying to see some way out, and you can see only one. That is to go back, face the creatures I hate, regain my freedom in the old way. And I, too, can see no other way. I came on impulse; I must return with impulse and madness burned out of me. And I am sorry. I dread it. I--would rather die."

"And I--" he began, then caught himself and pointed to the distant hills and mountains. "The herds are there," he said. "I am going to them. I may be gone a week or more. Will you promise me to be here when I return?"

"Yes, if that is your desire."

"It is."

She was so near that his lips might have touched her shining hair.

"And when you return, I must go. That will be the only way."

"I think so."

"It will be hard. It may be, after all, that I am a coward. But to face all that--alone--"

"You won't be alone," he said quietly, still looking at the far-away hills. "If you go, I am going with you."

It seemed as if she had stopped breathing for a moment at his side, and then, with a little, sobbing cry she drew away from him and stood at the half-opened door of Nawadlook's room, and the glory in her eyes was the glory of his dreams as he had wandered with her hand in hand over the tundras in those days of grief and half-madness when he had thought she was dead.

"I am glad I was in Ellen McCormick's cabin the day you came," she was saying. "And I thank God for giving me the madness and courage to come to *you*. I am not afraid of anything in the world now--because--*I love you, Alan*!"

And as Nawadlook's door closed behind her, Alan stumbled out into the sunlight, a great drumming in his heart, and a tumult in his brain that twisted the world about him until for a little it held neither vision nor space nor sound.

CHAPTER XX

In that way, with the beautiful world swimming in sunshine and golden tundra haze until foothills and mountains were like castles in a dream, Alan Holt set off with Tautuk and Amuk Toolik, leaving Stampede and Keok and Nawadlook at the corral bars, with Stampede little regretting that he was left behind to guard the range. For a mighty resolution had taken root in the prospector's heart, and he felt himself thrilled and a bit trembling at the nearness of the greatest drama that had ever entered his life. Alan, looking back after the first few minutes, saw that Keok and Nawadlook stood alone. Stampede was gone.

The ridge beyond the coulée out of which Mary Standish had come with wild flowers soon closed like a door between him and Sokwenna's cabin, and the straight trail to the mountains lay ahead, and over this Alan set the pace, with Tautuk and Amuk Toolik and a caravan of seven pack-deer behind him, bearing supplies for the herdsmen.

Alan had scarcely spoken to the two men. He knew the driving force which was sending him to the mountains was not only an impulse, but almost an inspirational thing born of necessity. Each step that he took, with his head and heart in a swirl of intoxicating madness, was an effort behind which he was putting a sheer weight of physical will. He wanted to go back. The urge was upon him to surrender utterly to the weakness of forgetting that Mary Standish was a wife. He had almost fallen a victim to his selfishness and passion in the moment when she stood at Nawadlook's door, telling him that she loved him. An iron hand had drawn him out into the day, and it was the same iron hand that kept his face to the mountains now, while in his brain her voice repeated the words that had set his world on fire.

He knew what had happened this morning was not the merely important and essential incident of most human lives; it had been a cataclysmic thing with him. Probably it would be impossible for even the girl ever fully to understand. And he needed to be alone to gather strength and mental calmness for the meeting of the problem ahead of him, a complication so unexpected that the very foundation of that stoic equanimity which the mountains had bred in him had suffered a temporary upsetting. His happiness was almost an insanity. The dream wherein he had wandered with a spirit of the dead had come true; it was the old idyl in the flesh again, his father, his mother--and back in the cabin beyond the ridge such a love had cried out to him. And he was afraid to return. He laughed the fact aloud, happily and with an unrepressed exultation as he strode ahead of the pack-train, and with that exultation words came to his lips, words intended for himself alone, telling him that Mary Standish belonged to him, and that until the end of eternity he would fight for her and keep her. Yet he kept on, facing the mountains, and he walked so swiftly that Tautuk and Amuk Toolik fell steadily behind with the deer, so that in time long dips and swells of the tundra lay between them.

With grim persistence he kept at himself, and at last there swept over him in its ultimate triumph a compelling sense of the justice of what he had done--justice to Mary Standish. Even now he did not think of her as Mary Graham. But she was Graham's wife. And if he had gone to her in that moment of glorious confession when she had stood at Nawadlook's door, if he had violated her faith when, because of faith, she had laid the world at his feet, he would have fallen to the level of John Graham himself. Thought of the narrowness of his escape and of the first mad desire to call her back from Nawadlook's room, to hold her in his arms again as he had held her in the cottonwoods, brought a hot fire into his face. Something greater than his own fighting instinct had turned him to the open door of the cabin. It was Mary Standish--her courage, the-glory of faith and love shining in her eyes, her measurement of him as a man. She had not been afraid to say what was in her heart, because she knew what he would do.

Mid-afternoon found him waiting for Tautuk and Amuk Toolik at the edge of a slough where willows grew deep and green and the crested billows of sedge-cotton stood knee-high. The faces of the herdsmen were sweating. Thereafter Alan walked with them, until in that hour when the sun had sunk to its lowest plane they came to the first of the Endicott foothills. Here they rested until the coolness of deeper evening, when a golden twilight filled the land, and then resumed the journey toward the mountains.

Midsummer heat and the winged pests of the lower lands had driven the herds steadily into the cooler altitudes of the higher plateaux and valleys. Here they had split into telescoping columns which drifted in slowly moving streams wherever the doors of the hills and mountains opened into new grazing fields, until Alan's ten thousand reindeer were in three divisions, two of the greatest traveling westward, and one, of a thousand head, working north and east. The first and second days Alan remained with the nearest and southward herd. The third day he went on with Tautuk and two pack-deer through a break in the mountains and joined the herdsmen of the second and higher multitude of feeding animals. There began to possess him a curious disinclination to hurry, and this aversion grew in a direct ratio with the thought which was becoming stronger in him with each mile and hour of his progress. A multitude of emotions were buried under the conviction that Mary Standish must leave the range when he returned. He had a grim sense of honor, and a particularly devout one when it had to do with women, and though he conceded nothing of right and justice in the relationship which existed between the woman he loved and John Graham, he knew that she must go. To remain at the range was the one impossible thing for her to do. He would take her to Tanana. He would go with her to the States. The matter would be settled in a reasonable and intelligent way, and when he came back, he would bring her with him.

But beneath this undercurrent of decision fought the thing which his will held down, and yet never quite throttled completely--that something which urged him with an unconquerable persistence to hold with his own hands what a glorious fate had given him, and to finish with John Graham, if it ever came to that, in the madly desirable way he visioned for himself in those occasional moments when the fires of temptation blazed hottest.

The fourth night he said to Tautuk:

"If Keok should marry another man, what would you do?"

It was a moment before Tautuk looked at him, and in the herdsman's eyes was a wild, mute question, as if suddenly there had leaped into his stolid mind a suspicion which had never come to him before. Alan laid a reassuring hand upon his arm.

"I don't mean she's going to, Tautuk," he laughed. "She loves you. I know it. Only you are so stupid, and so slow, and so hopeless as a lover that she is punishing you while she has the right--before she marries you. But if she *should* marry someone else, what would you do?"

"My brother?" asked Tautuk.

"No."

"A relative?"

"No."

"A friend?"

"No. A stranger. Someone who had injured you, for instance; someone Keok hated, and who had cheated her into marrying him."

"I would kill him," said Tautuk quietly.

It was this night the temptation was strongest upon Alan. Why should Mary Standish go back, he asked himself. She had surrendered everything to escape from the horror down there. She had given up fortune and friends. She had scattered convention to the four winds, had gambled her life in the hazard, and in the end had come to him! Why should he not keep her? John Graham and the world believed she was dead. And he was master here. If--some day--Graham should happen to cross his path, he would settle the matter in Tautuk's way. Later, while Tautuk slept, and the world lay about him in a soft glow, and the valley below was filled with misty billows of twilight out of which came to him faintly the curious, crackling sound of reindeer hoofs and the grunting contentment of the feeding herd, the reaction came, as he had known it would come in the end.

The morning of the fifth day he set out alone for the eastward herd, and on the sixth overtook Tatpan and his herdsmen. Tatpan, like Sokwenna's foster-children, Keok and Nawadlook, had a quarter-strain of white in him, and when Alan came up to him in the edge of the valley where the deer were grazing, he was lying on a rock, playing Yankee Doodle on a mouth-organ. It was Tatpan who told him that an hour or two before an exhausted stranger had come into camp, looking for him, and that the man was asleep now, apparently more dead than alive, but had given instructions to be awakened at the end of two hours, and not a minute later. Together they had a look at him.

He was a small, ruddy-faced man with carroty blond hair and a peculiarly boyish appearance as he lay doubled up like a jack-knife, profoundly asleep. Tatpan looked at his big, silver watch and in a low voice described how the stranger had stumbled into camp, so tired he could scarcely put one foot ahead of the other; and that he had dropped down where he now lay when he learned Alan was with one of the other herds.

"He must have come a long distance," said Tatpan, "and he has traveled fast."

Something familiar about the man grew upon Alan. Yet he could not place him. He wore a gun, which he had unbelted and placed within reach of his hand on the grass. His chin was pugnaciously prominent, and in sleep the mysterious stranger had crooked a forefinger and thumb about his revolver in a way that spoke of caution and experience.

"If he is in such a hurry to see me, you might awaken him," said Alan.

He turned a little aside and knelt to drink at a tiny stream of water that ran down from the snowy summits, and he could hear Tatpan rousing the stranger. By the time he had finished drinking and faced about, the little man with the carroty-blond hair was on his feet. Alan stared, and the little man grinned. His ruddy cheeks grew pinker. His blue eyes twinkled, and in what seemed to be a moment of embarrassment he gave his gun a sudden snap that drew an exclamation of amazement from Alan. Only one man in the world had he ever seen throw a gun into its holster like that. A sickly grin began to spread over his own countenance, and all at once Tatpan's eyes began to bulge.

"Stampede!" he cried.

Stampede rubbed a hand over his smooth, prominent chin and nodded apologetically.

"It's me," he conceded. "I had to do it. It was give one or t'other up--my whiskers *or her*. They went hard, too. I flipped dice, an' the whiskers won. I cut cards, an' the whiskers won. I played Klondike ag'in' 'em, an' the whiskers busted the bank. Then I got mad an' shaved 'em. Do I look so bad, Alan?"

"You look twenty years younger," declared Alan, stifling his desire to laugh when he saw the other's seriousness.

Stampede was thoughtfully stroking his chin. "Then why the devil did they laugh!" he demanded. "Mary Standish didn't laugh. She cried. Just stood an' cried, an' then sat down an' cried, she thought I was that blamed funny! And Keok laughed until she was sick an' had to go to bed. That little devil of a Keok calls me Pinkey now, and Miss Standish says it wasn't because I was funny that she laughed, but that the change in me was so sudden she couldn't help it. Nawadlook says I've got a character-ful chin--"

Alan gripped his hand, and a swift change came over Stampede's face. A steely glitter shot into the blue of his eyes, and his chin hardened. Nature no longer disguised the Stampede Smith of other days, and Alan felt a new thrill and a new regard for the man whose hand he held. This, at last, was the man whose name had gone before him up and down the old trails; the man whose cool and calculating courage, whose fearlessness of death and quickness with the gun had written pages in Alaskan history which would never be forgotten. Where his first impulse had been to laugh, he now felt the grim thrill and admiration of men of other days, who, when in Stampede's presence, knew they were in the presence of a master. The old Stampede had come to life again. And Alan knew why. The grip of his hand tightened, and Stampede returned it.

"Some day, if we're lucky, there always comes a woman to make the world worth living in, Stampede," he said.

"There does," replied Stampede.

He looked steadily at Alan.

"And I take it you love Mary Standish," he added, "and that you'd fight for her if you had to."

"I would," said Alan.

"Then it's time you were traveling," advised Stampede significantly. "I've been twelve hours on the trail without a rest. She told me to move fast, and I've moved. I mean Mary Standish. She said it was almost a matter of life and death that I find you in a hurry. I wanted to stay, but she wouldn't let me. It's *you* she wants. Rossland is at the range."

"*Rossland!*"

"Yes, Rossland. And it's my guess John Graham isn't far away. I smell happenings, Alan. We'd better hurry."

CHAPTER XXI

Stampede had started with one of the two saddle-deer left at the range, but to ride deer-back successfully and with any degree of speed and specific direction was an accomplishment which he had neglected, and within the first half-dozen miles he had abandoned the adventure to continue his journey on foot. As Tatpan had no saddle-deer in his herd, and the swiftest messenger would require many hours in which to reach Amuk Toolik, Alan set out for his range within half an hour after his arrival at Tatpan's camp. Stampede, declaring himself a new man after his brief rest and the meal which followed it, would not listen to Alan's advice that he follow later, when he was more refreshed.

A fierce and reminiscent gleam smoldered in the little gun-fighter's eyes as he watched Alan during the first half-hour leg of their race through the foothills to the tundras. Alan did not observe it, or the grimness that had settled in the face behind him. His own mind was undergoing an upheaval of conjecture and wild questioning. That Rossland had discovered Mary Standish was not dead was the least astonishing factor in the new development. The information might easily have reached him through Sandy McCormick or his wife Ellen. The astonishing thing was that he had in some mysterious way picked up the trail of her flight a thousand miles northward, and the still more amazing fact that he had dared to follow her and reveal himself openly at his range. His heart pumped hard, for he knew Rossland must be directly under Graham's orders.

Then came the resolution to take Stampede into his confidence and to reveal all that had happened on the day of his departure for the mountains. He proceeded to do this without equivocation or hesitancy, for there now pressed upon him a grim anticipation of impending events ahead of them.

Stampede betrayed no astonishment at the other's disclosures. The smoldering fire remained in his eyes, the immobility of his face unchanged. Only when Alan repeated, in his own words, Mary Standish's confession of love at Nawadlook's door did the fighting lines soften about his comrade's eyes and mouth.

Stampede's lips responded with an oddly quizzical smile. "I knew that a long time ago," he said. "I guessed it that first night of storm in the coach up to Chitina. I knew it for certain before we left Tanana. She didn't tell me, but I wasn't blind. It was the note that puzzled and frightened me--the note she stuffed in her slipper. And Rossland told me, before I left, that going for you was a wild-goose chase, as he intended to take Mrs. John Graham back with him immediately."

"And you left her alone after *that?*"

Stampede shrugged his shoulders as he valiantly kept up with Alan's suddenly quickened pace.

"She insisted. Said it meant life and death for her. And she looked it. White as paper after her talk with Rossland. Besides--"

"What?"

"Sokwenna won't sleep until we get back. He knows. I told him. And he's watching from the garret window with a .303 Savage. I saw him pick off a duck the other day at two hundred yards."

They hurried on. After a little Alan said, with the fear which he could not name clutching at his heart, "Why did you say Graham might not be far away?"

"In my bones," replied Stampede, his face hard as rock again. "In my bones!"

"Is that all?"

"Not quite. I think Rossland told her. She was so white. And her hand cold as a lump of clay when she put it on mine. It was in her eyes, too. Besides, Rossland has taken possession of your cabin as though he owns it. I take it that means somebody behind him, a force, something big to reckon with. He asked me how many men we had. I told him, stretching it a little. He grinned. He couldn't keep back that grin. It was as if a devil in him slipped out from hiding for an instant."

Suddenly he caught Alan's arm and stopped him. His chin shot out. The sweat ran from his face. For a full quarter of a minute the two men stared at each other.

"Alan, we're short-sighted. I'm damned if I don't think we ought to call the herdsmen in, and every man with a loaded gun!"

"You think it's that bad?"

"Might be. If Graham's behind Rossland and has men with him--"

"We're two and a half hours from Tatpan," said Alan, in a cold, unemotional voice. "He has only half a dozen men with him, and it will take at least four to make quick work in finding Tautuk and Amuk Toolik. There are eighteen men with the southward herd, and twenty-two with the upper. I mean, counting the boys. Use your own judgment. All are armed. It may be foolish, but I'm following your hunch."

They gripped hands.

"It's more than a hunch, Alan," breathed Stampede softly. "And for God's sake keep off the music as long as you can!"

He was gone, and as his agile, boyish figure started in a half-run toward the foothills, Alan set his face southward, so that in a quarter of an hour they were lost to each other in the undulating distances of the tundra.

Never had Alan traveled as on the last of this sixth day of his absence from the range. He was comparatively fresh, as his trail to Tatpan's camp had not been an exhausting one, and his more intimate knowledge of the country gave him a decided advantage over Stampede. He believed he could make the distance in ten hours, but to this he would be compelled to add a rest of at least three or four hours during the night. It was now eight o'clock. By nine or ten the next morning he would be facing Rossland, and at about that same hour Tatpan's swift messengers would be closing in about Tautuk and Amuk Toolik. He knew the speed with which his herdsmen would sweep out of the mountains and over the tundras. Two years ago Amuk Toolik and a dozen of his Eskimo people had traveled fifty-two hours without rest or food, covering a hundred and nineteen miles in that time. His blood flushed hot with pride. He couldn't do that. But his people could--and *would*. He could see them sweeping in from the telescoping segments of the herds as the word went among them; he could see them streaking out of the foothills; and then, like wolves scattering for freer air and leg-room, he saw them dotting the tundra in their race for home--and war, if it was war that lay ahead of them.

Twilight began to creep in upon him, like veils of cool, dry mist out of the horizons. And hour after hour he went on, eating a strip of pemmican when he grew hungry, and drinking in the spring coulées when he came to them, where the water was cold and clear. Not until a telltale cramp began to bite warningly in his leg did he stop for the rest which he knew he must take. It was one o'clock. Counting his journey to Tatpan's camp, he had been traveling almost steadily for seventeen hours.

Not until he stretched himself out on his back in a grassy hollow where a little stream a foot wide rippled close to his ears did he realize how tired he had become. At first he tried not to sleep. Rest was all he wanted; he dared not close his eyes. But exhaustion overcame him at last, and he slept. When he awoke, bird-song and the sun were taunting him. He sat up with a jerk, then leaped to his feet in alarm. His watch told the story. He had slept soundly for six hours, instead of resting three or four with his eyes open.

After a little, as he hurried on his way, he did not altogether regret what had happened. He felt like a fighting man. He breathed deeply, ate a breakfast of pemmican as he walked, and proceeded to make up lost time. The interval between fifteen minutes of twelve and twelve he almost ran. That quarter of an hour brought him to the crest of the ridge from which he could look upon the buildings of the range. Nothing had happened that he could see. He gave a great gasp of relief, and in his joy he laughed. The strangeness of the laugh told him more than anything else the tension he had been under.

Another half-hour, and he came up out of the dip behind Sokwenna's cabin and tried the door. It was locked. A voice answered his knock, and he called out his name. The bolt shot back, the door opened, and he stepped in. Nawadlook stood at her bedroom door, a gun in her hands. Keok faced him, holding grimly to a long knife, and between them, staring white-faced at him as he entered, was Mary Standish. She came forward to meet him, and he heard a whisper from Nawadlook, and saw Keok follow her swiftly through the door into the other room.

Mary Standish held out her hands to him a little blindly, and the tremble in her throat and the look in her eyes betrayed the struggle she was making to keep from breaking down and crying out in gladness at his coming. It was that look that sent a flood of joy into his heart, even when he saw the torture and hopelessness behind it. He held her hands close, and into her eyes he smiled in such a way that he saw them widen, as if she almost disbelieved; and then she drew in a sudden quick breath, and her fingers clung to him. It was as if the hope that had deserted her came in an instant into her face again. He was not excited. He was not even perturbed, now that he saw that light in her eyes and knew she was safe. But his love was there. She saw it and felt the force of it behind the deadly calmness with which he was smiling at her. She gave a little sob, so low it was scarcely more than a broken breath; a little cry that came of wonder-- understanding--and unspeakable faith in this man who was smiling at her so confidently in the face of the tragedy that had come to destroy her.

"Rossland is in your cabin," she whispered. "And John Graham is back there--somewhere-- coming this way. Rossland says that if I don't go to him of my own free will--"

He felt the shudder that ran through her.

"I understand the rest," he said. They stood silent for a moment. The gray-cheeked thrush was singing on the roof. Then, as if she had been a child, he took her face between his hands and bent her head back a little, so that he was looking straight into her eyes, and so near that he could feel the sweet warmth of her breath.

"You didn't make a mistake the day I went away?" he asked. "You--love me?"

"Yes."

For a moment longer he looked into her eyes. Then he stood back from her. Even Keok and Nawadlook heard his laugh. It was strange, they thought--Keok with her knife, and Nawadlook with her gun--for the bird was singing, and Alan Holt was laughing, and Mary Standish was very still.

Another moment later, from where he sat cross-legged at the little window in the attic, keeping his unsleeping vigil with a rifle across his knees, old Sokwenna saw his master walk across the open, and something in the manner of his going brought back a vision of another day long ago when Ghost Kloof had rung with the cries of battle, and the hands now gnarled and twisted with age had played their part in the heroic stand of his people against the oppressors from the farther north.

Then he saw Alan go into the cabin where Rossland was, and softly his fingers drummed upon the ancient tom-tom which lay at his side. His eyes fixed themselves upon the distant mountains, and under his breath he mumbled the old chant of battle, dead and forgotten except in Sokwenna's brain, and after that his eyes closed, and again the vision grew out of darkness like a picture for him, a vision of twisting trails and of fighting men gathering with their faces set for war.

CHAPTER XXII

At the desk in Alan's living-room sat Rossland, when the door opened behind him and the master of the range came in. He was not disturbed when he saw who it was, and rose to meet him. His coat was off, his sleeves rolled up, and it was evident he was making no effort to conceal his freedom with Alan's books and papers.

He advanced, holding out a hand. This was not the same Rossland who had told Alan to attend to his own business on board the *Nome*. His attitude was that of one greeting a friend, smiling and affable even before he spoke. Something inspired Alan to return the smile. Behind that smile he was admiring the man's nerve. His hand met Rossland's casually, but there was no uncertainty in the warmth of the other's grip.

"How d' do, Paris, old boy?" he greeted good-humoredly. "Saw you going in to Helen a few minutes ago, so I've been waiting for you. She's a little frightened. And we can't blame her. Menelaus is mightily upset. But mind me, Holt, I'm not blaming you. I'm too good a sport. Clever, I call it--damned clever. She's enough to turn any man's head. I only wish I were in your boots right now. I'd have turned traitor myself aboard the *Nome* if she had shown an inclination."

He proffered a cigar, a big, fat cigar with a gold band. It was inspiration again that made Alan accept it and light it. His blood was racing. But Rossland saw nothing of that. He observed only the nod, the cool smile on Alan's lips, the apparent nonchalance with which he was meeting the situation. It pleased Graham's agent. He reseated himself in the desk-chair and motioned Alan to another chair near him.

"I thought you were badly hurt," said Alan. "Nasty knife wound you got."

Rossland shrugged his shoulders. "There you have it again, Holt--the hell of letting a pretty face run away with you. One of the Thlinkit girls down in the steerage, you know. Lovely little thing, wasn't she? Tricked her into my cabin all right, but she wasn't like some other Indian girls I've known. The next night a brother, or sweetheart, or whoever it was got me through the open port. It wasn't bad. I was out of the hospital within a week. Lucky I was put there, too. Otherwise I wouldn't have seen Mrs. Graham one morning--through the window. What a little our fortunes hang to at times, eh? If it hadn't been for the girl and the knife and the hospital, I wouldn't be here now, and Graham wouldn't be bleeding his heart out with impatience--and you, Holt, wouldn't be facing the biggest opportunity that will ever come into your life."

"I'm afraid I don't understand," said Alan, hiding his face in the smoke of his cigar and speaking with an apparent indifference which had its effect upon Rossland. "Your presence inclines me to believe that luck has rather turned against me. Where can my advantage be?"

A grim seriousness settled in Rossland's eyes, and his voice became cool and hard. "Holt, as two men who are not afraid to meet unusual situations, we may as well call a spade a spade in this matter, don't you think so?"

"Decidedly," said Alan.

"You know that Mary Standish is really Mary Standish Graham, John Graham's wife?"

"Yes."

"And you probably know--now--why she jumped into the sea, and why she ran away from Graham."

"I do."

"That saves a lot of talk. But there is another side to the story which you probably don't know, and I am here to tell it to you. John Graham doesn't care for a dollar of the Standish fortune. It's the girl he wants, and has always wanted. She has grown up under his eyes. From the day she was fourteen years old he has lived and planned with the thought of possessing her. You know how he got her to marry him, and you know what happened afterward. But it makes no difference to him whether she hates him or not. He *wants* her. And this"--he swept his arms out, "is the most beautiful place in the world in which to have her returned to him. I've been figuring from your books. Your property isn't worth over a hundred thousand dollars as it stands on hoof today. I'm here to offer you five times that for it. In other words, Graham is willing to forfeit all action he might have personally against you for stealing his wife, and in place of that will pay you five hundred thousand dollars for the privilege of having his honeymoon here, and making of this place a country estate where his wife may reside indefinitely, subject to her husband's visits when he is so inclined. There will be a stipulation, of course, requiring that the personal details of the deal be kept strictly confidential, and that you leave the country. Do I make myself clear?"

Alan rose to his feet and paced thoughtfully across the room. At least, Rossland measured his action as one of sudden, intensive reflection as he watched him, smiling complacently at the effect of his knock-out proposition upon the other. He had not minced matters. He had come to the point without an effort at bargaining, and he possessed sufficient dramatic sense to appreciate what the offer of half a million dollars meant to an individual who was struggling for existence at the edge of a raw frontier. Alan stood with his back toward him, facing a window. His voice was oddly strained when he answered. But that was quite natural, too, Rossland thought.

"I am wondering if I understand you," he said. "Do you mean that if I sell Graham the range, leave it bag and baggage, and agree to keep my mouth shut thereafter, he will give me half a million dollars?"

"That is the price. You are to take your people with you. Graham has his own."

Alan tried to laugh. "I think I see the point--now. He isn't paying five hundred thousand for Miss Standish--I mean Mrs. Graham. He's paying it for the *isolation*."

"Exactly. It was a last-minute hunch with him--to settle the matter peaceably. We started up here to get his wife. You understand, to *get* her, and settle the matter with you in a different way from the one we're using now. You hit the word when you said 'isolation.' What a damn fool a man can make of himself over a pretty face! Think of it--half a million dollars!"

"It sounds unreal," mused Alan, keeping his face to the window. "Why should he offer so much?"

"You must keep the stipulation in mind, Holt. That is an important part of the deal. You are to keep your mouth shut. Buying the range at a normal price wouldn't guarantee it. But when you accept a sum like that, you're a partner in the other end of the transaction, and your health depends upon keeping the matter quiet. Simple enough, isn't it?"

Alan turned back to the table. His face was pale. He tried to keep smoke in front of his eyes. "Of course, I don't suppose he'd allow Mrs. Graham to escape back to the States--where she might do a little upsetting on her own account?"

"He isn't throwing the money away," replied Rossland significantly.

"She would remain here indefinitely?"

"Indefinitely."

"Probably never would return."

"Strange how squarely you hit the nail on the head! Why should she return? The world believes she is dead. Papers were full of it. The little secret of her being alive is all our own. And this will be a beautiful summering place for Graham. Magnificent climate. Lovely flowers. Birds. And the girl he has watched grow up, and wanted, since she was fourteen."

"And who hates him."

"True."

"Who was tricked into marrying him, and who would rather die than live with him as his wife."

"But it's up to Graham to keep her alive, Holt. That's not our business. If she dies, I imagine you will have an opportunity to get your range back pretty cheap."

Rossland held a paper out to Alan.

"Here's partial payment--two hundred and fifty thousand. I have the papers here, on the desk, ready to sign. As soon as you give possession, I'll return to Tanana with you and make the remaining payment."

Alan took the check. "I guess only a fool would refuse an offer like this, Rossland."

"Yes, only a fool."

"*And I am that fool.*"

So quietly did Alan speak that for an instant the significance of his words did not fall with full force upon Rossland. The smoke cleared away from before Alan's face. His cigar dropped to the floor, and he stepped on it with his foot. The check followed it in torn scraps. The fury he had held back with almost superhuman effort blazed in his eyes.

"If I could have Graham where you are now--*in that chair*--I'd give ten years of my life, Rossland. I would kill him. And you--*you*--"

He stepped back a pace, as if to put himself out of striking distance of the beast who was staring at him in amazement.

"What you have said about her should condemn you to death. And I would kill you here, in this room, if it wasn't necessary for you to take my message back to Graham. Tell him that Mary Standish--*not* Mary Graham--is as pure and clean and as sweet as the day she was born. Tell him that she belongs to *me*. I love her. She is mine--do you understand? And all the money in the world couldn't buy one hair from her head. I'm going to take her back to the States. She is going to get a square deal, and the world is going to know her story. She has nothing to conceal. Absolutely nothing. Tell that to John Graham for me."

He advanced upon Rossland, who had risen from his chair; his hands were clenched, his face a mask of iron.

"Get out! Go before I flay you within an inch of your rotten life!"

The energy which every fiber in him yearned to expend upon Rossland sent the table crashing back in an overturned wreck against the wall.

"Go--before I kill you!"

He was advancing, even as the words of warning came from his lips, and the man before him, an awe-stricken mass of flesh that had forgotten power and courage in the face of a deadly and unexpected menace, backed quickly to the door and escaped. He made for the corrals, and Alan watched from his door until he saw him departing southward, accompanied by two men who bore packs on their shoulders. Not until then did Rossland gather his nerve sufficiently to stop and look back. His breathless voice carried something unintelligible to Alan. But he did not return for his coat and hat.

The reaction came to Alan when he saw the wreck he had made of the table. Another moment or two and the devil in him would have been at work. He hated Rossland. He hated him now only a little less than he hated John Graham, and that he had let him go seemed a miracle to him. He felt the strain he had been under. But he was glad. Some little god of common sense had overruled his passion, and he had acted wisely. Graham would now get his message, and there could be no misunderstanding of purpose between them.

He was staring at the disordered papers on his desk when a movement at the door turned him about. Mary Standish stood before him.

"You sent him away," she cried softly.

Her eyes were shining, her lips parted, her face lit up with a beautiful glow. She saw the overturned table, Rossland's hat and coat on a chair, the evidence of what had happened and the quickness of his flight; and then she turned her face to Alan again, and what he saw broke down the last of that grim resolution which he had measured for himself, so that in a moment he was at her side, and had her in his arms. She made no effort to free herself as she had done in the cottonwoods, but turned her mouth up for him to kiss, and then hid her face against his shoulder--while he, fighting vainly to find utterance for the thousand words in his throat, stood stroking her hair, and then buried his face in it, crying out at last in the warm sweetness of it that he loved her, and was going to fight for her, and that no power on earth could take her away from him now. And these things he repeated until she raised her flushed face from his breast, and let him kiss her lips once more, and then freed herself gently from his arms.

CHAPTER XXIII

For a Space they stood apart, and in the radiant loveliness of Mary Standish's face and in Alan's quiet and unimpassioned attitude were neither shame nor regret. In a moment they had swept aside the barrier which convention had raised against them, and now they felt the inevitable thrill of joy and triumph, and not the humiliating embarrassment of dishonor. They made no effort to draw a curtain upon their happiness, or to hide the swift heart-beat of it from each other. It had happened, and they were glad. Yet they stood apart, and something pressed upon Alan the inviolableness of the little freedom of space between them, of its sacredness to Mary Standish, and darker and deeper grew the glory of pride and faith that lay with the love in her eyes when he did not cross it. He reached out his hand, and freely she gave him her own. Lips blushing with his kisses trembled in a smile, and she bowed her head a little, so that he was looking at her smooth hair, soft and sweet where he had caressed it a few moments before.

"I thank God!" he said.

He did not finish the surge of gratitude that was in his heart. Speech seemed trivial, even futile. But she understood. He was not thanking God for that moment, but for a lifetime of something that at last had come to him. This, it seemed to him, was the end, the end of a world as he had known it, the beginning of a new. He stepped back, and his hands trembled. For something to do he set up the overturned table, and Mary Standish watched him with a quiet, satisfied wonder. She loved him, and she had come into his arms. She had given him her lips to kiss. And he laughed softly as he came to her side again, and looked over the tundra where Rossland had gone.

"How long before you can prepare for the journey?" he asked.

"You mean--"

"That we must start tonight or in the morning. I think we shall go through the cottonwoods over the old trail to Nome. Unless Rossland lied, Graham is somewhere out there on the Tanana trail."

Her hand pressed his arm. "We are going--*back?* Is that it, Alan?"

"Yes, to Seattle. It is the one thing to do. You are not afraid?"

"With you there--no."

"And you will return with me--when it is over?"

He was looking steadily ahead over the tundra. But he felt her cheek touch his shoulder, lightly as a feather.

"Yes, I will come back with you."

"And you will be ready?"

"I am ready now."

The sun-fire of the plains danced in his eyes; a cob-web of golden mist rising out of the earth, beckoning wraiths and undulating visions--the breath of life, of warmth, of growing things--all between him and the hidden cottonwoods; a joyous sea into which he wanted to plunge without another minute of waiting, as he felt the gentle touch of her cheek against his shoulder, and the weight of her hand on his arm. That she had come to him utterly was in the low surrender of her voice. She had ceased to fight--she had given to him the precious right to fight for her.

It was this sense of her need and of her glorious faith in him, and of the obligation pressing with it that drove slowly back into him the grimmer realities of the day. Its horror surged upon him again, and the significance of what Rossland had said seemed fresher, clearer, even more terrible now that he was gone. Unconsciously the old lines of hatred crept into his face again as he looked steadily in the direction which the other man had taken, and he wondered how much of that same horror--of the unbelievable menace stealing upon her--Rossland had divulged to the girl who stood so quietly now at his side. Had he done right to let him go? Should he not have killed him, as he would have exterminated a serpent? For Rossland had exulted; he was of Graham's flesh and desires, a part of his foul soul, a defiler of womanhood and the one who had bargained to make possible the opportunity for an indescribable crime. It was not too late. He could still overtake him, out there in the hollows of the tundra--

The pressure on his arm tightened. He looked down. Mary Standish had seen what was in his face, and there was something in her calmness that brought him to himself. He knew, in that moment, that Rossland had told her a great deal. Yet she was not afraid, unless it was fear of what had been in his mind.

"I am ready," she reminded him.

"We must wait for Stampede," he said, reason returning to him. "He should be here sometime tonight, or in the morning. Now that Rossland is off my nerves, I can see how necessary it is to have someone like Stampede between us and--"

He did not finish, but what he had intended to say was quite clear to her. She stood in the doorway, and he felt an almost uncontrollable desire to take her in his arms again.

"He is between here and Tanana," she said with a little gesture of her head.

"Rossland told you that?"

"Yes. And there are others with him, so many that he was amused when I told him you would not let them take me away."

"Then you were not afraid that I--I might let them have you?"

"I have always been sure of what you would do since I opened that second letter at Ellen McCormick's, Alan!"

He caught the flash of her eyes, the gladness in them, and she was gone before he could find another word to say. Keok and Nawadlook were approaching hesitatingly, but now they hurried to meet her, Keok still grimly clutching the long knife; and beyond them, at the little window under the roof, he saw the ghostly face of old Sokwenna, like a death's-head on guard. His blood ran a little faster. The emptiness of the tundras, the illimitable spaces without sign of human life, the vast stage waiting for its impending drama, with its sunshine, its song of birds, its whisper and breath of growing flowers, struck a new note in him, and he looked again at the little window where Sokwenna sat like a spirit from another world, warning him in his silent and lifeless stare of something menacing and deadly creeping upon them out of that space which seemed so free of all evil. He beckoned to him and then entered his cabin, waiting while Sokwenna crawled down from his post and came hobbling over the open, a crooked figure, bent like a baboon, witch-like in his great age, yet with sunken eyes that gleamed like little points of flame, and a quickness of movement that made Alan shiver as he watched him through the window.

In a moment the old man entered. He was mumbling. He was saying, in that jumble of sound which it was difficult for even Alan to understand--and which Sokwenna had never given up for the missionaries' teachings--that he could hear feet and smell blood; and that the feet were many, and the blood was near, and that both smell and footfall were coming from the old kloof where yellow skulls still lay, dripping with the water that had once run red. Alan was one of the few who, by reason of much effort, had learned the story of the kloof from old Sokwenna; how, so long ago that Sokwenna was a young man, a hostile tribe had descended upon his people, killing the men and stealing the women; and how at last Sokwenna and a handful of his tribesmen fled south with what women were left and made a final stand in the kloof, and there, on a day that was golden and filled with the beauty of bird-song and flowers, had ambushed their enemies and killed them to a man. All were dead now, all but Sokwenna.

For a space Alan was sorry he had called Sokwenna to his cabin. He was no longer the cheerful and gentle "old man" of his people; the old man who chortled with joy at the prettiness and play of Keok and Nawadlook, who loved birds and flowers and little children, and who had retained an impish boyhood along with his great age. He was changed. He stood before Alan an embodiment of fatalism, mumbling incoherent things in his breath, a spirit of evil omen lurking in his sunken eyes, and his thin hands gripping like bird-claws to his rifle. Alan threw off the uncomfortable feeling that had gripped him for a moment, and set him to an appointed task--the watching of the southward plain from the crest of a tall ridge two miles back on the Tanana trail. He was to return when the sun reached its horizon.

Alan was inspired now by a great caution, a growing premonition which stirred him with uneasiness, and he began his own preparations as soon as Sokwenna had started on his mission. The desire to leave at once, without the delay of an hour, pulled strong in him, but he forced himself to see the folly of such haste. He would be away many months, possibly a year this time. There was much to do, a mass of detail to attend to, a volume of instructions and advice to leave behind him. He must at least see Stampede, and it was necessary to write down certain laws for Tautuk and Amuk Toolik. As this work of preparation progressed, and the premonition persisted in remaining with him, he fell into a habit of repeating to himself the absurdity of fears and the impossibility of danger. He tried to make himself feel uncomfortably foolish at the thought of having ordered the herdsmen in. In all probability Graham would not appear at all, he told himself, or at least not for many days--or weeks; and if he did come, it would be to war in a legal way, and not with murder.

Yet his uneasiness did not leave him. As the hours passed and the afternoon lengthened, the invisible something urged him more strongly to take the trail beyond the cottonwoods, with Mary Standish at his side. Twice he saw her between noon and five o'clock, and by that time his writing was done. He looked at his guns carefully. He saw that his favorite rifle and automatic were working smoothly, and he called himself a fool for filling his ammunition vest with an extravagant number of cartridges. He even carried an amount of this ammunition and two of his extra guns to Sokwenna's cabin, with the thought that it was this cabin on the edge of the ravine which was best fitted for defense in the event of necessity. Possibly Stampede might have use for it, and for the guns, if Graham should come after he and Mary were well on their way to Nome.

After supper, when the sun was throwing long shadows from the edge of the horizon, Alan came from a final survey of his cabin and the food which Wegaruk had prepared for his pack, and found Mary at the edge of the ravine, watching the twilight gathering where the coulée ran narrower and deeper between the distant breasts of the tundra.

"I am going to leave you for a little while," he said. "But Sokwenna has returned, and you will not be alone."

"Where are you going?"

"As far as the cottonwoods, I think."

"Then I am going with you."

"I expect to walk very fast."

"Not faster than I, Alan."

"But I want to make sure the country is clear in that direction before twilight shuts out the distances."

"I will help you." Her hand crept into his. "I am going with you, Alan," she repeated.

"Yes, I--think you are," he laughed joyously, and suddenly he bent his head and pressed her hand to his lips, and in that way, with her hand in his, they set out over the trail which they had not traveled together since the day he had come from Nome.

There was a warm glow in her face, and something beautifully soft and sweet in her eyes which she did not try to keep away from him. It made him forget the cottonwoods and the plains beyond, and his caution, and Sokwenna's advice to guard carefully against the hiding-places of Ghost Kloof and the country beyond.

"I have been thinking a great deal today," she was saying, "because you have left me so much alone. I have been thinking of *you*. And--my thoughts have given me a wonderful happiness."

"And I have been--in paradise," he replied.

"You do not think that I am wicked?"

"I could sooner believe the sun would never come up again."

"Nor that I have been unwomanly?"

"You are my dream of all that is glorious in womanhood."

"Yet I have followed you--have thrust myself at you, fairly at your head, Alan."

"For which I thank God," He breathed devoutly.

"And I have told you that I love you, and you have taken me in your arms, and have kissed me--"

"Yes."

"And I am walking now with my hand in yours--"

"And will continue to do so, if I can hold it."

"And I am another man's wife," she shuddered.

"You are mine," he declared doggedly. "You know it, and the Almighty God knows it. It is blasphemy to speak of yourself as Graham's wife. You are legally entangled with him, and that is all. Heart and soul and body you are free."

"No, I am not free."

"But you are!"

And then, after a moment, she whispered at his shoulder: "Alan, because you are the finest gentleman in all the world, I will tell you why I am not. It is because--heart and soul--I belong to you."

He dared not look at her, and feeling the struggle within him Mary Standish looked straight ahead with a wonderful smile on her lips and repeated softly, "Yes, the very finest gentleman in all the world!"

Over the breasts of the tundra and the hollows between they went, still hand in hand, and found themselves talking of the colorings in the sky, and the birds, and flowers, and the twilight creeping in about them, while Alan scanned the shortening horizons for a sign of human life. One mile, and then another, and after that a third, and they were looking into gray gloom far ahead, where lay the kloof.

It was strange that he should think of the letter now--the letter he had written to Ellen McCormick--but think of it he did, and said what was in his mind to Mary Standish, who was also looking with him into the wall of gloom that lay between them and the distant cottonwoods.

"It seemed to me that I was not writing it to her, but to *you*" he said. "And I think that if you hadn't come back to me I would have gone mad."

"I have the letter. It is here"--and she placed a hand upon her breast. "Do you remember what you wrote, Alan?"

"That you meant more to me than life."

"And that--particularly--you wanted Ellen McCormick to keep a tress of my hair for you if they found me."

He nodded. "When I sat across the table from you aboard the *Nome*, I worshiped it and didn't know it. And since then--since I've had you here--every time. I've looked at you--" He stopped, choking the words back in his throat.

"Say it, Alan."

"I've wanted to see it down," he finished desperately. "Silly notion, isn't it?"

"Why is it?" she asked, her eyes widening a little. "If you love it, why is it a silly notion to want to see it down?"

"Why, I though possibly you might think it so," he added lamely.

Never had he heard anything sweeter than her laughter as she turned suddenly from him, so that the glow of the fallen sun was at her back, and with deft, swift fingers began loosening the coils of her hair until its radiant masses tumbled about her, streaming down her back in a silken glory that awed him with its beauty and drew from his lips a cry of gladness.

She faced him, and in her eyes was the shining softness that glowed in her hair. "Do you think it is nice, Alan?"

He went to her and filled his hands with the heavy tresses and pressed them to his lips and face.

Thus he stood when he felt the sudden shiver that ran through her. It was like a little shock. He heard the catch of her breath, and the hand which she had placed gently on his bowed head fell suddenly away. When he raised his head to look at her, she was staring past him into the deepening twilight of the tundra, and it seemed as if something had stricken her so that for a space she was powerless to speak or move.

"What is it?" he cried, and whirled about, straining his eyes to see what had alarmed her; and as he looked, a deep, swift shadow sped over the earth, darkening the mellow twilight until it was somber gloom of night--and the midnight sun went out like a great, luminous lamp as a dense wall of purple cloud rolled up in an impenetrable curtain between it and the arctic world. Often he had seen this happen in the approach of summer storm on the tundras, but never had the change seemed so swift as now. Where there had been golden light, he saw his companion's face now pale in a sea of dusk. It was this miracle of arctic night, its suddenness and unexpectedness, that had startled her, he thought, and he laughed softly.

But her hand clutched his arm. "I saw them," she cried, her voice breaking. "I saw them--out there against the sun--before the cloud came--and some of them were running, like animals--"

"Shadows!" he exclaimed. "The long shadows of foxes running against the sun, or of the big gray rabbits, or of a wolf and her half-grown sneaking away--"

"No, no, they were not that," she breathed tensely, and her fingers clung more fiercely to his arm. "They were not shadows. *They were men!*"

CHAPTER XXIV

In the moment of stillness between them, when their hearts seemed to have stopped beating that they might not lose the faintest whispering of the twilight, a sound came to Alan, and he knew it was the toe of a boot striking against stone. Not a foot in his tribe would have made that sound; none but Stampede Smith's or his own.

"Were they many?" he asked.

"I could not see. The sun was darkening. But five or six were running--"

"Behind us?"

"Yes."

"And they saw us?"

"I think so. It was but a moment, and they were a part of the dusk."

He found her hand and held it closely. Her fingers clung to his, and he could hear her quick breathing as he unbuttoned the flap of his automatic holster.

"You think *they have come?*" she whispered, and a cold dread was in her voice.

"Possibly. My people would not appear from that direction. You are not afraid?"

"No, no, I am not afraid."

"Yet you are trembling."

"It is this strange gloom, Alan."

Never had the arctic twilight gone more completely. Not half a dozen times had he seen the phenomenon in all his years on the tundras, where thunder-storm and the putting out of the summer sun until twilight thickens into the gloom of near-night is an occurrence so rare that it is more awesome than the weirdest play of the northern lights. It seemed to him now that what was happening was a miracle, the play of a mighty hand opening their way to salvation. An inky wall was shutting out the world where the glow of the midnight sun should have been. It was spreading quickly; shadows became part of the gloom, and this gloom crept in, thickening, drawing nearer, until the tundra was a weird chaos, neither night nor twilight, challenging vision until eyes strained futilely to penetrate its mystery.

And as it gathered about them, enveloping them in their own narrowing circle of vision, Alan was thinking quickly. It had taken him only a moment to accept the significance of the running figures his companion had seen. Graham's men were near, had seen them, and were getting between them and the range. Possibly it was a scouting party, and if there were no more than five or six, the number which Mary had counted, he was quite sure of the situation. But there might be a dozen or fifty of them. It was possible Graham and Rossland were advancing upon the range with their entire force. He had at no time tried to analyze just what this force might be, except to assure himself that with the overwhelming influence behind him, both political and financial, and fired by a passion for Mary Standish that had revealed itself as little short of madness, Graham would hesitate at no convention of law or humanity to achieve his end. Probably he was playing the game so that he would be shielded by the technicalities of the law, if it came to a tragic end. His gunmen would undoubtedly be impelled to a certain extent by an idea of authority. For Graham was an injured husband "rescuing" his wife, while he--Alan Holt--was the woman's abductor and paramour, and a fit subject to be shot upon sight!

His free hand gripped the butt of his pistol as he led the way straight ahead. The sudden gloom helped to hide in his face the horror he felt of what that "rescue" would mean to Mary Standish; and then a cold and deadly definiteness possessed him, and every nerve in his body gathered itself in readiness for whatever might happen.

If Graham's men had seen them, and were getting between them and retreat, the neck of the trap lay ahead--and in this direction Alan walked so swiftly that the girl was almost running at his side. He could not hear her footsteps, so lightly they fell! her fingers were twined about his own, and he could feel the silken caress of her loose hair. For half a mile he kept on, watching for a moving shadow, listening for a sound. Then he stopped. He drew Mary into his arms and held her there, so that her head lay against his breast. She was panting, and he could feel and hear her thumping heart. He found her parted lips and kissed them.

"You are not afraid?" he asked again.

Her head made a fierce little negative movement against his breast. "No!"

He laughed softly at the beautiful courage with which she lied. "Even if they saw us, and are Graham's men, we have given them the slip," he comforted her. "Now we will circle eastward back to the range. I am sorry I hurried you so. We will go more slowly."

"We must travel faster," she insisted. "I want to run."

Her fingers sought his hand and clung to it again as they set out. At intervals they stopped, staring about them into nothingness, and listening. Twice Alan thought he heard sounds which did not belong to the night. The second time the little fingers tightened about his own, but his companion said no word, only her breath seemed to catch in her throat for an instant.

At the end of another half-hour it was growing lighter, yet the breath of storm seemed nearer. The cool promise of it touched their cheeks, and about them were gathering whispers and eddies of a thirsty earth rousing to the sudden change. It was lighter because the wall of cloud seemed to be distributing itself over the whole heaven, thinning out where its solid opaqueness had lain against the sun. Alan could see the girl's face and the cloud of her hair. Hollows and ridges of the tundra were taking more distinct shape when they came into a dip, and Alan recognized a thicket of willows behind which a pool was hidden.

The thicket was only half a mile from home. A spring was near the edge of the willows, and to this he led the girl, made her a place to kneel, and showed her how to cup the cool water in the palms of her hands. While she inclined her head to drink, he held back her hair and rested with his lips pressed to it. He heard the trickle of water running between her fingers, her little laugh of half-pleasure, half-fear, which in another instant broke into a startled scream as he half gained his feet to meet a crashing body that catapulted at him from the concealment of the willows.

A greater commotion in the thicket followed the attack; then another voice, crying out sharply, a second cry from Mary Standish, and he found himself on his knees, twisted backward and fighting desperately to loosen a pair of gigantic hands at his throat. He could hear the girl struggling, but she did not cry out again. In an instant, it seemed, his brain was reeling. He was conscious of a futile effort to reach his gun, and could see the face over him, grim and horrible in the gloom, as the merciless hands choked the life from him. Then he heard a shout, a loud shout, filled with triumph and exultation as he was thrown back; his head seemed leaving his shoulders; his body crumbled, and almost spasmodically his leg shot out with the last strength that was in him. He was scarcely aware of the great gasp that followed, but the fingers loosened at his throat, the face disappeared, and the man who was killing him sank back. For a precious moment or two Alan did not move as he drew great breaths of air into his lungs. Then he felt for his pistol. The holster was empty.

He could hear the panting of the girl, her sobbing breath very near him, and life and strength leaped back into his body. The man who had choked him was advancing again, on hands and knees. In a flash Alan was up and on him like a lithe cat. His fist beat into a bearded face; he called out to Mary as he struck, and through his blows saw her where she had fallen to her knees, with a second hulk bending over her, almost in the water of the little spring from which she had been drinking. A mad curse leaped from his lips. He was ready to kill now; he wanted to kill--to destroy what was already under his hands that he might leap upon this other beast, who stood over Mary Standish, his hands twisted in her long hair. Dazed by blows that fell with the force of a club the bearded man's head sagged backward, and Alan's fingers dug into his throat. It was a bull's neck. He tried to break it. Ten seconds--twenty--half a minute at the most--and flesh and bone would have given way--but before the bearded man's gasping cry was gone from his lips the second figure leaped upon Alan.

He had no time to defend himself from this new attack. His strength was half gone, and a terrific blow sent him reeling. Blindly he reached out and grappled. Not until his arms met those of his fresh assailant did he realize how much of himself he had expended upon the other. A sickening horror filled his soul as he felt his weakness, and an involuntary moan broke from his lips. Even then he would have cut out his tongue to have silenced that sound, to have kept it from the girl. She was creeping on her hands and knees, but he could not see. Her long hair trailed in the trampled earth, and in the muddied water of the spring, and her hands were groping--groping--until they found what they were seeking.

Then she rose to her feet, carrying the rock on which one of her hands had rested when she knelt to drink. The bearded man, bringing himself to his knees, reached out drunkenly, but she avoided him and poised herself over Alan and his assailant. The rock descended. Alan saw her then; he heard the one swift, terrible blow, and his enemy rolled away from him, limply and without sound. He staggered to his feet and for a moment caught the swaying girl in his arms.

The bearded man was rising. He was half on his feet when Alan was at his throat again, and they went down together. The girl heard blows, then a heavier one, and with an exclamation of triumph Alan stood up. By chance his hand had come in contact with his fallen pistol. He clicked the safety down; he was ready to shoot, ready to continue the fight with a gun.

"Come," he said.

His voice was gasping, strangely unreal and thick. She came to him and put her hand in his again, and it was wet and sticky with tundra mud from the spring. Then they climbed to the swell of the plain, away from the pool and the willows.

In the air about them, creeping up from the outer darkness of the strange twilight, were clearer whispers now, and with these sounds of storm, borne from the west, came a hallooing voice. It was answered from straight ahead. Alan held the muddied little hand closer in his own and set out for the range-houses, from which direction the last voice had come. He knew what was happening. Graham's men were cleverer than he had supposed; they had encircled the tundra side of the range, and some of them were closing in on the willow pool, from which the triumphant shout of the bearded man's companion had come. They were wondering why the call was not repeated, and were hallooing.

Every nerve in Alan's body was concentrated for swift and terrible action, for the desperateness of their situation had surged upon him like a breath of fire, unbelievable, and yet true. Back at the willows they would have killed him. The hands at his throat had sought his life. Wolves and not men were about them on the plain; wolves headed by two monsters of the human pack, Graham and Rossland. Murder and lust and mad passion were hidden in the darkness; law and order and civilization were hundreds of miles away. If Graham won, only the unmapped tundras would remember this night, as the deep, dark kloof remembered in its gloom the other tragedy of more than half a century ago. And the girl at his side, already disheveled and muddied by their hands--

His mind could go no farther, and angry protest broke in a low cry from his lips. The girl thought it was because of the shadows that loomed up suddenly in their path. There were two of them, and she, too, cried out as voices commanded them to stop. Alan caught a swift up-movement of an arm, but his own was quicker. Three spurts of flame darted in lightning flashes from his pistol, and the man who had raised his arm crumpled to the earth, while the other dissolved swiftly into the storm-gloom. A moment later his wild shouts were assembling the pack, while the detonations of Alan's pistol continued to roll over the tundra.

The unexpectedness of the shots, their tragic effect, the falling of the stricken man and the flight of the other, brought no word from Mary Standish. But her breath was sobbing, and in the lifting of the purplish gloom she turned her face for an instant to Alan, tensely white, with wide-open eyes. Her hair covered her like a shining veil, and where it clustered in a disheveled mass upon her breast Alan saw her hand thrusting itself forward from its clinging concealment, and in it--to his amazement--was a pistol. He recognized the weapon--one of a brace of light automatics which his friend, Carl Lomen, had presented to him several Christmas seasons ago. Pride and a strange exultation swept over him. Until now she had concealed the weapon, but all along she had prepared to fight--to fight with *him* against their enemies! He wanted to stop and take her in his arms, and with his kisses tell her how splendid she was. But instead of this he sped more swiftly ahead, and they came into the nigger-head bottom which lay in a narrow barrier between them and the range.

Through this ran a trail scarcely wider than a wagon-track, made through the sea of hummocks and sedge-boles and mucky pitfalls by the axes and shovels of his people; finding this, Alan stopped for a moment, knowing that safety lay ahead of them. The girl leaned against him, and then was almost a dead weight in his arms. The last two hundred yards had taken the strength from her body. Her pale face dropped back, and Alan brushed the soft hair away from it, and kissed her lips and her eyes, while the pistol lay clenched against his breast. Even then, too hard-run to speak, she smiled at him, and Alan caught her up in his arms and darted into the narrow path which he knew their pursuers would not immediately find if they could bet beyond their vision. He was joyously amazed at her lightness. She was like a child in his arms, a glorious little goddess hidden and smothered in her long hair, and he held her closer as he hurried toward the cabins, conscious of the soft tightening of her arms about his neck, feeling the sweet caress of her panting breath, strengthened and made happy by her helplessness.

Thus they came out of the bottom as the first mist of slowly approaching rain touched his face. He could see farther now--half-way back over the narrow trail. He climbed a slope, and here Mary Standish slipped from his arms and stood with new strength, looking into his face. His breath was coming in little breaks, and he pointed. Faintly they could make out the shadows of the corral buildings. Beyond them were no lights penetrating the gloom from the windows of the range of houses. The silence of the place was death-like.

And then something grew out of the earth almost at their feet. A hollow cry followed the movement, a cry that was ghostly and shivering, and loud enough only for them to hear, and Sokwenna stood at their side. He talked swiftly. Only Alan understood. There was something unearthly and spectral in his appearance; his hair and beard were wet; his eyes shot here and there in little points of fire; he was like a gnome, weirdly uncanny as he gestured and talked in his monotone while he watched the nigger-head bottom. When he had finished, he did not wait for an answer, but turned and led the way swiftly toward the range houses.

"What did he say?" asked the girl.

"That he is glad we are back. He heard the shots and came to meet us."

"And what else?" she persisted.

"Old Sokwenna is superstitious--and nervous. He said some things that you wouldn't understand. You would probably think him mad if he told you the spirits of his comrades slain in the kloof many years ago were here with him tonight, warning him of things about to happen. Anyway, he has been cautious. No sooner were we out of sight than he hustled every woman and child in the village on their way to the mountains. Keok and Nawadlook wouldn't go. I'm glad of that, for if they were pursued and overtaken by men like Graham and Rossland--"

"Death would be better," finished Mary Standish, and her hand clung more tightly to his arm.

"Yes, I think so. But that can not happen now. Out in the open they had us at a disadvantage. But we can hold Sokwenna's place until Stampede and the herdsmen come. With two good rifles inside, they won't dare to assault the cabin with their naked hands. The advantage is all ours now; we can shoot, but they won't risk the use of their rifles."

"Why?"

"Because you will be inside. Graham wants you alive, not dead. And bullets--"

They had reached Sokwenna's door, and in that moment they hesitated and turned their faces back to the gloom out of which they had fled. Voices came suddenly from beyond the corrals. There was no effort at concealment. The buildings were discovered, and men called out loudly and were answered from half a dozen points out on the tundra. They could hear running feet and sharp commands; some were cursing where they were entangled among the nigger-heads, and the sound of hurrying foes came from the edge of the ravine. Alan's heart stood still. There was something terribly swift and businesslike in this gathering of their enemies. He could hear them at his cabin. Doors opened. A window fell in with a crash. Lights flared up through the gray mist.

It was then, from the barricaded attic window over their heads, that Sokwenna's rifle answered. A single shot, a shriek, and then a pale stream of flame leaped out from the window as the old warrior emptied his gun. Before the last of the five swift shots were fired, Alan was in the cabin, barring the door behind him. Shaded candles burned on the floor, and beside them crouched Keok and Nawadlook. A glance told him what Sokwenna had done. The room was an arsenal. Guns lay there, ready to be used; heaps of cartridges were piled near them, and in the eyes of Keok and Nawadlook blazed deep and steady fires as they held shining cartridges between their fingers, ready to thrust them into the rifle chambers as fast as the guns were emptied.

In the center of the room stood Mary Standish. The candles, shaded so they would not disclose the windows, faintly illumined her pale face and unbound hair and revealed the horror in her eyes as she looked at Alan.

He was about to speak, to assure her there was no danger that Graham's men would fire upon the cabin--when hell broke suddenly loose out in the night. The savage roar of guns answered Sokwenna's fusillade, and a hail of bullets crashed against the log walls. Two of them found their way through the windows like hissing serpents, and with a single movement Alan was at Mary's side and had crumpled her down on the floor beside Keok and Nawadlook. His face was white, his brain a furnace of sudden, consuming fire.

"I thought they wouldn't shoot at women," he said, and his voice was terrifying in its strange hardness. "I was mistaken. And I am sure--now--that I understand."

With his rifle he cautiously approached the window. He was no longer guessing at an elusive truth. He knew what Graham was thinking, what he was planning, what he intended to do, and the thing was appalling. Both he and Rossland knew there would be some way of sheltering Mary Standish in Sokwenna's cabin; they were accepting a desperate gamble, believing that Alan Holt would find a safe place for her, while he fought until he fell. It was the finesse of clever scheming, nothing less than murder, and he, by this combination of circumstances and plot, was the victim marked for death.

The shooting had stopped, and the silence that followed it held a significance for Alan. They were giving him an allotted time in which to care for those under his protection. A trap-door was in the floor of Sokwenna's cabin. It opened into a small storeroom and cellar, which in turn possessed an air vent leading to the outside, overlooking the ravine. In the candle-glow Alan saw the door of this trap propped open with a stick. Sokwenna, too, was clever. Sokwenna had foreseen.

Crouched under the window, he looked at the girls. Keok, with a rifle in her hand, had crept to the foot of the ladder leading up to the attic, and began to climb it. She was going to Sokwenna, to load for him. Alan pointed to the open trap.

"Quick, get into that!" he cried. "It is the only safe place. You can load there and hand out the guns."

Mary Standish looked at him steadily, but did not move. She was clutching a rifle in her hands. And Nawadlook did not move. But Keok climbed steadily and disappeared in the darkness above.

"Go into the cellar!" commanded Alan. "Good God, if you don't--"

A smile lit up Mary's face. In that hour of deadly peril it was like a ray of glorious light leading the way through blackness, a smile sweet and gentle and unafraid; and slowly she crept toward Alan, dragging the rifle in one hand and holding the little pistol in the other, and from his feet she still smiled up at him through the dishevelment of her shining hair, and in a quiet, little voice that thrilled him, she said, "I am going to help you fight."

Nawadlook came creeping after her, dragging another rifle and bearing an apron heavy with the weight of cartridges.

And above, through the darkened loophole of the attic window, Sokwenna's ferret eyes had caught the movement of a shadow in the gray mist, and his rifle sent its death-challenge once more to John Graham and his men. What followed struck a smile from Mary's lips, and a moaning sob rose from her breast as she watched the man she loved rise up before the open window to face the winged death that was again beating a tattoo against the log walls of the cabin.

CHAPTER XXV

That in the lust and passion of his designs and the arrogance of his power John Graham was not afraid to overstep all law and order, and that he believed Holt would shelter Mary Standish from injury and death, there could no longer be a doubt after the first few swift moments following Sokwenna's rifle-shots from the attic window.

Through the window of the lower room, barricaded by the cautious old warrior until its aperture was not more than eight inches square, Alan thrust his rifle as the crash of gun-fire broke the gray and thickening mist of night. He could hear the thud and hiss of bullets; he heard them singing like angry bees as they passed with the swiftness of chain-lightning over the cabin roof, and their patter against the log walls was like the hollow drumming of knuckles against the side of a ripe watermelon. There was something fascinating and almost gentle about that last sound. It did not seem that the horror of death was riding with it, and Alan lost all sense of fear as he stared in the direction from which the firing came, trying to make out shadows at which to shoot. Here and there he saw dim, white streaks, and at these he fired as fast as he could throw cartridges into the chamber and pull the trigger. Then he crouched down with the empty gun. It was Mary Standish who held out a freshly loaded weapon to him. Her face was waxen in its deathly pallor. Her eyes, staring at him so strangely, never for an instant leaving his face, were lustrous with the agony of fear that flamed in their depths. She was not afraid for herself. It was for *him*. His name was on her lips, a whisper unspoken, a breathless prayer, and in that instant a bullet sped through the opening in front of which he had stood a moment before, a hissing, writhing serpent of death that struck something behind them in its venomous wrath. With a cry she flung up her arms about his bent head.

"My God, they will kill you if you stand there!" she moaned. "Give me up to them, Alan. If you love me--give me up!"

A sudden spurt of white dust shot out into the dim candle-glow, and then another, so near Nawadlook that his blood went cold. Bullets were finding their way through the moss and earth chinking between the logs of the cabin. His arms closed in a fierce embrace about the girl's slim body, and before she could realize what was happening, he leaped to the trap with her and almost flung her into its protection. Then he forced Nawadlook down beside her, and after them he thrust in the empty gun and the apron with its weight of cartridges. His face was demoniac in its command.

"If you don't stay there, I'll open the door and go outside to fight! Do you understand? *Stay there!*"

His clenched fist was in their faces, his voice almost a shout. He saw another white spurt of dust; the bullet crashed in tinware, and following the crash came a shriek from Keok in the attic.

In that upper gloom Sokwenna's gun had fallen with a clatter. The old warrior bent himself over, nearly double, and with his two withered hands was clutching his stomach. He was on his knees, and his breath suddenly came in a panting, gasping cry. Then he straightened slowly and said something reassuring to Keok, and faced the window again with the gun which she had loaded for him.

The scream had scarcely gone from Keok's lips when Alan was at the top of the ladder, calling her. She came to him through the stark blackness of the room, sobbing that Sokwenna was hit; and Alan reached out and seized her, and dragged her down, and placed her with Nawadlook and Mary Standish.

From them he turned to the window, and his soul cried out madly for the power to see, to kill, to avenge. As if in answer to this prayer for light and vision he saw his cabin strangely illumined; dancing, yellow radiance silhouetted the windows, and a stream of it billowed out through an open door into the night. It was so bright he could see the rain-mist, scarcely heavier than a dense, slowly descending fog, a wet blanket of vapor moistening the earth. His heart jumped as with each second the blaze of light increased. They had set fire to his cabin. They were no longer white men, but savages.

He was terribly cool, even as his heart throbbed so violently. He watched with the eyes of a deadly hunter, wide-open over his rifle-barrel. Sokwenna was still. Probably he was dead. Keok was sobbing in the cellar-pit. Then he saw a shape growing in the illumination, three or four of them, moving, alive. He waited until they were clearer, and he knew what they were thinking--that the bullet-riddled cabin had lost its power to fight. He prayed God it was Graham he was aiming at, and fired. The figure went down, sank into the earth as a dead man falls. Steadily he fired at the others--one, two, three, four--and two out of the four he hit, and the exultant thought flashed upon him that it was good shooting under the circumstances.

He sprang back for another gun, and it was Mary who was waiting for him, head and shoulders out of the cellar-pit, the rifle in her hands. She was sobbing as she looked straight at him, yet without moisture or tears in her eyes.

"Keep down!" he warned. "Keep down below the floor!"

He guessed what was coming. He had shown his enemies that life still existed in the cabin, life with death in its hands, and now--from the shelter of the other cabins, from the darkness, from beyond the light of his flaming home, the rifle fire continued to grow until it filled the night with a horrible din. He flung himself face-down upon the floor, so that the lower log of the building protected him. No living thing could have stood up against what was happening in these moments. Bullets tore through the windows and between the moss-chinked logs, crashing against metal and glass and tinware; one of the candles sputtered and went out, and in this hell Alan heard a cry and saw Mary Standish coming out of the cellar-pit toward him. He had flung himself down quickly, and she thought he was hit! He shrieked at her, and his heart froze with horror as he saw a heavy tress of her hair drop to the floor as she stood there in that frightful moment, white and glorious in the face of the gun-fire. Before she could move another step, he was at her side, and with her in his arms leaped into the pit.

A bullet sang over them. He crushed her so close that for a breath or two life seemed to leave her body.

A sudden draught of cool air struck his face. He missed Nawadlook. In the deeper gloom farther under the floor he heard her moving, and saw a faint square of light. She was creeping back. Her hands touched his arm.

"We can get away--there!" she cried in a low voice. "I have opened the little door. We can crawl through it and into the ravine."

Her words and the square of light were an inspiration. He had not dreamed that Graham would turn the cabin into a death-hole, and Nawadlook's words filled him with a sudden thrilling hope. The rifle fire was dying away again as he gave voice to his plan in sharp, swift words. He would hold the cabin. As long as he was there Graham and his men would not dare to rush it. At least they would hesitate a considerable time before doing that. And meanwhile the girls could steal down into the ravine. There was no one on that side to intercept them, and both Keok and Nawadlook were well acquainted with the trails into the mountains. It would mean safety for them. He would remain in the cabin, and fight, until Stampede Smith and the herdsmen came.

The white face against his breast was cold and almost expressionless. Something in it frightened him. He knew his argument had failed and that Mary Standish would not go; yet she did not answer him, nor did her lips move in the effort.

"Go--for *their* sakes, if not for your own and mine," he insisted, holding her away from him. "Good God, think what it will mean if beasts like those out there get hold of Keok and Nawadlook! Graham is your husband and will protect you for himself, but for them there will be no hope, no salvation, nothing but a fate more terrible than death. They will be like--like two beautiful lambs thrown among wolves--broken--destroyed--"

Her eyes were burning with horror. Keok was sobbing, and a moan which she bravely tried to smother in her breast came from Nawadlook.

"And *you!*" whispered Mary.

"I must remain here. It is the only way."

Dumbly she allowed him to lead her back with Keok and Nawadlook. Keok went through the opening first, then Nawadlook, and Mary Standish last. She did not touch him again. She made no movement toward him and said no word, and all he remembered of her when she was gone in the gloom was her eyes. In that last look she had given him her soul, and no whisper, no farewell caress came with it.

"Go cautiously until you are out of the ravine, then hurry toward the mountains," were his last words.

He saw their forms fade into dim shadows, and the gray mist swallowed them.

He hurried back, seized a loaded gun, and sprang to the window, knowing that he must continue to deal death until he was killed. Only in that way could he hold Graham back and give those who had escaped a chance for their lives. Cautiously he looked out over his gun barrel. His cabin was a furnace red with flame; streams of fire were licking out at the windows and through the door, and as he sought vainly for a movement of life, the crackling roar of it came to his ears, and so swiftly that his breath choked him, the pitch-filled walls became sheets of conflagration, until the cabin was a seething, red-hot torch of fire whose illumination was more dazzling than the sun of day.

Out into this illumination suddenly stalked a figure waving a white sheet at the end of a long pole. It advanced slowly, a little hesitatingly at first, as if doubtful of what might happen; and then it stopped, full in the light, an easy mark for a rifle aimed from Sokwenna's cabin. He saw who it was then, and drew in his rifle and watched the unexpected maneuver in amazement. The man was Rossland. In spite of the dramatic tenseness of the moment Alan could not repress the grim smile that came to his lips. Rossland was a man of illogical resource, he meditated. Only a short time ago he had fled ignominiously through fear of personal violence, while now, with a courage that could not fail to rouse admiration, he was exposing himself to a swift and sudden death, protected only by the symbol of truce over his head. That he owed this symbol either regard or honor did not for an instant possess Alan. A murderer held it, a man even more vile than a murderer if such a creature existed on earth, and for such a man death was a righteous end. Only Rossland's nerve, and what he might have to say, held back the vengeance within reach of Alan's hand.

He waited, and Rossland again advanced and did not stop until he was within a hundred feet of the cabin. A sudden disturbing thought flashed upon Alan as he heard his name called. He had seen no other figures, no other shadows beyond Rossland, and the burning cabin now clearly illumined the windows of Sokwenna's place. Was it conceivable that Rossland was merely a lure, and the instant he exposed himself in a parley a score of hidden rifles would reveal their treachery? He shuddered and held himself below the opening of the window. Graham and his men were more than capable of such a crime.

Rossland's voice rose above the crackle and roar of the burning cabin. "Alan Holt! Are you there?"

"Yes, I am here," shouted Alan, "and I have a line on your heart, Rossland, and my finger is on the trigger. What do you want?"

There was a moment of silence, as if the thought of what he was facing had at last stricken Rossland dumb. Then he said: "We are giving you a last chance, Holt. For God's sake, don't be a fool! The offer I made you today is still good. If you don't accept it--the law must take its course."

"*The law!*" Alan's voice was a savage cry.

"Yes, the law. The law is with us. We have the proper authority to recover a stolen wife, a captive, a prisoner held in restraint with felonious intent. But we don't want to press the law unless we are forced to do so. You and the old Eskimo have killed three of our men and wounded two others. That means the hangman, if we take you alive. But we are willing to forget that if you will accept the offer I made you today. What do you say?"

Alan was stunned. Speech failed him as he realized the monstrous assurance with which Graham and Rossland were playing their game. And when he made no answer Rossland continued to drive home his arguments, believing that at last Alan was at the point of surrender.

Up in the dark attic the voices had come like ghost-land whispers to old Sokwenna. He lay huddled at the window, and the chill of death was creeping over him. But the voices roused him. They were not strange voices, but voices which came up out of a past of many years ago, calling upon him, urging him, persisting in his ears with cries of vengeance and of triumph, the call of familiar names, a moaning of women, a sobbing of children. Shadowy hands helped him, and a last time he raised himself to the window, and his eyes were filled with the glare of the burning cabin. He struggled to lift his rifle, and behind him he heard the exultation of his people as he rested it over the sill and with gasping breath leveled it at something which moved between him and the blazing light of that wonderful sun which was the burning cabin. And then, slowly and with difficulty, he pressed the trigger, and Sokwenna's last shot sped on its mission.

At the sound of the shot Alan looked through the window. For a moment Rossland stood motionless. Then the pole in his hands wavered, drooped, and fell to the earth, and Rossland sank down after it making no sound, and lay a dark and huddled blot on the ground.

The appalling swiftness and ease with which Rossland had passed from life into death shocked every nerve in Alan's body. Horror for a brief space stupefied him, and he continued to stare at the dark and motionless blot, forgetful of his own danger, while a grim and terrible silence followed the shot. And then what seemed to be a single cry broke that silence, though it was made up of many men's voices. Deadly and thrilling, it was a message that set Alan into action. Rossland had been killed under a flag of truce, and even the men under Graham had something like respect for that symbol. He could expect no mercy--nothing now but the most terrible of vengeance at their hands, and as he dodged back from the window he cursed Sokwenna under his breath, even as he felt the relief of knowing he was not dead.

Before a shot had been fired from outside, he was up the ladder; in another moment he was bending over the huddled form of the old Eskimo.

"Come below!" he commanded. "We must be ready to leave through the cellar-pit."

His hand touched Sokwenna's face; it hesitated, groped in the darkness, and then grew still over the old warrior's heart. There was no tremor or beat of life in the aged beast. Sokwenna was dead.

The guns of Graham's men opened fire again. Volley after volley crashed into the cabin as Alan descended the ladder. He could hear bullets tearing through the chinks and windows as he turned quickly to the shelter of the pit.

He was amazed to find that Mary Standish had returned and was waiting for him there.

CHAPTER XXVI

In the astonishment with which Mary's unexpected presence confused him for a moment, Alan stood at the edge of the trap, staring down at her pale face, heedless of the terrific gun-fire that was assailing the cabin. That she had not gone with Keok and Nawadlook, but had come back to him, filled him with instant dread, for the precious minutes he had fought for were lost, and the priceless time gained during the parley with Rossland counted for nothing.

She saw his disappointment and his danger, and sprang up to seize his hand and pull him down beside her.

"Of course you didn't expect me to go," she said, in a voice that no longer trembled or betrayed excitement. "You didn't want me to be a coward. My place is with you."

He could make no answer to that, with her beautiful eyes looking at him as they were, but he felt his heart grow warmer and something rise up chokingly in his throat.

"Sokwenna is dead, and Rossland lies out there--shot under a flag of truce," he said. "We can't have many minutes left to us."

He was looking at the square of light where the tunnel from the cellar-pit opened into the ravine. He had planned to escape through it--alone--and keep up a fight in the open, but with Mary at his side it would be a desperate gantlet to run.

"Where are Keok and Nawadlook?" he asked.

"On the tundra, hurrying for the mountains. I told them it was your plan that I should return to you. When they doubted, I threatened to give myself up unless they did as I commanded them. And--Alan--the ravine is filled with the rain-mist, and dark--" She was holding his free hand closely to her breast.

"It is our one chance," he said.

"And aren't you glad--a little glad--that I didn't run away without you?"

Even then he saw the sweet and tremulous play of her lips as they smiled at him in the gloom, and heard the soft note in her voice that was almost playfully chiding; and the glory of her love as she had proved it to him there drew from him what he knew to be the truth.

"Yes--I am glad. It is strange that I should be so happy in a moment like this. If they will give us a quarter of an hour--"

He led the way quickly to the square of light and was first to creep forth into the thick mist. It was scarcely rain, yet he could feel the wet particles of it, and through this saturated gloom whining bullets cut like knives over his head. The blazing cabin illumined the open on each side of Sokwenna's place, but deepened the shadows in the ravine, and a few seconds later they stood hand in hand in the blanket of fog that hid the coulée.

Suddenly the shots grew scattering above them, then ceased entirely. This was not what Alan had hoped for. Graham's men, enraged and made desperate by Rossland's death, would rush the cabin immediately. Scarcely had the thought leaped into his mind when he heard swiftly approaching shouts, the trampling of feet, and then the battering of some heavy object at the barricaded door of Sokwenna's cabin. In another minute or two their escape would be discovered and a horde of men would pour down into the ravine.

Mary tugged at his hand. "Let us hurry," she pleaded.

What happened then seemed madness to the girl, for Alan turned and with her hand held tightly in his started up the side of the ravine, apparently in the face of their enemies. Her heart throbbed with sudden fear when their course came almost within the circle of light made by the burning cabin. Like shadows they sped into the deeper shelter of the corral buildings, and not until they paused there did she understand the significance of the hazardous chance they had taken. Already Graham's men were pouring into the ravine.

"They won't suspect we've doubled on them until it is too late," said Alan exultantly. "We'll make for the kloof. Stampede and the herdsmen should arrive within a few hours, and when that happens--"

A stifled moan interrupted him. Half a dozen paces away a crumpled figure lay huddled against one of the corral gates.

"He is hurt," whispered Mary, after a moment of silence.

"I hope so," replied Alan pitilessly. "It will be unfortunate for us if he lives to tell his comrades we have passed this way."

Something in his voice made the girl shiver. It was as if the vanishing point of mercy had been reached, and savages were at their backs. She heard the wounded man moan again as they stole through the deeper shadows of the corrals toward the nigger-head bottom. And then she noticed that the mist was no longer in her face. The sky was clearing. She could see Alan more clearly, and when they came to the narrow trail over which they had fled once before that night it reached out ahead of them like a thin, dark ribbon. Scarcely had they reached this point when a rifle shot sounded not far behind. It was followed by a second and a third, and after that came a shout. It was not a loud shout. There was something strained and ghastly about it, and yet it came distinctly to them.

"The wounded man," said Alan, in a voice of dismay. "He is calling the others. I should have killed him!"

He traveled at a half-trot, and the girl ran lightly at his side. All her courage and endurance had returned. She breathed easily and quickened her steps, so that she was setting the pace for Alan. They passed along the crest of the ridge under which lay the willows and the pool, and at the end of this they paused to rest and listen. Trained to the varied night whisperings of the tundras Alan's ears caught faint sounds which his companion did not hear. The wounded man had succeeded in giving his message, and pursuers were scattering over the plain behind them.

"Can you run a little farther?" he asked.

"Where?"

He pointed, and she darted ahead of him, her dark hair streaming in a cloud that began to catch a faint luster of increasing light. Alan ran a little behind her. He was afraid of the light. Only gloom had saved them this night, and if the darkness of mist and fog and cloud gave way to clear twilight and the sun-glow of approaching day before they reached the kloof he would have to fight in the open. With Stampede at his side he would have welcomed such an opportunity of matching rifles with their enemies, for there were many vantage points in the open tundra from which they might have defied assault. But the nearness of the girl frightened him. She, after all, was the hunted thing. He was only an incident. From him could be exacted nothing more than the price of death; he would be made to pay that, as Sokwenna had paid. For her remained the unspeakable horror of Graham's lust and passion. But if they could reach the kloof, and the hiding-place in the face of the cliff, they could laugh at Graham's pack of beasts while they waited for the swift vengeance that would come with Stampede and the herdsmen.

He watched the sky. It was clearing steadily. Even the mists in the hollows were beginning to melt away, and in place of their dissolution came faintly rose-tinted lights. It was the hour of dawn; the sun sent a golden glow over the disintegrating curtain of gloom that still lay between it and the tundras, and objects a hundred paces away no longer held shadow or illusionment.

The girl did not pause, but continued to run lightly and with surprising speed, heeding only the direction which he gave her. Her endurance amazed him. And he knew that without questioning him she had guessed the truth of what lay behind them. Then, all at once, she stopped, swayed like a reed, and would have fallen if his arms had not caught her.

"Splendid!" he cried.

She lay gasping for breath, her face against his breast. Her heart was a swiftly beating little dynamo.

They had gained the edge of a shallow ravine that reached within half a mile of the kloof. It was this shelter he had hoped for, and Mary's splendid courage had won it for them.

He picked her up in his arms and carried her again, as he had carried her through the nigger-head bottom. Every minute, every foot of progress, counted now. Range of vision was widening. Pools of sunlight were flecking the plains. In another quarter of an hour moving objects would be distinctly visible a mile away.

With his precious burden in his arms, her lips so near that he could feel their breath, her heart throbbing, he became suddenly conscious of the incongruity of the bird-song that was wakening all about them. It seemed inconceivable that this day, glorious in its freshness, and welcomed by the glad voice of all living things, should be a day of tragedy, of horror, and of impending doom for him. He wanted to shout out his protest and say that it was all a lie, and it seemed absurd that he should handicap himself with the weight and inconvenient bulk of his rifle when his arms wanted to hold only that softer treasure which they bore.

In a little while Mary was traveling at his side again. And from then on he climbed at intervals to the higher swellings of the gully edge and scanned the tundra. Twice he saw men, and from their movements he concluded their enemies believed they were hidden somewhere on the tundra not far from the range-houses.

Three-quarters of an hour later they came to the end of the shallow ravine, and half a mile of level plain lay between them and the kloof. For a space they rested, and in this interval Mary smoothed her long hair and plaited it in two braids. In these moments Alan encouraged her, but he did not lie. He told her the half-mile of tundra was their greatest hazard, and described the risks they would run. Carefully he explained what she was to do under certain circumstances. There was scarcely a chance they could cross it unobserved, but they might be so far ahead of the searchers that they could beat them out to the kloof. If enemies appeared between them and the kloof, it would be necessary to find a dip or shelter of rock, and fight; and if pursuers from behind succeeded in out-stripping them in the race, she was to continue in the direction of the kloof as fast as she could go, while he followed more slowly, holding Graham's men back with his rifle until she reached the edge of the gorge. After that he would come to her as swiftly as he could run.

They started. Within five minutes they were on the floor of the tundra. About them in all directions stretched the sunlit plains. Half a mile back toward the range were moving figures; farther west were others, and eastward, almost at the edge of the ravine, were two men who would have discovered them in another moment if they had not descended into the hollow. Alan could see them kneeling to drink at the little coulée which ran through it.

"Don't hurry," he said, with a sudden swift thought. "Keep parallel with me and a distance away. They may not discover you are a woman and possibly may think we are searchers like themselves. Stop when I stop. Follow my movements."

"Yes, sir!"

Now, in the sunlight, she was not afraid. Her cheeks were flushed, her eyes bright as stars as she nodded at him. Her face and hands were soiled with muck-stain, her dress spotted and torn, and looking at her thus Alan laughed and cried out softly:

"You beautiful little vagabond!"

She sent the laugh back, a soft, sweet laugh to give him courage, and after that she watched him closely, falling in with his scheme so cleverly that her action was better than his own--and so they had made their way over a third of the plain when Alan came toward her suddenly and cried, "Now, *run!*"

A glance showed her what was happening. The two men had come out of the ravine and were running toward them.

Swift as a bird she was ahead of Alan, making for a pinnacle of rock which he had pointed out to her at the edge of the kloof.

Close behind her, he said: "Don't hesitate a second. Keep on going. When they are a little nearer I am going to kill them. But you mustn't stop."

At intervals he looked behind him. The two men were gaining rapidly. He measured the time when less than two hundred yards would separate them. Then he drew close to Mary's side.

"See that level place ahead? We'll cross it in another minute or two. When they come to it I'm going to stop, and catch them where they can't find shelter. But you must keep on going. I'll overtake you by the time you reach the edge of the kloof."

She made no answer, but ran faster; and when they had passed the level space she heard his footsteps growing fainter, and her heart was ready to choke her when she knew the time had come for him to turn upon their enemies. But in her mind burned the low words of his command, his warning, and she did not look back, but kept her eyes on the pinnacle of rock, which was now very near. She had almost reached it when the first shot came from behind her.

Without making a sound that would alarm her, Alan had stumbled, and made pretense of falling. He lay upon his face for a moment, as if stunned, and then rose to his knees. An instant too late Graham's men saw his ruse when his leveled rifle gleamed in the sunshine. The speed of their pursuit was their undoing. Trying to catch themselves so that they might use their rifles, or fling themselves upon the ground, they brought themselves into a brief but deadly interval of inaction, and in that flash one of the men went down under Alan's first shot. Before he could fire again the second had flattened himself upon the earth, and swift as a fox Alan was on his feet and racing for the kloof. Mary stood with her back against the huge rock, gasping for breath, when he joined her. A bullet sang over their heads with its angry menace. He did not return the fire, but drew the girl quickly behind the rock.

"He won't dare to stand up until the others join him," he encouraged her. "We're beating them to it, little girl! If you can keep up a few minutes longer--"

She smiled at him, even as she struggled to regain her breath. It seemed to her there was no way of descending into the chaos of rock between the gloomy walls of the kloof, and she gave a little cry when Alan caught her by her hands and lowered her over the face of a ledge to a table-like escarpment below. He laughed at her fear when he dropped down beside her, and held her close as they crept back under the shelving face of the cliff to a hidden path that led downward, with a yawning chasm at their side. The trail widened as they descended, and at the last they reached the bottom, with the gloom and shelter of a million-year-old crevasse hovering over them. Grim and monstrous rocks, black and slippery with age, lay about them, and among these they picked their way, while the trickle and drip of water and the flesh-like clamminess of the air sent a strange shiver of awe through Mary Standish. There was no life here--only an age-old whisper that seemed a part of death; and when voices came from above, where Graham's men were gathering, they were ghostly and far away.

But here, too, was refuge and safety. Mary could feel it as they picked their way through the chill and gloom that lay in the silent passages between the Gargantuan rocks. When her hands touched their naked sides an uncontrollable impulse made her shrink closer to Alan, even though she sensed the protection of their presence. They were like colossi, carved by hands long dead, and now guarded by spirits whose voices guttered low and secretly in the mysterious drip and trickle of unseen water. This was the haunted place. In this chasm death and vengeance had glutted themselves long before she was born; and when a rock crashed behind them, accidentally sent down by one of the men above, a cry broke from her lips. She was frightened, and in a way she had never known before. It was not death she feared here, nor the horror from which she had escaped above, but something unknown and indescribable, for which she would never be able to give a reason. She clung to Alan, and when at last the narrow fissure widened over their heads, and light came down and softened their way, he saw that her face was deathly white.

"We are almost there," he comforted. "And--some day--you will love this gloomy kloof as I love it, and we will travel it together all the way to the mountains."

A few minutes later they came to an avalanche of broken sandstone that was heaped half-way up the face of the precipitous wall, and up this climbed until they came to a level shelf of rock, and back of this was a great depression in the rock, forty feet deep and half as wide, with a floor as level as a table and covered with soft white sand. Mary would never forget her first glimpse of this place; it was unreal, strange, as if a band of outlaw fairies had brought the white sand for a carpet, and had made this their hiding-place, where wind and rain and snow could never blow. And up the face of the cavern, as if to make her thought more real, led a ragged fissure which it seemed to her only fairies' feet could travel, and which ended at the level of the plain. So they were tundra fairies, coming down from flowers and sunlight through that fissure, and it was from the evil spirits in the kloof itself that they must have hidden themselves. Something in the humor and gentle thought of it all made her smile at Alan. But his face had turned suddenly grim, and she looked up the kloof, where they had traveled through danger and come to safety. And then she saw that which froze all thought of fairies out of her heart.

Men were coming through the chaos and upheaval of rock. There were many of them, appearing out of the darker neck of the gorge into the clearer light, and at their head was a man upon whom Mary's eyes fixed themselves in horror. White-faced she looked at Alan. He had guessed the truth.

"That man in front?" he asked.

She nodded. "Yes."

"Is John Graham."

He heard the words choking in her throat.

"Yes, John Graham."

He swung his rifle slowly, his eyes burning with a steely fire.

"I think," he said, "that from here I can easily kill him!"

Her hand touched his arm; she was looking into his eyes. Fear had gone out of them, and in its place was a soft and gentle radiance, a prayer to him.

"I am thinking of tomorrow--the next day--the years and years to come, *with you*," she whispered. "Alan, you can't kill John Graham--not until God shows us it is the only thing left for us to do. You can't--"

The crash of a rifle between the rock walls interrupted her. The snarl of a bullet followed the shot. She heard it strike, and her heart stopped beating, and the rigidity of death came into her limbs and body as she saw the swift and terrible change in the stricken face of the man she loved. He tried to smile at her, even as a red blot came where the streak of gray in his hair touched his forehead. And then he crumpled down at her feet, and his rifle rattled against the rocks.

She knew it was death. Something seemed to burst in her head and fill her brain with the roar of a flood. She screamed. Even the men below hesitated and their hearts jumped with a new sensation as the terrible cry of a woman rang between the rock walls of the chasm. And following the cry a voice came down to them.

"John Graham, I'm going to kill you--*kill you*--"

And snatching up the fallen rifle Mary Standish set herself to the task of vengeance.

CHAPTER XXVII

She waited. The ferocity of a mother defending her young filled her soul, and she moaned in her grief and despair as the seconds passed. But she did not fire blindly, for she knew she must kill John Graham. The troublesome thing was a strange film that persisted in gathering before her eyes, something she tried to brush away, but which obstinately refused to go. She did not know she was sobbing as she looked over the rifle barrel. The figures came swiftly, but she had lost sight of John Graham. They reached the upheaval of shattered rock and began climbing it, and in her desire to make out the man she hated she stood above the rampart that had sheltered her. The men looked alike, jumping and dodging like so many big tundra hares as they came nearer, and suddenly it occurred to her that *all* of them were John Grahams, and that she must kill swiftly and accurately. Only the hiding fairies might have guessed how her reason trembled and almost fell in those moments when she began firing. Certainly John Graham and his men did not, for her first shot was a lucky one, and a man slipped down among the rocks at the crack of it. After that she continued to fire until the responseless click of the hammer told her the gun was empty. The explosions and the shock against her slight shoulder cleared her vision and her brain. She saw the men still coming, and they were so near she could see their faces clearly. And again her soul cried out in its desire to kill John Graham.

She turned, and for an instant fell upon her knees beside Alan. His face was hidden in his arm. Swiftly she tore his automatic from its holster, and sprang back to her rock. There was no time to wait or choose now, for his murderers were almost upon her. With all her strength she tried to fire accurately, but Alan's big gun leaped and twisted in her hand as she poured its fire wildly down among the rocks until it was empty. Her own smaller weapon she had lost somewhere in the race to the kloof, and now when she found she had fired her last shot she waited through another instant of horror, until she was striking at faces that came within the reach of her arm. And then, like a monster created suddenly by an evil spirit, Graham was at her side. She had a moment's vision of his cruel, exultant face, his eyes blazing with a passion that was almost madness, his powerful body lunging upon her. Then his arms came about her. She could feel herself crushing inside them, and fought against their cruel pressure, then broke limply and hung a resistless weight against him. She was not unconscious, but her strength was gone, and if the arms had closed a little more they would have killed her.

And she could hear--clearly. She heard suddenly the shots that came from up the kloof, scattered shots, then many of them, and after that the strange, wild cries that only the Eskimo herdsmen make.

Graham's arms relaxed. His eyes swept the fairies' hiding-place with its white sand floor, and fierce joy lit up his face.

"Martens, it couldn't happen in a better place," he said to a man who stood near him. "Leave me five men. Take the others and help Schneider. If you don't clean them out, retreat this way, and six rifles from this ambuscade will do the business in a hurry."

Mary heard the names of the men called who were to stay. The others hurried away. The firing in the kloof was steady now. But there were no cries, no shouts--nothing but the ominous crack of the rifles.

Graham's arms closed about her again. Then he picked her up and carried her back into the cavern, and in a place where the rock wall sagged inward, making a pocket of gloom which was shut out from the light of day, he laid her upon the carpet of sand.

Where the erosion of many centuries of dripping water had eaten its first step in the making of the ragged fissure a fairy had begun to climb down from the edge of the tundra. He was a swift and agile fairy, very red in the face, breathing fast from hard running, but making not a sound as he came like a gopher where it seemed no living thing could find a hold. And the fairy was Stampede Smith.

From the lips of the kloof he had seen the last few seconds of the tragedy below, and where death would have claimed him in a more reasonable moment he came down in safety now. In his finger-ends was the old tingling of years ago, and in his blood the thrill which he had thought was long dead--the thrill of looking over leveled guns into the eyes of other men. Time had rolled back, and he was the old Stampede Smith. He saw under him lust and passion and murder, as in other days he had seen them, and between him and desire there was neither law nor conscience to bar the way, and his dream--a last great fight--was here to fill the final unwritten page of a life's drama that was almost closed. And what a fight, if he could make that carpet of soft, white sand unheard and unseen. Six to one! Six men with guns at their sides and rifles in their hands. What a glorious end it would be, for a woman--and Alan Holt!

He blessed the firing up the kloof which kept the men's faces turned that way; he thanked God for the sound of combat, which made the scraping of rock and the rattle of stones under his feet unheard. He was almost down when a larger rock broke loose, and fell to the ledge. Two of the men turned, but in that same instant came a more thrilling interruption. A cry, a shrill scream, a woman's voice filled with madness and despair, came from the depth of the cavern, and the five men stared in the direction of its agony. Close upon the cries came Mary Standish, with Graham behind her, reaching out his hands for her. The girl's hair was flying, her face the color of the white sand, and Graham's eyes were the eyes of a demon forgetful of all else but her. He caught her. The slim body crumpled in his arms again while pitifully weak hands beat futilely in his face.

And then came a cry such as no man had ever heard in Ghost Kloof before.

It was Stampede Smith. A sheer twenty feet he had leaped to the carpet of sand, and as he jumped his hands whipped out his two guns, and scarcely had his feet touched the floor of the soft pocket in the ledge when death crashed from them swift as lightning flashes, and three of the five were tottering or falling before the other two could draw or swing a rifle. Only one of them had fired a shot. The other went down as if his legs had been knocked from under him by a club, and the one who fired bent forward then, as if making a bow to death, and pitched on his face.

And then Stampede Smith whirled upon John Graham.

During these few swift seconds Graham had stood stunned, with the girl crushed against his breast. He was behind her, sheltered by her body, her head protecting his heart, and as Stampede turned he was drawing a gun, his dark face blazing with the fiendish knowledge that the other could not shoot without killing the girl. The horror of the situation gripped Stampede. He saw Graham's pistol rise slowly and deliberately. He watched it, fascinated. And the look in Graham's face was the cold and unexcited triumph of a devil. Stampede saw only that face. It was four inches--perhaps five--away from the girl's. There was only that--and the extending arm, the crooking finger, the black mouth of the automatic seeking his heart. And then, in that last second, straight into the girl's staring eyes blazed Stampede's gun, and the four inches of leering face behind her was suddenly blotted out. It was Stampede, and not the girl, who closed his eyes then; and when he opened them and saw Mary Standish sobbing over Alan's body, and Graham lying face down in the sand, he reverently raised the gun from which he had fired the last shot, and pressed its hot barrel to his thin lips.

Then he went to Alan. He raised the limp head, while Mary bowed her face in her hands. In her anguish she prayed that she, too, might die, for in this hour of triumph over Graham there was no hope or joy for her. Alan was gone. Only death could have come with that terrible red blot on his forehead, just under the gray streak in his hair. And without him there was no longer a reason for her to live.

She reached out her arms. "Give him to me," she whispered. "Give him to me."

Through the agony that burned in her eyes she did not see the look in Stampede's face. But she heard his voice.

"It wasn't a bullet that hit him," Stampede was saying. "The bullet hit a rock, an' it was a chip from the rock that caught him square between the eyes. He isn't dead, *and he ain't going to die!*"

How many weeks or months or years it was after his last memory of the fairies' hiding-place before he came back to life, Alan could make no manner of guess. But he did know that for a long, long time he was riding through space on a soft, white cloud, vainly trying to overtake a girl with streaming hair who fled on another cloud ahead of him; and at last this cloud broke up, like a great cake of ice, and the girl plunged into the immeasurable depths over which they were sailing, and he leaped after her. Then came strange lights, and darkness, and sounds like the clashing of cymbals, and voices; and after those things a long sleep, from which he opened his eyes to find himself in a bed, and a face very near, with shining eyes that looked at him through a sea of tears.

And a voice whispered to him, sweetly, softly, joyously, "Alan!"

He tried to reach up his arms. The face came nearer; it was pressed against his own, soft arms crept about him, softer lips kissed his mouth and eyes, and sobbing whispers came with their love, and he knew the end of the race had come, and he had won.

This was the fifth day after the fight in the kloof; and on the sixth he sat up in his bed, bolstered with pillows, and Stampede came to see him, and then Keok and Nawadlook and Tatpan and Topkok and Wegaruk, his old housekeeper, and only for a few minutes at a time was Mary away from him. But Tautuk and Amuk Toolik did not come, and he saw the strange change in Keok, and knew that they were dead. Yet he dreaded to ask the question, for more than any others of his people did he love these two missing comrades of the tundras.

It was Stampede who first told him in detail what had happened--but he would say little of the fight on the ledge, and it was Mary who told him of that.

"Graham had over thirty men with him, and only ten got away," he said. "We have buried sixteen and are caring for seven wounded at the corrals. Now that Graham is dead, they're frightened stiff--afraid we're going to hand them over to the law. And without Graham or Rossland to fight for them, they know they're lost."

"And our men--my people?" asked Alan faintly.

"Fought like devils."

"Yes, I know. But--"

"They didn't rest an hour in coming from the mountains."

"You know what I mean, Stampede."

"Not many, Alan. Seven were killed, including Sokwenna," and he counted over the names of the slain. Tautuk and Amuk Toolik were not among them.

"And Tautuk?"

"He is wounded. Missed death by an inch, and it has almost killed Keok. She is with him night and day, and as jealous as a little cat if anyone else attempts to do anything for him."

"Then--I am glad Tautuk was hit," smiled Alan. And he asked, "Where is Amuk Toolik?"

Stampede hung his head and blushed like a boy.

"You'll have to ask *her*, Alan."

And a little later Alan put the question to Mary.

She, too, blushed, and in her eyes was a mysterious radiance that puzzled him.

"You must wait," she said.

Beyond that she would say no word, though he pulled her head down, and with his hands in her soft, smooth hair threatened to hold her until she told him the secret. Her answer was a satisfied little sigh, and she nestled her pink face against his neck, and whispered that she was content to accept the punishment. So where Amuk Toolik had gone, and what he was doing, still remained a mystery.

A little later he knew he had guessed the truth.

"I don't need a doctor," he said, "but it was mighty thoughtful of you to send Amuk Toolik for one." Then he caught himself suddenly. "What a senseless fool I am! Of course there are others who need a doctor more than I do."

Mary nodded. "But I was thinking chiefly of you when I sent Amuk Toolik to Tanana. He is riding Kauk, and should return almost any time now." And she turned her face away so that he could see only the pink tip of her ear.

"Very soon I will be on my feet and ready for travel," he said. "Then we will start for the States, as we planned."

"You will have to go alone, Alan, for I shall be too busy fitting up the new house," she replied, in such a quiet, composed, little voice that he was stunned. "I have already given orders for the cutting of timber in the foothills, and Stampede and Amuk Toolik will begin construction very soon. I am sorry you find your business in the States so important, Alan. It will be a little lonesome with you away."

He gasped. "Mary!"

She did not turn. "*Mary!*"

He could see again that little, heart-like throb in her throat when she faced him.

And then he learned the secret, softly whispered, with sweet, warm lips pressed to his.

"It wasn't a doctor I sent for, Alan. It was a minister. We need one to marry Stampede and Nawadlook and Tautuk and Keok. Of course, you and I can wait--"

But she never finished, for her lips were smothered with a love that brought a little sob of joy from her heart.

And then she whispered things to him which he had never guessed of Mary Standish, and never quite hoped to hear. She was a little wild, a little reckless it may be, but what she said filled him with a happiness which he believed had never come to any other man in the world. It was not her desire to return to the States at all. She never wanted to return. She wanted nothing down there, nothing that the Standish fortune-builders had left her, unless he could find some way of using it for the good of Alaska. And even then she was afraid it might lead to the breaking of her dream. For there was only one thing that would make her happy, and that was *his* world. She wanted it just as it was--the big tundras, his people, the herds, the mountains--with the glory and greatness of God all about them in the open spaces. She now understood what he had meant when he said he was an Alaskan and not an American; she was that, too, an Alaskan first of all, and for Alaska she would go on fighting with him, hand in hand, until the very end. His heart throbbed until it seemed it would break, and all the time she was whispering her hopes and secrets to him he stroked her silken hair, until it lay spread over his breast, and against his lips, and for the first time in years a hot flood of tears filled his eyes.

So happiness came to them; and only strange voices outside raised Mary's head from where it lay, and took her quickly to the window where she stood a vision of sweet loveliness, radiant in the tumbled confusion and glory of her hair. Then she turned with a little cry, and her eyes were shining like stars as she looked at Alan.

"It is Amuk Toolik," she said. "He has returned."

"And--is he alone?" Alan asked, and his heart stood still while he waited for her answer.

Demurely she came to his side, and smoothed his pillow, and stroked back his hair. "I must go and do up my hair, Alan," she said then. "It would never do for them to find me like this."

And suddenly, in a moment, their fingers entwined and tightened, for on the roof of Sokwenna's cabin the little gray-cheeked thrush was singing again.

Made in the USA
Monee, IL
24 September 2020